L.T. Suzuki

Book Cover, graphic design and layout:
Scott White
Shinobi Creative Services
www.shinobicreativeservices.com

imagine...

There is a secret place that exists; unknown to most, forgotten by many, and lives on only for the few who believe.

Though you cannot look to a map to find this magical realm, it is still very real. In this world, lost on a plane that hangs in the twilight where one enters a dream as sleep takes over the mind and body, Imago lives on.

Here, as in all places where man dwells, the eternal struggle between good and evil plays out. In this land, there are places fair and foul, heroes that are larger than life and villains that one hopes exists only in our nightmares.

In this mystical world, life is an extraordinary adventure where revenge and redemption, betrayal and salvation, and love; lost and found, are woven together to create this rich tapestry of life.

Where is this realm you ask? To find Imago, all you must do is close your eyes and believe...

acknowledgement

Special thanks to my husband, Scott
for his undying support and patience,
martial arts advice, and his skill
with that trusty, red pen.

dedication

This book is dedicated to my mother,
whose warrior spirit lives on
and of course, to my muse,
Nia... with much love.

contents

prologue

"Imago Chronicles: Book One, A Warrior's Tale" begins at the height of the turmoil that shall determine if indeed there will be a Third Age of Peace. Besieged by enemy soldiers from the east and now immersed in war with soldiers of the Dark Army from the west, Nayla Treeborn and her people are already deeply entrenched in political upheaval in a land swept up in absolute chaos and anarchy. They are about to engage in the next great war that will decide the fate of all mankind and Elves in Imago.

In a desperate attempt to deliver word to the Elf king of Wyndwood and those of the Alliance for a call to arms, she is the last surviving messenger sent forth by her people. Now, trapped in a storm at the top of the world, she fights to survive the deadly elements in a strange land.

Despised by Elves and shunned by mortals, she must now find the courage to make her place in this world, and the compassion to save those who keep her at arm's length. This story recounts the defining moments in her life that had forged her into a deadly warrior, a great captain and a legend amongst the people of Imago.

This is Nayla Treeborn's story; this is her warrior's tale.

1
the end

Where you end in life has much to do with how you begin...

The words of her master came back to haunt her. After all she had endured, this was hardly the way she had imagined a warrior of her calibre would meet her end. Perhaps in the heat of battle, yes; but alone, succumbing to the freezing elements at the top of the world? It was not supposed to end this way.

Her teeth chattered uncontrollably as her body shivered with the ferocity of the cold. Drawing her cloak tightly around her small frame, she ploughed through the calf-deep snow. The cruel north wind howled unmercifully as it whipped the white flakes around her in a swirling, blinding flurry as she ventured on. Its cold breath chilled her through to the bones, freezing her inside out with each sharp lungful of air she struggled to gulp down.

Behind her to the east lay her war-ravaged country of Orien. As her eyes squinted through the blowing snow, gazing to the west she could make out the distant lands. Either way she turned, the smells of war were carried high on the inhospitable winds. Pursued by enemy soldiers to the east, there was a very likely chance that, as she ventured deeper into the Dark Lord's stronghold – into the dreaded land of Talibarr, other soldiers were advancing toward her.

The prospects were not good. In fact, they were downright dismal. And now that she had come so far, breaching these mountains, she was trapped by a freak blizzard engulfing the summit.

No wonder this place is called Deception Pass, she thought.

Her trembling hand shielded her eyes from the blowing snow. Less than one hour ago, there appeared no need for concern as she approached the summit. Though the winds did blow, the clouds were nowhere to be seen. The sun shone warmly on this early spring day.

Now, in a strange twist of fate, her shivering body fought to keep warm as she retreated, struggling back into the pass.

She scrutinized the many corpses littering the path before her. Soldiers, either too weak or cold to endure the elements succumbed to its icy grip. The bodies, frozen hard as the terrain they died in, were glazed in a crystalline layer of frost. They would now be buried beneath a mantle of snow if this weather were to persist. Soon she, like those that lay before her, would become one with the mountain, falling victim to its embrace.

There was no doubt had she been a full-blooded mortal she would have expired by now. This was one of the few times she was grateful to have the blood of the Elf-kind coursing through her veins.

Her fingers, though sheathed in leather gloves, were growing numb with the icy cold. In desperation, she struggled; hastily prying away the frozen cloaks still worn by several of the dead soldiers. Backing into a small recess carved into the mountain pass, she momentarily paused to consider the now-frozen corpse that had sought refuge here.

The dead soldier was sitting upright. His knees were drawn up tightly to his chest while his arms were wrapped around his legs. He appeared to be sleeping; his arched shoulders hunched up around his neck. The man's face, shielded from the buffeting winds, remained frozen between his arms as his forehead rested upon his knees. Though he was much larger than the mortal men from her country, this corpse looked as if his whole body shrank under the wind's deadly breath.

Quickly trampling down the snow, she compressed this layer beside the dead soldier before throwing her leather pack down next to him. Kneeling atop her pack, it provided her with an effective barrier from the frozen ground. She drew the three frozen cloaks up around her. Stiff as thin planks of wood, she propped them up - one between herself and the corpse as a windbreak, the others leaning in over her body. Digging the edges into the growing layer of snow, it'd only be a matter of time before she and this impromptu shelter would be buried.

With nothing more than the sounds of the howling wind to pierce the growing darkness, she wrapped her cloak tightly around her body before curling into a ball. With her extremities tucked beneath her, she bowed her head down low. Wedging her numb hands into her armpits for warmth, her breathing became short and fast. As though her lungs were bellows stoking an internal flame, she tried desperately to keep what little body heat she had mustered remaining inside of her.

Under normal situations, this warrior would be sitting upright, her back perfectly straight, her fingers woven together to summon the energy of fire. But this situation was far from normal. Her mind raced as she struggled to focus on keeping warm, on staying alive. How she managed to survive the trek thus far now seemed more a matter of sheer luck than skill. Perhaps this time, her luck had run out.

Huddled in a tight ball, her eyes slowly closed as the insulating layer of snow burying her beneath this makeshift shelter took the edge off the bitter, icy winds. Her warmed breath as she called upon the element of fire seemed to dull the teeth of the cold air gnawing upon her exposed skin. Exhausted by her ordeal, she soon lapsed into a strange twilight, the point just before sleep that claims the body and mind. Here, her soul hovered on this plane. Again, the words of her master echoed deep in her mind: *Where you end in life has much to do with how you begin...*

In her mind's eye she could see herself: a small child appearing no more than twelve mortal years of age. She was crouched beneath a large, flowering shrub. Her knees were drawn up to her chest while her thin arms wrapped around her legs. Had it been any other child, it would appear she was deeply engrossed in a fun, childhood pastime – a game of hide and seek. However, she was no ordinary child, nor was she engaged in harmless child's play.

Her eyes were clenched shut as the sounds of light footsteps drew closer.

"Where are you, Nayla? I know you are near!"

She trembled as a pair of dark brown, leather boots stopped just before her. Poised like a pheasant waiting to be flushed out of the undergrowth, Nayla prayed beneath her breath: "*Please, please, keep moving! Please, do not find me!*"

"You cannot hide forever! Where are you?" snarled a familiar voice.

To her horror, those dreaded boots slowly turned in her direction. Could those Elven ears hear the panicked beating of her heart? Nayla froze. She prayed, hoping against hope those big boots would just go away. Instead, a menacing shadow crouched low to the ground.

Peering up, she could see his large frame silhouetted against the impending night sky.

"You know you cannot hide! I can sense your fear! I can feel it!" growled the Elf. His large hand thrust down to yank her from her hiding place.

Nayla bolted. She burst out from beneath the shrub. With her frightened heart thundering and her little feet scrambling wildly, she made a desperate flight for the gateway. Her escape was short-lived.

His powerful hand reached out, seizing her by the end of her ponytail. Yanking on her hair so forcefully, it caused Nayla's feet to fly out in front of her. She came crashing down onto her back, landing hard on the unforgiving gravel footpath.

"You do this every time, and every time it is the same. You know you cannot escape me!"

Nayla's scalp burned. She felt the stinging sensation, strands of hair tearing away at the roots as she was hoisted up onto her feet.

"You are so pathetic; a sorry excuse for a mortal or Elf! It is a good thing that you are neither."

"But father, I did as you said. I stood up for what was right! I made a stand!"

"Yes. Indeed you did, but need I remind you it was at my expense?"

"But I thought – "

"You thought nothing! You are incapable of thought! It matters not what I said. The point is that you – a child, had the gall to disgrace me in front of the elders."

"You know I was right! You know those warriors will be doomed if you do not strengthen their numbers before sending them on this mission."

"How you even intercepted that message is beyond me, but listen now! You do not; I repeat, *DO NOT* tell me how to command my armies!"

"But father, do not let your pride stand in the way. It was a mistake; a mistake that can still be undone!"

"Then what? Claim before all that I, Dahlon Treeborn, a high Elf and the steward of Nagana was wrong and you, a half-caste, worthless child – a girl at that, was right? I think not!" he grunted in disgust.

"Tell them you only now received the message!" pleaded Nayla.

"It is too late. You have already made a spectacle of yourself when you burst into the meeting hall with your ludicrous claims!"

"Had you only listened rather than force me to confront you before the elders!"

"Listen to you? Listen to a child? How dare you? Why do I not take advice from the village idiot if that be the case?" growled Dahlon.

"Mother always warned me that you would take heed of a poisonous snake only after it had bitten you."

"It was bad enough when you hid behind your mother's skirt. Now you are as impossible and as dangerous as she was!"

"You were the one who told me to stand up for what is right, even when all others may disagree! You were the one who told me to stand up for what I believe in, even if it means standing alone! Now I stand before you *and* against you, for I know innocent lives will be lost because of your pride!"

"Damn you!" cursed her father. "Bite your tongue."

"You… you are a hypocrite," snapped Nayla; "a hypocrite of the worst kind!"

Dahlon Treeborn towered above his young daughter. Her tiny form was dwarfed; completely engulfed by his menacing shadow. His body trembled with rage as he listened to her vent unrepentantly.

Without warning, his right fist lashed out. It caught Nayla across her face. The impact instantly dislocated her lower jaw. Before she could stumble back from the force of the blow, he back-fisted her as he retracted his hand. Her misshapen jaw snapped back into place with the percussion that connected from the opposite direction. She was momentarily stunned, reeling from the powerful shockwave of the violent blow.

Defiantly shaking off the pain, she stood steadfast before her father, unwavering. She was determined not to yield to the hostile glare of his cruel, piercing blue eyes.

Though her jaw ached terribly, she shouted through clenched teeth: "I will not back down! I am not scared of you!"

"You insolent fool! I shall give you reason to be scared," snapped Dahlon.

Snatching her off the ground, he used one hand around her waist, the other to cover her mouth. He stormed out of the private garden, his quarry in his grip as his quick, deliberate steps delivered him to the deserted armoury. He hastily scanned the grounds for watchful eyes as he made his way.

Under the cover of night, the Elf struggled to subdue the small, thrashing figure. As he forced open the doors of the simple, wooden building, he threw Nayla to the dirt floor.

Like a frightened animal, she scrambled on her hands and knees to escape his wrath. Instead, Dahlon's foot came crashing down squarely onto her back. Her arms and legs collapsed under his weight; splaying out to her sides as she felt and heard the *'crunch'* of her ribs cracking as his boot deliberately and slowly crushed her small body down onto the cold, hard ground.

"Tell me you shall recant what you had said to the elders! Tell me you are sorry!" bellowed Dahlon, his foot pressing down harder.

"If the lives of our warriors shall be spared, I will not recant! I cannot be sorry for something I am not sorry for!" wheezed Nayla, struggling to breathe.

"By God, you *will* be sorry!" growled her father, picking her up by the scruff of the neck. "And you shall respect me as a child should respect her father, you worthless deviant!"

Nayla glared at him as she hissed: "I shall respect you when your deeds and words warrant respect, not because you feel you are deserving of it. You are no different than me. You must earn respect!"

"You wicked child! You are as stubborn and outspoken as your mother was!" shouted Dahlon, giving her a violent shake.

"And you are a coward to take on one so small!"

The Elf seethed in rage as he raised Nayla off the ground. Unable to contain his fury, he hurled her across the room as though she was nothing more than a rag doll.

With a resounding *'boom'* Nayla slammed into the wall with such force, swords and halberds rattled and bounced on the weapons rack.

She felt herself dissolving into a gray fog as the back of her head struck the wall. As she slowly slid down to the ground, Dahlon seized Nayla by her tiny wrist. She stumbled along in a daze as her father dragged her to the central support beam. Grabbing hold of a coil of rope, he tossed one end up and over the structure, high into the rafters. He worked swiftly to bind Nayla's wrists together. Taking the other end, he yanked sharply on the rope so she was forced up onto her feet. With her arms drawn high over her head, she was hoisted upright until her toes barely touched the ground.

Her body began to tremble, not from fear, but from the excruciating pain she now endured. Her damaged rib cage, fully exposed as she hung from this tether, strained as gravity worked against her. Her breathing became short and sharp, unable to take in full breaths.

The Elf snatched up a dirty rag that was balled up and tossed to the ground. Giving it a sharp snap, it unfurled to release a cloud of dust and desiccated rat feces.

"This will do," grumbled Dahlon.

He forced the filthy cloth between Nayla's clenched teeth, tightening a knot at the back of her head.

"You shall respect me, if it is the last thing you do!" growled Dahlon, snatching up a bamboo cane.

The first strike ripped across her back with such force the cane split on impact. Its sharp edges bit into her flesh. Nayla's eyes were thrown wide open in shock, her back flinching in agony, but she refused to cry out.

Just as Dahlon raised the bamboo cane once more, Nayla suddenly found herself standing across the room, watching this act of violence. Somehow her soul, no longer willing or able to endure the pain, had transmigrated from the trembling body that now hung from the rafters. Feeling no pain, she walked over to the little girl, completely unnoticed by her father.

"Do not cry," she whispered to the pathetic, trembling form. "Be brave now… Whatever happens, do not let Dahlon see you cry."

The little girl looked into Nayla's eyes; she weakly nodded in understanding. As the cane cracked down again upon her back, her teeth clenched together, biting down on the rag in her mouth to stifle her scream.

"It will be over soon. I promise," whispered Nayla. "Just do not let that Elf see you cry."

The little girl glanced up hopefully. As the cruel sting of the splintering bamboo cane bit into her flesh once more, she wondered morbidly: *Perhaps I shall be lucky this night. Perhaps he will kill me this time.*

"Hush! Mother would not like to hear you speak in this manner. Do not give Dahlon the satisfaction. He shall tire of this soon. You shall see. He will stop," promised Nayla, in a whisper as she huddled close to the girl to offer some comfort.

As the bamboo cane came down again and again in unmerciful repetition, Nayla felt her burning back grow moist with the blood seeping through her tattered clothing.

Her senses, both mind and body, were growing numb to the abuse. For a moment, she thought if she could only open her eyes, her nightmare would end, but her eyes were already open.

Perhaps if I close my eyes I can dream of places far and away from here, she thought in desperation. She could hear Dahlon gasping for his breath as he worked himself into an absolute frenzy. It would be the last thing she remembered as she faded into the darkness.

It was only when the Elf noticed that her body had gone limp, her chin dropping to her chest, lolling forward like a piece of driftwood bobbing on the tide, did he finally relent; ending his physical tirade.

Dahlon used the back of his arm to wipe away the beads of perspiration forming on his forehead. For a brief moment, he stood in silence to compose himself.

"You drive me to despair! Look what you force me to do," growled the Elf, his trembling hand still wielding the shattered cane.

Nayla did not respond, not even flinching in fear under his harsh tone.

He gave her lacerated back a deliberate prod, testing to see if she was still alive.

There was no cry of pain, only a pathetic whimper. But even at that, it was nothing more than raw nerves responding to his cruel touch.

Dahlon quickly released the rope from the rafters, causing Nayla to crumple to the ground in a bloodied heap. Securing one end of her tether to the center post, he tied it just high enough to be out of her reach should she come to. He used the toe of his boot to push back on her shoulder to ascertain that she was still indeed breathing.

"That should teach you, you insolent child. You shall remain here to contemplate what your actions have done to me!" The Elf grumbled beneath his breath as he bolted the door behind him.

In the cold light of the moon shining through the narrow, high windows, large brown rats with bare, scaly tails scampered silently over Nayla's prostrate body. Their twitching noses and nervously quivering whiskers skimmed over her, sniffing for signs of life.

The female rodents, plump with impending offspring, looking to supplement their diet of seeds with some badly needed protein proceeded to indulge. Their small, pink tongues lapped away at the blood that was beginning to coagulate on Nayla's shredded back. It was only when one brazen rodent sank its razor-sharp incisors into her flesh did she eventually stir from this unnatural sleep.

Only inches away from her face, a rat's black, beady eyes slowly came into focus. Nayla blinked hard; staring at the unsightly rodent as it nonchalantly groomed its whiskers and paws after sating its appetite on her.

Gasping in surprise and disgust, Nayla bolted upright. She sent the frightened rats scurrying in all directions. For a long moment, her bleary eyes took in the deep shadows of the armoury. All was silent except for the thundering of her heart pounding loudly in her ears.

After being bound so tightly for so long her hands had grown numb, now only prickling with sensation. Nayla flexed her fingers in a feeble attempt to increase the flow of blood to her extremities before attempting to remove the gag from about her mouth.

Her fingers pried and pulled at the filthy cloth, but to no avail. Her parched, chapped lips began to bleed as she struggled with the gag. Dahlon had drawn and tied it so tightly; it cut into the corners of her mouth, making her dislocated jaw throb all the more.

Nayla slowly rose up, staggering onto her unsteady feet. Her eyes followed the length of rope up along the post where Dahlon had secured it well out of her reach. At first, she made several attempts to jump up in a bid to access the knot, but the jarring pain rippling from her cracked ribs and coursing through her body made it a torturous exercise in futility. She took a moment to consider her limited options.

Several stacked, wooden crates were within her reach if she extended one of her legs. If she were able to maneuver one of them over, she can stand on it and perhaps, untie the rope from the post. Once done, any one of the swords in this room could easily slice through the knot binding her wrists together. She'd be free at last. Free to escape. Free to run away once and for all.

Straining against the tether that bit into her raw wrists, Nayla stood balanced on one leg as she reached with the toes of the other to snag onto the corner of a crate. Her toes caught the very edge, but the sheer weight of the other crates stacked on top was too much for her. In anger and frustration, her foot struck out, knocking the crates over. They toppled over with a resounding crash.

She cursed beneath her breath, realizing the impact sent all the crates well beyond her reach now. Slumping down to the ground in utter defeat, Nayla could feel the tide of despair and hopelessness. It lapped at her feet and now it threatened to wash over her completely, perhaps this time, to drown her in sorrow.

With a loud bang, the door to the armoury swung open.

Nayla's heart raced in sheer panic as the realization her punishment was about to resume overwhelmed her. Curling into a tight ball, her arms instinctively wrapped around her head as they always did to diffuse the blows to her face and skull. Her tortured body began to tremble uncontrollably as she braced herself for more torment.

She could hear light footfalls, too light to be that of a mortal's, making their way through the dark structure. As the Elf's steps neared, Nayla's eyes squeezed shut as she steeled her nerves.

The sound of an astonished gasp caused her eyes to snap open. Before her loomed an imposing shadow and a pair of dark brown, leather boots. In sheer terror, Nayla leapt onto her feet, scrambling to escape in the opposite direction.

Like a frightened animal taking flight, she ran, but once again, escape was impossible. Nayla's arms were thrown up high over her head. Her shoulders wrenched back as she came to an abrupt end on her short tether. She slammed down onto the hard ground, the dirt and pebbles embedding into her raw and bloodied flesh.

Ignoring the searing pain, Nayla immediately rolled onto her stomach. Drawing her knees to her chest, she rolled into a tight ball once more, her arms clamped firmly over her head.

"Good god! Nayla, is that you?"

A gentle hand touched her lightly upon the head. She began to tremble, waiting for it to strike her with a vengeance.

"He has gone too far," whispered a voice, quivering in shock at the sight of Nayla's bloodied, battered body.

Too frightened to move, she lay huddled in a quaking, crimson heap. Her eyes followed this shadow as he reached up to untie the tether from the post. As he knelt down before her, he struggled to untie the rope binding her wrists. The knot was so tight; he had no choice but to cut Nayla free with his dagger. Placing his weapon down so he could remove the cloth used to gag her; he gently peeled the filthy rag away from her mouth.

Nayla lunged for the dagger. She scrambled away on her hands and knees, retreating into the deep shadows of the armoury.

"Nayla! It is I, Joval Stonecroft," announced the Elf in a gentle tone, moving slowly toward her. His hands were open, raised to show he meant her no harm. "Put the dagger down, Nayla. Listen to me. I am here to help you."

The large Elf knelt before the little girl. The weapon created an imposing barrier, even in her small hands. The razor-sharp blade came to life, glimmering like liquid silver as a shaft of moonlight penetrated the darkness of the armoury. Joval could make out Nayla's eyes and what he saw tore at his heart and would haunt him for his remaining days. Dahlon Treeborn's actions not only mutilated her body, but he extinguished the very essence of her life from her eyes. They were dark and liquid, yet they showed no sign of anger, hate, sorrow or love. The only emotion that came to surface was pure, unadulterated fear.

Joval reached out to console the frightened child, but Nayla instantly recoiled from his touch, raising the tip of the blade toward him.

The Elf froze.

"Nayla, I promise, I will not hurt you."

He leaned in closer to gaze into her eyes, searching for a soul that now seemed to elude him.

"I am sorry, child. I have failed miserably in my promise to Lady Treeborn. I should have seen this coming."

Upon hearing her mother's name, Nayla began to tremble. Her gaze fell upon the dagger. Startled to see the glint of the deadly blade poised in her hand, her grip instantly loosened. The weapon tumbled to the ground as she drew her knees up to her chest. Her arms wrapped tightly around her legs as her forehead came to rest on her bended knees. She began to rock slowly, back and forth, back and forth, as though she was cradled in her mother's safe, loving arms once again.

Joval was rendered utterly speechless, watching this once exuberant, spirited child reduced to an empty husk. Her father had finally succeeded in breaking her. Stripped of all human emotions, devoid of any human feelings - she no longer had the ability to cry in pain or shed tears for her own agony and tortured existence. Joval slowly crawled over to her side, sitting himself down next to her broken body and shattered soul.

"Do wish to leave this city, Nayla? Do you wish for me to take you away from Nagana?"

Her head slowly lifted at the sound of her one prayer finally being answered. She nodded in response.

"So be it, child," said the Elf. "You shall endure no more at the hands of your father. If this is the only way I can hold true to my promise to your mother to keep you safe, then we shall leave immediately."

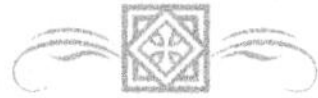

"Why all the secrecy, Joval? Why are we leaving Nagana at this ungodly hour?" questioned an Elf, hurriedly fastening his cloak over his shoulders as Joval Stonecroft guided him to an awaiting carriage.

"There shall be time for explanation later, my friend. We must make haste. We must be well on our way before the cock crows," insisted Joval. Large scrolls of parchment needed for this trek were tucked under his arm.

"Are we about to embark on some high adventure? Perhaps you have schemed up a plan to journey into western Imago to return to the enchanted forest of Wyndwood?" queried the Elf, the excitement rising in his voice at the prospects.

Joval motioned him to quiet down as he directed his friend to take control of the horses.

"No, Valtar. We are not making a trip into western Imago, but I can tell you this much; we are about to embark on a great adventure, one that you shall remember for all time," promised Joval. "Now, take the reins. Get us out of Nagana quickly. Head north."

"North? North to where?" asked the younger Elf.

"Anshen," replied Joval.

"Anshen? There is nothing there but the warriors of the Furai Mountains: the Kagai Warriors!"

"I know. Let us be on our way," urged Joval.

"Ah! We are on a secret mission of sorts."

"Yes, this is most definitely secret," admitted Joval, as he ducked into the carriage. "Now, go!"

Inside, with the curtains still drawn across the windows, Nayla waited nervously. She was hunched forward so her lacerated back would not bloody the upholstery. In a single glance, the Elf was able to take in her diminutive, pathetic form, perched upon the seat. She was so small her tiny feet did not even reach the floor.

As their carriage neared the west gate, the Elf removed his cloak. He moved closer to conceal the child beneath it, but once again Nayla instinctively recoiled in fear, backing into the far corner.

"Hide beneath this, Nayla. It is the only way to remove you from this city without your father's knowledge. You must remain still until we are well on our way."

She reluctantly obliged, huddling into a small ball upon the seat as Joval spread his great cloak over her. As they neared the gate, he quickly unfurled several of the large scrolls – maps of Imago, detailing the country to the east of the Furai Mountains. He draped them over Nayla's little form.

"Who goes there?" called a voice.

"Valtar Briarwood," answered the Elf, as he brought the steeds to a rolling stop before the guard. "I have one passenger: Captain Stonecroft."

"Captain Stonecroft?" repeated the guard, frowning in doubt.

"Yes, Joval Stonecroft," confirmed the Elf, leaning out of the open door to show his face.

"My apologies, Captain Stonecroft, I did not mean to delay your departure," responded the guard, glancing into the carriage to ensure all was fine. "Forgive me, but you know how Lord Treeborn is when it comes to movement in and out of Nagana during these times of upheaval."

"I understand completely," said Joval, acknowledging the warrior with a nod. "It is wise to remain vigilant."

As Joval stepped back inside, the guard motioned for the others to raise the portcullis. He waved Valtar on to proceed as the heavy iron grate slowly lifted. Moving through the open gateway, the Elf urged the steeds northward along Esshu Road.

With a loud clatter the portcullis fell back into place. It echoed behind them and with the steady gait of the horses pulling the carriage away from Nagana, Nayla breathed a great sigh of relief. Joval watched the slow rise and fall of his cloak as the tiny form beneath found a temporary sanctuary.

After a half hour of travel had passed, Joval leaned over to remove his cloak. He was not surprised to see Nayla was now fast asleep, although it was a disturbed sleep. She twitched and flinched, her face twisting into a scowl as though she was unable to escape her tormentor even in her dreams.

For a moment, Joval debated whether to wake her from this nightmare, or to let her sleep. Eventually, he resolved that nightmares were a regular occurrence for this child. Each time she closed her eyes, undoubtedly just as in her waking hours, she was unable to escape her fate. Joval decided to let her rest.

"You know you cannot hide! I can sense your fear! I can feel it!" snarled Dahlon, reaching down to pull her from her hiding place.

Nayla bolted, She burst out from under the shrub to knock the Elf over as she fled. Her heart was thundering in her ears and her little feet scrambled as she made a desperate flight to the gateway.

Dahlon immediately gave chase. With his much greater stride, he was quickly catching up to her as she raced from the garden toward the courtyard. Dashing as fast as she could, her body was poised like a bird ready to take flight. She leapt up, waiting for an invisible wind to catch her, to allow her to fly away. Instead, she tumbled to the ground.

Glancing behind, she saw her father fast approaching. Scrambling to her feet, she darted through the crowded courtyard where she was pushed and jostled by the people.

Once again, Nayla leapt into the air. Again, she tumbled to the ground. She struggled to her feet to the sound of laughter of those who watched her desperate flight.

Why can I not fly? Why can I not escape this time? Nayla wondered, as she looked at all the jeering, laughing faces that crowded around her. *Perhaps I need to be higher.*

She pushed her way to the stairs leading to the battlements surrounding the fortress city. *I must get higher!*

Nayla was gasping for her breath as she reached the rampart. Behind her, a crowd led by Dahlon Treeborn was in pursuit. She promptly turned, running to the edge of the battlement. Peering down, it was at least a thirty-feet drop to the ground below.

As her father veered ever closer, Nayla backed away from the edge.

Just as he lunged at her, she took a running start before pitching herself off the high wall.

For a brief instant, at the very moment her feet left the floor of the stone rampart, all she felt was air all around her, as though an invisible force suspended her in nothingness. Her outstretched arms waited for the wind to catch her, to allow her to soar, flying high above her pursuers to sail away from her troubles.

Nayla's triumphant smile was instantly transformed into sheer terror. It was a feeling of nothingness, as if one had stepped off the stairs not realizing there was no landing to offer a safe footing. There was only emptiness. She plummeted straight down to the ground below at a frightening speed. Her eyes gazed up to see Dahlon and the others mocking and laughing at her as she fell.

Just as her body was about to crash down onto the ground, Nayla bolted up from her sleep. Her eyes snapped wide open. They were wild with fear as her head turned to and fro, fighting to recognize the strange surroundings. They came to settle on Joval Stonecroft seated before her.

"Nayla, you were having a nightmare."

The little girl sat up very straight, almost proudly, yet her chin rested on her chest. Her eyes were downcast as she fought to regain her composure.

"Are you thirsty?" asked the Elf, holding forth an open flask. "Would you like some water?"

Nayla's eyes timidly peered up, considering the offer. She startled Joval as her small hands lunged forward, snatching the flask from his hand. Gulping down the water, she dribbled much of it down her chin in her haste to quench her thirst.

"Slow down, child! There is plenty of water to be had," advised the Elf, surprised by her actions. "In fact, you can keep the flask, if it pleases you."

When Nayla realized Joval had no intention of taking the water away from her, she was momentarily embarrassed by her pitiful behavior. She gingerly wiped the spilled water from her tender chin with the back of her hand.

Joval watched as she winced in pain as her wrist, burned raw by her restraints, made contact with her bruised and swollen jaw.

"Nagana is well behind us now," announced the Elf.

Nayla held the flask before him, motioning him to take it from her hand. As he moved to reseal it, she scooted across the seat, kneeling on it so she can gaze out the window. Drawing back the curtains, her eyes were wide open in awe as they took in the hills and valleys of the Takai Forest, the great bamboo forest of Orien. The tall, jointed stalks and the jade green leaves were a welcome sight to behold.

Even through her pain, a small smile creased her face as the realization that she was no longer a prisoner within the walls of the fortress city finally sank in. This Elf did indeed remain true to his promise. Joval Stonecroft did take her away from that wretched place, and most importantly, away from Dahlon Treeborn. At this point, she did not know where they were going, nor did she care. Anywhere was better than Nagana.

As Nayla marvelled at the ever-changing landscape, Joval could not ignore the cruel lashing this child had endured. The clothes on her back were tattered to shreds and deeply soiled with her own blood. The long, linear wounds marring her body were crusted with dried blood. Some of the wounds were weeping a clear, watery substance that would be the precursor to pus as infection set in.

In his long existence, Joval had seen many criminals caned, as it was a common form of corporal punishment in this part of Imago. He had seen grown men reduced to screaming, wailing, pathetic souls that would beg for mercy or would simply pass out from the brutality of the pain. How Nayla was able to endure this assault without the whole palace grounds alerted to her abuse, gagged or not, was a profound mystery to this Elf. Even now, with wounds so fresh, this child seemed able to distance herself from the pain, or at least, she was very convincing at concealing her misery and discomfort.

While Nayla's eyes drank in the lush, green surroundings as they journeyed northward, Joval silently moved closer. He raised his left hand, holding his open palm about an inch away from her body as he focused on her energy. Though the most obvious assault was to her back, the Elf closed his eyes as he concentrated on the task at hand. His hand skimmed just over her body. A disruption in the flow of her energy would indicate an injury, even if it was unseen by the eyes.

Joval's heart sank as it quickly became apparent that her jaw had been dislocated or broken and at least three of her ribs were damaged to varying degrees. He was momentarily startled as the palm of his hand could still feel an intense heat rising from her lacerated back.

Sensing his hand near to her, Nayla yelped in fright. She hurled herself into the far corner of the carriage to escape.

Joval raised both his hands in a gesture for calm as he reasoned with her: "You are hurt, Nayla. Let me help. I can heal your wounds if you allow it."

She peered into his clear, blue eyes, searching for signs that this was not some cruel trick.

"If your mother were alive, you know she would insist on it. Lady Treeborn would want me to help you and she would expect you to accept this help."

Nayla said nothing. She reluctantly nodded her head in agreement, moving away from the corner.

"Can you speak?

She answered '*no*' with a shake of her head.

Joval removed his cloak, folding it several times before placing it onto the floor. "Kneel on this," he instructed.

Nayla did as she was told. Kneeling before the Elf, her suspicious eyes were always watchful.

Joval raised his hands above his head. With a loud clap, the palms of his hands came together as his eyes closed. As he focused on harnessing his energy, his hands rubbed lightly, but briskly together, generating ample heat and the Elven power to heal.

Nayla fought the instinctive urge to recoil from his touch as his hands neared her face. Even before he made contact, she could feel immediate relief; the dissipation of the dull, throbbing ache of her lower jaw. As Joval recited a healing incantation, Nayla could hear the Elvish words he whispered just beneath his breath. These magical words and his soothing voice helped to calm her jittery nerves, allowing for his powers to work more effectively.

Somehow, when this Elf spoke in his native tongue, his words were gentle, almost lyrical. It did not seem like the same language Dahlon Treeborn used when he spoke in Elvish.

Her mother spoke to her in Taijina, the language of the mortals of Orien, as well as the common speech. Her father had a working knowledge of Taijina, but he preferred to use the common tongue. Elvish was only spoken in the presence of his own people. Nayla's own comprehension of the Elvish language was stilted at best. She had come to know every Elvish word of profanity her father would hurl at her, but it was nothing she could use in normal, day-to-day conversation with her father's people.

As her thoughts meandered, Joval continued to work on her. His healing touch and magical words did wonders to ease her aching ribs and she felt only a tingling sensation as he set about healing the lacerations on her back. When he was done, he was disheartened to see Nayla would be forced to bear permanent reminders of her last encounter with Dahlon Treeborn for the rest of her life. The open wounds were healed, but there remained many long, red marks that would eventually fade into silvery-white scars.

Had Nayla been an Elf, rather than one of mixed blood, Joval knew these scars would all but disappear. However, in his heart, he felt that even if these scars did vanish, no doubt she would carry a burden far worse.

Taking her raw wrists into his large hands, the Elf proceeded to vanquish the weeping wounds and broken skin.

Nayla watched in fascination.

Although Dahlon, a high Elf, had been gifted with greater powers to heal, he always allowed her to suffer the maladies, cuts and abrasions a mortal child must endure in the course of living. She only knew of the cruelties inflicted by his hands, never its powers to nurture and heal.

"Is that better now?" asked Joval, helping her back onto the seat.

Nayla responded with a nod, still marvelling at the faint, red marks left on her wrists after Joval worked his Elven magic. The throbbing, burning lacerations on her back were now tingling with sensation as the torn flesh continued to knit together beneath her newly healed, though scarred skin.

"Are you able to talk?" questioned Joval.

Again, she merely nodded.

"Are you afraid to speak, child?"

After a reflective pause, she answered in a small voice: "It is usually when I speak that I find myself in dire trouble."

"You know I would never harm you, Nayla," promised the Elf.

"I know…"

"And just how long were you locked up in the armory?"

"I do not remember," she answered, her slight shoulders shrugging in response. "No longer than usual I suspect."

"Your father has done this before?" questioned Joval, his brows furrowing into a frown of disapproval and surprise.

"I have spent many long hours in that armory. Consider it my second home, but this is the first time he had beaten me to this extent."

"Well, it was most fortuitous that I happened along when I did. Had I not heard you signal for help, I would never had found you."

"I was *not* signalling for help. I was merely attempting to facilitate my own escape when you came by."

"Whatever the case, no doubt your father is now aware you are long gone. If the fates conspire and luck is with you, he shall think you have merely run away," stated Joval.

"Fate has never treated me kindly."

The Elf considered the child's bitter words and with a sigh of resignation, in his own heart he had to agree with her. Although she has existed for thirty-seven years, she was still the physical equivalent of a prepubescent mortal child. She was aging much slower than a mortal, yet she was aging twice as fast had she been a full-blooded Elf.

Obviously her longer years of existence made her more worldly and knowledgeable than a mortal child of twelve. He noticed too, that she was much more precocious than other children, but all this made her an outcast. Unable to fit in with mortal youngsters, Joval had grave doubts that had there been Elven children for her to associate with, she would still be ostracized by his kind. And children, especially mortal ones, had a tendency to be cruel in their dealings with others who were different, whether the child be mortal or Elf.

Nayla had inherited her mother's dark, exotic looks and diminutive stature. She was darker than any other *dark* Elf that dwelled in western Orien, yet her small, delicate ears ascending into a recognizable Elven point made it clear to all that she was, as Dahlon and others less tolerant would describe, a half-caste.

"Thank you," she said, her voice barely audible.

"Thank you? For what?" queried Joval.

"For helping me," answered Nayla. "I know what you have undertaken is not without great risk to your own personal safety. I fear when Dahlon finds out what you have done, he will have your head."

Joval's eyebrows were raised in mock concern as he replied: "You do not say!"

"Oh, I do!" she exclaimed, her eyes wide-open to express her genuine fear. "He swore up and down that if I told a soul about his treatment, I would die and so would anyone who attempts to come to my aid."

"Do not be concerned, child," responded Joval. "He will not find out about this. As far as he and the elders are concerned, I have forged on ahead of the battalion he intends to send north to circumvent an invasion from eastern Orien."

The Elf was also well aware that if by chance he was found out, his punishment would still pale in comparison to anything Nayla would be forced to endure, for he knew in his heart Dahlon Treeborn had a great fondness for him. The high Elf always favoured Joval, even above his own child. In many ways, Dahlon considered him to be the son he never had, but always longed for.

"Do you wish to know where we are going?" asked Joval.

"Yes, please."

"I am taking you to Anshen."

"Anshen? I have heard my mother speak of this place before and yet, I could never find it on a map," she replied.

"All you need to know is that it is in a secret place, far to the north."

"Will I be safe?"

"Indeed, you will be quite safe."

The steady roll of the carriage came to a gentle stop. Light footfalls approached the carriage. In that instant, Nayla panicked. She leapt behind Joval, hiding behind his large form.

"Do not be afraid," assured the Elf. "It is only my friend, Valtar Briarwood."

As the door swung open, Valtar stood there, his mouth agape. His face blanched in horror as he recognized the girl peering out from behind Joval's shoulder.

"Tell me that I am dreaming!" gasped Valtar, as he pleaded: "Tell me that is not her."

"Yes, this child is Dahlon Treeborn's daughter, but you best forget her identity. Better yet, forget you ever saw her."

"What is going on here, Joval?" asked Valtar, mortified by his discovery. "I demand to know!"

"I am delivering Nayla to Master Saibon in Anshen," replied Joval, motioning him to calm down.

Valtar shook his head in dismay, gesturing his captain to follow him. "Come with me, Joval. I need to speak to you in private."

"Remain here, Nayla. Do you understand?" asked Joval. "Do not wander off."

She nodded in understanding as she watched Joval step out. He followed Valtar a way up the dirt road.

"What is the meaning of this, Joval?" Valtar demanded to know. "What have you gotten us into?"

"The less you know, the better it will be for all," responded Joval.

"Are you attempting to abduct Lord Treeborn's daughter? For if you are, it will be the death of us!"

"Abduct her?" snorted Joval, with a chuckle. "I hardly think so. I am helping her to escape her father's wrath."

"Joval, it is not your place to interfere where family issues are concerned, especially where it involves Lord Treeborn!"

"Valtar, you have no idea what Nayla was forced to endure last night. Lord Treeborn brutalized his own daughter in ways you would never want to imagine," explained the Elf, his voice hushed so the child would not hear his words.

"Your heart is too soft, my friend. Why should you be burdened with another man's problem?"

"Your heart is not soft enough. And *she* is not the problem; *he* is the problem," rebuked Joval. "Where is your sense of compassion, Valtar? She is a child without a mother. Her father torments and abuses her. She is scorned by mortals; shunned by our own people. Show some mercy for pity's sake."

"And you feel by taking her away from her father you can give her a chance at a normal life?"

"Normal or not, at least she will have a life to speak of," retorted Joval.

"And you speak of mercy!" groaned Valtar, his hand slapping his forehead in frustration. "What kind of mercy do you think Lord Treeborn will show us if he catches wind of this?"

"I speak to you now not as your captain, but as your friend, Valtar. Do not breathe a word of this to a soul, I beseech you," pleaded the Elf.

Valtar gazed into Joval's eyes, and then over his shoulder to spy upon the little girl peering at them through the open door.

"This is madness. I swear you have taken leave of your senses," whispered Valtar.

"Let me assure you, my senses are quite intact. I know what I do, and if you refuse to help me as a friend, then consider this an order from your captain," urged Joval.

"True, you are my captain, but first and foremost, you are my friend. And as a *friend*, if what you do shall jeopardize your rank and your reputation, then I will not be a party to this madness!"

"As a warrior, are you not sworn to protect the innocent? To uphold justice for the people of western Orien, whether they are Elf or mortal?" questioned Joval.

Valtar glanced at Nayla again before he muttered beneath his breath: "Look at her. She is neither. That child is an abomination of nature."

"Those are harsh words, Valtar. If this be your sentiment, perhaps you should be off. I shall complete this journey without you," replied Joval. "Though I know the risk I run in doing so, I will not entangle you in this affair."

"You would do this? You would risk your standing, possibly your life for this half-caste child?"

"Yes."

"I fail to understand why. You owe her nothing."

"It is not yours is to understand, Valtar. I have my reasons for doing so. Just know that I cannot, in good conscience, turn a blind eye to the situation any longer. Nayla is an innocent victim of circumstances far beyond her control."

Valtar stood in silence as he agonized over Joval's words. His hands ran through his long, brown hair as though he was on the verge of yanking it out in sheer frustration. Finally, he gazed up at his friend and with a weary sigh he replied: "This is not the adventure you had promised, nor I had envisioned…"

"Ah, but it is an adventure nonetheless!" countered Joval.

"Very well, I suppose it matters not whether we go down in defeat together in the field of battle or whether it be by Treeborn's own hands."

"Spoken like a true friend, Valtar! Let us take this time for the horses to rest and drink, and then we shall be on our way," responded Joval, with a broad smile.

"Just mark my words, Joval; you may very well live to regret this whole fiasco. This could be the beginning of the end for you – and for her!"

2

on to anshen

"It is as plain as day; he does not like me," stated Nayla, calling out from the carriage as she donned fresh apparel.

"Who does not like you?" responded Joval. He stood outside, waiting for the child to emerge.

"Your friend, the one taking us to Anshen."

"His name is Valtar Briarwood. And you do not know him enough to make such a claim," argued Joval.

"There is no need to lie, Captain Stonecroft. I heard his words." Nayla's own words were crisp, spoken with conviction.

"You heard us talking?" Joval's eyebrows arched up in surprise.

"Of course I did. I may only be half Elf, but I assure you, my hearing is almost as good as yours."

As she stepped out of the carriage, Joval gazed upon her. His hand flew up to his mouth in an attempt to stifle his laughter and to conceal a broad smile that creased his face. In his obvious haste to flee Nagana with this girl, Joval had stolen into her bedchamber, randomly stuffing articles of clothing into a pack. It was only upon seeing the child dressed in fresh clothing did he discover the errors of his ways.

Her mismatched apparel, some bright and gaudy, others in demure, earth tones; some meant for everyday wear, others for grand occasions had been thrown into the pack. She frowned at the Elf as he tried to contain himself. With an air of dignity, Nayla smoothed out her clothes with the flat of her hands.

"I suppose it is not everyday you see the daughter of a high Elf dressed up like a court jester," grumbled Nayla, as she made note of Joval's response. "I am just grateful you tried to do this for me."

"Forgive me, Nayla. It was not my intention to make fun. This was my first attempt at packing for a girl child. I suppose my knowledge of what is, and is not, fashionable leaves much to be desired."

Nayla's small shoulders shrugged in response. "At least I will not show up in tattered rags when we arrive in Anshen."

"Indeed! Perhaps you will start a new fashion trend," suggested Joval.

"How odd! An Elf with a sense of humour," noted the child. "Most unusual..."

"Just because we are reserved by nature, that does not mean we do not find humour in certain situations," remarked Joval.

As Valtar led the horses off to the side of the road to a creek meandering lazily alongside, Nayla considered him for a moment before turning away to head down the embankment to the edge of the great bamboo forest. Joval followed.

"As I said before, your friend does not like me."

"No... It is better to say Valtar just does not understand you."

"What is there to understand? Like he said, I am neither Elf, nor mortal. And he is correct. Though I may be blessed with longer life than a human being, I shall not live an eternity as your people do. I will be denied entry into the Twilight to pass on into your so-called Haven. Nor will I be able to join my mother when I meet my end."

"I take it then, Lord Treeborn had not blessed you with the eternal life of the Elf-kind," surmised Joval.

"No, he has not. Nor would I accept it from him if he had."

"But why?"

"Look at me. Do you not think that living with mortals or the likes of your kind, neither of whom accept me, would give me reason to embrace an eternity in this Hell?"

"Your mother accepted you. She loved you to the bitter end, with her dying breath she did," reminded Joval.

"She was the exception."

"I accept you."

"Do you? Is it only because your mother, though she was Elf and my mother, though she was mortal, were like sisters? That you are forced to accept me because your mother accepted me as an aunt would accept a niece, just as my mother embraced you as kin?"

"I accept you because your mother had always treated me with great kindness, dignity and respect, especially after my mother and father departed for the Haven. I believe somewhere in there, in your heart, you are very much like your mother. I do this to keep her memory intact. She was a wise and powerful woman, even more so than your father dared to imagine. The world is in need of more people like Kareda

Treeborn. Perhaps one day, you shall rise up to her greatness."

Nayla was momentarily taken aback by his words. Then a cynical laugh bubbled forth.

"I am nobody! I am a non-entity!" And in a whisper, she confided: "I can only wish to be like my mother."

"Well, with that kind of cynicism you are right. You sound much more like your father than your mother," commented Joval.

Nayla's eyes burned with rage as his words lashed at her soul. She lunged at the much larger Elf, knocking him backwards.

"How dare you?" she screamed as she pounced on top of Joval. Her little hands balled into tight, quivering fists, ready but unwilling to pummel him. "You take that back! I am not like Dahlon Treeborn. I shall die before I become like him."

Joval merely rolled to his side, dumping Nayla unceremoniously to the ground.

"If that is the case, then honour your mother's memory by behaving as she would see fit!"

Nayla struggled to right herself, sitting in a dejected heap. Her body trembled in anger and yet, her eyes were downcast in shame. Her soul wished to cry out in anguish, but for Nayla, there were no more tears left to shed.

"Do not underestimate yourself, child. Your father holds no sway in the course of your destiny now. Do not fall to the wayside and follow a bitter path for indeed, you will become worse than the man you dread."

Joval rolled up onto his feet, brushing off the dust. He stared down at Nayla who remained on the ground.

"Let us be off now. It is many days to Anshen," said the Elf, extending his hand before the child.

His swift movement, the hand coming toward her caused Nayla to instantly recoil in fear. Joval frowned, and then he realized that her reaction was instinctive, never knowing a kind touch since her mother had passed away.

"Come, child, we have far to go," reiterated the Elf, his hand still extended to her, inviting her up onto her feet.

Nayla gazed up at his tall form. For a moment, she considered the large, outstretched hand before her. Joval slowly retracted his hand as the little girl plucked herself up from the ground, unwilling to accept his offer of help.

Valtar was already waiting, reins in his hand as Nayla and Joval returned to the carriage. She opened the door and lacking the grace of an Elf, awkwardly clambered inside, sitting in silence as Joval took his place across from her.

For several long hours both said nothing, listening to the steady rolling of the wooden wheels against the dirt road as the carriage journeyed northward. As Joval gazed out the window, he could sense Nayla's eyes scrutinizing him.

In Nayla's young mind, it was easy to fear the Elf sitting before her. He was as tall as her father, but larger: broader shoulders, bigger muscles; overall, he was much more physically imposing. Like Dahlon and many of the so-called *dark* Elves, his eyes too, were blue. However, where her father's eyes were of an icy-blue to match his frosty disposition, Joval's eyes were a gentle blue; blue like the petals of the forget-me-not flowers that flourished in the valleys early in the spring. Even though he was a seasoned warrior who, in his long life had witnessed many calamities and survived many battles, his actions to aid her spoke volumes of his compassion. She could swear there was a kindness to them, unseen in her father's eyes, but clearly visible in this Elf's.

Her mother had often told her that the eyes reveal much about a person's character; *'the portal to one's soul'* as she had once said. Her mother had the uncanny ability to just gaze upon Nayla's little face, into her innocent, brown eyes to determine if the child was telling the truth, telling a little fib, or fabricating an out-and-out lie. And perhaps her mother was right, for when she reflected upon her father's own haunting eyes, they seemed devoid of compassion, and most definitely of love.

Joval's eyes on the other hand were ablaze with a passion for life and living. Set against his flowing, dark brown hair and finely chiselled features, Nayla surmised that even by mortal standards, perhaps this Elf was pleasing to the eyes based on her past observations of the Taijin women who would give him admiring glances as he strode by. However, to this child, he was nothing more than an overgrown man with pointed ears, but he did have eyes worth marvelling at. Perhaps part of her fascination was in the fact that she and the mortals of Orien all had the same, consistently dark brown eyes.

"You have pretty eyes," remarked Nayla, giving him an approving nod.

"Pardon me?" responded Joval, shifting uneasily upon hearing the first words to come out of her mouth in quite some time.

"I suppose girls have pretty eyes. Perhaps it is better to say that you have very *nice* eyes."

"I take it, you mean to pay me a compliment," determined the Elf.

Nayla shrugged her slight shoulders as she answered: "I am merely making conversation."

"Oh, so you are no longer angry? You are speaking to me again."

"Did I say I was angry?"

"No, you were so quiet for so long, I just assumed-"

Nayla was quick to interject: "One should never assume, Captain Stonecroft. Did it not occur to you that perhaps I was merely thinking?"

"Hmph," grunted the Elf. "Obviously you had much to think about."

"Indeed… I was wondering, what in heaven's name would compel you take it upon yourself to risk your own life to save mine."

"It was a promise I had made, one that I have every intention of keeping," answered Joval.

"You made no such promise to me," responded the child, her little brows furrowing in bewilderment.

"It was not to you, Nayla. It was for Lady Treeborn."

"For my mother?"

"Yes, it was a promise made to your mother. On her deathbed, she made me swear that I would watch over you, protect you."

Nayla was momentarily stunned by his words. "She told you about Dahlon, about what he would do to me?"

"She warned me that your father could be heavy-handed in his dealings with you and she feared that upon her death, a bad situation would only grow worse," answered Joval.

"*Worse*? That is an understatement if there ever was one!" retorted Nayla, her gaze falling to the floor of the carriage.

"So I take it, your father did not beat you when your mother was still alive?"

"There were times when he would try, but he was always mindful of my mother. He was always careful to act only when she was not in his immediate presence," reminisced the child. A small smile crept across her face as she added: "Dahlon was scared of her, you know?"

"Lord Treeborn was scared of that tiny woman?" asked Joval, mystified by her claim.

"Oh yes! Once, when I was small, much smaller than I am now, Dahlon decided to teach me a lesson about the dangers of fire. He took me by the right hand, holding the palm of my open hand upon the surface of a tin pot filled with boiling water that sat over a flame. I remember hearing the sound of my sweating palm sizzle against the metal… the smell of my flesh burning. He only ceased his torment when my mother heard my screams and came running."

"Good heavens!" gasped the Elf, horrified by Dahlon's cruel actions.

"That was nothing," stated Nayla, continuing her story. "I remember my hand was so badly burned, my entire palm was one large, silvery blister, so large it was; I could not even clench my hand into a fist. After my mother plunged it into a bucket of cold water, she promptly marched back into the dining hall where Dahlon was still warming himself in front of the fireplace. She took up the poker that lay amidst the burning logs and proceeded to take after him. I peered into the room upon hearing the crashing of chairs, just in time to see Dahlon trying to escape my mother's wrath as she decided to give him a taste of his own medicine!"

Joval chuckled as he responded: "Somehow, I can picture Lady Treeborn doing exactly what you had described. She had little patience for such asinine and cruel behavior."

"It was a sight to behold! The mere image of my father dashing to and fro, frantically trying to escape from my mother was enough to stop my tears!"

"I am sure that alone would have been enough to keep your father on his best behavior!" determined Joval.

"Well, needless to say, since that day, he was very careful in his dealings with me, for my mother seemed to sense when I was in trouble, but soon after she died…" Nayla's small voice trailed off as her eyes slowly closed, as though she was attempting to block out some terrible memory.

Joval could not help but feel great sympathy for the little child sitting before him. He reached out, taking her hand into his as he reassured her: "I swear, Nayla, on your mother's good name, you shall never be treated in such a manner by your father again."

Nayla's eyes slowly opened, gazing down upon the Elf's hand gently clasping hers. She abruptly pulled away from his touch.

"In all this time, I never suspected it was as bad as that. Perhaps, my own fondness for your father blinded me to the truth. If this be the case, I am truly sorry, Nayla."

"You have nothing to be sorry for, Captain Stonecroft. I know my father loves you. There is no denying that. I realize he holds you in the same regard as had you been his own son. My relationship with Dahlon has no bearing on what transpires between the two of you. As far as I am concerned, if you benefit from your relationship with him, then so be it. Good for you, I say."

There was something so pragmatic about her way of thinking. Joval was dumbfounded by such mature ideals coming from one so young.

A sudden wave of guilt washed over the Elf. He recalled moments in the past, moments that could have easily passed as nothing more than accidents, the trials and tribulations of a reckless, clumsy child making her way through a much larger world. He cringed internally; now realizing the bruises and the marks she bore were not self-inflicted or accidental.

"Why did you never tell anyone about what was really happening, Nayla? Why did you not tell one of the elders, or even me?"

"I think not… Who would believe the words of a child over that of a high Elf, a great leader like Dahlon Treeborn?"

"I would have believed you."

"Only after I had been beaten within an inch of my life did you believe," countered Nayla.

It was as though the child's words seized his heart, piercing it with the truth. His feelings of guilt seemed to permeate every inch of his body and mind.

"Besides, had I spoken the truth to anyone, do you not think I would merely be accused of ruining that Elf's good reputation, of betraying him and besmirching the Treeborn name?"

"But to endure such abuse…"

"Truth be told, there were many times when he had vented his wrath on me that I had wished he would just kill me. It would lead to his undoing. It would become his own testament of his treatment, and though I be dead, at least someone might have believed without having me *betray* that man."

After a moment of silence the Elf asked: "I am curious, Nayla. During all this time, did it not occur to you to just run away, to escape from Nagana?"

"I was warned that I would face far greater retribution outside the walls of the fortress city. Dahlon said the people would see that I was a *half-caste* as Valtar put it. He said outsiders failing to recognize me as the daughter of a high Elf would enslave me, perhaps stone me in hate, or worse…"

"Good heavens!" exclaimed Joval. "How you survived for this long, how you managed to endure under such desperate conditions is beyond me."

"In my life, it is all I have ever known," she answered in a small voice.

It was only when Valtar had opened the door, did both Nayla and Joval realize the carriage had come to a stop. The Elf peered in as he spoke: "I suggest we rest for the night. Though I may be able to continue on, the horses cannot. They must eat and rest."

Joval nodded in agreement, stepping out of the carriage. He stretched his dormant muscles, numbed by the long ride before accessing the back storage compartment of the carriage where food, bedrolls and other items were stowed for their long journey.

Gathered around a small fire, the three travelers sat beneath a starry sky of a beautiful, deep cobalt blue. They ate their meal in relative silence as a large, full moon slowly climbed above the tree line. High overhead, Nayla's eyes intently studied the tiny, black silhouettes of bats fluttering about in erratic flight. The creatures eagerly pursued nocturnal insects that filled the evening sky.

Valtar's eyes gazed up as the flapping of leathery wings passed over his head. The light of the fire attracted many insects, which in turn, drew more bats to hover above the trio.

"Detestable little vermin!" snapped Valtar, tossing a stone up into the darkness.

"Stop that! They have done nothing to you!" protested Nayla, brazenly catching the Elf by his wrist as he prepared to launch another projectile toward the bats.

"Those nasty little creatures do not deserve to live."

"And who are you to make such a judgment?" questioned the child, scowling at Valtar.

"The Maker of All was playing a joke when He created those vile little creatures. They are freaks of nature!" retorted the Elf.

"I disagree. And for a race that prides itself for living in harmony with nature, you, Master Briarwood, should be ashamed of yourself! You are a sorry excuse for an Elf."

"Those disgusting vermin serve no purpose other than to tangle themselves in one's head of hair," grunted Valtar.

"That is absolute nonsense. Have you ever known anyone to have a bat fly into his hair? I certainly never heard of this. How about you, Captain Stonecroft? In all your thousands of years of existence, have you ever heard of such a ridiculous thing?"

"Thousands of years?" Joval muttered his response. "I am barely over six centuries old!"

"Yes, yes, so you say! The point being; in all your years, have you ever known a mortal or Elf to have had a bat fly into his or her hair?"

The Elf cogitated on her question before he finally answered: "The child is quite right, Valtar. Never in all my so-called *'thousands of years'* have I ever heard of this happening."

"Well, I am sure someone must have had this happen for this story to come about," reasoned Valtar.

"It is nothing more than an old wives' tale, you fool," retorted the child.

Joval laughed at the stunned expression on his friend's face as Nayla's candor and insult caught him totally off guard.

"I shall tell you this now, young miss, I am more than willing to live in harmony with those flying rats if they actually served some good, but they do not!"

"Obviously, you have never taken the time to observe them. If you had, you would see these *'flying rats'* as you call them rid our night sky of bothersome moths that destroy our clothes, insects that devour our crops, as well as mosquitoes and flies that would eagerly drink our blood. In fact, I would say they serve a greater purpose than you do!"

"Why you little – "

Joval motioned for Valtar to bite his tongue. He was surprised by Nayla's observation, for she did speak the truth. "How do you know all of this?"

"All one must do is to open one's eyes to see what bats do under the cloak of darkness. They are fascinating little creatures," stated the child.

"Of all things for a child to be fascinated with, Valtar is quite correct, Nayla. They are rather detestable, loathsome creatures," responded Joval.

"And their night-time forays… It is rather sinister that they would choose the night over the day to be active," added Valtar.

"I beg to differ. Perhaps the Maker of All designed them for the night so they can rid us of all the pests not consumed in the daylight hours by the other animals," explained the child.

"Well, I tend to agree with Valtar. He is accurate in describing them as ugly and sinister, yet for some strange reason you seem to have a fascination for these creatures," noted Joval.

"Therein dwells my fascination. You regard them as being ugly and sinister, *'a freak of nature'* as Master Briarwood described them. Perhaps it is for this reason I can relate to them. I know what it is like to be regarded in the same manner. Though they may not be pleasing to the eyes, as far as I am concerned, they are merely misunderstood."

Both men were momentarily rendered speechless, not knowing how to respond to her statement. Valtar aimed another stone skyward, watching as the winged creatures deftly navigated around the projectile, even in this darkness.

A small stone suddenly hit Valtar square on the chest. He stared in Nayla's direction as she armed herself with another rock, this time slightly bigger than the last one.

"What do you think you are doing?" snapped the agitated Elf, glaring at the girl.

"I am doing what you are doing," she stated emphatically, defiantly selecting a larger stone yet.

"I hardly think so! I am shooing away those disgusting creatures," retorted Valtar.

"As I said, I am merely copying you. I, too, am attempting to shoo away a disgusting creature."

"Why you insolent – "

"Enough!" shouted Joval, rising to his feet. "Stop it right now, the both of you! Drop those stones. Valtar, leave the bats alone. Nayla, leave Valtar to be. I recommend we all get some sleep for tomorrow shall be another long day."

The journey north to Anshen was unhampered and uneventful. During this time, Joval came to realize that Dahlon Treeborn made no attempt to locate Nayla, as warriors and travelers they had encountered on route made no mention of this missing child. Or if he had, Dahlon must have made nothing more than a cursory effort to search for her within the walls of Nagana and perhaps the outlying villages. Whatever the case, the high Elf made just enough of an effort to appease the elders and his peers that he had made an attempt to locate his errant, wayward daughter.

"Are we there yet?" asked Nayla, gazing hopefully out the window.

"No, it is another fifteen-day journey," replied the Elf.

"Fifteen days! Perhaps there is somewhere closer than Anshen that we may go to," suggested the child.

"There are other places closer, but Anshen is the only place you shall be truly safe if your desire is to avoid detection by your father."

"But why would I not be safe elsewhere?"

"If your father has offered a reward for your return, or for word of your whereabouts, there is a very likely chance a villager in Saiyo or any of the other smaller settlements might divulge the information to collect the reward, no matter how small. If that be the case, it will be over for both you and me."

"And the people of Anshen, are you telling me that they would do differently?" queried Nayla.

"Absolutely, if I swore them to secrecy, they would honour their promise. They would never reveal to anyone outside of their village, mortal or Elf, of your whereabouts."

"How can you be so sure? They are probably no different from anyone else. They can probably be swayed just as easily if properly motivated."

Joval gave her a knowing smile as he recalled his time spent with the citizens of Anshen. "Rest assured, child, they are not like the average mortals of Orien. They are honourable and duty bound to do what is right. They are, for most part, considered to be holy men."

"You are sending me to live with holy men?" asked the child, stunned by this revelation.

"I assure you, they are not ordinary holy men, Nayla. They are the Kagai Warrior priests of the Furai Mountains."

"The Shadow Warriors?" asked the girl, her eyes wide-open in awe.

"Yes," answered Joval.

"But they are nothing more than legend – a myth! Unseen and unheard, they are merely phantoms; stories of apparitions used to drive back the Imperial soldiers…"

"They are unseen and unheard only when they choose to be so. I assure you, they are quite real. In fact, I have spent time learning from some of their greatest masters."

"Perhaps they will teach me… perhaps I can become a Shadow Warrior, too," hoped Nayla.

Joval smiled upon hearing her words. "I suppose there is always that possibility. If that be the case, you would not be the first girl they had ever recruited for their cause."

"And what is their '*cause*'?" questioned the child, fascinated by the possibilities.

"Theirs is to protect the religious centers that arose in western Orien after the so-called *'cleansing'* in the prefectures east of the Furai Mountains. Apparently, it happened long before my father and all the dark Elves arrived here after leaving their home in Wyndwood to avoid their own persecution. The Kagai Warriors protect all that is holy. They protect the lives of all those who fled eastern Orien to escape the famine and poverty that accompanied the tyranny brought about by the reigning royal family, by that descent into anarchy."

"How fascinating! I suppose I shall learn more about their kind once we arrive," stated the child. "Perhaps they will teach me how to go by unseen and unheard."

"Indeed, you shall learn all about these mortals in due time."

For the first time in the many days they had been traveling, Joval noticed a small spark of life return to Nayla's eyes.

Valtar allowed the steeds the opportunity to rest. They idly grazed by a creek as the Elf readied a midday meal.

Nayla used the opportunity to explore, following the little creek that bubbled, churned and splashed its way toward a small pond. She took a moment to gaze upon the sun as it danced, sparkling on the surface of the water. Slowly sitting down upon a log, she watched with fascination the life that flourished along the water's edge.

Turtles basked on a partially submerged log as a sulphur-yellow butterfly alighted upon the largest of the reptiles, its siphon-like tongue probing the moist corner of the turtle's eye. The winged insect was attempting to steal away with nutrients it could not obtain from a constant diet of nectar. Nayla giggled with delight, watching as the turtle blinked and flailed in a bid to drive the butterfly away. No longer able to withstand the insect's persistent, unwanted attention, the turtle finally slipped beneath the water.

All around her, large dragonflies hovered and darted, their large, transparent wings rattling loudly as they maneuvered effortlessly through the air, between the tall stands of bulrush. She admired their long, sleek, black bodies accented with bright, iridescent patches of blue and green.

Though mesmerized by their aerobatic feats, her mind began to wander. In no time at all, she was lost, deep in thought as she contemplated her fate. Joval moved silently through the tall grasses as he came to sit by her side.

"You seem deeply entrenched in your thoughts, Nayla. What can be going on in that young mind of yours?"

"My *young* mind was contemplating on how small and irrelevant I must be in the big scheme of things. Dahlon often told me that I was a mistake. He said I was never intended for this world. I cannot help but believe his words to be true. I have no purpose. Why else would he treat me as he does?"

"There is a reason and purpose for everything, Nayla. Whether fair or foul, good or evil, we are all placed here for a reason. Each one of us is like a thread in an elaborate tapestry of life. Woven together we tell a tale, we create an entire image. Separately, we remain but a plain bit of thread."

"So you believe I am part of this tapestry?"

"Indeed you are."

"Then why do I feel that I do not belong? I feel that I am nothing more than the tangled mess of threads that nobody ever sees on the back of the tapestry. Why do I feel so insignificant?" lamented the child.

"Nayla, you have only existed for a mere thirty-five years. You have yet to find your place in this world. Give yourself time. And just because you may feel small now, know that even something as small as a mosquito has the power to affect a being much larger than itself."

"A mosquito?"

"Yes, even a little mosquito," confirmed Joval. "Have you ever been driven to distraction by that ominous buzzing as it hovers around your head at night, waiting for you to sleep, so it may feast? It is something so small, yet it has the power to keep you awake for countless hours, until you are finally forced to act on it."

As if delivered by fate, a mosquito alighted upon the back of Nayla's hand. The ravenous insect inserted its proboscis into her skin to feast on her blood. Using her other hand to draw her skin tight, the mosquito was now trapped, unable to remove its needle-like snout from her taut flesh. Nayla held her hand aloft for Joval to observe.

"Watch what becomes of this mosquito," requested the child. No sooner than she raises her hand up that a large, hungry dragonfly hovered in closer to land upon her hand.

Snatching up the trapped mosquito into its forelegs, the dragonfly's mandibles made short work of its victim, rapaciously devouring this easy meal.

"That mosquito may have been capable of affecting one much larger, but see… there is always another, bigger and stronger, waiting to swoop down; to come in for the kill."

"That is a rather fatalistic point of view," groaned Joval, shaking his head in dismay.

"Perhaps, but it is true."

"So, you consider yourself no more significant than a mosquito," replied the Elf.

"What I am saying is that I am no more relevant or significant as a mosquito in the whole scheme of things."

"How can you say such a thing about yourself?" admonished Joval. "Do not give in to self-pity."

"It is not self-pity. It is the truth."

"Come now," Joval dismissed her words.

"If it were not so, do you not think my own father would treat me with more kindness? That he would not throw me to the wayside so easily?" asked Nayla, her slight shoulders shrugging with indifference. "Dahlon once said that as a half-caste and a girl, I am worthless. I am unworthy of the Treeborn name, unable to carry on the legacy of his people. He said that had I been a boy, even half mortal, at least I could show my worth in battle. Even as a girl, had I been great in stature like you, I might have proven my worth. But alas, I am small: small in stature, small in presence and small in… I am just plain small. I shall never amount to greatness. I will never be anything my mother would be proud of."

Joval shook his head in sadness upon hearing her disappointed words. "Size has nothing to do with greatness, Nayla. Do you not know that true legends are not born; they are made? Some of our greatest heroes were forged in the heat of battle, by the very edge of their sword. Others still, use the power of their words to hold sway over great men. Believe me, all that is needed to acquire greatness is to have the courage to do what others would deem impossible. You need not be great in size to possess that kind of courage."

"Courage is something I am lacking in."

"I beg to differ. It takes enormous courage to survive as you have. It takes incredible fortitude of both body and mind to endure what you have endured."

"Anyone with half a spine can endure a beating," she remarked, her tone flippant, cold and unfeeling.

"Believe what you will; I know differently. But did it not occur to you that to even flee from Nagana, from Dahlon Treeborn, and to venture into the unknown takes great courage."

Nayla answered with a small laugh: "You are the only person I know who would view the act of *running away*; the act of a coward, as being courageous."

"You are not listening, are you?" grunted Joval, his eyes rolling to the heavens.

"I have heard every word you said."

"You may have heard, but you certainly are not listening. If you were listening, you would know that I said; the act of running towards the unknown, to embrace the unexpected takes great courage. When you defied your father by leaving; that most certainly required tremendous courage."

Nayla silently considered his words before finally responding. "You are most unusual indeed, Captain Stonecroft."

"Just mark my words, Nayla. As I said before, just because you are not born into greatness, just because you may not be great in stature, it does not mean you are not capable of great things."

"Do not make fun of me!" snapped the child, weary of hearing his promising words that held no real potential for her.

"Fun? Who is making fun? I am quite serious. Perhaps you are destined for greatness! Do not be surprised if one day you find great and powerful men bending to your will; scraping and grovelling on bended knees before you."

"Do not patronize me, Captain Stonecroft, I may be young, but I am nobody's fool!"

"Ah, now you sound just like your mother," replied Joval, nodding in approval.

"Good!" she retorted. "I shall take your words as a compliment."

"Good!" he responded. "Then stay true to your mother's memory by not ignoring sound advice; the words of others who may be older and wiser than you."

Nayla's eyes peered up to meet his unyielding stare. Even in the dimming light of the day, his eyes seemed to burn with life. It suddenly dawned on her that although she had seen this Elf all her life, she really did not know him at all. He had always been a presence in the Treeborn household, yet his quiet, reserved nature always made him seem somewhat unapproachable.

"Exactly how old are you?" queried Nayla, now intent on learning more about this Elf.

"Where did that come from?" asked Joval, stunned by the abrupt change of subject.

"Never you mind," responded Nayla. "Just answer my question: How old are you?"

"I am a mere six-hundred-and-three-years-old," responded the Elf. "Why do you ask?"

"Somehow, I thought you were older."

"How old do I appear to be?" He gave her a disgruntled frown.

"*Old*." Her answer was succinct.

"How old?"

"I suppose you look to be the equivalent of a mortal in his late twenties, perhaps early thirties."

"That is because I am!"

"See, I told you. You are old."

"By your standards, perhaps I am. Most certainly by mortal standards, I am well beyond *old*, but let me assure you, by Elven standards, I am not."

"You *are* old," reiterated the child.

"Can we not change the subject?"

"Why?"

"We have already established that I am *old*, need I say more?" grunted the Elf.

"Then, for your benefit, I shall change the subject," decided Nayla. "Are you married?"

"Pardon me?" Joval gasped in exasperation.

"Now you are the one who is not listening," groaned the child. "I asked if you are married."

"Can you stop asking such personal questions?"

"Why?"

"Because it is none of your business," grumbled the Elf.

"Why?" she asked again.

"Because I prefer to keep my life private, if I may," responded Joval, unleashing a dreary sigh.

"Well, are you?"

Joval glared at her, realizing that she would persist until she received a satisfactory answer. Finally, he snapped: "Not only is it none of your business, but what is the relevance of this line of questioning?"

"I do not believe you are married," she surmised, as she gave him a thoughtful nod.

"And how did you come to this conclusion?"

"You are far too grumpy. What woman would want to marry a man like you?" answered Nayla.

"You insolent, little snip! Before this journey is through, you will be the death of me!" groaned Joval, his hand dragging down his flustered face.

"I do not believe my mother would appreciate you speaking to me in this manner," goaded Nayla, amused that she seemed to have hit a nerve.

"I do not believe your mother would appreciate your brashness," replied the Elf. "Enough talk!"

"Well, *you* shall be the death of *me* if you refuse to talk. I shall die of sheer boredom in your company!"

"I tell you what, suppose I ask Master Briarwood to keep you company while I drive? Yes, he can ride the rest of the trip inside here with you. I am sure Valtar will be more than pleased to answer all of your questions, personal and otherwise."

Nayla's back straightened, her eyes widened in dismay.

"Ha! I thought that would get your attention! Perhaps, I shall switch places with my friend right now."

"No! If you do, I will not be able to bear it!" pleaded Nayla, suddenly sincerely apologetic.

"Oh, so you admit that I make a better travel companion than Master Briarwood?" queried Joval.

"Yes, he is much grumpier than you are!"

"Pardon me?" He was becoming more exasperated by the minute.

"I mean to say, he is not as personable and understanding as you. I beg of you, Captain Stonecroft, I shall be more mindful of my words if you will only endure this long journey with me," promised Nayla.

"Do I have your word?"

"I promise."

Over the course of their travel, Joval learned much about the little girl, who as a young child would spend much of her time cowering behind her mother whenever he or other Elves were nearby. He came to realize that what initially appeared to be a child's innate shyness was actually a very real fear of any Elf who reminded her of Dahlon. All Elves, even the shortest were still markedly taller than the tallest Taijin man. With their great stature and flowing brown hair, other than the differences in eye color that ranged from brown or hazel to blue, all the Elf men looked alike to Nayla. Though her fear seemed extreme to him once, he now understood that it was not unfounded.

For Nayla, she gradually discovered this quiet and reserved Elf actually had a wry sense of humour and a true sense of valor and honour. Somewhere beneath his cool and aloof demeanour, there was much kindness in his heart. She never dreamed her salvation to escape the cruel hands of one Elf would be facilitated by the compassion of another. Aside from Joval and his own parents, Iaden and Jen-nel

Stonecroft, all other Elves minded their distance in their dealings with both Nayla and her mother. Though always respectful to Lady Kareda Treeborn, much of the respect was only due to the fact that she was the mortal wife of a high Elf and she was instrumental in their peoples' alliance.

Outwardly, the mortals and Elves treated Nayla with respect, being of Dahlon's blood. Unbeknownst to most, she also possessed the sharp ears of the Elf-kind. Nayla could make out the hushed words of those who whispered in her presence.

It was when Joval would speak of her mother that Nayla felt most at ease around him. Perhaps it was because she was the one thing they had in common, the one thread that entwined their two very separate lives. It was obvious to her that Joval had regarded Lady Treeborn with the greatest respect.

"Tell me more about my mother," pleaded Nayla.

Joval's head tilted in curiosity as he considered her words for a moment. "What do you remember of her?"

Her eyes rolled up as though she was hunting for long-forgotten memories buried deep within her mind.

"I remember she was very kind and loving," said Nayla, as a heavy sigh escaped her. "That is all."

"That is a fine memory you should hold fast to," recommended Joval.

"It has been almost seventeen years since her passing. I fear she will eventually fade from my memory as time goes by – and with it, the only sense of love, of any self-worth I ever had, shall fade, too."

"Your mother's love for you was strong. No matter what, it shall endure," promised the Elf.

"How do you know that?"

"My mother once told me that if a woman truly loves her child, all the teachings she instils so her child may grow to be a good and decent person would shine through in the end. Everything she imparts to make her child wise and strong, kind and compassionate, all these qualities will emerge, but must be nurtured. Just as a gardener must tend to his flowers or vegetables to reap the benefits of beautiful blooms or a bountiful harvest, it becomes a labour of love. The end product shall be a testament of her love."

"If that be the case, then what shall become of me? I am a garden abandoned," lamented Nayla.

"Though your time with your mother was cut short, Lady Treeborn has left an indelible mark on you. Up here and in there," stated Joval, as he pointed to her mind and to her heart. "You have your mother's inner strength and fire, I can sense it. I have no doubt you have many fond memories of her, and they shall sustain you for the rest of your life."

For a moment, Nayla silently reflected on his words. Eager to learn and remember more, she asked: "What did you admire the most about my mother?"

"Aside from the fact that she treated with me much kindness and respect, especially after my mother's parting from this realm, I would have to say it was her bold approach to life."

"How so?"

"I suppose the fact that she had defied her parents to pursue a life she wanted rather than to bend to their will was a prime example. She chose to run away from home rather than to be forced to bind herself to a man of their choosing; to marry because it was expected of her. Conformity did not sit well with Lady Treeborn. Apparently, she fled her village and eventually accepted a position in my father's household so she may live independently. That in itself created quite the stir amongst mortals and Elves alike! When all other young women were married off, she chose to forge her own path, to build a life of her own making. That is how she and my mother met and became the very best of friends. My mother always found Lady Treeborn's forthright manner, her ability to speak her mind, rather refreshing. In fact, it was my mother who introduced her to Dahlon Treeborn."

"So your mother was to blame for this pairing?"

"Blame? You really do not appreciate what Lady Kareda Treeborn did for the mortals of Orien as well as the Elves. She was the one who worked with your father so he may better understand the Taijins, their language, their customs, their policies and protocols. Though it is Dahlon Treeborn who sits in council with the elders, it was your mother who was directly responsible for putting him in that position. She is the one who was instrumental in uniting our two races."

"Now why was that even so important? Could your people not survive without this alliance?"

"As Imago entered the Second Age of Peace following the Great War, my parents, as did all the *dark* Elves departed from Wyndwood. After establishing a colony called Starwood in the Emerald Forest, they were forced to move on shortly after. They followed Lord Treeborn into this land to begin a new life far from the home of our forefathers. Many of your father's people were killed during that last uprising against the Dark Lord Beyilzon. Others, unable or unwilling, to face persecution by the *fair* Elves or live outside the enchanted forest chose to enter the Haven. When we finally arrived in this strange land, our numbers were few."

"What was it like to be in Wyndwood?"

"I do not know. I was born in the Emerald Forest of Carcross. I was still a babe in my mother's arms when they made the long trek into eastern Imago. It was not long after we entered this strange land that we were beset upon by unknown enemies. According to my father, at the height of this battle, when he thought all would be lost, we were aided by mortal warriors that seemed to materialize from out of nowhere, from the shadows of these great forests. The Elves and mortal warriors fought side by side and these warriors annihilated the enemy forces, so none lived to tell of this encounter. That was our introduction to the Taijins or more specifically, to the Kagai Warriors."

"So an alliance was not formed back then?"

"Oh no, the Taijins allowed us to dwell in their lands in peace, for they could empathize with our plight. The mortals living to the west of the Furai Mountains fled from eastern Orien due to the religious and political unrest brought about by the internal strife between members of the royal family. The need to form a strong alliance, to coordinate our efforts became more apparent after these past few centuries. As more Imperial Soldiers were sent by a corrupt Emperor to capture and destroy the leaders in a bid to quell their growing fears of a rebellion, a new evil made its way from western Imago in pursuit of Dahlon Treeborn's people."

"The fair Elves? They came after you?" Nayla's eyes were wide with wonder.

"Oh no! Far worse than that! The once mighty Wizard of the East, Eldred Firestaff, fled or was banished from western Imago. In retaliation, he has made the lives of the dark Elves, and all who aligned themselves with us, sheer hell. He carved a path of destruction, and in his wake; he randomly attacked villages, killed innocent, defenceless people, and destroyed the forests, always using fire, his natural element. In fact, I was there when he almost succeeded in killing your father from the back of his dragon."

"But why? What would drive this Wizard to do such a terrible thing?"

"It is my understanding that Eldred Firestaff was deeply disenchanted, bitter beyond words with mankind. The fact that mortal man seemed incapable of proper behavior drove him to the brink of madness. He felt that even after all that King Brannon, the savior of

Imago had sacrificed to bring peace to the lands, mankind was still innately evil, corrupt souls."

"But if his grudge is with the human race, why did he pursue the Elves?"

"Because Eldred Firestaff believed that mankind only flourished and prospered by hiding behind the cloak of the Elven race. As the healers and guardians of this realm, he felt that our compassion for the human race would lead to the corruption and downfall of civilization. He longs for the days before mankind came to being, when the lands consisted of only Elves, Fairies and the Wizards. As far as Eldred was concerned, mankind was an unsightly blight on society; a terrible mistake that was undeserving of life."

"So he believes that by bringing ruin to the race of Elves, mankind would fall."

"Exactly," answered Joval, nodding in confirmation.

"If that be the case, why did he not pursue the fair Elves?"

"That, I do not know the answer to. Perhaps, because our numbers are fewer, he felt that by removing us first, it would pose an easier task to confront the Elves in their stronghold of Wyndwood, after all, there are far more of the fair kind than of us dark Elves. Who really knows?"

"Do the fair Elves still exist?"

"Apparently so," replied Joval. "According to Lindras Weatherstone the Wizard of the West, when he last came by this way prior to your mother's passing, Lord Kal-lel Wingfield still ruled over his domain in Wyndwood."

"I remember the great Wizard! He came to Nagana seeking Dahlon. I remember how he looked so large and imposing in that flowing robe he donned. And that staff of his… In the glow of the crystal set atop his staff, he would show me many wonderful and faraway places he had visited."

"You remember Lindras Weatherstone?" marveled the Elf.

"I may have been the mortal equivalent of an eight-year-old child, but one does not forget meeting a special being of such wondrous, magical powers. Plus, I remember he was very kind to me. I do not forget the rare person who treats me with kindness."

"That is very true," admitted Joval. "I have not seen the Wizard since he last sought out your father, but it is my understanding he spends much of his time amongst the fair Elves in Wyndwood these days."

"Tell me about the fair Elves," requested the inquisitive child.

"My knowledge is limited to stories, legends and lore shared by my parents and the elders who have long departed into the Haven."

"So have you ever seen one of these fair Elves?"

"If I had, I do not recall. I do know that like me, they are of fair complexion, but their hair is like fine threads of spun gold and they all possess eyes of varying shades of blue."

"How very odd!" exclaimed Nayla. She gazed upon Joval's features, particularly his eyes. "I cannot imagine beings so fair."

"No more odd than how we must have appeared to the first Taijins we encountered," responded Joval, with a light laugh.

"Do you ever wish to see the fabled forest of Wyndwood?"

"When I was much younger, I often dreamed of seeing this enchanted place, the home of my father and grandfather, but now…" Joval's voice trailed off as his mind wandered to another place and time.

"Now this dream has changed?"

"It is far better to appreciate what you already have than to long for what will never be. And on this note, we should rest for the night. I am sure the steeds are weary by this day's long journey."

The early morning sun cast the land in a warm, golden haze as fingers of light crept over the Furai Mountains to vanquish the darkness of night. The trill songs of wrens and finches heralded the beginning of this new day; their melodious calls echoing through the sleepy valley as the three travelers readied for another long trek.

Nayla noticed the road becoming rockier, and obviously not as well-traveled, as they continued northward.

"This is the final leg of our journey; by nightfall we shall be in Anshen," stated the Elf.

Nayla's eyes gazed out the window at the landscape as it rushed by. "So we are almost there?"

"Indeed," answered Joval. "And remember, when we arrive, I want you to be on your best behavior. Understand?"

Her little face scowled at him, hurt by his insinuation that she would be anything but well behaved.

"Well?" prompted Joval.

"I understand."

"Will you do your utmost to fit in with these people?" queried the Elf.

"I shall do my best. However, I do not believe I will have a say in whether I shall be accepted, never mind fit in, with these mortals," replied the child, in a meek voice.

"All I ask is that you do not make it more difficult for yourself than it has to be," stated Joval.

"You make it sound as though I shall go seeking trouble for myself," answered Nayla. Her indignation flared as her small arms folded across her chest.

Joval's brows arched up on hearing her tone and then he laughed, but not unkindly.

"You, my little friend, are your mother's daughter!" declared Joval. "Let me just say there will be times when it will serve you well to bite your tongue; swallow your pride and allow yourself to follow the river's current rather than constantly swim against it. You shall soon discover there are some battles in life that are better to walk away from and others that are worthy of a fight. Learn to know the difference."

"How will I know the difference?" asked the girl, perplexed by this riddle.

"I believe in time you shall learn to discern for yourself which ideals and principals you should champion and which ones will ultimately be a waste of your time."

"So you are saying, I should select my fights."

"Yes, and select carefully. Remember, there shall be times in your life when there will be events or situations of which you shall lack the power to change, come what may. Also, there will be times when you shall have the ability to make profound changes; to be the master of your destiny. The secret is to know the difference. You must find the will and grace to accept what must be, as well as having the courage to rise to the challenge to change the things that you can."

"Hmm, it would seem that with your great age, comes great wisdom," observed Nayla.

"Are you again implying that I am old?" asked Joval.

"No. But if I were, then it would be wise for you accept the fact that there are some things that even *you* cannot change," answered the child, offering the Elf a smug smile.

Joval promptly reached up and knocked on the ceiling of the carriage, causing Valtar to bring it to a rolling stop. "I think I shall ride up top with Valtar for the time being, before *you* cause me to age faster than I already am."

"The choice is yours, Captain Stonecroft. I believe I have had enough of your chatter for the time being."

Nayla casually dismissed the Elf with a wave of her hand as he stepped out to join his friend. Joval shook his head in dismay as he secured the door behind him.

"So, Captain, you grow weary of your company," teased Valtar with a self-satisfied grin as Joval, wearing a tortured expression, sat down next to him.

"I shall tell you this; if the words she spoke were coming from the mouth of an adult rather than a child, it would be easier to bear. I must admit, for one so young, she has incredible insight, well beyond that of any mortal or Elf of equivalent age. Perhaps you should get to know her better, Valtar. I do not mind taking the reins for the time being," suggested Joval.

"I think not, my friend! The less I know about her and this insane mission you have embarked on, the better it be for me."

Joval thought upon his words and indeed, this Elf preferred to distance himself from the entire situation. Most evenings, when Valtar and Nayla were forced to share the same campfire, the two of them would say very little to each other. Valtar would quietly brood as he glared at her. For her part, Nayla would respond by merely glaring right back at him, undaunted by his cool demeanor.

"You are right," decided Joval. "It is probably for the better."

For several more hours, the horses plodded on at a steady pace. As the sun sat high in the near-cloudless sky, Valtar brought the carriage to a stop. He freed the horses of their harness and bridle to allow them to graze and drink unfettered. Valtar then prepared the midday meal.

As usual, Nayla would wander off in search of ponds or meadows, anywhere that wildlife congregated. Joval traced her tiny footprints to find her at the edge of a clearing. She was watching intently as two young bucks with nothing more than spindly, first-year growth of antlers, nervously eyed each other. Nayla could somehow sense the Elf's silent approach, motioning him to join her on the ground, surrounded by tall grasses.

"A fight shall ensue," observed the Elf, in a whisper.

"No, not this time," countered Nayla, her voice was barely audible as her eyes remained fixed on the wildlife.

"How do you know?"

"It is too early in the year. The rut does not begin until the fall," she reminded him.

"Oh, you have a point there." Joval nodded in agreement.

"They have other matters to be concerned about," whispered Nayla, motioning to a distant thicket as a mature buck in its prime with a fine rack of antlers still shrouded in velvet, confidently emerged from the vegetation. "He is about to drive them both on their way from his territory."

Sure enough, the buck angrily pawed the ground, lowering its crown of antlers as a bold warning before charging toward the two deer. The young intruders immediately bounded off into a grove of trees, unwilling to confront their much larger adversary.

"See…" the child stated.

"How did you know?" asked the Elf, pleasantly surprised by her prediction.

"I have seen this behavior many times before," answered Nayla, rising up onto her feet.

"Where? When?" queried the Elf. "I thought you were pretty much restricted to the palace grounds."

"Whenever I could sneak off, I would spend my time in the forest, away from the walls of the fortress city," admitted Nayla. "I would much rather spend my time amongst the animals of the wild than amongst the two-legged creatures that inhabit Nagana."

It was early on in their journey Joval had noticed Nayla had a fascination for the complexities of nature, taking every opportunity to study animals of all varieties. No creature, great or small, was too insignificant to pass by unnoticed, scrutinized by her eyes and curious mind. For an instant, he thought that perhaps she was more Elf than she cared to admit.

"You seem to know a great deal about plants and animals, Nayla. Why would a child be so fascinated by nature? You should be playing games…"

For a moment, she thought upon his words before she finally responded: "Animals, whether it be bird or beast, are far more trustworthy than people."

"How can that be so? Animals are wild – unpredictable."

"No, *people* are unpredictable. Animals by their very nature, especially under stress, are expected to be unpredictable; people are not. Whether mortal or Elf, people's behavior, though outwardly civilized, they are still capable of extreme cruelty, especially toward each other. In my mind, this would make them far more dangerous and unpredictable than the so-called '*wild*' animals you speak of."

He thought upon her words and it became clear that she was speaking of the high Elf.

"Besides," she concluded, "I have not the time for games, nor do I have friends to play with, if I had."

The Elf was taken aback by her comment, though she spoke the truth, oddly, there was not an ounce of self-pity in her words. She was merely stating a fact, nothing more.

Rising up on her feet, she tagged along behind Joval. She followed his large footsteps, leaping from one print to the next, her tiny feet landing in his impressions before they vanished. As they returned to the carriage, Valtar had readied their meal, waiting patiently for his passengers' return. They consumed their meal and after they were done, Valtar allowed the steeds another hour or so to replenish their energy before proceeding on their way.

The carriage rattled and creaked as the wooden wheels laboured in the ruts and irregular surface of the diminishing roadway. Nayla rocked to and fro, deliberately exaggerating the swaying motion of the carriage.

Joval's eyes followed her movements until he could take no more: "Do you mind?"

"Mind what?"

"Do you mind not rocking like that?"

"Why? Does it bother you?" asked Nayla, exaggerating her movements all the more as the wheels hit another rut.

"Yes, it bothers me!" snapped the Elf.

Nayla reluctantly stopped as she moaned: "I am so bored."

"Then keep your self amused; find something constructive to do," responded Joval.

"There is nothing to be done," lamented the child.

"Be creative," suggested Joval. "Surely you can think of something to occupy your time."

"I can ask you questions, and you can answer," replied Nayla.

"Oh no, you will not!"

"And why not?"

"Because you have a tendency to ask questions that are far too personal for my liking."

Nayla gave an indignant grunt as she sighed: "So we are back to the beginning, with nothing to do. Boorrinng…"

"Suppose I ask you questions, and *you* can answer?" suggested the Elf, turning the table on the child.

"That is a splendid idea!" praised Nayla. "But do not ask me questions of a personal nature."

"Really? Like what?"

"Do not ask me of my age or if I am married," teased the child, in mock gesture to the Elf. "That line of questioning is much too personal!"

"Fair enough," responded Joval, pausing for a moment to think of a question. "What will you miss the most about Nagana?"

"That is easy: *Nothing*!"

Joval stared at her with raised eyebrows, surprised by her terse response.

"I mean it! I certainly will not miss Dahlon Treeborn; that is for sure!" declared Nayla. Her voice scored by bitterness.

"No need to get testy! It was merely a simple question," stated the Elf, His hands were raised, motioning for calm.

"If he had treated me with even an ounce of respect, never mind with a grain of love, perhaps I would feel differently to that man." Her voice reached a higher pitch as her throat tightened in anger.

"Why do you suppose Lord Treeborn always treated you so poorly?" queried Joval.

Nayla's shoulders shrugged in response. "As I said before, he often told me that I was a terrible mistake, not worthy for this world."

"That is a terrible thing to say, especially since he is a direct cause for your existence."

"Whether that be true, or not, I hardly think it is a reason to treat me so cruelly. Besides, I never asked to be born."

"Perhaps he is bitter because you remind him so much of your mother," determined Joval. "The more I come to know of you, the more I see of Kareda."

"If that be the case, then I shall tell you now; my mother and father always had an uneasy alliance through their marriage. Much of it was a ruse; a means for Dahlon to secure his position in council as you had pointed out. It was also my mother's attempt to secure my position in his high house. She believed that by making it clear to all I was the daughter of a high Elf, one in a position of power, it would somehow protect me from the cruelties inflicted by others. Sadly, it did nothing to deter Dahlon."

"How do you know this to be true?" questioned the Elf.

"I just do."

"Have you always addressed your father as '*Dahlon*'?"

"No. Only when the proprieties that come along with being born his daughter are required will I address him before others as 'father' or 'my lord'."

"That is odd, would you not agree?"

"Not really. If he treated more like a daughter than like a despised acquaintance, then perhaps I would acknowledge him accordingly, but alas, he is only my father by blood and title, nothing more."

The carriage slowly rolled to a stop. Nayla looked up hopefully to Joval.

"Have we arrived?"

"No," answered the Elf, opening the door for both to exit. "As you can see, Esshu Road ends here. It shall be another three leagues through these forests before we reach Anshen."

"So we must walk?"

"We could, but as you can see, Valtar already prepares the horses," responded Joval, pointing to his friend as he unhitched the steeds from the carriage."

"I like to ride," said Nayla.

"Good, for by horseback, we shall arrive well before sunset," stated the Elf, his hand shielding his eyes as he scanned the western sky. The bright, golden orb now sat low over the Iron Mountains. Soon, dusk would settle upon the lands.

"You are not going to make me ride with Master Briarwood, are you?" asked Nayla, in a whisper as she scowled at Valtar.

Before Joval could answer, his friend responded: "Goodness, no! *You* shall be riding with Captain Stonecroft."

Assuming that Valtar always ignored her, the child was momentarily startled that the Elf's sharp ears detected her muted words.

"Good!" she responded in a crisp tone.

With that said, Joval gave Nayla a leg up onto his steed before hoisting himself onto the horse's bare back. They followed an invisible trail, heading northeast. Joval led the way through the forest, following the sounds of a river. Far off in the distance, still unheard by Nayla's ears, the coursing waterway was as clear to the Elves as a voice beckoning them on through the tall groves of bamboo.

Joval motioned for Valtar to stop.

"What is it?" asked Valtar, reining in his steed.

"Do you not hear that?" His voice was hushed as he turned about on his steed, cocking his head in every which way as he listened.

"I hear nothing."

"Exactly! Something is not right. I hear not a single sound of the forest creatures. They hide in fear!"

"You do not suppose…" gasped Valtar, sensing an invisible threat.

"Let us be off! We have not a second to spare!" ordered Joval, sinking his heels into the steed's flanks.

"What is happening?" asked Nayla. She turned to peer up, seeing Joval's eyes darken with concern.

"Something evil lurks here. We must get to Anshen!"

"I thought you said I would be safe up here!"

"In Anshen, yes, but we are not there yet. We are close to the Magare Valley; a route used by the Imperial Soldiers to access western Orien."

"Imperial Soldiers?" asked Nayla, stunned by this news. Her concern grew with the urgency in Joval's voice. "They are close to us?"

"Perhaps, but we will not remain to find out!"

The steeds charged through the forest, the landscape a blur as it rushed by. The pounding of the horses' hooves rang in their ears, drowning out the sounds of their own hearts racing in anticipation of the unseen evil. As though the air was charged with electricity, Joval could now sense the enemy's suffocating presence looming ever closer. Valtar's steed followed closely behind as they careened through the forest, racing towards the river.

"Nayla, if I do not make it, you will have to run! Run as fast as you can to the river. Head north; follow the river to Reyu Falls. Behind the waterfall is a hidden path. Follow this path to the other side. Continue eastward and you shall see a lake; the village is hidden in the forest just beyond its shores. Seek out Master Saibon. Tell him I had delivered you to him," instructed the Elf, glancing over his shoulder towards the impending evil. "Do you understand?"

"What do you mean, *'if you do not make it'*? What are you saying?" asked Nayla.

Again the Elf asked: "*Do you understand*?" His tone was brusque, his words emphatic.

"Yes, but-"

The angry hiss of an arrow sliced through the air directly above her head.

"Stay low!" ordered Joval, urging his mount onward.

Nayla immediately leaned forward, low over the stallion's withers. Clutching a fistful of mane, she instinctively turned her face to one side to avoid impact with the powerful beast's neck as its head bobbed rhythmically in time with its urgent strides.

Joval and Valtar directed their tiring steeds through the densest groves of bamboo, allowing the vegetation to take the brunt of the assault as they wove through, dodging and ducking the hail of projectiles. Soon, the all too familiar whine of arrows piercing the air subsided. The enemy's supply was depleted, but they continued their pursuit, now with swords drawn.

As if reading each other's mind, both Elves simultaneously wheeled their steeds about to face the onslaught. Arming themselves with their own bows, they rapidly dispensed their arsenal, downing the soldiers with deadly accuracy. But still the soldiers came, pouring forth from the ever-darkening forest.

With their arrows now depleted, Joval hastily lowered Nayla to the ground as he gave her final instructions: "Take cover! Run, Nayla! Run as fast as you can! Do not look back!"

Beneath her feet, she could feel the tremor of the ground as though the earth itself was quaking in fear. It reverberated with the pounding of the horses' metal-clad hooves and those of the soldiers' as they proceeded to encircle them. Nayla froze in sheer terror.

"*RUN!*" ordered Joval.

Still, she remained frozen as her eyes fixed on the advancing army. Without warning, the Elf raised his hand high as though he was about to strike out at her. Nayla instinctively leapt back, dashing away in fear. She raced off towards the sounds of the river that she could now detect in the distance.

Joval and Valtar leapt off their mounts. They stood back to back as the remaining thirty-one soldiers surrounded them. An eerie silence fell as the Elves stood their ground, swords poised in their hands. The men, like a pack of hungry wolves, closed in for the kill.

An ear-splitting sound that was neither a scream nor shout shattered the unnatural quiet, echoing through the dimming, twilight sky. The whole forest was reverberating with this noise. The Imperial Soldiers raised their weapons in terror as their eyes darted to and fro, scanning the darkening landscape for signs of this impending peril.

These soldiers were all too familiar with the legends surrounding this great bamboo forest. Many had ventured into these haunted woods, never to be seen again. None ever returned to tell the tale of what happens beyond the Furai Mountains. Only stories of ghostly apparitions that dwelled in these parts filtered down through the ages. Tales of long-dead warriors killed by Imperial Soldiers haunted these parts – specters hungry for revenge, willingly venting their wrath on all who dared enter their domain.

As abruptly as it started, the eerie calls stopped. The unsettling quiet gripped the soldiers in sheer panic. Their fear-filled eyes continued to search the impending darkness as they attempted to steel their frayed nerves. This silence was broken by screams of pain as a mysterious hail of arrows rained down upon the soldiers.

Those fortunate enough raised their shields just in time. Abandoning the dead and the wounded, they dispersed, taking cover behind trees.

In the confusion of the moment, Joval seized the opportunity, turning upon the nearest soldier. His deadly blade arced through the air, dispatching his first opponent. As he turned on his next adversary, the soldier skilfully parried his blows before countering with a swift barrage of his own. The Elf deftly angled and blocked in response, but with the last blow, his timing was slightly off as he maneuvered on the uneven terrain. The edge of the soldier's sword delivered a powerful upward cut, slicing into Joval's right bicep.

"Aaargh!" bellowed Joval. The Elf tumbled backwards as he screamed more in anger than pain.

He quickly rose up to his feet. Unable to wield his weapon in his right hand, he immediately took up the sword into his left, attempting to counter the next assault.

The soldier turned on Joval, charging toward him with his sword held high. As the blade came down on the Elf, Joval immediately raised his own weapon, turning the sword horizontally to block the incoming blow. The soldier's sword came down with such speed and power that Joval's left arm buckled from the force. The soldier's weapon spun down and outwards, sending the Elf's blade flying from his hand. The impact as the swords crashed together was enough to drive him down. Joval collapsed backwards. The jolting shockwaves coursed through his body, throbbing with excruciating pain as it raced down to terminate through his wounded right arm.

The soldier laughed mockingly in triumph as he stood before the Elf, his sword poised in his hands, preparing to deliver a swift death.

To his left, Joval could see Valtar was involved in his own battle, fending off two soldiers simultaneously. It was apparent that help would not be forthcoming. He glanced back up at the soldier, watching as the mortal rose up onto his toes to lift the sword higher so he could execute the death-delivering blow.

He growled in response as Nayla burst out from beneath the undergrowth, throwing herself over Joval. She stared up at the soldier hovering over them.

"My quarrel is with the Elf!" snarled the soldier, speaking in the native tongue of his people. "Out of my way!"

Nayla was undaunted, huddling low over Joval, she pleaded in Taijina, begging for his life: "Show some mercy! He is unarmed! There is no glory in taking the life of one who is defenceless!"

"I care not! I will show him mercy by killing him quickly!"

"Then you will have to kill me, too!"

"So be it, you little fool!" growled the soldier. Taking the sword into both his hands, he turned the tip of the blade down. Hoisting his weapon up high, he drew a deep breath as he prepared to impale both the girl and the Elf onto his sword.

3

the kagai warriors

Nayla's eyes squeezed shut, bracing herself to meet this horrific demise. She clung desperately to Joval, even as the Elf frantically pushed her trembling body away to safety.

"So child, you choose to die with this Elf! It matters not to me," growled the soldier. The muscles of his arms flexed, tightening as he prepared to ram the steel blade through his victims.

The soldier's body convulsed as he took a faltering step forward. Gurgling in agony as an arrow struck him from behind, tearing through the throat; his final words now decided by the arrow's tip. Still, his desire to kill was so intense, the adrenaline and hate coursing through his veins drove him on. With his dying strength and the gravitational pull of death drawing him closer to the ground, he managed to drive the sword down.

As the point of the blade slammed down, Joval immediately rolled to his side, taking Nayla with him. Coming within a hair's-breadth of his body as it tore through his cloak and vest, the sword continued onward to pierce the earth, stopping only after striking against rock. The soldier collapsed to his knees, and then toppled over, his lifeless body crumpling alongside of the Elf's.

Rising swiftly to his feet, Joval snatched the dead soldier's sword into his left hand. Bracing himself for his next foe, his eyes glanced about. Before him stood Valtar, trembling as he gasped for his breath. Exhausted and visibly shaken by the ordeal, Valtar's eyes were closed. His weary face turned skyward as his sword dangled limply from his hand. He seemed oblivious to the blood seeping from a slash on his left cheek.

Joval's eyes cautiously surveyed the carnage. All around them lay the dead soldiers of the Imperial Army. It was obvious arrows had downed most of the men.

Nayla crept up to Joval's side, shocked by the sight of the blood and dead bodies strewn about like broken dolls. She gasped in surprise as Joval grabbed her. Pulling the child away, he concealed her behind his large frame as his sharp eyes caught sight of silent shadows scurrying down from the surrounding trees.

Valtar turned abruptly, startled by the shadowy figures advancing soundlessly toward them. He took up his sword in both hands, anticipating another battle.

"Do not make any sudden movements, Valtar," ordered Joval, in a whisper. "Put your sword down. Do so slowly."

"And die defenceless? I think not!" protested the Elf, gripping the hilt of his weapon. "Not while I still stand."

"No harm shall come to us if you do as I say," urged Joval. He placed his sword on the ground before him, raising his hands up high to show he was now unarmed.

Valtar hesitated, watching as the shadows neared. Reluctantly, he lowered his weapon, placing it down before him. His hands rose up in surrender.

Nayla watched in stunned silence, peering out from behind her protector. Fifteen Taijin warriors stood before them. Their bows were drawn, arrows poised and ready to launch on command.

"I see we share a common foe," announced one of the shadowy figures, as he approached with caution.

"Kagai Warrior, I mean you no harm," said the Elf, opening his raised hands to show he bore no weapons.

"You are lucky to be alive. What business do you have here?"

"I am Captain Stonecroft, a warrior from Nagana," stated the Elf.

"*Stonecroft*! Joval Stonecroft?"

"Yes."

"Well! It has been a good long while since you have been in these parts," chimed a voice in the common speech. From the shadows, a warrior stepped forward from the others to come into full view.

"Chusai Saibon? You are looking well! You have not aged a day since our last meeting," announced Joval, both surprised and pleased to see a familiar face.

The warrior motioned his men to lower their weapons.

"If only that were true, my friend," lamented the man. "I believe you have mistaken me for my father. An easy mistake to make, for I was a young man when we last trained together under my father. That was over thirty years ago."

"Yaruke Saibon?" queried Joval, staring into the mortal's face as his eyes ignited in recognition.

"Indeed," said the mortal, nodding his head in confirmation.

"You have grown since I was last in your company," remarked Joval, clasping wrists in warm salutation.

The Kagai Warrior laughed heartily: "*Grown*? Grown old, most definitely! I am now about the same age as my father was when you were last here," acknowledged the warrior.

"It is still good to see you again!" exclaimed the Elf, embracing his warrior brother with a hug. "And how is your father? Is Master Saibon well?"

"As well as can be expected for a mortal in the winter of his life," responded Yaruke, with an affable smile. "You shall see for yourself!"

"Valtar, this is Yaruke Saibon," Joval introduced his friend to the Kagai Warrior.

The Elf nodded in acknowledgement as he stated: "Your arrival was most timely; we would never have survived the attack if it were not for you and your men."

"Timely? You Elves are like the mortals from the east. You seem to have an uncanny sense for heading directly into danger, if that was your intention," mused the warrior. "I was about to dispatch decoys to lure the Imperial Soldiers into our trap when you happened by."

"You already knew of the army's presence?" asked Valtar.

"Of course," replied Yaruke. "I held back on sending forth my own warriors when the two of you came crashing through the forest with the enemy in full pursuit. We merely waited for you to deliver them directly to us!"

"Whatever the case, I am grateful for your presence," the Elf thanked him, recalling that this was a typical ploy used by the Kagai.

"We were merely doing what our people have always done," smiled the warrior, eyeing the Elf with concern. "I suppose the two of you know that you are both bleeding… quite badly I may add."

Valtar's left hand touched lightly upon his slashed cheek. Closing his eyes, he began the process of healing his wound. Joval glanced down at his injury that sliced through his right bicep, rendering it useless.

"That is a rather nasty gash. Would you like my father to tend to it?" offered Yaruke, grimacing in empathy.

"Thank you, but no. That will not be necessary," said Joval. "If you can just help to press the wound together, I will mend it."

Yaruke moved to the Elf's side, his hands carefully ripping the bloodied sleeve wide open to give him access to the gaping wound. Gingerly, he pressed the two edges together as Joval's left hand concealed the torn flesh. His eyes closed as he whispered a healing incantation in Elvish.

Yaruke felt a tingling, warm sensation; a healing energy rising from the area of the wound as the tension of muscles tightened as fibres reconnected and fused together. The Kagai Warrior released his hold on Joval's arm. It was at this very moment, he set his eyes upon the tiny figure shielded in the shadow of the Elf's towering frame and flowing cloak.

"Well now, who do we have here?" asked the warrior, gazing down upon Nayla as her dark brown eyes peered up to meet his.

Yaruke escorted the unexpected visitors to Anshen as the other warriors worked quickly to conceal the bodies, hiding all evidence of the invading army. It would now appear that he soldiers on this scouting mission had vanished without a trace, whisked away from this realm by mysterious forces.

The mortals of the east were suspicious and superstitious by nature and the Kagai Warriors used this against them. By sowing the seeds of fear and doubt, they were able to hold large armies at bay. Many soldiers were unwilling to venture into the unknown, to confront the *invisible demons* that roamed the shadows of western Orien. Those who dared enter were motivated by avarice or driven by poverty to accept the promised financial rewards to track down and kill those accused of insubordination; potential rebel leaders who could one day return to the east to restore religion and order. Alas, none of these soldiers ever returned to collect their rewards.

Joval lifted Nayla down from his steed as all dismounted before Reyu Falls. She stood mesmerized by the thundering waters as it cascaded down a sheer cliff into a foaming, churning pool. High above, a massive rock formation projected from the river like a dragon's great head staring up to the heavens. The clear, icy water splashed against this rock, swirling and boiling as the river divided into two, before rejoining as one again as it plummeted downward.

"Come this way," ordered Yaruke, as he motioned the others to follow. Nayla watched as he and his horse vanished behind the curtain of water.

"Go ahead, Nayla. Follow him," instructed Joval, taking up his stallion's reins into his hands.

Against the wall of granite, she peered behind the waterfall to spy a narrow footpath. Again, the warrior waved her on. She followed the warrior's steps, her eyes straining to see through the translucent veil of water that served to conceal this path. Her skin tingled as the mist rising from the pool clung to her hair and clothes. As it touched her, she shuddered involuntarily, not from the cold, but from an invisible energy. It made her feel alive, her spirit invigorated – an inner cleansing of sorts. It was a feeling she had no recollection of ever experiencing before.

Emerging from the secret trail behind the waterfall, Yaruke escorted the group through a thick grove of bamboo. As they stepped out of this forest, they could see the lake, its glass-like surface reflecting the tiny, white stars that now dotted the evening sky.

Yaruke stopped. Cupping his hands to his mouth, he gently whistled the call of the nightingale. Across the lake, somewhere in the dark shadows of the forest beyond, a soft whistle answered his call.

"They know we are coming," announced the warrior, guiding them onward.

As they walked through a lush, green meadow past the lake, onward to the forest, Nayla could not help but feel a multitude of eyes staring at her. Her little head darted about, her eyes adjusting to the growing darkness. Finally, her eyes focused on the silent shadows that lurked in the surrounding forest.

Yaruke stopped to unbridle his steed, removing its saddle so the animal could rest and graze in comfort. The Elves followed suit, removing the horses' bridles before releasing them to join the other steeds that grazed down by the lake. As they turned to follow the warrior, the shadows that tracked them in the surrounding forest emerged from the darkness, making their presence known.

"Father! Look who I have brought back with me!" called out Yaruke.

"Well, this is a delightful surprise!" responded an elderly warrior, the people parting to allow him through. "If my old eyes do not deceive me, it is Joval Stonecroft."

"Indeed it is," said the Elf. He bowed in respectful greeting before this mortal.

"They were being pursued by the soldiers of the Imperial Army, delivering them directly into the trap we had laid," explained Yaruke.

"Ha! After all this time, trouble still follows you wherever you go,

Joval!" declared Chusai Saibon, stepping forward to welcome the Elf.

"In more ways than one, Master Saibon," attested Valtar on his friend's behalf, his head motioning towards the child.

Nayla stood in silence as she scowled menacingly at the Elf.

The old warrior stood before the girl, scrutinizing the child. "You brought your daughter, Joval?"

"Oh, no, no! She is not my child. This is Nayla, daughter of Lord Dahlon Treeborn."

"Hmph, you do not say! She looks more mortal than Elf – like a Taijin," stated Chusai.

"Look again," suggested Valtar. To Nayla's dismay, he lifted her long, dark tresses to expose the small, Elf-like points of her little ears.

She immediately turned on the Elf, swatting at his hand as she kicked him deliberately and hard on his shin.

"*OOOW*!" howled Valtar, hopping about on one leg as his left hand nursed the pain she inflicted on the other.

Those gathered before them laughed in amusement.

"Judging by her actions, I would say she is definitely the daughter of Lady Kareda Bansho," assessed the elderly warrior.

"That she is," acknowledged Joval, grabbing the child by her arm to pull her away from Valtar's reach. "Nayla, say good evening to Master Chusai Saibon."

"You know of my mother?" questioned Nayla, recalling her mother's maiden name.

"Know of her? Of course I knew her! She was one with us before heading to Nagana to start a new life," answered the elderly warrior.

"She lived amongst your people?"

"You could say that. But enough for now; let us go to my home. We can talk more. What say you?"

Inside the quaint log cottage, Master Saibon and his son welcomed the weary travelers. They were offered a modest meal and the opportunity to rest in the safety of this secluded village. Throwing more wood onto the fire, Chusai carefully stoked the flames before setting a large pot of water on to boil.

With their appetites appeased and the water finally hot, all relaxed over steaming bowls of fragrant tea. Joval recounted his time spent training with Master Saibon to Valtar and Nayla. He then informed his old Kagai friends of his forays into enemy territory, and his latest encounter with the Imperial Army as they ventured to Anshen.

As he spoke, Nayla listened with torpid interest as Joval's voice became nothing more than a distant drone. She began to drift off. Exhausted by the day's adventure, her eyelids grew heavy as she fought a losing battle to remain awake. Eventually, sleep laid claim to her body and mind as she slumped against Joval's arm. The Elf scooped her sleeping form into his arms, laying her upon a mat. The elderly warrior removed a blanket from a wooden chest, handing it to Joval. He spread the blanket over top of Nayla, leaving her to sleep.

Joval returned to sit with the others at the low, wooden table in the center of the room. Seated upon a cushion across from his old master, he glanced back at Nayla and released a weary sigh.

Chusai gazed over the Elf's shoulder as he asked: "So, my friend, tell me - and speak the truth - why are you here with Lord Treeborn's daughter?"

"I must ask a great favour of you, Master Saibon," confided Joval, speaking in a whisper.

"What is it?"

"I would not burden you with such a request if I had another option, but I do not."

"Yes, yes… what do you require from me, my friend?"

"You know her mother is dead, yes?"

Saibon shook his head in sadness as he responded: "Yes, I received word upon her passing long ago. It was most unfortunate… Kareda was like a daughter to me."

"Master Saibon, Nayla is in grave danger if she remains in Nagana. Valtar and I, we spirited her away from the fortress city."

"You stand corrected, Joval. *You* spirited her away. *I* was an unwitting and unwilling victim of circumstances," grunted Valtar, making his position clear to all.

"Fine! *I* removed Nayla from a treacherous situation. I feared that it would only be a matter of time before she would meet her demise if she remained in the fortress city."

"This sounds most dire. Who would want to do harm to the daughter of a high Elf?" questioned Saibon, thoroughly perplexed by these ominous words.

Valtar shook his head in response, averting his eyes from Joval as he still refused to accept his role other than that of driver.

"Her father," answered Joval.

Saibon was momentarily taken aback by his response. "Lord Dahlon Treeborn? I fail to understand."

"I cannot even begin to understand this mess, but she is a victim of Lord Treeborn's wrath. Kareda Treeborn made me promise to protect Nayla, for Lord Treeborn was heavy-handed in his dealings with the child. How dire the situation was, did not come to light until the night of our departure from Nagana, when I was made witness to her suffering."

"Lord Treeborn punished her? For what reason?"

"Punished is a gross understatement to describe what she had endured, master. Dahlon had bound and gagged her, thrashing her to within an inch of her life, all because she spoke up in a bid to ensure the safety of a battalion of warriors he was about to deploy on a dangerous mission."

The old warrior studied Joval's eyes as he mulled over his words. "You are not exaggerating the situation, are you?"

"No, master. This child is in very real danger if she remains with her father. She has already endured more than what is humanly imaginable and it is beyond me how she managed to survive in such misery for as long as she has."

"I take it Lord Treeborn does not know she is with you."

"I do not believe he has even made a concerted effort to seek her out. And even if the truth be discovered, what I shall be made to suffer will only pale in comparison to what she shall be forced to endure if he should ever get his hands on Nayla again."

"So you are seeking sanctuary for this child?"

"I do not know where else to take her, master. You are my last hope to redeem this life that Lord Treeborn so willingly casts aside."

Saibon considered the sleeping child for a moment. He looked to his son for his candid opinion.

"Father, she is the daughter of the one we once knew as Kareda Bansho. It is our duty to offer this child a safe sanctuary. Kareda had often risked her own life to assist our cause. I, for one, cannot turn my back on her daughter during her time of need," replied Yaruke.

"Joval Stonecroft, I know you well. You would not jeopardize your standing as a captain, nor break your code of honour as a brother warrior on a mere whim. You have always proven yourself to be honourable and trustworthy. I believe your concern for this child's safety is genuine. For this reason, I shall allow her to stay."

"Thank you, master!" Joval sighed in relief.

"We will keep her safe," promised Saibon.

"Your people, they will not breathe a word of Nayla's presence to outsiders?" queried the Elf.

"Of course not, my friend," promised Chusai Saibon.

"I beg that you be patient with her, master. She is very intelligent and mature; mature beyond her few years, but she is damaged."

"Damaged? How so?"

"Her will to survive is strong, but I sense that her last encounter with Dahlon Treeborn has crushed an already fragile spirit. I have healed her body as best I could; however, her soul is in disrepair. I lack the power to help her in this matter."

"By bringing her here, you have already taken the first step in helping her. The fact that Kareda was well-liked and respected, there is a chance my people will treat this child with the same regard."

"One can only hope. As a daughter of a high Elf, one who sits in council with the elders of Orien, her father's standing did little to shield her from disparaging remarks and the cruel treatment of others."

"With time, we shall see what happens," replied Chusai.

"You should know, master, though Nayla be half mortal, it would appear she is blessed with almost the same ability to see and hear as my kind," said Joval. "Given time, there is a chance she may revert to more human qualities, but perhaps with greater training, those senses could be honed and put to good use."

"Does she possess the eternal life of an Elf?"

Joval thought upon Chusai's question for a moment. He knew that his people did not actually possess immortality, but certainly by human standards, it would appear so. If he chose to remain in this realm, then he too would eventually perish, succumbing to old age many centuries from now. It was only when an Elf entered the Twilight to depart for the Elf Haven, the magical realm where his people originated, would he live for an eternity.

"No, she does not possess eternal life," confided Joval. "She shall be longer lived than a mortal, but it is apparent that she is aging much faster than an Elf."

"I see," responded Chusai, with a nod of understanding. "It shall pose an interesting challenge for me. In all my eighty years, Elves wishing to learn about warriorship from my people have always been a presence here, living and learning side-by-side with my warriors, but always departing for the outside world when their training was complete. This is the first child we have accepted from the outside, Elven or mortal, to actually live here. Obviously, her stay shall be much longer based upon her age and longevity. It shall be… interesting."

"I have no doubt it will be, master."

The elder Saibon glanced up at the Elves, offering to top up their bowl with fresh tea.

Joval's hand covered the top of the bowl as he thanked the old warrior: "I shall be retiring for the night, master. Tomorrow, Valtar and I wish to continue our journey northward to the pass in the Magare Valley before returning to Nagana."

"What awaits you to the north?"

"We received word that the Emperor had been directing his armies to this destination. It is my understanding they gather in strength. There are rumors they plan to invade our lands."

"I shall spare you a long, unnecessary journey, my friend. It is true they gather in force; I have sent my men to keep watch over the growing activity in this area. I will tell you this now; they are a superstitious lot. The soldiers fear entering our lands so instead, they send forth only small battalions, one at a time. Each time, they wait for their comrades to return, and each time, they do not. Now, these soldiers lie in wait in the Magare Valley. They are waiting for Lord Treeborn and the elders to push forth an army to invade the east. They have set up traps and snares to ambush our warriors in this valley, not knowing that if we should ever mount an attack on *them*, we would use the secret pass to the south; a much more direct route to the Imperial hordes in Keso."

"So Nayla was right then. She had somehow intercepted a message delivered to Lord Treeborn regarding the potential for a great calamity. Apparently, he had been warned to strengthen his forces before dispatching them on this mission. Treeborn dismissed this warning; stating that his informants were over-reacting. He was preparing to send forth a small battalion to search out and destroy those responsible for securing this region of the Magare Valley. Even as we speak, Lord Treeborn's warriors journey northward to do battle."

"As long as your warriors do not enter this area, there will be no blood-shed. We are that much closer to the valley, yet we cannot be bothered to drive back their efforts because we know that, at least for now, they are too fearful to enter western Orien to wage open war. Each time they send soldiers to scout out the lands as the Emperor await word of our location and numbers; his wait is in vain. None of his soldiers return to report back to their leader. The soldiers *mysteriously* disappear from the face of the earth," stated Chusai, with a knowing smile.

"Tomorrow, I shall journey southward. I must intercept my warriors before they advance much further. They must be warned; they must turn back," said Joval.

"How far away are they?" asked Yaruke.

"They are only four or five days behind us."

"If they be so close, why send them back?" inquired Chusai.

"Are you suggesting that we invade the valley, now knowing what fate awaits us?" queried Valtar.

"What I suggest is, since your warriors have come this far, my men already know the lay of the land; where the Imperial Army's *so-called* traps are hidden. Together, we shall have the upper hand."

"How many soldiers congregate in the pass?" asked Joval.

"It was last estimated at a mere two-hundred."

"Two-hundred!" gasped Valtar. "Lord Treeborn dispatched only fifty warriors! We shall be overwhelmed!"

"I will have another seventy-five warriors at your disposal in a day or two," said Saibon, with an encouraging smile.

"We will still be greatly outnumbered!" exclaimed Valtar.

"Rest assured, Valtar, Master Saibon would not suggest such a thing unless he knew we would have a definite advantage," advised Joval, contemplating their options.

"Indeed, my father would not intentionally and unnecessarily risk the lives of our men, being that there are fewer than one hundred of us left to protect our lands and people. I do believe he has a plan," assured Yaruke.

"And a grand plan it is indeed!" vowed the senior Saibon, with a twinkle in his eyes as he gave Valtar a reassuring wink.

"I shall leave tomorrow to meet up with my men. I will guide them into Hebeku Valley where we shall meet up with the Kagai Warriors."

"Do you not wish to spend at least one day here in Anshen? With the child?" asked Master Saibon, glancing over at Nayla as she slept.

"I do not want to miss my men and time grows short. Let us do away with the enemy before their numbers continue to multiply."

"Do we leave in the morn?" asked Valtar.

"Yes," confirmed Joval; "at first light."

Nayla's eyes slowly opened. In the dim light of morning, she glanced about the unfamiliar surroundings. In the fireplace, situated against the far wall, the still-warm embers of a long-dead fire continued to defiantly exude heat. The low table that she sat at last night was abandoned.

Where is everybody? Where is Captain Stonecroft? Nayla's mind raced as she came to the realization that she was alone in the cottage. Leaping to her feet, she peered out the window. The morning sky was a sombre gray as the first light cast by the sun barely made its presence known over the Furai Mountains.

Her eyes scanned the landscape that was still enveloped in an ephemeral veil of mist rising from the surface of the calm lake. In the meadow, down by the shores of Lake Anzan, she could make out Chusai Saibon and the two Elves. Joval and Valtar were preparing their horses; they were making ready to leave.

Nayla panicked. Throwing the door open, she ran bare feet across the dew-laden grass, running with all her might. The Elves bade farewell to their kind host as they mounted their steeds. As they turned their stallions about, Nayla screamed out: "Wait for me! I am coming!"

"Let us depart, Joval," urged Valtar, motioning his friend to turn away. "She is no longer your concern."

Joval glanced across the meadow to see the panic on the child's face as she raced toward them.

"Please wait!" pleaded Nayla, her voice echoed across the lake.

Her desperate pleas wrenched at his heart. Joval dismounted from his steed, turning to face her as she dashed past Chusai Saibon straight toward him.

"Do not leave without me," begged Nayla, her tiny hands grasped his arm. "I shall go with you!"

"The field of battle is no place for a child, Nayla," reasoned Joval. "We go to prepare for war."

"When will you return?"

"I cannot say."

She tugged at his arm as she pleaded: "Do not leave me with these strangers!"

"Once you come to know these people, they will no longer be strangers," promised Joval.

"Please, I beg of you, do not leave me!"

"I must, Nayla. If I do not leave now, the warriors you sought to protect could very well perish. Plus, there is a chance your father will dispatch men to search me out. I cannot risk this if you are to remain here, in secret."

"Were you not even going to say farewell?"

"You were sleeping."

"That is a sorry excuse! You were going to leave without so much as saying *'good-bye'*!" cried Nayla. "You are no different than my mother; she never said good-bye either. She abandoned me, just as you are doing now!"

"Your mother died, Nayla."

"Just as you shall be dead in my eyes, too, if you leave me!" wailed Nayla, her tiny clenched fists striking Joval on his chest. "You shall be dead to me, too!"

"Do not be so dramatic, Nayla!" admonished the Elf, seizing the child by her wrists.

Nayla angrily wrenched free of his hold as she asked: "When will you return? Will I see you again?"

Joval was silent as she stared up into his brooding eyes.

"Well?" she demanded an answer. "Am I going to see you again?"

"No," he whispered.

This single word resonated in her ears, stabbing her soul like a knife. Nayla crumpled to her knees before the Elf.

"See, you *are* like my mother, you will be nothing more than a memory – dead in my world."

Joval could see her eyes were dark and liquid, yet she succeeded in fighting back her tears as he knelt before her.

"I thought you were my friend…" she whispered sadly.

"I am," assured Joval, his hand resting gently upon her shoulders.

"Would you abandon *him*?" asked Nayla, her gaze turning to Valtar. "Would you leave Master Briarwood during his time of need?"

Joval was at a loss, his mind racing to find the right words to comfort the child.

"I thought not!" hissed Nayla, pushing his hands off her shoulders. "Well, I do not need you! You are like *him*! You are like all the Elves. You never cared for the likes of me!"

"Do not say such things, Nayla! You know it is not true!" protested Joval, embracing her in a hug.

She stood before him. Her arms hung limp by her side, unwilling or unable to reciprocate. The Elf could feel her small body trembling in rage as the helpless feelings of abandonment washed over her once again.

"Nayla, I have done as much as I could possibly do for you," whispered the Elf. "You will be safe here, away from your father. And for once, you shall have other children to play with. I promise you, it will not be that bad. You must give this new life a chance."

Nayla's heart was numbed by the very fact that he, the only person aside from her mother to ever show a grain of interest or concern for her well-being, was about to leave her in the company of strangers.

"Your mother was well loved and respected by the people of Anshen. Do her proud, Nayla; keep your chin up," ordered Joval, his hand gently lifting her face so their eyes could meet. "Be mindful of Master Saibon, for he has much to show and teach you."

"What can he teach me that you cannot?" asked Nayla.

"Did you not say you wished to become a Kagai Warrior?" queried the Elf.

Her eyes opened wide at the possibility.

"If you wish to learn the secrets of these great warriors, you would be wise to learn from the best. Do you not agree?"

Nayla nodded her head in understanding.

"Good," said Joval, with an approving smile. "In time, Master Saibon can tell you stories about your mother that will make your hair stand on end! You will soon discover how much of your mother lives on through you, through your words and your actions."

"Joval! We must be on our way," urged Valtar, his hand shielding his eyes from the golden rays of the sun that now burst over the distant mountains.

"Perhaps one day, we shall meet again, Nayla," said Joval, gathering his steed's reins.

The child shook her head as she replied, "No. If I become a Kagai Warrior, I shall go through this world unseen and unheard. I will be nothing more than a shadow."

Joval's head cocked in bewilderment, uncertain if these were the words of a bitter child or one who truly wished to pursue this treacherous vocation.

"Listen to Master Saibon, or you shall have to answer to me," cautioned the Elf, wheeling his stallion about.

Her shoulders slumped in dejection as she watched both Joval and Valtar charge off westward, disappearing into the early morning mist.

Chusai Saibon stood next to her, observing their departure. He gazed down at the girl as he spoke with a kind smile: "Today is the beginning of a new life for you, my child."

"If I am to begin a new life, then I no longer wish to be the daughter of a high Elf," decided Nayla. "I no longer wish to be cursed with the Treeborn name."

"Very well then," agreed the warrior priest. "What name do you wish?"

Nayla shrugged as she responded: "My father called me by many names, but none that is appropriate to repeat."

"What name did your mother call you by?"

"My Taijin name is Takaro," answered the child.

"Why do we not call you Takaro then?" suggested the old warrior, smiling down at his new charge. "It is a lovely name."

"I have not been called by this name since my mother died," she replied wistfully.

"Do you know what *Takaro* means in my people's language?" he asked.

"My mother once told me, but I do not remember," responded the girl, shaking her head in sadness.

"It means *Noble Child* and I do believe you have the character and fortitude to live up to the name," said Saibon, with a knowing smile.

"*Nobody's Child* would be more fitting. I am not destined for nobility or greatness. I am a nobody."

"Well, Takaro, it is my understanding that you wish to become a Kagai Warrior. Now, that is a grand aspiration indeed, especially for a girl!"

"Too grand?"

"Grand, yes, but it is not impossible," replied Chusai Saibon. "If that be the case, there is much work to be done, Takaro."

For seven years she toiled. Like the other females in the village, she was taught to cook and clean for the warriors and the boys training to one day become great warriors. For the longest time, she was quite satisfied, content just to be living without the constant threat of Dahlon Treeborn's presence. Neither was she subjected to the same level of scrutiny and unsavoury remarks cast in her direction by those less tolerant. She lived with Yaruke Saibon's family, and they treated her with the same regard as their own daughter.

She would help care for their two young children, both of whom grew and matured much quicker than she. Eventually, she was forced to deal with the fact that the youngsters she once cared for were now older, both physically and mentally, than she.

Yaruke noticed that Takaro was beginning to distance herself from his own children, unable to deal with the fact that although she had now lived for forty-four years, she was no older than a girl of perhaps fourteen mortal years. Standing not even five feet tall, she was miserably stunted for an Elf and was considered small even by Taijin standards.

During these years, Joval Stonecroft never did return. It was only through the stories repeated by warriors returning from battle did she ever learn about the Elf and his exploits, and that he was even still alive.

She knew his travels would bring him northward, yet he would never show his face, to see for himself, what had become of her. It made her bitter to know that he, too, had washed his hands of her. She had no doubt that once he felt he had kept his promise to her mother, fulfilling the task, and was no longer morally obligated to do anymore; she no longer existed in his world.

As time crawled by, more and more of her time was spent with Chusai Saibon, listening to his stories of old as well as his wisdom and the teachings of his people's beliefs. One day, as she delivered an armload of firewood to Master Saibon's cottage, she stopped to watch as the elderly warrior, now too infirm to engage in the physical aspects of teaching, sat upon a chair watching his son Yaruke instruct a new generation of warriors.

"Takaro, sit with me. Look at how these boys are still struggling with something as basic as body angling," Chusai Saibon snorted in disgust, watching as a bamboo training sword cracked down sharply upon one of the boys.

The new pupil had shifted his upper body away from the downward strike, but failed to move his leg as well. Yaruke's training sword smacked him callously just above the knee.

"See!" exclaimed Chusai. "Had it been a real sword Yaruke wields, the boy would be missing his leg now!"

Takaro nodded in agreement. Her eyes turned to the old warrior as she changed the subject: "Master Saibon, I have worked tirelessly doing what was asked of me so that I may earn a place amongst your people. I know these boys, all of whom were much younger than me when I first came here. Now, they all train as disciples of your art."

"And?" responded Chusai, suspecting where this comment was leading.

"When will my training begin?"

Chusai Saibon considered Takaro's words before he answered: "You, my child, began your training from the day you first arrived."

She frowned at the retired warrior as she questioned his words: "How so? You have relegated me to nothing more than a cook and servant."

"And what have you learned in all this time?" queried Chusai.

"Other than to cook and clean; to cater to the whims of the menfolk, nothing that pertains to training," answered the girl, heaving a disheartened sigh.

"Nothing, you say? I beg to differ! You have learned to live in peace with those around you; something I admit I had grave doubts about during your first few months. But aside from social skills, what else have you learned?"

Takaro's small shoulders shrugged in response.

"Think, child!" urged the old man, staring intently into the girl's eyes. Finally he stated: "Patience! In all this time, you have learned about *patience* and how to be patient."

"Patience?"

"Yes, indeed. That is why you did not ask if you can begin your training, the physical training, from day one."

"I did not ask sooner because I was certain you would say no to my request."

"And had I said *'no'*, it was only because your body was not ready for the rigors of training. Your mind, however, set to work all on its own."

"What do you mean?"

"In your heart, you knew you were not truly ready to endure the physical demands of a warrior's training regimen, yes?"

"I suppose."

"So instead, while these boys and the more seasoned warriors trained, what did you do, Takaro?"

"I would bring their food, their water, pick up after them…"

"And I noticed how you listened and observed as they trained! You listened to Yaruke's words of instruction, did you not?"

"Yes… but that is not the same thing as training."

"Again, I beg to differ." Chusai Saibon gave her a wry smile upon hearing her naïve words.

"How so?"

"Do what I do," requested the old Kagai master. Slowly rising to his feet, he held forth his walking stick as though it were a sword. With unexpected ease, he parried and countered an attack by an invisible enemy. "Now here, take my walking stick and do exactly what I just did."

Takaro took up his stick, and with the fluidity of a dog forced to walk on its hind-legs, she attempted to emulate her master. Embarrassed by her efforts, she slumped down in defeat next to him.

Taking the stick from her hand, he lightly rapped her on the head as he ordered: "Watch again; pay close attention."

Again, Chusai repeated the same motions, his last move effectively decapitating a flowering weed that grew before him. He handed the stick back to Takaro. "Now try again, but this time, close your eyes."

"Close my eyes? How can I see what I am doing?"

"Trust me, child. Now close your eyes. Visualize everything that you saw me do."

Reluctantly, she did as she was told. In her mind's eye, she could envision Chusai Saibon's deliberate strokes and fluid movements. She replayed them over in her head.

"Can you see how I made each strike, the way my wrists would turn to angle the blade – to change its direction? Notice how I would place my body behind each strike so the power came not from my hands or arms, but from my entire body?"

"Yes."

"Now this time, instead of seeing me go through the motions, visualize yourself, sword in hand, doing the exact same thing."

Takaro's hands automatically tightened their grip on the walking stick. Chusai observed as her muscles twitched as though she was maneuvering a lethal weapon. Beneath her closed lids, he could see her eyes following an invisible adversary.

"Now, open your eyes, Takaro. Show me what you know," prompted the old man.

Nayla rose up onto her feet. Again, her eyes closed for a moment as she replayed the images in her head. Suddenly, as though she was guided by an invisible force, the weapon she wielded in her hand came to life, parrying and countering against an invisible foe, coming down to separate a flower from its stalk.

Chusai clapped appreciatively as he praised her: "Not bad at all, my child!"

She stood before him, momentarily stunned by her own performance. Slowly, a small smile crept across her face as the realization that she was capable of learning by using her eyes, ears and mind, finally sank in.

"Now, my dear, you know these past seven years were not a waste of time. While the boys before us only began their training, you have been training all this while."

"So I am now ready to join them?" she asked hopefully.

"That shall be Yaruke's decision. You must just be patient."

"I must still wait?"

"Yes, and remember, patience is a virtue; something you have yet to discover, obviously."

"What does patience have to do with training?"

"In the warrior arts, patience has *everything* to do with training. *Patience* will allow you to not only know a technique or skill; it shall permit you to know all the intricacies therein. It will allow you to expand on your knowledge beyond the physical realm. *Patience* will allow you to assess a situation rather than to rush headlong, plunging recklessly into danger. Do not be in a rush to die. Death comes soon enough… And remember, *patience* will steady your hand and shall spare you the grief of taking an innocent life because you did not act in haste."

Takaro silently absorbed his words, feeling foolish. "Then I, too, shall be patient, master."

"Good, because unlike these youngsters, you have a good long time to hone your skills; to perfect the arts," said Chusai, with a knowing smile.

From that point on, Takaro spent all her free time, observing the others as they trained. She listened and watched, and for every new technique she studied, she would envision in her mind the minute details, all the subtle movements unnoticed by the young warriors in training. Whether it was basic avoidance or hand-to-hand combat techniques, Takaro rehearsed each one over in her mind, replaying how she would apply the techniques against opponents of varying sizes.

Although her presence was not welcomed by some of the older boys, Takaro continued to stay after delivering their meals and drinks, always watching and listening as she went about her daily business. One day, as the men waited for their lessons to begin, Takaro stood alongside them, watching as the boys trained.

Yaruke was teaching them how to break their fall to minimize injury when pushed or thrown to the ground. Her mind continued to assess each technique, rehearsing them over and over in her head. As she absentmindedly picked up the ladle and bucket, preparing to replenish it for the men, she turned away. She accidentally stepped into one of the boys as they were quickly dispersing.

The little bit of water left in the bucket splashed up, spilling onto the boy's trousers.

The boy's face reddened in embarrassment and anger as the others laughed for the placement of the water stain made it appear as though he had urinated on himself.

"Look at what you have done, you clumsy oaf!" shouted the boy, a fifteen-year-old that stood a good head taller than her.

"I am sorry," apologized Takaro, as the others chuckled at his misfortune.

"Is that all you can say?" he growled before giving her a hard, deliberate shove.

"How dare you!" shouted the girl, stumbling backward into the men. Lowering her right shoulder, she pushed back at the bully.

In retaliation, the boy's hands went to her small shoulders, shoving her with all his might. The ladle and bucket flew from Takaro's hands as she fell. Her hands came down to her sides, breaking the impact of her fall. To everyone's surprise, she quickly and smoothly rolled backwards over her left shoulder, rising effortlessly onto her feet.

The sound of laughter quickly turned to gasps of surprise as Takaro dove for the boy, tackling him about his waist. Both went to the ground as she leapt atop the boy's chest, pinning his arms with her knees. Seizing him by his hair, she wrenched his head about to force him to look at her as she demanded an apology.

"Say you are sorry!"

"Never!" shouted the boy, struggling against the much smaller girl that now sat perched on top of him.

"Say it!"

"To a girl? Never!" His answer was as defiant as the first time.

"Why, I will show you!" hissed Takaro, as she seized a fistful of his black hair.

As the boy cried out in pain, the sea of spectators parted as Yaruke intervened. Plucking the girl off her hapless victim, he reached down and seized the boy by his ear, pulling him up onto his feet.

"I do believe an apology is in order," stated the warrior.

"Sorry," grumbled the boy, his eyes pleading for forgiveness.

Yaruke cuffed him on the back of his head: "Not to me! Say you are sorry to Takaro."

The boy bowed and apologized once more, this time to the girl.

"Apology accepted," responded Takaro, knowing full well that the meaning of his words were hollow.

"You must learn to use your head before you use your fist," ordered Yaruke, scolding the boy.

"My apologies, master, I meant no disrespect to you," the boy lowered his head, humbling himself before Yaruke.

"We shall talk tomorrow, for now, think about your actions," rebuked the warrior. "Now, be off with you!"

The boy bowed once more before taking his leave, scurrying off with his young friends.

Takaro picked up the ladle and bucket, turning to replenish it for the men. Yaruke motioned for one of his senior disciples to lead the others through a punching drill as he turned his attention to the girl.

"We need to talk," said the warrior.

Takaro lowered her head in shame as she stated her case: "I did not mean to hurt him, Master Saibon."

"Oh, I believe you did, and I certainly believe you could have if you had set your mind to it."

"I am sorry."

"I am afraid an apology will not suffice this time. You need to learn a lesson; to redirect your energy and to control your temper."

"I shall accept my punishment," sighed Takaro, in resignation.

"Good! You shall be required to show up each day after your chores. And everyday, you are to train with the others."

"Wh… what?"

"Six hours a day, you will train with these boys. Are you ready for this?" questioned Yaruke.

"Yes… yes, of course!" stammered the girl, unable to conceal her excitement. "Thank you, Master Saibon! I will not disappoint you! Thank you so much!"

"Do not be so eager to thank me now, Takaro. You may live to regret ever wanting this."

4

in pursuit of perfection

On a somber, gray autumn morning, Takaro gathered with her adopted family and the other citizens of Anshen to lay Chusai Saibon to rest. The old warrior had passed away peacefully in his sleep at the ripe old age of ninety-three.

It was as though he had planned the day of his departure from this realm. He was very talkative the day before his passing. Yaruke remained by his father's bedside, listening as the old man retold countless tales of his youth. The elder Saibon shared in his great adventures, his moments of enlightenment as he trained with his own father, as well as the wisdom of the warriors of old. He also passed onto Yaruke some sage advice as to Takaro's own future and then, when he was done, when he had shared all he wished to impart, he fell silent. Chusai Saibon never spoke again, waiting quietly to begin a new chapter in the story of his life.

In the early morning hours, while the stars still shone and a hunter's moon still glowed brightly like a perfect, iridescent pearl against a cobalt sky, the senior Saibon passed from this realm.

In the eleven years she had known him, Chusai was the wise and compassionate grandfather Takaro always longed for. Though in his latter years he was too feeble to train her physically, he shared in his wisdom, patiently guiding the girl as she ventured into this bold, new world of warriorship.

Those around her wept, unashamed of their open display of grief. As the heavens opened up, the raindrops mingled with their tears of sorrow. For Takaro, the rain was welcomed. Although her grief was great, as deep as Yaruke's and the others, she did not shed a single teardrop. Even burdened with feelings of shame and guilt, she did not cry. It was as though an emotional well had dried up in her.

As time went by, she no longer marked her existence in years, but instead, measured it by the passages of those around her who were born, lived and died. And just as surely as spring followed winter, Yaruke Saibon was in the autumn of his life and his son Medaru stepped out from his shadow to come to the forefront. The small boy whom Takaro once cared for was now a mature man well into his twenties. He was responsible for all aspects of their physically demanding training while his father worked with the seasoned warriors; honing their mental skills, teaching them strategy, as well as the more esoteric aspects of their training that separated the legendary Kagai Warriors, the Shadow Warriors of the Furai Mountains, from all others engaged in warfare.

For the mortals of Anshen, Takaro was the eternal child, or more specifically, a teenager of fifteen mortal years. For her, these beings seemed to live and die in a blink of an Elven eye. She was often torn when she would hear the mortals tell her how grateful she should be that she was blessed with such longevity, for they had no idea of her suffering as she watched the ones she loved die; knowing full well that many generations of the Saibon family would come and go in her lifetime. It was a very discomforting feeling to know that she would outlive Yaruke's children, his grandchildren and even his grandchildren's children.

Her early years training under Yaruke Saibon's supervision, and then his son's, was as much a mental struggle as it was physically challenging. Lacking the size and the strength of the boys she trained with, Takaro was quick to learn how to adapt each technique to work to her advantage.

Much of her earlier training was fraught with much anguish as the boys would bully and intimidate her, each trying their best to drive her out. The more they pushed, the harder she pushed back, unwilling to relent to their torment. Her tenacity and unwillingness to give up eventually worked in her favor, garnering respect from her fellow students as well as Yaruke and the experienced warriors. She became as skilled as the men. Still, though she had lived longer than most of the men in her company, she was still physically the equivalent of a fifteen-year-old; too young to join her warrior brothers in battle.

For over two decades she perfected her skills. Takaro's abilities and knowledge was at such a level, she would assist Yaruke's son Medaru in instructing the boys that had now come of age to train. Now, she shared her knowledge with others although by mortal standards she was no older than the oldest boy in the group. Some of the foolhardy lads, assuming she was nothing more than a *weakling* girl would cruelly test her, pushing her whenever the opportunity arose.

One such occasion arose when Medaru left Takaro orders to oversee the class as they sparred while he tended to other matters. The largest of the boys immediately decided to ignore her instructions. He stood before her, his arms resting defiantly across his chest as he stared her down.

"Mekai, find a partner to work with, do so now," ordered Takaro, ignoring his icy stare.

"Look around you. Everyone is paired off. There is no one left, but *you*," stated the boy, annoyed that she refused to be intimidated by his presence and resistance to comply with her demands.

"Then I shall work with you," offered Takaro.

"*Me*, fight against *you*? A *girl*? Ha! You make me laugh!" scoffed Mekai, refusing to cooperate.

"We are not going to fight. We are going to train," corrected Takaro, rolling up her sleeves.

"Fight, train, what is the difference? You are a girl. You are weak like a girl, you train like a girl, and you fight like a girl," snorted Mekai in disdain, as he challenged Takaro.

His harsh tone and condescending words meant to humiliate caused all others to desist in their activities as they listened to the verbal exchange.

Watching as the other young disciples cleared a path for an anticipated brawl, Takaro responded by merely turning her back on the much larger boy. She chose to walk away from him.

"See! Master Yaruke Saibon might sing her praises, but that girl is a coward!" taunted Mekai.

Takaro's nerves bristled as his mincing words struck a chord, but still, she refused to fight him.

Keodai, Medaru Saibon's own son, stepped forward in her defense as he scolded his friend: "Mekai, do not be a fool. Takaro may be a girl, but need you be reminded that she has been training since long before you were even born."

"I am well aware of that, but all it means is that not only is she a girl, she is also a freak of nature," taunted the boy. He grabbed hold of Takaro by her hair, yanking back on her ponytail to show all her pointed ears.

Without warning, Takaro's hand reached up, seizing Mekai by his littlest finger. She squeezed. The boy yelped in pain, immediately releasing his grip on her hair. With one hand on his wrist, the other locking his arm out straight just above his elbow, Takaro pivoted and unceremoniously hoisted him over her right hip to dump him onto the ground.

With a loud *'thud',* Mekai landed hard on his back; the wind knocked out of him. Still controlling his locked arm, Takaro used her shin as a fulcrum, wrenching the boy over to flip onto his stomach. Pouncing onto his back, she plunked down hard; forcing out what little air he had left in his lungs. Seizing his other appendage, Takaro maneuvered the boy's arms behind his body, locking them between her knees. With both her hands now free, she reached for his hair, yanking back hard on his head.

"You owe everyone here an apology for disrupting their lessons," growled the girl.

"I owe nothing!" grunted Mekai.

Takaro released her grip on his hair, squeezing her knees together. This caused Mekai's arms to strain against their sockets.

"Do not make it so that you are unable to train, Mekai. Say that you are sorry," ordered Takaro.

"You would not do-"

"Oh yes, I would; just a little more and I shall dislocate both your arms from your shoulders," she warned him.

He groaned in pain as her knees squeezed together so his elbows almost touched behind his back.

"Sorry! I am sorry!" yelped the boy, unable to tap out.

Takaro immediately released her hold just as Medaru appeared to take control over the class.

"What happened here?" asked the warrior, watching as Mekai slowly stood up.

"Takaro attacked me. She pushed me to the ground, she did!" growled Mekai, pointing an accusing finger at the girl.

"I did no such thing!" protested Takaro.

"Yes, she did, Master Saibon. It was totally unexpected and unprovoked!" insisted the humiliated boy.

"Just as grabbing me by my hair or saying that I fight like a girl was unexpected and unprovoked," she countered.

"Well, you do fight like a girl!"

"Oh?" Medaru scowled upon hearing the boy's words. "So how was it that you were on the ground and she was not?"

"She cheated! She took me by surprise!" snorted Mekai

"That is a lie!"

"Father, Takaro speaks the truth," insisted Keodai, willing to face the boy's wrath after their lesson was done. "Mekai was the troublemaker in this matter!"

"I just refuse to be ordered about by a girl," explained the bellicose student, as he glared at Takaro.

"Mekai, you say that Takaro fights like a girl. Can you demonstrate how this is so?" asked Medaru. "Can you show us how her fighting techniques are different from the way you or any of the boys would fight?"

"I suppose…" Mekai answered with obvious reluctance.

"Good! Face me and bow," instructed Medaru, "and then, bow to each other in respect."

"Right now? Right this minute?" stammered Mekai, stunned by this order.

"There is no better time than the present! Show your fellow students this so-called '*girl*' fighting," insisted his master.

Both Takaro and Mekai complied, each bowing to the other. As she raised her head, her eyes locked with the boy's. She gave him a small, yet unmistakably menacing smile; an omen of what was to come.

Mekai's eyes opened wide in terror. He took a faltering step away from her as he gasped: "She is going to kill me!"

"She will do no such thing! This is just a demonstration," countered their master, pushing the boy to face his opponent.

Takaro waited for Mekai to make the first move. Each time his fist lashed out in her direction, she easily angled and pivoted out of harm's way. As he tired, she made her move, striking and then quickly maneuvering behind him.

For Mekai, it was becoming extremely unnerving. Each time he sparred, every boy he would come up against would constantly back away from him. He was the largest and strongest of them all, often using brute force rather than skill to overpower his opponents. He was not used to an adversary that did not fearfully back off. Instead, Takaro would *tag* him, and then vanish, only to reappear behind him as he turned around. This time, the boy panicked. His fist swung backward, blindly striking out behind him. He caught Takaro on her chin with such force; it sent her flying to the ground, her jaw dislocated.

Medaru and his disciples gathered around her as Mekai stood a respectable distance away, preparing to take flight in case his victory was premature.

Takaro picked herself up from the ground.

Keodai gasped as he exclaimed: "Takaro, your jaw! It is broken."

Takaro shook off her pain. Rotating her jaw, she used her hands to *snap* it back into place with grinding precision.

"No, it is not that bad," insisted the girl, through clenched teeth.

"Are you hurt, Takaro?" asked Medaru.

She was rather unfazed by the impact. It was nothing compared to the other injuries she had sustained as a young child. She dusted herself off as she answered: "I am quite fine, master. Let us finish this."

"Hear that, Mekai?" warned Keodai, eager for the boy to get his comeuppance. "She is going to finish you off!"

Mekai ducked behind Medaru as he declared: "She's going to kill me!"

"She will do no such thing," insisted Medaru. "But if you wish to concede, so be it."

Feigning his fear, the boy turned as though in surrender, knowing full well a true Kagai would never attack in such a situation. Takaro, in response, lowered her guard. Mekai immediately turned on her, this time kicking in her direction. She responded by angling away just enough to avoid contact. As his foot skimmed past her chest, she caught his ankle in the crook of her elbow. She quickly rose up to take away his balance.

As Mekai hopped about on one foot, struggling to remain upright, Takaro seized his foot in her hands, giving it a quick, hard twist. The torque was enough to cause the boy to flip in midair, going down face first. Once again, Takaro pounced on top of him, restraining him by pinning both his arms behind his back.

Yaruke, having just arrived in time to witness this bout and Mekai's humiliating defeat, leaned toward the boy. With a wry smile he announced: "Perhaps we should all learn to fight like a girl if this is the end result!"

"You have proven yourself, Takaro. You may get off of Mekai now," ordered Medaru.

As the boy brushed off the traces of dust and humiliation, the elder Saibon advised him: "Your number one mistake was to underestimate your opponent."

"Huh?" grunted Mekai, still bewildered and embarrassed by his defeat.

Yaruke unceremoniously rapped the boy on his head as he continued his reprimand: "Let this be a lesson to all, never believe for one minute that just because your opponent seems unworthy, that there is always the possibility that he; or *she* in this case, may be faster, smarter or more experienced than you. As Takaro had just demonstrated, size was not the determining factor in who won this contest. Come with me, young man!"

All watched as Yaruke seized Mekai by his ear, leading him away to further chastise the boy in private.

"As for you, Takaro, you shall no longer be training and working with these boys. You shall become my father's responsibility once more," said Medaru.

Her body began to tremble in fear as the prospects of being ejected from her lessons gnawed at her conscience and heart.

"But master, please do not remove me!" Takaro gasped in disbelief. "I am sorry! I swear; this will never happen again! I will do anything you ask. Please do not end my training! This is my life! This is all I have; all that I know."

Keodai and the other boys scowled in resentment at Mekai, knowing full well that he was to blame for Medaru's decision.

"Takaro, it would be foolish for me to allow you to continue in this manner. It is detrimental to you," explained the warrior, watching as her head fell in shame, her eyes cast down in disgrace. "I should have done this some time ago."

Again she pleaded: "I beg of you--"

Medaru raised his hand for silence as he spoke: "From this day forward, you shall train with the men."

A collective gasp of awe from the young disciples filled the air.

"The men? The *real warriors*?" asked Takaro, stunned by her mentor's words.

"Yes, I do believe you are more than ready to learn about the weapons of our trade from the best," stated Medaru, satisfied with his decision. "My father will be most pleased to share in his wealth of knowledge with you."

"This is most humiliating," groaned Takaro, holding forth her bow for Yaruke's inspection.

"And what is the problem? It looks like a longbow to me," answered her master in a dismissive tone, fastening a padded length of leather to her left forearm.

"But this bow is meant for a child! Look at it. This is *not* a *longbow*, this is a... a *shortbow*," she insisted. "This is a complete and utter travesty! I have been given a toy!"

Taking the bow from her hand, Yaruke placed the nock of the arrow onto the string. Drawing it back with ease, he took aim at the distant target. His fingers released the arrow, the string snapping forward to deliver the projectile with perfect accuracy, striking its mark.

"Hmm! I have never known a toy to do that!" exclaimed her master, handing the bow back to the girl.

She was silent as her face reddened with embarrassment as she grumbled: "Being cut-down, the bow just looked so ineffective."

"It was not cut down. Appearances can be deceiving; you know that. Look at my bow," ordered Yaruke, holding his weapon vertically. "It is taller than you, yes?"

"Yes," acknowledged Takaro.

"Take it in your hand. Take this arrow and see how far you can make the arrow travel with this much larger bow."

Holding Yaruke's bow before her, she immediately realized she was much too short to handle a full-sized weapon of this nature.

"Stand on this log," instructed her master. "From here, your draw shall be unimpeded by the tall grasses and anything that projects from the earth.

Elevated a good eight inches above the ground, Takaro positioned herself to face the target. With a much shorter draw length and lacking his strength, she was able to pull the arrow back only half as far as Yaruke did. Struggling to increase her draw-length, she pulled her right shoulder back causing her left shoulder to tilt in.

"I would not do that – " Before Yaruke could finish his sentence; Takaro released the arrow.

As the bow jolted back into its relaxed state, the string of deer sinew snapped forward, striking first across her left breast, and then along the length of her left forearm, totally bypassing the protective arm guard.

Takaro leapt off the log, howling in pain. She hurled the bow down like it was a white-hot lump of coal as her shoulders arched up and her chest caved in with the stinging pain inflicted by the string. She clutched her smarting breast and arm as Yaruke in turn, howled with laughter.

"That was not funny!"

"I tried to warn you," chuckled the warrior, wiping away his tears.

She struggled to remove the strip of leather that was meant to protect her forearm. To her chagrin, the string caught her on the underside, from her elbow down to her wrist, striking along the length of her forearm. A perfect, long, rectangular welt appeared before her eyes.

She had no doubt her left breast was marred with a nasty welt as fierce as the one rising up on her arm.

"How bad is it?" asked Yaruke, still attempting to regain his composure for her benefit.

"As bad as you had planned it," snapped Takaro, her right hand nursing her wound.

She shook her head in dismay as she watched his less than sympathetic reaction. These humans were so unlike the staid, reserved Elves. They were always quick to show their emotions and when they did, it was as though an emotional floodgate had opened. Whether they were unabashedly laughing with joy or weeping openly in sorrow, they unashamedly expressed their feelings.

Takaro assumed it was in their nature to do so because, comparatively speaking, their lives were only a fraction of that of an Elf. These people lived for the moment. Elves on the other hand were always in control of their emotions. The Elf maiden would cover her mouth as she discreetly giggled while the men seemed detached, almost aloof about every situation, until they were pushed to react. Perhaps, with their long lives, they became more jaded with the passing of time.

Yaruke grabbed her wrist, examining the raised, red welt. Unlike an Elf, Takaro would be rewarded with an ugly, dark bruise: a *Kagai tattoo* as the men liked to call it. "Well, that shall leave a nasty mark for a good, long time," assessed her master.

"I am fine," remarked the girl, pulling away from Yaruke's grip.

"Yes, you will be in a week or two," smiled the warrior.

"Let us get back to the business at hand," insisted Takaro, wishing to divert his attention from her embarrassing plight.

"Oh, yes," agreed her master. "As I was saying, the longbow – *your* longbow, was designed specifically for someone of your stature. Just as the sword you bear was made specifically for your draw length, so too was this bow."

Takaro's eyes fell to the blade concealed within the scabbard secured to her left hip. She recalled how she had complained bitterly that she did not wield a long, dangerous sword as the others did. It was only when Yaruke pitted her against another armed warrior did she realize that a longer blade was only good if you were able to draw it before your opponent could produce his weapon.

Her arm was far too short for a full-sized sword; forcing her to take a step back with her left foot as well as pulling her left hip back so the blade can be completely unsheathed. By that time, her opponent would *dispatch* her before she even had a chance to parry his first blow.

She eventually came to learn that the size of one's sword was not the determining factor of how dangerous the blade was. Instead, it was one's own skill in handling the weapon that determined whether one died by the edge of the blade, or not.

"You witnessed first hand what happens when someone of your size takes up a weapon that is far too big. My bow looks much larger than yours, but when you tried to use it, not only was it cumbersome, you were only able to draw your arrow part way. There was no power behind the projectile."

Her master pointed across the meadow where her arrow had fallen terribly short of its mark.

Takaro's sharp eyes made out the black and brown pheasant feathers that tipped the arrow, allowing it to stand out against the green grasses and weeds.

Yaruke observed as she released a slow, disheartened sigh. "Takaro, look at yourself. Your fellow warriors know that although you have yet to be tested on the battlefield, you have trained longer than most of them have been alive."

"And for this reason, I should expect more of myself," grumbled Takaro, in disappointment.

"Your abilities show," assured Yaruke. "The men all know, for they have felt the pain you are capable of inflicting. Because of your size, because you are a woman, you know you have had to train harder and longer than your brothers to be better than them. You had to be faster, more precise in the execution of your techniques. Believe me, all this shines through. This long, hard road you have laboured on has only served to steady your hand with the sword and has given you far greater control not to injure others when it is so very easy to do so. You have become one of the most feared of our warriors by virtue of the fact that you are more skilled."

Takaro's chin lifted as her eyes peered up at Yaruke. It was apparent she was ready to resume her training.

"Now, had you used a bow specifically designed for someone of your stature and your draw-length, the arrow would have traveled farther and faster. It would have had power behind it. And to add insult to injury, not only did you miss your mark, you will also receive a reminder as to why a little girl like you, should not be using a big bow like mine," stated Yaruke, pointing to her battered arm.

"Yes, I understand now," sighed Takaro, in resignation.

"Yes, I believe you do," nodded her master. "Do you know why you were struck?"

"The bow was too big for me?

"No. It was the manner in which you drew. When you pulled back on this string, you attempted to make up for the lack of draw-length by over extending yourself. You pulled your right shoulder too far back and at that very moment, you caused the string to rest against your body. When you fully extended your left arm, your left shoulder turned in causing your chest to be in the line of fire when you released the arrow, thereby snapping the string against your body. Now, let us start again. Pick up your bow."

Takaro silently absorbed his words. Staring at her bow with a degree of contempt, she cringed upon reliving the vicious assault inflicted by the offending weapon. She stooped to reclaim it from the ground.

"As for your forearm, raise the bow up again. No need to arm it, just hold the bow up as you would if you were taking aim."

She held the bow before her as Yaruke examined her grip and her arm positioning.

"Number one: There is no need for this death-grip. The bow is not about to leap from your hands and run away. Relax your grip. Do not allow all this energy to ball up into this tight fist."

Takaro instantly loosened her hold.

"Number two: Always line up these two bones. Position them, one above the other. Do not hold your arm so these bones are lying horizontally."

He held her hand in the same position as he slowly rotated her forearm so the bones, the radius and ulna, were now placed one above the other. "See... Now this wide part at the elbow no longer protrudes in the way. Notice too, how the arm guard is now in position to actually protect your forearm from the string as it is released."

Takaro nodded in understanding.

Plucking an arrow from her quiver, he handed it to her. "Now take aim."

She carefully positioned the nock onto the string, slowly drawing back. Her eyes homed in on her target.

"Pull back until your draw delivers the nock of the arrow and your fingers to the right corner of your mouth. Hold it steady... Now, do not release the string like you are plucking and pulling at a stringed, musical instrument. Instead, let the string *slide* smoothly off your fingertips."

Taking heed of his words, Takaro lined up her sights. Releasing the arrow, it sliced through the air to strike the tree trunk.

She smiled, pleased that this time, she hit the tree.

Yaruke assessed her targeting, "So tell me, did you mean to place the arrow so high up on the tree's trunk?"

"Yes."

Her mentor looked at her, one eyebrow raised in doubt.

"No." She changed her answer.

"I did not think so. But at least this time, your arrow flew with enough speed and power that it hit the tree, though it was well off your anticipated target. Try again. This time set your sights so you are aiming to strike the heart of a man, say about my size."

Takaro carefully took aim and once again, her arrow hit the tree but this time, well below her target.

"Again," ordered Yaruke.

She repeated this process until her quiver was empty. The warrior could see the mounting frustration as she eyed the tree, now riddled with arrows. Two came to within an inch or two of her desired mark, the rest embedded too high, too low, too far to the left or to the right of the target."

"Let us try that again," suggested Yaruke.

Takaro struggled to remove the arrows as he plucked the ones placed too high for her to reach. Embarrassed by her demonstration, she sheepishly replenished her quiver. They both moved to her original position.

"Again," ordered her master.

Taking up another arrow, she took aim and let it fly. The projectile lodged itself well off its mark yet again. For a lingering moment, both stood silent as she scrutinized her aim.

"Aarrgh! I hate this!" declared the girl.

Seething in absolute frustration and rage, Takaro threw down her bow and tore off the quiver that hung from her right hip. She promptly dumped the arrows out onto the ground, kicking them so they scattered before her. Snatching one from the ground, she gripped it into her trembling hands as she snapped it over her raised knee. When her tirade was done, Takaro's whole body was quaking in anger, her chest heaving as though this emotional and physical outburst expended the same energy as if she had run a long distance. She collapsed to the ground in a trembling, angry heap.

Her master knelt down before her as he asked in a calm voice: "Why do you rage so, child?"

She slowly raised her head and as their eyes met, he could see the pinpoints of anger and frustration burning in them.

"Because I want *this* to be perfect! *I* want to be perfect! I want to strive for perfection, but it is well beyond my grasp!"

"*Perfection*?" repeated her mentor, as he laughed, but not unkindly. "My child, to strive for perfection is beyond anyone's grasp. It is an unattainable goal. For both mortals and Elves alike, perfection does not exist. Instead, I recommend you strive for personal excellence. It is far more realistic and it is much more attainable."

Her heart stopped racing and her breathing calmed as she listened to his wisdom.

"Now, are you ready to strive for personal excellence?" he queried, his hand extended before her.

Takaro took his hand into hers, allowing the warrior to hoist her back onto her feet. She collected her scattered arrows, placing them back into the quiver. She assumed her position, ready to receive further instruction. To her dismay, Yaruke wandered out toward the tree, directly into her line of fire.

"Over here, Takaro," called her master, waving her to join him. "Stand over here."

The girl's brows furrowed in curiosity. She reluctantly moved forward, standing next to him.

"You wish for me to shoot from here? You jest, right?" quizzed Takaro.

Yaruke shook his head in all seriousness.

"I am but two paces from the tree," responded the girl.

Her mentor looked at her, and then measured out the steps to the tree trunk. Standing about seven feet away from the tree, he determined: "You stand corrected. You are now about two and one half paces from your intended target."

"You mock me!" retorted Takaro. "Even a blind man can hit the tree from where I stand."

Yaruke's brown eyes scrutinized the tree's bark. All over was evidence of Takaro's poor aim. "Perhaps you are correct, but from what I can see, of all the many arrows you dispensed, only two have come close to hitting your mark. When you can prove to me that your aim is better than that of a *blind man*, we will move on."

Taking the knife from his belt, he carved a small *'x'* onto the tree's trunk that measured about her shoulder height from the ground.

"I want you to hit this," stated the warrior, the tip of his blade retracing the mark. Once all of these arrows are grouped on this mark, you shall take one step back and repeat the process."

"But - "

"No '*buts*', Takaro," interjected the warrior. "This is no different than when I taught you how to use the throwing darts. I recall you had the same problem with your aim. Remember how I made you practice repeatedly until you hit your mark although you were but two paces away? Remember how, only after each and every one of those darts met their mark, that I would allow you to take a step back? "

"Yes," answered Takaro.

"Well, child, this is no different. The weapon has changed, but the training is still the same. Until you can group each and every arrow from where you stand, there you shall remain. Once you succeed, I will allow you to take a step back, and so on, and so forth."

"Very well, master."

"Now remember, at the very moment you hit your mark, think about how you stood. Think about the grip of the bow in your hand, the draw of the arrow – think of all the minute details that allowed you to hit the mark in the first place. Once you comprehend what you did to succeed, repeat everything exactly as how you did it. Do it until it becomes ingrained not just in your memory, but in your body, too. That way, it shall become as natural as any other movement that you make, just like walking or breathing."

Takaro's eyes closed. Her arms fell limp by her sides as her breathing became slow and deep as she concentrated on his words. When her eyes opened, she found renewed energy and greater focus as she took up her bow and arrow. Taking heed of her master's words, she dispensed her arrow, delivering it dead-on the mark where the two lines intersected. Soon, she released a rapid succession of projectiles until her quiver was empty. With Yaruke's nod of approval, she took a step back, repeating the process. Each arrow met its mark, and each time the arrows were compressed into a tighter and tighter grouping.

By dusk, under a diminishing sky, Takaro practiced relentlessly although her muscles were becoming fatigued. Yaruke stood up from the log he was resting on as he watched the girl. From twenty paces, her aim was now as accurate as it was from two.

Undoubtedly, her keen eyes aided her, but the warrior priest knew that above all else, it was her determination to better her skill that helped to steady her aim. Greatly encouraged by her vast improvement, he stated: "Takaro, take this to heart: unlike the rest of us, you have a good long time to improve on your skills. Like everything else you have been taught, this too will take time to master. One day you will be a great archer, mark my words."

With her final arrow in hand, she focused on the last one to hit its mark. As her eyes homed in on this projectile, to impress her master, she was determined to split its shaft with the last arrow.

Drawing in a deep, cleansing breath through her mouth, an errant gnat was suddenly vacuumed into her mouth and plastered to the back of her throat. Nayla's eyes were opened wide in surprise and her immediate response was to gag and cough. Clinging stubbornly to her now dry mouth, the small insect flailed helplessly, its tiny wings fluttering in vain as Nayla frantically coughed and jumped about to dislodge the unwelcome intruder. With her focus now completely lost, her fingers slipped from the string allowing the arrow to take flight.

To her master's dismay and surprise, he was forced to act. Yaruke pivoted his upper body just enough to allow the misguided arrow to fly past him. The warrior priest shook his head in disgust, issuing a reminder as he walked away: "As I said, Takaro, *one day* you will become a great archer."

5

# of women... and assassins

With the passage of time, the days dissolved into weeks, the weeks into months, and the months into years. Takaro continued her rigorous training in the warrior arts, becoming skilled in all forms of weaponry. From the small, benign-looking throwing darts to the deadly swords and spears, she became proficient with all the weapons she was exposed to.

Now, into his seventies, Yaruke had last seen battle seven years ago. His son, Medaru Saibon had stepped into training the seasoned warriors while Medaru's own son, Keodai, Yaruke's grandson, assumed the responsibility of training the future generations of warriors. With his advancing years, Yaruke now focused all of his energies instructing only his son and Takaro.

"I was only a boy, much younger than Keodai, when your mother first came to live amongst us," said Yaruke, between contemplative puffs on his pipe. "Though she never took to weapons as you did, she was still a force to contend with."

"How so?" asked Takaro, her eyebrows raised as he made mention of her mother."

"Kareda Bansho, as she was known in those days, fled her parent's home in the hills of Saijun to avoid an arranged marriage, apparently to a man much older than she was."

"Yes, I am aware she had fled her intended plight."

"It was quite by accident my father came across her. She was sixteen-years-old, no more the age that you are now, at least in mortal terms that is. And I assure you, she was as rebellious and stubborn as you were when Joval Stonecroft first brought you here."

"Was I truly that difficult?"

Yaruke merely stared at her with raised eyebrows. His mincing look caused her to refrain from seeking an answer.

"Even as a boy, I was not blind to Kareda's beauty and charms, if and when she chose to be charming, that is. My father knew this and although Kareda was unwilling to take up conventional arms, she was more than willing to learn the lesser known realms of warriorship."

"Lesser known? Are you implying there is more?"

"There is much more. Your mother used the natural assets she was born with, her mind and beauty, to accomplish what no man ever could. Together with a bit of training, ingenuity and her unwavering confidence, she became as dangerous as any one of our warriors. In many ways, she was even more dangerous, for she was perceived to be a harmless, innocent woman; incapable of dispensing death and destruction."

"What are you telling me?" queried Takaro, thoroughly mystified by her master's words.

"Your mother was a skilled spy and highly successful assassin," confided Yaruke.

"A spy and assassin? My mother?" repeated Takaro, in disbelief. "Why did Master Chusai Saibon never speak of this?"

"Indeed, it is true," revealed Yaruke. "I suppose my father never spoke of this because he felt you were not yet ready to accept this truth."

"Tell me more," pleaded Takaro.

"Your mother was well versed in the art of deception," continued Yaruke. "She would infiltrate enemy camps, even the Imperial Palace in Keso to gather information. In fact, it was she who was able to provide the layout of the palace."

"You do not say!" gasped Takaro, stunned by this revelation.

"Kareda was unwittingly invited amongst the enemy. We all knew her true vocation, but the enemy only saw a beautiful, young woman; a lovely flower amongst a bunch of weeds."

"Go on!" urged Takaro, eager to learn more.

"In fact, that was how your mother was introduced to your father, Lord Dahlon Treeborn."

"She was sent to kill Dahlon?"

"If need be, but it never came to that," responded Yaruke, drawing a deep draught from his pipe before he continued. "An elder, one in council in Nagana, sent forth word to my father that a high Elf, one Dahlon Treeborn, wished to form an alliance with the mortals that inhabited western Orien. For centuries we had lived side by side in peace and waged war together against the enemy to the east, but a growing threat from the west of the Iron Mountains forced his hand. Many of the Elves that followed him to Orien had departed for the Elf Haven, no longer wishing to exist in this realm. Lord Treeborn was faced with a greatly diminished population. The logical answer was to form an alliance with those in power. My father sent Kareda to, let me say, get better acquainted with your father. Her task was to learn more about this high Elf, to discover if his intentions were honourable, if he could indeed be trusted."

"And could he be trusted?" queried Takaro.

"Truth be told, he was probably more honorable and trustworthy than some of the elders he sought help from."

"Did he ever love my mother?"

"Who can say?" Yaruke's shoulders shrugged in response: "I believe Kareda loved the Elf, or perhaps his ideals. Whatever the case, she never returned to Anshen."

"Did you know my mother well?"

"Did any of us really know her well?" He laughed as he replied: "She was always very mysterious. My father and mother knew her best. As for me, I was only a boy when she first came to live amongst us. I do recall her being very kind so naturally, I developed a great fondness for her. Then again, she garnered the attention of many of the young men of our village. They followed her about like lovesick puppies; hanging on her every word. Yes, she was quite the lovely, young lady."

"I will never know this problem," said Takaro, with a disappointed sigh. "I am plain. I am ugly. I am just plain ugly."

The warrior sat upright upon hearing her claim: "And who told you this nonsense?"

"Dahlon used to tell me this all the time. And he is right."

"Well, if you believe his words, then you are a bigger fool than I ever believed," responded Yaruke, with a chuckle.

Takaro was silent.

Leaning forward from his chair, he stared into her deep brown eyes. He realized that the Elf's cruel words cut deep into her soul, even after all these many years. "No, Takaro, your father - "

"Do not call him my father!"

"Very well. Lord Treeborn was wrong, very wrong if he said such a terrible thing to you. It would take a being devoid of a soul to dispense such cruel words to an innocent child."

His hand gently patted her shoulder in reassurance. Takaro remained silent as she listened to his sympathetic words.

"Lord Treeborn was a fool for making such a statement, and I would still consider you a bigger fool if you believe him. He would be forced to eat his own words if he were to see the lovely, young lady you have become."

Takaro blushed. She shifted uneasily at his generous compliment. Never in her entire life had she been referred to as 'beautiful' or 'lovely' by anyone else but her mother.

Yaruke laughed at the irony of life: "It seems such a strange thing that when we first met, you cared for my children. Now Medaru's own son, my grandson Keodai, is fast-approaching manhood. You, my child took a good portion of my lifetime to see you mature into the young woman that you are now. Yes, this flower has finally blossomed. Perhaps it is time to teach you the lesser known, but the very lethal skills of -"

"An assassin?" interjected Takaro. Her eyes were wide open in fascination.

"Of a woman," concluded her old master. "Yes! Perhaps it is time for you to expand on your knowledge. Are you ready for such responsibilities? To learn all the secrets that made your mother the woman she was?"

"Oh yes, master," she nodded in confirmation. "Please teach me more. Teach me to become the formidable foe that my mother once was!"

"I shall warn you now, in all your life, you will never endure training of this nature," cautioned the old warrior, chewing thoughtfully on the mouthpiece of his pipe as a wisp of gray smoke dissipated into the darkness. "Are you positive this is what you desire?"

"Most definitely, master, more than anything."

"Be sure now, for once you proceed, there shall be no turning back…"

"Look at me! I look like a trollop," groaned Takaro, in despair as she gazed at her reflection in the hand mirror.

Her lips, like a dainty rosebud were painted with a vermilion colored cream. Her large, almond-shaped eyes accentuated by black kohl eyeliner were striking. It was a startling contrast against her skin, now made pale and translucent by a dusting of fine powder.

"Do not exaggerate," scolded Yumai, her fingers worked

fastidiously to undo Takaro's braided hair. "It is only because you are not used to looking as you should; like a proper, young woman that you complain."

"But I am a warrior," protested Takaro, appalled by this makeover.

"Like it or not, you are both," rebuked Yumai.

She eyed Keodai's sister with mild contempt as the young woman brushed her long tresses with a wooden comb. For some reason, this *look* seemed fine for Yumai and the other women of the village, yet somehow; Takaro was staring at a stranger as she glanced at her reflection once more.

"I look like a doll…"

"That is the idea; to look delicate – dainty like a doll."

"Well, I am nobody's plaything."

"No, no, no, Takaro! If you accentuate and refine your feminine qualities just so, men shall become *your* plaything, if you get my meaning?"

She shuddered in response as she wondered: *What would I ever want with a man?*

Yumai pulled and twisted the dark tresses, securing it with beautifully crafted hair ornaments. As she swept Takaro's hair up onto her head, the girl's hands instinctively flew upwards, tugging at wisps of hair so the small, but definite points of her ears remained hidden.

"That is much better," praised Yumai, giving her subject an approving nod.

"Are you done with me?" questioned Takaro, only to see Yumai's eyebrows were raised in dismay.

"Ha! You only wish!" she responded. "Remove all the trappings of a warrior."

"All of it?" gasped Takaro, stunned by her request.

"Now please!" insisted Yumai, the toes of her sandal impatiently tapping the floor in response to Takaro's resistance to change.

"But this is how I always dress."

"Change is good. Remove everything; from your toys," stated Yumai, pointing to her swords, "to those wretched boots you always insist on wearing."

Takaro reluctantly complied with her wishes. Yumai held forth a beautiful silk gown, trying to ignore the obvious scars that marred Takaro's back as she slipped her arms through the sleeves. Her eyes closed as she reveled in the luxuriant fabric caressing her bare skin. Takaro had not dressed in such finery since she was a child, when her mother had last dressed her for a special occasion at the palace.

"This was once my dress," Yumai announced proudly, her fingers working to carefully wind the long, silk sash around Takaro's tiny waist. "I, too, wore this on my sixteenth birthday, when I came of age."

"*Came of age*? Age for what?" questioned Takaro.

"By mortal standards, would you not say that you are now sixteen, perhaps seventeen years?" queried Yumai.

"I suppose..."

Yumai opened a wooden trunk. She rummaged through its contents until she found a small trinket box. "This belonged to your mother. She would want you to have this."

Takaro took the box from Yumai's hand. She cautiously opened it to peer inside. A sparkle of light immediately caught her eyes. Inside a pair of earrings, one of which was attached to a silver ear cuff by a fine thread of silver glistened before her. Takaro glanced up at Yumai, noticing it was similar to what she and all Taijin women wore.

"I remember this... How did it come to be here?" asked Takaro, her finger fondling the shining ornament.

"Upon hearing of your mother's death, my great grandfather, Chusai Saibon received, along with the condolences sent by the elders, this. I suppose they felt it would have sentimental value. He asked that it be stored away. Perhaps he knew that one day you would come."

Takaro carefully placed the silver ornaments into the palm of her hand for closer inspection.

"My mother wore this on her left ear. I remember how the design carved into the ear cuff and this slip of silver hanging down to join with the earring would sparkle and shine whether she be in the moonlight or the sunlight."

"It is beautiful," agreed Yumai. "Now it is for you to wear."

Takaro glanced up at her, noticing how she wore her ear cuff on her right ear. "Does it matter on which side it is worn?"

"Of course it does. If the ear cuff is worn on the right ear, it means the wearer is not yet betrothed. If worn on the left, it means she is married or has pledged her troth. Whether it is worn on the left or on the right, all Taijin women wear this."

"Why?" questioned Takaro.

"How else is a man to know a woman's status, of her availability?"

"And what symbol does a man wear so a woman will know of his *status*?" queried Takaro.

For a brief moment, Yumai was silent. A smile spread across her face as she responded with a giggle: "You are too funny, Takaro! Why would a man be in need of such a symbol when it is the man who does the courting?"

"So you are telling me this is worn so a man can determine, from the very first meeting, whether a woman is *available* to him, or not?"

"There is nothing worse than when a man unintentionally pursues a woman who has already pledged her troth to another. Believe me, more than a few lives have been lost over such feuds."

"And what if a woman becomes involved with a married man because she has no *symbol* to go by that would indicate that he is a married man?"

Yumai considered her words before answering: "Believe me, Takaro, a woman can tell quite easily if a man is bound to another, whether he be happily or unhappily married."

"So you are telling me that I am to wear this to allow all men to know that I am '*available*' as you so eloquently put it? Well, if that is the case, I refuse to don this symbol of… of…" stammered Takaro.

"If you choose not to wear it for this reason, then wear it as a show of respect to the culture of the people that took you in and raised you. If you cannot do it for this reason, then at least wear it in your mother's memory."

"But I am not Taijin," lamented Takaro, in a sad whisper.

"Your mother was Taijin. You have half her blood flowing through you," responded Yumai. "If not for the honor of our people, then wear it in honor of your mother."

Takaro's fingertip lovingly fondled the silver that lay in the palm of her hand. With a sigh and a nod, she removed the plain, silver studs from her ear lobes and proceeded to slip the small hoops of silver into the piercings.

Yumai smiled kindly at the little warrior, taking the ornate, silver ear cuff from her hand. She gently clipped it to the edge of Takaro's right ear, just below the small, but definite, Elven point.

"That is more like it," smiled Yumai. "Now you look more Taijin than Elf."

Takaro looked at her reflection in the mirror. Though she wore the same jewelry donned by all Taijin women, in her heart, she knew she was about as much Taijin as she was Elf.

"Your mother would have been so pleased to have seen you wearing her earrings; to know that you have come of age," said Yumai.

"But come of age for what? To go to battle?" queried the warrior-in-training.

"How many women do you see traipsing into battle with my father and brother? Think, Takaro!"

Her shoulders arched up, shrugging her response.

Yumai's eyes rolled in dismay: "You are of an age that, as a young lady, you should be considering your options."

"What options are you speaking of?"

"A man, silly! You should be considering suitors for betrothal."

"You jest!" scoffed Takaro. Her laughter stopped only when she realized Yumai was silent.

"I am quite serious," insisted Yumai.

Takaro was dumbfounded. She stared wide-eyed in disbelief.

"For most of your long life, my father and grandfather trained you to be a warrior. What I am attempting to do is to bring some sense of balance to your life. Every woman is in need of a man, Takaro."

"A *man*? Why would I need a man when I had already spent a good portion of my life cooking and cleaning for men?"

"Every woman needs a man; someone who will care for her, provide her with a roof over her head, food on the table…"

"I am perfectly capable of doing this, and more, for myself," protested Takaro.

Yumai rolled her eyes in frustration. "Yes, yes, I have no doubt you can, but that is not the point."

"Then what is the *point*?"

"The point is; that is what a man is for. That is their duty in life. It gives them a sense of purpose."

"Then what? When he dies or decides he is tired of this *duty* he abandons her? The woman shall be left helpless and alone, unable to provide and care for herself. That is truly a pathetic existence."

Yumai thought upon her words as she conceded: "Yes, it would be pathetic, but that is our lot in life."

"It does not have to be this way. And I, for one, will not bow down to such expectations!" declared Takaro.

"Need I remind you that men are able to fulfill other needs?" responded Yumai, giving her a coy smile.

"Like what?"

"Do not make me explain!" Yumai's face became flushed with embarrassment.

"Now I am truly curious. Tell me, what else men-folk are good for!"

"You know…. Love. And all the physical aspects thereof…" replied Yumai, blushing as she answered.

"*Love*? Love! You are trying to make my skin crawl!" protested Takaro, frowning in disgust as she feigned a shudder.

Yumai rolled her eyes yet again: "Mark my words, Takaro, one day *you* will fall in love with one special man."

"I will not!"

"Oh, you will! Like it or not, it shall happen when you least expect and probably with the man you least likely expect it to happen with!" retorted Yumai, her arms waving in the air in total exasperation.

"Well, if this whole exercise was a trick so I may merely ensnare a husband, I have had enough!" declared Takaro, stamping her foot in rebellion.

"Fine!" replied Yumai; stomping just as hard.

"Fine!" snapped Takaro, her arms crossed defiantly in front of her chest.

Embroiled in this standoff, both eyed each other in contempt as Yaruke knocked on the door before stepping into the room. His head cocked, nodding in approval as he walked in a circle around Takaro, admiring her drastic transformation.

"You did a wonderful job, Yumai," praised the old warrior.

"Thank you, grandfather. Unfortunately, Takaro does not feel the same way."

"Stand up straight, young lady! Uncross those arms!" demanded her master, his walking stick rapping impatiently on the floor as he continued his inspection.

Takaro sheepishly complied.

"Feet together! Chin up! Shoulders back!" barked Yaruke. As he quickly reviewed her posture, he responded with a smile: "Now, that is much better!"

"You... you tricked me!" sputtered Takaro, her arms defiantly crossed in front of her chest once again.

"Tricked you? When have you ever known me to trick you, Takaro?" questioned Yaruke.

Takaro thought upon his words and indeed, Yaruke Saibon had never been one to deliberately set her up for a prank.

"There is a first time for everything. Obviously, you use this opportunity now to make a fool of me!" whined Takaro.

"In all my years, Takaro, every single one of my disciples have treated and spoken to me with respect. You, however, are your mother's daughter. You have this inability to bite your tongue when you should. You are far too outspoken at times!"

Takaro bowed her head in shame: "I am sorry, Master Saibon."

Yaruke considered her apology, although she was outspoken, far more so than even the men, he never failed to notice that when she did speak out, it was always with good reason.

"Why do you believe I have tricked you, Takaro?"

"Look at me! How can dressing in this manner be part of my training?" queried his disciple, eyeing her master with great suspicion.

"Look at you indeed, Takaro! I do believe my granddaughter has done an exceptional job. I hardly think any of the men would recognize you if you were to walk through this village."

"But what is the point? I look like a fool!"

"I beg to differ. You look absolutely beautiful!"

Takaro reddened beneath the face powder. She could feel her cheeks burn as she realized that he was sincere in his compliment.

"With all due respect, master, thank you for your kind words, but what does beauty have to do with any of this training you had promised me?"

"My dear, most men are reduced to blithering idiots when faced with a beautiful woman. They only see what is on the surface, and as though all the blood from up here," stated Yaruke, pointing to his head, and then to his nether regions, "goes rushing down to here, their brain ceases to function as their desire gets the best of them."

The old warrior chuckled as he continued: "Believe me, once that happens, you shall have the definite advantage!"

"How so?" questioned Takaro, still trying to comprehend her master's mysterious words.

"Let me say that men are not designed to run from danger when their manhood is standing at full attention," chortled the old warrior. "In fact, his most vulnerable part is now an obvious target!"

The girl cringed inwardly as her mind visualized this image, sorry she had asked for an explanation.

"Now, walk toward me," demanded Yaruke.

"What?" gasped Takaro.

"For goodness sake, girl! For once, do not *ask*, just *do*!" responded the old warrior. With an impatient sigh, his walking stick rapped the floor.

Takaro walked toward her master. Her strides were deliberate and paced, as though she was marching onto a battlefield in dress sandals.

"What was that?" queried Yaruke, shaking his head in disgust. "It was as though you were stomping about a muddy field in your boots!"

"I did as you asked. I walked."

"You walked like you were marching into battle! Look at your clothes – your hair! Do you look like you are dressed for war?"

Takaro's shoulders drooped in defeat.

"Again! Chin up; back straight; knees together! Keep your steps small – dainty. Step lightly, as though you are treading on fallen leaves, but you do not wish to make a sound."

She stared vacantly at her master, as though all this was too much for her mind to take in.

"Close your eyes and relax, Takaro. Clear your mind. Take a deep breath in through your nose, and then exhale through your mouth. Now, do it again. Walk toward me."

Takaro's eyes slowly fluttered open as she focused on the task at hand. Her steps were smaller as she glided silently across the floor.

"That is much better, Takaro. Now do it again, but do not move like you are stiff as a piece of wood. Think of a willow branch swaying in the summer breeze," suggested Yaruke.

Takaro's frowned; confused by his description.

"Like so," demonstrated her master, moving away from her. His bony hips swayed with great exaggeration as both she and Yumai burst out in laughter as he gazed over his shoulder and coyly batted his eyelashes at them.

"You want me to walk like a hobbled mare with a bad limp?" asked Takaro, between gasps as she clutched her aching ribs.

"Well, I am not the best example of one exuding womanly charms," conceded Yaruke, in embarrassment.

"Like this, Takaro," said Yumai, as she walked before her. Her steps were delicate and small, but her hips swayed in a provocative manner, rolling ever so gently with each step she took.

"Yumai shall teach you how to dress, how to walk, talk, and even to eat like a lady of high breeding."

"But why is all of this necessary?"

Her master gave her a knowing smile as he answered: "Sometimes, the best way to learn a man's secret is to get close to him: Very close. Even the Imperial Palace is easy to penetrate if you are a skilled courtesan."

"A courtesan! You want me to bed strange men?" gasped Takaro.

"Bedding them shall be your choice, but I would highly recommend killing them before it gets that far."

"And how do you suggest I kill them? I hardly think a courtesan's attire includes a sword or a spear."

"My dear girl, there are as many ways for a woman to assassinate a man as there is for her to make love to him. The tools of your trade will be revealed to you once we can leap over this first obstacle."

"And what obstacle is this?"

"We shall see how the men react to you; this new you, so to speak," explained Yaruke.

"You want me to prance about, dressed like a trollop in front of the warriors I train with!" gasped Takaro, her eyes wide in horror.

"Oh yes! How else will we know if you have succeeded with your transformation?" responded her master.

"I cannot! I will not go out there!" Takaro protested vehemently.

"Yes, you will," ordered her master, his hands on her shoulders as he directed her to the door. "Consider this exercise to be mandatory. You are to walk to the well and return with a full bucket of water."

"But I-"

Before she could finish her sentence, Yaruke pushed her out the door and promptly slammed it behind her.

Takaro abruptly turned, her fists pounding angrily on the door as she demanded to be let in.

Her master and Yumai gazed out the window, grinning broadly at her.

"Go on, fetch me some water," urged Yaruke, waving her off. "And by the way, the louder you bang on this door, the more attention you will draw to yourself."

Takaro stopped her fists at mid-strike. From the corner of her eye she could see the villagers, making their way past the Saibon cottage, stopping to see what the fuss was about. Takaro drew in a long, slow breath to compose herself, the palms of her hands smoothing out the fabric of her gown. Slowly, and with great poise, she confidently stepped off the stoop as heads turned to watch her.

It quickly became apparent these people; the women, men and children did not even recognize her. They bowed and smiled in greeting at Yaruke's *guest* as she made her way past them. Her eyes remained fixed straight ahead as several young men, warriors that only earlier today she had sparred and fought with by sword, stopped in mid-stride as she glided by.

She sensed their eyes following her. Her sharp ears could make out their muted whisperings as all three men argued over who was going to introduce himself to the lovely stranger. Soon all three men were in pursuit, pushing and shoving each other as they jockeyed for position.

"Good day, my lady!" said the tallest of the men.

"Yes, welcome to Anshen," said another, jostling his comrades to push past them.

Takaro said not a word; she merely gave them a demure smile as she played along, mildly amused by their boyish antics.

The most handsome of the three grabbed the other two men by the scruff of the neck as he pulled them back and away from the object of his desire.

"My name is Hemashe," greeted the young man. "I must declare; I have never been witness to such beauty in all my life."

Takaro blushed beneath the face powder, but still, she said nothing.

"Yes, beauty indeed!" the other two men chimed in agreement.

She placed the bucket into the well; her dainty hands grasped the handle of the winch to lower it down to the water.

"Allow me," offered Hemashe, moving to her side to aid her.

His large hands covered hers as he turned the handle, his body pressing up against hers. Takaro moved to one side, allowing the warrior to work the winch to hoist the full bucket up. The young warrior used one hand to show off his physical prowess. He lifted the heavy bucket, emptying it into another for the young woman.

"Let me carry that for you," offered the tall warrior, pushing his way past his two comrades. "This is much too heavy for a delicate creature like you."

Takaro turned about to head back to Yaruke's cottage with three men following close behind while others, hearing that there was a strange and beautiful, young maiden in their midst, gathered and followed, too.

As Hemashe made his move, the other two men struggled over the handle of the bucket. They clamored over who should have the privilege of carrying the water for her.

"So, will you be visiting for awhile," inquired the handsome warrior, following at her heels.

Takaro nodded her response.

"Perhaps I will see you again?"

Upon hearing his words, his two friends, ceased their struggle. They realized Hemashe had already made his move as they foolishly fought for the right to carry the bucket of water.

Not knowing how to answer, Takaro did not respond.

"Will I see you again?" he asked hopefully.

His two friends both chimed in: "Yes, will we?"

She stepped up onto the stoop of the cottage as Yaruke and Yumai waited at the window, observing with great interest as the growing crowd of men, young and old, gathered outside his home. Takaro smiled sweetly at Hemashe, nodding her response as she took the bucket of water from his friend's hand.

"Never mind Hemashe! Why do you not join me?" inquired the tallest of the men, trying to shove his friends out of the way. "I can show you all the glories of our beautiful countryside."

"No, no! Better yet, I know of a beautiful ridge not far from here where one can watch a truly magnificent sunset," offered the shorter warrior, struggling to push Hemashe's hand away from his mouth so he may be permitted to speak.

"My lady, please ignore my friends. A woman of your beauty and obvious refined breeding should not be made to endure such boors," apologized Hemashe. "I shall see you later, but in the meantime, your name. What is your name, my lady?"

Takaro's head tilted in wonder; *he really does not know*.

She gave the young men a demure smile, causing Hemashe's friends to end their hormone-driven posturing.

"Takaro," she answered in a gentle voice.

"Takaro? That is lovely!" stated Hemashe, sighing as he breathed her name.

"Yes, indeed it is," agreed his companions.

"You fools! It is me: Takaro Bansho!

"Ta… Takaro?" stammered a stunned Hemashe. His eyes grew wide in surprise as recognition set in. "It is you!"

"You are like a bunch of disgusting dogs in heat! Be off with you!" growled Takaro, splashing the bucket of cold water into their astounded faces.

Drenching her hopeful suitors from head to toe, she tossed the bucket in their direction. Hemashe stood dumbfounded as his comrades leapt out of the way.

Removing one of her sandals, Takaro pitched it at the handsome, young warrior, striking him squarely upon his forehead.

"Be gone, all of you! Do not make me get my sword!" shouted Takaro, as she stormed into the cottage.

The door slammed soundly in his face as Hemashe picked up Takaro's tiny sandal. As the crowd dispersed, he held forth his prized possession in one hand as the other absentmindedly rubbed the red welt forming on his forehead as he whispered beneath his breath: "I do believe I am in love…"

After what seemed to be an exceedingly long training session, Takaro made her way to Yaruke's cottage. She banged loudly on his door.

"Come in, Takaro!" responded her master.

She peered into the austere room that was free of clutter.

Yaruke sat at the table pouring a bowl of tea.

"How did you know it was me, master?"

"I could feel your intention. I can sense your pent-up anger and rage. It is unmistakable; like a tidal wave, it is."

Takaro's arms crossed defiantly in front of her as she paced to and fro like a caged animal waiting to lash out.

"So, what is on your mind, Takaro?"

"That was most humiliating! Did you see them?"

"See who? The warriors?" queried Yaruke, pouring fragrant tea into a bowl for his agitated guest.

"They still treat me differently, like I am that… that…"

"Beautiful, young lady," finished Yaruke.

"Yes! Even as I am dressed now - as a warrior!"

"That is because they see you now for what you truly are, Takaro," stated her master, sliding a steaming bowl across the table toward her.

"I am a warrior!"

"You stand corrected. Like it or not, you are a sword-wielding, quiver-slinging, knife-throwing beauty," replied Yaruke. "You, my dear, are both: a warrior and a woman."

"It is queer, the men's behavior," she grunted in disgust.

"Why? They seem to be acting as any red-blooded male would behave before a beautiful, young maiden."

"I am the same person that trained with them the other day. Now look at them all. They stand and gawk at me like they are a bunch of slack-jawed dolts!"

"Takaro, do not be so harsh on these young men. You must admit; you did give them quite the surprise the other day. And yes, you are the same person you were yesterday, but even for you, your transformation was quite the metamorphosis. For the first time, you saw with your own eyes, your true beauty although you still prefer to hide behind your weapons."

"But I am ugly," sighed Takaro.

"Enough of that nonsense! That is Dahlon Treeborn speaking," scolded Yaruke.

"Master, this is most disconcerting. The men no longer train with me in the same manner. Apparently, they do not want to *hurt* me."

"And that is a problem?"

"I am no longer one of *them*," she whined.

"If you were wise, you would take advantage of their ineptitude," advised her master.

"What do you mean?"

"In the long history of the Kagai Warriors, at least long by human standards, women have always played an integral part in our family annals. Long before your mother joined forces with us, there were others. However, you my dear are the first to be trained as a full-fledged warrior, well versed in all of our weapons as well as hand-to-hand combat. Let me just say that at this moment the men, your brother warriors are a little awe-struck by you. I would say that if the men are foolish enough to take care not to injure you in the course of training, then take advantage of it. They all know exactly what kind of punishment you are capable of dispensing, and that being the case, why should it hinder the level of your training? So what if they are the ones being banged and bruised and you are not?"

"Are you telling me to go ahead and beat them, to pummel them into the ground if I wish?"

"Why not?" Yaruke's response was pragmatic. "If they are so willing to drop their guard, I would say they shall be receiving their just desserts. It would be a good lesson for them to learn, for one day, the enemy may well employ the same method to infiltrate our ranks. If that be the case, let them learn the hard way."

"I do suppose you have a valid point, master," conceded Takaro.

"Of course I do! And besides, when you first asked to be trained in the same manner as your mother, you accepted the consequences of this training, did you not?"

"Yes…"

"Well, my dear, this is exactly what was to happen if you had succeeded."

"I have only succeeded in alienating my brother warriors," lamented Takaro.

"Then you have succeeded," stated Yaruke. "And it would be wiser to say that they respect you from a whole new perspective."

"This whole thing is somewhat confusing."

"Perhaps this is confusing to you, but do you not realize that you have control over them?"

Takaro gave her master a frown as she responded with a shake of her head.

"You control them by having their puny, little minds believe that you are now a harmless little flower. On another level, they are fully aware that you are a capable warrior, as deadly as any one of them, but now, you have them believing that you are a delicate, dainty, young lady. You have disarmed their minds and that is the most dangerous thing for any warrior. They have effectively lowered their guard, making them most vulnerable to an attack, if you choose to do so."

She silently absorbed his words as her master chewed thoughtfully on his now cold pipe.

"Now Takaro, knowing full well what this transformation has done to your brother warriors, all of whom know you are accomplished in all aspects of warriorship, can you imagine what power you possess over an ordinary man who knows not of your true vocation? Because of this," stated Yaruke, his eyes gazing at her reflection in the bowl of tea, "you shall now gain entry into places and social circles where none of my men will ever be permitted. So, if you are wise, you will allow Yumai to continue to groom you. You shall learn to use your feminine wiles, so you may charm, disarm and beguile your unsuspecting victims."

Her master's words now made absolute sense to Takaro. She possessed something her fellow warriors did not and never will. The feeling of empowerment was almost overwhelming. Her own femininity was now a weapon she could use at will. She stood a little taller and prouder as she reveled in her newfound powers.

"As my father warned me before I took my wife and as I had warned Medaru when he wed: Never underestimate the power of a woman, especially a Kagai woman."

"This is an exercise in strategy and stealth," announced Yaruke. His son, Medaru stood by his side in the impending darkness after dividing the warriors into two teams. "As you are not permitted to use weapons, you may use whatever other means to subdue your *enemy*. Once you have been captured, your captor shall use a rope, of which each of you had been supplied with to restrain your *prisoner*. Once captured, you shall be excused from this exercise and shall be dealt with accordingly if your team be the loser."

"Yes," added Medaru, giving his father a knowing wink. "I know not what punishment shall be dispensed as of yet, but let me assure you, you do not want to be on the losing team!"

"We have marked off quadrants of this forest. At the opposite ends you will find a banner. The object of the exercise is to capture the *enemy's* banner and return it to your team's area. You may use any method of retrieving the banner; however, I must emphasize, no weapons shall be employed. Use your skills, use your ingenuity, but no weapons," reiterated Yaruke Saibon.

"Is that understood?" queried Medaru, addressing his students.

The forty eager disciples stood before their masters, bowing in understanding. Takaro was assigned to one team. Medaru's son Keodai was assigned to the other to equalize the teams' abilities and skill level.

"You shall have adequate time to stake out your area and to devise a plan of action. When you see my signal, proceed. Now go!" ordered Yaruke, waving them off.

Both teams vanished into the dark forest with nothing more than the moon and the stars to light their way. Takaro's keen eyes adjusted to the darkness. Her pupils were fully dilated as they amplified what little light there was to allow her to see almost as well as a full-blooded Elf. The warriors automatically followed Takaro as she easily made her way to their banner at the far end of the forest. The sounds of their movements were muted by the thundering crash of the not-too-distant waterfall.

As the team gathered around their banner, Takaro proceeded to give instructions.

"And just who made you the captain?" growled Mekai, in an abrasive tone. The bane of her existence came forward. The bully stood toe-to-toe with the little warrior.

"I assumed that-"

"Yes, you did assume! And you assumed wrong," retorted the young warrior, with a snarl of contempt. "We do not need a captain. It is obvious what to do. We storm the enemy, take them by surprise!"

"You want us to just attack?" asked one warrior.

"Without so much as conceiving a plan of action?" gasped another.

"We have not the time to argue and I, for one, do not wish to endure the *punishment* that shall be doled out to the losing team," confessed

Hemashe. "If we are to win, we will need leadership, not all us running amok through this dark forest. We need a captain."

All in attendance nodded in agreement, all except Mekai.

"So be it," said Mekai. He sounded reluctant until he decided to offer up his services. "Then I will be your captain."

"No," disagreed Hemashe, shaking his head. "You are a reckless buffoon! I suggest Takaro be our captain."

"Why? Because you are *fond* of her?" taunted Mekai, batting his eyelashes at Hemashe in mock adoration as Takaro's face reddened in the darkness.

"Fetch off, you imbecile! Takaro's experience far exceeds all of ours combined!" stated Hemashe, judiciously. "In fact, let us vote. If you choose Takaro as our captain, raise your hand now."

Instantly, all hands, with the exception of Mekai's, shot skyward.

"How many would choose Mekai?"

Just as quickly, all hands dropped as Mekai's darted up. The humiliated warrior slowly lowered his hand in defeat.

"Majority wins! Takaro is our captain," announced Hemashe. "So, what do you recommend, captain?"

"First, two warriors shall move ahead to assess the situation at the enemy camp," instructed Takaro. "We shall need a report as to how many remain to guard the banner."

Two young men stepped forward for the task.

"Very well, but know this; one of you may have to *sacrifice* yourself so the other can flee," advised Takaro.

"Ha! Your *captain* willingly gives you up to the enemy!" Mekai chided.

"Yes, I do, just as each and every one of you may one day be faced with such a dilemma. Remember, it is far better to sacrifice the life of one in order to spare the lives of many."

"Takaro is right," agreed Hemashe, scowling at Mekai with growing resentment. "Be on your way. Move with stealth and only advance as far as necessary to ascertain their numbers and movement."

The two anxious warriors bowed, and then turned into the darkness, disappearing into the shadows.

"One shall remain at the banner. Seven shall wait in the shadows over there," instructed Takaro, her finger pointing to the tall stand of trees about thirty paces before the clearing where their banner fluttered in the evening breeze. "Use your ropes to ensnare the enemy."

"But we were told not to use weapons," reminded one warrior.

Takaro raised her rope up as she spoke. "Can I stab or cut with this?" she asked, holding forth the limp cord. "I think not. And I am certainly not asking you to hang or garrote any of our *foes*."

"Ha, I see your point! Then ensnare we will!" nodded the warrior. "The rest of you shall follow me."

"Is it wise to leave only one to defend our banner?" queried Hemashe.

"It will be if the other seven *do away* with the enemy as they advance," stated their captain. "It shall be the seven largest, strongest warriors to defend the one guarding the flag, for I will require the ten fastest warriors for the last detail of this operation."

The young men quickly assessed each other. Six stepped forward, but the largest of them, Mekai, stood resolutely apart from the rest.

"Why should I remain here while the rest of you revel in the glory of seizing the enemy's banner? If I am sent forth, I shall guarantee our victory!" stated the cocky, young man. His hands rested on his hips as he proudly thrust his chest out.

"We are a team. It matters not who captures the banner," argued Hemashe. "We shall all be victorious, or we will all go down in defeat, whether you are the one to make it that far or not."

Their eyes glanced up as a flaming arrow launched into the velvet blackness of the night sky marked the beginning of the training exercise.

"There is no time to argue, Mekai. Come with us," ordered Takaro, turning eastward to the enemy camp as another warrior volunteered to take his place. "We must move ahead quickly and await word from the other two I had sent ahead."

"That is your strategy? To wait?" grumbled Mekai, rolling his eyes in frustration.

"That is exactly what we will do," stated Hemashe, turning to follow Takaro.

As she and the others were within one-hundred yards of the enemy camp, they took refuge behind the dark shadows cast by the trees, shrubs and fallen logs. All froze as two dark figures glided silently past them. Recognizing her teammates, even in the pale light cast by the moon, Takaro seized them by their arms, hauling them down into the shadows.

"Hush! It is I, Takaro," announced the little warrior, releasing her hold.

"Thank goodness!" exclaimed one warrior. "The enemy is on the move."

"How many?"

"All advance with the exception of three to guard their banner."

"Now that we know, you five shall remain here," decided Takaro, pointing to the men hidden behind the trees. Turning to Mekai and the three other warriors crouched behind the brambles of a red berry shrub: "You four shall take control of the banner. Give yourselves a wide berth advancing from the north and wait for my instructions to move in."

"What of the rest of us?" asked Hemashe, in a hushed tone.

Pointing to the two young warriors that had just returned from the scouting mission, she selected the smallest, most agile of them. "You shall hide in that tree. Position yourself where the moon shall be directly behind you. As the enemy advances past these five men, you shall draw their attention. Make sure their eyes are directed to the moon," instructed Takaro.

"Ha! I know what you are planning," smiled the warrior, as he nodded in approval.

"Good! Once they have caught an eyeful of the bright moon, then you," said Takaro pointing to the other warrior, "shall draw them away; act as a decoy. You will lure them away as though you plan to advance from the south. Once you have their attention, turning away from the bright moon to the darkness of the forest will temporarily blind them as they begin their pursuit."

"And then we shall attack," added Hemashe, nodding in understanding.

"Exactly! When the timing is right, once their group divides to pursue our decoy, we shall turn on them. As soon as we have them secured, be prepared to advance."

"And what shall you and Hemashe be doing at this time?" asked Mekai in a dismissive tone, now realizing that Takaro may indeed have a workable plan.

"Hemashe and I shall create a diversion that will allow you and the others to advance in order to seize the banner."

"What is this *diversion* you speak of?" queried Mekai, his eyes full of suspicion.

"You will see soon enough, just be sure that once I am done, no matter what you see or hear, you and the others move quickly and silently. Each one of you shall dispatch one of their three guards, while the fourth shall capture their banner. Take the banner and be off. Do not tip the enemy off that you have it, for you must still run the gauntlet to return to our camp," instructed Takaro. "No gloating that you have their banner. Is that understood, Mekai?"

Hemashe and the others glared at the young man to make sure, in no uncertain terms, he would comply with this order.

"Understood," conceded Mekai, with a grumble as he and the others rose to their feet.

"Good! As for the rest of you, remain hidden until the enemy has passed," instructed Takaro. "Be prepared to run. Do not look to the moon when the commotion begins. Just run, silently and quickly!"

All nodded in understanding as Takaro's sharp ears detected the movements of the advancing enemy. She motioned all to remain silent and still.

As the shadowy figures crept with great stealth through the stand of trees, Takaro could see that Keodai had indeed sent forth almost his entire *battalion* with the exception of the three left to guard the banner. He planned to overpower Takaro's team with sheer numbers before they neared their camp.

Overhead, the subtle rustling of leaves high above drew the attention of the opposing team members. Glancing upward, their pupils contracted as the cold glow of the moon filled their eyes with its bright light as they searched the crown of the tree for the source of this noise.

"Up there! Look!" announced one warrior. His finger pointed to a figure crouched high on the branch.

"So what do we have here?" asked Keodai, his eyes squinting at the figure silhouetted again the round, fat moon. "Your attempt to hide is rather futile. Why not come down and surrender? You know there is nowhere to run."

The treed warrior suddenly shouted, gesturing for his comrade to run, motioning him to dash southward.

The young warrior, already slinking toward a bamboo grove proceeded to noisily crash through the vegetation as though he was not one, but many, advancing to the enemy camp.

"Get them!" ordered Keodai, signaling five warriors to begin the pursuit.

"I cannot see!" shouted one warrior, blinking hard as the harsh light of the moon continued to dance before him like a bright apparition.

One warrior stumbled over another as he rubbed his eyes in an attempt to vanquish these smears of light.

"Damn it all!" cursed Keodai. "We have been duped."

Their pupils wreaked havoc with their night vision as the phantom specter of the moon continued to fill their eyes, temporarily blinding the men as the cold, celestial rays burned into their retinas. Takaro motioned for Mekai to begin his advance from the north with his three men. The warrior nodded in understanding before they dissolved into the dark shadows.

"They are getting away! Follow them!" shouted Keodai, urging five warriors southward. Shaking his head in disgust, he watched as they stumbled blindly into the darkness.

As his eyes slowly adjusted, he waved the others onward. Keodai forged ahead with the rest of his men, unaware that members of his party were under assault. Takaro, Hemashe and the others took from behind the last four stragglers, still blinking hard to refocus their eyes. Emerging from the shadows, with folded cloth in one hand, they quickly engulfed the faces of their prey, denying them both sight and sound in an instant. Their cries for help stifled, Takaro and her comrades attacked pressures points to effectively subdue them further.

Keodai turned to order his men to advance with greater speed, but to his dismay, his ranks were thinned. Only seven remained.

"Those fools! I suppose they took after the other five," grumbled Keodai, waving his comrades on to follow him.

With the opposing team moving on, after securing their prisoners, Takaro whispered her instructions for the five remaining warriors to hunt down Keodai's men, those in pursuit of their decoy. Without a word, the men slipped into the shadows of the forest to carry out her order.

"Follow me," whispered Takaro, as she led Hemashe in a straight line that would take them directly to the enemy camp. He followed, attempting to move with her speed and stealth.

As they entered a clearing, the white banner fluttered in the distance. Around it stood three guards, keeping a watchful eye.

"Now what?" asked Hemashe, his words spoken in a hush. He watched Takaro as she re-laced her leather boot before advancing.

"Just stay close," she whispered.

Before he could say another word, Takaro leapt up, charging toward the enemy line. The three young men posted to guard their banner immediately braced themselves for the attack. She laughed inwardly as her eyes made out their silhouettes, watching as all three relaxed upon seeing that it was she and only one other warrior.

"What is your plan, Takaro?" Hemashe asked again, as he rushed to her side. "Tell me you have a plan!"

"Just follow me!" she ordered.

They were running headlong toward the enemy when Takaro cried out as she fell hard. As though her foot had caught on an unseen tree root protruding from the ground, she flew forward, rolling over her shoulder and landing with a hard *'thud'*!

As the three warriors rushed in to capture Takaro and her comrade, Hemashe scrambled to her side as she writhed in pain, clutching her ankle.

"Let me see, Takaro," said Hemashe, pushing her hand away.

He gasped when he saw the sheen of wet blood in the moonlight and the strange protrusion jutting against the leather of her boot.

"She is hurt! Takaro is hurt!" called Hemashe, as the three men slowed their advance, approaching with great caution. As he touched her ankle, his hand instantly recoiled as she screamed out in pain.

"What happened?" asked one warrior, huddling over Hemashe to see.

"Is it not obvious? She has broken her ankle! Look at the blood! Look at that *bone*!" groaned Hemashe, as he grimaced in sympathy.

Another warrior stooped for a closer look. "This is not good! Remove her boot!"

Hemashe loosened her bootlace, but as he took hold of it, Takaro screamed out in pain, swatting the young man across his head.

"Owww!" shouted Hemashe, cringing from this assault.

"That was nothing! How do you think I am feeling!" snarled Takaro.

"We must get help! We must find Master Saibon!" shouted one of the young men, his concern mounting. "Can you stand, Takaro?"

"I can try," she answered with a groan.

Hemashe and the warrior helped to steady Takaro on one leg, her arms around their shoulders for support.

"Hemashe, I will assist you with delivering Takaro back for help. Tisai, you run ahead, fetch Master Saibon. Ask him to meet us," ordered Megoto, the leader of this small group. He turned to the last warrior with final instructions to guard the banner until he returned while Tisai crashed through the forest with utmost urgency in a bid to locate Yaruke Saibon.

Hemashe and Megoto struggled to assist Takaro. Being shorter than both the young men in her company, it was becoming difficult for her to hobble along on one foot. She clung to their shoulders as they stooped awkwardly to support her.

"This is taking much too long, Takaro," decided Hemashe. He suddenly scooped her up in his arms. "I will carry you."

"This is not necessary. I can walk," insisted Takaro, squirming in protest.

"Well, you are not doing a very good job of it," commented Megoto. "Allow Hemashe to help you."

"I am too heavy to be carried."

"You are as light as a feather, Takaro. Now stop struggling!" demanded Hemashe.

"This is embarrassing!"

"Swallow your pride and allow him to assist you," ordered Megoto. "Can you manage, Hemashe?"

"Yes, and you best get back to the game," suggested Hemashe, holding Takaro in his arms.

"Can you walk with us just a little further?" pleaded the wounded warrior. "I fear Hemashe will tire soon and drop me."

The warrior frowned at the young woman in his arms. "Are you saying that I am too weak to carry you?"

"No… I am saying I am too heavy," argued Takaro.

"And I am saying that you are both wasting precious time. Let us move on!" ordered Megoto, giving Hemashe as gentle shove in the right direction. "I shall go a little further, but I will have to turn back soon."

"Return to the game," ordered Hemashe. "I insist."

The warrior looked at Takaro for a moment. "You will be fine. Hemashe will see to it. I must return to my men, Takaro. I shall see you both later after your team had been doled out your punishment for losing."

"So be it," conceded Hemashe. "Luck be with you!"

"Yes, luck be with you," chimed Takaro, speaking with utmost sincerity.

The young warrior raced through the dark shadows of the forest, heading back to his post. As he emerged into the clearing where Takaro had met with misfortune, he spied the form of his teammate. He still stood where Megoto had left him.

As Megoto neared, he called out, but his call went unanswered. He dashed up to his friend and to his surprise; his comrade was gagged and bound to the staff from which the banner once flew.

His comrade frantically thrashed about; attempting to loosen the rope as Megoto removed his gag.

"This is not good…"

"Not good? Not good you say? We are doomed!" snapped the struggling warrior. "We have been duped! Takaro and Hemashe tricked us into lowering our defenses. Untie me now! We may still be able to retrieve our banner!"

As Hemashe entered a meadow near the edge of the forest, Tisai, who had been sent forth by Megoto to find help, met them. Yaruke and Medaru were both by his side.

"Thank you, Tisai," said Hemashe, grateful to the young warrior. "Now you best be on your way. Go finish the game."

Tisai nodded in agreement, dashing back into the forest to resume his post at the banner with his comrades.

Hemashe gently lowered Takaro onto the ground, his dark eyes wide with genuine worry.

"So Takaro, what happened here," queried Yaruke, bending low to assess her injury.

"It is really nothing, master," insisted Takaro.

"Nothing? You are bleeding! And look at that bone!" declared Hemashe, pointing to the strange protrusion from her boot.

"That?" responded the little warrior. "That is nothing. See." Her finger probed down into the side of her boot to remove the small, gnarled knot of a tree root.

"What?" gasped Hemashe. "What about this blood?"

"Blood? There is no blood," insisted Takaro.

"What do you speak of?" asked Hemashe, his trembling finger pointing to the dark, wet stain on her boot. "This blood!"

"Oh, it is nothing," dismissed Takaro, as she flicked a small object at Hemashe's forehead.

It bounced off his head, leaving behind a red stain. He wiped his forehead with the back of his hand, staring at the smudge of crimson liquid.

"Want one?" asked Takaro, offering him a red berry. "They are quite ripe this time of the year."

"A berry! You mean to tell me this is the juice of some berries?" asked the young man, startled by this revelation.

Yaruke and Medaru exchanged glances and both fell to the ground in laughter.

"I say, she even had us fooled, Hemashe," said the elder Saibon, slapping the young warrior on his back.

"I swear; you looked as frightened as Tisai did when he first sought us out!" chuckled Medaru.

"You mean to tell me that you were only pretending?" Hemashe gasped in exasperation. He collapsed to the ground in dismay as he stared in disbelief at Takaro.

"Did I not tell you that I was going to create a diversion to allow Mekai and the others a chance to steal away with the banner?"

reminded Takaro.

"You did, but you should have warned me! You should have told me what it was to be," rebuked the young man, shaking his head in embarrassment. "I was worried about you. I thought you were terribly hurt."

"But I am not."

"That is not the point. I truly believed you were hurt!"

Yaruke and Medaru rose up as shadows emerged from the edge of the forest.

Mekai waved the enemy banner in victory as his teammates led the opposing team members out, still roped and tethered. "We won!"

"We won?" asked Hemashe, stunned by this news.

"I knew we would," said Takaro, with a confident smile.

"Takaro's team is the victor!" announced Yaruke.

Medaru untied Keodai's wrists as his son stared down at the ground in embarrassment.

"So, what becomes of us now?" asked Keodai, smiling weakly at his grandfather and father, hoping for some leniency.

"For the victors, wine and food await before a roaring fire. For the losers, a quick plunge from Reyu Falls, and then a dash back to the village! If you are quick about it, there may still be wine and food left for you!" announced Medaru.

"But master, what Takaro did, was that not tantamount to cheating?" questioned Hemashe, glancing over at the warrior maiden as she laced up her boot.

"Did she or any member of your team use weapons?" asked Medaru.

"No."

"Did she, at any time, forfeit the game?"

"No."

"Well then, what can be the problem?" questioned Yaruke.

"But it is my understanding Takaro tricked us," continued Keodai, pleased that Hemashe was willing to side with him.

"She tricked me, too, and I was on her team," stated Hemashe, with an indignant huff.

"Call it trickery if you like, but I prefer to call it ingenuity. Personally, I thought it was quite clever and rather ingenious of Takaro to concoct this diversion. Besides, in a real battle situation, do you truly believe the enemy will care if one cheats or not, in order to survive or get the upper hand?"

Around a roaring fire Yaruke and Medaru Saibon as well as all the seasoned warriors joined the young disciples. As Mekai proudly retold the tale of their victory, Takaro sat back and listened, eating but drinking little.

Medaru handed her a bottle of wine that she passed on to Hemashe.

"You did well tonight, Takaro. Why do you not drink in celebration with your brothers?"

The little warrior glanced about at those sharing the fire. All the men, young and old were sharing in the camaraderie of this brotherhood. All were at various levels of sobriety as they indulged in the red wine.

"I have had my fair share for this night, master," answered Takaro, in a whisper. "And remember, I have been around long enough to know that tomorrow, you and your father shall call upon us early in the morn. You will have us engage in a rigorous training regimen. I have witnessed one too many of these warriors heaving on the wayside after a busy night of drinking, that is why I refuse to imbibe."

"A wise decision, Takaro," praised Medaru, as he indulged in another drink.

As the night wore on and the last of the wine consumed, the warriors staggered away from the dying embers of the fire to find a few hours of sleep before their early morning training resumed. Those too inebriated to make the short journey home fell asleep where they sat; slumped over in an alcohol-induced stupor.

Hemashe wavered as he rose up onto his unsteady feet only to topple backwards in his drunken haze. As he fell, his hands instinctively latched onto the closest object to him. He caught hold of Takaro's arm, taking her down with him.

He groaned in pain as she deliberately landed hard on top of his chest. As she struggled to right herself, he smiled stupidly as he gazed up into her face.

"Well, hel-lo there, Tak-ka-ro." His words were slowed and slurred as though his tongue was too swollen for his mouth. "What're yoou do-in' here?"

"You fool! You pulled me down when you fell!"

"I fell?" asked the young man. His glazed eyes glanced about. "Oh! What do ya know?"

"You fell over drunk," scolded the little warrior.

"Nah, actually, I'm just resting."

"You may be resting, but I am *not* your blanket! Unhand me!" demanded Takaro.

"Ah, come now, this is downright cozy," insisted Hemashe, tightening his embrace around her body.

"You want cozy? Then I shall fetch you a much bigger *blanket.* Why do I not throw Mekai on top of you? He is passed out right over there," offered Takaro, her thumb jabbing over her shoulder to where Mekai was sprawled out on the ground, obviously to the whole world.

Reaching behind, she grabbed hold of the smallest finger on Hemashe's hands. With a squeeze and a twist, she wrenched his paws off from around her waist.

"OW! OW! OW!" yelped Hemashe. Though his nerves were dulled by alcohol, Takaro's painful joint manipulation could still be felt.

The young man sat up, shaking his hands in painful response as he declared: "You are mean!"

"And you are drunk!"

He stared up at her through squinted eyes, as though her sharp words were just as harsh as the physical punishment she dispensed.

"Come on, help me up," Hemashe ordered, extending his aching hands to Takaro.

She eyed him suspiciously.

"Please, Takaro, be a friend," he pleaded, doing his very best to look helpless.

Taking him by his hands, Takaro abruptly yanked him up onto his feet. Hemashe wavered and staggered forward a bit before finally throwing his arm around her small shoulders in a bid to remain upright.

"Get off me!" demanded Takaro, attempting to lift his heavy arm from about her.

"Be a good friend, Takaro," requested the intoxicated, young man. "Just walk me back to my cottage."

"If it means to be rid of you sooner, then very well," conceded Takaro, supporting his dead weight as he staggered forward. She pivoted around, giving him a hard jerk as she corrected his steps. "You are going the wrong way, *I* live that way."

"Your place, my place; what does it matter? As long as we can be together, that's what really counts," he replied with a longing sigh.

"You are talking like an absolute fool. If I was not already holding you steady, I would use my hands to slap some sense into you," she grumbled.

"Come now, Takaro, I thought you were my friend. I thought you liked me," groaned Hemashe.

"I like you as a friend, and I like you more when you are sober!" She snapped as she struggled to send him off in the right direction.

"I'm not drunk," protested Hemashe.

"Your judgment is too impaired for you to even comprehend how truly drunk you are," corrected Takaro, as she glared at him.

"Well, perhaps I am a little drunk, but know this; I cannot help but speak my mind where you're concerned. It's your fault I talk as I do."

"You have the gall to blame me for your scrambled thoughts and idiotic words?" rebuked Takaro.

"Oh, yes! If you weren't sooo cute, I'd be treatin' you like one of the men. Thank goodness, you're one cute warrior. I mean girl. I mean warrior girl," stammered Hemashe.

"My goodness, you are absolutely drunk!"

"And you are absolutely cute!"

"Shut your mouth!"

"No! You shut your mouth, right on top of mine!" insisted Hemashe, pointing with an unsteady finger first to his nose, then to his lips. "Kiss me!"

"What?" gasped Takaro, as she dumped him to the ground. The drunken warrior crumpled into a pathetic heap before her.

"You heard me," answered Hemashe, struggling to right himself. "You're so cute, I want to kiss you."

"*You* kiss *me*? I would much rather kiss a filthy pig," growled Takaro, her anger mounting with each passing minute. "And what is this? I am not cute. Cute is unbecoming on me! I am a warrior."

"Excuse me, you're right. I stand corrected, Takaro," admitted the inebriated warrior. "You are not a cute girl. Oh, no! You are a *beautiful woman*. And I'll shout this out for the whole world to hear!"

Takaro stood before him, her eyes wide in dismay.

"Takaro is the most beaut-"

Her hand flashed out to cover his mouth, stifling his words. "Quiet, Hemashe!" scolded Takaro. "Get inside before you wake your family."

Hemashe removed her hand from his mouth as he snorted with a silly grin: "Ha! You are blushing! I made you blush."

"Not only are you drunk, you are blind! And if I am blushing, it is only because I am so embarrassed for you," groaned Takaro, pulling

Hemashe back onto his feet.

"What unkind words spout from that pretty, little mouth of yours," sighed the young man. "You can be quite mean when you want to be."

"I am only as mean as you make me to be."

"Oh, no! You do quite the fine job all on your own, Takaro," he stated judiciously, even in his intoxicated condition as he swayed and staggered up the stoop of his cottage. Suddenly, his hand balled into a loose fist, punching Takaro high on her arm.

"What was that for?" asked Takaro, propping him against the door.

"That was for being so mean to me on this night," sulked Hemashe. "You were bloody cruel!"

"Well, if only your addled-brain chatter was not so annoying, I would have been nicer to you," admonished Takaro.

"No! You were mean before we even began drinking on this eve!"

With an angry scowl, Takaro's eyes seemed to burn through his heart as she glowered at him.

"That's right, Takaro! Even before that, you were mean to me; when you tricked me into believing you were hurt!"

"It was only a game, Hemashe!"

"Game or not, you scared me!" he snapped in anger. "I thought you were truly hurt!"

"But we won, did we not?"

"I would rather lose that stupid game and be punished ten times over than to see you hurt!"

"I am sorry. I did not think you would care as long as we were victorious."

"Of course I care! How can I not care?" grumbled Hemashe, as he glared at her in disappointment. "I love you."

Takaro's face softened upon hearing his words. She smiled, and then she patted his cheek as she turned away.

"Now I know, you are truly and surely drunk, my friend," giggled Takaro, dismissing his words.

Hemashe caught her by the wrist, pulling her close to his body as he whispered into her ear: "I assure you, I may be drunk, but I do know what I speak of. I am in love with you."

Takaro's hands came up, pushing against his chest to escape his embrace and unwanted attention.

"I shall forgive you for this, Hemashe. This is nothing more than the wine speaking."

"No, this is my heart speaking," insisted the warrior.

"Do not talk to me of love – " Her words were stifled as he placed a finger over her soft lips.

"Hear me out, Takaro," pleaded Hemashe, as his facial expression changed, becoming quite serious. The drunken haze in his eyes seemed to fade, replaced by a moment of lucidity. "I have admired you from afar for much too long, always too afraid to tell you what I truly feel. If you insist that it is the wine, then perhaps it has only given me the courage to speak my mind. And I tell you now, my mind and heart, whether drunk or sober, cannot hide what it truly feels for you. I am in love with you."

Takaro was stunned to hear Hemashe's heartfelt confession.

"If you do not believe in my words, then look into my eyes and tell me that you cannot see the depth of my feelings for you," whispered Hemashe, drawing her closer.

She gazed into his dark, smoldering eyes and her heart began to race as the realization slowly sank in that he spoke the truth. Hemashe's fingertips gently brushed away the stray wisps of hair from her eyes.

"Do not do this, Hemashe. I am a warrior," said Takaro, in a soft voice as she tried desperately to resist his charms.

"True, you be a warrior, but you are also a woman," responded the young man, his hand now softly caressing her cheek.

She was taken aback by the gentleness of his touch.

"Most definitely, you are a woman," he whispered into her ear as he raised her chin. Her eyes slowly closed as his lips pressed lightly against hers.

Takaro's heart was pounding loudly in her chest. Her whole being felt a tingling sensation, as if an electrical charge was coursing through her body from that one touch, that single kiss. It was as though he was stealing away with her breath. She began to tremble in his arms as she rose up on her toes to answer his kiss, only to pull away from him in anger.

"How dare you? I am a warrior!" growled Takaro. "You need to sober up!"

With her fist tightly clenched, she delivered a blow, striking Hemashe in his midriff. The warrior stumbled back, falling against the door. Clutching his stomach, his eyes were wide open in shock as he reeled from this unexpected assault.

As Hemashe slumped against the door, Takaro pulled on the latch. The door flew open as the young man crashed backwards onto the wooden floor. She raced off into the darkness and as she did so, she glanced back to see the flickering of flames as candles lit up the cottage. In the distance, she could hear Hemashe retching terribly, heaving as much from her punch as the effects of too much wine as his mother and father groaned in disgust.

Against a dreary dawn sky, the young warriors stood before Medaru Saibon. He paced between the rows of bleary-eyed, weary disciples. It was clear to him these young men were still suffering from the ill effects of too much wine. He gave Takaro a knowing smile as he assessed the damage from last evening's celebration. The faces of some of the men had a sickly pallor. A few were trembling as they fought the urge to vomit before their master and fellow students.

"It is obvious that most of you indulged in perhaps a little too much wine last night. With this in mind, today's training session shall not entail hand-to-hand combat, throws, weapons training, and so on," announced Medaru.

His words were met with a great, singular sigh of relief from all the young men.

"Instead, today's lesson is totally devoted to rolling. That is right men: forward rolls, backward rolls, side rolls, dive rolls, handsprings!" decided their master, nodding judiciously.

This time, his words were met with a loud round of sorry groans.

With an unsympathetic smile, Medaru added: "And we will not confine this training to this one small area. I want you to roll and spring clear across this field. And back again. Any questions? Complaints?"

Medaru's only response came from Mekai as he abruptly dropped to his trembling knees, retching loudly.

As the students began the torturous regimen, Takaro gleefully went about her training; rolling and springing, always landing lightly back onto her feet again and again. She watched as the others struggled, groaned and vomited their way across the field. When she was done, Medaru asked her to fetch some water for the queasy students. Their night of drinking, heaving and the repeated rolling was no doubt making them very dehydrated.

She returned with a bucket full of cool, refreshing water. Hemashe was one of the first to complete the exercise, taking a deep draught from the ladle of water. He smiled as he stood next to Takaro, waiting for the others to finish. Her gaze turned away from him, uncomfortable after their late night encounter.

"Thank goodness I got sick last night," sighed Hemashe. "I would be far worse off had I kept all that wine inside of me."

"You were sick?"

"Oh yes, I retched my guts out until there was nothing left inside of me," replied Hemashe. "Needless to say, my parents were none too happy with me last night."

"It was that bad?"

"It would have been far worse in doing all these rolls without having first been sick," admitted Hemashe, his hand gingerly rubbing his sore stomach.

"Do you feel sick again?" she asked as she watched him wince in pain.

"No," answered Hemashe, raising his shirt for her inspection. "I have a bruise here. I think I must have fallen last night."

He pointed to the dark contusion on his hard, flat stomach.

Takaro released a sigh of relief. It was obvious Hemashe was much too drunk to remember that it was she who had punched him to leave this nasty bruise. No doubt, he had no recollection of his drunken words or of his ill-fated attempt to kiss her either.

As the group dispersed after their grueling lesson, Hemashe sidled up to Takaro. "Oh, yes, and thank you for last night," he whispered, giving her a sly wink.

Takaro's eyes flew wide open in shock.

"Last night?" she repeated.

As he turned away to head home, he answered: "Yes, thank you for getting me home instead of leaving me to waste away here with Mekai and the others." He smiled at her as he wandered off to join his comrades.

6

the mark of the kagai warrior

Many days had passed since Takaro first learned of the extent of her mother's involvement with the Kagai Warriors and her role as a spy. After she had gotten over her initial shock and accepted this new realm of warriorship, Takaro wholeheartedly immersed herself into all aspects of training.

During this time, Yaruke went to great lengths to teach Takaro how to distil plants to extract poisons and how to use the benign looking accessories carried by most women as deadly weapons. From easily concealed knives to the iron fan, she was trained on how to hide and use these tools of destruction. A great deal of her time was also spent in exercises that would allow her to memorize detailed maps and complicated messages.

"My head is throbbing," groaned Takaro, her hand pushing away the worn piece of parchment. "I do not believe I can memorize one more map."

"Now see here Takaro, it is most important to study these scrolls," insisted Yaruke.

"Why is it so important? Why can a person not just take one of these maps on a mission, instead of memorizing it?"

"Takaro, when you are ready to go on such missions, if by chance you are captured; maps, notes, messages, all these things can reveal to the enemy our location, our movements, our strategy. It is far too great a risk. If you are killed, all this information stored in your head shall die with you. Do you understand what I am saying?" asked her master.

Takaro nodded as she responded: "You speak the truth, master. I do understand."

"Good, for soon, you shall be asked to take up arms to join your brothers," said Yaruke. "Your task will be to memorize the areas; the lay of the land Medaru shall be leading our men into. If any of the men become separated, it will be your job to see the warriors to safety. And as you are now trained in the art of healing, your task is to administer to the care of the wounded until they can be delivered back to Anshen."

"Will I be ready?" asked Takaro. "Will I be leaving any time soon?"

"You are as ready as you will ever be. And yes, you will be leaving soon," answered her master. "I had received word from the east that the Emperor has sent forth another army to enter our lands. He plans to invade our country before the next full moon."

"And I shall be going this time?"

"Unfortunately, yes," answered Yaruke, with a dismal sigh.

"How can that be unfortunate? I have trained for this a good long time, master. I have seen too many of my brothers go off to battle, some never to return. I feel a need to go; to fight by their side."

"Are you not scared?" queried the warrior priest.

"I cannot deny that deep down, I am scared, but I am more scared of failing than I am of dying," she responded in a small voice. "I am afraid that I may not have the courage to face the enemy when the time comes. I worry that I may lack the bravery to rise up against our foes to do what you and your forefathers have done."

"What do you define as courage, Takaro?" questioned Yaruke.

"A warrior who is courageous is one who can boldly charge into battle and willingly slays the enemy, as quickly and as many as possible," she answered with conviction. "And he can rise up to each occasion to do battle again and again without wavering."

"No, my child, this is not courage. Any seasoned warrior can enter battle and not think twice about the situation he is about to face."

"Then what does it mean to be courageous?" asked Takaro, curious to learn more.

"The measure of one's courage is not dependent on the number of heroic feats one undertakes, or the number of foes taken down in battle," explained Yaruke. "Instead, true courage arises when one is forced to face his absolute worst fears, to be truly frightened, yet still find the courage to rise up and meet the challenge. Now *that* is true courage."

Takaro considered her master's words and with a sigh, responded: "Whether this type of courage is within me, it is yet to be seen. I suppose I will not know until the moment of truth."

"Let it not be said that there is not one of us; my father, his father, or his father's father who did not question this the first time we were asked to take up arms. It is like a baptism by fire, not until you are tried in the heat of battle will you discover your true courage," attested the elderly warrior. "For my part, I have shared with you all that I can of warriorship. I have imparted the wisdom of my forefathers on to you. And through you, I hope to keep our traditions alive for as long as it is needed to secure peace and justice in our realm."

"I will try to do you proud, master," promised Takaro, bowing deeply in respect.

"I know you will, little one. I hold great hope for you," said Yaruke. His eyes twinkled with pride as a smile creased his aged face. He gave her hand a gentle squeeze of reassurance.

Four days later, on a warm spring night Yaruke Saibon, breathing his last breath, passed from this realm. Yaruke's son, Medaru and his grandson, Keodai presided over the prayers for the dead as the funeral pyre was lit. Takaro consoled Yumai as she wept bitterly for her grandfather, as wounded by his passing as she was when her mother died.

Takaro lowered her head in silent prayer. Her heart ached upon Yaruke's passing, but mingled with her sadness was her own shame that she was unable to weep, to shed a single tear of grief for her master.

She embraced Yumai as her body shuddered with great sobs. Even her brother, Keodai wept for their grandfather.

As the villagers dispersed after the service, Takaro stood by Medaru's side before the roaring flames that rapaciously consumed Yaruke's body.

"My father lived a good, long life, Takaro. By mortal standards, ninety-one years is a long time to live in this realm," stated Medaru, taking a step back from the intense heat.

"I shall miss the old man," she responded wistfully.

"As I will too, but for now, there is no time to be burdened by grief. Tomorrow, we head north," stated Medaru. "Before we do, we shall rise at dawn to sprinkle my father's ashes into Reyu Falls. Water was always his favorite element. We will let the powers of the water claim what is left of his earthly remains."

"I shall be there to pay final respects to my master," promised

Takaro, in a solemn voice.

"My father asked that you reside in his cottage. It is yours if you wish to live there," offered Medaru.

"His home should remain in the family. It should be for Keodai or Yumai, not for me," insisted the little warrior.

"You *are* family, Takaro. My father held you in the same regard as a daughter, just as I do now," answered Medaru.

"I am most honoured, master. In light of what we face tomorrow, it is best to let fate decide. If I survive my first battle, then I shall return to Master Yaruke's home. I will care for it and maintain your father's cottage in his memory."

"I suppose many of us shall have our fate decided tomorrow, Takaro," said Medaru, in a gentle voice as he led her away from the funeral pyre.

Against a crimson dawn, ninety-five warriors armed with bows and swords gathered in the great field by Lake Anzan. Now donning the dark, earth-tone battle raiment of her warrior brethren, Takaro fell into line with the men. Their cloaks rippled and billowed in the brisk, morning breeze as Medaru gave the warriors final orders before heading out of Anshen.

The Kagai leader stood proud and erect, still a commanding presence for a man in his fifty-sixth year of existence. His once raven-black hair, now peppered with gray strands, was the only sign of his age.

"For many of you, this shall be your first battle, and possibly your last. Be warned now, no amount of training can prepare you for the horrors of war, but God be willing, we shall endure and return all the stronger for it. I pray that each one of you remember all the various scenarios we have incorporated into your training. I pray each of you find the strength and courage that will allow you to aim your arrow straight and true, and to wield your sword with a steady hand. And always remember, if you are captured, as a Kagai Warrior, there is honour to be found in death. You must not think only of yourself. You are only one. The lives of many shall be counting on you. Your fellow warriors, the women, the children, you must keep them safe. They *must* remain safe. Is that understood?"

"Yes, Master Saibon!" the warriors shouted in response.

Takaro glanced down at the short sword thrust into the knot of her belt. Not only will it become her secondary weapon, she knew it would become her best solution for a hasty death should she be captured.

"This morn, we shall journey north to Magare Valley. We will travel all morning into the afternoon. We shall rest at midday, and then continue on until darkness falls. At the first light of dawn, we will journey on and then prepare to attack the enemy at nightfall. It is my understanding, Lord Dahlon Treeborn and the elders of Orien have sent forth a large battalion to aid us with this incursion. Whether they shall arrive in time is doubtful, but we will do what we have always done. We shall keep the Imperial Army at bay! We will deliver death to all who enter our lands!" stated Medaru. "Are you ready, warriors?"

"Yes, Master Saibon!" they answered, their voices ringing with pride and unwavering confidence.

"Let us be on our way!" shouted Medaru, as he mounted his steed.

The women, children and the warriors too old or injured from previous battles saw them off, watching as Takaro and her brother warriors disappeared into the morning mist as they marched out of Anshen.

The warriors journeyed through the rugged terrain, covering a good distance that by day's end, their trek delivered them around the edge of a swamp as they ventured northward. Medaru urged the warriors to eat and to rest while rest could be afforded to them. They would rise at dawn and continue on until dusk.

The following day as their march came to an end, Medaru and several of the warriors ventured ahead to meet up with the other warriors previously assigned to monitor enemy activities in the Magare Valley.

As dusk descended, Medaru returned with more warriors. All gathered around their master as he gave instructions. Using a stick to etch into the sand, he hastily drew out the mountains, forests and fields. This was to represent the backdrop, the landscape that was to play host to this hostile encounter.

"The enemy gathers at the mouth of the Magare Valley. None have yet to set foot onto our lands. They await more soldiers and will prepare to invade in the light of day," announced Medaru.

"How many," asked Takaro.

"There are at least five-hundred," answered her master.

"Five-hundred?" gasped Keodai. "We are greatly outnumbered!"

"If all goes as planned, we shall engage in battle with only half that number," stated Keodai's father, with smile to reassure him.

"Still…" responded Keodai.

"My son, need I remind you, in the past we have faced far greater numbers with fewer warriors. We will endure. We always do."

"Are we to enter the Magare Valley under the cover of night?" asked Keodai, as he scrutinized the diagram.

"We shall attack by night, but we will not be going to them. They shall be coming to us," stated Medaru.

"But you said that they will only engage in war in the light of day," continued Keodai.

"We will force their hand. We, on horseback, shall offer ourselves up as decoys. We will lure the soldiers to us," explained their master. "By eluding our own snares and traps, we shall lead the Imperial Army directly into the pine forest. I estimate that perhaps, one-hundred-fifty to two hundred soldiers will pursue our decoys into this field."

His stick pointed to the base of the mountain slope at the mouth of the valley. "Once they reach this point in the field, we shall set off the trip-lines that shall unleash an avalanche to seal off the mouth of the valley. I anticipate the deluge of rocks and boulders will crush a good number, while the rest shall be separated and sealed off in the valley by this landslide. They will be unable to come to the aid of their comrades and when they do finally penetrate this wall of rocks and earth, it shall be over. We will be gone and so will the bodies of their dead comrades," stated Medaru.

"I see now," replied Keodai.

The father smiled with confidence at his son as he continued to brief his men.

"And there is more. As they cross this field, they shall be greeted by concealed pits of which, the floors are lined with many sharp, wooden stakes," announced Medaru, his stick pointing to four strategic locations outlying the forest. "These pits will undoubtedly dispatch a number of the soldiers as they surge forward, unable to stop due to the crush of men advancing from behind. Those that do survive will be drawn into the forest where we shall engage them in battle."

"With our swords?" asked Takaro.

"No, with our bows," responded Hemashe, edging in closer to the little warrior's side to observe Medaru's depiction of the battlefield.

Medaru smiled at his young, yet-to-be-tested warriors as he responded: "Hemashe is correct. Bow and arrow first, and then we fight with sword, but we will only take on those who survive entering this grove of bamboo growing along the perimeter of the pine forest."

Their master pointed to the multitude of snares lining the footpaths as he continued on: "Here, our warriors have manipulated strong, flexible canes of bamboo and ropes to ensnare the enemy. The first line of soldiers to advance into the pine forest shall be met with a barrage. Logs have already been secured high into the trees. They cannot be detected in the darkness. As the soldiers pour into the forest in pursuit of our decoys, lines shall be cut to release these logs. They will swing down, knocking over the enemy and crushing those that get caught between them. And then, we shall dispense a volley of arrows from high above, in these trees."

"I do not believe we may even have to confront them head on," assessed Hemashe, marveling at Medaru's ingenuity and resourcefulness.

"You would be surprised, young warrior. There are always some that elude our snares and traps, but rest assured, none has ever lived to tell the tale of meeting up with a sword wielded by a Kagai Warrior," averred Medaru.

The warriors all nodded in agreement.

"Does everyone understand this mission we are about to embark on? Does everyone remember where we have placed our snares and traps?" asked Medaru. He silently took stock of all the faces before him.

"Good! We will be on our way to meet the enemy. The warriors responsible for the traps and snares are already lying in wait. When we reach this pine forest, I shall assign each of you to your post. Those of you to bear arms for the first time should remain close to those who have already seen battle. The experienced warriors will help you if they can, but always be mindful of your backside, and always look before you strike. In the heat of battle, all too often it is easy to instinctively lash out first, before knowing what one is lashing out at. You do not want to find yourself on the end of your brother warrior's sword. Understand?" cautioned Medaru. "And none will begin the assault until you receive the signal."

"Yes, Master Saibon!" The warriors answered collectively.

"Let us be on our way," said Medaru, waving the warriors on to follow him into the growing darkness.

As the sun withdrew its last, dying rays, the forest was cloaked in the deep shadows of the impending night, enveloped in an unnatural

hush. The creatures of the forest, sensing danger, scurried away to hide in fear. Their movements and calls were stifled. In its place, Medaru and a number of warriors called out randomly, using the sounds made by the nightingales to give the forest and the surrounding mountains a sense of calm. To the untrained ears, the enemy soldiers could only detect the sounds of a forest as it came alive with the creatures of the night. Lulled into a false sense of security, they settled down as darkness slowly descended upon the land.

High up in the trees, the warriors watched and waited as they mentally braced themselves for the battle to begin. Takaro was perched on a branch, her back resting against the tree trunk. She glanced over to see Hemashe. He nervously stared down at the forest floor. In the other trees, her sharp eyes could make out the dark silhouettes of her brother warriors. She could see Keodai and Mekai concealed in the tree next to hers. Below, Medaru and a dozen warriors on horseback prepared to run the gauntlet from this pine forest to the enemy camp. Without a word, they dissolved into the blackness, swallowed up by the great shadows of the forest.

Against a rising full moon, from their high vantage point, Takaro could see Medaru and his men deftly weaving their way through the snares set up in the stands of bamboo and onward, between the cleverly hidden pits. These pits, though easy enough to spot in the light of day, were nigh on impossible to see by moonlight. The large gaping holes, concealed by heavy tarps of rough burlap that were pegged into the ground at each corner, and then covered with a thin layer of soil and grasses waited patiently for their unsuspecting guests.

Takaro continued to watch as her master and his loyal warriors advanced toward the mouth of the valley at an easy pace, their horses trotting to the enemy camp, still unnoticed. As they neared, soldiers posted to sentry duty suddenly became aware of their presence. Before they could call out in warning, Medaru and his men, clad in dark, flowing hooded cloaks, launched a series of arrows to down these guards. With a great roar, he and the others charged directly into camp, dispensing arrows as they stormed through the crowd of startled soldiers.

Medaru's cry, neither a scream nor shout, echoed through the valley, rattling the soldiers' nerves and alerting his warriors that the battle was about to begin. Steeds careened and reared as the dark clad riders sent soldiers scattering for their weapons.

Medaru and his warriors charged back, retreating toward the open field. As he did so, he sent aloft an arrow consumed in flames to pierce the night sky. In response, the warriors hidden on the slopes of the mountains that reduced the entrance of the valley into a narrow 'v' shape, prepared to trigger the trip-lines.

Like angry wasps agitated from their hive, Imperial Soldiers spilled out from tents, swords and halberds at the ready.

"After them!" shouted the captain, frantically urging his soldiers on. "Kill them all!"

From where Takaro was perched, she could see the great, black swarm as they poured out from the valley in pursuit of the Kagai Warriors. Medaru released another bone-rattling call. She stood up for a better view just in time to see the sides of the mountains collapsing as supports securing the weak points of the slope gave way with a resounding '*crash*'.

She could make out the frightened screams of soldiers caught in the wake of the landslide and the angry shouts of those now separated from the rest of the army. They were now trapped in the valley with no way to aid their fellow soldiers on the other side.

Undaunted by the calamity, the captain of the Imperial Army ordered his men to continue their pursuit. Takaro watched as soldiers gave chase on foot.

"How many come, Takaro?" asked Hemashe. "Can you see?"

"I would say almost two-hundred," whispered Takaro, as she continued to watch as Medaru and his men beat a hasty retreat for the forest.

"We are outnumbered two to one," responded Hemashe.

"We do not know that yet," answered Takaro, sensing his rising fear.

She and her comrades listened as screams of agony filled the night air. Soldiers on the front line had run headlong into the pits. They tumbled in, only to be impaled on the many wooden stakes. Many of them halted their advance, only to be pushed forward to meet their demise due to the insurgence of those pressing forward, unaware of the traps that lay before them.

Still, the captain was unmoved by the plight of his hapless soldiers, his sword waving angrily in the air as he urged the men on. The rustling of bamboo was immediately replaced by the screams of men catapulted into the air as they set off the many snares.

When it became evident all the deadly snares had been tripped, the captain waved his remaining men onward, motioning them to advance. The soldiers entered the so-called *haunted* forest with great trepidation, their swords and halberds pointed forward as they blindly forged ahead.

In a blur of movement, Medaru charged past them. Emitting another unearthly call, he signaled to his men to release the logs. Like massive, wooden pendulums, the logs swung down, bowling over the unsuspecting soldiers. Many were crushed, caught in between the colliding logs, while other men were slammed against tree trunks. With a wave of his sword, Medaru signaled all the warriors to release their arrows. The deadly projectiles hailed down upon the soldiers like a rain of death, pinning some of the unfortunates to the still-swinging logs as they attempted to escape.

Adrenalin coursed through her veins. Her body trembled in nervous anticipation. Takaro unleashed a relentless flurry of arrows. One after another, soldiers reeled and tumbled to the ground with the impact of her unerring aim. With arrows spent, Medaru gave the warriors the signal to descend from the trees to finish off the soldiers still standing. Soon, the entire forest reverberated with the calls of the Kagai Warriors echoing off the surrounding mountains. The soldiers glanced about in fear, unsure of the direction and numbers of their unseen assailants.

With great agility, the warriors moved like silent shadows, pressing in on the frightened soldiers. As she landed lightly onto the ground, Takaro drew her long sword in preparation for battle. Rushing in with her weapon held high, she froze as an enemy soldier turned to face her. Her mind raced and her heart panicked as her muscles refused to budge.

Fight, damn it! Fight! Takaro cursed at herself.

By her response, the soldier quickly realized the little figure before him was an inexperienced warrior. He gave a defiant snarl as he lunged at Takaro. As she angled out of the way of his blade, an arrow skimmed past her, slamming into her assailant's chest.

The soldier tumbled backward from the impact, his sword falling from his dying grip. Takaro glanced back to see that it was Hemashe's arrow that had downed the soldier. She breathed a sigh of relief, but her eyes grew wide in horror as a soldier silently rose up behind Hemashe, halberd raised high to quickly dispatch him.

"Hemashe!" shouted Takaro, as she flung her sword like spear in his direction.

As the young warrior hit the ground and rolled, the great axe came down narrowly missing him. Takaro raced to his side. Before her lay the soldier, writhing in his final death throes as her sword pierced straight through his chest, just missing his heart.

As the realization that she and the others were now engaged in an all-out war, with one foot braced against the chest of the writhing soldier, Takaro seized her sword into her hands. With a deliberate and fatal twist, she severed the already damaged artery to finish the job. Yanking it away from the corpse, she quickly twisted her wrist, flicking away the blood coating the blade of her sword as she turned on the next soldier charging toward her.

This time, there was no hesitation. Takaro raced toward the much larger man. Just as he came over top of her, she abruptly turned sideways, dropping down onto her right knee. Rising up, her right arm went between his legs, throwing him over as she pivoted. The soldier crashed down hard on his back as Takaro's blade arced down upon him, effectively eviscerating the man. He lay in a quivering, screaming heap. As she stepped over his convulsing body, her blade swung down, quickly and deliberately slashing his throat to end his life.

Through the chaos of battle, she spied Keodai. Two soldiers had him cornered. He parried the incoming sword of one while dodging the halberd of the other. Takaro dashed to his aid, diving below the sword of an enemy soldier. As she rose up onto her feet behind Keodai's foes, her sword slashed upwards from her left to the right, slicing through the man's back. Turning her attention to the other soldier, her sword swung around in her hands as it turned horizontally, instantly decapitating the soldier. Blood pulsated from one of the severed arteries, spraying both Keodai and Takaro in a hot jet of crimson. She leapt back just as Keodai's sword rammed straight through the soldier's body, coming out of his back, almost impaling her in the process.

As the soldier fell over, Keodai yanked his sword out, giving the little warrior a nod. His eyes widened in fear, but before he could scream out, Takaro could sense an energy closing in behind her. Instinctively, she dove down and rolled. A soldier's blade skimmed over her, barely missing her. Keodai lunged at the man as the frustrated soldier slashed out once more.

Rolling over her shoulder, Takaro rose up onto her feet, but in the midst of the confusion and darkness, she lost her sword. As she rose up, she found herself standing directly before an Imperial Soldier. This hulk of a man immediately seized Takaro by her throat, easily lifting her clear off the ground. The metal gauntlet he wore on his hand cut into her neck as he squeezed. Takaro gasped as she fought for her breath, struggling to unclench his fingers and thumb.

The man's eyes burned with unadulterated hate as his left hand continued to tighten about her throat. Takaro watched as his right shoulder flexed backwards, telegraphing his intent. She knew he was retracting his sword in preparation to ram it straight through her body.

A painful gasp escaped his lips. His eyes opened wide in dismay as he released his grip. Takaro fell to the ground as the soldier toppled over. She scrambled over his dead body, reclaiming her short sword that now pierced his throat.

A loud groan of pain caught her attention. Glancing up, she watched as Hemashe was slammed against a tree. His assailant attacked with a vengeance, pinning the warrior against the trunk. Fending off this brutal assault, Hemashe struggled to remove the handle of a broken halberd pressing unmercifully against his throat.

Takaro raced to his aid. Dive rolling to the ground; she scooped up her long sword into her hand as she somersaulted, coming to a stop directly behind the soldier. With a sword in each hand, she instinctively cross-slashed, slicing through the unprotected tendons at the back of the soldier's knees. The enemy screamed out in pain as his own weight caused his legs to buckle. As he collapsed backwards, Takaro's blades slammed down, one piercing the soldier's throat as the other plunged into his heart. Hemashe was gasping for his breath as he fell to the ground, still clutching the handle of the halberd as the little warrior darted off into the darkness, in search of her next foe.

No sooner than it started, the battle was done. In less than fifteen minutes, the Kagai Warriors had all but annihilated the Imperial Army.

An eerie silence smothered the land. The only sound that could be heard was the rapid beating of their hearts and the loud gasping as the weary warriors fought to regain their breath.

Takaro glanced about in stunned silence. Her keen eyes could make out the many dead, dismembered and decapitated bodies scattered about the forest floor. Everywhere there was blood. And as she gazed down upon her raiment, she could see the dark, random splatter of crimson splashed across her. As the beating of her heart calmed, the groans of wounded warriors and the squelched cries of enemy soldiers raked at her nerves.

She could see Medaru and other warriors darting from soldier to soldier, finishing off those that were still alive, but mortally wounded. As much as this final act seemed to be done out of mercy, it was as much to ensure the enemy soldiers would not survive long enough to speak of what had happened.

Takaro's breathing came to her in short, sharp gasps as her chest tightened with every beat of her heart. Her sword, now bathed in blood from the tip to the guard, slipped from her grasp as she collapsed to her shaking knees. Her flesh was raised as if an icy chill enveloped her, as though the souls of the soldiers she herself had downed, now crowded around her, suffocating her. Takaro's eyes were dark and liquid as the horrifying images of her own deeds replayed in her mind. Her whole body began to tremble as she stared down at her bloodied hands.

"Takaro! Are you hurt?"

Her eyes blinked hard as these words buzzed like a distant echo in her ears that still rang with the cruel sounds of war.

"Takaro?"

She peered up to see Medaru and Keodai kneeling before her.

"You are covered in blood, Takaro," said Medaru. "Are you hurt?"

She merely shook her head in response as Keodai helped her onto her feet. She could feel the surface of her skin tighten as the splattered blood coagulated and dried. Her parched mouth began to salivate as the taste of copper filled the back of her throat as her nostrils breathed in the air, now rife with the scent of freshly spilled blood. Takaro pulled away from Keodai, running only a few steps. She collapsed onto her knees by an old tree stump, retching and coughing.

Her eyes watered as she stood up, wiping her mouth with the back of her hand only to smear the drying blood across her face.

"If you are not hurt, you must tend to the wounded," ordered Medaru, his hands shook her slight shoulders in attempt to break this trance she was in. "Do you understand, Takaro?"

She merely nodded her head. Her trembling hands wiped the blood off her sword onto her cloak before struggling to sheath her weapon in its scabbard.

"Then quickly, Takaro, help your brothers. Tend to those in most dire need first," instructed Medaru, as he led his son and the other warriors to gather up the dead.

Their next task was to fill the pits with the dead bodies of enemy soldiers. With so many corpses, it would not take long for the warriors to fill the hollows; bury the bodies; and to replace the grasses, shrubs and other vegetation to effectively conceal the graves. When the enemy soldiers eventually break through the landslide, their comrades would have all but vanished, spirited away by mysterious forces.

Her eyes followed the shadows of the warriors as they worked quickly, gathering bodies and weapons. Those who were trained in the healing arts as well as the warriors too hurt to assist with the task of concealing the dead, set about to gather their wounded comrades.

"Make haste, Takaro! You are needed now!" a voice called out from the darkness. “Quickly!”

As she made her way forward, men waited in silence as those more experienced than she quickly assessed the injuries. Most had superficial cuts and contusions to accompany their nasty gashes. One warrior cried out in pain as two others worked to reset his broken arm and dislocated shoulder.

Wandering through the carnage, her gaze fell upon a wounded warrior. The man was doubled over and convulsing in agony. To her horror, the enemy’s sword still protruded from his body. It had entered from the front just below his left rib cage to pierce straight through his body. As the warrior coughed, blood and vomit spewed from his mouth and nostrils as he quaked violently from the trauma of his injury.

Takaro knelt before him. Removing her pack containing bandages and salves, she prepared to aid him. This help was short-lived as another healer seized her by the wrist, pulling her away from the warrior.

“Come Takaro! Leave him be,” he ordered her.

“Can you not see he is hurt?” She yanked away from his grip. “I can help him!”

“No, you cannot. None of us can,” he whispered angrily in his impatience. “He is dying as we speak. Your time is better spent helping those that will live through the night.”

“But I cannot leave him like this!” insisted Takaro.

“You must! Your help is needed elsewhere. Now quickly, come with me!” ordered the healer.

Takaro glanced back at the dying warrior. She raced over to his side as she whispered to him: “I will not leave you like this, impaled upon the enemy’s sword.”

The warrior gave her a weak nod as he braced himself for more pain. Takaro seized the weapon by the handle and as quickly and smoothly as possible, she extracted the lethal blade.

The warrior groaned as he collapsed to his side, his pained eyes glanced up at the little warrior as she removed her cloak, throwing it over his trembling body to warm and comfort him.

“Thank you,” he whispered in a weak voice.

“I shall return,” promised Takaro, as the healer seized her by the wrist once more to lead her away.

“I know you think me callous and I know you mean well, Takaro. All these men are deserving of our aid, but they are many and we are few. You must learn to help only those that will survive,” explained the healer. “The ones with minor wounds can wait; the others in need of immediate attention shall die if they do not receive care first. As for the dying, Master Saibon will deal with them. For now, we must get to work."

He led her through the worst of the wounded until they came across a warrior lapsing into shock from the trauma of his injuries.

"Hold this lantern steady," requested the healer, as he set his medicine bag down.

The groaning warrior bore a gaping wound inflicted by a halberd; his left thighbone was smashed by the impact. The healer tore open his legging to better assess the wound. There was blood, and plenty of it, but he knew immediately that the axe had not severed the femoral artery.

"He is lucky," determined the healer.

"You call this *lucky*?" gasped Takaro, grimacing as she endured the grisly scene before her.

"He will not bleed to death. It is a pretty clean break and if infection does not set in, neither will he lose his leg," stated the healer, his hand pressing the two edges of the wound together. "Put the lantern down. Give me your hand. I need you to hold this together. Apply pressure to the wound. It will help to staunch the flow of blood."

Takaro asked no questions. She did as she was told. As her palm pressed down on the wound, the heat emanating from the injury and the blood that continued to flow startled her. She trembled as the man let out a gasp of pain.

Bracing one hand behind the warrior's knee, the other around his ankle, the healer slowly raised the wounded leg, bending it forward.

She knew the healer was intent on realigning the shattered bone as best he could.

With a swift and powerful jerk, he snapped back on the leg.

The warrior bolted upright, howling in excruciating pain as Takaro fell backwards from the force. She watched as the warrior's eyes rolled up into the back of his head, the shock of the pain too much to bear.

"I shall apply a splint as soon as we are done. Have you ever stitched up a wound?" asked the healer.

"None like this," gasped Takaro, staring at the bloody mess.

"You are a woman. You know how to sew. Just apply the same skills to this wound," ordered the healer.

"Sewing a torn pair of trousers is not the same as sewing flesh and skin together," argued Takaro.

"I beg to differ," replied the healer, as he rummaged through his bag for a ball of fine, silk thread and a needle. "Your fingers are smaller than mine. I shall hold the wound open so you can access his muscle.

Stitch together the worst of it. Leave enough thread so it can hang outside his leg so we may remove it once the muscles have mended sufficiently."

"But it will hurt him! I do not wish to inflict more pain!" protested Takaro.

"Believe me, the sooner you are done, the better. Thankfully, in this state, he shall not feel a thing. Get to it, Takaro. You do not want to be half way done when he wakes up," insisted the healer.

Three hours passed quickly and during this time the worst of the wounds were tended to. Medaru and the others returned to lead the warriors back to Anshen. As he approached, the warrior priest found Takaro resting against a fallen log. Upon her lap, lay the head of the dying warrior. Though having been impaled upon an enemy sword, death was slow to make its claim. The man's body, still draped in Takaro's cloak, rose and fell with each laboured breath he struggled to gulp down.

Medaru knelt before them.

"He wishes to relinquish his life," whispered Takaro, in a sad and weary voice.

The warrior struggled to right himself, feebly clutching his short sword in his bloodied hands.

Medaru leaned in close over the dying man, supporting his trembling body. He could feel his energy ebbing away.

"Does she speak the truth, my brother?" he asked.

The warrior answered back between pained breaths: "Yes, master. I do not… wish to linger… in this state."

"Very well, so be it," responded Medaru. He signaled the able-bodied warriors to gather around him.

As Takaro rose up, the warrior seized her hand. "Do not leave… my side now, Takaro. Please… help to remove my cloak."

"Of course, I will not leave," promised the little warrior, her voice trembling as she slipped her cloak back over her shoulders as she helped to remove his.

"I wish to die with my pride intact, and yet, I cannot hold… myself steady," he said in a whisper.

"Then I will help to steady you," she offered.

"Thank you, Takaro," he replied as he slowly sat upright,

sword poised at his chest as her small hands rested on his quaking shoulders.

Medaru and the warriors formed a circle around the dying man. Their fingers were woven into the configuration to summon the energy of the air. As he led the incantation, a warm, gentle breeze swirled around them as though waiting to deliver home the warrior's spirit. Medaru offered the warrior a final blessing whereupon, without hesitation, the warrior rammed the tip of his short sword upwards to strike his heart. Stifling his cry of pain, before he could slump forward, Medaru's sword came down with blinding speed.

The light of the fading moon danced off his blade as it swept past Takaro's ashen face. She immediately turned away, averting her eyes as the sword decapitated the warrior, cleanly severing his head from his neck.. With a heavy *'thud'* the warrior's head tumbled to the bloodstained ground, rolling away with a final sense of peace, and a look on his face that was now devoid of pain.

The man's body lurched forward, away from Takaro's grasp. Still, she could not force herself to look as Medaru and Keodai administered the prayers for the dead. Hemashe came to her side, his arm around her shoulders as he led her away so the other warriors could prepare the body for the journey home.

Under a pre-dawn sky, Medaru escorted the warriors back to Anshen. Those unable to walk were carried out on horseback. A litter was quickly constructed to carry out the body of their dead brother and for the warrior with the badly wounded leg. It pleased Takaro to see that the man had eventually come to, groaning and complaining intermittently as he was transported over the rough terrain.

As the morning sun climbed high into the sky, Medaru gave orders for the warriors to stop by a large pond. "We shall eat and rest for a few hours, and then we shall continue on until dusk."

Many of the weary warriors collapsed in exhaustion where they stood. The wounded men rested beneath the shade of the trees as those with still the energy to do so, delivered food and water to all. The others were posted to sentry duty.

Takaro gathered as many water flasks as she could carry. Heading off to find the stream that fed the pond, she planned to replenish the flasks for the others.

Hemashe caught up to her, taking some of the containers. "Let me help you, Takaro."

She said nothing, surrendering an armload of the flasks to him.

He noticed that she had said little, not uttering anything more than single word responses since assisting in the dying warrior's honourable death. As he gazed into her eyes, they were strangely vacant.

As they knelt down by the water's edge, Hemashe glanced at her reflection. "You look a bloody mess."

Takaro's gaze turned to her comrade's blood-splattered face and raiment, and then to her own reflection. Her face, neck, and across her entire body, there was blood. It was as though she had been immersed in a vat of crimson liquid. Dried clots of blood, both of the enemy's and her warrior brothers' caked her hair and seeped deep beneath her fingernails. For the first time, she caught a frightful glimpse of her image. She just stared; rendered speechless by what she was forced to look upon. Her heartbeat hastened as her mind raced: *That is not me! That cannot be me!*

"Let us get some of this blood off you, Takaro," suggested Hemashe, holding forth a flask to pour its contents into her hands.

She cupped her hands, catching the water as it streamed out. Splashing it onto her face, she watched as the diluted blood splattered onto the ground in front of her.

She rinsed again, and again; red droplets ran down from her hands and face.

"It is not coming off!" she gasped, staring down at her stained hands. "This blood is not coming off, Hemashe!"

Before he could stop her, Takaro bolted up and dashed into the pond. Diving beneath its surface, her cloak, pack and clothes quickly became saturated, absolutely waterlogged. Soon, she was pulled down by its weight.

"I am not amused, Takaro!" ranted Hemashe, standing by the edge of the pond. "Come out right now!"

All he could see was the surface of the water as it settled back to its calm, the ripples subsiding as it reached the shore. The dazzling reflection of the sun and the sky made it impossible for him to see through the water.

As she sank, Takaro's eyes gazed upwards. She could see the sun's light sparkling upon the pond's smooth surface. Staring down at her hands, she began to scrub, desperately attempting to remove the blood clinging stubbornly to her skin. As her efforts became more frantic, the water began to churn and cloud around her as the blood dissolved from her skin, hair and clothing.

Keodai and his father slowly stood up as they heard Hemashe's distressed shouts and watched as he anxiously paced the water's edge.

"Takaro! Come out this instant!" hollered Hemashe. Panic filled his heart as he watched bubbles rise, breaking the surface.

Medaru and Keodai raced to his side as Hemashe threw down the flask he held in his hand. He tore off his cloak and swords as he dove into the water.

Keodai threw down his weapons as he followed Hemashe. Though the pond was small, it was deceptively deep. In the now murky depth they spotted her. It was as though she had given up. Her arms floated above her head as a steady stream of bubbles slowly escaped her lungs as she sank further. Keodai and Hemashe reached down, each grabbing a hold of her wrists as they quickly pulled her to the surface.

On the shore, warriors gathered along the edge. Takaro coughed and sputtered as she surfaced for her first breath of air, still struggling with the weight of her waterlogged raiment and pack. Keodai and Hemashe helped Takaro back to dry land where Medaru waited, his cloak held open to wrap her trembling, wet body.

She dropped to her knees, gasping and coughing as Hemashe knelt before her. He threw his arms about her, holding her close as he whispered: "What were you thinking, Takaro? Tell me this was an accident."

"No need for concern, men! Get back to your duties. Catch some rest while you can, for we shall be on the move in a few hours," ordered Medaru, as he waved the warriors off to disperse.

Hemashe bent forward to look into her dark eyes as he asked: "It was an accident, right?"

Her eyes remained downcast as she answered in a small voice: "There was so much blood. It would not come off."

"I know, I know. It was a pretty gruesome sight," admitted Hemashe, trying to comfort her. "But it is gone now."

He held forth her small hands for her to inspect. There were only traces of blood still trapped beneath her fingernails and dark stains that permeated deep into the leather of her boots and her vest.

"What little is left will fade with time," assured Keodai, as he helped to lift Takaro onto her feet.

She nodded in understanding, praying that he spoke the truth.

"I know you can stay beneath the water's surface longer than any of us, Takaro, but do not ever do that again," pleaded Hemashe.

"Yes, you gave us all quite the scare," added Medaru. "For now, dry out in the warmth of the sun. Get some rest and food. We shall speak later."

"Yes, master," responded Takaro. Keodai escorted her to a sunny clearing, away from the others.

"Hemashe, you are one of Takaro's closest friends. Stay near to her," ordered Medaru. "I can sense she is greatly troubled by the events of last night. Stay close to her side for the time being."

"Of course, master," replied Hemashe. He bowed in understanding before turning away to join Takaro.

As the sun's waning light surrendered to the coming of the night, the warriors settled down for the evening. The campfire peeled back the darkness of the forest as warriors gathered around to share food and stories of the latest battle.

Takaro sat at the outer edge of the group. Medaru observed her from a distance. She would occasionally offer a weak smile and a nod, but it was apparent to him that she was oblivious as to what she was smiling and nodding about. It was as though she was so deeply mired in her own thoughts that the words of the others were nothing more than jumbled fragments of sentences. Her response was merely out of courtesy.

Medaru stood up before his company to make an announcement: "Last night was an excellent example of how we work. We first pare down the enemy's numbers before engaging in hand-to-hand combat, and then we strike hard and fast. We get in and out as quickly as possible. For many of you, it was the first time you faced the enemy. It pleases me to no end that all of our young warriors endured. Although many of you received injuries that will heal in time and we did lose one of our brothers, take comfort in knowing that the enemy was taken down in defeat. Our suffering and loss has not been in vain."

The warriors all cheered in agreement as Medaru raised his hands for silence as he continued: "Each one of you had shown incredible valor and courage in the heat of the battle and upon our return to Anshen, the newly initiated shall receive the mark of the Kagai Warrior." His hand patted the dark tattoo he proudly wore high upon his right arm.

Another boisterous round of cheers filled the night.

"Master, why did we not receive this mark before we went into battle?" asked Mekai. "Did you not think I had the makings of a great warrior?"

"Oh, I had little doubt that each one of you would find your courage and will to take up arms against the enemy, but if by chance you did not survive your first battle, you would have received this tattoo needlessly," answered Medaru.

"Master Saibon is quite right, young sir," interjected a senior warrior standing to Medaru's left. "This mark of our brotherhood is not to be worn lightly. It not only says who we are, it also represents what we are willing to die for. Besides, tomorrow night you shall find out for yourself exactly how painful the tattooing process is. If you can endure it, you will understand why we wait until we are tested in the field of battle before we subject ourselves to this ordeal. Believe me; you would not want to suffer through this lengthy process only to be killed the first time out."

"Well, I for one shall be proud to bear the mark of the Kagai *brotherhood*," declared Mekai, as he glared at Takaro. "Too bad there is not one for a *sisterhood*, but mind you, what is the point when there is only one."

A discomforting hush filled the air. The warriors grew silent upon hearing the young warrior's ignorant and abrasive words directed to Takaro. She merely glared at him as she quickly withdrew from their company, retreating into the shadows of the forest.

Mekai glanced up at the many scowling faces staring back at him.

"What? What did I say?" grumbled Mekai.

"You've said too much!" growled Hemashe.

"I only spoke the truth! Takaro is not meant to be a warrior; to be one of us," snapped Mekai, speaking in his own defense.

Hemashe's response was immediate. He tackled Mekai, knocking him backwards to the ground. Straddling his body, he grabbed Mekai by his collar as his other fist was clenched and raised, poised to strike. "Take back your words! Apologize to Takaro!"

"Come now, Hemashe, be reasonable! Who would you rather have by your side in a real battle situation, her or me? Which one of us is more capable of coming to your aid? To save your life if need be?" snarled Mekai.

Hemashe's trembling fist rose up to slam into Mekai's face, only to have Keodai catch it as he responded: "Last night was a real battle situation, Mekai! Takaro held her own. She stood up to this ordeal as good, if not better, than any one of us!"

"Well, if that is the case, why do you not explain her conduct today?"

Mekai hissed, his voice full of malice. "Why do you not tell Master Saibon what really happened? Why she went for her little *swim*?"

"Why you!" shouted Hemashe. He struggled against Keodai's grip so he may strike Mekai.

"Last night, Takaro saved my life," stated Keodai, glaring down at the prostrate warrior.

"And mine, too," added Hemashe. "Where were you, Mekai? Were you so engrossed in saving your own skin or taking down as many enemy soldiers that you were blind to the fate of your brother warriors? Did you come to the aid of any of your brothers?"

Mekai was silent, his trembling hands still held before his face to intercept Hemashe's angry fist, should it fly.

"I thought not," growled Hemashe, releasing his grip as Keodai hauled him off of Mekai.

"He is not worth the trouble, my friend," stated Keodai.

"I pray the day will never happen that she must come to your aid," snapped Hemashe. "So help me, if it does, I will make you choke on your own words. I swear I will make sure you are at her beck and call until you have repaid her for sparing your worthless life!"

As Hemashe and Keodai backed away, all the warriors, one by one, stood up, turning his back to Mekai.

The young warrior rose up to his feet, startled by the hostile response he was met with.

"As far as I am concerned, Takaro has earned a rightful place in the Kagai brotherhood. She has proven herself worthy, willing to die for a fellow warrior," declared Keodai. "I have yet to see this quality in you, Mekai. You may have killed your share of soldiers last night, but I have yet to hear from one brother that you had come to their aid. I, for one, am proud to fight by Takaro's side."

Mekai glanced at all the backs of those turned against him. Brushing off the dirt and humiliation, he looked to Medaru for his support, only to have his master turn his back to him as well.

The dejected warrior soon came to the sorry conclusion that his words soundly offended all in his presence.

"Master Saibon, please accept my humble apology. I meant not to offend you or my brothers," repented Mekai.

"True you have offended all of us, especially me, for I am Takaro's mentor – her teacher. When you dispute or question her abilities, then you ridicule my teachings," admonished Medaru.

"That was not my intention, I was merely - " responded Mekai, biting his tongue as his master motioned for silence.

"As offended as I am, it is Takaro that is deserving of an apology," rebuked Medaru, as he turned to face his young disciple. "Though you believe you are now a grown-up because you bear arms and march into battle alongside my men, you still have much to learn about being a *man*. You shall soon discover that to bear the mark of the Kagai, to be a true member of this *brotherhood*, it will take more than your ability to wield a sword."

Mekai shrank back from his master's harsh words as his eyes lowered in shame.

"I shall fetch Takaro, master," offered Hemashe.

"No, remain here with the others," instructed Medaru. "I feel a need to speak to Takaro in private."

Huddled beneath the shadow of a tree, Medaru found Takaro brooding in her solitude. He sat down by her side, staring up into the starry sky. For a moment, neither spoke.

"I recall the first time you and Mekai had an altercation. You were so small and yet you stood toe-to-toe against this much larger boy. You exuded no fear, only a strong need for justice," reminisced Medaru. "I remember pulling you off of Mekai, for I was sure you were going to throttle that young man."

"I should have when I had the chance," whispered Takaro. "He has been the bane of my existence from the day he was born."

Medaru laughed as he listened to her words. "In all this time, Takaro, Mekai has not changed, yet you have."

"How so, master?" queried Takaro, her gaze still fixed onto the celestial bodies adorning the deep, cobalt sky.

"I was only a young child when you were first brought here to live and learn from Chusai Saibon. My grandfather and my father shared many tales of your *adventures* in these earlier years. It was through these tales that I had gained a better understanding about you and the complexities of life you were faced with, and still continue to face. Even as I grew up, and now, grow old in your presence, I had witnessed some of your outbursts that can only be attributed to your youth and inexperience," answered Medaru, with a knowing smile. "That is Mekai's problem now."

"What do you mean?" asked Takaro.

"Mekai is still a young man with limited knowledge and experience in life. You on the other hand, in your earlier days you would not have thought twice about turning on a bothersome boy. In light of what ignorant words spewed forth from Mekai's mouth tonight, I believe you surprised us all when you chose to walk away than to engage in a senseless fight with that young man."

"It would not have been worth the effort, master," replied Takaro.

"True, but you cannot deny that had this happened a few years earlier, in all likelihood, Mekai's face would have met up with your fist," stated Medaru. "You are learning self-control and you are also learning to conserve your time and energy for fights that are worthwhile than to expend energy on a fool and his words."

"I cannot help but to believe that Mekai is right. I shall never belong in this brotherhood," lamented Takaro. "I will never be one of *them*."

"No, you will not," confirmed her master, giving her a reassuring smile. "Instead, one day you shall *lead* them, Takaro."

"I think not, master. Perhaps Mekai is right," said Takaro, with a sigh of resignation. "I am not meant to be a warrior."

"Did you hear his words?" asked Medaru, his eyebrows furrowing with concern.

"Of course I did. You know I did. These cursed Elven ears of mine tend to hear more than I ever care to hear. They seem to hear only what is said of me that is cruel and unkind."

"If that be the case, do not tell me that your own heart will be guided by the asinine words spewing from the mouth of one so young and ignorant," said Medaru. "In your own heart, do you truly believe that you do not have the makings of a great warrior?"

Takaro's eyes were downcast in shame as she responded: "The very moment I faced my first Imperial Soldier, I froze."

"And what made you freeze? Were you scared to fight? Were you scared that you might die?" questioned Medaru.

"I was scared to take his life," revealed Takaro. "It was so strange. The moment our eyes met, although I knew he had every intention of killing me, for that split second, I was thinking that this man was somebody's son or brother; or he was someone's husband or lover; perhaps he was a father. Suddenly, he was not some faceless enemy."

Medaru gave her an understanding smile as he responded: "Takaro, you hesitated not because of fear, but out of compassion for a fellow man. It is only human."

"I am *not* human," reminded Takaro.

"Human, Elf, it matters not. The point is; you are a caring being. There is nothing wrong with that," stated her master.

"But my inactions could have cost the lives of our men," said Takaro.

"Inactions? By all account, according to my son and Hemashe, as well as the other warriors fighting by your side, you fought with as much courage and valor as they did. Keodai and Hemashe both claimed before all that your fast actions and quick thinking spared their lives," countered Medaru. "I would say, today you found your courage, little warrior. As far as I am concerned, you held up very well considering the fact this was your first real battle. You endured far more than Mekai was forced to, for you also tended to the wounded and it was you to come to the aid of a brother warrior in his hour of need, when he relinquished his life. Believe me; it was far more than Mekai endured."

"But why do I feel such a void. It is as though a terrible emptiness now fills my heart and consumes my soul as I took his life and the lives of the other soldiers. Why?"

"If there is an ounce of compassion in you, Takaro, you will appreciate the value of life. It is never easy to take the life of another, even the life of an enemy. It is when you no longer feel this '*emptiness*' that there is cause for concern. Just keep in mind, what we do, we do out of compassion. We fight to keep our people safe and to ensure that a measure of justice shall always prevail. If you lose sight of your purpose as a warrior, if taking a life is as easy for you as breathing, if you wantonly kill because you thirst for revenge or lust for the blood of others, then you are no longer Kagai. You are nothing more than a cold-blooded, ruthless murderer."

Medaru gave her shoulder a gentle squeeze. She released a weary sigh as she absorbed his words of wisdom.

"I fear for Mekai," confided Medaru. "When it becomes easy to take a life, and when you no longer respect or value life, it is easy to go astray. One is no longer motivated to do what is proper and right because there is a profound lack of compassion."

"Will I always feel this way? Each time we go to war?" asked Takaro.

"I pray to God you do, little warrior, but rest assured, each time we engage in battle you shall rise up to find the courage and the strength to protect those weaker than you. Yes, each time it will become easier, but do not lose sight of the importance of life. When all is said and done, show your respect by praying for their lost souls, just as you hope that one day, should you be cut down in battle, your enemy too shall say a prayer for your soul."

"I will do that master," promised Takaro.

"And believe me, Takaro, there are far worse things to happen to a warrior the first time he goes to war," attested her master.

"So you too froze the first time you faced the enemy?"

"No, worse than that," confessed Medaru, with a wry smile. "I was so terrified, I wet myself!"

Their return to Anshen was marked by a great celebration. Takaro and all the young men shared in the wine and food with Medaru Saibon and the more experienced warriors. When the festivities came to an end, each young man anxiously waited for the initiation to begin.

"You have earned the right to wear the symbol of the Kagai Warrior; to be one with this respected brotherhood. In bearing this symbol, each of you will be bound by an allegiance that cannot be broken by time or distance," stated Medaru, pointing to his own tattoo. "This ancient character means *for justice.* Below this symbol, this character means *for peace.* Always keep in mind, what we do; we do to uphold justice for our people so that we may have peace. Once you wear this mark, you have made a pledge to each other and shall be honour bound to stand by your brother warrior in life and in death. You shall willingly relinquish your life to preserve the life of another. Are my words and this oath understood?"

"Yes, Master Saibon!" answered the young warriors, speaking in unison.

"Before you, the tools used in applying the tattoo and the dye that will create this ever-lasting symbol. A brother warrior already bearing the mark of the Kagai Warrior shall be the one to initiate you. As I warned you before, it is a far from pleasant experience and it is a lengthy process, but once you bear this mark, even if you should die in the field of battle, devoid of your head, we will still know you and shall claim your body for proper burial or cremation."

Medaru turned to his veteran warriors, nodding to them to choose a young disciple to begin this rite of passage. To Takaro's mortification, all the warriors took their place next to a young man. She was left, sitting alone.

Hemashe's eyes quickly turned away, sensing her disappointment and embarrassment. She slowly rose up to depart when Medaru approached her.

"I would be honoured to be the one to initiate you into our brotherhood, warrior maiden," said her master.

Takaro knelt before him, rolling up her sleeve.

"No, Takaro, for you, you shall bear this mark elsewhere. Your arm is much too small and because of the manner in which my father had trained you, you must keep this tattoo concealed. It shall go over here," he said as his finger tapped her back, high on her right shoulder blade.

"I shall warn you now; the application will hurt significantly more on your back than had it been placed on your arm. Do you still wish to proceed?"

"Yes, master. It makes no difference to me. I believe my back has endured worst things than what I am about to be subjected to," responded Takaro, as she removed her vest and loosened the ties of her bodice so she could lower the back of her blouse down around her shoulders.

As Medaru knelt behind her, he was momentarily taken aback by the multitude of long, silvery scars that peered over the edge of her blouse. He suddenly understood her words, applying this tattoo would only pale in comparison to the pain she must have endured when she received this lashing.

"Are you ready, Takaro?"

"Yes," she answered in a small voice.

As her hand clutched her bodice, closing it in front of her, the thumb and index finger of each hand joined and linked together. The tips of her other fingers touched with the corresponding finger of each hand. Her head bowed down as she summoned the energy of the earth. With each long, deep breath she inhaled through her nose and slowly expelled through her mouth, her soul sank deeper into the earth, becoming one with this natural energy.

Although she was trained in all of the breathing cycles to call upon the powers of the various elements, it was in this realm that Takaro always felt the most focused and centered. Although her mind and soul meandered on this plane, she was still very aware of her surroundings.

After tracing the Kagai symbol onto her shoulder blade with a fine brush, Medaru picked up a slender, six-inch piece of bamboo stem. One end was splintered into many tiny, sharp, needle-like shafts. This was the end that was dipped into the indigo blue dye and inserted into the flesh.

In his other hand, her master held a small, wooden mallet; this was used to pound the other end of the bamboo so the needle-like end can be forced through her skin and into the muscle on her shoulder blade. As Medaru's tool worked its way into her flesh, the only sign she gave to indicate she felt the bamboo as it bit into her shoulder was a short, quick breath in; nothing more.

For almost two hours, Takaro and the other young warriors endured. Her eyes remained closed, her breathing deliberate and controlled as Medaru used rapid, sharp strikes with the mallet to drive the small tip of the bamboo into her skin over and over again. He only stopped to blot away the blood that would seep forth and mingle with the blue dye.

Hemashe winced in pain as a warrior worked the bamboo into the muscle high on his arm. He glanced over at Takaro to notice that her face was graced with a look of utter serenity as Medaru completed his work.

He smiled inwardly as his gaze shot over to Mekai, wishing that Takaro would open her eyes, even for a moment, to see how Mekai's eyes watered and his face reddened as he endured the process.

Although he was the largest of the young warriors, the well-developed muscles on his arms seemed to push all the nerves high to the surface of his skin. Mekai seemed far more sensitive to the tattooing process than any of them. His discomfort was clear to see as a warrior methodically and deliberately forced the bamboo into Mekai's flesh; each strike, biting and burning his muscle as the dye permeated deep beneath his skin.

When Medaru was finally done, he concealed the still bleeding wound with a clean dressing. Pulling Takaro's blouse back over her shoulders, he whispered into her ear: "You are one of us, Takaro. You are now a Kagai Warrior."

7

under a harvest moon

For a week since their return to Anshen, Takaro helped care for the injured men still in need of attention. During this time, the warrior giving her the greatest concern and the most grief was Shenyu, whose leg had been badly shattered by a halberd during the battle.

A mild infection resulted in a low-grade fever, but it was nothing that could not be remedied by the medicines she had at her disposal. Takaro kept the wound clean and had to deal with the outbursts of profanity as Shenyu cursed when she removed the stitches, tugging at the threads that helped keep his thigh muscles together to better facilitate healing. His tirades were quickly stifled when she would offer to amputate his leg with her sword rather than bothering to remove the sutures if he continued complaining.

After each session with this warrior, Takaro would raise her hands over her head. Clapping them together once, she would briskly rub the palms of her hands to generate a healing energy. When she felt this pulsating sensation emanating from her hands, she would rest them gently over the wound. The warrior felt instant relief as the warmth of her hands helped to better the circulation of blood to this area, thus speeding the healing process.

During this time, Medaru and Keodai were off with some of the other warriors to deliver the enemy's swords and halberds collected from the battlefield. Their journey took them to the outlying villages where these weapons were retooled and used by the men in case they were called to war.

The young children, always excited to see the warriors return to Anshen ran to greet the men, offering to take the horses to the stable for them. Hemashe smiled as he rode in to see Takaro fetching some water from the well. He dismounted and passed the reins on to an eager, young boy.

"Let me help you with that, Takaro," offered the returning warrior, taking the full bucket from her hands.

"Thank you, Hemashe, but it is not necessary," she insisted.

"I know it is not necessary," he responded with a gentle smile, turning to follow her. "Have you been well?"

"As well as can be expected," she answered as she walked back to her cottage. "I see your tattoo is healing quite nicely."

Hemashe glanced over at his right arm, switching the heavy, water-laden bucket into this hand so he would have an excuse to flex his muscles in front of her.

"Yes, it was a relief to see that after the dressing was removed and the crust of blood washed away, that I was left with the actual mark of the Kagai rather than a symbol of profanity inscribed by a warrior too drunk to know what he was doing," chuckled Hemashe.

Takaro giggled lightheartedly at his words.

"And how about you? Does your tattoo heal?"

"As far as I can tell by the reflection in the looking glass, it is fine now, but it certainly did burn for the longest time," she admitted, subconsciously rolling her right shoulder.

For a moment, they walked side by side in silence.

"Master Saibon is hosting a feast tonight," said Hemashe. "Everyone will be there."

"What is the occasion?"

"Does our master ever need a reason to share in food and wine with his friends and family?"

"True enough," answered Takaro. "Yumai will not be pleased that she and the other women were not given more notice."

"Yumai always comes through. She has her father's uncanny ability to command and orchestrate those around her," responded Hemashe. "You will see; she shall have the women-folk preparing a wonderful meal in no time."

"You think highly of Yumai, do you not?" questioned Takaro, searching his dark brown eyes for the truth.

"Of course I do," insisted the young warrior. "She is Master Saibon's daughter and my best friend's sister."

"Well, perhaps one day she shall make a wonderful wife for you, Hemashe," said Takaro, stepping up the stoop of her cottage. "I know she has her eyes cast in your direction."

Hemashe laughed nervously as he set down the bucket of water. "Though Yumai be a fair and delicate flower, *my eyes* are certainly not cast in her direction."

"Please do not tell me you wish to become a warrior bound to only his sword and shield; existing day to day for the next battle? That is a rather pathetic and lonely existence," responded Takaro.

"I suppose it depends on who shall be there to go to battle with me, by my side," answered Hemashe.

"If that is the path you choose, I should warn you now, your best friend, Keodai Saibon will not be by your side forever. Eventually, his thoughts shall turn to taking a wife and having a family, to carry on the Saibon legacy," stated Takaro, as she set some water over the fire to boil for tea.

"I was not thinking of Keodai," answered the warrior, pacing nervously across the floor.

"Well, you can count Mekai out, too. Boorish as he can be, even he has already set his sights on Shenyu's youngest sister. And believe me, she shall keep him on a short tether!" replied Takaro.

"Mekai? Do not even mention that buffoon's name in my presence," grumbled Hemashe, cringing at the thought of the large, lumbering warrior as his constant companion. "He may be strong and powerful with his sword, but he is lacking in something up here."

His index finger tapped his own head as he continued: "I swear; Master Saibon's only motivation to allow Mekai to become a warrior is that his large size alone permits us to use him effectively as a shield."

Takaro laughed in agreement, almost falling backwards as she knelt to stack some wood by the fireplace.

"It is good to hear you laugh, Takaro," commented Hemashe, offering his hand to assist her. "It is not often a sound I hear from you."

As she took hold of his hand, he easily lifted her on to her feet. She smiled in appreciation as she released her grip only this time; Hemashe did not let go as he gazed down at her small hand in his.

Takaro abruptly pulled away. Her action seemed to break his momentary trance.

Hemashe smiled nervously at her as she turned away to fetch some tea for him.

"So, will I see you tonight?" he asked.

"Tonight?"

"Yes, Master Saibon's celebration, remember? This evening?"

Takaro shook her head as she responded: "I do not believe so, Hemashe, not this time."

"Come now, Takaro, you are expected to attend. You must come!" pleaded Hemashe.

"I have other things to do that are more pressing than to revel in celebration with a bunch of drunken warriors when there is no reason to make merry," replied Takaro.

"What do you speak of? There is plenty to celebrate!" responded Hemashe, his eyebrows raised in dismay.

"Like what?"

The young warrior's eyes rolled upwards as he collected some random thoughts: "We can celebrate the fact we survived our first battle…"

"We already did that."

"Then, we shall celebrate the end to another beautiful day," suggested the young man.

"Now you are grasping at straws," insisted Takaro.

"So, you will not be coming?"

"Not this time."

"But you are expected, Takaro. Please come, even for a little while," urged Hemashe.

"I will not even be missed. You go ahead. You are part of the brotherhood. You are expected to partake in whatever festivities Master Saibon organizes."

"If that is the excuse you wish to use, then keep in mind that you are now part of this brotherhood, too. You will be expected to be there," insisted the young man.

Takaro could see that Hemashe would be sedulous, persisting until she folded to his will.

"Very well," conceded Takaro. "I suppose I can go, at least long enough to let my presence be known, and then I shall leave."

"No, I highly recommend that you stay until the bitter end, Takaro," advised Hemashe.

"Why so?" she asked.

"I may need you to walk me home again," he answered with a knowing smile as he slipped out the door.

"Fifty years ago today, when I was a mere child of eight, our village received an unexpected guest. To this very day, this *guest* has remained in our company much to the delight of my grandfather and father. She has been a constant source of inspiration for many of our up-and-coming warriors and recently, she had become a very welcomed addition into the Kagai brotherhood," stated Medaru, before the exuberant crowd.

Takaro was speechless as Yumai took her by her hand, pulling the little warrior into the center of the gathering. Though she always regarded this to be her day of re-birth, when she shed her identity of Nayla Treeborn to begin a new life as Takaro Bansho, it was something she always chose to push to the back of her mind.

"Yes, today we celebrate Takaro's *birthday* so to speak, for she has shared in our lives for the past fifty years, and I am pleased to say, unlike myself, she certainly does not look her age!"

"Well, that is a good thing, because this year would mark my eighty-seventh year of existence," remarked Takaro.

A gasp of surprise rose from the younger members of the group who had no idea of exactly how old she really was.

"You are most fortunate, Takaro. The years have been kind to you. May you never have to face the ravages of time as we mere mortals do," said Medaru, raising his goblet on high to toast her.

"Here! Here!" chanted those in her company.

Takaro's face was flushed with embarrassment as her fellow warriors raised their goblet in her honour.

"Yes, here is to eternal youth," added Mekai, his voice full of spite. "May you find peace of mind as those around you fade and die while you remain forever young with nothing more than memories and loneliness as your constant companion."

Takaro's eyes were dark and liquid as she glared at Mekai. Yumai scowled angrily at the young man, clutching her friend's hand to prevent her departure. Instead, Takaro pulled away, storming off rather than subjecting herself to more of this mortal's scorn.

An angry silence befell the crowd. Mekai was met with a round of hostile scowls and groans of resentment.

"You cannot keep your damned mouth shut, can you?" shouted Hemashe. His fist slammed into Mekai's midriff, causing the warrior to double over in pain. Hemashe then dashed off after Takaro.

"What is wrong with you, Mekai?" snarled Keodai, shaking his head in disgust. "Why is your dislike for Takaro so intense? She has never done anything to you!"

"Are you all blind?" groaned Mekai, as he righted himself. "Can none of you see that she is not like us? It is unnatural that she should live so long, untouched by the cruel hands of time as the rest of us fade in our spent youth, dying a slow death as we age."

Medaru stood before Mekai, admonishing the warrior: "You have no idea the level of cruelty you speak with. And your words cut as surely as the edge of a knife when you said that she will be alone, for that indeed shall be her fate. Whether Takaro expires many years from now or dies by our side in the field of battle, her soul will be condemned to a realm uninhabited by Elves and mortals. Yes, she will be alone. And until you, Mekai, can learn to deal with others with some degree of compassion, you too shall be forced to live alone, outside of Anshen, stripped of your standing as a Kagai Warrior."

"But… But master…" stammered Mekai. He was stunned by this news.

"We have all stood by for too long while you grew up bullying those you deemed smaller and weaker than you. I believe your animosity is seated in the fact that Takaro had been the only one to ever have the courage to stand up to you!" snapped Keodai.

"My son is correct, Mekai. I will no longer condone such appalling and impetuous behavior that is unbecoming of a Kagai Warrior. If you cannot hold your tongue when common sense dictates, how can you be trusted not to divulge vital information? How can you be trusted not to let that tongue wag under duress if you be captured by the enemy?" queried Medaru, his dark eyes scrutinizing the young man.

"But this is different, Master Saibon," protested Mekai.

"No, it is not," argued Medaru. "You had already been warned on more than one occasion to be mindful of your dealings where Takaro is concerned. It is obvious that my warnings are dismissed. They continue to go ignored by you. Is this indicative of how it shall be in battle, too? Will you not take heed of my words, my warnings at the expense of your life and the lives of others?"

"But we are not in the field of battle," argued Mekai.

"No, we are not. But know this now, if there is dissension in our ranks, if there is discord between us, the enemy will see it and use it to their advantage. Each of us can be thought of as a link to a length of chain. A weak link shall cause us to break. It is my responsibility to ensure that either this *weak link* be removed or be reinforced," stated Medaru. "Just as Takaro is expected to stand up for each and every one of her brother warriors, I fear that you cannot be depended on in the same manner. Tell me now, Mekai, do I remove this link, or do I make another bid to improve and strengthen it?"

When Hemashe finally caught up to Takaro, she was standing alone at the top of a ridge overlooking the village. Her small figure was silhouetted against the dimming sky as the sun slowly slipped behind the distant mountains. Her cloak fluttered and billowed behind her as her arms were outstretched to her sides, as though waiting for a wind to carry her away. Though Takaro's back was turned and her eyes were closed, she could sense the young warrior's approach.

"Are you waiting for the wind to fly you away from here?" asked Hemashe, as he stood by her side, gazing out over the green landscape.

"Only in my dreams, but it has been a lifetime ago since I had last dreamed I could fly, for even that had been taken away from me," answered Takaro in a solemn voice, her arms slowly dropping to her side.

"If one could only fly away from all of life's problems," agreed Hemashe. His hand shielded his eyes from the glare of the golden sun as it withdrew its waning light from the darkening, twilight sky.

For a moment, both said nothing.

"I am sorry about Mekai. He is such an arrogant and thoughtless sod. Sometimes I pity him as much as I dislike him," stated the young warrior.

"You should not be apologizing for Mekai's behavior. After all, his words are true."

"True? In what respect?" queried Hemashe.

"It is unnatural that I should live so long while those I care for diminish with the years. Keodai and Yumai are the fourth generation of the Saibon clan I have known since coming here fifty years ago. I remember their father, Medaru Saibon as a small child when I first arrived, and now look: He quickly approaches his sixtieth year and I have aged nothing more than the equivalent of five or six mortal years in all this time," admitted Takaro, her voice meek.

"Consider it a blessing, Takaro," he responded with a reassuring smile.

"It is truly a blessing, Hemashe? How would you feel if it was you to outlive all whom you care for while enduring the scorn and abuse from the likes of Mekai?"

"Mekai is but one. His words are those of a fool. You would be wise to dismiss his ignorant ranting," advised Hemashe.

"Under most circumstances, yes, I would choose to ignore his words, but even I must admit that he does speak his mind and perhaps, he should not be reprimanded for doing so. After all, where others only dare to speak of me behind my back, Mekai has the stupidity, and the courage, to speak his mind directly to my face," replied Takaro, sitting down on the grassy ridge to take in the last of the evening light.

"What makes you believe others speak of you in the same manner?" questioned Hemashe.

Takaro shook her head. A little giggle escaped her lips as she pulled back on her long, dark hair to expose the small points of her little ears. "Remember, not only am I cursed with long life, I am also cursed with these Elven ears. I hear what the others say."

"Are you saying you can hear those people speaking down below in the village?"

"Oh, no, just as I am not as long-lived as an Elf, neither do I possess eyes and ears as sensitive as an Elf. As I understand, I can see and hear much better than a mortal, but only half as well as an Elf."

Hemashe's face momentarily blanched as he recalled some of his own words he had whispered to his friends regarding this warrior maiden. "So, have you ever heard me speak of you?"

Takaro smiled as she answered: "There were times when I have heard you speak up in my defense. At the risk of being regarded as an outcast too, I know you and Keodai, Medaru and Yumai constantly work to dull the barbed words cast in my direction."

"I do not believe anyone, save for Mekai, speaks ill of you, Takaro. If anything, they just do not understand the Elf-kind."

"It is funny to hear you say that, Hemashe. The *Elf-kind* you speak of chooses to view me as a mortal, while the mortals tend to view me as an Elf. Alas, I am both, but neither," stated Takaro. "Tell me, what do you see when you look at me?"

Hemashe knelt down before her to gaze into her deep, brown eyes. He looked long and hard, as though searching her soul before he answered: "When I look into your eyes, I see a beautiful, young woman with a will of steel and a heart of gold. I see a kind and compassionate soul carried within this youthful body, and yet, in your eyes, I see the wisdom of the ages. I see the soul of one who has lived long, and has seen and endured much. That is what I see, Takaro."

"You have always been kind to me, Hemashe. You have always been a true friend."

"Is that all you see when you look at me, Takaro?" asked the young warrior. "Am I nothing more than a friend to you?"

"What are you asking me?" questioned Takaro, her gaze turning away from him to the darkening sky.

"Do you not feel anything more for me than friendship? Do you hold me in the same regard as Keodai and the other young men in the village?"

"It can never become anything more than friendship, Hemashe. You know that," whispered Takaro.

"Why? Why can it not be more?"

"Because I am not like you, I am not a mortal."

"Then what am I to do?" lamented Hemashe.

"I do not understand. What do you speak of?"

"Remember that night in the spring when we all drank and you walked me back to my cottage?"

"Goodness, you were so drunk that night," recalled Takaro, with a smile as she remembered his inebriated words.

"I admit I was drunk, but I cannot deny those words I spoke were all true."

"Come now, Hemashe, you were so far gone you do not even recall any of our conversation," countered Takaro.

"Think what you will, but I remember *everything* I said. I even recall how you punched me, *hard* may I add, after I kissed you."

"You remember…" gasped the little warrior.

"How can I forget," admitted Hemashe. "I thought it was all very nice until you punched me. For some reason, I never thought the first time I would kiss a girl I would get such a violent response."

Takaro's heart pounded loudly in her ears as she fought her urge to run, to flee before she could hear anymore of his confession.

"In fact, I knew I was in love with you the very first time I saw you dressed up… at the well, fetching water for Master Saibon."

"You did not even know it was me at the time. You did not even recognize me."

"When I first saw you like that, I remember how you stole my breath away. My heart was racing so fast, and my eyes were absolutely bedazzled by your radiant beauty."

"That was not me," insisted Takaro.

"Oh, yes it was. You try to hide behind your battle raiment and your weapons, but I know you, Takaro. And I have seen the side of you that you keep hidden away," insisted Hemashe. "I remember how your eyes burned with anger as you doused the three of us with the bucket of water. And how you struck me right in my forehead with your sandal, but I did not care."

Takaro's little hand covered her mouth as she gasped in surprise.

"Somehow, I never imagined falling in love with you would be so painful, in so many ways," admitted Hemashe, one hand dropping to his stomach as the other rubbed his forehead.

"Do not speak to me of love, Hemashe. It is a mistake; a terrible mistake..."

"For the longest time, I had wanted to tell you how I truly felt, but I was such an idiot to confess my feelings to you in a drunken haze. When all was said and done, I knew you would believe it was nothing more than the ramblings of an inebriated fool. I was embarrassed for it was not supposed to happen that way. I always thought it would happen on a warm, summer night, under a canopy of sparkling starlight. I would confess my love for you on a night not unlike this night. Of course, I would be sober and I would find the courage to tell you exactly how I feel; how much I love you."

Takaro's eyes slowly closed and an audible sigh escaped her as she absorbed his words.

Hemashe's hand caressed her cheek, raising her chin to allow him to gaze upon her face. She responded by pulling away from his touch, rising up to her feet so she could escape, but he would not allow it, catching her hand.

"So tell me, Takaro, you still have not answered my question: What am I to do? I do not know of anyway to stop feeling for you as I do. I do not know how to stop from falling in love with you."

"Hemashe, I am like you. I am a warrior. I am part of the brotherhood," whispered Takaro.

"Do not use this excuse on me again, Takaro. You are just as much a woman as you are a warrior. Just because you wield a mighty sword as well as any man, it does not mean that you are any less a woman."

"You do not know what you speak of," protested the little warrior.

"Oh yes, I do. And if I believed in your logic, it would lead me to believe that if I chose to don a gown, in your eyes, it would suddenly make me a woman," reasoned Hemashe.

Takaro was taken aback by his words, and then a small smile crept across her face as she envisioned this handsome, young man standing before her, dressed in a lovely, silk gown.

"I know what you are thinking. You best be rid of that image from your mind," he suggested, still refusing to let go of her hand.

Unable to hold back any longer, Takaro began to giggle.

"Now you are laughing at my expense. It is a good thing that I am confident in my masculinity," sighed Hemashe. "And I must admit; if it allows me to bask in your luminous smile but for a moment, then it is well worth it."

Again, the back of his hand caressed her soft cheek, causing Takaro to cease her giggling. He drew her close; holding her in his arms as he peered into her eyes.

"Do not do this," pleaded Takaro. "This time, you will not be able to hide behind the wine."

"Even now, with words untainted by drink, you still refuse to believe me. How do I convince you that my words are true?"

"In all honesty, Hemashe, how can you be in love with me? I am a half-caste."

"So you somehow believe that it makes you less worthy of love?" questioned the young man. "Or perhaps you are trying to tell me that *I* am unworthy of your love. Is that it, Takaro? Are you waiting for an Elf to come riding into our village to proclaim his love for you? For if that be the case, it has been a good long time since we have had Elves amongst us."

"That is not what I am not saying, Hemashe. You know it," protested Takaro. "I am as much accepted by the Elves as I am by the mortals."

"I accept you," declared Hemashe. "But why is it so hard for you to believe? Why can you not see that I speak the truth? I do love you. To the very depth of my soul, I do love you."

"It cannot be," replied Takaro, her voice wavering.

"Why not?" cried Hemashe. "Is it because you feel nothing for me? Is that what it is? For if that be the case, look into my eyes. Tell me that you feeling nothing for me. If you can do this one thing, then I shall never bother you again."

Takaro's eyes gazed reluctantly into his as she answered: "I like you."

"Wrong answer."

"I like you very much."

"That will not suffice."

"I am quite fond of you."

"Again, *wrong* answer," stated Hemashe, lifting her chin so their eyes could meet. "Look me in my eyes and tell me exactly what you feel."

Her eyes locked onto his as she struggled to find the words to express her true feelings. Hemashe refused to release her from his embrace, waiting for her reply.

"I can very well stay here all night, holding you like this until I get an answer," insisted the young man.

As she stared into his kind eyes, it was as though his soul offered her a safe sanctuary, a reprieve from the cruelties of her day-to-day existence. She could feel her heart and soul slowly melting into one with his, surrendering to his warm embrace and gentle voice.

Finally, she answered in a whisper: "I do love you."

"Yes!" exclaimed Hemashe, then his eyes narrowed in suspicion. "Wait one moment, you do not mean like a brother or a friend, right?"

"I said, I love you," answered Takaro.

"Yes!" he exclaimed once again. "Hold on here, you are not saying this so I would let go? And then you can run off to leave me standing here like some fool?"

"How dense can you be?" gasped Takaro, exasperated by his constant second-guessing. "I love you like this." Taking his face in both her hands, she planted a kiss upon his lips. "Now would I do that to a brother?"

Hemashe stood before her, completely dumbfounded. He was rendered speechless and his eyes blinked hard as though he had just dreamed he had been kissed.

"Am I mistaken or did you just kiss me?"

"What is wrong with you?" groaned Takaro.

"I do believe I am dreaming. You better kiss me again… just to make sure," insisted Hemashe. He gently lifted her chin, pressing his lips softly against her full, sensuous mouth. As a sigh of relief escaped him, he whispered into Takaro's ear: "You are not going to punch me now, are you?"

As time went by, it became apparent that a special bond was developing between Hemashe and Takaro. Though both were discreet in their words and actions, it became obvious to Medaru that Hemashe was always by her side as they trained, during social gatherings and when they were called upon to take up arms. In the field of battle, they not only watched the backs of their fellow warriors, they kept constant watch over each other. For Medaru, this bond went well beyond that of any brotherhood.

Upon returning from the north after defeating yet another incursion into western Orien, Hemashe trudged along by Takaro's side. She and the others trained in the healing arts had taken care of their wounded, and as always, Takaro tended to her injuries last.

As the group of warriors came to a halt to rest and prepare for the impending night, Hemashe sat next to Takaro as she wearily slumped down to the ground. He noticed the drying blood that had trickled from a nasty gash inflicted by an enemy's blade. The crimson trail traveled down the entire length of her left arm, terminating where the blood dripped from her fingertips. Having used up all of the clean dressings on the other warriors, she used nothing more than the palm of her bare hand to staunch the flow of blood. Hemashe drew back her cloak to examine the extent of her injury.

"Let me see," insisted Hemashe, prying Takaro's hand away from the bloody wound. High on her left bicep, a diagonal slash, now encrusted with drying blood greeted his eyes. "This is not good, Takaro. You will need this stitched up. I shall fetch a healer for you."

"That will not be necessary," stated the little warrior, placing her hand back over her cut. "In my pack, there is still some thread and a needle. Fetch it for me, will you?"

"You do not intend to sew this up yourself, do you?" gasped Hemashe. "There are others here that can tend to you."

Takaro's eyebrows arched up in dismay as she whispered to him: "I have seen their handiwork. Believe me, I would much rather do this myself and minimize the scarring than to subject myself to their less than dexterous abilities with the needle."

Hemashe mulled over her words as he reflected upon the many men tended to over the course of their battles. Those whose wounds had been administered to by Takaro were eventually left with smaller, neater scars. Those hastily stitched together by the men trained to heal bore jagged, larger, more obvious marks. Eventually, all those who came to know Takaro's steady hands and quick, neat stitching would often wait for her assistance than to allow another healer to close their wounds.

"Are you sure you want to do this?" asked Hemashe, as he threaded a needle that was encrusted in dried blood.

"Given the choice, what do you think?" answered Takaro, as she struggled to widen the tear in her sleeve. She stared at the gash for a moment as she reached for her water flask.

"I must clean some of this blood off before I proceed. Pour this water over my arm," ordered Takaro, passing the flask to Hemashe.

He winced in empathy as Takaro flinched, the cold water streaming over her wound and down her arm. The wound seemed to pulsate as it came alive with renewed pain.

She tilted her shoulder inward so her right hand could begin the work of closing the wound. "Press the edges together," instructed Takaro, as she steadied the needle she held in her trembling hand.

Hemashe grimaced in discomfort, anticipating the pain, as he pushed the two sides of the gaping wound closed. He watched Takaro's face as she closed her eyes and slowly drew in a long, slow breath through her nose, and then exhaled slowly through her mouth. Repeating this breathing cycle several more times, her hand ceased its shaking as she focused on the task before her. She quickly set to work, breathing in this cycle.

Hemashe noticed the only sign she gave of the pain she was inflicting upon herself was that her cleansing breath was forced out through clenched teeth, yet during this whole process, not once did she cry out, not even a whimper, at her discomfort.

As Hemashe cut the thread on the last stitch, Takaro appeared satisfied at her suturing skills, pleased to see that the bleeding had subsided. As she clapped her hands together to harness the energy to heal, she felt the immediate jolt of pain course through her damaged arm, terminating at the wound. Undeterred, she continued to rub her palms together, generating ample heat. Placing her right hand over her wound, she sighed in relief as the warmth and pressure seemed to dull the throbbing pain.

"I must admit, this is one of the few times I wished I had been a full-blooded Elf," lamented Takaro.

"Why do you say that," asked Hemashe, storing the thread and needle back into her pack.

"Elves have this remarkable ability to heal; quickly and without these nasty scars."

"You do not say," remarked the young warrior.

"Oh yes, a wound such as this would all but disappear in a very short span of time."

"How do you know this?" asked Hemashe.

"I was once badly hurt when I was a child. An Elf used his powers to heal my injuries," admitted Takaro.

"Badly hurt? How badly hurt? What happened, Takaro?" Hemashe's eyes darkened with concern.

"It was so long ago, it is not even worth remembering, but see these marks?" she pointed to the faint scars left on her wrists. "These would have been much worse if I had not been healed by an Elf."

Again he asked: "What happened to you?"

"What happened is not important. What is important is that had I been an Elf, I would have the power to heal the others almost instantaneously, to better ease their suffering – to speed their recovery."

As she removed her hand, he could see the disappointment etched onto her face as she gazed at the still present wound. Although it was still there, the blood had now coagulated, sealing the cut together. It was well on the way to healing.

"Much better," sighed Takaro, drawing her cloak to conceal the wound.

"Night comes quickly now as winter's cold breath draws ever nearer with the passing of each moon," said Hemashe.

Keodai delivered some cured venison, stale bread and dried fruit to his comrades, sitting down by Takaro's side.

"Yes," agreed Keodai. "Soon, it will be too cold for Imperial Soldiers to make the long trek north. My father said that this was to be our last battle until the coming of the spring, when the Magare Valley opens up again."

Takaro gazed skyward. A thin veil of clouds drifted lazily before the half moon as it shone its cold, pale light upon them. As she exhaled, her breath was suspended in the frosty, night air.

"Yes, we shall see what the new year brings," replied the warrior maiden. *The weather shall be much too cold for the mortals to endure,* she thought as she observed the men gathering in a tight circle. They huddled around several campfires to stay warm.

The trek to Anshen seemed longer than usual as Takaro and the men trudged homeward, following behind Medaru and the seasoned warriors on horseback. As they passed behind the curtain of water at Reyu Falls, she knew it only seemed more arduous because night was stealing away with the light of day sooner with the approach of winter. As the weary warriors dispersed to their homes, Hemashe walked Takaro to Yaruke's old cottage. Opening the door, the interior was cold and dark. He closed the door behind Takaro and quickly lit several candles.

"Sit and rest, Takaro. I shall get a roaring fire going to stave off the chill in here," offered Hemashe, arranging a handful of kindling and dried wood shavings into the stone fireplace.

As she lowered herself down onto a cushion, a loud rap on the door caused her to rise.

"Sit," demanded Hemashe, making his way across the room. Throwing the door open, before him stood Medaru Saibon.

"Good evening, Hemashe. Is everything fine?" asked Medaru,

peering over the young warrior's shoulder at Takaro.

"I am helping Takaro settle in. I do not want her handling an axe to split her own firewood," stated Hemashe.

"So it is true. Keodai mentioned that she was hurt," stated Medaru, stepping around him to enter the room.

"I am quite fine, master. It was really nothing more than a minor flesh wound."

"Takaro, you should know by now when I ask for a full accounting of our warriors, especially when I ask about the wounded, you are not excluded from this. If I send you out, unaware that you are already incapacitated in some way, it can bring grievous results to all," explained Medaru.

"I am sorry, master. You worry needlessly. My injury is minor compared to the others. I am still fit to do battle," insisted Takaro.

Without warning, Medaru tossed his sword to her, forcing her to catch it with her left hand. Takaro's reflexes were slowed, hampered by the muscles straining at the sutures as she moved to catch the sword. It fell to the floor with a loud clatter.

"Well, I beg to differ where your fighting abilities are concerned," responded Medaru, with a shake of his head. "And it is for this reason you shall remain here this winter while Keodai, Hemashe and four other warriors shall be sent back north to guard the pass at Magare Valley."

"But, master, I will be fit to travel in a few days. My arm shall be healed sufficiently," argued Takaro.

"I am afraid not. Keodai will be leading the men out at first light tomorrow," stated Medaru.

"Tomorrow? But Master Saibon, Keodai claimed there would be no more battles until the coming of spring. He said that as winter draws near, the Imperial Army will withdraw; the Emperor will refrain from sending any more soldiers," stated Hemashe.

"Yes, that is how it has been for many years, my young friend, however, word had been received in our absence that a new threat looms from the east," warned Medaru.

"Whatever do you speak of, master?" asked Takaro.

"Apparently, the elders of Orien and Lord Dahlon Treeborn have informed us that the foul and despicable Sorcerer has resurfaced. He has been collaborating with those to the east. It would appear that Eldred Firestaff is in the midst of securing allies in his bid to do away with the Elves."

"If his grudge is with the Elves, why should it affect us?" asked Hemashe.

"In exchange for the manpower to defeat the Elves, the Sorcerer has promised to deliver the dissidents that protect those in western Orien. He has promised to destroy all who are not loyal to the royal family," revealed Medaru. "Besides, we have a long-standing alliance with Lord Treeborn and his people. We shall continue to honour this alliance."

"Are you saying the Sorcerer plans to lead an attack? In the dead of winter?" asked Takaro.

"Right now, there is no substantial proof to indicate such an attack will take place, but we cannot take any chances. We must remain vigilant. I have no choice but to send out a handful of our warriors to keep watch over the valley. Provisions, enough to last into the spring have already been gathered. Tomorrow, horses and the necessary supplies shall be made ready."

"Master, I assure you, I can go. Let me go in the place of another warrior who will be needed by his wife and children. I have no ties to bind me to this village," pleaded Takaro.

Medaru gazed at Hemashe, then back at Takaro. "Not this time, little warrior."

"But master, I – "

Medaru raised his hand for silence. "Tell me, Takaro, in your condition, what will you do if the men's lives are at stake? What will you do if you and the others are attacked? You could not even grasp my sword that was tossed to you. How do you expect to fight if that is the case?"

Takaro slumped in defeat, knowing full well that Medaru could not be swayed to change his mind.

"Hemashe, be ready to leave at first light. I recommend you spend this evening with your family. Say your farewells, for it shall be a long winter," suggested Medaru, as he turned to leave.

"I understand, master. I will be ready to leave in the morn."

"Very good," replied Medaru, shutting the door behind him. As he stood outside the cottage, enveloped in the darkness of the night, Medaru shook his head in sadness.

I am sorry, Takaro, but this relationship with Hemashe must come to an end now. Perhaps this long separation will place some distance in both of your hearts, thought Medaru, as he slowly walked away from her cottage.

Hemashe was quiet as he stoked the flames, positioning the burning logs in the fireplace. He placed a pot of water on to boil for tea. Takaro watched him as he went about this business.

“So you are leaving then?” she asked, breaking the silence.

“I have no choice in this matter. You know that,” replied Hemashe.

Her chin dropped to her chest, her eyes lowered in sadness.

“Come now, Takaro. Take comfort in knowing that I shall return. As surely as the cherry trees will blossom once more with the coming of the spring, I, too, will return,” whispered Hemashe, gently raising her chin so their eyes could meet. He kissed her gently upon her lips.

“But you shall be away for at least four months,” she groaned. “That is such a long time to be apart.”

Hemashe smiled as he listened to her words. “For one as long-lived as you, I thought four months would amount to nothing more than a blink of an eye in your lifetime.”

“The passing of this winter shall be long and torturous in your absence, Hemashe. I despair to be apart from you for this length of time.”

“Will you wait for me?” asked the young warrior.

“Of course, I will wait.”

“Good. When I return, I shall tell Master Saibon of my intentions to take you as my betrothed,” stated Hemashe. “I know he holds you in the same regard as a daughter, so it is only fitting that I receive his blessing.”

“But Hemashe, we have not even disclosed our relationship to your mother and father, not even Keodai or Master Saibon is aware of our feelings for each other.”

“I have only been discreet about this because you had asked that it be kept secret. Well, they shall find out soon enough how I feel about you,” answered Hemashe, holding her in his arms.

“But what of Yumai? You know she has set her eyes on you,” asked Takaro.

“I know you think of her as a sister, Takaro, but I have made it clear from the start, I have no interest in Yumai. My eyes and my heart are set on you,” answered Hemashe.

“I do not want to see her disappointment.”

“Nor do I, but at least now, in all fairness to her, she can turn her attentions to other possible suitors,” he replied, kissing Takaro once more.

She melted into his arms and held him tightly.

“I should be off now, Takaro.”

“No, not yet,” she pleaded in a soft voice. “Please, stay the night, just this one time.”

"Long have I desired to hear you speak these words, and long have I fought this desire to do so. I know if I were to bend to my will, this secret would be secret no more. You are as pure and chaste as the first snow of the winter, and you shall remain as such until we have honoured our union. I do you a grave disservice by giving in to my desires, to steal this moment – this one night, only to abandon you at first light. I would much rather wait until the night we are wed, under the next harvest moon," stated Hemashe, as he held her close to his chest.

"But that is almost a year away," groaned Takaro.

"I know, but I wish to honour our Taijin tradition, and I wish to honour you," he answered. "And to take you as anything less than my wife, will not suffice. You deserve better than that, Takaro."

She wrapped her arms about his neck as she drew his mouth to hers. She kissed him slowly and passionately, rubbing up against his body in a sensuous manner.

Hemashe groaned in response. "You are torturing me."

"And deliberately so," she purred into his ear as she gently kissed his neck.

"I do believe you are trying to seduce me," assessed the young man, reveling in the attention.

"Me?" asked Takaro, her long, dark eyelashes fluttered innocently at Hemashe.

"As tempting as you are, your virtue shall remain intact until we are wed."

"Hemashe," groaned Takaro, in disappointment. He smiled at her as he held her close. She could hear the hastened beating of his heart.

"Takaro, call me old-fashioned if you wish, but I shall not have others question your virtue. You know that you will be under even greater scrutiny, especially by my parents, when I make it clear that we wish to be together," reasoned Hemashe. "Do you understand?"

A heavy sigh escaped her as she gazed into his eyes. "Yes."

He held her close and kissed her with great passion. "I promise, I will return to you."

"I shall pray for your safe return, Hemashe," whispered Takaro, tightening her embrace.

Winter swept down upon the lands with a vengeance, its cruel breath freezing lakes and ponds, shrouding the landscape in a thick mantle of snow. Takaro counted the passing of each day, watching the bleak skies for signs of spring. Never in her life had time crawled by so slowly as she thought upon Hemashe and his long absence.

As the months passed and the lands began to thaw under the warmth of the impending spring sun, another group of warriors were dispatched to the north to replace those who endured the harsh elements of winter. Riding in on horseback, Keodai escorted the men into the village. The citizens poured out of their warm cottages to greet the returning warriors. From her window, Takaro watched as the men dismounted and were soon surrounded by their loved ones, wishing to welcome them home. Takaro resisted the urge to race out, to embrace Hemashe in an exuberant hug and to kiss him lovingly upon his lips. She observed Hemashe as his mother and father embraced their only son, leading him to their cottage. As he walked away, Hemashe glanced back and smiled at Takaro, knowing full well that she would patiently wait for him.

Almost two hours elapsed before Takaro finally received the highly anticipated knock on her door. Throwing it wide open, she seized Hemashe by his hand, yanking him into the cottage. The door slammed shut as she threw the returning warrior against it, throwing her arms about his neck to wrap him in a long awaited, welcoming embrace.

She kissed his face, lips and neck with fervent passion as Hemashe commented with a lighthearted laugh: "What a greeting! Perhaps I should go away more often!"

"Not without me," whispered Takaro, as she held him close.

He smiled warmly upon her face, his eyes drinking in her beauty.

Gazing into the dark recesses of his eyes, she could see that time spent in isolation, in such inhospitable conditions aged his soul.

"You removed your beard," she finally observed.

"Lest I be killed on your front stoop, mistaken as one of the barbarians from the east; yes, I thought I should make myself presentable before I came to your door," answered Hemashe, his hand rubbing his clean-shaven face.

"Beard or not, I shall always know you by these eyes," she replied in a soft voice as her hand caressed his face.

Hemashe took her small hands into his, kissing each before pressing them to his heart. He released a weary sigh as he said: "It is good to be home, as much to be by your side as to get away from Mekai's incessant snoring and obnoxious demeanor."

"How you endured his company for so long, in such close quarters, is beyond me," teased Takaro.

"To listen to the constant drivel of swill from his mouth was absolute torture. Sometimes, it was more than any of us could bear. The only comfort I now derive from his constant droning is how your lovely voice sounds all the sweeter to these ears," responded Hemashe. "But enough about Mekai; have you been well?"

"Aside from missing you terribly, I am well and all the better now that you have returned."

"Well, we shall never be apart again, Takaro. Tonight, I will announce to my father and mother, Master Saibon too, of our intentions to wed."

Takaro's eyes darkened with concern. "They will certainly be surprised. Perhaps I was a fool to insist we keep our love secreted away."

"Do not be concerned with the past, instead, let us look forward to the future, to our future," insisted Hemashe. "No doubt they will be surprised, but I have little doubt they shall be easily convinced to bless our union."

"Do you wish for me to be there?"

"No," answered Hemashe. "Tradition requires that I address my parents and your appointed guardian alone. Once the deed is done, we shall announce our betrothal to the world. Our love will no longer be a secret."

Hemashe's mother poured the piping-hot tea as her son served it first to Medaru Saibon, and then his father. Placing a cup before his mother, he took his place by his father's side.

Hemashe's father smiled proudly at his son as he announced to his guest: "It is obvious that my son has called for this meeting with you as he wishes to marry."

Medaru gazed over at the young man, watching as Hemashe shifted nervously on his cushion. The warrior priest asked: "Is this so, young man?"

"Yes, Master Saibon, I do seek your blessing to marry," admitted Hemashe.

"Yes, Medaru, our son wishes to unite our family," added the young warrior's mother. "You have known Hemashe since the day of his birth. You have seen for yourself what a fine, young man he has grown to become. Dependable, honest… he has already proven to be a great warrior. Now he shall be a great provider to a wife and family."

Medaru nodded in agreement. "I cannot dispute that Hemashe is everything you say, and more."

"Thank you, master," said Hemashe, bowing his head in appreciation of his kind words.

"I promise you, Medaru, Hemashe will make a wonderful husband," stated his father as his mother listened hopefully.

"Hemashe, you are Keodai's closest friend. This brotherhood you share with my son runs deep and true, and now, through marriage, you shall truly be brothers," said Medaru, with a congenial smile. "I welcome you into our family."

"Thank you, Master Saibon," said Hemashe, with a sigh of relief.

His mother clapped her hands in glee as she exclaimed: "Yumai is such a lovely, young lady, Medaru. We shall honour her as a daughter – one of our own!"

"Yumai?" gasped Hemashe. "It is not Yumai I wish to wed, mother. I am asking for Takaro's hand in marriage."

All were momentarily silent, and then nervous laughter filled the air.

"This is not the appropriate time to jest, Hemashe," scolded his father. "Forgive my son, Medaru. His long absence and isolation has obviously played havoc with his mind. He is not thinking straight. Of course he means Yumai."

"No, I do not mean Yumai, father. I wish to wed Takaro," reiterated the young warrior.

Medaru stared at Hemashe.

"Now son, you cannot marry that girl," gasped his mother. "Yumai is a more sensible choice."

"What do you mean; a more sensible choice? It is Takaro I love, not Yumai," explained Hemashe.

"You cannot be in love with Takaro," argued his father. "She is… She is different."

"You mean she is a half-caste," stated Hemashe. "Is that the word you were looking for, father?"

Hemashe's mother crumpled into a weeping, quivering heap as her husband consoled her. He apologized on behalf of his son: "I mean no offense to you, Medaru. I know you hold Takaro in the same esteem as a daughter, but Hemashe cannot marry that girl."

"That *girl* you speak of father is the girl I love."

"This is most unnatural, Hemashe, she is not one of us! She is not a mortal," argued his father.

"Her mother was a mortal!" countered Hemashe.

Medaru raised his hands in a gesture for calm. "It is true, her mother was indeed a mortal, a Taijin like us, but do not forget Hemashe, Takaro's mortal blood is mingled with that of the Elf-kind. She is not meant to wed a mortal, or even an Elf, for that matter."

"What are you saying, master? Are you telling me that she is fit for neither?"

"Hemashe, it is not a matter of whether she is unfit for man or Elf, truth be told, in an ideal world she would bind herself to another like her, another 'half-caste' as you said it. But alas, for her, there are none. She is the only one of her kind."

"I do not care! I love Takaro. Whether she be mortal or Elf, I cannot change the way I feel for her," declared Hemashe.

"You should care, for her sake and yours!" retorted Medaru. "I do not need to remind you that she shall outlive you by a good many years. You will be an old man, worn and tired with the years, unable to fulfill her needs as she remains youthful. Do you not think that there will be other young men who will be better able to meet her needs when she grows tired of an old husband?"

"We are in love!"

"Love can wax and wane, as surely as the tide, and given time, this love you speak of shall exist only in your memory as you fade with the years and watch her with your diminishing eyes as she goes off to war in the company of men whose youth is not yet spent."

Hemashe rose up from the table. His fist slammed down hard as he angrily denounced these words. "Master Saibon, how can you do this to Takaro? Why will you not allow her to find some happiness? If you care for her as much as I believe you do, you will allow her to bind to me."

"I care for both of you," confessed Medaru. "And it pains my heart to no end that Takaro is bound to this fate, to this existence; never to know the love of a man, whether he be Elf or mortal."

"I swear, Master Saibon, I can be the one to give her a life, to provide her with home and family," responded the young man.

Medaru shook his head as he listened to his desperate words. "Should you have children, they, too, shall be long-lived. No doubt, you shall be well past your prime when a son is old enough for you to share in the wisdom and teachings of his father. You will be too old to teach him the skills of the bow and sword, too feeble to show him how to hunt. People will think your children are your grandchildren. And eventually, time will rob them of a father."

"Listen to Master Saibon, Hemashe," pleaded his mother. "He knows what he speaks of. Do not subject yourself to such a life."

"What kind of life shall I subject myself to without Takaro by my side, mother?"

"Then, if not for yourself, think of your mother and me; what such a union will do to us. The people's tongues shall wag as they speak of us, and our son, and his choice of wife," warned Hemashe's father.

"Then we shall leave Anshen," vowed Hemashe.

"So you will turn your back on your own family," gasped his mother, as great tears tumbled down her flushed cheeks.

"If you go through with this Hemashe, you are no longer welcome in this home. It grieves me beyond words, for you are my one and only son, the one our entire family legacy shall hinge on. And now you are prepared to throw away your life, a life full of promise for the love of a half-caste woman," growled his father, rising up to challenge his son.

"Please Hemashe, even if she were not a half-caste, do not forsake our love for that of a woman who is trained in warfare and lusts for the blood of others. She will prove to be an unfit wife," cried his mother.

"But mother, I thought your wish was to one day see that I marry; to give you grandchildren… that you wished for me to find happiness in my life."

"Of course I do, that is why your father and I attempt to speak some sense to you now. Your infatuation with Takaro must end if you ever wish to find true happiness, with a mortal," she hissed in bitterness.

Hemashe slumped back down onto his cushion, his spirit felt as deflated as the wind escaping from the sails of a tall ship caught in the doldrums.

"Your parents speak in your best interest, Hemashe. It is only because their love for you is great that they willingly speak out to you. As I said before, I was merely a child of eight when Takaro arrived in Anshen and look now: I am in the autumn of my life while she remains relatively unchanged with the passing of time. Yes, you may have the distinction of having a *young* wife, but when you die and Takaro is still the mortal equivalent of a woman in her twenties, in the prime of her life, how do you feel right now to know that you may be only the first in a succession of husbands because she has grown dependent on a man?" asked Medaru.

"I never thought of that," answered Hemashe.

"Why would you? After all, you are in *love*. Rarely is a man in love capable of coherent thoughts," smiled Medaru, in genuine sympathy.

"Your mother and I love you, Hemashe. It would not be by our choice that you would be forced out of this home and driven from our memories if you choose to throw your life away," added his father.

"Do not make this choice based on the romantic notion of love. Think of what is best for you, your family, even for Takaro."

"And think of Yumai," his mother chimed in. "Think of what this will do to Yumai."

"I have never led Yumai to believe that I was interested in her," swore Hemashe.

"Obviously, you have been so engrossed with this infatuation with Takaro that you have been blind to Yumai's attentions," groaned his father, slapping his own forehead as if he wished to knock some sense into his son's.

"As her father, I have long been aware of my daughter's desire to bind to you," admitted Medaru. "And for the longest time, I chose to ignore this *friendship* you share with Takaro in hopes that you would come to your senses and see Yumai's love for you."

"Yes, think of poor Yumai, Hemashe," pleaded his mother. "You know if she does not wed a warrior, one already living in Anshen by her twenty-first year, Medaru shall have to abide by Taijin custom. He will have to consider suitors from the outlying villages. Although Master Saibon will choose a husband wisely for his daughter, Yumai will have to wed a stranger. She will have to leave Anshen to be with her husband's family. You know how Yumai loves Anshen. You know her desire is to remain in this village, close to her father and brother… and to you."

"My son, please, Yumai is a lovely girl. She shall make a wonderful wife and mother to your children," added Hemashe's father.

"I know with all certainty that Yumai shall be crushed to hear that you have chosen Takaro over her. Though Yumai has always held Takaro in the same regard as a loving sister, what do you think your choice shall do to their relationship if you bind to Takaro?" queried Medaru. "There is no question in my mind that jealousy will destroy their kinship. Do you truly want to be responsible for this?"

"Please Hemashe, it will be selfish of you not to consider what it will do to Master Saibon's family," insisted his mother.

"Hemashe, as much as I care for and love Takaro, do not think that it is beyond my ability or conscience to send her off to the north, to post her permanently to guard the Magare Valley in a bid to spare both she and Yumai heartache," warned Medaru.

"You would not do this," gasped Hemashe. He felt his overwhelmed soul being swallowed up in a tide of despair as he listened to the words of his parents and master. "You would not exile Takaro!"

"Exile would seem like such a harsh word, but I shall be forced to act on this if you give me no choice."

"But master, if she is stationed to the valley, she and those posted with her will be the first to see war – to do battle," stated Hemashe. "She will be forced to fight more than any of the other warriors."

"I am aware of that!" retorted Medaru. "As cruel as it may seem, I believe she is far better off to die on the field of battle than to diminish and pine away for a love that is not meant to be."

Hemashe glared at his master as he responded with a weary sigh, "You have no intention of allowing us to marry, do you?"

"When I consider how it shall affect your mother and father, Yumai, Takaro and even you, it is for the best. And if you are the man that Takaro admires so, then you will not think only of what you desire. You will think of the greater good for all."

Hemashe studied the look of woe and despair clearly etched across his mother's face as great tears continued to roll down her reddened cheeks. He cast his gaze towards his father's face only to be met by a severe scowl of disapproval.

"Think, my son, you have been absent for close to four months. What would ever compel you to believe that you are suddenly in love with Takaro?" questioned his father.

"I have been in love with Takaro for a good, long time," confessed Hemashe.

"If that is so, then why all this secrecy?" he snapped, his patience for his son wearing thin.

"Takaro asked that I do not disclose our relationship, no doubt for this very reason I am faced with now," answered Hemashe.

"Or perhaps Takaro wished it to remain secret because she had no intention of allowing it to evolve beyond anything more," responded Medaru.

"That is not so," protested Hemashe. "She was always more concerned of how it would affect Yumai."

"Then can you not see how you will come between them?" asked Medaru.

It was as though the walls of a steep canyon were closing in around the young warrior; his mind raced as he fought to find the words to convince those in his presence to grant his wish.

"So what will it be, Hemashe?" questioned Medaru. "I willingly give my consent if you wish to take Yumai's hand in marriage. However, if you do not abandon this foolish notion of binding to one such as Takaro, then I shall have no choice but to post Takaro far from here, much closer to danger before you act on this imprudent whim."

It was at this very moment Hemashe came to understand that Medaru could not be swayed. And though his master did indeed love Takaro as she had been his own daughter, it was evident that his first priority was to Yumai, his daughter by birth.

The following morning, Takaro knew things had not gone well. Hemashe was slow to appear at her door and when he did, he could barely face her. He could not look her in the eyes.

Hemashe did not have the heart to tell her what had transpired; only that he had been hasty in his words and actions. As this was only his twentieth year, he wished to remain unattached until the customary age of marriage for a young man. He wished to remain free of marital concerns, but she was free to consider other suitors if she wished to do so.

Takaro was absolutely heartbroken, and though she trembled upon hearing Hemashe's words, she did not shed a single tear of self-pity.

"I foresaw this, yet I foolishly chose to believe that some way, some how, I would find love in your arms," she said in barely a whisper.

"You shall find love one day Takaro, it will happen," promised Hemashe.

"No, I cannot help but believe all the whisperings that take place behind my back will always keep me apart from your people. I know what they say about me, and they are right. I am not fit to be seen with anybody's son," lamented Takaro.

"Do not despair, Takaro," cried Hemashe, holding her close as the tears welled in his eyes. "Please understand I never meant to hurt you."

"I know," sighed Takaro. "Do not blame yourself, for I have existed more than four times your life. I should have known better. Where I know how fickle love can be, you have much to experience yet. It is easy to mistake infatuation for first love. I was just a fool to believe that any man can fall in love with me."

Hemashe's heart continued to sink with the weight of her words. He was filled with both anger and sadness that he now felt compelled to allow Takaro to believe his love was feigned, only a passing fancy. In his own heart, he knew he would always love her.

Though Takaro and Hemashe continued to fight side by side, Medaru was especially watchful now, always ensuring that they were never posted together to conduct sentry duty. Nor would he permit them to conduct surveillance or deliver messages and supplies to warriors in the outlying areas. All the while, he encouraged Yumai to be more attentive to Hemashe.

Takaro had no choice but to accept her tasks and postings, all the while watching in silence as Yumai sought her sisterly advice on garnering the young warrior's attention while Hemashe slowly distanced himself from the little warrior.

As one day melted into the next and the passing of time was only noticed by Takaro with the coming and going of each season, the day she dreaded the most finally came to pass. Hemashe asked for Yumai's hand in marriage.

Her happiness for Yumai's good fortune could only be surpassed by her own sadness. In true fashion of one trained in the art of deception, Takaro stood by Yumai's side, displaying her joy as the man she once loved was now joined in matrimony to Medaru's daughter. Under a glowing harvest moon, the festivities wore on long into the night.

With the diminishing congregation, Takaro took the newlyweds aside to offer to Yumai and Hemashe a gift, Master Yaruke Saibon's former cottage. She had no desire to remain in Anshen any longer. She had no reason to prolong her misery, pretending to be happy.

"But Takaro, where do you plan to live?" asked Yumai, touched by her kind offer.

"I have already disclosed to your father that I shall be leaving tomorrow," answered the warrior maiden.

"So soon?" asked Hemashe, stunned by this unexpected news.

"Yes, I have put this off for far too long. I intend to travel to Saijun, to live amongst my mother's ancestors."

"Takaro, you are a Kagai Warrior," stated Hemashe. "You belong in Anshen."

"I shall remain loyal to this brotherhood. Medaru Saibon shall call upon me when I am needed," promised Takaro. "The next time I see you, it will be in the field of battle. In the meantime, I shall work to train others to take up arms. There is no point in delivering swords, halberds and shields to men if they are not properly trained to use these weapons."

"Will you not change your mind, Takaro?" asked Yumai.

"No, my presence is now better served elsewhere," she responded.

8
the return of the elf

Not once during her lone existence outside of Anshen did Takaro regret her decision to leave. Though her first winter went by slowly, she remained focused on her role as a warrior and a healer.

Those living in the foothills of Saijun, just north of her cottage minded their distance. They were at first leery of this mysterious woman warrior, for Takaro chose never to disclose her true identity and the fact that she was related to the Bansho clan that still existed in this area.

She spent her time teaching young men how to fight while working with local healers to better her understanding of medicinal herbs and remedies, as they would apply to mortals. Other than that, she deliberately distanced herself from the local citizens.

Periodically, Medaru would arrive with his son Keodai to deliver word of life in Anshen and anticipated battles she may be called upon to assist. As for Hemashe, Takaro did not see him again until they were brought together on the battlefield to engage in war.

Word was received from Medaru's network of spies in the eastern capital of Keso that the Emperor was sending forth a vast army, larger than ever before, north through the Magare Valley.

In the past, scouting parties of fifty to two or three hundred always entered western Orien, never to be seen again. This time, the Emperor rallied a huge army in a bid, once and for all, to face and banish the so-called demons of the haunted forests and to gather the rebel leaders and those who protected the religious centers to promote religious freedom.

In response, the elders of Orien mustered the warriors stationed in Nagana and many more from the surrounding countryside and villages lining Esshu Road to answer this call to arms. A large contingent of men were racing northward to meet the enemy as Medaru Saibon gathered the Kagai Warriors in preparation for war while Takaro readied the villagers of Saijun to join the battle.

On an early summer morn, against a predawn sky, Medaru and his men waited patiently as an army of Elven and Taijin warriors gathered in the shadows of the pine forest. The captain of the army dismounted from his steed, bowing before the Kagai leader.

"Welcome, captain! Am I mistaken to believe that you are Lord Dahlon Treeborn?" questioned Medaru, speaking in the common tongue. He gazed down at the Elf, bowing in respect before him.

As he straightened up, standing at his full height, he presented a large and commanding figure amongst the smaller Taijin men.

"Indeed you are, good sir. Lord Treeborn continues to work with the elders in Nagana. I am Captain Joval Stonecroft," answered the Elf.

"Stonecroft! I know this name. I am Medaru Saibon, my grandfather, Chusai Saibon and my father, Yaruke spoke often and most kindly of you!" stated Medaru, bowing in respect. "Though we have fought in some of the same battles, I suppose amidst the chaos, we have never been formally introduced."

At one glance, Joval could see by this warrior's age that his father, Yaruke Saibon was long laid to rest. "Yes, I knew your father and grandfather well. Great warriors they were."

"I remember I was a child, no older than eight years when you brought Takaro to Anshen," recalled the warrior.

"Takaro?"

"Yes, the young girl, neither Elf nor mortal," reminded Medaru.

"Oh, yes, I was the one to deliver her to your grandfather," nodded Joval. "How does Nayla fare? Is she well?"

"She is no longer with us," admitted Medaru.

"She is dead?" gasped Joval, stunned by this unexpected news.

"No, she lives alone, outside of Anshen," replied Medaru.

"How can that be?" queried the Elf. "She is only a child."

"I assure you, Captain Stonecroft, the one you speak of is no longer a child. Though she is long-lived, it would seem her mortal blood has accelerated her growth and aging. By mortal standards, she would be a young lady now of perhaps, nineteen years of age whereby had she been a full-blooded Elf, she would still indeed be a child."

"You do not say," stated Joval, his curious eyes now searching the group of Kagai Warriors standing behind Medaru Saibon.

"If your eyes mean to seek her out, she is not amongst us,"

revealed Medaru.

"So she did not become a Kagai Warrior?"

Medaru gave a gentle laugh as he answered: "Indeed she is Kagai, one of the best may I add. However, she commands an army of civilians when they are called to do battle by our side. She is not here now, but she will be here soon enough."

Hemashe stepped forward, introducing himself as he studied the tall Elf. "So you are the one Takaro had spoken of."

"If it was anything said in a derogatory manner, then I shall deny being that Elf," quipped Joval, as the young Kagai Warrior intently scrutinized him in the pale light of dawn.

"Her words were never derogatory, yet somehow, you are much younger than Takaro had always made you out to be," answered Hemashe.

Joval smiled as he responded: "When I first brought her here, she was a child. In her eyes, anyone who appeared to be over twenty mortal years was deemed old."

Medaru motioned for silence, standing up very straight as he listened. The call of a nightingale sounded in the distance.

"What is it?" asked Joval.

"They are coming. Brace your men for war, Captain Stonecroft. Our conventional means of destroying the enemy cannot be employed due to the timing and the number of soldiers dispatched to attack."

"Assault by bow and arrow first?" queried the Elf.

"Of course, position your best marksmen in the shadows of the bamboo forest that fringe the battlefield. We shall dispense our arrows without letting the enemy know what our numbers are. Nor will they have a clear aim at our warriors as they advance across the open field. Once our arrows are depleted, we shall wait until they enter this pine forest. Do not, I repeat, *do not* allow your men to be drawn into doing battle in the open field. We have adapted to fighting in the close confines of this forest. The Imperial Soldiers are trained to fight in the open; many shall bear the large and cumbersome halberds. It shall prove most difficult to fight in close quarters. If anything, our natural surrounding may be the defining factor that shall determine the victor."

"I understand, Master Saibon," nodded Joval. "Although it has been almost a century since I last trained with your father under Master Chusai Saibon's guidance, your grandfather's teachings have not been forgotten."

"Remember, time the volleys. As soon as the soldiers raise their shields overhead, have your frontline of archers aim horizontally to take down the enemy," instructed Medaru. "It is crucial that we destroy as many as possible before we engage in hand-to-hand combat."

"It will be done," acknowledged the Elf, as he mounted his steed. With a wave of his hand, his army advanced.

As the night silently surrendered to the sun's impending light, Kagai Warriors hidden amongst the boulders high on the rocky slopes at the mouth of the Magare Valley waited and watched. Below them, the Imperial Soldiers had cleared the landslide triggered by the warriors many moons ago. Just enough of the rocks, earth and other debris were cleared to allow them to penetrate into western Orien.

In the receding darkness, they could see an army, one thousand men strong gathering their arms and falling into line. Twice as many soldiers had been dispatched at this one time. Still, with this many men, it was evident to the Kagai Warriors that these soldiers felt that safety in numbers would still only be effective by the light of day. One too many rumors of night demons spiriting away their comrades under the cloak of darkness weighed heavily on their superstitious minds. Even if the warriors were to instigate an attack to lure the soldiers into the pine forests, they knew that even with their greater numbers, the soldiers would be hard pressed to pursue them at night. The soldiers would rather fight in a *safe* and familiar territory in darkness than to venture out into the unknown where their brothers have all mysteriously vanished.

As the first fingers of light stretched across the silent landscape, the Imperial Army began their march. Led by a captain and his most experienced soldiers on horseback, the infantry followed behind, their steps were confident and proud as they marched onward.

The Kagai Warriors, cleverly hidden against the rocky terrain, waited patiently, their bows were drawn and their arrows poised for the moment they were to mount their attack. As the soldiers taking up the rear cleared the entrance to the valley, following the others across the field, a warrior signaled for the assault to begin.

Attacking from the rear, the warriors knew the soldiers would flee from the direction of the arrows, away from the valley and into the pine forest. Another hail of arrows showered down upon the surprised soldiers as the orderly lines quickly disintegrated as panicking men charged forward to seek non-existent cover.

As the captain shouted orders for the men not to disperse, from the dense stands of bamboo a volley of arrows rained down upon them like a swarm of locusts, descending hungrily on the unsuspecting crop of men below. This initial assault caught most soldiers by surprise. Few had the opportunity to raise their shields as Joval's men launched an immediate strike, releasing a torrent of arrows horizontally to down many of the soldiers on the frontline.

With the ensuing pandemonium, the captain was unable to regain control of his soldiers. It was every man for himself as those who attempted to retreat back to the valley were met by the arrows unleashed by unseen enemies from up high. Those fleeing into the forest ran headlong into Joval's army and the Kagai Warriors. With a thunderous crash, the ground quaked in fear as mortals and Elves collided together in battle.

Medaru's men fought valiantly alongside Joval's warriors, desperately slashing, hewing and hacking at the Imperial Soldiers. As the Elf captain parried and then countered the blows of an enemy, he found himself locked, sword against sword. Raising his foot, he slammed it hard into the soldier's breastplate. As the man toppled backwards, Joval did not hesitate to ram his blade through the soldier's throat. Withdrawing his bloodied blade from the writhing figure, the Elf quickly glanced about. Immediately, he could see they were still greatly outnumbered.

He dashed to Keodai's aid as a large Taijin soldier raised his halberd on high to dispatch him. Medaru's son eyed his fallen sword where it lay on the ground now, well behind his foe. Joval dove forward. His hand easily scooped up Keodai's sword as he rolled. He came to an abrupt halt directly behind the soldier. Keodai dodged the halberd as it came down, but the soldier almost toppled right over him. As Keodai rose up, Joval pointed to his sword, now deeply embedded in the soldier's back.

"I believe this is yours!" shouted the Elf, as he dashed off to help another warrior.

Keodai wrenched his sword free, turning to face his next foe only to have the soldier fly past him. The soldier's body slammed hard into the side of a tree as another soldier that was catapulted through the air struck him. Keodai glanced over to see Mekai in action. He was like a crazed, wild man, throttling two soldiers with his bare hands. The large warrior spun in circles using the hapless soldiers to strike down their comrades as they ran to their aid. Mekai was whooping and hollering with glee, bowling over any soldier that stood in his way. It was obvious he was in no need of help.

A frightened soldier suddenly dodged around Keodai, running for his life. Hemashe dashed past Keodai. He was in pursuit of this soldier to prevent his escape. Keodai took one step forward to help his friend when an overwhelming surge of energy enveloped him from behind. For a split-second, Keodai froze in his tracks. He turned as a sinister laugh caused the hairs on the back of his neck to stand on end.

An Imperial Soldier towered before him. The tip of his sword was poised, ready to pierce Keodai's heart. As the soldier lunged forward, Keodai had no choice but to fall straight back to avoid the blade. He landed hard on his back, his own sword pointed forward to deflect the next blow. The soldier released another sinister laugh as he raised his weapon once more, the muscles on his arms and shoulders flexing to signal his intent. Trapped between the raised roots of a large tree; Keodai had no choice but to kick his feet forward to snap himself back into an upright position. It would bring him dangerously close to the warrior's deadly blade. He knew he would have to strike first with his sword as he landed back onto his feet.

Just as he kicked up, his body snapping forward, an arrow skimmed over him, just inches above his face and chest. The projectile slammed into the enemy, his thundering heart rupturing as the arrow tip continued through the soldier's body.

Keodai fell to the ground once more as the enemy spun from the impact, and then collapsed forward on top of him. As he struggled to remove this dead weight, he glanced up just in time to see Takaro unleash another arrow at a soldier running in Keodai's direction to finish him off. This time, her arrow caught this soldier square on his forehead with a loud *'crack'*. As he pitched backwards and reeled from the impact, the already dead soldier collapsed. He crashed down hard on top of his fallen comrade.

Keodai cried out in pain as the arrow lodged in the soldier's forehead plunged downward with the full force of his weight, slamming into the young warrior's right shoulder directly below his collarbone. The shaft of the arrow snapped as the soldier came down on top of Keodai, its broken shaft piercing through his clothes, skin and flesh. The dead and the living joined together briefly as one.

Takaro seized the dead soldier by his shoulder, rolling him off of Keodai. Again, the warrior cried out in pain as the shaft of the arrow embedded into his flesh was suddenly yanked free of his body as the soldier's head rolled off to the side. She then kicked the other body that still lay over top of Keodai, pinning him to the ground. Leaning forward, she handed back his sword as she recommended: "Pretend it is one very large sliver."

Takaro and her men seemed to appear out of nowhere. They gave the warriors already entrenched in war a surge of energy and renewed hope as she and the others shored up their numbers. The warrior maiden moved with ease and confidence as her sword came alive in her hands. She moved swiftly and deliberately as she deflected and angled away from the enemies' blades and halberd while dispensing punishment to all those who dared confront her.

It had been her experience that many soldiers upon seeing her, elected to ignore her, turning their attention to more *worthy* opponents. At first she was insulted by their actions, but as Medaru advised her, it was wiser to take advantage of their stupidity. If they chose to deliberately ignore a woman wielding a sword to take on a man because a male warrior poses a greater threat, then she should use this opportunity to help her brothers by taking down as many soldiers as she could from behind. And this was a matter of war. There would be no shame in dispensing death in this manner, for the soldiers should be the ones shamed for making such a foolhardy assumption to begin with.

As Takaro dashed from warrior to warrior in a bid to aid them, she raced forward to the assistance of an unarmed Elf. He was pinned against a tree trunk; the staff of a spear crushing unmercifully against his throat as he struggled to gain control.

Takaro moved silently behind the soldier who was so engrossed in his task that it was only when he felt the sensation of her sword puncturing through his breastplate to protrude outside his chest did he gasp in shock as he relinquished his hold. The spear tumbled from his dying grip as he slumped against the Elf. Throwing this dead soldier off to the side, for the first time Joval realized his rescuer was none other than Nayla Treeborn. Her face was devoid of expression as their eyes locked for a brief instance. She did not say a word to the Elf as she disappeared into the melee.

With reinforcement from Takaro's men as well as the Kagai Warriors that had earlier guarded the Magare Valley to unleash the first volley of arrows, the combined forces emerged victorious. All were exhausted by this ordeal, for never had the Kagai Warrior's engaged in a battle that went on for so long. Normally, they relied heavily on their traps and snares to pare down the enemy numbers before engaging in combat. They were usually done in fifteen minutes or less. This time, even with the aid of the army from Nagana, the last enemy was not laid down until almost twenty-five minutes into the battle.

Medaru and Joval quickly assessed the damage, directing the able-bodied warriors to finish off the dying enemy soldiers. Joval and his Elven warriors immediately set to work, assisting Medaru's healers to tend to the wounded. With the combination of the Elves' miraculous touch and the mortal's herbal remedies, mortal and Elves alike were quickly relieved of pain, their injuries healing rapidly.

Several Kagai Warriors too wounded to recover were tended to by Medaru and Keodai. They administered the rites of the dying before assisting them with their departure from this realm.

For the Elves, wounded and condemned to the ghost world of this realm if they should die, Joval released their souls so they may enter the Twilight, joining their loved ones already dwelling in the Elf Haven. Here they would be free of their pain and suffering, living an eternal existence in a land free of war and strife.

In a short span of time, the warriors removed the enemy soldiers from the forest, depositing their bodies in a hidden ravine to the north. Medaru asked Keodai to arrange for their dead to be returned to Anshen as Joval prepared to bury the dead men and to wrap a shroud around the fallen Elves as they were much too far from Nagana to return with the bodies of their fallen comrades.

Takaro finished tending to her men before turning her attention to helping the others to gather materials to construct litters to carry home the dead and those recovering from grievous injuries. Joval spied her as she quietly made her way through the swarm of busy warriors.

"Nayla!" Joval shouted, racing after her as she stepped into the shadows of the forest.

She ignored his call, walking away swiftly.

The Elf caught up to her, seizing her by the arm as he addressed her once more: "Nayla Treeborn!"

Yanking her arm free from his grasp, she slowly turned to face him as she responded: "Nayla Treeborn is dead."

"My eyes do not deceive me," said Joval, as he smiled in recognition. "It is you! I know it is you!"

Her head tilted ever so slightly as she stared into the Elf's excited, blue eyes.

"Do you not remember me? I am Joval Stonecroft."

"Of course you are," stated the warrior maiden, turning away to join her men.

"I take it; you do not remember me?" assumed Joval, following behind her.

"Did I say that I did not remember you?" responded Takaro; her tone was devoid of emotion.

"Well, you certainly did not act as if you recognized me."

She stopped, turning to confront the Elf: "What were you expecting from me? A welcoming hug? Fond words of salutation?"

"I just thought – "

"You thought nothing! I have heard tales of you and your men doing war with Yaruke Saibon, and yet in all the times you were up here, not once did you come back to Anshen. Not once did you come back to see me!" snapped Takaro, glaring up at the much larger Elf.

"You know why I did not return," responded Joval, taken aback by her hostile tone. "You know I swore to keep you safe; to keep your whereabouts a secret."

"That is a sorry excuse," hissed Takaro. "I have long since passed from the memory of those in Nagana."

"Well, had this been the type of reception I would have been met with, it is a good thing I had kept my distance," grunted Joval. "All I wanted to do was to thank you."

"Thank me? Thank me for what?"

"For saving my life back there," answered Joval.

"I was merely doing my job," replied the little warrior. She abruptly turned away from the Elf.

"Takaro!" hollered Keodai. He dashed to her side as panicked words spilled from his mouth: "Takaro, all the men are not accounted for! We are missing one!"

"How can that be? Who is missing?"

"Hemashe!"

"No! You are mistaken," gasped Takaro, shaking her head in disbelief. "Where did you last see him?"

"He was in pursuit of an enemy soldier. He was dashing after him toward the bamboo groves fringing this forest," answered Keodai. "That was the last time I saw him."

Medaru stepped forward, his brows furrowed with obvious worry as he shouted his orders: "Check the forest one more time. Check amongst our wounded and our dead! Look everywhere!"

Joval ordered his men to join in the search. As the warriors dispersed, looking for signs of Hemashe, Keodai and Takaro retraced his steps. As they followed the path Hemashe last traveled, the footprints delivered them to the edge of the open field. Amongst the trampled grasses and hoof prints left by the enemy on horseback, Hemashe's trail abruptly vanished.

"He has been captured!" Keodai groaned in despair. "Hemashe had been taken prisoner."

"We must save him!" responded Takaro. "Regroup your warriors, we must move swiftly before they take him far!"

As they retreated to gather their men, Medaru and Joval stood before them.

"Father, Hemashe has been captured by the enemy!" exclaimed Keodai.

"That is apparent," acknowledged Medaru.

"Master, I shall aid you in retrieving him," offered Takaro, pushing past Joval Stonecroft to reclaim her steed.

"No, you will not," countered Medaru.

"But father, if we leave now, we can catch up to the enemy. We can still save Hemashe," argued Keodai.

"That is exactly what the enemy anticipates. If we do this, we shall be playing directly into their hands. I will not risk the lives of any more men; not for the life of one," said Medaru.

"Master Saibon is correct in his thinking," added Joval. "If this warrior is true Kagai, you know he will take his life before speaking to the enemy."

Takaro stared into her master's eyes, searching for even a single sign of compassion that would allow her to pursue the enemy, to rescue their missing brother. It was painfully evident that Medaru was willing to sacrifice Hemashe for the safety of the others.

"So you are prepared to allow Hemashe to die?" queried Takaro.

"Yes." Medaru's answer was succinct.

"But this is your son-in-law we speak of. This is Yumai's husband!" cried Takaro.

"That is why my decision is so much more difficult," responded Medaru, turning back to join his men.

9

a journey into the unknown

Takaro never dreamed her next meeting with Yumai since leaving Anshen would be to console her in her grief. Though Takaro's heart was numbed by Hemashe's decision to forsake her to marry Yumai, she could not help but to share in Yumai's despair as she wept for her missing husband.

"What happened, Takaro?" asked Yumai, through the tears. "Hemashe always said you kept him safe in battle. What happened this time?"

Her words pierced Takaro's heart.

"It was not her fault, Yumai," stated Keodai, in her defense. "There were many soldiers, more than twice as many as there normally were. It was absolute mayhem. But if you seek someone to blame for Hemashe's demise, then the blame should fall upon my shoulders, for I was the last one to see him. I should have been the one to come to his aid."

Medaru shook his head and with a weary sigh responded: "My son, it serves no purpose to cast blame, or to accept blame, for what had happened to Hemashe was beyond our control. The fates decreed it. It was only a matter of time before one of our own would be captured in such a manner."

"It is most unfortunate indeed," agreed Joval. "However, we must count our blessings. Our losses could have been so much worse."

"So I am to be comforted by your words," sobbed Yumai, staring at the Elf. "I am to merely be grateful that others did not die. Well, this is my husband you speak of!"

"I am deeply sorry," apologized Joval. "I did not mean to minimize your loss. I merely speak as a captain. I am responsible for the lives of many, so when our losses are fewer than anticipated, especially when we are faced with such a daunting force, I am just grateful for the ones that did survive the war."

"Father, please, I beg of you, if there is a chance that Hemashe lives, please save him!" pleaded Yumai.

"You know I will not risk the lives of the others needlessly on such a perilous and impossible quest," answered Medaru, his eyes lowering, unable to meet hers.

In desperation, she turned to her brother, clutching his hands as she begged to him: "Please Keodai, Hemashe is your dearest friend. Honour your friendship by sparing his life. Help him, please!"

"Yumai, I must take heed of father's advice," responded Keodai. "As much as I am willing to sacrifice my own life for Hemashe's; I must follow father's orders."

"If not you, then Takaro will help me," decided Yumai, turning to the warrior maiden.

All eyes turned to her as Yumai dropped to her knees to make an impassioned plea.

"You have always been like a sister to me, Takaro. I beg of you, this one favor and I shall never ask for another thing from you again. Please, if you are such a dear friend as Hemashe claims you to be, if your allegiance to your brother warrior is as strong as he once said, then save him," begged Yumai.

Her words touched Takaro's heart, for she could see how deeply Yumai's love and devotion for her husband truly ran. "Yumai, you know Hemashe. If he has not already been put to death, then he has already taken his own life."

"Do not speak these words, Takaro! In my heart I know he still lives," cried Yumai, groveling on her knees before her. Clasping her trembling hands, Yumai pleaded again. "Please Takaro, if not for me, if not for Hemashe, then for this child I now carry."

"You are with child?" gasped Takaro, lifting her sister to her feet.

"Yes, and I cannot bear the thought of raising this child alone, without Hemashe by my side," sobbed Yumai.

Medaru shook his head in pity, but Takaro knew his daughter's tears or her desperate pleas for help could not persuade him. She held Yumai as she wept bitterly.

"Do not despair, sister," whispered Takaro. "I shall seek out the enemy. I will return with your husband."

"Thank you, Takaro!" gasped Yumai, kissing the little warrior's hands in gratitude. "Thank you!"

"You cannot do this alone, Takaro. You shall need a vast army if you wish to enter enemy territory," cautioned Keodai.

"This is what the enemy desires, Takaro. They want us to invade their lands, to do battle on their terms. It is dangerous and foolhardy to undertake such a task," warned Medaru.

"If that is what they expect, then I shall go alone," responded Takaro. "I will slip past them, unnoticed."

"If you insist on doing this, then I am forced to go against father's orders. I, too, shall accompany you," decided Keodai.

"You are full of valor and courage, my brother, but I shall be counted as a fool to take you on such a mission," countered Takaro. "Though your shoulder recovers nicely thanks to Captain Stonecroft's ability to heal, you shall be useless to me unless you can properly wield a sword or a bow. I best be on my own. Besides, I can travel much farther and faster, with or without a horse, if I am alone."

"She speaks the truth, Master Saibon," agreed Joval. "If indeed they are expecting an army, one or two shall slip by unnoticed. And an Elf can certainly travel tirelessly, for much longer."

"Captain Stonecroft, if this is your attempt to mock me, you know I am not an Elf," hissed Takaro, glaring at Joval.

"I was not speaking of you. I was speaking of myself," responded Joval.

"You?" asked Takaro, staring in disbelief.

"Yes," answered the Elf.

"Why would you risk your life for a mortal?" questioned Takaro, dismissing Joval's gallant offer.

"I believe my men and I are indebted to the Kagai Warriors, for long have Master Saibon's people honoured this alliance," replied Joval.

"And you would do this?"

"I honour my promises. I am always true to my words," stated the Elf, unmoved by her cynicism.

"Your promises mean nothing to me. Your deeds shall speak more loudly than your words," grunted Takaro.

"Tell me, little warrior, when did you last pass through enemy lands?" questioned the Elf.

"This shall be my first foray into enemy territory," answered Takaro.

"It is courageous of you to willingly journey into the unknown, but it may very well be your last venture, unless you have someone who knows the way," stated Joval.

"And you are telling me that you know the way?"

"I have journeyed into eastern Orien on a number of occasions," responded the Elf.

"Hmm, you may come in useful after all, Captain Stonecroft," determined Takaro. "We will leave tomorrow at first light."

Under a pale dawn sky, Takaro and the Elf prepared for the journey. Joval's sharp eyes gazed up, following a tiny form as it circled high above before descending rapidly from the sky, winging its way toward Medaru Saibon's cottage.

"A message," noted Medaru, turning to retrieve the small parchment attached to the falcon's jesses. "Do not leave just yet. Let us first see what word comes from the east."

With a heavy heart torn between despair and relief, Medaru returned to the group that had gathered to see Takaro and Joval off.

"Hemashe is still alive. He is well guarded as soldiers advance southward. Apparently, there has been specific instructions that he is to be kept alive at all costs, until he is delivered to the Imperial Palace in Keso," announced Medaru.

"I knew it! I knew he was still alive," gasped Yumai, her eyes gleamed with renewed hope. "Please Takaro, make haste. Find him. Bring Hemashe back to me!"

"I shall certainly do my utmost," promised Takaro, as Yumai gave her a grateful hug.

Joval mounted his steed as he turned to Medaru. "We are better off to head south now, along Esshu Road. We shall attempt to intercept the soldiers before they reach the palace."

"That would be wise, Captain Stonecroft," agreed Medaru.

"If you do not receive word in a month's time, do not waste any time or men to seek us out," advised the Elf.

Medaru nodded in understanding as he spoke: "Captain Stonecroft, I shall send word to those in the east of your coming."

"Your people to the east can be trusted?" queried the Elf.

"Upon my life," promised the warrior priest. "The one you should seek out if your travels do indeed take you to Keso shall be my cousin's nephew. He goes by the name of Nome Mewaku."

"And how will we find him?" asked Joval.

"He works within the walls of the Imperial Palace as a *cook*," revealed Medaru. "Long has he and his kin aided us, sending vital information that would affect those to the west. He can be trusted and he shall be prepared to help you and Takaro in whatever way he can."

"Very well," responded Joval.

As Takaro said her final farewells to Keodai and the others, Medaru whispered to the Elf: "If you are unable to facilitate Hemashe's rescue, you know Takaro will be forced to kill him. As distasteful as this task promises to be, you must ensure she carries through with this, before Hemashe is tortured and reveals to the enemy our numbers and whereabouts. If she fails to do so, it will be up to you to complete this mission. Is that understood, Captain Stonecroft?"

"Understood," answered the Elf, turning his steed westward. "Let us be on our way."

"Why do we venture south?" questioned Takaro. She urged her mare on to keep pace with Joval's steed. "There is no access into eastern Orien through the Furai Mountains to the south."

"There is one way," answered the Elf. "But for now, we shall not speak of this. It is a secret passage known only to a few. When the time comes, it will be revealed to you."

"How long will this trek take?"

"If we are unhindered in our travels, it shall take us twenty-four or twenty-five days to access the pass and perhaps another week of travel through eastern Orien to intercept the soldiers on route to Keso."

Without further questioning, Takaro followed Joval southward, the lush, green landscape rushing as their horses galloped on. The only time they stopped was to allow their mounts sufficient time to rest, drink and graze. It was only during these breaks did she and the Elf take in sustenance.

As the first day of travel came to an end, Joval led the steeds off the road to set up camp for the night. Before a small campfire, he and Takaro shared a modest meal under the light of the stars and the moon. The Elf's eyes caught sight of a sparkling glimmer. It was the slip of silver that hung from her ear cuff down to the small ring adorning her right ear.

"So little warrior, I see that you have yet to marry," determined Joval.

Takaro scowled at the Elf as she growled: "Whether I be married or not, it is none of your concern. Truth be told, I willingly forsake the love of a man so I can be loyal to my duties as a Kagai."

"No need to get angry," grunted Joval, his hands raised in a gesture for calm. "I was merely making an observation."

"You are better to keep your observations to yourself where I am concerned, Captain Stonecroft," cautioned Takaro. "If it were not for the fact that you know the way to Keso, I would be going forth on my own without being made to dull my mind and ears by listening to the idle chatter of an Elf."

"My! The passing of time has made you rather bitter," noted the Elf; "even more so than I thought possible."

"If you take my truths as bitterness, you are best to steady that tongue of yours if you wish to hear no more."

Joval's eyebrows arched up in dismay. He then chuckled at her hostile retort.

"What is it?" asked Takaro.

"You amaze me," answered the Elf, with strained affability. "The last time we passed along this route you begged for me to talk to you. For days on end, you insisted that we converse because you were *'bored beyond all reason'* if I recall your words correctly. I had to endure a barrage of questions, personal and otherwise, that you threw at me."

"Hmm, that is odd… I do not remember this."

"Yes, how convenient it is to forget when the shoe is the other foot," observed the Elf. "So, I am to assume I will not be subjected to a battery of questions on this journey?"

"There is nothing I wish to speak about with you, Elf!" snapped Takaro, dismissing his words and presence.

Joval shook his head as he groaned: "Why is it that you insist on making this journey an absolute excursion to hell for me? Frankly, I believe you were far more tolerable as a child. At least back then, I was able to manage your unruly behavior with the threat of my good friend, Valtar Briarwood's company."

Takaro involuntarily shuddered at the thought of the absent Elf. It was apparent to Joval she still detested Valtar after all this time.

"Does your friend still live?" questioned Takaro.

"Indeed he does! In fact, Valtar shall be leading my men back to Nagana in a day or two," answered Joval. "I am surprised you did not notice him when we did battle together with your Kagai brethren."

"What can I say? All you Elf men look alike to me," responded Takaro, her slight shoulders shrugging with indifference.

"That is a rather biased comment coming from the likes of you," rebuked Joval.

"How can it be unfair? Are you not all *freakishly* tall? Do you not all possess flowing, brown tresses and those pointed ears?" snapped the warrior maiden.

"Freakishly tall? We are quite the normal size for Elves," replied Joval, as he glared at the little figure sitting across the fire from him. "I believe you are just jealous because you are a runt, even by Taijin standards!"

"I will have you know I am taller than the average Taijin woman," retorted Takaro.

"You do not say! By how much, the width of a few strands of hair?" sniffed the Elf, unimpressed by her claim.

"You are an ass!"

"And you are a runt!" growled Joval.

"Giant!" countered Takaro.

"Pip-squeak!"

"You… You… Elf!" stammered Takaro.

"Ah! Finally, a compliment!" responded Joval, glaring at her with a self-satisfied grin.

"It was not meant to be a compliment!"

"Well, I can now see by your demeanor, you are definitely more human than Elf!" grunted Joval.

"How so?"

"Some humans have a way of bringing out the very worst in me," grumbled the Elf, glaring with evident hostility at his present company.

"Well, I can hardly say you do anything positive for my demeanor," retorted Takaro.

Joval drew a weary breath as he scowled back at her. "Tell me little warrior, do you wish for me to assist you on this misadventure you so willingly volunteered to undertake? For if you do, I strongly suggest you mind your words. And may I remind you; I am a captain. You are not. I will not tolerate any insubordination or words spoken in disrespect that are meant to challenge me. Do I make myself clear?"

Takaro was taken aback by his harsh tone. She was momentarily rendered speechless.

"You may be a Kagai Warrior, but if any of Master Saibon's words of wisdom have sunk into that thick skull of yours, his teachings would also include having due respect for other warriors, especially those of higher rank than you," admonished Joval.

She stared at the Elf in wide-eyed silence.

"Now, do I make myself clear?" he asked once more.

Takaro considered his words for a moment. Her head hung in shame as she realized Master Saibon would indeed be shocked and appalled by her conduct toward this captain.

"I am sorry. I should never have spoken to you in such a manner," apologized Takaro. "I foolishly addressed you not as a captain, but as a friend."

"A *friend*?" scoffed Joval, with a disgruntled frown. "Well, I would certainly hate to be considered an enemy if that is the case."

"I said I was sorry," snapped Takaro, "but if you expect me to beg for your forgiveness, I would sooner put out my own eye with a burning stick!"

The Elf's eyes rolled up to the heavens. He grumbled beneath his breath as he turned away from her to retrieve his bedroll: "By God, this trip will be the death of me..."

On their twenty-third day of travel, Joval noticed that Takaro grew more anxious as they neared the fortress city of Nagana. The Elf dismounted, allowing his steed to drink from a creek.

"Does any of this look familiar to you?" queried Joval.

"Vaguely so. It seems like a lifetime ago since I last passed this way," answered Takaro, in a small voice. "We are not heading directly to Nagana are we?"

"No," replied Joval. "From this point forward, we shall travel east."

"Good," she responded, hopping down from her saddle. "The farther away we are from that forsaken place, the better."

"Do not tell me this mighty warrior maiden still fears her father?" questioned Joval.

"Do not call him my father. And I am not scared of Dahlon Treeborn!" snapped Takaro, her words terse.

"Well, you could have fooled me."

"What makes you say I am scared of that Elf?"

"I always believed that if you had even an ounce of your mother's courage and will, you would have returned to Anshen some time ago to claim your rightful place in the House of Treeborn," said Joval, with a shrug of indifference.

"Why would I want a place in *that* house?"

"Because, like it or not, you *are* a Treeborn. You *are* the daughter of a high Elf," reminded Joval. "And because that is where Lady Kareda Treeborn would have expected you to be."

"Do not bring my mother into this. She is long dead!" snapped Takaro.

"Fair enough," responded Joval, leading his stallion from the creek. "For some reason, I just always expected more from the daughter of Lady Treeborn."

"Enough talk," ordered Takaro, staring up to the bleak sky. "Soon, night shall be upon us and the rains will fall. Let us get a move on."

Turning eastward, Joval led the way ever closer to the dark clouds looming high over the Furai Mountains. The thick, billowy masses latched stubbornly to the peaks, growing darker as the invisible sun withdrew what weak light penetrated the cloud-cover.

As they approached the base of one of the mountains, Joval dismounted from his stallion.

"A cold rain shall descend upon us soon," determined the Elf, watching the gray veil of precipitation move steadily down the mountain slope.

Takaro quickly removed an object no bigger than her bedroll from her mare's saddle. Unrolling the object onto a thick layer of tree boughs to keep it elevated off the soon-to-be-moist earth, she secured the small wooden pegs into the ground. Taking two slim, but sturdy pieces of bamboo, she positioned it at the opposite ends of the tent to support the peaked roof. This heavy tarp was treated with a special oil and bee's wax preparation to make it water-repellant.

"Perfect timing," announced Takaro, as big, fat droplets of rain darkened the earth.

She crawled inside her tent, the dry bedroll tucked beneath her arm. Laying out her bedroll, she then lit a candle with a small firestick that had been dipped into wax to protect it from moisture. The sting of sulfur in her nostrils quickly dissipated as the thin, gray wisp of smoke rising from the smothered firestick wafted away into the night air. As the rain fell in a torrent, drumming loudly against the roof, Takaro lifted the flap of her small tent to spy the Elf huddled beneath the dripping canopy of a tree. His bedroll was wrapped about his shoulders as he leaned in close to the tree's trunk to stay dry.

"Do not stand there like a fool!" called Takaro. "Get in here! There is room enough for both of us."

"I do not wish to impose," stated the Elf.

"You shall be imposing if you insist on staying out there. I will be forced to join you in the rain," answered Takaro.

"Are you sure?"

Takaro released a disgruntled sigh: "Of course I am sure. And I shall only make this offer but once. Take it or leave it!"

"Very well," shouted Joval, dashing to the tent. He quickly crawled in by her side. "Thank you."

"You are welcome," she responded, passing a small piece of bread to the Elf.

"What is this? It does not look like Elven bread," assessed Joval. "Did you make it?"

"Yes, I did. And it is similar to Elven bread, but Elven bread is flatter and in my opinion, bland, to put it bluntly. I have added honey, dried fruits and nuts, and though it looks heavier than the bread you may be used to, I assure you, this shall appease your appetite just as well without leaving you feeling heavy," promised Takaro.

"Hmm, it is good!" agreed Joval, sampling a small piece of bread. "Very good in fact."

"What is this? Do my ears deceive me or does the good captain pay this lowly warrior a compliment?" marveled Takaro, as she lay back on her bedroll to eat.

"Can you not just accept a compliment and leave it at that?" groaned Joval.

"Yes, I can," answered Takaro, breaking off another small piece of bread and wrapping the rest up for later. "I was just so overwhelmed by your show of kindness."

Joval gazed over at the little warrior. The soft glow of the candle softened her features. For an instant, she looked like the young girl he had left behind in Anshen almost sixty year ago. Her head slowly turned in his direction, feeling the steady gaze of his eyes.

"Is there a problem?"

"You will never forgive me for leaving you in Anshen, will you?" responded Joval.

Takaro rolled over, propping her head up by her elbow to face him. "Whatever made you think of this?"

"I can sense great bitterness in your voice when you speak to me," answered the Elf. "I can see it in your eyes when you look at me."

"It was silly of me to spout off as I did. If it had not been for you, I would still be in Nagana, or worse," confessed Takaro.

"For the longest time, I was haunted by the notion I had made a terrible mistake leaving you in Anshen," admitted Joval. "Back then, I had no other place to take you, nor could I allow you to suffer as you did. Yet, for many years my conscience plagued me as to whether I did the right thing. Was your life made worse by my actions?"

She could see by his eyes the Elf was sincere in his words; there was genuine concern… and guilt. She smiled kindly at him as she responded: "It has not been easy, but ultimately, I chose this path that I walk, not you. I wanted to be a Kagai Warrior. Now I am."

"But are you happy?"

"Happy? That word means so many different things to different people. It is merely a phase, an emotion that tends to wax and wane, like love. More often than not, it is as elusive as love," answered Takaro. "All I will say is that I am alive, thanks to you. And I have purpose in my life."

"To have purpose is good," said Joval, with an approving nod. "There is nothing more wasteful than life without purpose."

"And what of you? In all this time, have you found happiness?" questioned Takaro.

"As you so eloquently put it, happiness can be elusive," answered Joval. "I suppose we have more in common than you care to admit, for I, too, am a warrior bound to my sword and shield as I fulfill my purpose in this realm."

Takaro giggled as she lay back down.

"What is it?"

"We are both rather pathetic, are we not?" she answered with a smile.

Safe in the small, dry tent, the pair passed the night, sharing tales of battles they had endured and Takaro's life in the secret Kagai enclave of Anshen. In the many hours that passed, not once did Takaro ask Joval of Nagana or Dahlon Treeborn. When sleep finally did come, Joval, in typical Elven fashion, required only two or three hours of rest to feel refreshed. He readied the horses and scouted out the trail ahead while Takaro slept for two more hours.

When he returned, Takaro was awake and in the midst of compressing the tent back into a small bundle to secure to her saddle. She turned to see him appear from the shadows of the forest.

"Did you sleep well?" asked Joval, as he dismounted from his steed.

"Not bad considering all the rain," answered Takaro. "Have you been up for long?"

"Long enough to venture forth to see what awaits us beyond this mountain," replied the Elf.

"In what direction do we travel?" she asked.

Joval's finger pointed as he spoke: "We head about two leagues east beyond this mountain. From there, we access the secret pass."

Takaro glanced first to the north. Once she established her location, her eyes carefully scanned the lands to the west, south and then the east. Finally, she responded: "That would take us to Borai Mountain."

Joval gazed down at the little maiden, stunned that she guessed correctly. "How did you know? Did Master Saibon divulge the whereabouts of this secret passage to you?"

"Oh, no! In my time training with Medaru's father, Yaruke Saibon, part of my instructions included memorizing details of maps. I studied maps of both eastern and western Orien, so it was merely a matter of gaining my bearings and recalling natural and man-made landmarks," revealed Takaro.

"That is remarkable," marveled Joval. "Do all the warriors train in the like manner?"

"You would think, but no."

"What do you mean by that?" questioned Joval.

"You would think all the men would be made to memorize maps, for I have noticed the ones who rarely venture far from Anshen had a tendency to aimlessly wander about lost, for a good long time at that, than to ask for directions," stated Takaro, in a matter-of-fact tone.

"So you know the east as well?"

"Of course I do. Unless mountains have formed, lakes have dried up and rivers have altered course in the past twenty years or so, yes, I should know my way," she replied with utmost confidence.

"Then you truly do not need me to find your way about," determined the Elf.

"If need be, yes," admitted Takaro, as she mounted her mare. "However, it would make for a much faster trek with you leading the way, for if I was to venture forth alone, I would be forced to stop regularly to ascertain my location and direction."

"Ah well, the truth comes out," lamented the Elf, with a chuckle. "And here I thought you desired my presence because you were taken by my charm and dashing good looks."

Takaro's face momentarily reddened as he smiled at her.

"My, you are so full of self-importance," she mocked him. "I do not recommend standing too close to the tip of my sword lest it deflate that over-blown ego of yours!"

He feigned a gasp of disappointment: "Your words wound me, my lady!"

Takaro could feel her cheeks burn as they deepened a shade. It was the first time this Elf ever addressed her in such a manner. She was always referred to as 'warrior maiden', 'little warrior' and at one point, even a 'runt', but never '*a lady'*.

She wheeled her horse about, sinking her heels into its flanks as she galloped away.

"Wait! I thought you said you needed me to lead!" shouted the Elf, as he steered his mount to follow behind her.

For seven days, the pair journeyed northeast, keeping to the shadows of the forests, well off the main roads. The farther east they ventured, Joval gradually shifted their routine so they traveled by night and rested during the daylight hours. Whereas Takaro's vision at night was exceptional to that of a mortal's, she was truly amazed at the Elf's ability to see in even the darkest of nights, guiding their horses effortlessly through the blackness as they passed the hills surrounding the estate of the royal family in Shesake, now interned while the present Emperor ruled Orien.

As the travelers came to a stop high on a ridge overlooking the countryside, Joval's far-seeing eyes scanned the distant road under the impending light of the morning sun. All was quiet.

"If my calculations are correct, those holding the Kagai Warrior shall come by this way in three to four days if they travel by horseback," assessed Joval.

"So we have not missed them?"

"Definitely not. If the soldiers travel by foot, depending on how many and their condition, it shall be at least another week before they come by this way."

"Then we wait here?"

"That is the plan. We shall have to keep a constant vigil, take turns sleeping," stated the Elf. "I will take first watch, for I require only half the sleep you do."

Without the comfort of a campfire, Joval and Takaro sat in the darkness, waiting and watching. On their third night of the watch, as Takaro gazed down on the lands below, Joval lay on his back, staring up to the millions of tiny, twinkling stars dotting the heavens from horizon to horizon. He marveled as a shooting star blazed across the sky, its long tail quickly fading into the darkness.

"Did you see that?" gasped the Elf, still in awe.

"See what?" asked Takaro, reluctant to pull her eyes from the road below.

"A shooting star," replied Joval.

"*A* shooting star? Just *one*? That is nothing! Wait until the full moon of this summer month, for three nights the skies will be filled with them. It shall look as if it is raining fire in the heavens."

"One, one-hundred, it matters not to me. That brilliant flash of light traveling across the night sky has always captivated me. I have always wondered about its origin; where it goes and why its light is so fleeting," responded the Elf.

"The Taijin people believe that wishes are made on such stars. If the wish is made and the star travels in the direction of the wish-maker, it shall come true. If the star travels away, then the wish will remain just that, a wish," said Takaro, her eyes returning to the dark landscape below.

"Yes, I have heard of this Taijin lore," replied Joval, his eyes still fixed to the heavens. "So have you made many wishes?"

"From the time you first left me in Anshen, I had but one consuming wish. But this wish eventually played out only during my infrequent dreams and have long since faded to the back of my memory, until of late," stated Takaro.

"What is this one wish?"

"It is silly," replied the little warrior.

"I promise, I will not laugh, no matter how silly it is," vowed the Elf.

"Promise?"

"Upon my life," swore Joval. She watched as he raised his hand, placing it over his heart in solemn promise.

"For all these long years I have not wished this wish, no longer even dreaming about it until recently; since meeting you again," began Takaro, apprehension filling her small voice.

Joval rolled over onto his side, listening intently to her.

"Go on," he insisted.

"I swear you are a bad influence, Captain Stonecroft! Why else would these dreams fill my head once more?" sighed Takaro.

"Now I am truly intrigued. Go on, I say."

"Since the time I was a child, I cannot deny I had dreamed of returning to Nagana; to rise up against my father and reclaim my place in this house, much to his chagrin."

"Ha! I knew it was still in you! I knew you were your mother's daughter!" exclaimed the Elf.

"Alas, it is but a dream. It was something I had always hoped for;

to prove that I belonged, that the daughter of Kareda Bansho could indeed rise up to greatness. Now I am haunted by these long forgotten dreams once more, no thanks to you."

"You speak as though it is a bad thing," responded Joval.

"Dreams and wishes are a waste of time. Never had one dream ever come true for me."

"Well, it pleases me to see that you have not lost the ability to dream, for it is within these dreams that hope remains alive. When you cease to dream, then hope, too, dies," stated Joval.

"What good are they when they will never come true?" lamented Takaro, in a sad whisper.

"Why can it not come true?" queried the Elf.

"Do not mock me, Captain Stonecroft! I am a fool to cling to such desperate, pathetic hopes and dreams."

"Let me share some words of wisdom handed down to me by a mortal I once greatly respected: One can wish and dream an eternity away. However, if you want a dream to come true, not only must you believe; you must also strive to work hard to acquire this dream, to make it a reality. Otherwise, it shall always remain just that, a dream."

Takaro reflected on Joval's words, and then she asked: "And who was this venerable sage to share this wisdom with you? Was it one of the elders of Orien?"

Joval gave her a knowing smile as he responded: "No, in all honesty, it was your mother."

"My mother!" replied Takaro. She felt a small smile curl her lips as a warm energy filled her heart.

"Yes, your mother," reiterated the Elf. "And I do believe she would be pleased to know you still possess the desire to reclaim your rightful place in this world."

"Some things are better left as a dream; left to thrive only in one's imagination," replied Takaro, her smile fading from her face.

"Why limit this to your imagination? Why only dream about this? Your mother used to tell me that a life spent wishing for what could have been, is to live a life filled with regret. Lady Treeborn never regretted living her life as she did, making the choices she had made. She was never one to wonder what would have happened if she had only tried to change her circumstances," revealed Joval.

"I recall one time when I was a child my father scolded me when I said that I wished to be a great leader; one who might one day unite our lands in peace. Dahlon laughed first, and then he said that *'one who is a nobody and yet, still attempts to strive for greatness shall face far greater ridicule and scorn if he fails than one who is known and respected'*. I was crushed by his words, but my mother countered by saying that *'the greatest failure in life is to have never tried'*. In hindsight, I suppose that is what she meant about not living with regret."

"Well, for myself, I would much rather fail attempting to make a dream come true than to pine away in old age wondering *'what if I had only tried'*, that is for sure," attested the Elf. "I would rather live my life as your mother did; with no regrets."

"Oh, I am sure she did have at least one regret," speculated Takaro.

"What might that be?"

"Marrying the likes of Dahlon Treeborn."

"You are so wrong," stated Joval, in a firm voice. "She never regretted binding herself to your father."

"How so?"

"Through this union, you were begat. You were the joy of joys in Lady Treeborn's brief life. You filled a void in her heart that could be filled by no other," answered the Elf. "No, she never regretted marrying your father."

"Nayla! Wake up!"

A voice droned in her ears like a distant echo calling to her from the past. She stirred from her sleep as a voice called to her once more.

"Nayla! Rouse yourself! Imperial Soldiers are coming!"

Instinctively, the warrior maiden reached for her sword she kept under her bedroll as she leapt to her feet. As her eyes came into focus in the harsh light of day, she squinted at Joval's tall form gesturing her to follow him up the rise.

She quickly composed herself as she joined the Elf at the top of the ridge to gaze down into the valley. Far off in the distance, the tiny figures of men on horseback journeying southward with great urgency caught her eyes.

"How many?" she asked.

"Still too far away to be certain," replied Joval, his eyes straining to see. "Just be patient."

After a few more minutes had passed, the men drew closer. Joval announced: "There are forty-four soldiers, and indeed, the Kagai

Warrior is still alive, but just barely."

From what the Elf could see of Hemashe, he was securely bound and gagged. The Kagai Warrior appeared to be gaunt and haggard from his long trek.

"Forty-four soldiers… Even if we both mounted an assault with bow, in all likelihood, our efforts shall be in vain," determined the little warrior. "There are too many for the two of us to confront."

"Thank goodness, common sense reigns supreme," whispered the Elf. "If you were to suggest charging down to do battle in a bid to save your friend, I would be forced to abandon both you and this mission."

"Because you are scared?"

"Me? Scared?" laughed the Elf. "No, I just refuse to align myself with a fool, for a fool and his head shall soon be parted."

Her brown eyes rolled in dismay as she, too, now made out the advancing party of soldiers. In their midst was indeed Hemashe.

"I made this journey to save my brother warrior, not to get us all killed," she stated. "There is another way."

"What do you suggest?" queried Joval.

"We shall follow them into Keso."

"You mean to let the soldiers deliver your friend to the Emperor? To allow them to take him into the walls of the Imperial Palace?"

"Yes."

"And then what?" asked the Elf.

"Then I shall go in after him."

"And how do you intend to do that? Rattle on the portcullis and demand to be let in?" groaned Joval.

"That is not a bad idea, Captain Stonecroft!"

"Are you serious?" gasped the Elf.

"Deathly serious," answered the warrior maiden. Her eyes sparkled with the prospect of walking amongst the enemy. "I have a plan."

"Now I am truly scared," grunted Joval.

Avoiding the roads, the Elf led the way through forest and streams, cutting a direct route to Keso.

"It shall be an eight-day journey to the palace," stated Joval, as he waited for his steed to finish quenching its thirst from a stream.

"It is critical we arrive before the soldiers do. Is that a possibility?"

she asked.

"Most definitely, at the very least by a good day or so," responded the Elf. "The route the Imperial Army takes, though it be well used, it winds and twists southward to Keso. Plus, the men are weighed down with armor; their mounts shall tire more quickly. And do not forget, they also require more sleep than you or I."

"Very well, Captain Stonecroft," she replied. "It shall give me adequate time to gather together what I shall need before I enter the gates of the palace."

"I sense you intend to go in alone?" queried Joval.

"Absolutely."

"Are you not concerned that there will be four-hundred soldiers waiting inside rather than the mere forty-four heading there now?" questioned the Elf.

"When I enter, I shall hardly be viewed as a threat. I will not even require my swords when I venture on to the palace grounds."

"Please tell me you have not been touched by a temporary bout of insanity," pleaded Joval, eyeing her with a degree of suspicion.

"I assure you, I am quite sane, Captain Stonecroft. Yaruke Saibon had taught me much about the ways of the Kagai Warrior, but my training extends beyond that of using conventional arms."

"How so?" queried Joval.

"As a spy, I have been trained to adopt a number of disguises, from cook to courtesan. It will allow me to move about amongst the enemy so I may infiltrate their otherwise impenetrable domain."

"That is truly amazing," marveled the Elf.

"Not really, I merely follow in my mother's footsteps," she revealed to Joval.

"Lady Treeborn was a spy?" gasped the Elf, truly surprised by this bit of information.

"I wish you would refer to my mother as Lady Kareda Bansho, not Treeborn. And yes, apparently, she was sent to Nagana on the request of the elders to see how legitimate Dahlon's claims were for peace and to formalize the alliance between his people and the citizens of western Orien."

Joval was stunned.

"You did not know this about my mother, did you?"

"I had no idea. I knew she was pivotal in the bid to secure an alliance, but never to this extent, or by those means!"

"It just goes to show you how adept she was in her vocation. In fact, it was she who infiltrated the palace in Keso to steal away with the floor plans."

"These plans shall certainly come in useful. Do you have them?" questioned Joval.

"Yes."

"May I see?"

"No." Her tone was crisp.

"And why not?"

"It is up here," she answered, her index finger tapping her head.

"You have the floor plans memorized, too?" queried the Elf.

"What do you think would happen if I was caught by the enemy with maps and these plans? It would become very apparent to all what our ultimate destination is," replied the warrior maiden.

"You do have a point," admitted Joval, mounting his steed. "So what is your grand plan to enter the palace grounds?"

"I do believe they will be in need of a new cook when I arrive at the palace," she answered.

"And then what, you will roast and boil the enemy into submission?" he teased her.

"Very amusing, Captain Stonecroft," she smirked. "Let me just say I have the ingredients to do away with a good number of the soldiers."

"Well, this shall prove to be most interesting. And just how do I fit into all of this?" asked the Elf.

"You certainly cannot pass by unnoticed. Your tall, *gawking* height alone will be enough to turn heads. You best stay out of sight, for Elves are drawn and quartered if they set foot in this country. You will wait on the outside for me."

"That is it?"

"What more can you do? Just be ready to expedite our departure on my signal. I would strongly advise creating some kind of diversion that shall direct the enemy away from us when we take flight."

"That I can do," acknowledged the Elf.

Under a dark sky, Joval guided their steeds to the top of a hill. Here he stopped.

"Behold, the Imperial Palace," announced the Elf, in a whisper as his gaze turned directly eastward.

Before them, the spires of the great watchtowers pierced the cobalt night sky. The battlements were well guarded as soldiers patrolled the perimeter of the palace grounds.

"I suggest you get some sleep, I shall take the first watch," recommended Joval, leading his stallion into the deep shadows of the forest bracing the hillside.

The first fingers of light stretched lazily into the receding darkness as the sun peered over the horizon to touch the lands. Joval woke with a start as a pheasant unwittingly stumbled into the Elf's sleeping form. The bird burst into the sky in a small explosion of brown, red and iridescent green feathers. The Elf glanced about. Both horses were tethered and still grazing nearby, but the little warrior was nowhere to be seen.

"Bloody hell! She has gone to the palace, that fool!" gasped Joval, springing to his feet. "I cannot believe she can be that stupid."

"I assure you, I am not," said a voice from behind him.

The Elf turned to see the warrior maiden. In her hand, she carried the bag that once concealed her tent, but now, it was filled with a variety of plant parts.

"While you slept, I had been collecting the items I will need," she explained.

"Is this what you will use to annihilate the enemy? Vegetation?" queried Joval, with a frown on concern. "Or do you intend to don the greenery and sneak in under their noses as a shrub of some sort?"

"An Elf with a sense of humour. You *are* an odd one," she noted smugly.

"Did I say these words in jest?" replied Joval, eyeing her collection with serious doubt.

"These are no ordinary plants," replied the little warrior, ignoring his comment. She held forth a flowering spike almost as tall as her, of rose-colored, thimble-shaped blooms. The pale green, fuzzy leaves grew sparsely along this single flower spike that arose from a rosette of leaves that hugged the ground. "The flowers, stems and leaves of this plant are highly poisonous. Even a small quantity will wreak havoc on the heart. I shall be serving this up to the soldiers."

"And what is this?" queried the Elf. He examined the cluster of deep purple berries still attached to palm-sized, distinctly oval-shaped leaves with perfectly parallel venation extending from the central leaf vein.

"I was unable to gather sufficient poison, only enough to feed to a good number of the soldiers. So, for the Emperor and his esteemed guests, they shall be served up fruit tartlets made with these."

"It will kill them?" asked Joval.

"Alas, no. The best I can do is to make them extremely ill, very quickly. Those already in poor health can certainly die, but the others will be incapacitated in the most agonizing way."

"And it is not a poison?"

"That is a matter of opinion," she answered with a smile. "The bark and fruit of this tree can be used to make an extremely powerful laxative. It shall make for some severely agonizing bowel movements, if you get my meaning?"

"Nasty!" Joval laughed in response. "Does Master Saibon realize what a monster he has created?"

"He taught me everything I know," she replied with obvious pride.

The Elf rummaged deeper into the bag. "I know these to be rose hips, but what root is this?"

"I have a feeling the prisoners are in poor health, no doubt suffering from, at the very least, scurvy. The rose hip steeped in a tea shall do wonders for them, plus it shall dull the flavor of this root. It will work to lull them into a restful sleep."

"You intend to sedate all the prisoners?"

"Well, I certainly have no intention of killing them. Many are innocent men thrown into the prison garrison because they denounce the Emperor's inhumane treatment of his subjects," explained the little warrior. "Besides, if I do not take this precautionary measure, I assure you, once I make a bid to free Hemashe from his cell, all of the prisoners shall be clamoring for me to do the same for them. I cannot draw that kind of attention to us, nor can I risk freeing legitimate criminals."

"I cannot dispute that your plan may actually work, Nayla," stated the Elf, with a nod of approval.

The little warrior cocked her head. She stared at him as she asked: "Why do you insist on doing that?"

"Doing what?"

"You have been addressing me as Nayla since the beginning of this mission. Why?"

"Because that is your name," replied the Elf. "And it is the only name I ever knew you by."

"I abandoned that name the day you left me in Anshen. As I said before, Nayla Treeborn is dead – long dead."

"To the contrary, little warrior," countered Joval. "I would say Nayla Treeborn has experienced a rebirth of sorts. I have witnessed you in the heat of battle, and the more I learn from you and about you, the frightened little child I left behind has grown up to become a formidable force to contend with, even by Dahlon Treeborn's standards."

She silently absorbed his words before responding: "I suppose there have been worse things that you have called me."

"Like what?"

"Like '*runt*'!" exclaimed the little warrior.

Handing her weapons over to the Elf, she loosened her braid to let her dark tresses tumble down around her shoulders, concealing the small points of her ears.

"See," she said. "Now I can pass as a Taijin woman."

"Are you positive you want to go through with this?" asked the Elf, inwardly stunned at this sudden transformation. "It is not too late to change your mind."

"I will not leave a brother warrior to suffer in the hands of the enemy. If there is a chance I can help Hemashe, then I will."

"Hold on here! If you are true Kagai then you shall bear the mark of this brotherhood. I hardly think you will be able to constantly wear that cloak as you prepare food with the others. They will see your arm," cautioned Joval.

"No need for concern, Captain Stonecroft. I do indeed bear the mark of the Kagai, but I do not wear it on my arm."

"You do not say! So, where *do* you wear this mark?" queried Joval, his eyebrows arched up with great interest.

"That you shall never know," she answered with a coy smile.

He stood back and eyed the small figure before him, attempting to ascertain where this tattoo was concealed. The little warrior frowned in disgust as she felt his eyes undressing her.

"If you must know, it is on my right shoulder blade."

"Oh," replied the Elf, with an approving nod, his eyes quickly shifting from her stare.

"I demand to be let in!" she demanded. Her small hands rattled defiantly on the iron grate securing the entrance to the palace grounds. "Open up!"

For one so small, she certainly is not meek, thought the Elf, listening to her rant from where he hid.

The captain eyed this stranger with suspicion as he approached the portcullis. "What business do you have here, woman?"

"The Emperor seeks a new cook, one who specializes in catering extravagant, royal events," she answered. "I am here to answer this calling."

"I was not aware of this," grunted the captain.

"Are you an imbecile? Of course you would not know of this, unless you are the captain of domestic duties! Why would you know?" She snapped with impatience. "Look here! My ingredients will not remain fresh forever. Either you address this with the Emperor immediately, or you shall find someone with a better grasp of the situation than you! Now get to it!"

The captain blinked hard as though her abrupt words and sharp tone slapped him across his face as surely as her own hand had assaulted him.

"So you can cook?" questioned the captain.

"Come closer so I may box those cloth ears of yours!" she offered as she gestured for him to step a little closer to the iron grate separating them. "Are you deaf as well as intellectually challenged? Why else would I be requested to come to this forsaken place?"

Joval shook his head. *Goodness, she is both scary and irksome at the same time. I wonder how long it will be before the captain decides to just run his sword through her.*

"So, what will it be?" she asked in a huff. "I just as soon head home than be forced to waste my talents on the likes of you, but it will not be my head served up on a platter if I am turned away now, will it?"

Joval cringed as the captain endured her verbal assault. Then, much to the Elf's surprise, the captain ordered the portcullis to be raised. He watched as the little warrior disappeared through the gateway, escorted directly to the palace.

The captain reluctantly led her into the palace kitchen where one of the domestics directed him to the root cellar.

"Follow me," ordered the captain.

Down in the cool, dank cellar with nothing more than a coal oil lamp illuminating the storage room, a Taijin man wrestled with burlap bags filled with root vegetables.

"Mewaku!" called the captain, into the dim-lit hole in the ground. "There is someone here to see you."

"Send him down, captain. I have little time to waste today, for we are short-staffed in the kitchen," he shouted as he hefted a sack of carrots to stack with the others.

"Well then, consider this a god-send to you," laughed the captain, shoving the little woman toward the steps of the root cellar. "And if she is not, let me know, for I shall be more than glad to show her out."

"I can see myself out," insisted the new cook, giving the captain a deliberate shove back.

"You are a feisty one, woman. You best mind your manners if you wish to remain on staff," snapped the captain, as he turned away.

As she stepped down into the gloomy cellar, she stopped momentarily as her eyes adjusted to the glow emanating from the single lantern. She could feel the damp air clinging to her skin as she surveyed the earthen walls surrounding her. The man stopped to wipe his brow with his forearm as he considered the woman before him.

"That is odd, I did not think the Emperor had sent out word so quickly of my need for additional help. So, by whose recommendation were you sent forth?"

She knelt to the ground. With her finger, she etched into the sandy floor: MEDARU SAIBON.

He bent closer to the floor, examining the name. His hands quickly swept over the sand, destroying the letters. His eyes scrutinized her as he whispered: "So you are the one sent forth by Master Saibon?"

She nodded her response.

He introduced himself: "I am Nome Mewaku. And it is better that you do not reveal your true identity to me. It is safer that way."

"I understand," she nodded in agreement.

His shoulders slumped and a weary sigh escaped him as he advised her: "You could not have picked a worse time to enter the gates. The Emperor plans a great banquet tonight. He has many guests, including a number of warlords who even now, descend upon the palace. The grounds shall be crawling with soldiers."

"Believe me, it was not by choice that I enter these grounds now. The Kagai Warrior I mean to rescue shall be delivered to the prison garrison by late this afternoon or early this evening."

"So how do you intend to facilitate his removal from a well-guarded prison?" queried Nome. "There shall be many eyes watching from the grounds and along the battlements."

"Can your staff be trusted?"

"Absolutely! I hand-picked each one myself," stated Medaru's kin, with a confident wink of an eye. "We may be employed by the Emperor, but our placement here is two-fold. How can we assist you?"

"What I plan will not jeopardize your posting here. When I am done, it will be considered nothing more than extremely back luck that I was invited in by the Emperor's captain," she responded. "I take it the Emperor's guests dine first, followed by the army, with the captains and higher ranking officers eating next."

"Yes," answered Nome. "We cater to the guests, and then we serve up the slop for the soldiers. Of course, they do not dine on the same foods as the Emperor and his company."

"And what of the prisoners?"

"If the army has any food left over, the prisoners are made to fight for what is tossed to them. More often than not, they are left with mere scraps," stated Nome.

"Well, let us hope the soldiers are hungry this night, for we shall prepare a meal that they will not soon forget," she said with a smile.

Nome Mewaku worked by the little warrior's side as he instructed other kitchen staff to prepare the pheasants for roasting and vegetables for boiling. As he prepared the tart shells, she prepared the purple berries to fill the exquisite, miniature pies.

With the delectable scent of roast pheasant wafting through the air, Nome skimmed off the fat that floated to the top of the roasting pans. The excess juices were poured off into large, iron cauldrons to form the stock of the soup he prepared to feed the army. Along with the various vegetables, spices and salt, a poisonous ingredient was finely minced and blended into the soup. As it simmered over the flames, the warrior maiden reminded the staff not to sample the food, especially the soup. Turning her attention to the rose hips and the strange roots at the bottom of the bag, she bolted up as the sounds of soldiers hollering and horses stampeding in through the palace gateway shattered the still of the evening air.

She and the others stood at the doorway, watching as the captain of the returning battalion arrived victorious with prisoner in hand. There was much excitement and commotion as this captain was the first to ever survive entering western Orien.

Hemashe was yanked down from his horse, falling to the ground with a heavy *'thud'*. With his hands bound behind his back, he was unable to break his fall. Two soldiers immediately pounced on him, hauling the warrior up onto his unsteady feet.

The little warrior's heart sank upon her first real glimpse of Hemashe. He was dirty and bloodied, weak and gaunt from his horrific ordeal. The captain proudly paraded him through the courtyard to the prison garrison.

Marching off, the other soldiers muttered in discontent to their comrades as they dispersed.

"We watched from the valley, holding back until we received word to attack. We saw our *brave and fearless* captain lead the others into a death trap while he pranced about at the fringe of the forest while the others met their end," snarled one disgruntled soldier.

"Now he shall receive all the praise and glory for securing this prisoner when all he did was to nab this warrior and scurry out of enemy territory, leaving our brothers to die," grumbled another soldier.

Satisfied that it was only by sheer luck that the captain had escaped and it was only he that made it out alive from the battle, she hastily resumed her work. Setting a large pot of water to boil, she prepared a special brew for the prisoners. She quickly showed the others how to cut the rose hips, scraping away the small seeds from the center of each fruit. Though easily swallowed, these tiny seeds were covered with fine hairs that irritated the palate and the intestinal tract. The seeds were discarded before dicing up the rest of the rose hip fruit to toss into the water to steep. She then washed and grated the roots, straining the juice from the pulp through a cloth before adding the cloudy liquid into the special *tea*.

With the banquet well underway, the kitchen staff delivered the soup and bread to the soldiers' quarters. It pleased the little warrior to see that the jubilant captain, his chest still puffed out in pride as he sang his own praises of his harrowing escape with his prisoner, stood at the front of the food line along with the captain that had *welcomed* her entry at the gateway. They would be the first ones to sample her cuisine.

Slipping back into the kitchen just as Nome's assistant prepared to deliver the tea to the prisoners; she and the young woman carried the large vat. Takaro's nostrils were immediately assaulted by the stench of decay and human waste hanging heavily in the foul, dank air. She gagged as her hand covered her mouth and nose, attempting to filter out these rancid particles. Somewhere in here was Hemashe. She forced herself to forge on.

"Halt!" demanded a guard. "It is not time to feed the prisoners; the soldiers are still eating!"

"It is not food we bring, sir," answered the cook's assistant. The lid was removed to show the guard its content. "It is merely a tea to help stave off their hunger."

The guard picked up the ladle, stirring the steaming brew as pieces of rose hip swirled in a circle. "I have never seen the likes of this tea before. What is in it?"

The warrior maiden answered: "Your Emperor stated that the prisoners were in deteriorating condition. They grow weak with scurvy. This is a tonic, an herbal tea designed to remedy their ills. It is nothing more than rose hip steeped as a tea, flavored with a touch of honey."

"Hmph! The Emperor grows soft. Since when has he shown compassion for these upstarts?" grumbled the guard.

The guard scooped up a ladle full of the sweetly scented brew, sniffing it first before sampling it. His eyebrows arched up in surprise. "This is quite good, I must say!"

He waved his two comrades to come over, inviting them to partake in the steaming tea.

"Now sir, this tea is not meant for you and your comrades, it is to be served to the prisoners, by order of the Emperor," cautioned the little warrior. The more she pleaded with the guards, the faster they gulped down the hot beverage.

"There is plenty to go around," grumbled the guard, wiping his sopping beard with the back of his forearm. With a wave of his hand, his fellow guards returned to their post at either end of the garrison as he resumed his watch at the entrance.

Together, she and Nome's assistant lugged the heavy vat to the first cell overcrowded with male prisoners, young and old. They were filthy and emaciated; their thin arms and dirt-encrusted hands held forth their battered tin cups and bowls through the iron bars as they eagerly awaited the promise of some type of sustenance.

They worked quickly, serving up the tea as the warrior maiden's eyes studied all the sad, gaunt faces, searching for Hemashe. As they moved down to the next cell, there was still no sign of the warrior. They continued to ladle out the tea.

Finally, in the last cell, too weak to stand any longer, Hemashe rested on the floor against the bars as the other prisoners clamored all around him, impatiently waiting for what little was left for them. The warrior was so weak and dehydrated he had barely the strength to raise his bowl.

Pouring a small quantity into his tin cup, she whispered to him: "Do not drink it."

She quickly turned away to continue dispensing the tea, but to her horror, Hemashe in his delirious condition drank the liquid, spilling most down his soiled raiment. Grabbing hold of Hemashe, she gave him a quick shake as she ordered him to spit it out. The warrior, too dazed and weak, ignored her words, slumping into a ball on the cold, filthy stone floor. As she slowly stood up, one by one, starting with the guards, the men teetered backwards against the stone wall to slowly slide down, embraced in a drug-induced sleep.

Glancing about, the prison block grew deathly quiet. The still was only broken by the distant sounds of painful groans and loud retching as guests spilled out of the dining hall. Some were doubled over in agony as though their bowels had twisted into great knots, while some staggered and others dashed in a desperate search for the closest, unoccupied privy where they can be assaulted by waves of nausea followed by explosive bowel movements as their bodies fought to purge itself of the tainted food.

High above on the battlements, soldiers still on duty and untouched by this culinary revenge looked down in bewilderment as vomiting guests were joined by their fellow soldiers as they collapsed into fits of convulsion in the courtyard.

Everything was going according to plan. Dashing over to the unconscious guard, she removed his sword as he lay in a drug-induced stupor. Her hands moved swiftly along his leggings and vest until they came across a large, metal ring festooned with keys. She stared at it for a moment. Not only were there keys to the cells, this ring contained every key for every room in the palace and on its grounds. Realizing it shall take far too long to try every single key, she tossed the heavy ring down upon the guard's chest. Yanking off his cloak and stealing away with his sword, she ran back to the cell where her friend lay, now fast asleep.

Waving the young woman off to return to the kitchen, the little warrior took up the soldier's cumbersome sword, hacking at the heavy padlock. White sparks flew with each strike as she worked desperately to smash the lock. Finally, it broke apart, falling to the floor with a loud clatter.

She quickly stepped over the other sleeping bodies. Although Hemashe consumed very little of the concoction, in his dehydrated state, the tea sedated him as quickly as the guards that had guzzled down a good helping. Lifting his head to pry open one eye, she noted that his pupil was fixed and fully dilated. He was out, completely oblivious to the world. Propping him up, she quickly switched cloaks, throwing the guard's cloak bearing the royal family's emblem onto the warrior. Knowing that Hemashe was completely incapable of walking, let alone stand on his own two feet, she was given no other choice but to carry him out.

Taking a deep breath in through her nose, she slowly exhaled through her mouth as she called upon the energy of the earth to give her the power to lift her friend from the floor. Like a mountain rising up from the ground, just as she expelled her breath, she took hold of Hemashe's limp form. He flopped against her right shoulder and with surprising ease; she rose up with the warrior draped over her arm and shoulder. In his condition, he had lost a surprising amount of weight so it was relatively easy for her to lift and carry Hemashe out.

Tromping across the grounds, she was unfazed by the ruckus and confusion as guests spewed, soldiers wracked by convulsions died, and other men dashed about in a panic, searching for a captain not overcome to give them instructions.

Making her way to the gate, she felt a hand seize her ankle as a man toppled forward with a loud groan. It was the captain that had welcomed her into the palace. In a dying bid to warn the guards at the front gate to drop the portcullis, the captain staggered with his waning strength.

She abruptly kicked away the man's dying grip.

"It was you!" he groaned as his glazed eyes stared up at her, not even noticing the man she had slung over her shoulder. "I thought you said you could cook!"

"Indeed I did, but I never said I was any good at it!"

She leapt back as the captain dropped down on his hands and knees, violently spewing forth his stomach contents from his mouth and nose.

"That was rather disgusting!" she grunted, kicking him in his midriff. "And there is no need for thanks."

The captain collapsed into a tight ball, writhing in his own vomit as his heart began to fail.

With Hemashe still over her shoulder, the little warrior marched straight out the gateway. From out of the darkness, Joval charged forward to meet them. Taking hold of Hemashe, the large Elf easily hoisted the warrior over his steed's withers. Taking the reins of her mare, the warrior maiden threw herself into the saddle as her horse raced after Joval's.

It did not take long for the soldiers to realize that this whole situation was a ruse to distract them while the prisoner was freed from the garrison. Soon, a hail of arrows delivered by the soldiers stationed along the battlements descended upon them as they raced northward on the roadway.

The many arrows aimed recklessly into the deepening shadows of the night shattered upon striking the packed surface of the road. The horses careened about to avoid the exploding shards of wood.

Like a bolt of lightning coursing through her being, a jarring blow caused Takaro to be pitched forward. Slamming hard against her mare's neck, the impact of an arrow pierced her cloak and raiment. It burrowed on through her skin and into her flesh.

Her eyes flew wide open in shock as the arrow only stopped its forward momentum when it became jammed between the joint where her arm attached at the shoulder. The reins immediate fell from the grasp of her numbed, right hand. The projectile, wedged firmly into place, not only caused the wound to throb with excruciating pain, her arm was locked, unable to move as the arrow was now firmly embedded between the humourous bone and the shoulder socket.

Joval's steed veered sharply, forcing the stallion to take a great leap from the roadway, westward into the surrounding forest. Even with the reins hanging slack, her mare instinctively followed Joval's stallion, even without her master's urging or guidance. With her left hand knotted into a tight fist, clenching the mare's mane to remain seated, her steed sailed through the air, landing far off the road as it followed the stallion.

Racing westward, Joval could hear far off in the distance as the Imperial Soldiers, now on horseback, charged northward, believing their prisoner had been whisked away to whence he came via the Magare Valley.

10

the long road home

Joval knew immediately that something was seriously wrong. Dismounting from his steed, he glanced over at the warrior maiden. She sat motionless atop her mare, drawing a deep breath through clenched teeth. Her face was pallid, the color gradually draining from her cheeks. Her eyes were glazed and vacant as she began to tremble.

"Nayla, what is wrong?" asked Joval, as he carefully lowered his still unconscious passenger to the ground.

She did not answer as she slowly climbed down from her mount. It was only when she stood on the ground leaning heavily against her mare's sweat-stained withers did he see the long shaft of the arrow projecting menacingly from her back.

"I cannot move my arm," she finally answered in a small voice.

Running to her side as she crumpled to her knees, Joval grimaced as he noted the trajectory of the arrow and the fact that it did not pierce through to the other side. Unlike the Elven and Taijin arrows used in the west, the enemy used arrows tipped with a single barb. She had taken one such arrow before. It penetrated through the muscle of her left thigh, entering about four inches above her knee, narrowly missing the femur bone as it protruded out the back of her leg. As painful as it was to snap off the tip of the arrow to extract the offending weapon, it was far less pain than retracting the barbed, steel bodkin from the entry wound. She dreaded the thought of dealing with this new injury, for there would be no choice but to pull out the arrow, barb and all, from her shoulder.

"It could be worse," assessed the Elf.

"How can this be any worse? My arm is stuck! I cannot move it!"

"You could be dead," responded Joval, his words matter-of-fact.

"Point well taken."

"I can help, if you let me," offered Joval.

"Help Hemashe first," she ordered. "He is weak and thirsty. At the very least, get some water into him."

The Elf glanced down at her with great concern.

"Go on! I assure you; I am not dying. He will, if you do not help him immediately," insisted the wounded warrior.

"Are you sure?"

"It is not as though I am mortally wounded. A day from now, a week from now, it matters not. I hardly think this arrow is going anywhere. It is not as though it can travel any deeper into my body."

Propping the unconscious warrior against a tree trunk, Joval slapped his face, attempting to wake him up. Hemashe merely groaned in response, his eyes still firmly shut.

"Is he near death or did you serve him up some of your *witch's brew* as well?" questioned Joval.

"He drank before I could stop him," she answered.

The Elf tipped some water into Hemashe's open mouth. Most of it spilled over his parched, chapped lips as the warrior sputtered and coughed.

"I said to help him, not drown the man," groaned the disgruntled little warrior.

"He will be fine, just mind your own business," snapped the Elf, pouring some more cold water from the flask onto the warrior's swollen tongue.

Gathering only the driest pieces of wood, Joval prepared a small, but inviting fire. The flames crackled and popped as the smokeless flames drove back the darkness of night.

"This shall prove to be most interesting," mused the little warrior, wincing in pain as she turned her gaze over her right shoulder.

"What is interesting?" responded the Elf, assessing the damage.

"I feel like a pincushion. I never tried sleeping with an arrow sticking out of me before."

Joval frowned as he witnessed her morbid sense of humour, even at her own plight.

"We best deal with this now, before infection sets in, Nayla."

"We might as well." She lowered her forearm, but she was unable to rotate her arm at the shoulder with the arrow painfully wedged into the joint. "I suppose I am rather useless in this condition."

"I can remove the arrow, but not without pain, so *do not* scream. Cry if you must, but do not alert the enemy to our whereabouts by screaming," ordered the Elf, as he knelt by her side.

"*Cry*? I never cry!" snorted the little warrior, indignant that he would even suggest it.

"Never?"

"Perhaps when I was a child, but not since," she snapped in defiance.

"There is no shame in crying, Nayla," retorted Joval. "And besides, there is always a first time for everything."

She struggled to unfasten the clasps of her cloak with her left hand as Joval widened the hole torn through her cloak by the arrow. With great care, he slipped the shaft of the arrow through this hole.

Doing the same with her vest, he cautiously maneuvered it off her back. Beneath, blood from the wound caked and dried to her skin. She sat motionless as the Elf used his dagger to slice through the fabric of her blouse. She did not even flinch as he peeled the material away from the wound.

"So? What do you see?"

"I see there is an arrow in your back," responded Joval, stating the obvious. His keen eyes could not help but notice the edge of the deep blue tattoo peering over the slash he made in her blouse to better access the offending projectile.

"You do not say! I thought it was nothing more than a very large sliver piercing my skin," she replied, her voice dripping with sarcasm.

"Yes! Yes!" exclaimed the Elf, his eyes rolling to the heavens at the cynical tone of her voice. "You know I am not exaggerating when I say this will hurt. You do understand I will have no choice but to pull it out?"

"Do what you must and be quick about."

Joval knew it was not a simple matter of yanking the arrow out of the original entry wound. The feathers fledging the shaft caused the projectile to rifle, spinning as it was released, allowing the arrow to fly straight and true. He knew that, at least to a certain extent, the arrow continued to rifle even as it hit her and probably did not stop doing so until it came to an abrupt halt upon striking against bone. He would have no choice but to inflict her with more pain; even more than when the arrow entered her body. The cruel barb would tear at her flesh once more.

Bracing his left forearm against her small back, Joval gripped the offending arrow in his right hand. He leaned forward, gazing into her face.

"Are you ready, Nayla?"

"When you hear my heart beat slow, then do it. Just pull it out."

Her eyes closed as she slowed her breathing and steadied her heart. Her fingers were entwined to summon the calming energy of the earth. With each cleansing breath, Joval's sharp ears heard her heartbeat slowing substantially as she focused and steeled her nerves.

"One… two… THREE!" counted the Elf. His grip tightened around the shaft and with a mighty tug, he yanked the arrow free from her shoulder.

She released a loud gasp as she fell forward and cursed: "You bastard! That bloody well hurt!"

Blood flowed fresh from the entry wound that looked to be twice the size now.

"Keep still!" ordered the Elf, as he tossed the arrow away.

Joval raised his hands high over his head. Clapping once, he rubbed his palms briskly to generate healing energy. Placing his left hand directly over the wound, he closed his eyes as he spoke in Elvish, using the powers of a healing incantation to mend her injury. Her eyes slowly closed as she felt instant relief from the throbbing, searing pain. His soft voice, the words spoken in his people's tongue, lulled her rattled nerves. Within a few minutes he was done. The wound was nothing more than a red mark where fibers of muscle and skin continued to fuse together. When it is completely healed, she would be left with a scar, but at least she would regain the full use of her arm.

"Is that better, Nayla?"

"Much better!" She answered with a sigh of relief as she cautiously rotated her arm in its socket. "Thank you."

Joval smiled in response, pleased that he was able to relieve her suffering.

"Is your threshold of pain tolerance so high that you truly can endure injuries of this nature?" queried the Elf. "I was sure you would cry."

"Tears are for the weak," she responded, slipping on her vest before draping the cloak over her slight shoulders.

"Do not tell me! Let me guess: this is according to Dahlon Treeborn. Am I correct?" queried Joval.

"He gave this lecture to you, too?"

"In case you were not aware, just because he is a high Elf, it does not mean he is all-knowing and all-wise," stated Joval. "There are tears and there are *tears;* not all tears are shed in self-pity or are meant to be self-serving. Sometimes, it is merely a show of compassion for others and sometimes it shows that one still has a soul."

She was silent as she considered his words.

"Perhaps I am lacking in compassion and a soul," she finally retorted, unmoved by his sentiment.

Joval watched Hemashe stir momentarily, but the exhausted warrior settles back down for much-needed sleep.

"Speaking of compassion, tell me Nayla, what compelled you take on such a dangerous mission to save this man?"

"He is a Kagai Warrior, a brother-in-arms. I have taken an oath to keep my fellow warriors safe."

"Come now, what was your true motivation? Master Saibon, Keodai, all the Kagai Warriors, for that matter are bound by this same oath. Yet, it was you to endanger your life to spare his. Why?"

Her dark eyes glanced over at Hemashe's sleeping form.

"You would not understand," she whispered in a small voice.

As Joval stared at her, he could see the sadness in her eyes and it became instantly apparent to him: "You love this man. You did it for love."

"You know not what you speak of. Hemashe is a married man."

"He was not always married, Nayla," responded the Elf, stooping to gaze into her now downcast face. "I can see it in your eyes. This was not out of loyalty and compassion for a fellow warrior that you had risked your life. It is love. I can sense it."

"Then your senses deceive you!" she snapped as she turned away from his stare.

"And he broke your heart when he married another," added Joval.

"You are wrong! I have no heart to be broken." She abandoned the fireside to fetch her bedroll.

Hemashe's bleary eyes fluttered open. As the unfamiliar surroundings came into focus, his eyes darted about uneasily. He recoiled in fear as a towering form loomed before him.

"You are safe, my friend," greeted Joval. He spoke in a soothing tone as he held forth a flask of water.

"I know you," said Hemashe, his voice dry and raspy from his long sleep. His trembling hand took hold of the flask.

"Indeed, the battle up north… Remember?"

"Captain Stonecroft…" Hemashe responded in recognition, as he struggled to sit upright. "Where are we?"

"We are in the Medore Forest in eastern Orien. We journey westward," answered the Elf. "You are going home."

"Were you the one to rescue me?" questioned the warrior, allowing himself a sip of refreshing water.

"No, I did not. *She* rescued you." His finger pointed to the warrior maiden as she slept by the now cold campfire.

"Takaro? She came for me?" gasped Hemashe, stunned to see the little warrior. He crawled over to her side, gazing down at her.

Sensing an energy pressing down on her, her hand instinctively reached for her sword as she rolled to her side to escape. She was both stunned and relieved to see it was only Hemashe.

"You know better than to do that to me!" she scolded him as she lowered the tip of her short sword.

"Thank goodness, Takaro! I never dreamed I would look upon your face again!" exclaimed Hemashe, embracing her in a grateful hug.

She winced in pain as he held her tightly; her right arm pinned between their bodies.

"I know you are pleased to see her, but you might want to resist holding her so tight," recommended Joval. "Her shoulder still heals."

Hemashe immediately released her, gazing down at her arm now supported in a sling the Elf had cleverly fashioned with the cloak she wore. "What happened, Takaro?"

"I was hit by an arrow, but no need for concern. Captain Stonecroft was able to assist me. I will be fine in no time."

"I suppose you will insist it was nothing more than a flesh wound?" inquired Hemashe, relieved to see her familiar face.

"If it does not shatter bone or pierce vital organs, then yes, as far as I am concerned, it is nothing more than a flesh wound." Her words were matter-of-fact as she down played her condition.

"Are you sure you are fine?" queried Hemashe. His concern was clearly etched across his weary face.

"Yes."

"Nayla will be fine in a few days. She mends well considering the fact that she is only half Elf," added Joval.

"Nayla?" Hemashe glanced over at the Elf, frowning in bewilderment. "Why do you call her Nayla? Her name is Takaro."

"I keep telling him that, but Captain Stonecroft insists on using this name," grunted the warrior maiden, shaking her head in frustration.

"Only because it is the only name I ever knew you by," replied Joval. "And because, in my heart, I feel you have every right to bear the name of a high Elf. You are as much a Treeborn as you are Bansho."

"Treeborn?" gasped Hemashe. His eyes grew wide with wonder. "There is only one Treeborn that I know of. Are you telling me that Takaro is a descendant of Lord Dahlon Treeborn's bloodline?"

She motioned for Joval to cease his talking. Her left index finger dragged across her neck as though she was threatening to slit his throat if he persisted in divulging any more information than he already had.

"To say she is a descendant of the Treeborn bloodline is a gross understatement," responded the Elf, ignoring the little warrior's frantic gesturing. "She is the *daughter* of Lord Dahlon Treeborn."

Hemashe sat back. His gaze slowly returned to the woman he once loved, as though the only thing familiar to him now was her face.

"Long have rumors circulated that you were indeed the daughter of the great Kareda Bansho. And though I knew you were half Elf, but I had no idea you were the daughter of a high Elf."

"That was more than a lifetime ago, Hemashe. In this day and age, most in Anshen do not recall or know of this. If anything, I prefer not to speak of my past. Forget these words were ever spoken to you."

"But why, Takaro? You should be proud to bear this distinguished name. Lord Dahlon Treeborn is a wise and great leader, showing great compassion not just for his people, but for the mortals of western Orien, too. His name is honoured and revered throughout our lands," responded Hemashe, totally perplexed by the little warrior's desire to abandon her identity.

"One does not choose to walk away from such a namesake without good reason, Hemashe. Believe me, I had very good reason to leave my past behind."

"I fail to understand this," stated Hemashe, his eyes turning to Joval for some answers.

"You will never understand. We shall not speak of this again. Forget everything this Elf told you." She made this order clear as she secured her short sword through the knot of her belt.

Hemashe knew no answers would be forthcoming as Joval merely shrugged his shoulders in response to her demand.

"Enough about me, Hemashe," she said, as she rummaged through her pack to offer him some bread. "Are you hungry?"

"Very much so," admitted the warrior.

"This shall have to do for now," she replied almost apologetically, placing a small piece of bread and some dried fruit into his hand.

"Thank you," said Hemashe, fighting his urge to wolf down the food to quell his pangs of hunger. "I am most grateful for this offering."

"You are in need of water as much as you are in need of food," noted the Elf, passing the flask of water back to Hemashe.

The warrior nodded his thanks as he savored the sweet, leathery, dried slices of apple as though it was the most wonderful morsel to cross his palate in a very long time.

As they shared this austere breakfast with the famished warrior, Hemashe shared in the details of his ordeal. He started his tale with his capture by the captain of the Imperial Army when, in his eagerness to do away with an enemy soldier, he ventured out onto the open field.

There, the captain had ordered his men into the forest while he waited like a coward, determining if he should retreat or order the remaining army holding back in the valley to attack. Momentarily distracted as he charged after the fleeing soldier, Hemashe was taken by surprise. He was roped and dragged back to the enemy camp. From that point on, all his attempts to end his own life were dashed. Stripped of his weapons, he was then bound and gagged. Heavily guarded at all times, even his attempts to starve to death were stymied as he was force-fed just enough to be kept alive until he could be delivered to the Imperial Palace in Keso where the Emperor wished to oversee his torture and interrogation.

It touched and saddened her heart to hear Hemashe's desperate tale and the abuse he was forced to endure. She could see by his eyes that he was not the same man who once fought by her side. Something died inside him during his long, terrible ordeal.

Joval went on to explain to Hemashe how they had facilitated his rescue from the palace. The young man was not surprised that her determination alone would allow her to brazenly walk in, and then walk out with him in the midst of the chaos she had instigated.

"I knew if anyone could accomplish the impossible, Takaro, it would be you! Somehow, I knew it would be you," stated Hemashe, with a broad smile.

"I had little choice. Yumai pleaded to me to expedite your rescue, for she refuses to raise a child without her husband."

"Well, we shall both be grateful to you, for now the possibility of family can be realized," said Hemashe, his head bowing gratefully to her.

"Time it just so and you shall return well before the baby's arrival."

The color drained from Hemashe's face as he gasped: "Are you telling me that Yumai is with child?"

She offered him a knowing smile: "Yes, you are going to be a father, Hemashe."

The warrior gave her an exuberant hug, forgetting her damaged shoulder in his excitement, and then turned his attention to Joval, even embracing the Elf in a great hug. Now, more than ever, he was grateful to be alive.

"Are you ready to go home?" she asked.

"Most definitely," stated Hemashe, with an enthusiastic nod.

Traveling under the cover of darkness, for twelve nights Joval led the way westward. With the approach of dawn, the Elf recommended resting during the light of day and crossing the Furai Mountains at night. With home now within their reach, he was not about to risk capture by chancing a daytime dash to freedom via the secret pass, especially now that all the soldiers were on high alert to scour the lands for the escaped prisoner and those who aided in his flight.

With each passing day, Hemashe regained his strength. Fueled by his desire to return to his wife and the promise of their first child, the fire in his eyes burned brightly once more. He slept more fitfully the greater the distance placed between him and the prison in Keso. As he slept, the warrior maiden sat on a high bluff watching over Hemashe and the surrounding landscape for signs of danger. As she gazed down, she noticed the Elf was nowhere to be seen. For a moment, a look of panic clouded her eyes.

"Were you looking for me?" asked Joval, as he appeared at the top of the bluff. "I thought you could use some company as Hemashe sleeps."

"Why do you not get some rest, too?"

"I am quite fine for now," said the Elf. "It should be you seeking some sleep, for we shall travel a good distance when night comes if we wish to cross into western Orien before daybreak."

"I cannot sleep now, even when I try," she said in a whisper.

"What troubles you, Nayla?" questioned Joval. He stooped to gaze into her eyes, searching her soul for answers.

"Tomorrow we breach Borai Mountain, and well before dusk we shall be in Nagana. It is strange. I do not relish the idea of setting foot in that forsaken place, and yet, it is as though a voice is calling to me, beckoning me back to the fortress city… I feel like a moth being drawn to the flame of a candle."

"It is a sign," determined Joval; "one that should not be ignored."

"We all know what happens to the moth when it gets too close to fire," she answered in a small voice.

"I see your mother's spirit in you more and more with each passing day, Nayla. I see her courage, the fire and determination that once burned in her eyes and soul, surfacing in yours. Perhaps it is her voice calling you home. Perhaps it is time for you to confront your past; to reclaim your rightful place in your father's house."

"I am torn, Captain Stonecroft. My first instinct is to run, to avoid Nagana all together, and yet, something in my heart tells me to stand my ground."

"I have a feeling it is not Nagana that you wish to run from. Instead, it is Dahlon Treeborn," decided Joval. "Although your mind remembers all the anguish of your troubled childhood, I do believe it is your heart telling you there is no need to run anymore. You are not the small, terrified child Lord Treeborn once controlled. You are a warrior and not just any warrior; you are Kagai: the best of the best in all of Orien."

"You say it is time to confront my past. Why bother when the past cannot be changed?"

"True enough, history cannot be rewritten, but Nayla, you have the power to alter the course of your destiny."

"You believe this?"

"I believe there are those who allow things to happen to them; those who *let life happen*. And then, there are those who *make life happen*. There are those with the courage and will to grapple control over their destiny. Remember, we are all shaped by the events of our past. Ultimately, what shape our lives take depends wholly on whether you view yourself as a victim or a survivor of ill fortune. So, the question is; will you allow life to happen to you? Or will you take control of your life and be the one to effect changes? Do you choose to be a victim or a survivor?" queried Joval.

"And you believe I have the power to do this? To change my destiny?"

"I think the better question is; do *you* believe you have the power to do so? I have already witnessed what you have accomplished and what you are capable of doing when you have set your mind to it. You should know that your mother did not have an easy life either. She was beset by her share of problems, but she had a way of facing these problems with grace and courage, never viewing the difficulties in her life as insurmountable obstacles. To her, life's problems were nothing more than challenges to be conquered. Did you not face challenges in your fight to become a Kagai Warrior? To be accepted into this brotherhood?"

"The *challenges* were many and often. I did indeed think they were insurmountable at times."

"And yet, look at you now. Tell me, Nayla, why did you wish to endure everything you did to become Kagai? What fueled this desire?"

"In my heart, I wanted Dahlon Treeborn to see what I had become. I always wanted him to see that I *am* a worthy warrior; fit to do battle next to any of his men. I wanted him to know that his desire to see me crushed beneath the weight of his fist did not break me. Instead, it has made me a force to be reckoned with."

"If that be the case, what was the point of all the pain and suffering you had endured if he never knows what became of you? It will be a terrible waste if Lord Treeborn never sees the results of all your hard work. You shall receive nothing more than a false sense of gratification if you do not follow it through."

"To you it may seem false, but to me, my accomplishments are quite real."

"Think on it, Nayla. Do you not believe your sense of accomplishment; this gratification would leave a far sweeter taste in your mouth if your father is forced to confront the child he wronged many years ago? Think of how he will feel to know his iron fist only served to reshape you; not into a pathetic, groveling shell of a being, but instead, one of the best Kagai Warriors to come out of Anshen."

"This taste you speak of would be bittersweet…"

"You are no longer a child Lord Treeborn can easily lock away, for the elders shall certainly welcome the return of Lady Kareda Treeborn's daughter. Her role in the forging of this alliance between man and Elf has never been forgotten. And I know they will be accepting of you by virtue of the fact that you are the daughter of a high Elf. Yes, Dahlon will be forced to welcome his long-lost daughter into the palace. He will have no choice but to do so."

"It does pose a very interesting dilemma for Dahlon…" she replied, her mind wandering in thought.

"If by chance Lord Treeborn has mellowed with the years, if he should welcome you back, would you stay?" questioned Joval.

"I believe making the assumption that he has mellowed where I am concerned would be akin to saying a wild boar can be tamed," scoffed the little warrior, as she speculated on the likelihood of such a thing ever happening.

"But if he is accepting, do you believe that you can ever find it in your heart to forgive your father?"

For a lingering moment, she was silent as she cogitated on his question.

"Well? Can you forgive him?" asked the Elf, once more.

"Perhaps in time, I can forgive," she answered in a small voice. "But to forget the years of torment I endured? Never."

As the sun withdrew the last of its golden light from the twilight sky, the three travelers prepared for the final leg of their exhausting journey westward to freedom. High above, northeasterly winds blew clouds in an ever-thickening mass. Under overcast skies, there was not even the faint light of stars or moon to show the way. The darkness was unsettling, cloaking the lands in deep shadows. In some pockets of the forest, it was so black, Joval's steed forged on with nothing to guide him but his master's Elvish whisperings to direct him through the consuming darkness. The mare, bearing the weight of two riders, followed the pounding hoof beats of Joval's stallion, remaining close behind.

Stopping only long enough to allow the steeds sufficient time to rest and replenish their energy, they would travel on through the night. The Elf's sharp eyes constantly scanned the shadows for signs of danger as they advanced homeward. As the Furai Mountains loomed before them like giant sentinels against the pre-dawn sky, they pressed on. Joval led the way through the forest, up the slope of Borai Mountain. Behind a ridge protruding from the mountainside like the spine of a long-dead dragon, the rocky projections effectively concealed a narrow passage. They began their ascent.

The early morning call of songbirds echoed through the forest that grew along the lower elevations of the mountain slope. Joval's far-seeing eyes watched as a small herd of white-spotted deer dissolved into a thicket upon their approach. He knew immediately that all was quiet. Their ride home should prove uneventful.

Hemashe gazed to the east at the impending light of a pale sun as it burned through the clouds, and then to the western horizon where the night still refused to relinquish its hold on the sky.

"Home…" sighed Hemashe, filling his lungs with the cool, damp air as his senses absorbed the sights, sounds and smells of western Orien.

"Soon," responded Joval, urging his steed down the slope. "First, we go to Nagana, and then you shall receive an escort home."

"We can go from here. I am well enough to make the journey home," insisted Hemashe.

"I have no doubt you are, but Captain Stonecroft is quite right, a visit to the local healer is in order first. We must be sure you are fit enough to endure the long trek north. I will not have you die from some malady triggered by your long incarceration because you ignored your condition in your eagerness to return home. It would be a prudent after all we had endured to rescue you. It will also give us adequate time to gather proper provisions as the first frost of autumn shall be upon us as we journey home."

"But Yumai will be concerned about us. She will be consumed with worry as to our whereabouts," protested Hemashe.

"No need for concern, my friend," said Joval. "Upon our arrival in Nagana, I shall send word by falcon to Anshen. Master Saibon will be alerted to your condition and imminent return."

Nearing the walls of the fortress city, the little warrior felt an uneasy tide of familial discomfort rising around her as though long forgotten ghosts from the past peered at her, watching her arrival from atop the battlements. Joval could see in her eyes the growing anxiety as their horses trotted at an easy gait up the road beneath the row upon row of cherry trees lining the way to the west gate. No longer young saplings the trees were now in their full glory, each crowned with a thick canopy of green foliage as the leaves began to wilt and fade in surrender to the autumn winds.

Joval directed his steed off the roadway, heading to a small cluster of cottages that surrounded a lake to the east of Nagana.

"Where are we going? Are we to enter through the east gate?" inquired the little warrior.

"No, I wish to go to my home first," replied the Elf.

"You do not live within the confines of these walls?" questioned

Hemashe.

"Many of my warriors live in Nagana, but I had elected to reside just outside the walls of the city," explained the Elf. "I recommend we freshen up before we make a grand entrance at the palace."

"But we do not wish to impose on you or your wife," said Hemashe.

Joval smiled in understanding as he replied: "I have no wife to impose upon."

"Oh…" Hemashe responded, almost apologetically.

"Yes, I was once told many years ago that I was much too '*grumpy*' to be the object of any woman's desire," he said, directing his gaze at Nayla who merely looked away, pretending to not hear his comment.

Joval dismounted and tethered the horses to a hitching post by a large watering trough. He motioned for Hemashe and Nayla to follow him in. As he pushed the door open, dust particles, disturbed by the sudden movement of air, swirled and spun in the shafts of sunlight streaming in through the windows. On the bare, wooden table and along the mantle over the stone fireplace, a thin layer of dust settled back down.

"Sorry, for the condition of my humble abode, but I was in a hurry when I left. As you can see, I have been away for a good, long time," apologized the Elf, removing some clothes that were tossed onto the crumpled counterpane of his unmade bed. He discreetly dumped it into a small heap onto the floor. With the toe of his boot, he casually pushed it beneath his bed, hoping his guests would not notice.

"No need for apology. I understand completely," said Hemashe. His eyes rolled in dismay as he smacked the little warrior's hand as she used her finger to write in the dust on the table's surface: *DIRTY*. He gave her a disapproving scowl as she smiled back like a mischievous child.

In no time, an inviting fire roared in the stone fireplace as pots and a large kettle of water were boiled to fill a tub situated in a small room just beyond the wall where Joval's bed rested.

"Ladies first," offered Hemashe, handing the little warrior a towel.

Her nose wrinkled in disgust as she insisted: "Oh no, you first. Believe me; you are in dire need of this bath, more so than I. Besides, I would like to wash my raiment and cloak. I shall do so at the lake."

Hemashe knew better than to argue with her. He closed the door and proceeded to disrobe.

"Have you any soap?" she asked the Elf as he topped up the kettle of water to heat up for his bath.

He opened a cupboard and removed a cake of yellowish soap rendered from animal fat. Taking it from his hand, her nose wrinkled in disgust as she sniffed it.

"I would recommend adding some lavender or the attar of rose to your soap," she suggested.

"Do you want it, or not?" grumbled Joval.

"I suppose it will have to do," she answered with a sigh as she headed out the door to the lake.

Weaving her way through the shrubs lining the shore, she removed her weapons, boots and belt. She felt the soft, cool moss between her toes. Her eyes gazed at the pristine lake and its shores that were once familiar to her. Removing the clasps of her cloak, she waded knee-deep into the water before plunging in.

Maintaining a slippery grip on the cake of soap, she proceeded to slather her apparel in tiny, foaming bubbles that turned a dirty gray as she worked it through the material. Once adequately rinsed, she tossed her cloak to shore. One by one, she methodically shed her clothes; washing, rinsing and tossing the clean raiment onto land to dry until her body was free to be embraced by the cool, clean water. Removing the small, strip of leather holding her braid in place, she tipped her head back into the water. Her dark brown hair changed to raven-black as the long strands became saturated. She used the same soap to lather her hair.

When she was done, she clambered back to shore with the dwindling cake of soap in her hand. Her flesh was raised and she shivered as a breeze enveloped her, chilling her skin as the water evaporated under the gentle, invisible wind. Ringing her cloak out once more, with a flick of her wrists she snapped it open. The cloak unfurled before her. She hastily wrapped it around her body, and then gathered the rest of her raiment to dry by the fireplace.

As she moved to open the door, Hemashe was surprised to find her there, dripping wet with nothing more than her cloak wrapped about her body. He was refreshed and dressed, donning some of Joval's clean clothes. The little warrior began to giggle as she looked at her friend. He was almost drowning in the Elf's apparel, for Joval stood almost a good six inches taller than this Taijin man.

Hemashe glanced at her still-wet cloak that clung to her body to outline every curve of her naked form. "Goodness, Takaro, cover yourself!"

She smiled quite innocently as she answered: "I am covered."

"Not well enough!" he countered as he dashed over to Joval's bed, stripping it of its counterpane. He quickly threw it around her shoulders as he steered her to the fireplace.

"Captain Stonecroft's bedding will get wet," she argued, shrugged it off her shoulders.

"I hardly think he will mind," insisted Hemashe, picking it off the floor to cover her once again.

"But my cloak shall dry faster if I wear it like this."

"Not fast enough for my liking, Takaro," stated Hemashe. "Please show even a modicum of modesty. We are in the presence of an Elf."

"I have known Captain Stonecroft since I was a child," she retorted, dodging his efforts to hide her beneath the counterpane.

"All the more reason to cover yourself, Takaro. You are not a little child anymore," argued Hemashe.

"I hardly think you have reason to worry. Rumor has it; he is not interested in women, if you get my meaning?"

"You jest, right?" Hemashe's eyebrows arched up in surprise at this news.

"Do not be so naïve, Hemashe. Why do you think he is not married after all this time?"

"Oh…" responded Hemashe and in a whisper, he added: "How odd, I never knew Elves were like *that.* He just seemed quite… you know… manly."

She whispered back: "Yes, a real man's man, if you get my drift? Just do not breathe a word of this to another. Promise?"

"Not a word," swore Hemashe.

Their eyes turned to gaze upon a freshly cleaned and dressed Elf stepping through the doorway. He glanced up as he secured his belt, only to be met by two pairs of eyes staring intently at him.

"Is there something the matter?" he asked, smoothing back his flowing, brown hair with his hands.

"Oh… nothing," they both responded nonchalantly.

By the warmth of the fire, her cloak slowly peeled away from her body as it dried. Hemashe observed the Elf's eyes were always averted away, even when the damp material hugged her naked form to leave little to the imagination. The young warrior assessed this to one of two things: either Joval really was not interested in the opposite sex; or he was just very well mannered and respectful, choosing to be mindful where his eyes wandered.

"When will you be ready to go?" queried the Elf.

"As you can see, my clothes are not dry yet. You and Hemashe are welcome to go right ahead though."

"Takaro, it shall be a good long time before your clothes will be adequately dried," stated Hemashe, his hand touching the damp vest.

"As I said, feel free to venture forth without me."

"Hemashe, tend to our horses, I wish to have a word in private with Nayla," said the Elf.

"Very well," responded the warrior, heading out the door. "Just hurry up, Takaro, please! The sooner we are done, the sooner we can leave for home."

Joval turned to the small figure, now draped in a dry cloak. "You have no intention of going to the palace with us, do you?"

She shook her head in response.

"Nayla, you have come so far, do not let this opportunity pass you by," urged Joval. "Even if you leave tomorrow, just to gaze into Dahlon Treeborn's eyes just once, to tell him unequivocally how well you have survived without him, shall release you of all the memories of his past torment. You shall be purged of all your demons."

She turned away from the Elf.

"I know in my heart, Nayla, if you do not do this, you will regret this for the remains of your days on this earth. You were so close... and to leave now, like this, Dahlon has won yet again."

"I am not leaving," she answered in a small voice.

"Pardon me... Did I hear you correctly?"

"I said, I am not leaving, but neither will I meet with Dahlon tonight. The time is not right," she replied.

"And when will the time be *right*?" queried the Elf.

"After you have recruited me into your army, here in Nagana. I am about to force his hand, to make it so he can no longer deny me. And he will accept me not because he has no other option, but because I am about to prove my worth as a warrior."

11

the battle of magare valley

Joval and Hemashe were received with great celebration that night. Prior to their entry into the palace, the Elf warned the warrior not to breathe even a word of Nayla's return to Nagana. Hemashe abided with his wishes, mindful never to speak of her in the presence of others. Once inside, Joval had one of the servants dress Hemashe in proper apparel for his first meeting with the officials of the city.

They were greeted in the great dining hall where the elders of Orien and Dahlon Treeborn hosted a lavish banquet to honour the returning captain and the Kagai Warrior rescued from the clutches of the Emperor. Both bowed in respect and greeting, but it became apparent to Hemashe as Dahlon embraced the Elf in a warm hug reserved for family and close friends, that Joval was much more than just the captain of his army.

"I had grave concerns regarding your latest exploit, Joval," stated Dahlon, as he motioned for both men to take a seat. "Your ventures into eastern Orien had always been restricted to reconnaissance missions, never to be seen or heard as you traveled the lands to gather information. Although your quest to retrieve this warrior proved successful, it was with great trepidation that we waited for news of your safe return."

"You worried needlessly, my lord. None to the east was aware and still do not know of my presence or part in this mission," assured Joval.

"How can that be so? How did you ever facilitate this warrior's escape from Keso?" queried the senior Elf.

"It was not me," confided Joval. "I entered eastern Orien in the company of one of Master Saibon's most skilled warriors. It was critical that we remove Hemashe from the situation he was in, for it was only to be a matter of time before he would be tortured and made to speak of our numbers and whereabouts."

"Yes," added the warrior. "Try as I might, all my efforts to do myself in were hampered. I was afraid that the weaker I became; the more confused and delirious my state of mind would become. Had I been tortured and interrogated, I would not even know if I was giving the correct answers in my deteriorating state."

The elders conversed amongst themselves before the senior member of the council asked: "And where is this great Kagai Warrior you spoke of, the one who rescued you? And how did he manage to walk into the palace, of all places, to accomplish the seemingly impossible?"

"The warrior in question merely went in disguised as a cook and quickly proceeded to prepare food for guests and soldiers alike. The special menu the warrior had concocted had debilitating and deadly consequences for all who partook in the meal. After rendering prison guards helpless by administering a tea that would induce sleep, the warrior made good his escape. Hemashe was carried out," explained Joval.

"What a bold and brazen move on the part of this warrior!" exclaimed Dahlon. "We should like to meet this man! Where is he now?"

"I am sorry, my lord," answered Joval. "Perhaps one day you will, but as we speak, this warrior rides back to Anshen."

"That is a pity!" declared Dahlon. "I suppose it is all for the best though. His skills will be needed in the north, for we are about to be invaded once again."

"When did you receive word of this?" asked Joval.

"Two days ago," responded Dahlon. "In fact, our warriors are prepared to leave at first light in the morn. Whether you were here to lead them into battle or not, they are prepared to leave."

"Is the Sorcerer behind this incursion again?" queried Hemashe.

"Indeed he is," answered the senior member of elders. "He has convinced the Emperor to double his forces and it was not difficult to do. The Emperor is reeling from the humiliation that his prized prisoner had been whisked away from his own palace. In fact, our contacts to the east have warned us that as the army advances northward, it gains in strength and numbers."

"Double their forces! They intend to send forth thousands of soldiers this time?" gasped the Kagai Warrior.

"Apparently so. The Emperor's liaison with this madman has made him just as rash and malevolent as the Sorcerer. The Emperor is more determined than ever to break the resistance, especially now that he has lost face when this young warrior was successfully spirited away from Keso. The Emperor is now bent on penetrating western Orien," answered Dahlon.

"Never have we had to face so many…" said Hemashe. "The Kagai number fewer than two hundred now. It shall take great ingenuity to bring down an army of this size."

"Master Saibon has been forewarned. I have no doubt he already works to plan their demise," stated Dahlon.

"When is the anticipated incursion to take place?" asked Joval.

"At the rate the Imperial Army advances, their anticipated arrival would see them in the Magare Valley during the rise of the hunter's moon," announced the senior Elf.

"They mean to attack before the first snows of winter block the valley," assessed Joval.

"Will we arrive in time to aid my brother warriors?" asked Hemashe, his eyes clouded with worry.

"Only if we leave at first light and move swiftly," replied Joval. "A smaller army can move much faster than a large force on foot. We shall arrive in time, but just barely."

"No sooner than you return to our fair city that you must set forth yet again to do war," said Dahlon, his heart was heavy at the prospect of seeing Joval off once more.

"When you assigned me to the post of captain, I willingly accepted all the responsibilities and duties that come with this designation, my lord. I am sworn to uphold justice and to see that the enemy never sets foot on our lands," stated Joval. "And I am proud and honoured to lead such a courageous band of warriors into battle."

Smiling upon hearing his words, Dahlon praised him: "Just as I would be proud and honoured had you been my son, Joval. I would have passed from this realm a happy man knowing that the legacy of this high house would live on with pride and dignity. Alas, there are none to carry on, to bear the Treeborn name. However, the pride and courage of our people shall rest with you."

Hemashe exchanged glances with Joval as the high Elf raised his goblet to honour the captain.

"I wish to make a toast: Here is to the pride and courage of all the free people of Orien;" declared Dahlon, "and may the House of Treeborn always have a place in this realm when we call upon the courage and strength of our people to fight evil."

"Here! Here!" All chimed in unison, goblets raised high.

"I pray we have the strength to bring the enemy down upon their knees," said Dahlon, in a solemn voice.

"If we should survive this war, I have a request to make that may help our warriors greatly for future battles," said Joval.

"Go on, what is it," responded Dahlon, intrigued by Joval's words.

"For many years, some of us were sent to train with the Saibon clan so we may be better prepared to engage in warfare with the enemy encroaching upon these lands," replied the Elf.

"Yes, continue," urged Dahlon.

"It is a well-known fact that our best warriors are the ones that have trained side-by-side with the Kagai Warriors, is that not agreed?" continued Joval.

All present nodded in concurrence.

"Then why is this practice not continued to this day? It has been ninety years since I last trained with the Kagai Warriors. Though there is much I still retain of this training, there is still much that can be improved upon," stated the Elf.

"Are you suggesting we send our armies to train once more with Master Saibon's people?" queried the most senior mortal on council.

"This would only work if we sent a small contingent in at a time, for Anshen cannot support such a show of numbers at any one time," reminded another elder.

"That is why I propose we request that one of their best warriors be sent to Nagana to instruct our men," suggested Joval.

"It is certainly worthy of consideration," admitted Dahlon, as he turned to the elders. Conversing in Taijina, he consulted with the three men.

"So be it, Captain Stonecroft, your request has been approved. If Master Saibon is willing to relinquish his best warrior to share in the wisdom of his teachings, by all means, we shall welcome this warrior to begin training our men immediately upon their return from the north. We shall be better prepared for the next battle after winter releases its grip and the lands thaw," promised Dahlon. "We will be more than ready for the next confrontation."

"So, am I to understand this warrior shall be commissioned to assist in the training of *all* our warriors?" queried Joval.

"Most definitely! If it will give us the upper hand when we are forced to do battle alongside the Kagai Warriors, our men shall have a better grasp of how to deal in warfare with Saibon's people. We feel it will be most beneficial for our young warriors who have yet to see battle," said the senior Elf on behalf of the elders. "In fact, if it is at all possible, you must convince Medaru Saibon to appoint the brave warrior, the one who had ventured to the east with you to facilitate Hemashe's rescue, to this station."

"Very well, my lord, if you insist," complied Joval. "I shall write a letter of this commission for Master Saibon so he will know what your intentions are. I am sure he will be pleased to aid us in this manner."

"Yes, I shall leave the details for you to contend with when you meet with Master Saibon. This I know I can trust you to do. But for now, enough talk of war and training, Joval," ordered Dahlon, motioning for the servants to deliver and serve the wine and food. "Tomorrow, you leave to fulfill your duties, so on this night, let us feast and enjoy each other's company."

When the men finally dispersed from the dining hall, the moon was high in the sky. Hemashe was invited to stay in the palace as an honoured guest. Joval escorted the warrior to his bedchamber.

"I will see you in the morning, Hemashe. Here, I thought I would send you home in the company of two of my men. It would now appear we shall be heading north towards Anshen with our entire army to do battle for one last time before winter sets in," said Joval.

"Let us hope that winter arrives early to impede their progress. Perhaps an unseasonably early winter will strike to seal their fate," hoped Hemashe.

"Has winter ever arrived this early in the north? By the hunter's moon?" asked the Elf.

"If I remember correctly, only twice in my lifetime," responded Hemashe. "But one can always hope and pray."

"That I will do. Sleep well, my friend," said Joval. "I now have the task of telling Nayla of this impending war."

"Yes, I shall see you in the morn," responded Hemashe.

Joval quickly disappeared down the corridor and across the courtyard to the stable. Mounting his steed, he made his way out of the city on to his cottage. As he neared, he could see the soft glow of candles burning through the windows. Nayla was still awake.

Entering the small room, Joval was stunned to see that Nayla had taken it upon herself to wash both Hemashe and the Elf's clothes, including the laundry he had discreetly hidden beneath his bed. Most of it was now neatly folded and stacked while the rest hung by the fireplace to dry. She had also wiped down the table, fireplace mantle and any other dust-covered surface, as well as washing and drying the few dishes he did not have a chance to tend to prior to his last hasty departure. On the table, there was even a cluster of wild flowers she had collected and arranged in a cup.

As he walked around the room, Nayla was nowhere to be seen.

"Where is she?" Joval grumbled under his breath.

"Up here," a voice called from above.

The Elf turned his gaze up to the loft as he asked: "What are you doing up there?"

"I do not wish to impose on you. I wish to sleep up here if it is alright with you," she answered, peering down at Joval.

"Come down here, Nayla," the Elf requested. "We must speak."

She glanced at him, her eyes narrowing in suspicion. Joval flexed his index finger, motioning her to come down.

She reluctantly made her way down the ladder.

"What is it? Are you angry that I did some tidying? That I washed your clothes? I knew of no other way to thank you for all you had done for Hemashe and me."

Joval's eyes surveyed his humble surroundings. "I should be the one to thank you, Nayla, for it was not necessary for you to do this. And no, I am not angry. I want you to know what transpired tonight."

"I cannot deny that I am curious," she replied.

"Let us have some tea, yes?" offered Joval, as he folded his cloak over the back of a chair.

Nayla poured some boiling water from the kettle into a small, earthenware teapot. The aromatic scent of brewing tea filled the air. She set it down on the table, placing two mugs by its side.

"Sit," said Joval, pulling out a chair for her.

She complied.

The Elf sat across from her and proceeded to pour tea first for her, and then for himself. "This is nice."

"The tea?" she asked.

"Yes, and I was speaking of these flowers, too. My home is seldom graced by a woman's touch," smiled Joval, his fingertip stroking the soft petals of a wild rose.

"The table just needed something…" she responded nervously, hearing him use the word 'woman' to describe her.

"Well, thank you. And it really was not necessary to launder my clothing. I am perfectly capable of doing that myself," stated the Elf.

"I know. I just felt a need to keep my mind and hands occupied," replied the warrior maiden. "Where is Hemashe, by the way?"

"For this one night, he is a guest at the palace."

She gazed into the Elf's eyes, searching for the truth: "What happened? I sense all did not go well tonight. Does Dahlon know of me? Is that what you wish to speak to me of?"

Joval shook his head in response.

"Then tell me, what happened?"

"I told the council that it was not me, but a Kagai Warrior who rescued Hemashe. I told them how you got in and out of the palace, but never did I mention your name, even when they requested a meeting with you."

"I know there is more. Go on," she insisted.

"Indeed, there is more. Tomorrow we leave for the north. We have been called to war," revealed Joval.

For a lingering moment both said nothing.

"So we shall face the enemy once more. Before the coming of the winter, we shall rise up to do battle again," responded the little warrior.

"How do we rise up against an army that is reputed to be twice as large as the last, Nayla?" asked the Elf, unleashing a weary sigh. "Even with the combined forces of my men and the Kagai Warriors, as well as any man willing to take up arms by our side, we shall be lucky if there is eight or nine-hundred of us to do battle."

She took a sip of tea from her cup as she thought upon his words.

"Yet again, we are outnumbered," she stated. "This is nothing new. My intuition tells me the Sorcerer is behind this invasion. Is this so?"

"Your intuition serves you well. Unfortunately, *my* intuition tells me that Eldred Firestaff shall continue to send larger armies and more frequently, until we have met our demise."

"We may well be outnumbered, but the enemy can still be outwitted and out-maneuvered. All is not lost," said the little warrior.

"You have a plan. I can see it in your eyes," declared the Elf.

"I know Master Saibon. I know how he thinks, how he will strategize. If I am correct, he shall plan an ambush of a grand scale."

"That is nothing new," stated Joval.

"True enough, but never have we attacked the enemy before they set foot on our lands. We have always waited until they came to us. This time, I have a feeling we shall be going to them. We will take them totally by surprise, attacking while their defenses are down, when they least expect it."

"The element of surprise may be our greatest ally in this impending war," agreed Joval.

Her head tilted ever so slightly as she studied the Elf's lucid, blue eyes. "There is more, Captain Stonecroft."

He nodded his head in response.

"Yes, your request to be inducted into the army will not be. You shall not march into battle alongside my men," revealed Joval.

Her eyes fell away from his steady gaze, dropping away in disappointment.

"You were the one to preach to me the importance of '*confronting my past*' as you put it. So now, you will not help me?"

"I know this is not exactly what you had in mind, but I have convinced your father and the elders to commission you to instruct our armies in Kagai warfare here, in Nagana," stated the Elf.

"You did what?" asked the little warrior, astounded by his claim.

"You heard correctly. They have commissioned you to teach the great warriors of Orien. When the battle is done, if we should return home, you will be posted, with their blessings and Master Saibon's, to instruct my men in the art of war."

The Elf was taken totally by surprise when the warrior maiden leapt from her chair. She threw her arms about Joval's neck, embracing him in a grateful hug. "Thank you! Thank you so very much, Captain Stonecroft!"

"No need for thanks," responded the Elf, reciprocating with an awkward hug of his own.

"How did you do this? How did you manage such a feat?"

"It really was not that hard," insisted Joval. "It made perfect sense to the elders when I explained the rationale behind this."

"And that was all?"

"Well, at this time, they do not know it is *you* to be posted to this position," replied the Elf.

"What do you mean *'they do not know'*?"

"They did not give me a specific name of a warrior, only that they wished to post the Kagai who accompanied me to the east in Hemashe's rescue bid. They asked the appointment go to Master Saibon's best warriors. And that is exactly what they will be getting. I am merely fulfilling this request."

The little warrior beamed with delight as she responded. "How very ironic for Dahlon Treeborn."

"How so?" queried Joval.

"One of his last words to be said to me on the night we fled to Anshen all those many years ago was that I would *never* tell him how to command his armies."

Under the fading warmth of a late summer sun, Joval and Hemashe led an army northward from Nagana. An infantry of three-hundred warriors followed behind the two-hundred on horseback. They moved at a steady, determined pace, for they all felt the urgency of this call to arms.

Their warmed breath condensed like tiny clouds, suspended before the men as they exhaled into the crisp, early morning air. Though the leaves of the trees had yet to change to their brilliant autumn hue of red and gold, Joval knew that the cool touch of fall would soon crystallize the morning dew into frost and the night air would bring with it the sting of cold to herald the coming of winter. They were leaving the city just three days prior to the harvest moon that would herald the first day of autumn. That would give them exactly thirty-two days to reach Magare Valley, before the rise of the hunter's moon.

Joval knew it would not be a problem for those on horseback, but his mind was burdened with the thought that the warriors of the infantry may not make it in time unless they could press on at this merciless pace.

Marching onward, the walls of the fortress city vanished from their sight. The Elven warriors riding at the frontline with Joval all turned their heads to the east as a horse and rider emerged from the shadows of the forest lining the road. Valtar Briarwood drew his sword as he urged his steed forward to intercept the stranger.

"Approach no further!" demanded the Elf, his sword pointed at the hooded figure. "Can you not see an army goes to war? Stand aside and let us pass!"

"Fetch off! My business is with your captain, not with you!" growled an angry voice. The rider deliberately wove around the Elf's sword.

Valtar seized the stranger by the arm to halt his advance. With a sharp yank, the Elf pulled the rider off the steed to impede him.

Tumbling to the ground, the rider grabbed hold of the Elf, causing Valtar to fall from his mount. With his sword still in hand, the Elf attempted to impale his much smaller assailant as he came down.

The figure easily rolled out of the way as the tip of Valtar's blade pierced the ground. In absolute rage, the stranger's leg swung out, catching the Elf from behind, high above his right ankle, sweeping his leg from beneath him.

Valtar tumbled backwards, his sword flying from his hand as he crashed to the ground. Before the final shockwaves of the impact coursed through his body, his foe immediately rolled forward, landing squarely upon Valtar's chest. The Elf's arms were firmly pinned to the ground by his assailant's knees.

As Valtar's sword spun and tumbled, his assailant's gloved hand snatched it from mid-air as the deadly blade came down with great speed. When Valtar's eyes opened, they were met by the glint of cold steel flashing in the morning sun. He was held at bay by his own weapon; poised to slash his throat. All around him, the entire army came to a standstill. A circle of arrows and swords were drawn, pointing at his assailant.

"After all these years, you are still an ass, Valtar Briarwood!" hissed an unfamiliar voice cloaked in the shadow of a hood.

"Takaro! Release him!" ordered Hemashe, as he dismounted from his horse to come to the Elf's aid.

Joval leapt off his steed as he instructed his men to put away their weapons. Dashing over to his friend's side, he plucked the little warrior from Valtar's prostrate form as he demanded her to return the sword to its rightful owner.

"You know this ruffian?" asked Valtar, rising up from the ground with Hemashe's help.

"As you do, too," stated Joval, yanking back the warrior's hood.

Valtar's eyes grew wide in shock as recognition set in: "It is you! How can this be? Joval, what is going on here?"

"Your eyes do not deceive you, Valtar. This indeed is Nayla Treeborn," whispered Joval.

"Lord Treeborn's daughter!" gasped the stunned Elf.

Like a pebble breaking the surface of a still pond, a ripple of whispers spread through the throng of warriors: *Treeborn's daughter! Lord Treeborn's long missing daughter! She has returned!*

"Captain Stonecroft, we need to speak, in private!" demanded Valtar, brushing off the dust from his assault by the hands of this diminutive woman.

"Hemashe, keep the men moving. We shall catch up to you," ordered Joval. With a wave of his hand the Kagai Warrior motioned for the men to fall back in line and proceed forward.

Valtar angrily seized both Joval and the little warrior by their arms, leading them both well off the roadway.

"How long did you know of her? How long has she been here?" questioned Valtar.

"I traveled with Nayla into eastern Orien to rescue the Kagai Warrior. She has only been in Nagana since yesterday," confided Joval.

"Why did you not tell me upon your departure that it was *she* you traveled with? Why did you not disclose this information to me?"

asked Valtar.

"As your *captain*, I did not feel it was necessary to divulge this information to you at the time. It was not necessary for you to know who was deployed on this mission with me."

"As my *friend*, I thought you would have the decency to warn me that she was gallivanting about! With you no less! You know what will become of us both if Lord Treeborn catches wind that we were the ones to spirit her away to Anshen!"

The little warrior watched in silence, her head turning to and fro as the Elves bantered back and forth.

"If you recall, it was *I* who did this. *You* washed your hands of the entire fiasco. You were merely an innocent, a warrior forced to follow his captain's orders. Remember?" countered Joval.

"Does Lord Treeborn know of her? Do the elders?" queried Valtar.

"No one knew, until you tried to accost her," replied Joval. "Now the entire army is aware of her identity and presence."

"No thanks to you!" growled the little warrior. Her face screwed up in anger as she stood toe-to-toe against the much larger Elf, glaring up at Valtar.

"If you had only listened to my orders in the first place!" countered Valtar, glaring right back down at her with unabashed loathing.

"If you had not seized me as you had!" she snapped back.

Grabbing them both, Joval pulled them apart to end the standoff. "Enough! Both of you be quiet! If this is what I shall be forced to endure for the entire trek, then kill me now!"

"Why can I not just kill *him* instead?" offered the little warrior, her hand resting on the hilt of her sword. "Or at least poke him until he bleeds a little."

"Why you – !"

"Watch your mouth, Elf! I may be smaller than you, but rest assured, I can still have you drawn and quartered with my sword before you can even unsheathe your weapon!" she declared.

"This is a fine mess, Joval!" protested the Elf. "No longer is she an obnoxious, mouthy little child; you have created an obnoxious, mouthy, sword-wielding, high-strung Kagai Warrior! She is both crazy and dangerous!"

"Your tongue wags like the tail of a dog in heat. If you persist with your insults, I shall be more than glad to offer your flapping tongue a taste of my sword."

"If you both persist, I will draw and quarter both of you myself!" declared Joval.

Valtar and the warrior maiden reluctantly ceased their bickering as Joval seethed in his anger.

"Unfortunately, I am in need of as many warriors as possible for this upcoming battle. If we survive, by all means, feel free to kill each other for all I care. For now, I wish to keep my sanity intact," grumbled Joval. "If you cannot be civil to one another, then I recommend you give each other a wide berth. Stay clear of each other if you cannot stay your tongue!"

"As you wish, captain," responded the warrior maiden, turning to retrieve her steed. She suddenly turned about, feeling the Elf's intention as Valtar's hands reached out in a motion to throttle her.

"Watch yourself, Elf…" she cautioned him as she sauntered away.

"Valtar, I mean it! Mind your distance and your words where Nayla is concerned!" cautioned Joval. "Her tongue may be sharp, but her blade is sharper still. Do not rouse her ire!"

"But what if she tells Lord Treeborn the truth? We will be stripped of our rank, ousted from this army, or worse!"

"There is no need for concern. Believe me, she will not breathe a word of this to anyone, especially Dahlon Treeborn," responded Joval.

"How do you know that? How can you be sure?"

"She is a Kagai Warrior through and through. Honourable, both on and off the field of battle," averred the Elf. "Need I say more?"

For twenty-seven days, the army moved at a relentless pace. Rising with the sun and stopping to sleep only when the lands were cast in deep shadows, the warriors continued this daily grind, uttering not a single word of complaint as they contemplated the urgency of their mission.

A near-full moon peered through the massing of clouds high in the sky as the warriors settled down for the night. This glowing orb seemed to mock them from on high, its cold light streaming down from a ghostly, pocked face.

"The time of war shall soon be upon us," determined Joval, as he gazed up to the impending hunter's moon. "This journey has taken far longer to travel because of the dwindling hours of daylight. If we continue at this pace, we shall arrive in time to watch our Kagai brothers fall in defeat."

"You know what you must do then, Captain Stonecroft," said the little warrior. "You have no choice but to advance with those on horseback. Take all the Elven warriors and only those mortals that have already seen war. Leave the infantry."

"I do not relish leaving my men behind," stated Joval. "Yet, I know we shall cover greater distance without them. We would even have time to meet with Master Saibon to formulate a plan of attack."

"Then do so," she ordered. "Take my horse, give it to another warrior. Ride on at first light in the morn."

"But what will become of my men? I cannot abandon them in hopes that they can make their way northward on their own," stated the Elf. "Many have never been away from Nagana or their villages, let alone do battle against the enemy."

"Nor can you condemn our fellow warriors to the north to certain death," she replied. "Take my steed. I will lead the infantry to the Magare Valley. I shall take your men into battle. Whether we rise victorious or fall in the shadows under a crushing defeat, we will stand as a united front against this evil."

Under the bleak light of dawn, Joval addressed his warriors as they stood, row upon row, at attention.

"Today, I shall advance with only those seasoned warriors on horseback. Time is now a luxury we can ill afford. We have no other choice in this matter," stated the Elf.

Murmurs of confusion rippled through the crowd.

"For the rest of you, you shall continue northward in hopes that it will not be too late. I know for many of you, this will be your first time to engage in war against the enemy. Fear not, for you shall be led into battle by a Kagai Warrior who has faced the enemy many times and each time, had the skills and the courage to walk away victorious."

The warriors erupted into cheer as they turned their gaze to Hemashe.

Joval raised his hands for silence so he may continue: "From this point forward, you shall follow your new captain. Nayla Treeborn shall lead the march and you will follow her every instruction."

A round of surprised gasps met his words.

Fully expecting such a reaction, the warrior maiden was unmoved by their response.

Again, Joval raised his hands for silence. "I assure you, Captain Treeborn is one of the best Kagai Warriors to come out of Anshen. She has seen and survived far more battles than all of you mortals combined. Her knowledge of the lands, its terrain you are about to enter; her skill with the sword; and her expertise in strategy cannot, and will not, be questioned or disputed. Is that understood?"

"Yes, Captain Stonecroft!" the warriors answered collectively.

"You shall follow her directives and you will not waver in your loyalty to her, as hers will not falter as she leads you into battle. Her word is law. Anyone who rises up against her, to ignore her orders, shall be made to deal with the consequences of their actions. Keep in mind; if you foolishly choose to disobey her, then consider your actions to be in direct insubordination to my orders, for Captain Treeborn has been appointed under my authority. Understood?

"Yes, Captain Stonecroft!"

"From this point forward, you will address her as Captain Treeborn or Lady Treeborn. Is that understood?"

Once again, the warriors answered in unison: "Yes, Captain Stonecroft!"

"Be ready to move out on Captain Treeborn's orders!" commanded Joval.

As the men dispersed to gather their weapons and belongings, the Elf glanced down at the warrior maiden, whispering to her: "Are you positive you wish to do this? Many of the young men have yet to be tested on the field of battle."

"Absolutely, I will see you there," she answered, turning to face her assigned battalion.

Joval led the way with Hemashe and Valtar by his side as the infantry watched the mounted warriors charge northward, leaving them behind in the morning mist.

"Are you ready, warriors of Orien?" called out the warrior maiden.

"Yes, Captain Treeborn!" the men shouted in answer.

With this eager response she began the long, grueling trek. Setting the pace like a long-distance runner, she began their first leg of the journey at a steady run. For the mortals and the handful of Elven warriors, with their much longer stride, her gait was set at an easy pace for them. Her saving grace was that she had great stamina; it was almost comparable to that of the Elven warriors'. She was able to run tirelessly for long durations.

For four days, she kept the men moving at this relentless pace until they reached the Reyu River. As night fell, she instructed the men to rest. They would be safe as they were now in Kagai territory. She slipped away into the darkness, disappearing behind a veil of water behind Reyu Falls. Dashing through the bamboo forest and onward to the cottages near Lake Anzan, her racing heart slowed as she saw the steady glow of candles from the familiar homes she once knew. She stood on the stoop of a cottage, pounding loudly on the door.

As the door flew open Yumai immediately recognized the little warrior. She shouted her name out in joy as she threw her arms about her: "Takaro! It is you! Thank God it is you! I prayed for the spirits to watch over you!"

The little warrior embraced Yumai in a warm hug. She smiled at Yumai, now great with child as she waddled slightly in her gravid condition.

"I thought I would never see you again, Takaro," she began to weep. "I wanted so much to tell you how grateful I am that you rescued Hemashe from the enemy. He told me everything. He told me what you did to deliver him from their hands."

"It was nothing, Yumai. Any of our brothers would have done the same," she replied.

"That is not so, Takaro! Perhaps under any other circumstance it might have been the case, but it was you who did what no others would or could do," praised Yumai.

"I wish I had more time, but you know what is advancing from the north. Where are your father and brother? Have they left?"

Yumai quickly rifled through some worn and tattered scrolls. Her small hands quickly unfurled a rolled section of parchment to reveal a map of the northern reaches of Orien.

"Father and Keodai have led the men northward. They wait in ambush here," she said, her finger pointing well within the Magare Valley.

"I knew it! I knew my master would change his strategy!"

"Yes, father believes that because their numbers are so great, his only chance was to attack the enemy within the valley than to wait in the pine forest," acknowledged Yumai. "Had it been only a small scouting party sent forth as often had been the case, you know my father would let the enemy wander in as far as the Hebeku Valley than to waste our warriors' time and energy marching northward to face them."

"The element of surprise shall work in our favor. Long have the enemy felt secure in the Magare Valley, for never in my lifetime have we waged war in this manner," she nodded in approval. "Did other warriors come by this way?"

"Yes, Takaro. A large contingent of mostly Elves led by Captain Stonecroft arrived. Hemashe brought them here first. They came by three days ago. The Elf is probably with my father as we speak. Hemashe escorted them northward to meet with the Kagai Warriors. Our people to the east have sent word the Imperial Army shall arrive late in the day of the full moon. When the hunter's moon graces the nighttime sky, they plan to invade western Orien at first light."

"So they are still too frightened and superstitious to tread on our lands by the shadows of the night," she responded. "There is little time left. I cannot linger here for long, Yumai. I have an army of my own to escort to the valley."

"You are a captain?" Yumai gasped in surprise.

"Yes, I lead a battalion of three-hundred warriors from Nagana. I must go now."

"Will I see you again?" called out Yumai, as the little warrior rushed out the door.

"If the fates conspire and luck is with me, we shall meet again," she shouted back.

"Stay safe, Takaro! And please, this time, keep an eye on Hemashe!" hollered Yumai.

"That I shall do!" she promised.

"And Takaro!" Yumai called out once more. "Snow has come early to the valley. The Kagai Warriors shall be dressed in their white battle raiment!"

"I understand!" she shouted, disappearing into the night.

The nights were long and drawn-out, too dark and cold for the mortals to march on. The daylight hours came and went much too quickly with winter fast approaching. Two days before the rise of the hunter's moon and the newly appointed captain knew she and her men would have no choice but to press on hard and fast. She glanced over at all the weary warriors huddled around the fires that blazed. It would only get colder as they ventured further north, especially with the early onset of snow. In all her years in Anshen, rarely did it snow during the height of autumn.

Is this a sign of things to come? Will our lands and people be cast into the shadows of a long, cruel winter made worse by the plight of our enemy? She pondered these questions as her eyes gazed up through the tree branches laid bare by the icy breath of the north wind.

Through the veil of high clouds pushed about by an invisible wind, a near-full moon bathed the frozen land in its silvery light.

Come dawn, she would have no choice but to forge on. With still another day or two of travel to complete the trek, time was quickly running out with the impending full moon due to rise the following eve.

She would be forced to run the warriors farther and harder than ever before. Or, she could take a short cut across the swamplands. At this time of the year, with the unseasonable cold, she was confident the ground would at least be firm, if not already frozen solid. If they cut through this forsaken tract of land, they would shorten their trek by perhaps a good six to eight hours.

Had it been spring or summer, this was something she would never consider subjecting the men to. With the heat of the sun, the foul air would be rife with the odor of decay and thick with blood-sucking insects breeding in this quagmire. Though the waters here were not deep, they were dark with fermenting peat. This primordial soup of stagnating water was thick with slimy, green algae and veiled in a constant miasma that floated above its surface like the thin, gray noxious vapor of a dragon's breath. This was to be their route.

A phantom moon rose into the dimming sky. Its full, round face was yet to radiate the true intensity of its cold, silvery light. With the setting of the sun, clouds far on the western horizon were bathed in crimson as the pale sky turned a deepening mauve, casting the world into a strange twilight. In another hour or so, darkness would swallow up the lands.

Advancing westward like an orderly procession of ants, dark-clad Imperial Soldiers poured into the valley. Row upon row, they marched in until thousands of soldiers dotted the white landscape below. The captain shouted orders for the men to fall out of line and to make evening preparations, for in the morning, they begin their invasion.

As the soldiers put aside their spears, halberds and bows to proceed with the business of setting up camp, the solitary call of the owl drifted across the valley. The soldiers nervously glanced about, searching for this nocturnal bird. Like many creatures of the night, it was regarded with fear for it was believed to be the harbinger of death.

The captain angrily shouted orders for the men to hurry, for darkness would soon descend, and with it, the possibility of more snow. As another owl call floated across from the opposite slope of the narrow valley, an eerie hush fell upon the lands. This unnatural silence forced the soldiers to work with greater haste to set up their temporary shelters.

The silence was broken by the whine of hundreds of arrows cascading from the surrounding slopes of the valley. Many soldiers fell dead as they scrambled for their shields and weapons. Those more fortuitous closed their ranks, holding forth their shields on high to deflect the incoming projectiles. Just as suddenly as it started, the hail of arrows ceased. The captain ordered his men to lower their shields and take up their bow in retaliation.

An anxious soldier called out to the captain: "Where do we aim? The enemy cannot be seen!"

As the many eyes anxiously scanned the slopes leaning into this valley, all was strangely quiet and still. There was only the glistening mantle of snow and the deep shadows of the trees to greet their eyes. The Kagai Warriors, donning their winter raiment were impossible to see in the dimming light.

"Those blasted rebels are up there! Divide into two groups; take to the slopes!" ordered the captain. "Hunt them down!"

Just as soon as the soldiers began their advance, once again, they were met with a steady volley of arrows. Those taken by surprise were quickly dispatched, while the others closed their ranks again, holding their shields on high to deflect the onslaught.

The captain changed his strategy: "Men! Advance to the northern slope, keep your shields up and forward. We shall take them out one side at a time!"

Like a great black wave surging forth, the army closed in. Protected by the overlapping shields held overhead, the soldiers advanced towards the slope to pursue their unseen assailants.

A volley of arrows rained down from the opposite slopes, downing the soldiers taking up the rear as the captain gave orders to reposition their shields.

The captain wheeled his steed about. With sword drawn, he commanded his men to charge up the northern slope. A mighty roar echoed through the valley as the soldiers rallied their forces and summoned their courage to counter the assault. With adrenaline and hate coursing through their veins and fueling their souls, the soldiers charged across the valley with their shields held high.

To their horror, rising from the foot of the slopes before them, almost two hundred Elven warriors emerged from the snow like ghostly apparitions, launching an assault by bow and arrow to take down the soldiers on the frontline. Joval and his keen-eyed Elven marksmen quickly dispatched the advancing mob as Medaru ordered his warriors to charge into the valley to join the battle.

The ground shook and the valley echoed with the screams and battle cries as the Imperial Soldiers and the warriors of Orien collided headlong into war. Though the Imperial Army was now thinned to half their original force, the warriors were still outnumbered.

Whether Nayla arrived now with the infantry was a moot point as they braced for a bloodbath. With the hunter's moon now high in the sky, bathing the land in its pale light, the hot blood that splattered the snow to melt into the frozen landscape appeared black. Keodai and his battalion raced down from the southern slopes and across the valley to attack from the rear as Medaru and the other Kagai Warriors fought side-by-side with Joval's men.

In the midst of the chaos, Hemashe charged toward the captain of the Imperial Army. Slashing at the other soldiers who dared to get in his way, this Kagai Warrior continued his advance, determined to take down the man orchestrating the attack.

As the steed wheeled about before Hemashe, the captain reined his mount in, causing the stallion to rear up. The horse struck out at Hemashe as he dodged and weaved, avoiding the ironclad hoofs. The captain yanked on the reins once more, attempting to trample the warrior.

Hemashe lunged forward with his sword, slashing at the reins.

The captain toppled backwards off his steed, the broken reins still in his hands as he sank into the snow-covered ground.

With his sword, Hemashe dove at the captain as he struggled to draw his weapon from the scabbard trapped beneath his body. Hemashe's blade came down with speed as the captain rolled to his side just enough, and just in time, to avoid the razor-sharp tip of the sword.

Hemashe raised his weapon again, but a soldier standing directly behind, too close to swing his halberd, but not so close that he could not ram the butt end of the handle between the warrior's shoulder blades, assaulted the warrior. The violent impact rattled Hemashe's senses. The blow caused him to stumble toward the fallen captain.

As the warrior collapsed, the captain drew his knees up to his chest, kicking forward with both feet as Hemashe fell down on him. Striking the warrior in his chest, Hemashe was pitched backwards to the soldier who had struck him with the halberd.

The soldier laughed as a dazed Hemashe fell right into his arms. The captain rolled up onto his feet, striking the warrior hard across his face with an angry fist. Both Hemashe and the soldier bracing him stumbled back with the force of the punishing blow. The soldier struggled to hold Hemashe up as his captain drew his sword to finish the warrior off.

With a triumphant grunt, the captain prepared to lunge forward to slash Hemashe diagonally across his midriff to usher in a slow, painful death. As he pivoted to deliver the lethal blow, a single arrow skimmed past his face, striking the soldier holding Hemashe. The arrow narrowly missed the warrior, his cheek feeling the wake of the arrow as it flew past him. The projectile sank into the soldier's right eye socket and onward into his brain. The soldier collapsed to the ground, convulsing in the bloodstained snow. He pulled the Kagai Warrior down with him as he fell.

Hemashe's eyes opened wide in shock as the captain's blade glinted in the moonlight as he rushed in to finish him off. Instead of delivering the killing blow, the man shrieked as he toppled forward. His blade slammed down between Hemashe's parted legs, coming to within a hair's-breadth from the warrior's manhood.

The captain fell over quite dead, a Kagai arrow protruding from his back. To Hemashe's surprise, the warrior maiden unleashed it.

"Takaro! Thank goodness!" he exclaimed, checking his groin as she yanked him up onto his feet.

"No time to talk!" she responded, motioning the infantry on. Hemashe picked up his sword to take on his next foe as the little warrior disappeared, swallowed up in the noise and the mayhem.

Medaru released a haunting, ear-splitting call that pierced the air and caught the soldiers by surprise. The Kagai Warriors took advantage of this moment of confusion that was meant to alert them of the reinforcements as three hundred warriors joined their ranks.

As Joval fought back against the soldiers, he was relieved to see that Nayla honoured her promise, arriving with the infantry just in the nick of time. His warriors fought with renewed energy as the surge of power abruptly swayed in their favor. He watched as Nayla, parried and ferociously countered each assault, weaving easily between the warriors and soldiers to cut down the enemy from behind.

Turning on the warrior maiden, an Imperial Soldier's eyes burned with hate and revenge as he hacked and slashed at her. As she countered his strikes with her sword, the impact rang through her body like great shockwaves as the soldier's adrenaline fueled his assault. Turning her blade horizontally to slash at her assailant from his right to his left, the soldier charged toward her, his own sword held high.

Pivoting her left leg back, she now became a more linear target, but the soldier's sword tracked her. Just as she turned to strike, his sword missed her body, but smashed down on her left hand. The metal crossguard of his sword instantly shattered her wrist. Nayla's left hand fell away dead, but the momentum from her right hand continued to swing the blade forward and across the soldier's back and side. Taking her sword up in her right hand, she gave the enemy one final thrust with the deadly point of her blade. With her damaged left hand clutched against her body, the little warrior was undeterred. She took off after her next quarry.

In the midst of this chaos, Joval watched as a bloodied Valtar collapsed forward onto his hands and knees as an enemy soldier raised his halberd to decapitate him. Joval screamed out in warning as he scrambled over fallen bodies to his friend's aid.

Turning upon hearing Joval's cry, the warrior maiden immediately hurled her sword at the soldier. As the fearsome blade spun through the air, the soldier screamed in agony as it severed his raised right arm just above his elbow. The sword continued on with such velocity, it sank deep across his wide-opened mouth, cutting him down in mid-scream. As the body crumpled to the ground, the halberd fell from his hand. The flat edge of the blade struck Valtar on the back of his head, rendering him unconscious. The Elf collapsed on to the ground.

With no time to search for the weapon she threw, drawing her short sword, she shouted at Joval: "Leave him be! The enemy will think he's dead!"

The Elf scrambled over to Valtar's side, wrenching him around to flip him onto his back. Joval glanced up as the little warrior screamed out: *"Move!"*

He ducked low over Valtar's body as Nayla dove over him. Coming up over her shoulder, she deliberately slammed into the knees of the soldier standing directly behind Joval. The soldier had his halberd raised high, poised to cleave the Elf's head. As the force of her momentum carried her forward, the soldier toppled onto his back as she landed onto his chest. Without hesitation, her deadly blade spun around in her right hand as she rammed the tip of her short sword straight through his throat, pressing down with all her might until only snow and earth offered resistance.

The little warrior leapt up onto the dead soldier's chest. Using one foot for leverage, she pushed down on the soldier's head, rearranging his face into a final snarl of defiance as she yanked out her sword with her one good hand. She quickly twisted her wrist, flicking the blood off the blade.

Glancing behind her to see if Joval was unharmed, she turned to right herself, only to meet with the toe of a great, black boot as it caught her under her jaw, slamming her teeth together. Her brain felt the jarring impact of the blow as she was sent flying backwards to the ground.

Joval leapt up, intercepting the sword meant for Nayla. The Elf countered each blow as she rolled back onto her feet and silently circled behind the soldier. She disappeared from Joval's sightline as the soldier howled in pain, crumpling down onto his knees. The little warrior had sliced through the tendons at the back of his legs. Unable to support his weight, the soldier collapsed. She immediately impaled him through his back as Joval raised his sword, lopping off the soldier's head with one clean blow.

Nayla immediately leapt back to avoid a spray of hot blood erupting from the carotid arteries as the head tumbled to the crimson snow.

The sounds of crashing swords and halberds were now replaced with the painful moans and eerie cries of the dying and the wounded. Rising to her feet, Nayla glanced about. Something was not right. She could feel it. It was as though the air was charged with electricity, like the build up of static prior to a great lightning storm.

Joval, too, could sense this strange sensation. His eyes hurriedly scanned the battlefield, searching for the unseen evil, when, from out of the blackness, a great fireball erupted through the air. Warriors leapt out of the way as Joval and Nayla seized their startled men, knocking them out of its path.

"The Sorcerer!" shouted Joval, hoisting Nayla onto her feet.

"He must not get away!" ordered Medaru, waving his men forward as a dark silhouette took form on a high, rocky knoll overlooking the battlefield. All dodged and leapt from the path of another blazing ball of energy blasted at them. Joval seized Nayla's arm, directing her to follow. It became instantly clear to her that the Elf was attempting to take down the Sorcerer from behind as Medaru and his men closed in from the front.

Yanking her short sword from the dead soldier's body, she followed Joval into the tree line as the warriors scattered to avoid another fireball launched in their direction. Ducking into the forest, the two warriors raced through the darkness to capture the Sorcerer.

With demented delight, Eldred Firestaff gleefully bombarded his foes with another barrage of fire. Though the battlefield was becoming pocked with craters and lit up with the blazing, orange flames, the wilted grasses buried beneath the snow covered ground did not burn as the Sorcerer would have liked, had it been a dry, hot, summer day.

Reveling in the confusion brought on by his fiery display, the Sorcerer continued with his assault. He attempted to kill the warriors, even doing away with Imperial Soldiers too slow, weak or wounded to move away from this deadly barrage. Eldred released a maniacal laugh as he lowered his staff yet again only to turn with a start as the crystal orb atop his staff revealed the reflection of Joval and Nayla creeping up from behind. His response was immediate. Eldred spun about, aiming his staff at Joval. A bolt of blue light surged from the crystal, striking Joval in his chest. The Elf flew backwards, convulsing from the painful energy coursing through his body.

Nayla was undeterred by this violent display. She held her sword before her, poised to attack the Sorcerer.

"What is this? There are so few men in western Orien they now force women take up arms?" chortled Eldred, leaning upon his staff as this warrior cautiously pressed in.

"I may be a woman, but I do know how to use this," hissed the little warrior, veering ever closer.

"Men, women, Elf or mortal, they are all fair game to me," snorted the Sorcerer, his voice oozing with contempt.

He turned his attention away from her to hurl another fireball at the incursion moving forward to trap him. Nayla rushed at the Sorcerer, her sword held high.

Eldred gave a disgruntled snort of contempt as he aimed his crystal at her. A surge of energy knocked the sword from her grasp as it enveloped her in a paralyzing hold. It felt as though her body was as heavy as lead. She was unable to move – to fight back. The Sorcerer stepped in close, staring into her eyes. The little warrior glared back, but was momentarily alarmed, for as she stared into the dark, recessed orbs of his eyes, except for an eerie, red glow, it was as though she gazed into the soul of one already dead.

As he lowered his staff, his paralyzing magic was released. His gnarled fingers seized her by the throat, raising her off the ground. She struggled against his grip, dangling helplessly above the ground as the Sorcerer held her forth for the advancing warriors to see.

"I am about to make an example of this little warrior! Watch carefully!" demanded Eldred. "Behold the strength of my powers!"

The Kagai Warriors momentarily froze. Then, to Eldred's chagrin, Medaru motioned his warriors to advance quickly.

"You willingly sacrifice her life!" shouted the Sorcerer.

"She is Kagai! She knows about sacrifice!" answered Medaru, motioning Keodai and Hemashe forward.

"But she is our captain," protested a young warrior of the infantry she had led into battle. "We will not allow Captain Treeborn to be killed in this manner. We owe her our allegiance!"

"Treeborn? There is only one Treeborn and Dahlon Treeborn is too cowardly to rise up against me!" shouted the Sorcerer. He shook the little warrior as she kicked and wrestled to break this ungodly, powerful grip. "You are not an Elf, you are Taijin!"

"Unlike my father… I am not… afraid to face you!" growled the warrior maiden, sputtering through his choking grip.

The Sorcerer's lifeless eyes widened with surprise. He glowered at her. His eyes locked with hers, searching her soul for confirmation.

"That cannot be!" snapped Eldred. "Long have there been rumors that Treeborn's only child met an untimely demise long ago."

"You are… a fool to listen… to rumors," gasped the warrior maiden.

"Ha! How fortuitous indeed!" shouted the Sorcerer, giving her another violent shake. "I wonder what Dahlon Treeborn would sacrifice in exchange for the life of his daughter?"

"This will be one life… he shall willingly surrender… to see you… brought down!" snarled the warrior. Just as the Sorcerer turned to wave his prized possession before the army, she reached into her vest pocket. She rammed a poisoned throwing dart into a precise point on his exposed neck.

The Sorcerer screamed out in pain, his cry echoing across the valley as he dropped Nayla to remove the dart imbedded into the side of his neck. Taking advantage of this moment, the young warrior from her infantry ordered the others to attack. Without hesitation, the angry mob rushed forward to corner the Sorcerer.

Eldred screamed in anger, lowering his staff. Nayla rolled away as a circle of flames erupted around the crazed Sorcerer. As the great flames disappeared, so did Eldred. The Sorcerer had vanished.

The warrior maiden knelt over Joval, shaking him. Lightly slapping his face, the Elf slowly opened his eyes.

"What happened?" he groaned in pain.

"The Sorcerer escaped," she answered. She put her arms around

Joval's shoulders to prop him up. "Can you stand?"

"I feel numb, like my whole body is asleep; prickling with sensation," answered Joval.

"Stand up," ordered the little warrior, placing his arm around her shoulders. "I will help you."

With nothing more than the moonlight to work with, Medaru ordered the injured warriors be gathered and tended to. Others set about slitting the throats of the wounded enemy soldiers. For many of the young warriors uninitiated in warfare until this night, they were revolted by this action, but they understood the Kagai Warriors were trained to kill. They were not trained to maim or mutilate, nor did they believe in prolonging the suffering of the dying.

Keodai ordered all able-bodied warriors to gather up the dead soldiers. Burial was not an option in this frozen terrain, and with so many bodies, they would have no choice but to deposit them into a ravine to the north of the pine forest.

All through the night, dead bodies were roped together and dragged off by horses as the Elves and Kagai Warriors trained to heal worked together on their wounded comrades.

Among those in the crowd was Valtar Briarwood, now conscious and tending to the gash high across his left shoulder and across his chest. Joval could see Valtar was bleeding very badly and would require the healing powers of another Elf to see the wound closed.

With the wounded on horseback or resting in litters, Nayla escorted the warriors from the blood-soaked battlefield of the Magare Valley. Gazing to the north, with the approach of a bleak dawn, their misery was about to be compounded.

Joval gazed up at the somber, leaden sky. He sniffed the air, sensing the moisture mingling with the biting cold.

"The wind blows from the north. There will be snow and plenty of it before tomorrow morn," assessed the Elf.

"My warriors are dressed for this weather, Captain Stonecroft, and though I know the Elf men can endure this bitter clime, your mortal warriors will not survive unless we can beat the storm and take refuge in Anshen," advised Medaru. He knew it would now be a race against time and the elements.

Joval surveyed the recuperating and able-bodied men, trudging through the calf-deep snow. Even though the wounded were well on the way to healing, it was guaranteed to be a grueling test of will and human endurance.

"We cannot outrun this storm," determined the Elf.

"Yes, we can, or least we can avoid the very worst of it," argued the little warrior. "There is a faster route home, Master Saibon."

Medaru frowned in confusion as he gazed at her.

"And which way might that be?" he queried.

"The swamplands are frozen. I led the warriors this way on our trek north, for it was the only way to make it in time to the valley," she responded. "It shortened our trip by almost a good half day."

"Of course!" exclaimed Medaru. "Why did I not think of that?"

She offered him a smile as she answered: "Because you are not me."

"Lead the way, Takaro," ordered her master.

As the little warrior called out to gain the men's attention, she quickly explained the route they were to embark on and the urgency with which they would now be forced to advance with the impending storm.

To her surprise, the young warrior from the infantry that urged the others on to attack the Sorcerer called out: "You heard Captain Treeborn! Fall into line!"

Immediately, the warriors of the infantry assembled into an orderly manner. The young warrior called out again: "We are ready to move, Captain Treeborn!"

Medaru gave her an approving nod as he noted: "It is obvious you have earned their respect, Takaro. Let us go. Lead the way."

12

into the high house

The first severe storm to herald an early winter hit unmercifully hard. As they entered Hebeku Valley and raced eastward to take shelter in Anshen, the temperature continued to plummet while the driving snow raged around the warriors in a blinding flurry.

Joval's men were grateful to be taken in by their Kagai brethren who were more than willing to share their hearth and home. Safe and secure, they were offered a hot meal to warm their chilled bodies. They thankfully occupied chairs and floor space in the small cottages, appreciative to be spared another icy night outdoors.

Nayla carefully picked her way through the exhausted bodies as the weary men fell asleep on whatever floor space was vacant. There was barely enough room to maneuver around Yumai and Hemashe's humble abode.

Slinging her pack and bedroll over her shoulder, the little warrior made her way to the door.

"Takaro, where are you going?" Yumai demanded to know as she set down a tray of tea she was about to serve.

"I am going to find a place to sleep."

"You know all the homes are filled to capacity," reminded Yumai. "There is nowhere to go."

"I am going to the stable. I can sleep up in the hayloft."

"In the company of horses? I think not, Takaro. It is freezing out there. This was once your home, please stay," pleaded Yumai.

"No, Yumai. It is more than generous that you and Hemashe have opened your doors to give these men a warm place to stay. Especially the men who are recovering from their injuries, it is more important they stay warm. They shall recuperate much faster."

"And what about you, Takaro?" asked Yumai. "I can see your wrist still gives you grief."

"I will be fine. I just need to rest and the loft is dry and sheltered. And remember; I can tolerate the cold better than most."

"Hemashe, talk some sense into Takaro! She insists on sleeping in the stable," stated Yumai, turning to her husband to do something.

"Yumai is quite right, Takaro. You must stay the night," insisted Hemashe. "This was once your home."

"I have no home. I wish for you to keep these men warm; for soon they will be made to move on. Allow them some warmth and a good night's rest while it can be afforded to them," stated Takaro, as she stepped out into the blowing snow.

Hemashe watched in silence as the glow of the coal oil lamp she carried before her disappeared in the consuming darkness. He knew her well enough to know she could not be persuaded to stay.

The horses snorted in recognition as the little warrior made her way through, passing the rows of stalls. She climbed up the ladder into the hayloft. Hanging the lantern from a nail head protruding from the central support beam, she proceeded to spread out her bedroll over a thick layer of hay.

Much better than sleeping on hard floor, she thought, as she stretched out.

The insulating blanket of snow on the roof and the dry hay beneath her body made the loft comfortable. Even by human standards, a man, once wrapped in his bedroll, would find adequate warmth here. She lay in her solitude, contemplating the events of the past few days.

"Ha! So it is true, you beat me to it," said Joval, appearing at the top of the ladder.

"Whatever do you mean?" she asked, propping herself up on her elbow to look at the Elf.

"I was going to sleep here tonight. It is much too crowded for my liking in Master Saibon's cottage," stated the Elf. "Do you mind the company?"

"As long as you do not snore as long and as loud as Master Saibon does," she replied.

Joval laughed at her words as he responded with a smile: "I am an Elf. I do not snore."

"Then you are welcome to stay, Captain Stonecroft."

"Please call me Joval," he insisted as he tossed his bedroll onto the hay. "After all, you are a captain now."

"You have always been Captain Stonecroft for as long as I can recall," she responded. "It is like being called Nayla again. It shall take some getting used to."

"Now you make me feel so *very* old," laughed the Elf.

"Consider yourself lucky! I must admit, the first time I lay eyes on you after all these years I was quite surprised. You appeared unchanged with time, perhaps aging barely two or three mortal years in the duration of your absence."

"Well, I too must admit, I was very surprised to see you, Nayla. The last image I carried of you in my mind was that of a child no more than twelve mortal years. I was stunned to see that in sixty, short years you had transformed so drastically. I never dreamed that you would change as you had."

"How do you mean, *change*? Into a Kagai Warrior?" she queried, watching the Elf as he unfurled his bedroll.

"Into a warrior… and into a beautiful, young woman," answered Joval, spreading his bedroll out onto the layer of hay.

Nayla was momentarily speechless. She was taken totally by surprise, never expecting to hear such a compliment from this Elf. Her cheeks burned, flushing when a bright shade of red.

"Well, what do you know?" marveled Joval, with a lighthearted laugh. "I do believe I made this fearsome Kagai Warrior blush!"

"I do believe you received a blow to your head or your encounter with the Sorcerer somehow impaired your vision," she responded, laughing off his comment.

"Speaking of the Sorcerer, I was told you actually inflicted pain on that dastardly fiend. Is it true?" asked Joval. He lay down upon his bedroll.

"I stuck him with one of my poisoned throwing darts," she replied, pointing with a finger to her neck. "I have my doubts the dart had any lasting affect on the Sorcerer, but at least it was enough to make him drop me from his clutches and flee. After doing battle with the Imperial Army, I hardly think the warriors were in any condition to take on another foe, especially one that deals in the black arts."

"Perhaps you are right," said Joval, rolling onto his side to prop his head up on his elbow. "And thank you for coming to my aid, and for saving Valtar's life too. If you did not act as you did, we would both be dead."

"No need for thanks, just keep an eye on my back the next time we go into battle."

"That I can certainly do," promised the Elf. He noticed as she gingerly rubbed her left wrist. "How do your bones mend? Does it still give you grief?"

"No more so than your friend does. And as for Valtar Briarwood, it was merely a mistake my sword escaped my grasp to down the soldier. Your friend was just extremely lucky," she replied with a smug smile.

"Then he was lucky indeed that you had met with such a mishap. Let me see your wrist," ordered the Elf.

Nayla rolled up onto her feet, and then sat next to Joval. He examined her inflamed wrist, gently bending and twisting it all the while, watching her face to see if she flinched in pain.

"The bones mend nicely. However, had you been a full-blooded Elf, this process would not have such an affect on you. It is merely your body adjusting to this quick Elven healing. It is also aggravated by this cold."

He raised his hands high over his head. Clapping once, he briskly rubbed the palms of his hands together to generate ample heat. His large hands completely sheathed her wrist and tiny hand into his. The soothing energy melted away the gnawing pain as her bones, rapidly fused together under his healing touch continued to mend. Her eyes closed as she felt instant relief.

Joval gazed upon her face as her brows, clenched in obvious discomfort, slowly relaxed with the diminishing pain. The Elf knew Nayla spoke in jest about his closest friend, but he felt compelled to ask: "Tell me, Nayla; why do you despise Valtar as you do?"

"Why does he despise me?" She answered his question with a question of her own.

"I do not believe Valtar actually despises you. He is just fearful of Lord Treeborn's wrath. He is only concerned that my involvement in your disappearance will only lead to my dismissal from the army," speculated Joval.

"He never liked me."

"He does not even know you, not as I do. Valtar is overly concerned we shall be implicated in your flight from Nagana and we will be dealt with accordingly if the truth is revealed. You know that."

"Then I suppose my dislike for him is due to the fact he lacked the compassion to assist a child in need."

"Captain Treeborn?" a voice called out from beneath the loft.

"Up here," she responded, pulling her wrist away from Joval's hands.

From the top of the ladder, the head of the young warrior who had rallied the others to attack the Sorcerer to free their captain appeared before her.

"We heard you had taken shelter here to allow the recuperating men the comfort of staying with our hosts," said the young man.

"Yes, they should be afforded this one, simple comfort before we are forced to face the bitter elements again," she answered.

"Well, I discussed this with the others and we see the logic in your reasoning. If it is not too much to ask, we wish to remain with you, Captain Treeborn," requested the warrior.

She glanced over to Joval.

With a shrug of indifference he responded: "I have yet to relinquish you from your post as their captain. They are your men. You decide."

"Very well," responded the warrior maiden, motioning the warrior to join them.

The warrior threw his pack and bedroll up, clambering up into the loft. But to her surprise, behind him, another and another, and more warriors still, made their way up to join their captain.

"It appears you have a loyal following, Captain Treeborn," commented Joval, from his now crowded confines.

As abruptly as the early winter engulfed the lands in an icy stranglehold, her cold grip thawed as the cool, mild fall weather returned. After three days in the care and company of their Kagai hosts, Joval prepared to lead the army southward, optimistic that the unseasonable arrival of winter would be kept at bay until they neared Nagana.

With the warriors recuperating nicely, the women worked to bake bread and gather dried fruit, cured venison and salted, smoked fish to sustain the warriors of Joval's army for their long journey home.

The day before their departure, Joval met with Medaru, presenting him with a scroll. The parchment, written in the common language for both parties to understand, contained the request from the elders of Orien to commission a Kagai Warrior to train their men stationed in Nagana.

"In the past, Lord Treeborn and the elders always sent warriors to train with us. Why are they making this request now?" queried Medaru, studying the details outlined on this parchment.

"The logic is that our best warriors have always been the ones to receive guidance from your forefathers. Now, more so than ever, this training is of vital importance, as it would appear the alliance between the Emperor and the Sorcerer is resulting in more frequent attacks.

You know first hand an army is sent that is larger than the last. You know our numbers are not great. The advantage of training all of our warriors in the like manner as the Kagai Warriors may be a matter of survival for our people now," answered Joval.

Medaru cogitated on these words before asking, "And who is this warrior you wish to commission?"

"Nayla Treeborn."

The Kagai leader's eyebrows arched up in surprise. "You mean to say Takaro Bansho."

"She must assume her real identity if she wishes to accept this posting," replied Joval.

"Why do I believe your motivation is two-fold?" queried Medaru.

Joval smiled as he responded: "You are as insightful as your father and grandfather, Master Saibon. Indeed I requested Nayla to this posting because she is a most competent and experienced warrior, but you are aware that she is the daughter of a high Elf. It is time for her to return home, to reclaim her place in her father's house."

"Of all the people to make such a request, Captain Stonecroft, you were the one to bring her here. You are more aware than any of us why she was forced to dwell amongst my people for almost six decades. Do you truly believe that her sudden appearance in Nagana will force Lord Treeborn to accept Takaro into his home? Do you wish to subject her to rejection once again?"

"That is not my intention, Master Saibon. My first duty is to fulfill the elders' request to commission your best warrior for this posting. You cannot deny Nayla Treeborn is your best."

"True, her long training and numerous confrontations has made her one of the best warriors we have had the fortune of employing in battle. Still…"

"You and your forefathers not only trained Nayla, but it is obvious you raised her with the same consideration and care as a father for his daughter. It was something she was in dire need of in her earlier years, but now, it is time for her father, Lord Treeborn to face his past and accept responsibility for his deeds," replied Joval.

"Why do you feel so compelled to fix the past?" queried Medaru.

"Her past cannot be *'fixed';* instead, my attempt is to secure her future," replied Joval.

"But why do you insist on doing this? You have no duty or obligation to her. You are not bound by blood."

"That is true, but my oath, my pledge; this is what binds me to her as strongly as the ties of blood. Did Nayla ever disclose to you what had transpired on the night she fled from her father?"

"No," answered Medaru. "It must have been extremely traumatic, for she chose never to speak of that event in her life."

"For good reason, Master Saibon. The night I found her, she was thrashed to within an inch of her life. To bear the pain and humiliation of such a beating was one thing, but to know that it was her own father that inflicted her with such cruelty was a greater burden for her to bear. For my part, I swore to Lady Kareda Treeborn on her deathbed that I would keep her daughter safe. I had no idea what torment Nayla was subjected to until that night. I failed miserably in keeping my promise to Lady Treeborn."

Medaru released a heavy sigh as he shook his head: "The scars on her back, they were inflicted by her father?"

"Yes. I attempted to heal her wounds, but being only half Elf, she is now forced to bear the marks of Lord Treeborn's cruel treatment for the remains of her days," confided the Elf. "Since that night, I continue to be haunted by what I saw. When I looked into her eyes, it was as though her father had finally succeeded in killing her spirit, crushing her soul. All I could see was fear in that child's eyes. There was no hope, no fire, no life; only fear and emptiness."

"So, this is as much to relieve your soul of guilt as it is to redeem hers in her father's eyes," assessed Medaru.

"Lord Treeborn can be kind and compassionate to those he feels are deserving, but this show of compassion cannot be reserved to a select few. He must be made to re-think his attitude when it comes to his dealings with his own daughter," stated Joval.

"So tell me, Captain Stonecroft, what happens if you succeed in posting this warrior in Nagana only to have her father, before all, refuse to acknowledge her as his own? Are you willing to subject her to more torment and further rejection?"

"Nayla is no longer the child Lord Treeborn once knew. I have a feeling it will be she to have Lord Treeborn groveling, to have her acknowledge him as her father once she is done. Besides, I feel in my heart, unless she can be rid of her past demons, she will be forced to live a long life in self-doubt and bitterness."

Medaru dipped the nib of the quill into a small jar of indigo blue ink. "Where do I place my authorization?"

Joval pointed to the bottom, right-hand corner of the document.

Medaru obliged, etching his name on the line provided. Joval signed beneath as his witness.

"Why do I feel as though I have sealed her fate in doing so?"

wondered Medaru, setting the quill down.

"Nayla's fate is in her own hands now. And for your part, as far as Lord Treeborn and the elders are concerned, they requested that you forward your best warrior for this task. In your own heart and mind, you know Nayla Treeborn *is* the best."

Winter nipped at the heels of the army as they hastily journeyed southward. As they neared Nagana, the city received its first snowfall of the year. Joval ordered Nayla to lead the infantry into the fortress city as he, and those on horseback, rode on ahead to deliver news of their impending arrival.

Under a gentle fall of snow floating down like white confetti to greet the returning heroes, the trumpeting of horns from high atop the battlements announced their return. Nayla escorted the warriors through the west gate into the courtyard before the palace. Her men fell into line, row upon precise row before their captain, standing proudly before a throng anxiously waiting to welcome them home.

From atop the stairs of the palace the elders of Orien and Dahlon Treeborn greeted the heroes of the war, offering words of gratitude and congratulations as well as encouragement and support, particularly to the young men who had faced the enemy for the first time to return victorious. When the dignitaries were done, Joval stepped forward to add his own words of praise for one warrior in particular.

"Our request to Master Medaru Saibon the great Kagai leader to deliver his best warrior to aid in the training of our army has been granted and I am pleased to say, this very same warrior's skill and leadership aided in our victory in the battle of Magare Valley. This Kagai Warrior's unwavering determination to guide the infantry to war, to lead these young men into battle with courage and valor, and in the process, saving the lives of myself and other fellow warriors has set an example by which all warriors should live and die by. It is with great honour I present to you the daughter of Lord Dahlon Treeborn and Lady Kareda Bansho: Captain Nayla Treeborn."

Stepping forward, she knelt and bowed before the council as she drew back her hood for all to see her face.

Loud gasps of surprise filled the air as Dahlon took a faltering step back. His face blanched as though he had seen a ghost. He was absolutely mortified as he fought to remain composed. Standing before her father, the awkward silence that followed was overwhelming.

Dahlon took several slow, deliberate steps toward his daughter and then he stopped.

"You return to our city as a captain, therefore, I shall greet you accordingly," stated the senior Elf in a low, impassive tone as he bowed briskly.

Nayla merely nodded her head once in acknowledgement.

The young warrior who had been Nayla's most ardent and loyal supporter since she took command of the infantry suddenly dropped down on his knee, bowing in respect and honour. One by one, the entire army joined him in paying tribute to their captain as the elders bowed in acknowledgement to the returning daughter of this high Elf.

Nayla stood up to face her warriors. She ordered them to fall out of line upon which, friends and families rushed them, eager to greet their loved ones.

The eldest mortal of the council smiled as he personally welcomed Nayla: "Long have we and our forefathers wondered what had become of you. And never had we dreamed that we would be graced with such good fortune to have the daughter of Lord Treeborn return to our city. Tonight, there shall be a grand banquet to mark this wonderful occasion, for not only did our warriors return victorious, our daughter is now home."

Nayla's eyes turned to gaze upon her father as he stood before her. Though she remained composed, inside she was trembling, for he looked just as he did during their last hostile encounter. She gave him a small, knowing smile as she responded: "Yes, there shall be much to speak of tonight. For now, I wish to freshen up before I am to be honoured with your presence."

"Of course, Lady Treeborn, and we are the ones to feel honoured," responded the elder, guiding her up the stairs. "Your father kept your room just as it was when you had disappeared; in hopes that one day you would return."

Joval caught up to her as he made an offer: "It would please me to escort you to the banquet this evening, my lady."

"Oh, that you will do, my friend," whispered Nayla. "If I am to be subjected to delighting in my father's company, then you shall be party to this event."

"I will see you this evening, Lady Treeborn," said Joval. With a polite bow, he then whispered as he departed: "Be mindful of your manners, little warrior. Remember, do nothing that will bring dishonour to your mother's good name."

She watched as Joval turned to join Dahlon Treeborn in the meeting hall. The captain of the returning army was now to brief the high Elf of the events up north, and to deliver the agreement signed by Medaru Saibon of Nayla's posting in Nagana.

Gowns befitting the daughter of a high Elf were delivered immediately to Nayla's bedchamber on the elders' request. Lavish silk dresses arrived as the domestic staff, eager to please, hurried to ready her room. A bath was drawn and perfumed soap delivered.

Nayla sat before her dresser, watching the reflections of the staff as they went about their business. For a fleeting instance, she could have sworn she saw her mother's reflection in the mirror, smiling back at her. She shook her head and blinked hard. The apparition had dissolved as a servant approached to apologize that because of her unexpected return, there was no lady-in-waiting to assist her.

Nayla smiled in reassurance as she responded: "That will not be necessary. I am more than capable of readying myself."

"Very well, my lady. We shall be close at hand if you require our assistance."

"Thank you," she said as she closed the door behind the servant.

As she gazed about, the bed her mother once tucked her into each night, the dresser and looking glass she once sat before so her mother could comb her hair momentarily overwhelmed her with a flood of memories and raw emotions. She fought against the feeling that she was a child once more, locked into her bedchamber while Dahlon vented his wrath. And then she laughed inwardly as her eyes took in this mock shrine Dahlon had preserved in the memory of his long-lost daughter. She shook off these old feelings as she stepped into the adjoining room where a steaming tub of water awaited her.

The once-dried rose petals floating on the surface of the water released a delicate, floral scent. This fragrance filled her lungs to seduce her senses. She eagerly disrobed, stepping into the tub. The warm, inviting water engulfed her body and soul in a welcoming embrace as the days of toil and wear dissolved away from her skin and hair as she submersed herself. Her long hair floated around her, drifting lazily like dark seaweed in a tidal pool. She had no desire to leave this tub anytime soon. When she resurfaced, she relaxed against the sloping back of the tub. Her hand languidly stirred the now re-hydrated rose petals into a swirling kaleidoscope of pink and red floating before her. Here she remained until the water became lukewarm.

Wrapping a towel around her body, she peered into the wardrobe. There, a number of beautiful, silk gowns for her to select from was scrutinized by her discerning eyes. Her hands caressed the sensuous fabric, admiring the fine detailing and embroidery. As she admired the painstaking, meticulous work she could not help but notice that pushed far to the back of the wardrobe were clothes she had last worn as a child. For a moment, she was tempted to pull them out to look at them, and then she resisted, as though by doing so she would only stir up long forgotten memories that were better left to rest.

Selecting a scarlet gown with chrysanthemum blossoms beautifully embroidered throughout, Nayla tossed the long, tapered sleeve around each arm to enable her to wind the long, silk sash around her waist before reaching about to secure it in place with a bow.

Sitting before the mirror of the dresser, she picked up the wooden comb her mother once used to detangle her hair. Her eyes closed as she worked it through her damp tresses, recalling a time long ago when she enjoyed the simple pleasure of having her hair combed by her mother each night before bedtime. Nayla quickly twisted and rolled her hair up onto her head, securing her hairdo in place with ornaments adorned with tiny, silk flower blossoms. In doing so, she deliberately exposed the small but noticeable Elven points of her ears and the silver ornament that once belonged to her mother that now adorned them. Her greatest desire at this point was to make it perfectly clear to Dahlon Treeborn of who she was.

Her eyes scanned the various creams, powders and lip paints delivered by the servants. She was quick to put Yumai's teachings to work, first dusting her entire face with a fine, white powder, accentuating her large, brown eyes with the black kohl liner, and then painting her lips with a vermilion lip color. Her transformation now complete, she felt ready to meet with the council.

As she slipped her tiny feet into a pair of silk brocade sandals, she heard a loud knock on her door. Greeting the Elf at the doorway, Joval's eyes widened in surprise as he gazed upon the warrior maiden. With a pleasant smile and a gracious bow he declared: "I am here to escort Lady Nayla Treeborn to the banquet. Can you please tell her that Captain Stonecroft is here?"

"Do not tease, Joval!" she scolded the Elf as she held the door open for him to enter. "I am nervous enough without you making fun of me."

"Who said I was making fun?" responded the Elf, as he strolled into her room. "With all sincerity, I must admit you look as fetching in this gown of silk as you look fearsome in your battle raiment."

"Somehow, coming from your mouth, it did not sound like a compliment."

"Believe what you will. All I am saying is that you no longer appear to be the little ragamuffin that once haunted these corridors looking for mischief," responded Joval. He admired her elegant silk attire. "Are you ready for your audience?"

"I suppose I will be required to put on a show, so to speak," she replied, making final adjustments to her hair.

"No need to primp, you look absolutely lovely," insisted Joval, impatient to leave for the banquet.

"Tell me, Joval, you have already met with my father. What words were exchanged?"

"Truth be told, naturally he was shocked to see you and to discover that it was you who led his infantry into battle and on to victory."

"Go on. What else was said?"

"If you are asking if he was pleased with your return, in all honesty, I cannot say. We were joined by the three elders soon after, so whether his pleasure was feigned for the benefit of his company, I do not know," responded Joval.

"You know as well as I do, I was the last person he would suspect to be posted to this commission. I am as welcomed here as a rat is welcomed in a granary during a wheat famine."

"Dahlon did express his surprise that you were indeed alive after all these years. He reiterated to the elders how he had searched in vain for you after your disappearance and if you had been abducted for ransom, a request for an exchange of money for your life was never received so all assumed you had met an untimely demise."

"How convenient for him," she commented. "So tell me, how did you explain my reappearance after all this time?"

"I merely told him that I was as surprised as he was when I came across you during our initial battle that led to our trek into eastern Orien to rescue Hemashe."

"Then he knows it was me that ventured forth with you?"

"He knows now. And he did question me as to why I had not disclosed your identity when we returned to Nagana with Hemashe."

"How did you explain this matter?"

"I told your father that I was honour-bound, one warrior to another, not to reveal your identity at the time, for you felt the shock of this news would only serve to upset him."

"Was he convinced?"

"In the eyes of the elders, he certainly seemed distraught that his daughter failed to make her presence known then. They appeared to be sympathetic to his plight, offering to make this transition to unite father and daughter as easy as possible."

Nayla shook her head in disbelief and began to giggle at the absurdity of it all.

"I suppose we shall see for ourselves how welcoming he will be to his wayward daughter. Let us go."

"After you, my lady," invited Joval, opening the door for her. Arm in arm, he escorted Nayla to the great dining hall.

Illuminated by the warm glow of the many candles, the flickering flames danced off the fine china and crystal goblets gracing the silk tablecloth. As they neared the entranceway, a servant announced the arrival of Joval Stonecroft and Nayla Treeborn. The elders, Lord Treeborn and the well-heeled members of Nagana's elite all rose to welcome the honoured guests. A servant escorted them to their seats, pulling a chair out for Nayla by her father's left side. Joval took his place next to her.

As the senior member of the elders introduced Nayla to the company sharing their table, she politely nodded in acknowledgement. With this formality done with, the great room was filled with the savory aromas wafting in from the kitchen as servants delivered the epicurean delights for the feast to begin.

Nayla had little opportunity to eat as she was met with a barrage of questions from all wishing to know how she came to be in Anshen and whatever compelled her to take on the deadly vocation of a Kagai Warrior.

In response, she took great pleasure in fabricating a suspenseful yarn of her abduction from the city by two unknown and unseen assailants, and her escape from her captors after a long journey to the north. She continued on by concocting a not-so-far-fetched tale of her rescue by the Kagai Warriors as she stumbled upon Imperial Soldiers in the Hebeku Valley. As the night wore on, she concluded her tale with her acceptance into the village where the legendary Kagai Warriors dwelled and her desire to serve the people as a warrior trained in the tradition of the best fighters in Orien.

All present nodded in appreciation of her bold and noble gesture, sacrificing her life of privilege as the daughter of a high Elf to serve a greater good. Joval laughed inwardly as he listened to her tale of high adventure. The Elf only spoke when he wanted to remind those in their presence of Nayla's skills as a warrior, her ability to lead men into battle and her desire to train the next generation of warriors.

Ironically, the members of high society lavished Dahlon Treeborn with great praise for his decision to commission such a talented and courageous Kagai Warrior for this posting in Nagana. They also congratulated him on his turn of good luck that the warrior sent to do so was none other than his long-lost daughter.

The three elders on council were just as pleased as their guests. In their excitement, they would abandon the common speech, often reverting to Taijina as they addressed Nayla. They openly rejoiced at her return and Lord Treeborn's good fortune, finally being reunited with his daughter. They reminded the high Elf that the spirits that aid their God obviously kept Nayla safe, returning her only after forging her into this great warrior.

Nayla spent much of her time smiling pleasantly and nodding; listening to the conversation around her while all the time sensing a growing hostile energy emanating from her father's being. It was obvious the elders' gratitude and appreciation of her role with their military forces and more importantly, her status as the daughter of the late Lady Kareda Bansho had as much, if not more, relevance to these Taijins than the fact that she was Lord Treeborn's daughter. Though she maintained her composure throughout the evening, inwardly, she reveled in Dahlon's discomfort for indeed, he had no choice but to accept the fact that she had returned.

For Dahlon Treeborn, the unsettling knowledge that his daughter had reappeared in Nagana was a reality he was now forced to contend with. It became apparent to him that Nayla was not about to divulge the disturbing facts of his cruel treatment prior to her disappearance from the city. Perhaps it was the shame associated with being punished for *her* unruly, child-like behavior that prevented her from admitting the nature of their turbulent, violent relationship, or perhaps she elected to purge that part of her memory. Whatever the case, it was apparent his daughter was not about to speak of this.

As the night wore on, the elders marveled at the turn of events that would see Nayla's return to the fortress city, deciding that this was predestined by fate. They believed that she was guided by destiny itself to serve a greater good.

"Fortune smiled upon me when I was found by the Kagai Warriors. It was my destiny to take up arms for the cause of our people. And though I be the daughter of a high Elf, first and foremost, I am a Kagai Warrior. If it is your desire to have your men trained in the same manner, then you must keep in mind that my standing as a captain has far greater significance than my title as Lady Nayla Treeborn. I am a warrior and a captain first."

"I am sure that your request is understood and appreciated by all," agreed Dahlon, rising up from his chair. "This has been a very long day for the returning warriors and I am sure this captain is weary from her long trek, too. Before the evening goes on much further, I wish to have a word in private with Nayla before she retires for the night."

"Of course, Lord Treeborn," the senior member of the elders nodded in agreement. "It was rude of us to monopolize so much of your time in this manner. You, of all people, should have the opportunity to enjoy your daughter's company."

"Thank you for understanding, Master Sonkai" said Dahlon. "I would appreciate this moment to catch up with Nayla."

All rose to exit the room, thanking their hosts as they prepared to depart.

"No need to abandon the dining hall. Feel free to finish your food and wine at your leisure," offered Dahlon. "I shall retire into the meeting hall to speak to my daughter so there is no need to make haste."

Nayla followed behind her father, glancing back to see Joval was still seated, enjoying his wine in the company of a female guest. She entered the meeting hall as Dahlon secured the door behind them. Her eyes took in the once familiar room. This was the very chamber she was in when she confronted her father before the past elders to warn them of the plight of the battalion being sent north. Somehow, this room was now smaller than she remembered.

Dahlon sauntered over to take his place at the head of the great table.

"Sit!" ordered the Elf.

Nayla stared at him, tilting her head in disapproval of his sharp tone.

"Please," he insisted.

She sat directly across from him, noting his obvious discomfort as she now forced his hand to deal with her unexpected return.

"Never did I dream I would see your face again within the walls of this palace," stated Dahlon, his voice was devoid of emotion.

"Never did I dream I would desire to be in Nagana - in this palace again," she responded. The tone of her voice was just as impassive as his.

"I would be a fool to believe your cockamamie story. I know you ran away from this city. Now tell me, what brings you back?" growled the Elf, his caustic tone did little to intimidate her.

"Is it wrong for a daughter to want to see her father again?" she asked with a shrug of indifference.

"Do not mock me! If you mean to torment me with your presence, if you have the audacity to believe you can blackmail me with stories of my past dealings with you, you are sadly mistaken! The mortals that once worked here when you lived in Nagana are long dead. There will be none to back your claims. And if you utter one word to discredit or disgrace me, be warned now, none will believe you. It shall be the word of a murderous Kagai Warrior against that of a trusted high Elf. You may be the hero of the hour, but remember; I am known and respected by all, Taijins and Elves alike. I am Dahlon Treeborn, a high Elf, a leader to my people and a member of this council. *You* are nobody!" reminded her father, as a look of complacency settled on his face.

"For one so respected, you must be involved in far more heroic pursuits than what can be found in the field of battle. I do not recall ever seeing you lead your army to meet the enemy, in all the times I have waged war with my brother warriors," stated Nayla, leaning forward across the table to meet the intense stare of his icy, blue eyes.

"My job is to administer to the needs of this city and its people, to strategize the movements of my armies. And why I must even explain my actions and motives to you is uncalled for. I owe you nothing, I am beyond reproach!" snarled Dahlon in obvious contempt as his fist slammed down on the table to punctuate his mounting anger. "Now, I ask again. Why did you return? What do you want from me? Do you mean to bring me to my ruin?"

"The one thing I desire from you shall never be forthcoming so I shall not even bother. And my return to Nagana was not to incite your ruin, for if that is to be your fate, then *you* will be the one do so, not me. I am here because you and the elders requested my presence by asking my master, Medaru Saibon to send his best warrior," retorted Nayla.

"My conscience warns me that your true motives are merely disguised behind this purpose."

"Perhaps it is your conscience feeling the pangs of long-forgotten guilt," hissed Nayla.

"*Guilt*?" bellowed Dahlon, rising up from his chair. "I have no reason to feel guilt where you are concerned! You were deserving of every beating, of every profane word hurled at you because you were a belligerent, incorrigible child."

Nayla rose up to challenge him as he chastised her. Her eyes were unwilling to yield to his vengeful stare.

"That is what was so troubling. I was a child. Whether my behavior was deemed as belligerent and incorrigible, or brazen and foolhardy, *I* was just a *child*. *You* were the *adult*! You were the one who should have had the patience and the wisdom to deal with a child as an adult should, not as a bully and a tyrant! What grown man finds gratification in beating a child, answer me that?" she asked, her voice was now curdling with spite.

Even as she stood, the little warrior's small form was completely engulfed by his great shadow as the Elf erected himself to his full, imposing height. She leaned in closer still, almost reveling in the frenetic energy of his growing rage as it swelled like the rising tide as the realization that she was neither intimidated nor repentant became ever more apparent to Dahlon.

"In all these years you have not changed," he growled.

"I have you to thank for that. I am what you made me," she retorted as her eyes blazed.

"You wicked child! How dare you speak to me in this tone?"

"I may be wicked, but I am no longer a child. And how dare *you* speak to *me* in this tone?"

Dahlon began to tremble and his eyes grew dark with anger. Suddenly, he lunged at her. The back of his fist caught her across the face. The impact sent her crashing to the floor.

The Elf watched as Nayla's hands appeared at the top of the table as the little warrior pulled herself back onto her feet. She stubbornly shook off the pain. Her tongue tasted the blood that slowly trickled down from the corner of her mouth as her eyes locked with his once more, still refusing to be intimidated by his hateful stare. A small smile curled her lips.

"Judging by your actions, I would say that you are the one who has not changed with the passing of the years. However, this time it is *you* who fears *me*," she stated with all certainty.

"Fear you?" shouted Dahlon, as he charged toward her. "Fear a worthless, ugly, half-caste girl that was loved by none but her mother? You are as pathetic now as you were then!"

"You are the pathetic one! Look at you. Look at what you do, and what you have become. Oh no, you are most definitely the pathetic one," averred his daughter, wiping the blood away with the sleeve of her gown.

"You always thought you were so strong as a child, let us see how strong you are now, warrior maiden!" roared Dahlon.

His great hands attacked, striking her small shoulders. He easily bowled her over and yet, she made no effort to stem his assault, smashing into the chairs behind her. Once again, she rose up in defiance, standing before her father.

"What kind of warrior are you? For a Kagai you cannot even defend yourself!" grunted the Elf, in disgust as he advanced towards her.

"As a Kagai Warrior, I have a sense of honour. I will not fight you. As a father should never strike his child, a child should never raise her hand to her father!"

"What honour is there in dying without a fight? Defend yourself!" challenged Dahlon.

"Kill me if you wish, but I will never stoop to your level. I shall die first before I raise my hand to one who should be more pitied than punished."

"Pitied you say? You are the one who will be begging to be pitied when I am through with you!" snarled her father. Raising his right fist, it flew in directly to strike her face.

Nayla angled away, allowing the angry fist to skim past her cheek. Dahlon reacted by hurling his left fist to her face only to have the little warrior angle and deflect his blow. The Elf seethed in rage as his fists continued to fly at her, and each time she merely intercepted his attempts, angling away until he had her back against the wall.

Nayla stared up at her father's trembling form. His eyes were burning with unadulterated hate as he raised his fist yet again. However this time, Dahlon lunged forward with his left hand, seizing her by the throat. He pinned her against the wall as his right hand balled into a rock hard fist. Nayla braced herself for the impact, still unwilling to fight him.

"You shall beg for mercy, or you will fight!" declared Dahlon, trembling in his fury.

"There is no dignity… in doing either," she gasped as the Elf tightened his grip around her throat; raising Nayla up onto her toes as he bashed her hard against the wall.

She watched as he chambered his arm to deliver a debilitating blow when two hands seized Dahlon from behind, grabbing him by his shoulders. To her surprise, it was Joval. He wrenched her father off her to slam Dahlon into the wall. Turning the senior Elf about to face him, Joval grasped his collar, ramming him into the wall again as his forearm pressed unmercifully against Dahlon's throat.

"Lord Treeborn! What is the meaning of this?" growled Joval. He was both angered and shocked by this hostile display he was witness to.

"Unhand me, Joval!" wheezed Dahlon, struggling against his hold. He was absolutely flabbergasted by this Elf's impromptu appearance. "What happens behind closed doors between father and daughter is no concern of yours!"

"You are wrong, my lord. It *is* my concern. Though I am sworn by an oath to protect those on council, I am also bound by my duty to protect my fellow warrior," countered Joval. He glowered menacingly into Dahlon's eyes.

"Look here, Joval, you do not know what had transpired to lead up to this altercation," reasoned the senior Elf, as his attempts to palliate only served to raise Joval's ire.

"There is never a good reason to strike a lady. Of all things, my lord, a high Elf such as you should know better! There is no justification for what you subject Nayla to, not then, and not now!"

"You know…" gasped Dahlon. "Do not listen to her lies!"

He instinctively turned on Nayla only to have Joval tighten his grip as he thrust Dahlon against the wall, pinning him securely in place.

"Nayla said nothing. Long have rumors, whisperings of your ill deeds floated through the corridors of this palace. Oh yes, my lord, though your daughter attempted to spare your dignity by biting her tongue than to prattle on to others, her silence served to protect you. Did you think we could not hear your outbursts of rage? Did you think those on council could not hear your tirades as you vented your wrath upon her? For the longest time, I chose not to believe that you, a high Elf, was capable of such cruel and malicious behavior. I chose to close my eyes and turn a deaf ear to your daughter's anguish," snarled Joval. "Not anymore! This has gone on far too long. All eyes shall be watching you, my lord; watching and waiting to see how you will *welcome* your daughter into your high house. No longer can you lock her away, and no longer has she reason to protect your good name. If I were you, my lord, I would be mindful of your deeds and words where Nayla is concerned. Even if you foolishly refuse to acknowledge her as your daughter, keep in mind, she has been commissioned by the council to train your warriors."

Joval slowly released his hold as Dahlon continued to scowl in contempt at Nayla.

"Do we have an understanding, my lord?" asked Joval.

The high Elf smoothed out his ruffled attire, sweeping his long hair back into place as he regained his composure. Without a word, as though nothing out of the ordinary had just happened, he marched out of the meeting hall with a dignified air.

"Pompous, arrogant ass," grumbled Joval, muttering under his breath as he watched Dahlon calmly stroll away to rejoin his esteemed guests.

Joval turned as Nayla slowly slid down the wall, crumpling into a small heap onto the floor. Her knees were drawn up to her chest as her arms wrapped around her legs. Her forehead rested on her bent knees as her body began to tremble, and then shudder with great sobs.

Joval knelt before her, alarmed by her condition. It raced through his mind that Dahlon had somehow wounded her grievously, for never had he witnessed her cry out in pain, never shedding a single tear no matter how severe the nature of her own injury.

"Nayla, what is wrong? Did he hurt you?" asked Joval, stooping to gaze into her eyes. As he touched the crown of her head, she suddenly pulled away from his hand. "Nayla, speak to me. Are you hurt?"

"No," she answered in a quaking voice that was barely audible.

"Do not lie to me," demanded Joval, his hand slowly lifting her chin. As her eyes met his, the Elf was startled to see great tears roll down her rubicund cheeks, and the thin trail of crimson at the corner of her mouth. "What has he done? Where are you hurt?"

"I… I am fine," she whispered between her sobs.

"You are not fine, Nayla! I can see your tears," said Joval, becoming more distressed. "I can see you are hurt, there is no shame in crying. Now please, tell me where you are hurting."

She struggled to her feet as Joval's arms steadied her. "Speak to me, Nayla. What has Dahlon done to you?"

"I am not hurt, Joval."

"Come now! Speak the truth, for these tears I see are quite real."

"I do not cry in pain," she answered in a small voice. "My tears are for you."

"For me? I do not understand. I was not hurt in the altercation," stated the Elf.

"In all my life, never has anyone stood up to my father as you had. Not since my mother had anyone had the courage to step forward and put a stop to his insane tirades," replied Nayla, in a solemn voice.

"You tried to protect me from him."

Joval's heart sank as her tears flowed again. He now understood his simple act of common decency; this small show of kindness and compassion overwhelmed her, touching her to the very depth and breadth of her soul as none had ever done before. His hand touched her cheek as he gazed into her eyes. This time, there was no longer that haunting look of fear clouding her eyes, only boundless gratitude for this kind act of chivalry. His arms slowly wrapped around her small, trembling body, drawing her close to his chest as he consoled her.

"I certainly could not allow him to carry on as he did," responded Joval. "Someone had to stop him."

"That *someone* was you," she replied. Her head rested against his chest as she listened to the steady beat of his heart. As though her soul found temporary respite from the storm that raged around her, she released a weary sigh as she whispered: "Thank you."

"Let us leave this room," said Joval, his arm guiding Nayla toward the door.

"No, not like this, I cannot allow the others, the warriors, to see me like this," stated Nayla. Her small hand covered the contusion and drying blood at the corner of her mouth.

"That shall be easy enough to remedy. Sit down," ordered Joval, righting a chair that had toppled over during the violent melee.

As she sat down, the Elf knelt before her. The middle finger of his left hand gently concealed the small cut at the right corner of her mouth.

"I feel so ashamed," she whispered, fighting to hold back fresh tears.

"Why should you feel any shame?" queried Joval, deeply perturbed by her comment. "If Dahlon Treeborn had even a single shred of decency in his soul, he should be the one to feel shame, not you."

He closed his eyes and murmured an Elvish healing incantation as Nayla studied his perfect Elven features: his high, defined cheekbones and strong jaw line. It slowly dawned on her as she listened to his soothing voice that behind his usually stoic demeanor, sharp wit and large size, this Elf actually wielded a very kind and caring heart.

"There now, that is much better!" announced Joval. As his bright blue eyes sparkled in the candlelight, he smiled kindly at her.

"Thank you," she said as her finger touched the corner of her mouth that still tingled from the sensation of his healing energy.

"I shall escort you to your room," offered the Elf.

"I cannot stay here, not now."

"Are you saying that you wish to return to Anshen?" queried Joval, taken aback by her words.

"No, I mean I cannot stay here in the palace – not under the same roof as Dahlon."

"But if you leave now, Lord Treeborn will feel that he has once again crushed you, driven you out. Do not give him the satisfaction!" exclaimed the Elf.

"Joval, I know you mean well, but understand this, my first duty is that of a warrior, not as Treeborn's daughter. I am here to train your men. Whether he can accept it or not, that shall be Dahlon's problem to bear, not mine. But if I am to undertake this task, I must remain focused. I do not wish to be distracted by Dahlon's apprehensions and misgivings of my presence. I intend to honour Master Saibon and all Kagai Warriors by sharing my skills and teachings to the best of my abilities. With the coming of the spring, your men shall be prepared for war as never before. They will be a force to reckon with, even by Kagai standards. That is my first priority."

"But where will you stay?"

"If I must, I shall stay in the quarters where the warriors are housed," decided Nayla.

"I suppose that makes sense but Nayla, these quarters are designed to house the *men*. The open rooms with row upon row of cots, the less than private facilities shall drive you to distraction. And even if you are not bothered by it, the men will certainly feel ill at ease with a woman in their midst, especially one of higher rank. None of the captains dwell in these quarters and neither should you."

"Fine, then! I shall spend tonight at one of the inns, or in the stable if I must, and tomorrow I shall seek accommodations elsewhere."

"The inns will all be closed at this time of the night, and you are not spending the night in the stable with the horses, Nayla."

"Then what would you suggest, Joval?" queried Nayla. "There is no other option."

"There is one: Stay with me. You are welcome to spend tonight in my cottage," offered Joval.

"Are you positive?"

"I would not make such an offer if I was not being sincere," stated the Elf. "I shall ready our horses. Pack what you need, and then meet me in the stable."

13

the warrior way

Smothered beneath billowy drifts of snow the sparkling, white landscape reflected an eerie, bluish glow as the cold light of the moon and stars shone down from a cobalt sky. A deep quiet insulated the world as two on horseback plodded through this strange darkness from the east gate of the fortress city.

As they neared Joval's darkened cottage, the Elf ordered Nayla to dismount and take their packs in as he turned their steeds into the stable. The little warrior wandered into the Elf's cottage. It was as cold in here as it was outside as she watched her warmed breath condense into a small cloud before her as she exhaled a weary sigh.

The silver moonlight streamed in through the windows to illuminate the cottage. She easily made her way about the dim-lit room to the fireplace mantle where she quickly lit several candles and then proceeded to make a roaring fire to drive back winter's icy grip on the cottage. As the flames grew and the logs began to crackle with the intensity of the heat, Nayla removed the kettle that hung over the fire. The water had evaporated long ago. She ducked outside and quickly filled it with snow, returning to suspend the kettle over the fire.

Removing her cloak to hang on a wooden peg on the back of the door, her eyes glanced about the room. The flowers she picked to adorn the table prior to their departure about two months ago were now brown and desiccated, barely recognizable. The discolored petals lay scattered about the base of the cup. Her small hands quickly scooped up the wilted vegetation, sacrificing the crisp remains to the fire. The flames eagerly consumed the dry offering and in return, infusing the air with the faint, lingering scent of the flower's perfume.

Nayla stood before the fire, watching as the snow quickly melted as the flames licked the bottom of the kettle. She turned as Joval entered, securing the door behind him.

"Sorry for taking so long. I wanted to make sure the horses had plenty of fresh water and hay to last the night," explained the Elf, as he removed his cloak and hung it next to hers.

"I put some water on to boil. May I make some tea?" she asked meekly.

"Make yourself right at home, Nayla. In fact, I will join you," he replied, blowing the dust out from two cups before setting it down on the table. He searched in his sparse pantry until he found an earthenware jar sealed with a large cork, still half full of dried tea leaves. "Ah, here it is!"

Shaking some of the tea from the jar into the teapot, the Elf filled it with boiling water. Soon the fragrant blend of tea, barley and jasmine blossoms wafted into the air, filling the cottage with a light, floral scent like a meadow in the springtime.

"By the fire? Or at the table?" asked the Elf.

"Pardon me?" Nayla answered, as her mind jumped back to the present.

"Your tea. Would you like to drink it by the fireplace or at the table?" asked Joval, holding forth a steaming cup.

"Oh…um, by the fire," decided the little warrior. "Thank you."

He handed her both the cups as he moved two chairs in front of the fireplace, offering her a seat.

After a long silence, Joval finally spoke: "So did the events of this evening unfold as you had expected?"

"I knew from the start that Dahlon would not greet me with open arms. And yes, I knew a confrontation of sorts was imminent. However, I must admit, I was surprised he had turned on me as quickly as he had," confided Nayla, her hand subconsciously touching the corner of her mouth where she received the first blow.

"What amazed me more was your degree of self-control," replied Joval, still in awe. "In light of the fact that as a Kagai Warrior, with your skills and training, even without a sword, you could have killed Dahlon in a dozen different ways, and yet you chose not to retaliate."

"As I said to him, I was not about to stoop to his level."

"Still, I must say, even for me, I was so very mortified by Lord Treeborn's actions I could have throttled him myself," confessed the Elf, unleashing a disheartened sigh.

"I appreciate what you did for me tonight, Joval. I just hope that by intervening on my behalf, you have not jeopardized your standing in his eyes," hoped Nayla.

“I suppose we shall see what transpires over the next few days, but truth be told, at times it seems to be his way to overlook my actions.”

“So, he still holds you in the same regard as a son?”

“Right there, things are skewed. I am not his son and yet he chooses to treat me with greater kindness and courtesy than he does his own daughter. This is so wrong, Nayla. Do you feel any bitterness towards me because of this?”

“If there is any bitterness, it would be directed at him for his callous treatment, not at you. If you are the recipient of his kindness and generosity, so be it. You would be a fool not to take advantage it,” reasoned the little warrior.

“You speak with the wisdom and nobility of a high Elf,” stated Joval, as he absorbed her pragmatic words.

“I would rather think that I speak as a Kagai Warrior,” corrected Nayla, inhaling the sweet, floral scent emanating from her cup.

“Fair enough,” acknowledged Joval, with a smile as he tossed another log onto the fire. “When you are ready for sleep, you are welcome to use my bed.”

“Joval, you have been more than gracious and accommodating to me since my arrival. I do not wish to impose on you any further. I was quite comfortable in your loft when I was last here.”

“Tonight, you are a guest in my home. I would not have it any other way,” insisted the Elf.

She gazed into Joval’s eyes as she responded with an appreciative smile: “Why are you so kind to me? You know as well as I do that your promise to my mother had been fulfilled. And yet, you go above and beyond what is called for, even now. Why?”

His large shoulders arched up in a shrug as he answered: “When you are not being bossy and a know-it-all, you are actually quite tolerable.”

“Was that supposed to be a compliment?” queried the little warrior.

Under a bleak, early morning sky, Valtar dismounted from his steed and stepped up onto the stoop of Joval’s cottage. His eyes noted the two sets of footprints left in the snow. One was much smaller than the other. His eyebrows furrowed in curiosity, and then he realized that his friend must have spent the night with his mistress. Whether Joval was preoccupied, or not, with the impending light of the morning, he had no choice but to interrupt his friend. As Valtar raised his fist to knock lightly on the door, Joval suddenly appeared before him.

Valtar gave him a knowing smile as he coyly asked: “So my friend, which one is it this time?”

“That is none of your business,” stated Joval, as he hurriedly attempted to close the door behind him only to have Valtar block the way with his foot as he peered over Joval’s shoulder at the small form asleep on the bed.

Valtar’s face instantly blanched as Joval forced him from the entranceway to close the door.

“That was her! That was Nayla Treeborn!” gasped Valtar. “What is she doing in your bed?”

“Shhh!” Joval raised his hands, motioning the Elf to quiet his tone.

“Good god, Joval! What have you gotten yourself into now?” questioned Valtar.

“Let me explain,” offered Joval.

“No! Do not tell me, I do not want to know!”

“It is not what you think, Valtar.”

“What I *think* is that you have utterly and completely taken leave of your senses, Joval! Who in their right mind would bed the daughter of Lord Treeborn?” groaned Valtar, grabbing Joval by his lapel and giving him a disconcerting shake.

“Listen to me, Valtar. She had nowhere else to go last night. She is here as a guest, that is all.”

“Are you telling me that the palace was too good for her? Or was her welcome short-lived?”

“Neither,” retorted Joval, in Nayla’s defense. “She felt that to earn the respect of the warriors she is about to engage in training, it was better for her not be thought of as the daughter of a high Elf. She asked that she receive no special privileges and treatment. That means she is to distance herself from the palace and all the trappings that come with the *prestige* of being Lord Treeborn’s daughter.”

Valtar’s shoulders slumped in relief. He released an audible sigh as he cautioned his friend: “Thank goodness, Joval! You had me worried. You already risked far too much when you took her from Nagana, and now you risk even more in bringing her back. Do not make the mistake of embroiling yourself in her life. It is best to keep your distance from her as both a warrior and especially as a woman.”

“I shall take heed of your words, my friend,” promised Joval. “Now what brings you here so early in the morn? The sun has barely shown its face.”

"I was sent forth by the elders to deliver word to you that the warriors' training shall be canceled because *you know who* was missing from the palace. I suppose I shall return with word to call off the search," stated Valtar.

"Please do so, but I have a letter for you to deliver to the council and you are to see to it that Lord Treeborn reads it before the elders so there is no misunderstanding," instructed Joval, motioning Valtar to follow him back inside the cottage.

As the Elves entered, Nayla was no longer asleep in the bed. Joval snatched up a piece of parchment and a writing quill as he sat at the table to jot down a brief note. Valtar glanced about nervously, almost as though he was expecting the warrior maiden to pounce on him from out of nowhere.

Instead, Nayla casually strolled out of the adjacent room. Her face was freshly scrubbed and her long tresses, neatly braided back as she secured it in place with a short strip of leather.

"Well, good morning, gentlemen," she greeted the Elves.

"Good morning, Nayla. Did you sleep well?" asked Joval, glancing up briefly from the parchment.

"Yes, thank you," she responded politely as she stepped closer to Valtar. "Your bed was *very* comfortable!"

The Elf responded by turning away and muttering beneath his breath: "I know nothing. I see nothing."

Again she greeted Valtar in a syrupy sweet voice full of good cheer that only served to agitate him all the more: "I said *good morning*, Master Briarwood."

The Elf's brown eyes searched the ceiling of the cottage in a futile bid to ignore her as he continued to mutter: "I hear nothing. She is not here. This is but a bad dream."

She tugged at the Elf's sleeve like a small child trying to get the attention of an adult as she whispered gleefully: "If this is a bad dream to you, it is about to turn into a nightmare. Today is the first day of training with me."

Valtar glared at the little warrior as he yanked his sleeve free from her grasp.

"Nayla, please stop tormenting Valtar. He has an urgent errand to run for me," grumbled Joval. "Apparently the elders are up in arms. They think you had either mysteriously disappeared or had been *abducted* once again when the servants found your bedchamber unoccupied this morning. I am sending word that you are safe, and that you wish to seek accommodations outside of the palace during your tenure to this posting."

"And your choice of words to explain the situation?" queried Nayla, with great interest.

"I merely stated that you asked not be given preferential treatment, nor do you wish to take advantage of any special privileges offered to the daughter of a high Elf. That it is your desire to be treated with the same courtesy and respect given to all captains, thereby earning the respect of those you willingly undertake to train."

"And that is it?" queried Nayla.

"I explained that you felt by assuming all the trappings of a person of privilege, it will only hamper the training process by driving a wedge between you and the men. Instead of responding to you as Captain Treeborn, they shall regard you as *Lady* Treeborn."

"That sounds reasonable to me," responded the warrior maiden.

Joval signed and folded the parchment. Before handing it to Valtar, he dripped the molten wax from a red candle onto the parchment to seal it. As the wax began to congeal, he pressed the ring he worn on the index finger of his right hand into the wax, leaving the seal of the Stonecroft family emblem stamped on the letter.

Passing it on to Valtar, he gave him further instructions to divide the men into two groups for the training, one to begin in the morning and the second half to commence training in the afternoon. The first group was to meet in the training hall in one hour's time.

The Elf respectfully bowed in understanding, turning to leave just as Nayla called out: "Do you care to join us for a cup of tea before you go, Master Briarwood?"

Valtar stopped and momentarily cringed at the thought, and then left the cottage to deliver Joval's letter.

"This is most impressive," praised Nayla, as she paced the length of the great training hall. Her eyes scanned the high ceiling, the many weapons racks mounted to the walls, and the wooden floor so carefully crafted, there was an obvious *give,* a slight spring to the surface if a man was thrown down hard.

"Only the best training facility will do for our warriors," responded Valtar, as he proudly showed her around.

"Heated in the winter, cool during the summer," continued the Elf, pointing to two wood-burning stoves situated at opposite ends of the training halls and the push-out windows and sliding doors that allow air to circulate freely when it became too warm.

"All the comforts of home," she noted thoughtfully as she turned to the two-hundred warriors standing at attention before her. "However gentlemen, when you go to war, you shall be as far away from home as you can ever imagine. There is no heat except what burns inside you as you charge into battle. There will be no comfortable wooden floors, only unforgiving earth, and there shall be no roof to spare you from the scorching sun or the freezing rain. The Kagai Warriors do not train in such buildings. Our training is conducted outdoors, in weather fair or foul, for that is where we engage in battle. Master Briarwood, lead the men outside, into the courtyard."

The warriors exchanged suspicious glances, not knowing if her demand was serious.

"Pardon me?" asked Valtar, just as bewildered by her request. "This hall was specifically designed for training our warriors."

Nayla glanced about the great room, and then she responded: "This hall is merely a wooden structure. It is a building. And I assure you; it is not capable of doing any sort of training. *I* am here to train these men."

"You heard Captain Treeborn. Lead the men outside, Master Briarwood," ordered Joval, as he slid the doors open.

As the men filed outside, Joval leaned over and whispered to Nayla: "Though the sun shines this morn, it is still bitterly cold. The mortals shall freeze out here."

"No need for concern, Captain Stonecroft. I will not allow your men to *freeze.* In fact, they shall be so engrossed in training, they shall soon forget about the cold. It is when they stop moving and lose focus on the training that they shall feel winter's cruel bite," assured the warrior maiden. "Just trust me."

Beneath a brilliant, winter sun, braced by the cold, crisp air, Nayla strolled to the frontline to address the warriors: "Before we commence, are there any questions about my methods or practice?"

One young warrior slowly raised his right hand. There was apprehension in his eyes as he screwed up his courage to confront the new instructor.

"What do you wish to ask?" queried Nayla.

"I mean no disrespect, sir… I mean, my lady… um, captain," stammered the young man, "but how do we benefit from the wisdom of your teachings if we are too busy freezing to death. The Elf men may be able to endure this cold, but need I remind you, they do not call us humans, mortals for no reason."

"Fair enough," answered Nayla. "Just do as I do."

She removed her leather gloves and tucked them into her belt.

A voice in the crowd shouted out sarcastically: "So you wish us to suffer in the cold by compounding it with frostbite?"

"Listen to Captain Treeborn!" ordered Joval, removing his own gloves. His sharp tone was met with instant cooperation. "Do as she says!"

Raising her hands high over her head, the palms of her hands slapped sharply together. Holding them before her, the friction of her palms briskly rubbing together began to generate heat; so much so, the warriors at the frontline were surprised to see steam rising from her hand, dissolving into the frigid air.

"If you are cold, this shall warm you quickly," advised Nayla. Immediately, all the warriors raised their hands, a singular, loud clap echoed through the courtyard as the men began rubbing their palms together. As they did so, the warrior maiden continued with her instructions: "Now, close your eyes. Visualize this heat rising from your palms. See it as a ball of white hot energy growing in your hands. Now, picture a burning, hot ember, deep inside your belly. It flickers and glows, but you must fan this ember to make it into a great flame. Now, join your third finger and thumb to form rings using these rings to join your two hands. The fingertips of your remaining fingers shall come together, pointing to the heavens."

As she watched the warriors weave their fingers together to summon the energy of fire, she then instructed the men to change their breathing cycle. Demonstrating with short, sharp breaths through the nose and equally quick breaths exhaled through her mouth, she told the men to visualize their breath like a bellow, stoking life into the small ember. She asked the men to visualize this ember as it glowed and burned in intensity, erupting into a great flame. As the warriors focused on this breathing cycle, she ordered the men to picture it in their mind's eye as this internal flame crackled white-hot, their breathing fanning the fire within.

In a short span of time, the warriors were adequately warmed. She could see steam rising from their bodies as though they had just exerted a great amount of energy from strenuous exercise. They were ready for their training to commence.

"Never has a war been waged within the pristine, sterile confines of a training hall. Instead, I shall teach you how to use your surroundings and the *gifts* nature readily provides to your best advantage. The element of surprise shall be your greatest ally when you are outnumbered as we usually are. Whether you tread through grass, mud, sand or snow, you can use these elements to confuse and surprise the enemy."

Selecting the twelve men at the front line, she asked that each follow in her footsteps, placing their impressions directly over hers. As they followed, Nayla asked them to observe the single set of tracks they left behind.

"See how this gives the illusion there was only one man walking across the courtyard when in reality, twelve men had crossed over with me."

Taking the same men, she had them dash across the courtyard in a random fashion, and then she instructed them to cross the courtyard again, but this time, moving backwards. As they reached the other end, she asked them to dash forward again.

"By the tracks these men left behind, though we know it was made by only a dozen men, to the enemy, how many men do you think they believe crossed this area, twelve or thirty-six?"

The warriors nodded in understanding.

"Depending upon what you want the enemy to believe, they can be fooled into thinking they are about to take on a single man when in fact, they are about to walk into a trap of many. By the same token, they may be forced to rethink their attack if a few men gave the illusion that there are many more in their company, too many for the enemy to consider mounting an attack on."

The warriors absorbed her words, now gaining a better understanding of how the Kagai Warriors had, time after time, defeated the Imperial Armies sent forth to destroy them.

Nayla deliberately selected three of the largest warriors for the next demonstration, asking that they try to contain her.

The largest of the Taijin warriors laughed in dismay: "Captain Treeborn, spare yourself the embarrassment. It will not require the three of us to contain you!"

"If I cause embarrassment to myself, then so be it. Please, indulge my request," insisted the little warrior.

As two Elves, with the Taijin warrior between them, closed in on Nayla, the Taijin warrior lunged at her. In response, she leapt away from his grasp and rolled backwards. Unsheathing her short sword with her right hand as she rose up to her feet, she held it forth as her left hand clutched the scabbard.

All three warriors dove forward to capture her.

Once again she leapt back, but as she did so, her left hand bearing the scabbard swept out from her right to her left. The startled warriors stumbled backwards as a blinding flash of snow she had scooped into the scabbard flew into their faces. The frozen crystals stung as it struck their eyes. Hastily wiping the melting snow away from their faces, to their surprise, Nayla was gone.

The Taijin warrior yelped in astonishment, falling backwards as a small hand seized him by the scruff of his neck, easily hauling him down. She leaned over his prostrate body. The blade of her deadly sword glinted before his eyes.

"Had my scabbard been full of sand, water or blinding powder, the effects would have been the same. Again, the element of surprise, and the elements provided by nature itself, worked in my favor."

No longer wishing to bore the men with theory, she went on to the more practical aspects of warriorship: hand-to-hand combat. The warriors were asked to put aside their swords for this session.

"Unless you take to sleeping, bathing and eating with your sword as your constant companion, there will be times you are forced to fight, but a weapon may not be at your disposal. Even in the field of battle, your sword can be broken. It can be lost or your assailant may be faster and you are unable to draw in time to counter his attack. First, we shall deal with unarmed combat; and then we shall go on to armed-against-unarmed combat and, time permitting, we shall deal with multiple attackers."

Beginning with the most basic of grappling techniques, she called upon Joval to assist her. Knowing that she was well versed in break-falls and how to minimize the impact as she hit the ground, the Elf had no qualms about repeatedly picking her up and tossing her over his hip. After the warriors had ample opportunity to practice this basic hip-throw, she called upon Joval again.

Asking Joval to demonstrate the throw again, he positioned himself to toss her over his right hip. Nayla immediately sank her weight to lower her center of gravity. Her right hand pushed against the small of his back, jamming his movement so he was unable to execute the throw. The forward thrust of her right hand and the pull of her left on his back collar caused Joval to come crashing down onto his back into the well-trampled snow.

Intrigued by this move, the warriors asked to see it again.

Again, just as he attempted to execute the throw, Joval went down, just as hard as the first time.

Nayla strolled through the group, observing and instructing as the warriors applied this counter to the throw. Wishing to expand on this technique, she asked for another volunteer. None stepped up to her request until Joval gave Valtar an encouraging shove forward.

Instructing Valtar to apply the same hip-throw, the Elf was now wise to her ways. He moved swiftly to ensure that Nayla was unable to execute the same counter she had demonstrated on Joval. Valtar smiled in triumph as he easily picked up the little warrior, flipping her hard and fast over his right hip.

A loud round of surprised gasps filled the air as Nayla's right arm shot through between his legs. Her hand reached through, grasping the back of his trousers. His own momentum caused Valtar to somersault forward, landing hard on his back. Nayla merely tucked and rolled, landing squarely on his chest while holding him down in a cross-choke.

"Master Briarwood, fancy meeting you here!" she said with a broad grin as she leaned into his face. The other warriors chuckled as Joval plucked Nayla off Valtar's body. He pulled the winded Elf back onto his feet.

"Do not volunteer me for such demonstrations again," groaned Valtar, as he grasped Joval's wrist.

"We are here to set an example, Valtar. Besides, if I must subject myself to this abuse, so do *yooouu*!" shouted Joval, as he flew through the air.

Nayla had locked out his left arm high against her right shoulder and then dropping down onto her right knee, she sent the much larger Elf sprawling onto his back before her.

Valtar began to laugh at Joval as he groaned in pain.

"You are next," said Nayla, seizing Valtar by his wrist as an eager group waited for their chance to test their newfound knowledge.

Through the sun, snow and freezing rain, Nayla trained the men day after day in the outdoors. Conditioning them to endure the elements they may be made to face in the future, the warriors grew to accept this practice. As the days grew longer and warmer, she also trained the warriors to fight in the darkness of night, teaching them to move silently in the shadows as they engaged in mock battles.

Oddly enough, the warriors seemed to thrive on her abuse and the rigors of training, eager to incorporate more and more of the way of the Kagai Warrior into their own training regimen.

During this time, efforts to find appropriate accommodations for Nayla outside of the palace failed miserably. The only rooms available were situated over the public drinking establishments; hardly the appropriate place for the daughter of a high Elf or a captain of an army.

Other homes that normally boarded warriors from distant villages suddenly became unavailable when it became known whom the room was to be boarded to. It was apparent that Nayla's reputation as a rabble-rouser and pugilist, though rather unwarranted, preceded her. The good people of Nagana, as well as the citizens of the outlying villages, frowned upon her less-than-lady-like vocation. It only served to stir the imagination of young girls and rouse the fascination of young boys.

Under these trying circumstances, Joval felt compelled to share his cottage with her, renovating the small loft to provide Nayla with suitable living space and a degree of privacy.

For the warrior maiden, she found the Elf to be quite tolerant and amiable as far as Elves went. Joval became the voice of reason between she and her father while paving the way to acceptance with his more seasoned warriors, for initially they were reluctant to take instruction from a female, even if she was Lord Treeborn's daughter.

For the Elf, Joval did not mind Nayla's presence and company. He found her strangely amusing at times and at others, discovered she was capable of comments and observations that were quite profound and thought provoking. He eventually grew used to Nayla's severe looks of consternation when he'd return late after a night of carousing with Valtar and other senior ranking warriors, for he knew it was only her concern for his safety that she worried about him.

The one element of their living arrangement that was particularly disconcerting to Joval was that his privacy was severely compromised, especially when a female companion came to spend the night. On more than one occasion he had to endure the incessant groans of complaint as Nayla lay in her cot, loudly tossing in restlessness with a pillow firmly clamped over her head and around her ears to extinguish the sounds of the lovers' noisy coupling.

At other times, during the throes of passion, Joval's libido was soundly squelched by the rain of footwear, articles of clothing, and accessories that would *accidentally* fall from the loft to land at the foot of his bed. More often than not, the courtesan would dress in haste, leaving in a disgruntled huff, swearing never to return until Joval's *guest* was gone.

Despite their differences, over the course of time Joval and Nayla forged a friendship bound by mutual respect, one warrior to another. For her part, Nayla willingly took on most aspects of domestic duties; cooking, cleaning and so on in exchange that Joval be her escort when she was summoned to the palace to engage in social affairs.

Though she enjoyed dressing for these special occasions, she took no pleasure in attending these events. Her sharp ears always picked up the subtle whisperings of those Taijins and Elves who spoke respectfully to her face, but willingly exchanged disparaging remarks behind her back.

Joval appeared to detest these functions as much as Nayla did. Although he seemed to begrudge this arrangement he had with her, protesting as he was forced to don formal apparel for these events, secretly he did not mind. It allowed him to keep father and daughter at bay, thereby upholding the peace. Plus, he noticed that once Nayla was dressed in a silk gown, her hair and face done up in a feminine fashion, she also changed her demeanor from that of a feisty warrior to a well-mannered, young lady. It was actually a pleasure to be in her company during these rare times.

During the days not devoted to training, Joval would spend countless hours tutoring Nayla. In a bid to enlighten and educate her, and to make her appear less boorish in her father's eyes, Joval would teach her how to speak and write the Elvish language.

Though her grasp of Taijina and the common speech were impeccable, her working knowledge of the Elvish language suffered greatly due to the lack of use during the long years of her absence from the fortress city. Joval had made the mistake of asking Nayla to recite everything she knew in Elvish to determine her level of understanding. The most commonly used words and phrases to spew out of her mouth were liberally peppered with Elvish profanity. A barrage of expletives that would make a grown man's ears burn assaulted him. Joval knew these were merely insults permanently etched in her childhood memories; hostile, demeaning words hurled at her by Dahlon when he'd spiral into one of his many fits of rage.

Joval also shared in his knowledge of the lore and customs of the Elf-kind as well as the protocols and unspoken rules used in the palace and in dealing with the members of society and the council. Though he could see her reluctance to embrace her Elven heritage, he could also see how quickly she absorbed the information he shared with her. As driven as she was to be a great warrior, he could tell she was just as determined to master the language and learn of the customs of his people, no doubt to her father's chagrin.

One spring day as he and Nayla returned from studies down by the edge of the lake, they crossed the meadow leading back to his cottage. The lush, green grasses splashed with the vibrant colors of wild flowers gave promise of an early end to the winter. The bright yellow butterflies with delicate wings accented with a spot of black burst from their chrysalis. Prompted by the warming weather, the winged insects emerged from their winter slumber to fly low over the meadows in search of nectar and a mate. With child-like abandon, Nayla bounded like a graceful deer through the tall grasses and flowers, gazing skyward as the butterflies fluttered away upon her approach.

Joval watched in fascination as this hardened warrior's eyes sparkled with delight. She opened her arms to her sides as she twirled beneath the yellow cloud of wings floating above her. For a moment, there was an innocence about her that startled the Elf. Perhaps Dahlon had not fully succeeded in crushing the child out of her soul after all. He laughed as Nayla collapsed to the ground, dizzy with her spinning. She instantly disappeared in the grasses as she went down.

"Come, Nayla! There is much to be done. Let us be on our way. We have a banquet to ready for," called Joval, as he waded through the tall grasses. He stared down at the ground only to find that she was gone.

"Nayla?" he called, kneeling down to better examine the ground for her small impressions.

She leapt out from behind him, bowling Joval over to send the books, parchment and inkwell flying from his hands.

"Why you incorrigible, little ruffian!" scolded the Elf, as he struggled to sit upright, laughing that he allowed himself to be set up in this manner.

"Shame on you, Captain Stonecroft!" she gleefully chided him as he rolled to his side to dump her to the ground. "I cannot believe you allowed yourself to be ambushed in this manner."

"You caught me off guard," protested Joval. "We were engaged in mental exercises, not in physical training."

"As a warrior, you know you should always be aware of the possibility of attack," cautioned the warrior maiden, "especially when I am about."

"Yes, *especially* when you are about," agreed the Elf, as he gathered the study materials. He released a dreary sigh as he picked up the inkwell. The cork seal had popped off when it hit the ground, spilling out half the ink. "Look at this mess."

The indigo blue ink spread from the side of the inkwell onto his hand as he examined the remaining contents.

"Sorry," said Nayla. Her voice was meek and contrite as she picked up the cork seal to place it back onto the inkwell he held forth. "Yuck! It is sticky!"

She glanced at the blue ink staining her fingertips, and then, a mischievous grin curled her lips.

"Take that!" she exclaimed, her fingers flashing out to smear the ink onto Joval's face.

The Elf was momentarily stunned by her childish behavior. She began to giggle as she examined the blue ink liberally smudged across his left cheek and the bridge of his nose.

"I am not amused, Nayla," grumbled Joval, frowning in disapproval of her conduct.

"Oh, you would be if you could see yourself now!" she laughed heartily.

"Believe me, this is not amusing at all," denounced the Elf. "However, *this* is amusing!"

He dropped the inkwell to smear the dark residue on his fingers onto her forehead and down her little nose. He began to chuckle as Nayla sat before him with a stunned expression on her own face.

"I suggest you close your mouth before a bee flies into it!" laughed Joval, as her mouth gaped open in disbelief. "Ha! It would appear that this time, you were the one to be taken by surprise!"

Nayla's eyes opened wide in horror as she gasped, her gaze shooting over Joval's left shoulder. The Elf instinctively turned to see what had caught her attention, quickly glancing behind him. As his eyes scanned the tall grasses, he could see nothing of danger. Turning his head about to face Nayla again, she squealed with delight as her fingers accosted his right cheek, generously smearing more ink onto his face.

"Ha! Now it matches the left side!"

"What is the matter with you?" scolded Joval.

"With *me*? I am not the one with ink all over my face!" giggled Nayla, as she stood up to abandon the flabbergasted Elf.

"Well, I can remedy that!" countered Joval.

Just as Nayla turned away to head back to the cottage, Joval seized her by the ankle. She tripped, stumbling forward. Instinctively, her hands flew in front to break her fall. Rolling onto her back to confront her assailant, Joval moved swiftly. His stained fingers went straight to her face. Using both her hands to fend off his colorful assault, she began laughing uncontrollably. In this weakened state, it was easy for the Elf to pin her tiny wrists together with his left hand as his right hand set to work smudging big, blue *freckles* across her cheeks.

He leaned in close to her face as he studied his handiwork. Satisfied with the revenge he had exacted, Joval began to laugh at her. By this time, Nayla was laughing so hard, tears streamed down from the corners of her eyes. Joval lay on top of her, taking in the hilarity of the moment and feeling the rush of exuberant energy emanating from her smile.

"I surrender! Truce! Let us call a truce," begged Nayla, fearing that he would tickle her as she lay pinned to the ground. "Accept my offering of peace."

Reaching over, she plucked a single stem of forget-me-nots growing amidst the shade of the tall grasses.

"Is this the best you can do?" snorted the Elf, in feigned disgust. "Say something nice to me!"

He leaned in close to her face, his fingers poised to continue his artistic assault.

"You have… You have…" gasped Nayla, struggling to squeeze the words out during this fit of laughter.

"I am waiting," stated Joval, pretending to become impatient with her.

She thrust the tiny cluster of blue flowers into his face as she declared: "You have beautiful, blue eyes, like these flowers!"

Joval was momentarily taken aback by her compliment. He was expecting a wisecrack, an insult, or a facetious remark – not a compliment. He stared into her deep brown eyes that sparkled with life. As he gazed into her soul, he could see that she was like a multi-faceted gemstone. From whatever angle he gazed upon her, he saw something new and different. She was a seasoned warrior, but she was also a woman. She exuded incredible strength and yet, there was a vulnerability to her. She was a skilled and commanding leader and still, she had the innocence of a young child. She was truly an enigma.

"Do you mind getting off of me," asked Nayla, bouncing the sprig of dainty flowers against his nose.

Her words went unheeded as Joval continued to stare into her eyes.

"Hel-lo! Can you hear me? Is there anybody home?" she asked as her finger tapped on his forehead.

"Pardon me?" asked the Elf. Her words seemed to echo from the distance.

"You are crushing me, you big brute!" laughed Nayla, squirming beneath him.

"Oh! I am sorry!" the Elf apologized, quickly rolling off of her body.

He proceeded to gather the books and parchment from her studies as Nayla secured the lid of the inkwell.

As they both stood up, they turned to look upon each other in silence. Both warriors were liberally smudged and smeared with dark blue ink all over their faces. All attempts to regain their composure fell to the wayside as Joval and Nayla burst out laughing once more.

"This is much better!" exclaimed the little warrior.

"What is better?"

"You! Your demeanor," she answered. "You do not smile and laugh often enough."

"I usually do not have anything to smile or laugh about," responded the Elf, wiping his face with the back of his hand.

"I would not do that if I were you," recommended Nayla. "It will only serve to spread that ink all the more."

"Damn it!" cursed the Elf, as he examined the back of his stained hand.

Nayla began to briskly walk away from the Elf. She headed straight to the cottage.

"Where do you think you are going in such a hurry?" Joval called out.

"I wish not to hear foul words spout from that mouth of yours," she shouted back, placing greater distance between her and the Elf.

"Sorry! I shall watch my language," promised Joval.

"I do not think so, not when I tell you that there was only a small slip of soap left. There is only enough to clean the first person who can get to it," she announced as she raced away from him. "And that would be me!"

Joval groaned as the realization the banquet to be hosted by Dahlon and the elders was to commence in a few hours.

"Come back here!" he demanded as he gave chase.

His much larger strides allowed him to almost catch up to Nayla. She dashed up the stoop of the cottage and as Joval raced up close behind, she soundly slammed the door in his face. He could hear her laughing in triumph as she fled to the backroom, dancing about with the last bit of soap in her hand.

Joval burst into the cottage, racing to the secured door. The thick planks of wood bounced and reverberated as he pounded hard, shouting his displeasure: "Nayla, open this bloody door this instant!"

"Sorry, busy washing up!"

"Nayla! You better not use up all that soap or you *will* be sorry!"

"Soap? What soap? There is no soap!"

"Come now, Nayla! Open this door!"

He could hear her giggling as water splashed about in the washbasin. "See here, Nayla, if you do not spare me some soap, then I shall not spare you my time. You can go to the banquet on your own."

His threat was followed by profound silence. The door promptly opened and before him, the little warrior gazed up at the Elf. Joval's eyes widened in surprise as he began to laugh. The obvious smudges and splotches of indigo blue ink were now spread evenly across her face, from ear to ear. In an attempt to wash the ink away, she only served to dilute it, spreading it across her entire face.

"It is not coming off," she said in a small voice.

"Serves you bloody right!" snorted the Elf, with a laugh. He was unsympathetic to her plight.

Joval tipped away the blue tinted water Nayla had washed with. Topping up the basin, he quickly splashed his face with the clean, tepid water. Taking what little soap remained, he began to scrub. As the water turned an ever-darkening tint of blue, he gazed into the looking glass. The large, obvious splotches of ink gave way to spread across his entire face, bathing it in a pale shade of blue. The Elf's efforts became more frantic as he scrubbed in vain.

"See! I told you it was not coming off," chided Nayla, peering at his reflection in the mirror.

"Well is this not grand? Look what you have done!"

"I warned you this would happen, but would you listen to me? No!" groaned the little warrior.

"We are expected at a banquet in a few short hours. We cannot appear before the council and the guests like this!"

Joval tipped away the tainted water, topping up the basin again as both jockeyed for position to wash and grapple control for the last wafer of soap.

After several more attempts, until the soap had all but dissolved, both Nayla and Joval were still looking a pale tint of blue, giving their skin a rather sickly pallor.

"This is not good. How do we explain this to everyone?" asked the Elf, blotting his face on a stained towel.

"Why are you so concerned? At least your skin tone goes quite nicely with those blue eyes of yours!" commented Nayla. Her mischievous smile caused her teeth to flash unnaturally white against the hue of her tinted skin.

Under the warm glow of candlelight, Nayla and Joval received the guests in the great dining hall. They stood side by side, greeting the members of high society as the elders and Dahlon looked on with concern as their distinguished guests pretended they did not notice their unusual skin tone.

Even under a dusting of face powder, Nayla's skin was still an ever-so-pale tint of blue. After the guests paraded through, Dahlon approached Joval, questioning the captain: "What is going on here? You both look sickly."

"We are feeling a bit under the weather, my lord, a little *blue* you might say," answered Nayla, speaking with all seriousness.

Dahlon frowned at his daughter as he whispered: "You might fall to illness, but Joval does not. What happened?"

"Nothing really, my lord," answered Joval. "It was nothing more than an unfortunate mishap with some spilled ink."

Dahlon's eyebrows arched up in dismay.

"Mishap or not, I do not expect the captains of my army to appear in public looking… looking… blue!" stammered the Elf, as he attempted to stifle his angry tone.

"Then may we be dismissed from this function?" Nayla asked hopefully.

"Not on your life," her father growled beneath his breath as he nodded at his guests strolling by to take their place at the table. "I shall have the servants remove some of the candles where you two sit. And if this *mishap* should ever happen again, both of you will be banned from attending such functions."

"Understood, my lord," answered Joval, with a contrite bow of acknowledgement as Dahlon turned away to join his guests.

"Have we anymore ink left?" asked Nayla in a whisper, smiling up at the Elf as his eyes rolled in dismay.

As the days grew longer, Nayla devoted more and more of her time to training the warriors. This was not so much because the men required more work, but because they took great pleasure in learning from this Kagai Warrior. The training was hard and rigorous, but it was her approach of encouraging rather than badgering; offering constructive advice rather than criticism; and training for the sheer joy of movement that motivated these men. There was also an added reward: the sense of empowerment bestowed to those with the patience to learn the Kagai ways. They were driven to do better, to excel so they can achieve their own level of personal excellence.

Though smaller in stature than all of the Taijin men and dwarfed by the Elven warriors, Nayla still issued a powerful presence. Her life force was so overwhelming at times many could sense her approach before even setting eyes on her. Her small size served as inspiration to the young, still-growing adolescent males who grappled with their teenaged awkwardness as they struggled to find their place amongst the seasoned warriors.

Nayla instilled in them that size was not a determining factor in one's ability to defeat the enemy. They admired her flowing movements and the ease with which she dealt with her opponents. Though her skills and training methods raised the eyebrows of more than a few of the experienced warriors, in due time she had earned the respect of all the men. Those who unwittingly or foolishly insisted on challenging or scoffing her methods did not have to deal with the wrath of her words. Her actions spoke volumes, as the men were soundly humbled before those who knew better than to question her abilities.

Though it seemed harsh to publicly humiliate the nay-sayers, Nayla knew these men could not be swayed by mere words. It was only through her deeds and actions did they finally come to understand the true essence of her teachings.

Each training day found Nayla to be the first to arrive in the morning and the last to leave in the evening. As the warriors dispersed, Nayla remained behind to make sure all the training weapons were stored away in their proper place. It was during these moments of solitude did she take the opportunity to practice the lesser known weapons used by the Kagai Warriors such as the throwing darts, the iron fan and inoffensive items such as a simple wooden staff that would double as a benign walking stick and a deadly striking tool.

Nayla's eyes were closed as she parried and countered an invisible foe, striking and thrusting with the three-foot staff. As she moved and visualized her assailant, an unmistakable surge of energy could be felt at the entranceway to the training hall.

Joval Stonecroft, she thought as she turned to face the source of this powerful life force.

There stood the Elf. He gave her a smile as she ceased her exercise. "What was that you were doing?"

"It is easier to show than to explain with words," answered Nayla.

"Then show me," insisted Joval, stepping closer.

"Very well. Try to punch or grab me," ordered the warrior maiden, inviting an assault.

Joval swung out to punch with his right fist, only to have Nayla angle away and strike his biceps with the tip of the staff. Her strike was timed and so precise, allowing him to basically run into the staff, jamming into it so the hard tip separated the muscles and struck down to the bone. The resulting shockwave that coursed through his arm and into his body was immediate and painful.

Undeterred, Joval swung out with his left fist. Again, Nayla angled back and struck his left biceps, effectively jarring his senses as wood met with bone.

Changing his strategy, the Elf pivoted towards Nayla, seizing her by the lapels of her vest. He smiled in victory as he pulled the little warrior toward him so she was unable to strike out with her weapon.

The wooden staff she held in her right hand passed under Joval's arms, coming up and over top. Her left hand crossed her right beneath the Elf's arms, catching the staff so his wrists were now trapped between her own wrists as the wooden staff bit into his flesh and ground into his wrist bones from over top.

Joval grimaced in pain as Nayla suddenly rammed the staff horizontally across his chest, thrusting the Elf against the wall and effectively pinning him.

"That was most painful," groaned Joval, as the little warrior held him against the wall. She looked quite pleased with the execution of her technique. "May I try?"

"Would you like me to demonstrate again?" she offered.

"Oh no, that will not be necessary. I do believe I got the gist of it," stated the Elf.

Nayla mimicked Joval's moves, first punching with her right, then her left and then seizing the Elf by the lapels of his vest. She cringed, wincing in pain as Joval countered with the same speed and impact as she used on him.

"Not bad," complimented Nayla, as Joval pressed her against the wall, the staff pinning her high across her chest and shoulders.

She placed her hands on the staff to either side of the Elf's hands, attempting to push him off.

"Not bad? I would say that I did pretty darn good," gloated Joval, with obvious pride as he leaned in close to make sure the little warrior was not going anywhere.

"It was not bad," reiterated Nayla, less than generous with her compliment.

"That is not what I wanted to hear," said Joval, with a laugh. "I believe you are now at my mercy. Say it; tell me how good I did."

"You force me to lie just to feed your over-inflated ego? Never!" protested Nayla, as she did her best to look indignant.

She gazed up at the large Elf as he leaned in closer still to meet her eyes. "Admit it! I did *very* well!"

"Yes, you did very well," conceded Nayla, she batted her long, dark lashes as she stared into Joval's bright, blue eyes.

He found her innocent, fawn-like expression, those dark, soulful eyes blinking back at him totally disarming. She looked rather helpless pinned to the wall. As he gazed into her eyes, he felt his soul being seduced into these deep, limpid pools. He felt his heart begin to race as his gaze fell upon her soft, full lips that seemed to pout in surrender. He slowly leaned closer; his lips hovered over hers as he wrestled with an irresistible desire to kiss Nayla. Just as his lips could feel the warm, magnetic draw of her mouth to his, he released a loud bellow of pain.

Using the instep of her right boot, she raked it down the front of his left shin. Catching Joval completely off guard, Nayla's grip on the staff changed. Allowing her left arm to fold in, it caused the Elf to suddenly tilt to his right. Nayla's right arm rose, pushing toward Joval as his weight shifted and his balance was broken. She easily pivoted, using his own weight and momentum exerted by his pressure to slam him into the wall. The warrior maiden knew instantly that Joval's greater size and strength would easily push her off. Still grasping the staff, she sank to the floor, placing her right foot against his left hip. As easily as sitting down, she threw her arms up simultaneously, heaving him up and over her body so he landed flat on his back.

In his attempt to wrestle the staff away from her, Joval had a death-grip on the piece of wood so Nayla merely used his momentum to deliver her as she rolled over him. As she landed on his chest, she made no effort to soften the blow as she deliberately and forcefully landed on him, knocking the wind out of the Elf. With a self-satisfied grin, she leaned into the Elf's face and began to laugh.

"That was not fair!" protested Joval, gasping for his breath.

"In war, nothing is fair," reminded the warrior maiden, unmoved by his sentiment.

"Need I remind you, we are not at war, nor am I the enemy,"

countered the Elf.

"You are just sore that I beat you and beat you good!" teased Nayla, as she laughed.

"Fine! If that is the attitude you wish to take and you choose not to fight fairly, then neither will I!" declared Joval, as he rolled to his side to pitch Nayla off his body. She crumpled into a heap, overcome by a fit of laughter as the Elf pounced on top of her. "Now you are in *big* trouble!"

He began to tickle her with a vengeance as she shrieked and laughed at the same time.

"Ha! The warrior maiden has a weakness after all! She can be defeated!" declared Joval. He knew he had the upper hand as Nayla thrashed and struggled, weakened by her own laughter. "I will show you no mercy!"

Nayla was rendered completely helpless, tears rolled from her eyes as she fought desperately to curb her urge to surrender to the Elf's brand of punishment. Both came to an abrupt halt when they took notice of a dark pair of boots standing only a few feet away from them, the toe of one boot tapping impatiently on the wooden floor.

"Ah-hem!" Valtar grunted loudly as he frowned in disgust, his arms folded across his chest in disapproval. "What is this? Can it be a new form of torture to extract vital information from the enemy?"

"Forgive me, Valtar," Joval apologized as he pulled the still-giggling Nayla to her feet. "Someone was in dire need of a lesson. We got a little carried away; that is all."

"I can see that," he muttered, making no effort to hide his disdain. "I come with word from Lord Treeborn. He wishes to see the both of you immediately. We have been called to war."

14

a season of war

Nayla and Joval knelt, bowing before the members of council before taking their place at the table.

"The early spring brings with it yet another season of war," announced Dahlon Treeborn. "Though word of an incursion from the east have yet to be verified, those who oppose the rule have sent words of warning that the Sorcerer continues to conspire and manipulate those in power."

"So we are to act on unsubstantiated rumors?" queried Joval.

"Our eyes in the east state that notification of conscription had been issued to every village and town in eastern Orien. Every able-bodied man, young and old, capable of wielding arms have been called to war. Even as we speak, the armies mass in Keso, Hegashe and Hetai. There is no doubt there shall be war on a grand scale. It is only a question of when the Emperor will deploy his armies," stated Dahlon, his fingers pointing to these places on the map set before them.

"So when are we to depart?" asked Joval.

"How soon can your men be ready?" questioned Dahlon.

"If the Imperial Army has yet to set forth, there is no apparent rush," reasoned Joval. "We can easily be ready to move by the fortnight, if not sooner."

Nayla rose up from her chair to address those present: "I mean no disrespect to Captain Stonecroft, but it would be my recommendation that we move out immediately."

"I was not asking for *your* recommendation," growled Dahlon, leaning forward to glare at his daughter.

"Then why was I summoned to this meeting?" she asked tersely.

Joval raised his hands for calm.

"Lord Treeborn, I would like to hear Nayla's reasoning for this," interjected Joval; "as I am sure the elders would like to consider her words, too."

The three mortals nodded in agreement, forcing the high Elf to slowly recline in his chair and listen to his daughter.

"There is no reason we cannot leave earlier, even in a day or two," stated Nayla. "If we are called to war, let us not race to arms at the last minute, arriving with men exhausted by the long trek. Whereby the Elven warriors can travel long and tirelessly, the Taijin warriors cannot."

"What does it matter as long as they arrive in time to do battle?" grunted Dahlon, dismissing her words.

"I have no doubt we shall be greatly outnumbered again. Let us have the advantage of rested troops ready to engage in battle," responded Nayla. "Our early arrival shall allow us to work closely with Master Saibon's people to build better snares and traps to aid in the defeat of the enemy. In fact, I would recommend leaving only a small force here to secure the fortress city while the rest of the army ventures northward to take residence in the Hebeku Valley until the turning of the leaves. Your warriors shall return before the coming of the winter."

The elders conversed amongst themselves in Taijina, carefully considering the little warrior's words."

"Lord Treeborn, perhaps your daughter is wise to make such a suggestion. It must be tiring for the warriors to make this journey to and fro," said one of the elders.

"Perhaps it is better to allow our army to take residence up north while the possibility of war looms before us. All evidence points to the fact that none, not even the Sorcerer is aware of the secret pass through Borai Mountain. This being the case, a small show of force here in Nagana shall suffice," stated the senior member of the council. "Besides, if the Emperor is intent on conscripting the citizens of eastern Orien to do war, I have no doubt Eldred Firestaff shall orchestrate wave after wave of assault on our lands."

Dahlon was pensive as his fingers thoughtfully rubbed his chin as he mulled over this suggestion.

"Where before, we have maintained half our troops in this city, sending forward and replacing men as need be, it is apparent from the growing number of soldiers being sent from the east, it would better serve us to move as many men as we can afford, to do battle alongside with the Kagai Warriors," determined Dahlon. "Let us take heed of Captain Stonecroft's sage advice. We shall move our army northward. They will leave the day after tomorrow!"

"It was your daughter's- " Before Joval could finish his sentence;

Dahlon raised his hand for silence.

"Prepare your warriors, Captain Stonecroft. See that they are ready to go to war," ordered Dahlon.

Under a somber morning sky, the citizens gathered to see the warriors off. Many families wept as young men, prepared to serve and die for the cause, marched off to war for the first and what could be their last time. Joval Stonecroft escorted the warriors on horseback through the west gate as Nayla Treeborn led the infantry consisting of the new recruits and young warriors that have already seen war by Nayla's side. Although three warriors on steeds accompanied the infantry, Nayla chose to march with her men, setting the pace for their long, grueling exodus from the fortress city.

As they passed through the west gate and onward along Esshu Road, the cherry trees lining the way swayed in the gentle brace of a zephyr wind. Their branches, though still bare of foliage, were laden with dense clusters of pink blossoms. Nayla breathed in the delicate perfume mingling in the air. She savored this floral scent for soon it would be replaced with the malignant odors of war; of the blood and sweat spilled in the heat of battle. Her eyes gazed skyward as papery, pink petals floated down, swirling and fluttering in the invisible breeze like a gentle, pink snowfall.

Glancing back at the men in her company, she felt confident these warriors were better prepared than their predecessors to do battle against the enemy. Within four short, intense months, Nayla had the warriors of Orien trained. They were well versed in all aspects of warfare, even engaging in mock ambushes and learning to fight in the close confines of the forest as they may be forced to do so once they are engaged in battle. Whatever the outcome, she and the men were ready to meet their fate. With Joval and those on horseback charging on ahead, the infantry moved at a steady, determined pace to their final destination to the north.

With the summer solstice still a month away, Nayla and the warriors of the infantry made good timing, taking advantage of the lengthening hours of daylight. As Esshu Road gradually deteriorated until it became nothing more than a foot trail, the warrior maiden escorted the men into Hebeku Valley just west of Anshen.

As they entered the deepening forest, her sharp eyes watched for signs of movement. She raised her hand. Without a word, the men immediately came to a halt, silently waiting for her orders.

Her keen ears listened. There was an unnatural hush that settled on the lands; the sounds of beasts and birds were stifled. It was much too quiet. With a flash of her hand, the warriors armed their bows, staggered their lines as those at the front dropped down on one knee below the line of fire of those behind them.

There was a very real possibility that enemy soldiers were in the area. Nayla's hands cupped her mouth as she whistled. For a long moment, she listened. Finally, in the distance to the northeast, a whistle responded to her call. She motioned for the men to put away their weapons and to advance.

Following the sounds of the whistle, it took them towards the Reyu River. Through the forest, Nayla could hear the sound of horses approaching quickly, the dappled sunlight streaming through the tree canopy made it difficult to ascertain how many moved in their direction.

"Captain Treeborn, this is most unexpected! We did not think that you would be arriving for another three days!" shouted a familiar voice.

Nayla was pleased to see Joval coming through the forest to meet them. In his company were Valtar, Medaru and Keodai.

"Takaro!" shouted Keodai, excited to see her again as he leapt from his saddle and ran to greet her with an exuberant hug. "It is good to see you again!"

She embraced Keodai in a warm hug reserved for family, pleased to see her brother warrior.

"You are looking well, Takaro! Life in Nagana must agree with you," commented Medaru, giving her a welcoming embrace as she rose up after bowing in respect to her master.

"In my heart, Anshen will always be home to me. I am only bound to Nagana by duty," replied the little warrior.

For the first time she noticed Medaru was beginning to show signs of his age. Though he still moved with the same confidence and grace as he always did, his black hair was now markedly gray, his face was now creased with more obvious lines and the fire in his eyes seemed somewhat dimmed.

"It is good to be with family again," greeted Nayla. "Have you been well, master?"

"As well as this mortal body can be as I approach the autumn of my life," answered Medaru, with an affable smile. "You on the other hand have not aged a day in all this time."

"Sometimes it is more a curse than a blessing, master," she answered resolutely.

"Nayla, you made excellent time. We are surprised to see you so soon," stated Joval, as he dismounted from his steed. He handed the reins to Valtar so he could walk alongside the little warrior. "I take it; all went well during this trek."

"Your men are fit and in good spirits," she responded, motioning the warriors to follow. "And for you, how was your journey?"

"Aside from one horse falling lame, it was thankfully uneventful," replied the Elf. "I must say, we were pleasantly surprised for when we arrived, Master Saibon and his men were already busy constructing shelters for our warriors in this forest."

"Yes, we received word from Lord Treeborn of his intention to station an army in this valley during the months that bring enemy incursions to western Orien. It makes good sense for these warriors to remain here for the duration than to make this long and arduous trek several times a year," attested Medaru. "Lord Treeborn was wise to make this decision."

Nayla and Joval exchanged glances, laughing inwardly, for both knew who made this original suggestion. In his typical fashion, Dahlon was credited for this idea.

Not far from the Reyu River, a seasonal camp had been constructed to house the warriors. Though the shelters were simple, they would provide this army with adequate protection from the elements and a readily accessible supply of fresh water, game and fish as well as firewood. The location of this temporary settlement placed these warriors less about one league away from the village of Anshen.

As the infantry poured into this encampment, their fellow warriors that had made the journey with Joval greeted them. Nayla breathed a sigh of relief as it became clear that the young warriors would now have time to adjust to their new surroundings; have the opportunity to work first hand with the Kagai Warriors; and to be well rested when they are finally called upon to take up arms.

"Will you be residing in Anshen during this time, Takaro?" queried Medaru.

"No, I wish to stay with the men I am responsible for."

"I understand," nodded her master.

"Takaro, you must come this night. I am an uncle now!" declared Keodai, eager to show off his infant nephew.

"Yumai had her baby?" asked Nayla.

"Yes! Almost two months ago now," stated Keodai. "She gave birth to a healthy boy!"

She gave Medaru a congratulatory pat of his shoulder. "So you are now a grandfather, master."

"Oh yes, this is long overdue! But soon I shall be doubly blessed for Keodai's wife is due to give birth in about three months," said Medaru.

"You are going to be a father, Keodai?" asked Nayla, excitedly.

Keodai's proud smile said it all as he nodded in confirmation. The little warrior gave him a warm, congratulatory hug.

"And your wife, who is she? Do I know her?"

"You shall meet her tonight. She is not from Anshen. She is from Saijun," explained Keodai. "Apparently, she said her brother knows you, that he was trained to fight by you."

"I cannot wait to meet her and to see Yumai's baby. She must be so pleased," said the little warrior.

"Indeed, Yumai and Hemashe are both very proud of their son," stated Keodai.

Nayla's smile slowly dissolved upon hearing Hemashe's name.

"Enough about babies and such," said Medaru, wishing to change the subject as pangs of guilt over his involvement to end Takaro and Hemashe's relationship resurfaced. "How is life in the great city, my child?"

"It is a city. How great it is, is a matter of opinion, master. I choose to reside outside the walls of Nagana."

"You do not dwell in the palace?" asked Medaru, his brows furrowed in concern.

"I prefer the tranquility of the forest than to be surrounded by stone, brick and mortar," she explained.

Medaru glanced over at Joval, only to have the Elf avert his eyes from his questioning stare. The old warrior knew immediately that she was only telling him half the truth.

"Lord Treeborn did not respond to your return as you had hoped," determined Medaru.

"He responded just as I had anticipated," she replied, her gaze falling to the ground.

Though Nayla remained untouched with the passing of time, so much had changed in Anshen. Since she departed to live outside of Saijun two years ago, and then moved on to Nagana, what would have amounted to nothing more than a blink of an eye by Elven standards, the mortals of this little village marked this brief passage of time living, aging, dying and being born. Many, if not all, of the young men who had set off to war for the first time with this warrior maiden, Keodai and Hemashe included, were now married with families of their own.

All around her, the laughter and delightful squeals of children and toddlers at play and the ravenous cries of babies demanding to be fed, filled the evening air as Medaru played host to a gathering in honour of Nayla's return and to welcome Captain Joval Stonecroft.

"So Takaro, have you adjusted well to life with your kind?" asked Mekai.

"My kind?" queried Nayla, staring at the large Kagai.

"Yes, the Elves," the bully of a warrior responded.

"I am as much an Elf as I am a mortal. There is none of my *kind,* as you so eloquently put it, to be had."

"I figured by now there would be other *half-castes* such as yourself roaming the countryside," stated Mekai, shrugging with indifference.

Joval's head tilted ever so slightly. His eyes narrowed in suspicion as he scrutinized the large Taijin warrior as he blatantly accosted Nayla with his words. Nayla could not tell if it was a look of contempt or pity that was etched across this Elf's face.

Joval leaned over to Nayla as he whispered: "He seems a rather ignorant sod. Is he a moron or is he just inebriated?"

"I am afraid he is a little bit of both," whispered Nayla, almost apologetically. "It is rumored that Mekai has taken one too many blows to his head, maybe even some that were self-inflicted."

Medaru shook his head, embarrassed by this mortal warrior's dim-witted comments.

"It is nice to know how some things do not change with the passing of time," stated Nayla, as she stared at the stocky warrior.

"How so?" asked Mekai.

"Where you have matured physically; your mind has yet to catch up with your body. You are still as boorish and as insensitive as ever!" noted Nayla, whose comment was met with a round of laughter.

Mekai had indeed grown greater in brawn, but his pea-sized brain seemed to selectively decipher only Nayla's comment of his *mature physique*. He proudly puffed out his barrel chest and flexed his great biceps for all to admire as he gloated: "Oh yes, one look at me and the enemy quake in fear and the women swoon with desire!"

"What women?" Mekai's wife demanded to know as she hurled a chunk of bread at her husband.

The great warrior seemed to shrink into the crowd, cowering more from her shrewd glare than the laughter that ensued as the bread she threw bounced off his forehead, leaving behind a small smear of butter.

"I suggest you bite your tongue lest you meet with the wrath of your dear wife," cautioned Medaru. "The nights are still rather cool to be forced from your bed, if you get my meaning?"

Mekai nodded meekly, wiping away his embarrassment with his sleeve.

Nayla gazed up as the crowd parted, allowing Yumai and Hemashe to step forward. Yumai greeted the little warrior with a warm hug as she thanked her: "Because of you, my son has a father to see him through the years."

Hemashe smiled as he proudly placed the small baby in Nayla's arms. He gave her a grateful hug as she cradled the tiny infant.

In her heart, she was so very pleased for Yumai and Hemashe, and yet, deep down, Nayla could not help but feel the cruel sting of jealousy, knowing that if fate had for once looked kindly upon her, this baby she held in her arms would have been hers, not Yumai's. She blinked back her incipient tears as she whispered to Hemashe: "My hands know only how to grip a sword. They are not meant to hold something as delicate as a baby."

Hemashe's face saddened as he took his son back into his arms. He could see the tears of joy mingled with that of sorrow.

With a *'clang'* on a cooking pot, the revelers were called to a great table where the women presented a cornucopia of foods of every flavor and texture to appease even the fussiest palate. Under a canopy of stars, Medaru gestured for all to partake in the celebration as wine flowed freely.

Three weeks had passed since the arrival of the falcon from the east bearing a message the enemy forces were pressing on to the north. The warriors braced for the first war of the year. And for the first time, in a bid to seek out the Sorcerer in case he came in advance to see what might lie in store for the Imperial Army, Medaru posted sentries throughout the Magare Valley rather than just the few that kept watch at the mouth of the valley leading into western Orien.

This time, as the only survivor from the confrontation of last year was the Sorcerer, Medaru decided to change his strategy. The warrior priest anticipated Eldred Firestaff would warn the troops heading northward of a possible ambush in Magare Valley. Instead of launching an assault in this location again, the Imperial Army was to be drawn into war, luring the soldiers deep into the Hebeku Valley. Medaru decided to allow the anxious soldiers to spend a sleepless night anticipating an attack under the cover of darkness as before. Knowing full well the Emperor's army would avoid entering western Orien during the night, the weary soldiers would be forced to launch their invasion at first light. Medaru also knew that as they approached Hebeku Valley, dusk would be settling upon the land. This would be the most opportune time for the Kagai Warriors to menace the superstitious soldiers before beginning their first wave of assault.

Just as Medaru predicted, the enemy arrived in the Magare Valley late in the afternoon. The Kagai Warrior posted to this area immediately sent word to Medaru that the forces were even larger than the last and were camped out in the valley. These soldiers endured a very long and unsettling night. Even with sentries posted to guard the perimeter of the large encampment, sleep was still elusive.

Kagai Warriors, skillfully blended into their surroundings, began to imitate the call of the male gray owl and in no time, the whole valley echoed with the eerie call of these nocturnal birds, eagerly answering the challenge to defend their territories. Eventually, the answering calls ceased when the owls realized imposters were fooling them.

An eerie silence prevailed over the valley, but as soon as it became evident the soldiers were now ready to settle down for some sleep, the Kagai took to howling like a pack of wolves that were waiting and watching their hapless quarries from the mountain slopes. So convincing they were at mimicking the birds and beasts, when dawn finally broke, the exhausted soldiers were forced to advance even though they were sleep deprived.

As the army proceeded to head into enemy territory, a Kagai Warrior released his falcon. The bird delivered a warning to Medaru that the army was advancing. Watching the soldiers march out of the valley, the warriors settled down for a bit of sleep before following this army westward. Their job was now to capture and kill any of the soldiers that escaped the battle and were attempting to retreat back into the Magare Valley.

With the sun's waning light diffused by the encroaching darkness, the cautious soldiers advanced into an area of thinly treed forest. Apprehension filled their eyes as they took in the unfamiliar landscape. Many wondered if any other soldiers wandered this far into enemy territory before meeting their demise. The captain ordered the men to set up camp for the night. As he assigned soldiers to sentry duty, many of the nervous men began to jockey for position in the middle of the encampment while the less fortunate where forced to claim a space on the edge of the clearing.

As soon as weapons were laid down so the soldiers could go about the business of preparing for the night, the sharp crack of a whip followed by the thundering of hooves caused the soldiers to take notice. Struggling to focus in the dimming light, they spied the form of a number of dark horses galloped toward them. Perplexed by the presence of steeds without riders, the soldiers noticed only too late that each pair of horses was hitched to a great log mounted on a wooden wheel attached to each end. As the horses charged forward, the log would roll with the wheels, but to the men's horror, the branches protruding from the log were cut down and reshaped into sharp spikes. These deadly protrusions rotated with the same velocity as the wheels it was mounted to, spinning as fast as the horses were racing through the confused crowd.

Many of the soldiers did not even know what hit them as the men blocking their view scrambled and shoved to escape the path of this deadly attack.

Above the screams of agony and shouts of fear, the captain fought to restore calm, shouting at his men to rally together than to panic and flee. As they gathered their weapons to face their unseen foe, a strange silence smothered the forest. The frightened soldiers glanced about, searching for the supposed demons haunting this region, listening as the horses delivering the first assault vanished into the darkness.

"Hold steady, men!" demanded the captain, his anxious eyes scanning the deepening shadows.

He strained to hear through the unnatural quiet when suddenly, a *'whoosh'* broke the foreboding silence. Pandemonium ensued as soldiers were bowled over. A log suspended horizontally from ropes, swung down from high above.

Before they could flee, invisible foes released a series of logs to descend upon the unsuspecting soldiers. Some were crushed as logs came smashing together while others were hurled through the air upon impact.

In a matter of minutes, the aerial assault ended as quickly as it started. Once again, a eerie hush enveloped the forest. The remaining soldiers were more than ready to flee, their swords and halberds poised to fend off the unseen enemy as they made good their escape.

Fighting to remain composed, the captain mounted his steed. Drawing his sword he shouted: "Be prepared to attack, men!"

"Attack what!" shouted one frightened soldier. "How do we fight invisible demons?"

"Close your ranks! Draw your – " Before the captain could finish his sentence, a single arrow pierced his throat, the impact throwing him from his saddle.

Attacking from the west, Joval's warriors silently emerged from the shadows of the forest as the keen-eyed Elven marksmen easily downed the soldiers before them with a steady barrage of arrows.

As those on the frontline released their arrows, they immediately dropped down on one knee to nock another arrow. Below the line of fire, the subsequent row aimed and fired, dropping out of the way for the next line of archers so they may have an unobstructed shot at the enemy. This repetitive wave of assault was devastating for the Imperial Army, as line upon line of soldiers fell dead to the ground. The soldiers that still had their wits about them immediately set up a wall of shields to defend against this attack.

Confronted by this imposing barrier of shields, Joval ordered his warriors to cease this assault. Pointing his sword skyward to reflect the cold light of the moon, the Kagai Warriors responded to his signal. Those hidden high in the trees released a volley of arrows from overhead. Their deadly projectiles rained down on the unsuspecting soldiers. Those who were not downed by this barrage raised their shields to protect themselves from the arrows that cascaded down upon them from all directions. As soon as the soldiers hoisted their shields overhead to intercept these projectiles, Joval motioned his warriors to resume their assault, picking off one soldier after another at will.

Unable to return this volley, the soldiers huddled in a tight mass, their shields held aloft and forward in a bid to deflect the incoming arrows. In this formation, the soldiers found relative safety, but all knew they could not hold out forever. They would be forced to fight or flee.

With their quickly dwindling forces, their captain dead and the number of foes still unknown, the remaining soldiers agreed to fall back, edging eastward in this haphazard formation. With shields held to shelter them from above while those facing Joval's warriors to the west continued to hold their shields forth, they proceeded to retreat.

As abruptly as they first appeared, the Elven marksmen suddenly withdrew into the deep shadows of the forest as the Imperial soldiers slowly backed away. As the army neared the eastern edge of the clearing, thinking they could make a break into the forest, they turned to flee. A lethal volley of arrows met them as Nayla instructed her men to attack.

More screams of pain and panic erupted as the soldiers, now tripping and stumbling over their dead and wounded comrades were forced back into the clearing where they were met with another overhead barrage of arrows.

Adding to this frightening moment of confusion, Medaru on horseback came charging through the clearing. With a nerve shattering call echoing through the night air, he signaled his warriors to descend from their treetop hiding places to engage in combat. Like ghostly shadows creeping silently down from their lofty perches, the Kagai Warriors raced into battle to join Joval and Nayla's men on the ground.

Hemashe slashed, punched and kicked his way through the mayhem as he made his way to Nayla's side. As though nothing had changed since they last went to war together, the warrior fought close by her side as he always did.

Mekai was in the maelstrom of the conflict, wallowing in the pride and glory that he was the biggest and mightiest of the Taijin men to do battle. With reckless abandon, he hacked, slashed and hewed at any soldier who dared stand up to him. His eyes were wild and filled with bloodlust as he reveled in the chaotic excitement.

The adrenalin coursing through Mekai's veins only served to heighten his savagery. Seizing the soldier attacking Keodai, Mekai's monstrous hands grasped the man's head, helmet and all. With a swift and deliberate twist, he easily snapped the soldier's neck with enough force that the head now stared lifelessly backwards. Barely acknowledging Keodai, Mekai tossed the body aside as he stormed off to seek out his next victim.

The hulking warrior roared in defiance as he turned on two soldiers. They were assaulting one of Nayla's young recruits, attacking the warrior with a vengeance. Mekai plucked them up from the ground by the scruff of the neck. Smashing the soldiers' heads together, he flung the unconscious men to the ground like they were rag dolls.

The steaming heat of a hot breath snorted down on Mekai. The hairs on the back of his neck stood on end. He slowly turned to face an Imperial Soldier even bigger than he. This soldier was tall for a Taijin, as tall as an Elf! Standing just over six feet tall and just as wide, this man stood a good four inches taller than Mekai. His massive, muscle-bound arms and legs were as stout as a tree's trunk. His huge chest and shoulders, well plied with bulging, rock-hard muscles made his neck all but disappear.

With a deafening roar, the men attacked each other. Mekai punched the soldier square in the mouth with all his might. The soldier barely flinched, only spitting out blood and then laughing at the warrior's bold, but foolish attempt at taking him down.

Mekai felt a pain biting into his knuckles. To his surprise, embedded quite deeply was the man's front tooth! Never in Mekai's entire life had any man remained standing after such a devastating blow. The soldier spat once more, growling in defiance as his hands wrapped around Mekai's throat. He slammed the warrior hard against a tree.

In desperation, Mekai reached across with his right hand to draw his sword. Before he could do so, the soldier used his free hand, balling it into a great fist to drive into the warrior's midriff. The force was so great, Mekai groaned, folding with the pain of internal organs colliding together.

The soldier laughed mockingly as the Kagai Warrior collapsed onto his knees. Kicking Mekai over onto his side, the soldier used his massive bulk to knock the wind out of the warrior. He smashed down on Mekai's chest with both knees. His ribcage shifted and painfully creaked with the tremendous strain crashing down on him.

Straddling the warrior's body, the soldier decided to display the true might of his strength by strangling Mekai with his bare hands. In response, Mekai's neck grew taut as his muscles swelled and tightened as he tucked his chin in to break the soldier's hold.

The soldier was unrelenting, pressing down with all his weight to choke the life out of Mekai. The warrior struggled for every breath as he fought against his foe's suffocating grip. Repeatedly slamming his knees up against the soldier's massive, well-muscled back, it did nothing more than rock the larger man higher onto his chest, crushing him beneath his weight. Mekai felt an overwhelming sense of panic grip his heart. Never before had he been placed in such a desperate situation. He had always been the one to easily overpower his enemy.

Raising him by the throat, the soldier repeatedly pounded Mekai's head into the ground. The dazed warrior gasped for air. His resolve and strength were quickly ebbing away as the soldier unmercifully strangled him. He released a stifled groan as the soldier's weight became more unbearable. Unbeknownst to Mekai, Nayla had leapt upon the soldier. Wielding her short sword in both her hands, she repeatedly rammed the blade through the soldier's back.

The adrenaline coursing through this man's hulking frame, pumping through his veins and surging through every fiber of his muscles numbed his senses to Nayla's brutal assault as she continued to drive her blade deep into his back. Dwarfed by his great size, his only acknowledgement of her presence was when he shrugged his hefty shoulder to knock the warrior maiden off his back to the right.

Mekai could make out Nayla's small form rising up onto her feet. He caught a glimpse of her crimson blade held before her as his eyes began to roll into the back of his head. He was starting to lose consciousness.

With a bone-chilling cry resonating from deep down inside her small body, Nayla's right hand spun her sword once before she pivoted slightly, dropping back on her right knee. With frightening speed, her sword slashed upward, skimming dangerously close past Mekai's neck. The blade continued on, slicing through the soldier's throat and onward through cervical vertebrae to shear his spinal cord.

Nayla leapt back as a crimson spray of blood erupted from the severed arteries.

"Damn it!" cursed Nayla. The little warrior groaned in disgust, managing to avoid the worst of the gore.

Mekai abruptly came to as the combination of the soldier's dying grip and the jet of hot blood spraying into his face served to jolt his senses. He gasped loudly, rolling away as his opening eyes took in the still-menacing scowl permanently etched onto the face of the soldier's disembodied head. It had tumbled to the ground with a heavy *'thud'*, landing right next to Mekai's.

"Get up! Get up and fight, Mekai!" ordered Nayla. She dashed off, sheathing her short sword to call upon the keen-edged blade of her long sword to do battle.

Struggling to his feet, Mekai watched as the little warrior disappeared into the mayhem, cutting a swathe through the enemy soldiers as she came to the defense of her brother warriors.

Hemashe breathed a sigh of relief as his adversary suddenly dropped dead before him. He knew immediately the warrior maiden was close at hand, glancing up just in time to see her turn her attention to the soldier venting his rage on Keodai. It was apparent to Hemashe that she continued to watch his back as she always had.

Without hesitation, Nayla rammed her sword straight through the soldier's back until it protruded from his chest. She held onto her sword with both hands as the dead man toppled to the ground to release the blade. She gave Keodai a reassuring smile, spinning the sword in her right hand to flick off the liberal slathering of blood as she turned to take down the next soldier.

An icy chill coursed through her veins as an invisible hand squeeze around her heart. She heard Joval scream out her name as an image of the Elf flashed through her mind. Joval was injured and overwhelmed by several Imperial Soldiers. Nayla could feel the Elf's heart racing. A sense of panic filled his embattled soul. It was as though she could read his thoughts; hearing his voice cry out in defeat: "*This time, I die!*"

Hemashe saw the look of sheer panic in her eyes as she abruptly spun about, searching for someone. Leaping over fallen bodies, dodging the slashing swords and swinging halberds, she vanished from his sight.

Nayla angled and wove her way through the melee, guided by nothing more than her intuition as she navigated through the darkness and utter confusion. Approaching the edge of the clearing, to her horror, there indeed was Joval. He was painfully slumped over on his hands and knees. Three Imperial Soldiers encircled him like rabid wolves.

One soldier kicked him hard in his ribcage to send the Elf flying over onto his back. She could see that Joval had somehow lost his sword. From the corner of her eye, she spied Valtar struggling against his own foe. Without hesitation, she charged straight for the soldiers assaulting Joval. The largest of the men turned upon hearing Nayla's rushed footsteps. He was met with a poisoned throwing dart sailing from her hand. It struck him in his jugular vein. Before he could yank the dart from his neck, the man fell over dead.

The second soldier faced the warrior maiden. With sword poised high over his head, he waited for her to come within striking distance. Just as he brought his sword down with all his might, Nayla's sword came up; the blade held horizontally over her head to intercept his blow. With one broad, circular motion coming up from the right and sweeping across to her left and downwards, her body pivoted as her left leg swung out to give her greater power and momentum. Putting her entire body weight behind her countering strike, in this single motion, the tip of her blade sliced through the man's raiment, skin and flesh.

The impact sent the soldier's sword flying from his hands. The weapon sailed through the air coming to a stop only when it impaled an Imperial comrade. The stunned soldier stood before his tiny adversary, collapsing to his knees. His trembling hands fumbled about, struggling to contain his entrails spilling out from his lower midriff.

Nayla spun about to deliver a devastating kick with her right foot to the soldier's throat. She did not even wait for him to hit the ground before she turned her attention to the soldier continuing his assault on the Elf.

Joval rolled from his back onto his left side, avoiding the enemy's sword as the tip of the blade slammed down. Unleashing a bellow of pain, dazed and reeling from the many blows, Joval did not move away fast enough. The sword pierced through his right side just below his ribcage. Driving him hard onto his back, the tip of the blade sank through the Elf's body, pinning him to the ground.

A ferocious smile curled the soldier's lips. He tightened his grip on the sword to yank it from the earth and Joval's body. As he crouched down to free his weapon, the soldier's eyes flashed open in surprise as a blur like liquid silver flew in his direction. The soldier staggered back with the impact. Nayla's short sword sailed through the air striking him dead-on in his chest. Stumbling backwards, the man fell hard to the ground as Nayla dove on top of him.

Straddling his body, she ruthlessly wrenched her sword from the dying soldier's chest. Filled with rage, she began plunging the blade into his body again and again, stopping only when a blood-filled scream gurgled from the man's throat.

Nayla stood up from the corpse. Her eyes followed the few remaining soldiers fleeing into the forest, racing away northward. She glanced about as the other weary warriors near to her struggled to regain their breath and composure. There was no need to pursue the retreating soldiers, for they were about to run headlong into a battalion of Kagai Warriors arriving from their post in the Magare Valley. Their sole purpose was to kill the escaping soldiers.

A mournful groan caught her attention. Nayla turned to see Joval as he attempted to grasp the handle of the sword protruding from his body. Still firmly skewered to the ground, the Elf struggled to remove the blade.

Dashing to his side, she called his name: "Joval!"

Gazing up at her, Nayla slugged him just hard enough to stun the Elf. With his senses reeling, as his attention instantly shifted to this new source of pain, Nayla grasped the hilt of the sword. She carefully and swiftly extracted the offending weapon, pulling it straight out.

Joval gasped at the sudden, burning pain as the weapon withdrew from his body. His left hand immediately covered the bloody wound. Nayla rolled him onto his left side. Placing her hand on the exit wound, she applied pressure, attempting to staunch the flow of blood.

Valtar raced over to his friend's side, roughly shoving Nayla aside as he did so.

"Get out of my way! You are not an Elf!" Valtar bellowed in anger as he knelt by Joval. "You cannot help him!"

Nayla sat up, watching in stunned silence as he tore open Joval's vest, struggling to pull up on his raiment to access the wound.

Joval grimaced in obvious pain. His chest was heaving as he fought to steady his breathing and racing heart as the blood continuing to pool beneath him. Nayla crawled up to the Elf, gently raising his head onto her lap. As Joval's left hand pressed down over his wound, his eyes squeezed shut as he began uttering an Elvish healing incantation. Valtar, too, was busy at work. His left hand lay over the wound on Joval's back as he joined him in calling upon the powers that heal.

Nayla continued to cradle Joval's head. She watched as the color slowly drained from his face. Overwhelmed by an utter sense of helplessness, she leaned in close as her soft voice pleaded to him: "Do not die, Joval. Please do not die."

Her body began to tremble in fear. Tears of sorrow spilled from her eyes, trickling down her burning cheeks. As her tears fell onto Joval's face like gentle raindrops, his eyes slowly opened. Hearing Nayla's heart anxiously pounding in her chest, he could feel the desperation in her arms as she cradled his head. There was a look of absolute anguish as he gazed upon her sad face.

Her eyes fluttered open as Joval's hand touched her cheek to gently wipe away the tears. A weary sigh of relief escaped her as she threw her grateful arms about the Elf's neck, holding him close. In that instant, he could feel all her despair and woe melt away as he embraced her in his arms.

"Can you stand, Joval?" questioned Valtar. He attempted to pull his friend onto his feet and away from Nayla's arms as Keodai, Hemashe and the other warriors gathered around them.

"I will be fine, Valtar," assured the Elf, nodding in confirmation.

Valtar rested Joval's arm over his shoulders for support. Leaning unsteadily against Valtar, Joval watched as Nayla rose up before him. She hastily wiped away the tears from her face with the back of her hands so none would see as she glared at Joval.

With her hands balled into fists, she angrily slammed them against Joval's chest causing him to fall against Valtar's body. She growled beneath her breath: "You reckless fool! I may not be there to help the next time you call for me!"

The Elf was as startled by her words as her acerbic tone, watching as Nayla stormed off in search of Medaru.

Working through the night and well into the early morning hours, Elves trained to heal battle related injuries worked side by side with the Taijin healers to care for the wounded. Four Elves met their demise during the war, succumbing before they could be delivered to the Twilight to join their kin in the Elf Haven while nine mortals met their end instantly. Medaru and Keodai administered last rites to three Kagai Warriors so mortally wounded they chose to relinquish their lives than to linger until death made its claim.

Late the following morning while the able-bodied warriors went about the morbid task of concealing the corpses of the many enemy soldiers in mass graves, Nayla took a break from her duties to visit Joval as he recuperated in his shelter. She peered in through the open flap of his tent to see Valtar standing by Joval's cot as he waited for the Elf to finish writing a brief report.

"May I come in?" asked Nayla.

"Captain Stonecroft is not receiving visitors and well-wishers at this time," responded Valtar in a crisp tone, his hand moving to drop the tent flap on her.

Joval grabbed Valtar's arm to stop him. He motioned at Nayla to enter, inviting her in: "This visitor is welcome, Valtar. Come in, Nayla. Just bear with me as I finish this message."

She watched as he rolled the piece of parchment, stuffing it into a small metal tube to be fitted to the leather jesses of a falcon. "You are sending word to Dahlon?"

"Indeed, the usual information: size of the enemy army, our losses and so on," answered the Elf. "Valtar, please see to it that Master Saibon sends this message off immediately."

"Of course," replied Valtar, accepting this duty. As he turned to leave, he deliberately snubbed Nayla, pushing by her as though she was not even there.

"And a good day to you, too, Master Briarwood," muttered the little warrior, as the Elf existed the tent.

"So what brings you here, Nayla?" questioned Joval, struggling to sit up on his cot.

She adjusted his pillow, easing him back down. "I came to see how you fare. You had me quite worried you know."

The Elf was touched by her concern.

"With adequate time I shall heal completely. Though broken bones mend and torn muscles and tissues repair, it is the loss of blood, the very essence of life that can kill an Elf, as you may well know. Thankfully, that soldier did not succeed in putting a big enough *hole* in my body to drain me entirely of life."

"Are you in pain?"

"Not really, just a bit weak," replied Joval. "I will be fine in a day or two. Mind you, had a high Elf like your father been here, his ability to heal would see me fully recuperated in a fraction of the time."

Nayla shook her head in shame as she responded: "It is a pity he chooses to hide behind the safety of the walls of Nagana. Even if Dahlon did not go to war as we do, his presence, even to heal the injured, to preserve life, would be put to good use."

"I can understand your sentiment, Nayla, but you know Lord Treeborn's place is to mind our stronghold, to protect the surrounding villages if the southern range of the Furai Mountains be breached by the enemy. He cannot be at all places at all times."

"You, my friend, are far too generous in defending my father's *good* name and reputation," grumbled Nayla.

Joval smiled at the little warrior as he responded: "Speaking of reputations, it is my understanding mine had been severely tarnished thanks to you coming to my rescue."

"A little humility goes a long way, Captain Stonecroft. It is far better for even an Elf such as you to be humbled and be alive than to be proud and very dead."

"Well, I not am ready to enter the Twilight or to be condemned to the ghost world of this realm," replied Joval. "I mean to thank you. You placed yourself at great risk by coming to my aid."

"You were lucky I heard you call for me above the din," she said as she gave his hand a consoling pat.

"I do not understand, Nayla. I did not call for you."

"Do not tease me, Joval. I heard you call out my name," stated the little warrior.

"I assure you, I did no such thing," reiterated the Elf.

"But..." Nayla frowned as a look of confusion clouded her eyes.

"Even if I had called for you, I still cannot understand how you, even with your sharp ears, could hear me above all the noise. And how you knew where to even begin looking for me is a complete mystery," admitted Joval, his eyes studying her face.

Nayla did not respond. She looked pensively at his large hand as it gave hers a gentle squeeze.

"What are you thinking? What is going on in that head of yours?" queried the Elf.

Clearly baffled, she reflected on the events of the night: "I swear Joval, the moment I heard your voice, it was as though…"

"As though what? Go on Nayla," insisted the Elf, becoming more intrigued.

"No. This is all too strange," she answered in a small voice.

"Speak please, do tell," he prompted her again.

"When I heard your voice call out for me, at that very instant, it was as though I could feel your pain, hear your thoughts… It was as though I could see exactly what was happening to you at that very moment."

Joval's brows furrowed with curiosity as he responded: "Truth be told Nayla, though I do not remember calling out your name, when I realized that I might very well die, for a fleeting instant, I did think of you."

"How can that be? How can you reach out to me, to enter my thoughts in this manner? Is this some kind of Elven magic I am not aware of?"

"It is said the Elf-kind to first arrive in Imago from the Haven possessed this ability, similar to that of the Watchers."

"The Three Sisters watching over this realm from a distant mountain far to the west?" asked Nayla.

"Yes, and even some mortals have this power; this sense to see what is yet to be or to pick up the thoughts and feelings of others."

"But why me?"

"Why not you? You are your mother's daughter, Nayla."

"Are you saying my mother was gifted with this power?"

"Yes, but to what extent, I am not sure," stated Joval, in all seriousness.

"That cannot be."

"Think Nayla! You said yourself there were times when you were in dire trouble that Lady Treeborn appeared from out of nowhere to come to your aid."

She was quiet for a long moment as memories from her life long ago replayed in her mind. "I must admit there were times when Dahlon was in the midst of venting his wrath when my mother would seemingly appear from out of nowhere, as though she knew I needed her…"

"No doubt your bond with your mother was strong; strong enough that she could feel you reach out to her in your moment of need."

Her head lowered as she recalled the darkest moment in her life when her mother had passed away. Though at that very moment when Kareda Bansho breathed her last breath, while Nayla was forced to wait in the corridor as the healers tended to her, she knew before word was delivered her mother had died.

That night, alone in her room, Nayla tucked herself into her bed. Pretending her mother was drawing the counterpane around her shoulders and neck to keep her warm, Nayla took great comfort in seeing her mother standing before her. She seemed luminous. The color that had drained from her face in death now seemed to radiate with life. Though Kareda spoke no words, it was as though she touched her daughter's heart, offering comfort and her undying love as she promised Nayla her life would change; that she was to hold out for hope. Although her life had come to an end, Nayla's life was only about to begin.

Joval broke the silence: "Nayla, I for one knew your mother had a premonition of her own death. She knew she was destined for a short life in this realm. It was for this reason she so greatly cherished her time with you. It was also the reason why she had made me swear I would watch over you in her passing."

"Let us not speak of this… this…" stammered the little warrior, bewildered by this new knowledge.

"This gift?" concluded the Elf.

"How can it be a gift?"

"If it were not for this *gift*, I would be dead now, Nayla," stated Joval. "It was your premonition that caused you to act as you did."

She glanced up as a great shadow loomed at the entrance of the tent. A familiar voice called out: "Captain Treeborn?"

Nayla was stunned. The voice definitely belonged to Mekai, but never had he addressed her as Captain Treeborn, nor with such respect.

"I am in here, Mekai," she responded. "What is it?"

"Captain Treeborn, I do not wish to disturb you, but I was wondering. Is there anything that you need done? Is there anything I can assist you with?" asked the great warrior, his head bowed in humility as he addressed Nayla.

Her startled eyes gazed at Joval. The Elf had a quizzical look on his face as he shrugged his shoulders in response.

"This is a trick, right?" asked Nayla. A broad smile of amusement was stretched across her face.

Mekai's eyes grew wide in dismay as he insisted: "Oh no, Captain Treeborn! This is no trick at all. Is there anything I can do for you?"

"Who put you up to this? Keodai? Hemashe? Was it Master Saibon?" queried Nayla, her eyes narrowing in suspicion as she scrutinized Mekai.

"I am here as your humble servant," answered the warrior; "for I am indebted to you, Captain Treeborn."

"You received a nasty blow to your head last night, yes?"

"Yes… It was quite bad," admitted Mekai, thinking back on his ordeal.

"Aha! So you are not thinking straight!" declared Nayla.

"Captain Treeborn, I mean no disrespect, but I assure you, my thinking is not any more impaired than it normally is," replied Mekai. His face suddenly flushed with embarrassment as he realized his words did not come out exactly as he had planned. "What I am saying is: I am thinking more clearly than ever before. I am here to make amends to you for my past behavior. I owe you my life."

"You owe me nothing, Mekai. What I did for you, I would do for any of the warriors. I would come to the aid of any of my brothers," vowed Nayla.

"Please, Captain Treeborn, for even this one day, I am your servant," insisted Mekai. "I am at your service."

Nayla began to giggle: "This is absolutely preposterous, Mekai! You are not my servant, you are a warrior."

Mekai was unmoved by her comment. Standing before her, he waited for her first order.

"Nayla, I do believe this warrior is quite serious," commented Joval, gazing over at the large mortal.

"Mekai, there must be other things you can do? Perhaps your help is needed elsewhere? Have you checked with Keodai or Hemashe?"

"Hemashe is the one who told where to seek you out," answered Mekai.

"Aha! So it was Hemashe who had put you up to this!" exclaimed Nayla, shooting an accusing stare at the warrior. "I knew it!"

"Oh no, Captain Treeborn! He merely directed me to your whereabouts. I am here on my own accord," explained Mekai, anxiously wringing his large hands. "Now please, what can I do for you? Do you need fresh water delivered to your tent? How about more firewood? Fresh clothes? I can wash your clothes for you, if you wish."

"*Nobody* washes my clothes, thank you very much! Though you seem quite sincere Mekai, something is mighty odd about all of this."

"Come now, Nayla, since when did you last have anyone offer to launder your clothes?" asked Joval. "Take advantage of this opportunity."

"I repeat: *Nobody* touches my *things,*" stated the little warrior. "Mekai, if you are so intent on having me order you about, here is one order I am sure you can follow quite easily: Leave me be! Go bother Hemashe instead. Please!"

"If you insist," said Mekai, unleashing a disheartened sigh.

"Oh, believe me, I *do* insist. I am sure Hemashe can use a man-servant for the day."

"Are you sure?" asked Mekai.

"I am positive!"

"You will not change your mind?"

"What have I said that you did not understand? Just leave me be!" she growled as she shoved the hulking warrior out of the tent. "Go bother Hemashe!"

Joval observed Mekai sulking as he sauntered off, looking somewhat morose that he was unable to fulfill his good deed.

"Do not be so hard on him, Nayla. He is trying to show his gratitude."

"If you ask me; Mekai's strange display was above and beyond a show of gratitude," responded Nayla, shaking her head in disgust.

"He is like an over-grown puppy. He merely wishes to please you," explained Joval.

"I have been known to kick puppies that get in my way," grunted Nayla.

"Good gracious!" groaned the Elf, rolling his eyes in frustration. "You certainly do have a mean streak about you!"

"It is my *mean streak* that keeps the likes of you alive, my friend," responded Nayla, flashing Joval a knowing smile.

"What are you doing back so soon?" queried Hemashe, lifting his horse's forefoot as he began cleaning the clump of dried mud from the frog of the hoof. "We had an agreement: If she ever saved your miserable hide, you shall be at her beck and call for the *entire* day. This day is far from over."

"Deal or no deal, the only order Captain Treeborn asked that I obey was to spend my time assisting *you,*" explained Mekai.

"Really now?" responded Hemashe, as he lowered his steed's hoof. "Takaro did not accept your offer?"

"No. In fact, she was quite adamant that she be left alone. At the risk of rousing her ire, I chose to honour her request by assisting you."

Hemashe stood before the warrior, scratching his head in bewilderment.

"Well, if she is unwilling to use your services, I have no qualms in doing so," replied Hemashe, as he placed the pick into Mekai's hand. "You can finish this task: check the fitting of these shoes; file down any part of the hoof that is overgrown and removed any debris that is stuck in the frog."

"Is that it?" asked Mekai, hopeful that his life debt would be paid off so easily.

"After you are done with my horse, all those need to be serviced too," answered Hemashe, pointing to another two-dozen stallions, mares and geldings tethered to the hitching post.

"What?" gasped Mekai, glancing at all the horses waiting their turn. "All of them?"

"All of them," Hemashe nodded in confirmation, smiling as he walked away.

"This is not fair," groaned the warrior.

"Sure it is! And just think, it could be a lot worse, Mekai," responded Hemashe. "Instead, you could be relegated to the lowly task of washing Takaro's dirty laundry!"

For over a month, the Magare Valley lay quiet. Medaru continued to post warriors deep into the valley to watch, not so much for approaching military forces, but for the Sorcerer, Eldred Firestaff. When word was received of encroaching hordes marching northward, this time three-times as many as the last, once again the warriors of Orien joined forces with their Kagai brothers to do battle.

Though the days were still long and warm, the nights were beginning to feel the chill of autumn as the men braced for war. Facing an army of unparalleled magnitude, Medaru called for a meeting with Keodai,

Joval and Nayla and the decision was made to lure the enemy into battle. With such staggering numbers to oppose, the old Kagai Warrior felt it would be to their greatest advantage to mount an attack by the cover of night.

With the weeks leading up to this next assault, the warriors went to great lengths to excavate and cleverly conceal a number of pits. Large tarps carefully camouflaged by sod and small vegetation, were pegged over the gaping holes in the earth where a series of sharp, pointed stakes waited to impale the unsuspecting men stumbling into this trap. A series of these pits were carved into this field leading into the groves of bamboo that fringed the pine forest. Staggered in a seemingly random pattern, the only safe passage through this death trap was a narrow corridor, a direct line from the mouth of the valley, straight through the center of this field.

The backbreaking task of moving earth and stone high up onto the slopes of the mountains that narrowed the entrance of the valley into a '*V*' shape took a number of days to complete. The warriors carefully braced stones and rocks against boulders to set up an easy to trigger landslide. By merely removing several strategically placed pieces of wood, the warriors would now be able to instigate a great avalanche of earth, rocks and boulders to effectively seal off the valley again, killing any soldiers caught in the wake of the landslide.

In the groves of bamboo lining the open field, the warriors took advantage of these tall grasses. The spring rains and the plentiful sun created a lush growth that allowed these plants to shoot up from the ground at an astonishing rate. Where the soil was most fertile, the jointed canes of bamboo were able to grow as much as four feet in a single day. Still full of moisture, the canes were incredibly flexible and springy. The warriors carefully lowered the crowns of these massive stalks to the ground, tying them down with a length of rope. At the top of each cane were long, wooden spikes anchored by more ropes. Once the ties were cut, the tension created would send the canes of bamboo whipping forward to deliver the wooden spikes with deadly force.

With the traps set into place, Joval's warriors, under Nayla's leadership, would be the first line of defense as the marksmen would release an unrelenting torrent of arrows at the enemy while all the while retreating further into the pine forest. As these warriors fell back, the surviving soldiers would be lured deeper into this forest where Medaru and his warriors would present the second line of defense. Only when the ranks of the enemy soldiers were adequately thinned would the warriors engage in hand-to-hand combat.

Then one fateful summer day, the enemy arrived in the Magare Valley just as anticipated. By late afternoon, their numbers swelled to fill the valley floor. Immediately, sentries were posted along the perimeter of the encampment to keep watch through the night as the remaining soldiers set up camp, resting in preparation to launch an invasion at dawn.

The Kagai Warriors, hidden along the mountain slopes overlooking the valley, patiently bided their time as the sun worked its way across the sky to rest low over the western horizon. Its light bathed this land in a strange glow; the sky seemed ablaze in an eerie crimson. Tall trees quaked and shuddered in the invisible wind, casting eerie shadows that stretched across the landscape. Like long, dark fingers of a gnarled hand, these shadows crept ever closer to the encampment. As the sun slipped behind the distant mountains, the waning light of day surrendered to the coming of the night as one by one, tiny stars dotted the steadily darkening sky.

On this night, not a single creature stirred. There were no sounds of crickets, no chorus of frogs, not even the ominous call of the dreaded owls to break this unnatural silence.

Instead, an oppressive hush blanketed the valley; a suffocating silence that was as thick and heavy as the humid night air. The soldiers made attempts to ignore the quiet, but it bore down on them like an invisible hand, stifling their breath and slowing their movements as the heat and humidity climbed.

The captain, riding high on a great dark steed, roamed the perimeter of the camp, giving the guards posted to sentry duty final instructions as a velvety darkness settled on the lands. With row upon row of tents neatly set up, the captain steered his horse to the large tent situated in the midst of all the smaller ones. Handing the reins to a soldier, the captain prepared to retire for the night. He glanced up, staring into the darkness as the loud clatter of thundering hooves echoed through the valley.

A volley of arrows set ablaze lit up the nighttime sky as Medaru, Joval and seven warriors on horseback targeted the many tents and the guards posted at the mouth of the valley. They deliberately charged through the confused crowd as unwary soldiers poured forth from their tents. The less fortune ones were met with an arrow as the Kagai Warriors taunted the enemy before retreating into the darkness from whence they came.

The captain seized the reins from the soldier, mounting his steed as he shouted orders to pursue their assailants.

Instead, the soldiers picked up their weapons, but they faltered, balking at the prospect of entering the cursed land in the cover of darkness.

"You cowardly fools!" screamed the captain, waving them on. "The enemy is getting away!"

"But captain, the night… the demons that haunt those forests by night!" protested one soldier, staring off into the blackness engulfing the open field before them.

Gasps of surprise sounded as the sea of soldiers parted. They made way for a hooded figure clad in a dark cloak, watching as he turned upon the soldier.

"Afraid of demons, are you? Afraid of the night?" he hissed in disdain. He lowered his staff at the quaking soldier. "You should be far more afraid of me!"

The soldier's eyes grew wide with terror. He dropped his shield and sword as he backed away to flee. A bolt of blue energy emanating from a crystal orb burst forth, striking the frightened man down. The soldier collapsed before his stunned comrades, writhing in agony as the energy coursed through his body. As though being cooked from the inside out, they watched in horror as thin, gray smoke curled from the soldier's open mouth and nostrils as he screamed in agony.

"I have seen the enemy! They are not demons. They are of flesh and blood just like all of you!" snarled the Sorcerer. He pointed his staff at the soldiers, his hands trembling in rage. "And if you cowards are frightened of these beings, then I shall give you something to be truly frightened of!"

The soldiers cautiously backed away from this terrifying entity, their eyes turning to their captain for support and guidance.

The captain warily eyed the Sorcerer, and then glanced out into the darkness where the Kagai Warriors awaited them. He knew he had no other option. Drawing his sword, with a wave of his hand, the captain motioned for his men to advance.

"Yes! Go to it! Kill the enemy! Kill them all!" shrieked the Sorcerer, goading them on into the darkness. "Show them no mercy, for they will show you none!"

Working the soldiers into an absolute frenzy, driving their courage with sheer bloodlust, Eldred reveled in the excitement of the moment.

Rallying his forces, the captain ordered the soldiers to charge across the field. As the silhouettes of Medaru and the other warriors stood out against the dark sky, the captain ordered the soldiers to advance like a great black tide, their eyes firmly set on their quarry.

Medaru, Joval and the warriors held steady, watching as the Imperial Army poured out of the valley onto the open field. As the soldiers neared, as though to taunt them, Medaru boldly charged toward the overwhelming force, thundering past them in a wide circle, just out of their reach.

Insulted by this brazen and vagrant display, the captain shouted at the soldiers to attack. The ground reverberated with the pounding of thousands of footfalls as the men gave chase, driven on by both fear and adrenaline.

Medaru escorted the others on a straight course through the field, following a narrow strip of land that presented the only safe passage back into the pine forest.

As the soldiers taking up the flank exited the valley, they stopped in their tracks. A low rumbling sound filled their ears as a great tremor shook the earth beneath their feet. To their horror, they were instantly swallowed up in a landslide, crushed beneath tons of earth and boulders.

The captain and his soldiers knew immediately they had been set up. They had wandered directly into a deadly trap. With the valley sealed off, their only escape route gone, they had no choice but to forge onward.

The sudden whine of arrows piercing the night sky was followed by the screams of pain as soldiers toppled over, either dead or wounded. The captain ordered those at the rear to raise their shields, but pandemonium ensued as invisible Kagai Warriors hidden high on the slopes continued their assault. Instead of holding their ground, the soldiers at the rear panicked, pressing forward to escape the barrage. Those on the frontline were forced ahead, carried along by the crushing tide of the advancing surge.

This time, screams echoed from the frontline. The earth swallowed up the soldiers. Falling one atop the other as the ground opened up to bite them, the hapless souls were impaled upon the many wooden stakes lining the floor of these pits.

In desperation, the captain ordered the men to retreat. Amidst the screams and the deafening clamor of weapons and armor, his words were lost, drowned out in a sea of mayhem. He watched helplessly as the soldiers attempting to avoid the air assault from the rear continued to drive the men on the frontline forward, unaware of their plight. The first row of pits filled with bodies, that if not impaled, the men were soon trampled and crushed. More screams followed as the forward surge pushed more men into the next row of awaiting pits as the level of panic amplified.

Unable to stem this horrid tide, the captain urged his steed on to the very front of the line. Charging through the chaos, he bellowed over the noise and confusion to be heard. But his soldiers only heard his scream of horror as both he and his horse disappeared, tumbling into one of the pits at the edge of the field.

As the soldiers at the frontline attempted to brace themselves, to push back against the panicking mob coming up from behind, all attempts to contain this flow failed. More screams followed as soldiers met a quick death, their own comrades forcing them over the brink with their suicidal stampede.

As those in the rear were now well out of range from the aerial assault, the soldiers gathered before the great groves of bamboo that fringed the open field. With only the sounds of their panicked breathing to fill the air, the surviving soldiers stood motionless, unsure of how to proceed. With no captain and no hope of retreating to the Magare Valley, they were at the cruel mercy of fate.

The silence was abruptly shattered. The Kagai Warriors released calls that echoed through the mountains to make their numbers artificially higher than it really was.

Once again, panic seized the soldiers' hearts as the realization they were about to be attacked from the rear by an unseen evil caused these men to flee towards the cover of the pine forest.

Nayla gave the order for the lines to be cut. The immediate snapping and rustling of vegetation and the swift movement of air surprised the soldiers on the frontline. Canes of bamboo sprang to life, whipping forward with incredible speed to smack down the soldiers like hapless flies, swatted by crowns studded with wooden spikes.

Soldiers lucky enough to avoid this deadly assault began to back away from the dense groves of bamboo, but their efforts were thwarted. Those in the rear continued to press forward. Driven on by fear as the calls of the Kagai resounding from the Magare Valley grew louder and grew to be many, the soldiers were ready to chance dispersing into the forest in hopes it would offer some respite from these demons.

Summoning his courage, one soldier's voice rose above the others as he shouted orders to take cover in the forest. From this position, they could face the approaching enemy that now pursued them from across the valley. Now, they would be safely shielded from view as the Kagai Warriors were forced to make their way across the open field if they wish to engage in war.

With renewed hope and a deafening war cry to drive them on, the army charged headlong through the towering stands of bamboo into the pine forest. The soldiers crashed through the dense vegetation that abruptly gave way to a dark forest. They dared the enemy to give chase.

Immediately, Nayla gave the orders for the archers to begin the assault. The familiar whine of arrows pierced the air, claiming the first line of soldiers to emerge before them.

Unable to see what lay in store, the other soldiers continued to pour out from the bamboo groves only to stumble over their fallen comrades as they, too, were met by the lethal projectiles.

With each line of marksmen taking aim and unleashing their arrows, they moved steadily backwards, withdrawing deeper into the pine forest.

"Look, their lines grow weak! They are retreating!" shouted a soldier.

Led into believing the warriors before them drew back in defeat as they were unable to stem the advancing tide of the army, this soldier was confident these rebels were only a few hundred strong. With the possibility of victory now swaying in their favor, the soldier rallied his forces, ordering the men emerging into the pine forest to hold their shields forward to deflect the volley of arrows.

Nayla gave orders for the warriors to retreat. They instantly turned, running westward, straight into the deep shadows of the forest. On her mark, the warriors divided into two groups, one moving to the south, the other circling in from the north. As the Imperial Army poured into the pine forest, the warriors had all but vanished. The soldiers glanced about nervously, their anxious eyes darting about in a desperate bid to determine where their foes had disappeared to.

"Cowardly dogs! They are all a bunch of shameful cowards! They run like frightened mongrels with tails tucked between their legs when they see the true might of our force!" gloated the soldier. "They know they are no match for us! We will crush them!"

"Shall we head back to the valley?" a voice called out.

"I am your leader now! I am your captain!" declared the soldier, waving his sword aloft for all to see. "We will not retreat! We have come too far and have lost too many to turn back now! That is exactly what the enemy wants us to do! No, my brothers! We shall flush them out! We shall hunt them down! And then, we will kill them, one by one!"

Greeted by a roar of support, the new captain motioned the soldiers to disperse into the forest to seek out their quarry. Before they could take another step, the call of a solitary owl echoed through the treetops.

The soldiers glanced up; searching for this harbinger of death when suddenly, Kagai Warriors hidden high in the crowns of the trees released a hail of arrows. Many were downed by the first wave of assault, while those who desperately scattered to seek refuge behind the trees were the next to be brought down. The soldiers who did not falter, instinctively drawing up their shields to deflect the arrows, were the only ones to remain standing as they sought cover.

With fewer than twelve hundred Imperial Soldiers left standing, Medaru's ear-splitting call summoned the warriors to engage in battle. Nayla and her men, having already encircled the soldiers, charged out from the shadows as the Kagai Warriors nimbly raced down from their treetop hiding places. Within seconds, the crash of steel against steel and the screams of pain and horror filled the forest. The earth trembled in fear as it sopped up the freshly spilled blood.

Joval, Medaru and all those on horseback hewed and slashed at the heads and necks of the enemy as they careened through the pandemonium. Though the Imperial Army still outnumbered their warriors, the soldiers were now overcome with the devastating realization they had played right into the hands of the enemy from the start. With no choice but to fight, their energy seemed to ebb as their confidence and the last chance of victory slipped away from their grasp.

As Nayla battled against a soldier, she swiftly parried his blows, always angling away, for she knew she lacked the strength to lock weapons with this larger, more powerful man. Countering his assault, she rolled away from him. Rising up onto her feet, a foreboding sense of danger filled her heart. She felt his energy, his overwhelming intention to kill, sweep over her. Without turning or retreating, as though in her mind's eye she could see exactly where he stood as he raised his blade, Nayla stepped back directly into him. She rammed her sword backwards into the soldier's chest. Delivering a hard back-kick to the soldier's midriff, he toppled over as she retracted her sword. Without missing a beat, she turned to aid Keodai as he fought for his life.

She ran swiftly and silently. The soldier gasped in surprise, feeling the cold steel of her deadly blade drive through his torso. Keodai gave him a death-delivering slash across his throat as the dying man crumpled to the ground.

"Keodai!" shouted Nayla, as she pointed to the east. "It is the Sorcerer!"

He turned to see the warrior maiden give chase as a shadowy figure retreated into the grove of bamboo, darting away with unnatural speed.

"Hemashe!" called out Keodai. "Takaro pursues the Sorcerer!"

Hemashe quickly yanked his sword from the soldier's body as he followed Keodai. Guided by the sounds of rushed footsteps and rustling vegetation in the wake of her pursuit, they raced after her through the northern edge of the forest fringing the open field.

They stopped dead in their tracks as they caught up to Nayla. She stood before them, motioning for silence as her head turned to and fro. She attempted to pinpoint the location of her quarry.

"Where is he, Takaro?" asked Keodai, his sword poised cautiously before him as he stood to her right.

"He is near. I can sense him," whispered the warrior maiden, her eyes piercing through the deep shadows of the forest.

"Are you sure it was the Sorcerer?" queried Hemashe, in a hushed tone as he edged his way to her side.

"I am positive it was him."

With a loud whistle, an arrow skimmed by, narrowly missing her. Both she and Hemashe instinctively dove to the ground, but Keodai remained standing.

To her horror, the arrow had missed her, but pierced through the leather vambrace Keodai wore. Though it did not penetrate into his flesh, the arrow traveled through one of the straps and buckles to pin the warrior's right forearm against the tree trunk directly behind him. The impact as his arm hit the tree caused the sword to tumble from his grip.

Nayla glanced up to see Keodai yanking desperately at the deeply embedded arrow, trying to free himself. The warrior cursed as another arrow struck the tree, barely missing his head as he ducked.

She immediately leapt up, slamming her body hard against Keodai's back. As his chest folded against his forearm, the pressure snapped the shaft of the arrow where the tree would not give up its hold. The strap of the vambrace tore, setting the warrior free as Nayla pushed him to the ground.

She fell heavily, landing on top of Keodai as a burning sensation ripped through her. In a blur of movement, she could see Hemashe as he wrenched her onto her back, seizing her by the shoulders as he pulled her to safety behind the tree. Keodai scrambled on all fours as he knelt by Hemashe's side.

Nayla gazed up to see Hemashe staring down at her. He was

visibly shaken as the color drained from his face. It was only when she struggled to sit up did she realize what had happened. An arrow protruded from her chest, just below her left breast. It sank deep into her body, stopping only after it shattered the bone at the back of her ribcage.

Along with this realization, the sharp pain abruptly became all too real. She groaned in agony as the wound seemed to pulsate with a heartbeat of its own.

"Do not move, Takaro," ordered Keodai. "I shall go for help."

Nayla seized him by his collar, pulling him down close as she ordered: "No! Get the Sorcerer!"

"But Takaro - "

"Listen to me, Keodai. We cannot allow him to escape! Go!" she demanded as she shoved him away.

The warrior reclaimed his sword as he instructed Hemashe to stay by her side. They watched as Keodai resumed the chase, disappearing eastward.

"This is not good, Takaro," whispered Hemashe, his quaking hand gently touching the shaft of the arrow. "Not good at all."

Nayla did not respond as she fought to remain focused. All efforts to quiet her racing heart were hampered by her inability to breathe. The arrow had ravaged her left lung.

"You need the help of an Elf, Takaro. I shall go for help!" offered Hemashe, his eyes were filled with fear and concern for her. "I will seek out Captain Stonecroft."

Seizing his sleeve, she halted his movement: "No, Hemashe! Do not leave me. It is too late."

"What do you mean *'it is too late'*?" gasped the warrior, wrenching his sleeve free of her grip. "I will get the Elf."

"I am dying," whispered Nayla. "I do not intent to die with an enemy's arrow stuck in my body like this. Help me to remove it."

"This is an arrow used by the Imperial Army. You know it is barbed. You know what it will do if I remove it."

"Yes, but it makes no difference how grievous this wound be, I am dying," she gasped. "Please, pull it out."

Hemashe's trembling hands wrapped around the shaft. He grasped it as close to her body as he could. As he tightened his grip, Nayla's eyes closed as she focused on her breathing cycle. Her attempts to call upon the energy of the earth to calm her heart and soul failed as her left lung began to collapse from the puncture wound.

The warrior knew what she was attempting to do and he understood her failing lungs would not allow her to call on this power.

Her eyes opened again as she pleaded to him: “Just do it, Hemashe! Do it now.”

He watched as her fingers sank into the earth as she braced herself for the unthinkable agony he was about to inflict on her. Hemashe’s heart raced as rapidly as hers as he knelt by her side. Nayla could feel the burning sensation as the arrow shifted slightly inside her as the warrior firmed up his grip.

“Now!” she shouted as her eyes squeezed shut.

Hemashe yanked the arrow straight out of her chest cavity. He quailed as he felt the tearing, the cruel barb snagging onto the thin membrane of the air sacs and flesh. He cast the arrow aside as his despair grew, watching as blood began to flow freely from her wound. Air mixed with the blood, bubbling forth as she exhaled. She flinched as she pressed her left hand over the small but fatal wound.

“Takaro, please, let me find Captain Stonecroft,” he insisted once more. “I beg of you!”

With the injury now further traumatized, she fought for each breath she gulped down.

“Hemashe… you will never find him in time,” she gasped. “I am drowning… in my own blood.”

“I will not let you die like this!”

“You have no control… over who lives… and who dies.”

“There must be something I can do?” groaned Hemashe, wallowing in a sense of absolute helplessness.

“Take up your… your sword,” she answered.

“What are you asking of me?” Hemashe whispered as his eyes grew large with apprehension.

“I wish… to relinquish my… my life,” she gasped between each laboured breath.

“No…” groaned the warrior, as he cradled her in his arm. “Do not ask this of me, Takaro.”

“If I am to die… I wish to choose… how and when,” she wheezed. The taste of copper rose in the back of her throat as the blood continued to fill her left lung. “The time… is at hand. Please, Hemashe… this is my last and dying wish.”

Hemashe held her head to his chest as he sobbed. Great tears spilled from his eyes and rolled down his burning cheeks as he despaired: “No, Takaro! Please, please let me help. I shall fetch Captain Stonecroft. He can help you. I know he can!”

“You do not… know… know where he is. He may… well… be

dead," gasped the little warrior.

Hemashe rolled her onto her side as she coughed up blood. He could feel her life force ebbing away as he held her in his arms.

"Do not speak as though there is no hope," pleaded the warrior, placing his own hand over hers as she continued to press down on the wound.

"There is… no hope," she whispered, her voice becoming feeble as she slowly closed her eyes. "I am dying."

"Keodai!" shouted Hemashe, gazing up to see the warrior emerge from the stand of trees. "See, Takaro. Keodai is here. He shall remain with you while I go for help."

Her eyes barely opened, even as Keodai knelt before them, touching her ashen face.

She reached up with her right hand to touch Keodai's as she pleaded with him: "Help me… Keodai. I wish… to relinquish… my life."

"Takaro, you are Kagai! You are strong! Just allow me to – " Before Hemashe could finish his sentence, Keodai motioned him for silence.

"Are you sure you wish to do this, Takaro?" asked the warrior.

"She is delirious, Keodai. She does not know what she speaks of!" argued Hemashe.

"Hemashe, surely you can see. Takaro is dying!"

"Do not… allow me… to suffer like this… Keodai," pleaded the warrior maiden. Her right hand fumbled as she slowly unsheathed her short sword. Her ebbing strength caused her to drop her weapon. "I am too… too weak… to take up my… my sword. Help me… Hemashe."

"You cannot ask me to do this, Takaro!" gasped Hemashe. "I cannot – I will not do this to you!"

She struggled to sit upright as she squeezed out with her dying breath: "If you cannot… wield my sword… then I beg of you… hold me… so Keodai… may wield his."

Hemashe gazed up at Keodai as the warrior unsheathed his long sword from its scabbard.

"No, Keodai! Please, you cannot do this to Takaro!" pleaded Hemashe, as he wept.

"She is dying, Hemashe. Can you not see Takaro is dying," whispered Keodai, as his own eyes began to well with tears. "Though I wished not to be the one to be called upon for this task, I do not intend to allow her to suffer needlessly."

"Thank you… Keodai," gasped the little warrior, as she tried desperately to hold herself upright.

"Please, Hemashe, hold Takaro by her arms so that I can deliver one clean blow," ordered Keodai. "So she can be dispatched swiftly."

"Takaro, please, let me find the Elf," pleaded Hemashe again, tears spilling shamelessly as he stooped to gaze upon her face.

Her eyes seemed strangely vacant now as she slowly shook her head in response.

"Let me die… Hemashe. Please… just allow me… this," she said in barely a whisper.

Hemashe began to tremble as he knelt behind her, bracing her arms so she was kneeling upright. He began to sob as her head lolled forward, fighting to gulp down some air as her chin rested on her chest to fully expose the back of her neck to receive the blade.

Hemashe gazed up as the moon's cold light danced off Keodai's blade as he held it aloft. He could see the tears now streaming down his friend's face as the warrior attempted to steady the tremors of his quaking hands.

As Keodai issued her the last rites of passage, he rose up on his toes, for he had no intention of faltering now. Just as she slipped into a calming, warm blackness, she could hear the last words whispered by Keodai while in the distance, the warrior maiden heard the faint echo of her name: *Nayla!*

It was followed by the whip-like sound of the warrior's blade as it sliced through the heavy night air to come down upon her neck.

15

the gift of life

"NAYLA!" Joval's voice bellowed across the forest.

He charged toward Hemashe and Keodai just as the warrior's sword came down with blinding speed. Simultaneously, Hemashe wrenched Nayla away from the path of Keodai's keen-edged blade.

The tip of the sword slammed down, biting into the earth as Hemashe's desperate bid to spare Nayla's life was met with success.

Joval leapt off his steed, racing to her side.

"Is she still alive?" asked the Elf.

"She barely clings to life," answered Hemashe, gently turning her onto her back. "Takaro was downed by an arrow."

Her breathing was now shallow; barely perceivable as tiny bubbles of air and blood gurgled from the wound.

"She is dying – drowning as we speak," determined Joval, tearing at her wet, bloodstained raiment to access the wound.

"Can you help her?" asked Keodai, as he sheathed his sword.

"I do not know," answered Joval.

"What do you mean *'you do not know'*? You are an Elf! Of course you can save her!" declared Hemashe. "Takaro once told me you could perform such miracles."

"She has already lost much blood. It fills her left lung and soon it shall flow into the right side," announced Joval.

The Elf tore off his cloak, thrusting the bundle beneath her shoulders so her chest was elevated to stem the rising tide of blood. She lay in a lifeless heap as her head lolled backwards.

"I must get this blood out before it is too late," said Joval.

In a desperate move, he sealed his mouth over hers. Pinching her nostrils closed, the Elf blew a long, steady stream of air into her. They watch as her chest inflated and blood spewed out of the wound. Again,

Joval filled his lungs as he forced another breath of air to drive the pooling blood out. With a final, deep breath, the Elf watched as her chest slowly rose, and then fell as the blood now slowly oozed from the wound.

Joval moved swiftly, placing his left hand over the puncture. Calling upon the healing powers, he closed his eyes as he recited Elvish incantations. Hemashe and Keodai knelt by his side praying for a miracle.

After several excruciatingly long minutes had passed, Joval finally removed his hand from her body. The wound had effectively sealed, leaving only a nasty red mark. He watched as her breathing slowly returned to normal; the rising and falling of her chest was steady and even. He leaned in over her body, listening to her lungs as she breathed.

Instead of the steady rush of air swirling through, he could hear the lining of her left lung, vibrating like the rattling purr of a cat. It was the residual blood still trapped within.

Joval rolled her over onto her right side. Raising his hand to hit her back in an effort to make her cough up the remaining blood, his hand stopped at mid-strike as it neared her body. A disruption in the flow of her energy alerted him that the arrow had traveled straight through her chest to strike up against the back of the ribcage, shattering the bone. Removing her cloak and pulling up on her raiment, he quickly placed his left hand on her back over the lower left ribcage. As he set about the task of healing her broken body, he heard a faint gasp of horror as Keodai and Hemashe noticed for the first time the many linear scars marring her small back.

When he felt the bones were adequately mended, he smacked her high across her back with an open hand.

"What are you doing? You mend her, and then you try to break her again?" shouted Hemashe, grabbing the Elf by the wrist as he held it up to strike her again.

"There is still blood trapped inside," explained Joval, pulling away from the warrior's grasp.

"Hemashe! Leave him be!" ordered Keodai, pulling the warrior away. "Captain Stonecroft knows what he is doing."

As Joval hit her hard across the back again, Nayla began coughing and sputtering as her lungs spasmodically expelled the blood. She lay gasping for her breath, but still remained unconscious.

"She will live, yes?" asked Hemashe hopefully.

"At this point, that will be entirely up to her," stated the Elf, as he gently blotted away the blood from the corner of her mouth with the edge of his cloak. "Keodai, fetch my horse."

Scooping her limp body up into his arms, he easily lifted her onto his steed as he took his place behind her. Holding her steady against his chest, he turned his steed westward.

"I shall deliver her back to safety," offered Joval. "You two will be needed by Master Saibon. There are bodies to be rid of and the injured in need of care are many. Return immediately."

"We shall do that, Captain Stonecroft," replied Keodai. "And thank you for coming to our aid. If it had not been for you, Takaro would be dead."

"Yes, Captain Stonecroft, how you found us way out here is no small feat," praised Hemashe, grateful for the Elf's unexpected arrival. "It was a miracle you found us in time."

"It can hardly be called a miracle," replied Joval, as he turned his steed away. "I heard her call. I merely followed the sound of her voice."

Keodai and Hemashe exchanged confused glances as the horse galloped away.

"I did not hear Takaro call out," stated Keodai, scratching his head in bewilderment.

"That is because she did no such thing," replied Hemashe, as he watched the Elf disappear with the little warrior.

Through the long hours that ensued, Joval remained by Nayla's side. Sleeping for only four or five hours at a time was normal for her, but it had been over twenty-two hours since she was felled by the enemy's arrow. With each passing hour, Joval's concern grew. Now with the lengthening shadows stretching over the canopy of this tent, he knew the sun was low over the horizon. Dusk would soon settle upon the lands.

During this vigil, the only comfort the Elf could find was in the fact the color had returned to Nayla's cheeks and her breathing was no longer hampered by the injury and resulting seepage of blood into her lungs.

Joval gently raised her head as he carefully tipped a healing tonic of water steeped with the analgesic properties of the willow Medaru Saibon had left for him to administer to her. Though his Elven ability to heal worked to repair the damage, he now relied on the medicinal remedies used by mortals to counter the resulting pain that often occurred when a mortal experiences the rapid healing brought about by this miraculous touch.

"Is she awake?" asked a hushed voice.

Joval turned to see Hemashe standing at the entrance of the tent. He motioned for the warrior to enter as he shook his head in response.

The Elf slumped back in his chair as Hemashe sat upon the edge of the cot, gazing down upon Nayla's sleeping face. He gently picked up her small hand into his as his eyes darkened with worry.

"Why does she not wake?" asked Hemashe. "Why does she still linger in this unnatural sleep?"

"Perhaps she was so confident that she was going to die, she had already embraced this fate," answered the Elf.

Hemashe stroked the stray wisps of hair from her eyes. He still felt an overwhelming sense of helplessness as his fingers entwined with hers as Joval looked on uneasily.

"So tell me; do you still love her?" inquired the Elf.

Hemashe could not look Joval in his eyes as he answered: "I have a wife and child, Captain Stonecroft."

"Yes, but do you still love her?"

"Your question is rather inappropriate."

"Why? Because you are married to another though your heart is still bound to hers?"

"You do not know what you speak of, Captain Stonecroft," insisted Hemashe. He slowly released Nayla's hand.

"I believe I *do know* what you speak of, Hemashe," responded Joval. "I know with all certainty the perilous trek Nayla endured to rescue you from Keso last year was done more out of love and compassion for you than to answer the pleas of help from your wife. Nayla risked everything, her own safety and life, to save you. One does not take on such a monumental task for no good reason."

"She told you this?"

"Perhaps in not so many words, but it was evident her motivation was driven by more than a need to save a brother warrior," answered Joval. "So I ask again, do you still love her?"

"Why is that so important now? I have pledged myself to another. I have a wife and a child to think of."

"Though Nayla may be long-lived compared to other mortals, her existence in this world has been a lonely one. She almost died last night. To pass from this realm believing she is not loved is a cruel burden to bear, even for one as strong as she is," stated Joval. He could now see the sadness and shame in Hemashe's dark eyes. "Why did you forsake her for another when I sense in your heart, you still long for her? What happened?"

The young warrior mulled over the Elf's words and then he answered: "It was the most difficult decision I had ever had to make where Takaro was concerned. I never wished to cause her hurt or grief."

"Go on," prompted Joval.

"The night I requested Takaro's hand in marriage, Medaru Saibon and my parents argued vehemently against my wishes. Master Saibon had threatened to assign Takaro to sentry duty, to guard the Magare Valley indefinitely."

"He threatened to exile her?" Joval was shocked by this revelation.

"It was not a threat, captain. Master Saibon was more than prepared to oust Takaro from Anshen, to subject her to a most difficult existence to the north. Most definitely did she face the prospect of a life in exile if I did not abandon my desire to bind to her."

"Fate has truly been unkind to her," responded Joval, with a dismal sigh. "Does Nayla know of this?"

"I dare not tell her, for her own love for Master Saibon is that of a daughter's for a father. If I told her the truth, the sanctity of their relationship will be put asunder. The only family she ever knew, she ever loved and trusted had also been the one to alter the course of her destiny. How do you think she shall take to this news; that she was betrayed by the one man she loved and trusted as not just a mentor, but as a father? Lord Treeborn had already cast her off. How do you think this shall sit on her conscience, knowing what Medaru Saibon was prepared to do to her?"

"I understand," nodded the Elf, these troublesome words weighing heavily on his mind.

"Besides, with each passing year as I age, she remains forever youthful. In time, what would she have done with a husband all shall mistakenly look upon as her grandfather? Though my love for her shall be undying, the harsh reality of this fact is that ultimately, I shall be in the winter of my life and will die long before the spring of her youth has been spent. I will be an old, worn, useless man; a mere shadow of the warrior I once was. This is not the man she fell in love with and it is not a fate I wish to bind her to," explained Hemashe, knowing full well all his parents and Medaru had counseled him on would come to be with the passing of time.

Joval sympathized with Hemashe as he thought aloud: "What will become of this warrior, neither mortal nor Elf?"

"Tell me, Captain Stonecroft, is there not one Elf that has shown interest in Takaro?" asked Hemashe.

"She is the daughter of a high Elf, Hemashe. I would assume it is safe to say none step forward to claim her hand because none feel worthy to be bound to Lord Treeborn's one child. Besides, though she is long-lived, she shall pass from this realm never to enter the Twilight to be united in the Haven with the Elf of her liking, for she is not gifted with the eternal life of my people."

"But can she not be blessed with eternal life?" pondered Hemashe. "She is half Elf after all."

"Only a high Elf like King Kal-lel, the Lord of Wyndwood can do so," answered Joval.

"But you said Lord Dahlon Treeborn, too, is a high Elf. Can he not bless Takaro with eternal life?" queried Hemashe.

Joval breathed a weary sigh and with great regret he replied: "Lord Treeborn has the power to do so. However, he has yet to offer this blessing. And truth be told, it is questionable if he ever will."

"What would motivate Lord Treeborn to offer this gift to Takaro? What would sway him to act out of compassion for his daughter?"

"There lies the problem, Hemashe," stated Joval. "He has no compassion or love for his daughter. His heart has grown cold and only grows colder still with the passing of time. I know of not one thing that would persuade him to act out of compassion where Nayla is concerned."

"Captain Stonecroft, it is apparent to me Lord Treeborn holds you in the highest regard and with the greatest esteem. Perhaps you would hold sway over him. Surely you can influence him to see the logic in this," insisted Hemashe.

"What logic?"

"It would be a shrewd move on his part to offer her eternal life, for as long as she is present, so shall his standing in the council of Nagana, for she is the daughter of Kareda Bansho," reasoned Hemashe. "And there is always the fact warriors and captains, great leaders such as Takaro, do not rise up from the ranks so easily. Surely Lord Treeborn will act upon the best interest of the people, to preserve their lives and homes by any means possible."

For a brief moment Joval silently digested the warrior's words. "Perhaps you have a point, Hemashe. My relationship with Lord

Treeborn is such that I know he will act on what he believes would present him in a favorable light. I shall give your words serious consideration."

"Please do, captain," said Hemashe, as he gazed down at the little warrior. "You have been here for a good many hours. Perhaps you would care to leave this tent, to see how your men fare? I can watch over Takaro."

"I am quite fine," whispered Joval.

"It is no bother, really," insisted the warrior.

"I prefer to wait by her side should Nayla wake."

Hemashe was mildly surprised by his response. He studied the Elf's blue eyes, noting his look of genuine concern as he continued his vigil.

"Tell me, Captain Stonecroft, how deep does your own love for Takaro run?" asked Hemashe.

"Pardon me?" replied Joval, his brows furrowing with concern.

"I may be a mere mortal, but I assure you, I am no fool," answered the warrior. "I have seen you on and off the field of battle, always close to her side. Your interest and concern for Takaro is more than that of one warrior for another."

Hemashe's observation took Joval by surprise. The Elf only offered a small smile.

"I know of this bond you have forged with her," continued the warrior, as he rose to leave the tent.

"What bond do you speak of?"

"Last night when you saved her life, you said in passing that she had called for you."

"Yes?" responded the Elf.

"I was there the whole time. Even when she knew she was going to die, not once did she utter your name. And yet, you claimed you had followed the sound of her voice. Perhaps it was the magic of the Elf-kind that delivered you to her, but above all the noise and the confusion, you were able to find her," replied Hemashe, ducking beneath the tent flap as he walked away.

As the pale light of the morning sun filtered through the canopy of trees, Nayla's eyes gradually opened. The mellifluous call of songbirds heralding the rising of the sun carried through the encampment.

She came to recognize the surroundings of her tent as she glanced about. To her right, in a deep sleep while sitting in his chair as Joval Stonecroft.

She reached over, her finger weakly tapping him on his leg. The Elf's eyes snapped open. It was as though he was always awake and merely resting his eyes.

"Well, it is about time," said Joval, with a pleased smile as he leaned forward in his chair to greet Nayla.

"How long have I been asleep?" Her voice was low and raspy from her long rest.

"You had us most concerned. You had been asleep for about thirty hours or so, if you need to know."

"I have never slept for this long before, not even when I had been taken ill with fever," said Nayla.

"Obviously, your body was in dire need of rest; to recuperate from the trauma it received. How do you fare this morn?"

Her small hand rubbed her chest. Her throat was still raw from both the air he had forced through her lungs and from coughing up blood.

"My lungs ache. It feels as though they were made ready to burst."

"Hmm! That is mighty odd. I wonder what brought that about," responded Joval, as he passed her a flask of water to quench her thirst.

Nayla took a sip, swishing the water about to moisten her dry mouth before swallowing it to soothe her parched, aching throat. "How did I come to be here? Did Hemashe or Keodai deliver me to camp?"

"I brought you back."

"You? How can that be? I do not recall you being there."

"It does not surprise me. But believe me, I was there. I arrived in the *nick of time*," said the Elf. He made play on words as he pointed to his own neck. "Excuse the pun if you will, but Keodai was in the midst of dispatching you."

"You healed me," said Nayla.

"I did what I could for you," replied Joval. "You seem to be on the mend now."

"I have certainly seen better days, but at least I am not dead yet," said Nayla.

"If that is your way of saying *'thank you'*, then you are most welcome," responded Joval.

"I did not ask for your help, Joval. I was quite prepared to die," stated the warrior maiden.

"If that be the case, then why did you call for me? You know I would not allow you to die if I could help it," responded Joval.

Nayla slowly sat up as she peered into his eyes. She looked momentarily bewildered.

"Are you going to tell me that you did not call for me?" queried Joval.

"I admit when I realized I was going to die, moments of my life seemed to flash before my eyes. Though I recall images of you in my thoughts, I do not remember calling out your name."

Joval's brows furrowed with curiosity. He gazed into her eyes as he struggled to understand. "You were under great duress, Nayla. Perhaps you just do not recall doing so."

"Perhaps," she agreed, drawing off her blanket.

"Where do you think you are going?" queried the Elf.

"Surely, you do not expect me to spend one more second on this cot?" grumbled the little warrior.

"Well, it is not as though there is a war to be fought. All is quiet on the front," countered Joval.

"I am a captain, Joval. If I am confined to this bed any longer than need be, what do you think the warriors will think of me? They shall treat me like I am a *girl.*"

"No offense, Nayla, but in case you have forgotten, *you are a girl,*" reminded the Elf.

"You know what I mean. They shall think me to be weak."

"No, they will think their captain is recovering from a serious injury, nothing more."

"Perhaps if the tables were turned they would think that of you, but believe me, I must work twice as hard to earn and keep their respect," said the warrior maiden. "I wish to earn my keep and retain my dignity."

"Come now, Nayla, there is no need to rush your recovery," argued Joval.

"I have recovered sufficiently. To lie here will do me no good," insisted Nayla.

"You are so bloody stubborn!" declared Joval.

"No more so than you are," she retorted.

"I am just worried about you."

"Then it is not my fault you choose to worry so much, and to do so needlessly."

"Then do not give me cause for worry," argued the Elf.

Joval rose up before her as though his much larger form would somehow intimidate her back under the warm blanket.

Her lackluster eyes peered up at him. She could sense his genuine concern for her welfare.

"Look here, Joval, it is not as though I intend to jump off this cot and run for several leagues. I just grow weary of this tent and cot. I promise, I shall not engage in any activity that will impede my recovery," she promised.

"I cannot stop you, can I?"

"Have you ever?" answered Nayla, giving him a knowing smile.

"Well, if you insist on mucking about, let me gather our steeds. We shall head to Anshen. Master Saibon and your Kagai brothers have been here often to visit as you slept and recuperated. They will appreciate seeing you up and about."

"That, I can do," replied the little warrior, as she stretched her dormant muscles.

As they shared a celebratory meal with the clan, Hemashe quietly observed the interaction between Nayla and Joval. Although he was aware this Elf maintained a constant vigil by her bedside, he noted that Joval continued to be watchful of Nayla, always remaining near to her side even now.

At first he thought it was his concern for her health that kept him there but soon, he noticed this Elf was also very generous with his praise where her abilities as a warrior and captain were concerned. She would modestly brush aside his kind words, but it was apparent to Hemashe that Joval seemed to come alive in her presence, basking in the warmth of her radiant smile as she reveled in the camaraderie of this brotherhood.

Medaru motioned for Joval to sit by his side so they may converse without the need to shout to be overheard above the boisterous group. Master Saibon was in a festive mood, throwing a fatherly arm around Joval's shoulders as he thanked him for taking care of the little Kagai Warrior.

Hemashe watched as Nayla withdrew from the crowd, retreating into the forest. He knew exactly where she was going and he could feel the burn of Joval's intense stare as he stood up to follow her.

Just as Hemashe had predicted, he found her at the top of the ridge overlooking the village. Her eyes sparkled as the sunlight reflected off the mirror-like surface of Lake Anzen. Without turning to face him,

Nayla knew immediately it was Hemashe.

He stood by her side, his hand shielding his eyes from the radiant glare of the sun. For a lingering moment, both said nothing as their eyes drank in the infinite horizon sprawling out before them from this high vantage point.

"It has been long since I last stood here," reminisced Hemashe.

"The last time I was here, it was when you confessed your love for me," she said with no bitterness to her tone.

Hemashe smiled as he recalled that moment. It seemed like it was only yesterday. "I have not been up here since that day."

"I suppose there are some things better left in the past."

"Yes. And some things are easier said, than done," Hemashe added with a sad sigh.

She gazed over at the handsome, young man, studying his familiar brown eyes as she asked: "Are you happy, Hemashe?"

"Happiness is a state of being that is in constant flux. I often wonder if I would have been happier under different circumstances. If I had only…" his voice trailed off. "What about you, Takaro? Are you happy?"

She gave him a forced smile as she answered: "I command my own army."

"Yes, but are you happy?"

"I am respected by the elders of Orien," she added.

"But are you happy, Takaro?"

For a moment, she sat back, reflecting on her life. "At one time, I thought I knew what happiness was. I thought I found happiness in your arms, but it was as fleeting and as elusive as love itself. I now find comfort in my sword and I have purpose in my life commanding the best warriors to come out of Nagana."

"To find fulfillment in duty is one thing, Takaro, but it does not fill the void in one's heart if there is no love or happiness," attested Hemashe, glancing over at the little warrior as her cloak fluttered in the breeze.

"I have found my true calling, Hemashe. That is all I need in my life."

"Well, I hope this *calling* of yours does not blind you to other possibilities," cautioned the warrior.

"There are no other possibilities for me."

"Do not be so sure of that Takaro. You seemed to have developed a very close friendship with Captain Stonecroft."

"He has been instrumental in my commission to Nagana," nodded the warrior maiden. "Yes, he has been a most reliable ally."

"An ally you say?" His voice was raked with annoyance. "There is no need to be coy with me, Takaro. I sense the captain is much more than just a mere *ally* to you."

Her head tilted as she stared at Hemashe, baffled by his comment: "Whatever do you mean by that?"

"Come now! I am not blind to his words and actions. It is as plain as day he is more than a friend to you!"

She stood before Hemashe, her eyes blinking hard as she shook her head in dismay, not believing his words.

"This so-called *ally* of yours came from out of nowhere to save your life. This *ally* chose to sit by your bedside, night and day, as you recovered from your injury. He is never far from your side. And I have seen how his eyes follow you, watching your every move. They come alive when you are in his presence."

At first, she was dumfounded by Hemashe's observations, and then she began to giggle.

"I am quite serious, Takaro."

"Do you even realize what you are saying, Hemashe? That Elf you speak of is over five-hundred years older than I am. As I approach my one-hundredth year and appear to be the mortal equivalent of nineteen or twenty years of age, Joval Stonecroft, I believe is over six-hundred-and-fifty years old now. He is the mortal equivalent of a man into his thirties."

"So he is ten mortal years my senior," grunted Hemashe. "That hardly means that he is too old to admire the charms and grace of a woman."

"Do you not recall what I said about that Elf? His disinterest in the opposite sex?"

"Do not feed me more cockamamie tales, Takaro! He leans in that direction as much as the sun travels across the sky from west to east."

"That is an interesting analogy, Hemashe," said Nayla, turning to hide her embarrassment.

"Do not change the subject, Takaro. If you are too blind to see the obvious, then take heed my warning: It would be ill-advised to allow Captain Stonecroft to believe he could possibly be the object of your affections when you are in no way romantically interested in him."

"I have done nothing to make him believe so."

"If that is so, you should know that more often than not, a man can easily mistake the kindness and generosity, even common courtesy shown by a woman, as a sign of love – a romantic overture, if you will. If he is already enamored with you, it would be so very easy for him to believe such displays are genuine shows of a woman's love," cautioned Hemashe.

"He is a warrior, as I am!" rebuked the little warrior.

"That is a rather feeble excuse, and you know it. It did not stop me from falling in love with you, did it?"

"Obviously, it was enough to make you think better of binding yourself to me," she retorted in bitterness.

Hemashe hung his head in sorrow as he replied: "Takaro, if it is of any comfort to you, though I am bound to Yumai by marriage, and now by this child we share, my heart will always belong to you. Though I care deeply for Yumai, for she has proven to be a loving and devoted wife, I cannot deny I never stopped loving you. In my heart, I sense Yumai can feel this too, yet her own love for me allows her to look the other way."

"Why do you tell me this now?"

"Guilt? Undying love? I do not know, Takaro," whispered Hemashe. "I feel a void, a great void that cannot be filled even with the passing of time and your long absence."

"Perhaps it is nothing more than jealousy you feel, envy that I might choose to give my heart to another."

"I cannot deny there are pangs of envy I feel in knowing that Captain Stonecroft may be the recipient of your affections, but I have no say in this matter."

"As I said before, Joval Stonecroft is a friend – an ally. He does not love me. In fact, he barely likes me. We have learned to tolerate each other," she stated emphatically.

"I hate to say this, Takaro, but I believe your skull is as dense as Mekai's. Do you not comprehend a single word I say? Captain Stonecroft has feelings for you that you choose to ignore, or you are inexplicably blind to. Are you oblivious to his attention?"

"You read far too much into Captain Stonecroft's chivalrous gestures," she quickly dismissed his warning.

"He is a man, Takaro. You can deny it all you want, but he can be influenced by the feminine charms of one as beguiling as you."

"Joval Stonecroft is a great warrior and a great leader. He is an Elf of unquestionable virtue and integrity," explained the warrior maiden. "He is above such frivolous feelings. He has also proven to be a great ally and a friend, nothing more."

After a moment of awkward silent, Hemashe continued: "Rumor

has it you live with him. Is that true?"

"We share the same cottage."

"Aha! I knew it!"

"You know nothing! Joval is a perfect gentleman as far as that goes for an Elf."

"Right…" Hemashe looked smugly at her as his head nodded in mock agreement.

"What are you insinuating?"

"I am not insinuating anything," replied the warrior. "Just answer me this: Do you share his bed?"

"That is none of your business! And if I did, what concern is it of yours?"

"You are right. It is none of my business if you choose to lead him astray; if you choose to mislead his heart."

"I do declare; I detect a note of jealousy after all! I can hear it in your voice and see it in your eyes."

"That is neither here nor there, Takaro."

"If that is so, then where are you going with this conversation?" she snapped with annoyance.

"All I wish to say is that you are making a grave mistake if you mean to toy with the captain's affections. He may be an Elf, but I am sure he is just as susceptible to all the angst and sorrows of heartache as we mortals are," warned Hemashe. "It is unfair of you to allow Captain Stonecroft to believe there is far more to your relationship than you care to admit. If you give yourself freely to him, so be it, but I have no doubt he believes that when you do so, it is not only with your body, it is with your heart and soul as well."

"He is not a fool, Hemashe."

"Any man who believes he is in love can easily be played for a fool. If you respect him as you claim you do, then do not toy with his heart and his emotions."

"As you did with mine?" she asked.

"That is not fair! You have no idea why I had to give you up as I did. You have no idea at all what drove me to do this."

"There is nothing you can tell me that will allow me to believe you threw away what we had for good reason. Nothing you can say now will un-break my heart," sobbed Nayla.

For the first time in his life, Hemashe saw tears well up in her eyes and spill down her cheeks, as though the wounds he left long ago were freshly drawn open once more.

He held her to his chest as he vowed: "On my life, Takaro, I swear my love for you is undying. It has not waned with the passing of time. Fate has dealt us a cruel blow and we are now forced to reckon with it."

"Then tell me; what happened to us? If you still feel as strongly as you do, then tell me," she pleaded through her tears.

Hemashe held her trembling body in his arms. As she wept, he whispered to her: "One day, the truth will be known. I only pray you have the heart to forgive me."

The golding of the leaves arrived with the cool breath of autumn as the early morning dew crystallized into a sparkling, crisp blanket of frost. The horses grazed on the grasses now wilting beneath this chilling brace of fall. Their steaming, hot breath condensed in the morning air, becoming one with the ephemeral veil of mist rising above the placid lake and the surrounding meadows. The steeds munched lazily as their masters were busy bidding farewell to Medaru Saibon and the Kagai Warriors.

Having received confirmation from their allies to the east that the season of war had come to an abrupt end with the last deadly incursion, it was time to go home. The remote chance of another attack before the Magare Valley was closed off by snow with the onslaught of winter was now an impossibility. The disturbing disappearance of the entire Imperial Army sent ripples of fear coursing through the rattled nerves of those to the east. Apparently, the loss of this army was so devastating, an adequate force to penetrate the Kagai stronghold would only be met with defeat yet again unless the Emperor was able to more than double his forces. To rally an army of over four or five thousand soldiers that were combat-ready was nothing more than a dream for those in power to the east.

Master Saibon and his people made sure the departing warriors were well stocked for the journey that lay before them. He embraced the warrior maiden in a fatherly hug.

"Are you certain you wish to extend your commission in Nagana, Takaro?" queried Medaru.

"There is more reason to be in the fortress city than to stay here, master."

Medaru released a heavy sigh as he hugged her once more. "If that be the case, if the fates conspire, I shall see you next spring."

Yumai and Hemashe both embraced the little warrior as she kissed their son's plump, rosy cheek. In response, baby Tadashe gurgled with delight, his tiny hands reaching out to touch her face.

Keodai and his wife, too, were there with their newborn son. She gently kissed the baby atop his head, finding comfort in knowing her efforts to defeat the enemy forces were to protect the lives of these innocents. As she turned away to join her warriors, Mekai pushed his way through the villagers. To the surprise of all, he gave Nayla as great hug, picking her up clear off the ground.

"We shall go to war again, Captain Treeborn. Until then, take care," said the large warrior, speaking with utmost sincerity.

"Mekai, to you, I am just Takaro."

"No. In my eyes, you are a great captain and I shall be honoured to fight by your side when we are called to face the enemy once more," declared Mekai, as he knelt and bowed with newfound respect before the warrior maiden.

"Until next year, my friend," said Nayla, bowing her head in mutual respect. "Keep well and stay safe, Mekai. Do not go looking for trouble. It will always seek you out."

With a wave of his hand, Joval motioned for the warriors to move out. They were ready to begin the long and arduous trek back to Nagana. With Nayla fully recovered from her injury, she refused Joval's offer of taking one of the horses. She preferred to march along with the warriors of the infantry.

Beneath a blue sky dotted with golden-yellow and deep crimson leaves that gently floated down, the trees surrendered their greenery to the coming of autumn as the army moved with great speed as they journeyed homeward. No longer dogged by the threat of war, their steps were light. Fate looked kindly upon them as they made this long trek. They were met with cool, but unseasonably dry weather; forced to endure only four intermittent days of torrential downpours.

Seven days after the rise of the harvest moon, the army was fast approaching the walls of the fortress city. Joval sent forth one of the warriors on the fastest steed to deliver a message of their impending arrival.

Under great fanfare, the army marched through the west gate of the city as horns trumpeted and bells pealed to announce to all the return of the warriors of Orien.

As the warriors fell into line in the courtyard, they stood at attention. Joval and Nayla knelt and bowed before the elders and Dahlon Treeborn.

Speaking on behalf of the elders, amidst the cheers of the growing throng, Dahlon took great pleasure in welcoming back the heroes of war. A medallion of gold was presented to both Joval and Nayla for guiding the warriors on to victory against overwhelming odds.

The Elf graciously accepted this merit of recognition as Nayla turned to face the men of the infantry. Holding the medallion forth for all to see, she declared with all sincerity that this medal of honour was deserving of all the warriors in her company. She was only one, relying on the might of many to face the enemy.

In response, under the thunderous applause and cheers from the concourse, row upon row of warriors fell on bended knee, bowing to their captain as all of Joval's warriors dismounted from their steeds and bowed in respect to the warrior maiden.

Nayla motioned for the warriors to refrain from this display only to find Joval, too, knelt and bowed before her.

"Joval, this is not necessary. Do you forget you are a captain, too?" she whispered, embarrassed by his actions.

"No, I have not forgotten, but sometimes you do. I am merely giving respect where respect is due."

"Captain Stonecroft is correct," admitted Master Sonkai, the most senior of the elders. "We received word of your heroic feats to the north in a bid to defeat the enemy."

"My feats were greatly exaggerated," dismissed Nayla, downplaying her role in the victory.

"Captain Stonecroft is not one to exaggerate," responded the elder. "Your actions will not go by unnoticed or unrewarded, for such courage and valor is not easily come by. Our warriors were faced with a vast army greatly outnumbering them. It is clear your ties to this brotherhood only strengthened our alliance with the Kagai Warriors. The fact that our losses, especially of the young warriors in the infantry were kept to a minimum can only be accounted to you. For the first time in our warring history we are doubly blessed with a magnificent victory and to have so many of our men return home. This is in great part to you, Captain Treeborn."

With a wave of his hand, Master Sonkai motioned for a servant to step forth to deliver a gift.

"As a token of our appreciation, we would like to present you with the following," announced the elder. With great pride, he held before her a glittering vest of chain mail. "This is a vest of legend. It is no ordinary chain mail. It is Elven mail."

"Take pride in wearing this, Nayla," said Joval. "There are few who are gifted in this manner, for this protective vest was crafted by the

Elves in the forest of Wyndwood."

Nayla recalled stories of old about this magical vest made by the Elven craftsmen for the warriors of Wyndwood. Blessed by the high Elves, this incredible, light armor of silvery, metal rings could easily withstand the impact of a sword, whether it be struck by the broadside or the keen-edge of the blade.

A number of the Elven warriors wore such vests, handed down from father to son. Joval, too, wore a vest gifted to him by his father Iaden Stonecroft. Truly a rare commodity, the only such Elven vests existing now are those relinquished by Elves entering the Haven where armor and weapons of war are unheard of and unneeded.

The elder held it forth for Nayla to accept. For a moment she was awe-struck as the small rings glistened in the autumn sun.

"Of course, we had to modify the fit, for no vest of mail comes in a size small enough to outfit a warrior of your stature. Please accept it."

"Thank you, Master Sonkai," said Nayla, nodding in appreciation.

"You are most welcome, and there is more," he said with a generous smile as he presented her with another gift. "On behalf of the council and the people of our country, I would like to present you with this sword."

A magnificent weapon encased in a black, lacquered scabbard was balanced in his hands. "This was specially crafted for you."

As she took it into her hand, her mind was already fooled, thinking it was as weighty as her own weapon. Instead, it was light, as though the scabbard did not conceal a deadly blade at all.

"Go ahead, examine it. See that it is to your liking," encouraged the elder. "Just do not allow the blade to touch the scabbard as it shall cut clean through."

Cautiously unsheathing the sword, the blade silently glided out of the scabbard, coming alive as the sun's dazzling light bounced off the flat edge of the weapon.

"This is truly a remarkable sword! It feels as though it is one with my hand. And the weight and balance… it is incredible!"

"Do not be deceived by its weight, or lack thereof, warrior maiden. This weapon was crafted by the best swordsmith in our lands. Made from forged steel, pounded and folded one-thousand times to make this weapon light and effortless to wield, it still carries a formidable blade of razor-sharpness. I assure you, the enemy shall quail upon seeing such a sword. See here," said Master Sonkai, his finger pointing to the flat edge of the blade close to the hilt. "These five score marks indicate the strength and sharpness of this blade. Each score represents a body."

"You are telling me this sword can hack through five bodies in a single stroke?"

"*Hack* is hardly the appropriate word to use. It can easily slice through five grown men if the wielder of this sword wishes to do so."

Nayla bowed as she graciously accepted this prized weapon.

"Wield it with honour, Captain Treeborn," said the elder, handing her the matching short sword. "I pray these weapons serve you well in battle, may these swords always keep you safe."

Nayla turned to face the warriors still standing at attention. She held her sword aloft for all to see as the anxious crowd waited to greet their loved ones. Lowering her new weapon, she ordered the men to fall out of line. She smiled to see the families reunited as excited wives rushed to the open arms of their loving husbands; children gleefully wrapped their little arms around their long-absent fathers' legs; while mothers and fathers welcomed their young sons, relieved to see they had survived their first battle.

Before turning to depart, Master Sonkai offered words of congratulations to the captains: "There will be a great banquet this evening. As the guests of honour, we expect to see both of you there."

"Of course, Master Sonkai. We will be there," promised Joval.

"Very well," said the elder, as he ambled up the stairs to join Dahlon and the others as they retired into the palace. "Yes, there will be much to discuss tonight!"

As if they had never left, the two warriors settled into their usual routine. With logs ablaze in the stone fireplace, several pots and a large kettle were filled with water to boil. Nayla set about making tea and tidying, removing all traces of dust that had gathered in their absence while Joval filled the bathtub with boiling water, topping it up with the cold, spring water to bring the temperature to a comfortable level.

He always allowed Nayla to bathe first, not so much because he was being courteous as he was being practical. In the length of time it took for him to bathe and dress for these functions, the warrior maiden would still be fussing with her gown, make-up and hair. It made far more sense to allow her to bathe first that way, usually by the time he was done; Nayla would almost be ready to go.

Rinsing his long, flowing mane, Joval's hair appeared almost black in this saturated state. He relaxed in the calming brace of the warm water, leaning against the sloping back of the tub. He momentarily closed his eyes; unwinding as the realization another season of war had thankfully come to an end. His eyes snapped open as a light, but urgent rapping on the closed door caught his attention.

"What is it, Nayla?"

"I need to speak to you."

"About what? Can it not wait until I am done in here?" responded Joval, his voice tightened with annoyance.

"Please," she pleaded.

Before the Elf could deny her entry, Nayla invited herself in.

"I could do with a little privacy right about now. Do you mind?" asked Joval.

"No, I do not mind," she answered quite innocently as she stepped in, crouching by the edge of the tub.

"I can see that," responded Joval, as he closed his eyes again, trying to ignore her presence.

Her silk gown puddled around her as she knelt down. Her arms were balanced on the edge of the tub as she rested her chin on her entwined fingers. She seemed totally oblivious to the fact this large Elf was naked beneath this water, now clouded with a thin film of soap.

"What do you suppose Master Sonkai meant when he said there was much to discuss tonight?" asked Nayla. Her eyes absentmindedly followed a raft of soap bubbles drifting aimlessly on this tide-less water. They came to cling to Joval's bent knees protruding above the waterline like two islands in a minuscule, finite sea.

"Strategy? Training of new recruits? Who can say? Your guess would be as good as mine," responded Joval. His eyes opened to gaze upon her face. It was clear to see she was greatly vexed by the elder's words. "Why are you so concerned?"

"I find it perplexing Dahlon was more distant than usual today. Normally, he seems to thrive on the pomp and pageantry of such public displays, especially when the crowds are in force, but today…" Her voice trailed off as she recalled the impassive stare he gave her as Master Sonkai honoured her. "He is up to something. I can sense it."

"Your little head may worry all for naught, warrior maiden," replied Joval. "Perhaps it is *something*, and then again, it may be absolutely *nothing*. What is the point of investing your time and energy worrying about this matter?"

"I suppose you are right," admitted Nayla, raising her chin from her hands. Her gown drooped open slightly to reveal the soft curves and deep shadows that formed the valley between her breasts. Joval averted his eyes, closing them once more as Nayla made no effort to draw the silk gown closed.

After a moment of silence, she spoke again.

"You wield a mighty weapon, Joval. Long have I admired it," confided Nayla.

"Pardon me?" gasped the Elf, startled by her comment. He struggled to sit upright in the tub.

"Is it true size and heft have little to do with how effective it is? That its power comes from the skill possessed by the wielder?" she continued.

Joval's face was flushed with embarrassment as he gasped: "What in the world do you speak of?"

"Your sword, of course."

"Oh… Of course," responded Joval, sighing with relief as he eased himself back against the tub.

"Where most Elves bearing arms wield the double-edged swords crafted by your people, my new sword is identical to the one gifted to you in all respects, except it is a good span shorter than yours," answered Nayla, as she opened her hand wide to show him how much longer his sword's blade measured against hers.

"The swordsmiths were given specific instructions to create a weapon similar in draw length to what you wield now. You know as well as I do the difficulties in extracting a sword that is beyond your capability," reminded the Elf, as he relaxed in the water once more. "And trust me; though the Elven sword is legendary and much sought after by the mortals in western Imago, the Taijins to the west of the Furai Mountains have admittedly forged a formidable weapon that is lighter and far superior in many respects. Keep it close to your side, for it will serve you well."

"I suppose I shall find out how well the swords perform when they are put to the test on the field of battle," replied Nayla, her chin resting back upon her hands.

Her eyes stared at the large, flat plates of well-developed pectoral muscles high on Joval's chest. Though she had caught fleeting glimpses of this Elf in the nude when she would interrupt his trysts as she hurled items down at he and his lover to stifle their noisy coupling, it was the first time she looked upon him this closely. His skin was smooth; absolutely devoid of any hair as was typical of the Elf-kind. She also noticed the wounds from past battles had all but disappeared on his flawless form. This momentary distraction was interrupted as Joval attempted to sink deeper into the tub to avoid her probing eyes.

"Will you stop staring?" ordered Joval.

"I was not staring, I was thinking."

"I am afraid to ask," groaned the Elf.

"And what of the Elven vest of mail? I am flattered I was honoured with such a vest, but is its power not greatly exaggerated? After all, it did not protect you when you were felled by an enemy sword during our first battle of the year."

"I can safely say you *underestimate* the power of this chain mail, Nayla. True it did not stop me from being wounded; but it is a matter of how one is attacked. These rings can take repeated, powerful blows from a sword or a halberd, not even marring the metal however, each link is forged in such a manner that only the tip of an arrow or the sword brought down with great force can weaken the link to penetrate the vest," confided Joval. "Mine has served me well on many occasions however; admittedly, it did not protect me on all counts."

"I suppose some protection is better than none. At least it is not cumbersome like the metal breastplates worn by the soldiers of the Imperial Army. I am confident it will allow me to move effortlessly, unimpeded by weight and the inflexibility of an armor shell."

"And on that note, do you not think it would be wise to finish dressing?" asked Joval, his eyes falling to the silk gown. It lay open to offer a tantalizing glimpse of the pale orbs of her breasts that were partially concealed by the sensuous fabric."

Nayla rose up, her small hands clutching the front of her gown. Nodding in agreement, she turned to part from the small room. As the Elf's dripping, wet form stepped out of the tub; he glanced down. He could not help but to notice that even the now tepid water did little to banish this unwanted desire.

Every person of importance, whether they be Elf or mortal, gathered for the banquet in the great dining hall. The elders were in an unmistakably jovial mood as they celebrated their good fortune with the defeat of the Imperial Army. Throughout the night, as Joval and Nayla shared tales of their adventure to the north, the warrior maiden could not help but notice that Dahlon Treeborn was withdrawn – clearly subdued for most part. Though he readily engaged in conversation when another initiated it, it was more out of courtesy and necessity than out of the enjoyment of entertaining members of high society. In Nayla's mind, Dahlon was definitely up to something. It was only a question of what.

With appetites well sated, the high Elf rose before all to make an announcement. Dahlon raised his hands to gesture for silence as the elders looked on in anticipation.

"Today, we were blessed with the return of our brave warriors from the frontline of battle. Led to victory by Captain Joval Stonecroft and my daughter, Captain Nayla Treeborn, they led our men to defeat the mounting enemy forces."

A rousing round of applause echoed through this great room as the Elf motioned for silence so he may continue.

"Today, the elders gifted Nayla with items deserving of a great warrior, leader and captain," said Dahlon.

Somehow, hearing the Elf refer to her as his daughter made Nayla cringe inwardly. Even his words of praise seemed rather hollow after all this time.

"The swords and the vest of Elven chain mail that were bestowed upon her shall aid her in the fight to protect our lands and our peoples," continued Dahlon; "but what I am gifting to Nayla on this day will allow her to face our rivals, to keep justice and peace for a good long time to come. Today, Nayla shall be blessed with the eternal life of my people!"

The high Elf's words were followed by surprised and appreciative murmurs from the guests as well as a polite round of applause.

Joval was pleased and relieved to finally hear these words. He reached beneath the table to give Nayla's hand a gentle squeeze. No longer will she face the ravages of pestilence and sickness; no longer will she be made to carry the scars she now bore; and now, if she so desired, she will have the chance to retreat to the Elf Haven rather than to linger in this realm for centuries before old age laid claim to her failing, aging body. His smile slowly dissolved as Nayla rose up to respond to her father.

"Thank you, Lord Treeborn. Though your offer is generous and I am sure, well intended, this is an offer a humble half-caste cannot accept," responded Nayla, as she stared directly into her father's eyes.

All in attendance gasped in response, shocked by her refusal of this wonderful blessing.

Dahlon glared at her. His back became rigid as her words raised his hackles and his ire. He raised his hands for silence as he questioned her: "Are you saying you refuse to accept this blessing?"

"Yes." Nayla's answer was concise. There was no hesitation to her response.

Guests froze in shock, and then jumped as Dahlon's fists slammed down hard on the tabletop to send cutlery, dishes and goblets rattling. Leaning across the table to confront her, he snarled in rage: "Are you a fool? Who in their right mind would refuse such a gift, a blessing such as this?"

"I assure you, I am no fool," replied Nayla, unwilling to fold to his unyielding stare and hostile tone. "And though I mean you no disrespect, believe me, for a person such as myself, an eternal life is hardly what I would call a blessing."

Dahlon threw back his chair as his trembling finger pointed to the doorway.

"To the meeting hall! Now!" demanded Joval, as he slammed his chair against the table before storming away from the dining room.

Nayla politely excused herself from the table, encouraging the guests to carry on in their absence. She smiled at the elders as they looked on, an expression of absolute mortification etched onto their faces.

As she turned away, Joval seized her by the arm to issue a warning.

"Be mindful of what you say and how you say it, Nayla," whispered the Elf. "Be *very* careful."

She gave him a small smile of understanding and a reassuring pat on his hand.

Turning down the corridor, she entered through the open door of the meeting hall. As she stepped inside, the door immediately slammed behind her. To Dahlon's chagrin, she did not even flinch. She already knew he was close at hand. His manic energy, stoked by his boiling rage emanated from his being like the heat rising from a white-hot coal.

Nayla calmly stood before him, waiting patiently for the Elf to speak his mind.

Dahlon paced the length of the room, eyeing his daughter with undeniable contempt that was fueled by her complete indifference. He angrily picked up a chair, slamming it down onto the floor as he growled: "What is the meaning of your ungrateful, arrogant display before our guests? Was it your intention to embarrass me?"

"I am sorry if you view my refusal of this so-called *gift* as a source of embarrassment."

"You are my daughter. How dare you not accept this blessing?"

"I am only your daughter when it suits you. And this *blessing* is meant to appease the elders, otherwise you would have gifted me with this on the day I was born, not now when you see my potential to lead your armies on to victory," she replied, unaffected by his caustic tone.

"You are determined to publicly humiliate me before my peers!" Dahlon's arms defiantly crossed his chest.

"That was not my intention, but it would appear you do this quite well all on your own." Her voice was matter-of-fact.

"How dare you?" he bellowed in rage as he threw the chair across the room.

"Now, now, Dahlon! Tantrums are rather unbecoming, especially for a high Elf," she noted, setting the chair upright to push it back against the table.

"You will address me as Lord Treeborn! Is that understood?" growled Dahlon, as he stood before her. He rose to his full height making every attempt to intimidate his daughter as his great shadow engulfed her little form.

"And you will accept this gift of eternal life or I will… I will…" stammered the Elf, as he allowed himself to be consumed in his bitterness and anger.

"Or you will kill me?" finished Nayla, as she stood steadfast before her father.

In absolute rage, his right hand lunged out, seizing his daughter by the throat.

"Do not tempt me!" snarled Dahlon, as he rammed her hard against the door.

"Kill me if you wish, but I will tell you now, I will never disgrace myself as you do. I shall never allow myself to stoop this low. Though there is no love lost between us, I will never raise my hand to you."

"Am I to blame because you drive me to despair? Am I at fault your wicked tongue forces me to instill respect?"

"For an enlightened being I am appalled you believe respect can be garnered in such a manner."

"You are a thankless, wretched deviant! If I am made to dole out punishment to teach you to be respectful, then my actions are warranted!" he ranted as his hand began to slowly tighten around Nayla's throat.

"If you feel your actions are so justified, then why do you not dole out this *punishment* in full view of the elders? Why behind closed doors?"

Dahlon slowly released his grip only to turn on her once more. Her head slammed against the door as his hand squeezed around her throat.

"Come now, little warrior," goaded the Elf. "Let us see if you have nerve enough to fight for your life, to rise up against your own father."

"I will not fight you," gasped Nayla, raising her hands before her in surrender.

"How pathetic! The mighty Captain Nayla Treeborn, unable to defend herself," taunted Dahlon, his right hand continued to tighten as his left hand secured the latch on the door so none may enter.

"I shall not raise my hand to you, but neither will I allow you to run rough-shod over me ever again!" declared the little warrior.

As his suffocating grip clamped like a vise around her throat, Nayla's left hand seized Dahlon's little finger while her right hand grabbed his thumb, prying his large hand off. Working against the vulnerable joints, she pulled back on these pained digits until he was forced to unhand her.

In one swift movement, she wrenched his hand over, applying a wrist-throw. The Elf crashed to the floor, landing on his back. Before he could move another muscle, Nayla locked out his right arm. Using her shin as a fulcrum, she worked Dahlon's arm against her right leg, wrenching the Elf over to flip him from his back onto his stomach. Pinning his arm behind his back, he was now immobilized.

"I will never fight you, but make no mistake, you shall never treat me like I am some kind of animal to be beaten into submission!" declared the little warrior. "I am not some dog you can kick because you are angry at the world!"

Dahlon gasped in surprise as a loud pounding on the door was followed by Joval's call: "Lord Treeborn, what is going on in there?"

"What will it be, Dahlon?" asked Nayla, in a whisper as her left hand reached for the latch. "I can quite easily open the door without releasing my hold on you. Is this how you wish to be found?"

"No," grunted the Elf, as she applied a little more pressure. He groaned more so in embarrassment than pain as he called out in response to Joval: "I am sorry, Captain Stonecroft, I am temporarily indisposed."

Again, Joval pounded on the door. "Nayla! Are you in there?"

"Yes, Joval," she called back. "We are just having a little father/daughter discussion."

"And how do you fare?" queried the Elf, pressing his ear against the door to listen for signs of distress on her part.

"Things could not be better," answered the little warrior, her words sounding confident. "Run along now, Joval. I will not be long."

"Very well," responded Joval, as he issued a warning for Dahlon to heed: "I will be close at hand, if need be."

She could hear Joval's soft steps disappear down the corridor.

"Now, where were we before we were so rudely interrupted?" asked Nayla. "Oh yes! Shall we finish our conversation here on the floor, or do you prefer to sit at the table like two civilized, mature people?"

Dahlon struggled momentarily, but the more he struggled, the more agony he inflicted upon himself. He came to the appalling realization his much smaller daughter had him effectively restrained; helplessly pinned to the floor.

"The table! We shall sit at the table!" yelped the Elf, wincing in pain.

"Are you going to behave?" questioned Nayla, sounding much like a mother reprimanding an errant child.

Dahlon grumbled some Elvish words of profanity under his breath. He ceased only as Nayla's knee pressed down on his arm that was trapped against his back.

"I will behave!" promised the Elf, his face contorting into a grimace of pain.

"That is more like it," said Nayla. She rose up from Dahlon's prostrate body to pull a chair out for him.

"Sit!" she ordered.

The high Elf smoothed back his ruffled attire, brushing off the invisible dust as well as the traces of humiliation. His large hands swept back his dark, disheveled hair as he approached the table. Like a big dog that had been soundly smacked across his snout by a much smaller master, Dahlon reluctantly took his place. This time, it was *his daughter* sitting in *his chair* at the head of *his table*.

Nayla sat back, her hands behind her head, reclining in Dahlon's great chair as the Elf sat before her. She appeared calm; completely unruffled by their hostile altercation.

"Why are you so adamant about refusing this gift of eternal life?" asked the Elf, as he struggled to regain his composure before her.

"Perhaps the more appropriate question is: Why you are so adamant I accept this so-called gift?"

"I admit I do so upon the request of the elders. They believe it is their insurance you shall exist for as long as you are needed to drive back the enemy forces," confided Dahlon, inwardly reveling in the hopes that perhaps his daughter would be wounded to know even the well meaning elders acted on their own best interest. "Otherwise, I feel it is a terrible waste to squander such a blessing on the likes of you."

Nayla's intense stare seemed to burn a hole through his heart as she mulled over his words. Sensing his growing discomfort, she remained unmoved, now impervious to his callous tone and harsh treatment. Instead, she chose to enjoy this momentary repose.

"So answer me this, warrior maiden. Why do you decline this blessing when it is yours for the taking?" questioned Dahlon.

Nayla was silent. A dozen different answers ran through her head and each one was just as significant as the next. Finally, she replied: "I cannot deny that in my life I had dreamed of possessing the eternal life of the Elf-kind. Alas, it shall remain but a dream, for I am trapped in an unending nightmare that will not cease even in my waking hours. Forever will I be trapped between two worlds and two cultures; shunned by one, denied by the other and despised by both. I have as much desire to lengthen my existence in this realm as I do to enter the Twilight and endure an eternity with the Elves in the Haven."

"You willingly condemn yourself to the unknown?" queried her father. "For if you die now, you know your soul shall be set loose into a realm uninhabited by those of mortals' and Elves'. Is that what you choose?"

"What I choose is a finite life of my own making. What I choose is not to be bound to you by this so-called gift, for I know it shall bear a heavy price, one of which I am unwilling to pay with my life, especially for an eternity," responded Nayla. "I wish to owe you nothing."

"If you feel this fate, to pass from this realm alone, is better than to show some gratitude and consideration for your father, then so be it," grunted Dahlon, scowling in resentment.

"It matters not to me if I were to leave this realm alone, for I am alone."

"Then I shall tell the elders *you chose* to decline this gift," stated Dahlon.

"You are at liberty to tell them whatever you please. It makes no difference to me," replied Nayla, as she rose up to depart the room.

"I am not yet done with you," growled Dahlon, rising from his chair to continue his tirade.

Nayla slowly turned to gaze upon the high Elf.

"I am most certainly done with you," retorted Nayla. "If you wish to address me further, you shall have to do so in the company of our esteemed guests."

Dahlon watched as her silk gown twirled in a palette of color. She turned, heading for the doorway to breeze out of the meeting room. As Nayla made her way down the corridor, Joval seized her by the arm, pulling her into the vestibule. He gazed intently at her face, looking for signs she may have been accosted once again.

"He did not hurt you, did he?" asked Joval, his blue eyes shone, burning with resentment for Dahlon.

"Oh no!" she responded. "I had the situation well in hand."

The Elf's eyebrows arched up in wonder as he asked: "Alright, what have you done?"

Nayla gave him a telling smile as she responded: "As I said once before, I shall never raise my hand to my father, but I dare say, he will think long and hard before he scrounges up the nerve to confront me again."

Joval's eyes narrowed as he scrutinized her. "Please do not tell me that if I should walk into the meeting hall I will find Dahlon a broken and bleeding man."

Nayla casually sauntered away from Joval as she whispered to him:" "Bleeding no, but most definitely broken."

16

# of love and war

Sitting before the fireplace, Nayla's hands wrapped around a piping hot cup of tea. Joval pulled a chair up next to hers. He could see she was mired deep in thought.

"So tell me, little warrior, exactly what had transpired during that private meeting with your father? Have you thought better of Lord Treeborn's blessing of eternal life?"

"Indeed, I have thought upon his offer and it was no epiphany his actions were merely to appease the elders," replied Nayla. "But I am most disheartened in knowing the elders are motivated by their own interests to keep me alive and in their service."

"Perhaps it is not the most prestigious means by which to be bestowed with this gift, but it matters not," responded Joval, trying to sound cheerful. "What matters most is that you shall be granted passage to the Elf Haven if you should tire of the strife and turmoil of this world or should you be grievously wounded. There, you will not be made to suffer in pain."

"That holds little comfort for me," stated Nayla.

"What do you mean?" questioned Joval.

"I refused Dahlon's *gift,* if you can call it that."

"No, Nayla!" the Elf groaned in disbelief. "That is not what I wanted to hear from you! What were you thinking? I will have to speak to your father. I shall tell him you made a mistake – a grave mistake."

"It was no mistake, Joval." Her eyes did not leave her cup, staring wistfully as bits of tealeaves floated to the surface. "As much as Dahlon despises me, he is also a vexation to *my* spirit. He has become the bane of my existence. I am already bound to that Elf by blood and name; I do not wish to live my life in servitude, ingratiating myself to him for a gift I do not desire. I would rather live a finite life of my own design than to be obligated to him; to be at his mercy for an eternity."

Joval was shocked by her decision. He knelt down before her, staring into her dark, liquid eyes that reflected every spark crackling in the fireplace.

"Nayla, you know this chance will not present itself again," stated Joval, frustrated by her indifference. "You know Dahlon will never repeat this offer, especially now that you have publicly declined this gift. Of all things, Nayla, you have affronted him in the presence of his peers, before all on council!"

"Even if I were to be *blessed* with the immortality of the Elf-kind, it will not make my presence in the Haven any more bearable. I am a half-caste. That is something that will never change. Your people will never accept me. With the passing of time and through my deeds to protect the people of this land, I am tolerated. However, I know mortal man or Elf will ever love me. I have no place in either world."

Joval was disheartened to know Nayla would now be doomed to languish in this realm. She would be made to suffer as the unmerciful hands of time ravaged her body and mind until her life was spent, only to cast her soul to the four winds when the end came.

Almost four weeks before the arrival of the solstice, winter's deadly grip wreaked havoc on the lands. Snow fell thick and heavy to smother the world already stripped bare by the cruel north winds. And with this bitter cold crept in an insidious and silent killer unseen by all.

One by one, villages far and wide fell victim to a strain of influenza of pandemic proportions that laid claim to many lives. The very young, those already weakened by cold or disease as well as the elderly, were the hardest hit. They succumbed to an inflammation of the lungs and a raging fever. They would die within only a few days of contracting this virus.

In a bid to contain the spread of this deadly infection, all those inflicted were quarantined. In Nagana, the empty training hall was converted into a house of healing where the citizens of Nagana and the surrounding villages were brought to recover, or to die.

As the numbers of Taijins swelled and crowded into the training hall, the quarters housing the warriors were used to handle the overflow, forcing the men not infected to seek room and board elsewhere.

Dahlon Treeborn assigned the Elves to travel the countryside to assist those unable to make the arduous trek to Nagana for assistance. Unaffected by such pestilence, and able to endure this foul weather far better than the mortals, the Elves set forth to administer herbal remedies as recommended by the Taijin healers.

In this situation, Elven powers, this ability to miraculously heal had no affect on the ravages of this viral infection. Though all the Elves have the capacity to heal, and some were more specialized in this art to mend traumatic injuries such as broken bones, weapon damaged tissue and flesh, they were now powerless. Because they do not fall victim to disease, none had the ability to remedy this condition. They were now relegated to the role of offering comfort to the dying, medicine to those still strong enough to recover, and to cremate the corpses, in hopes of putting a halt to the rampant spread of this plague.

It soon became apparent to the Elves tending to the sick and dying the only relief these mortals found came from a substance in the willow plant. Its medicinal properties worked to calm the fever and to reduce the inflammation of both joints and lungs. Large cauldrons of water steeped with the inner bark of the willow tree were produced, but as fast as the batches could be made and distributed to those in need and delivered to the outlying villages, they were faced with a quickly depleting supply of willow. There was no choice but to venture westward towards the Iron Mountains. It was only here that the willow grew in abundance, flourishing in the shadows of these formidable mountains along the Reyuzan River and along the western shores of Safiya Lake.

Unable to tend to the sick, as she was just as susceptible to this infection, Nayla volunteered to lead an expedition to collect more of this healing plant. She estimated the journey would take two weeks to get there and back if heavy snowdrifts did not impede them.

Under a bleak winter sky, Nayla and six Taijin warriors ventured westward. They would race against time and the elements to harvest what they could of this plant.

Joval, Valtar and the other Elves remained to administer to the needs of the ill and to deal with the grim task of cremating the dead. It seemed that for each dead man, woman and child, another was brought in to fill the vacant cot. Their only consolation came from those they were able to return home with the promise of restored health.

On the fortnight since their departure, Nayla and her party finally returned to the fortress city. Their journey home was marred with illness as the warrior maiden contracted the infection. She ordered the other warriors to mind their distance around her as she isolated herself from their camp. Upon their arrival, she instructed the men to return to their home. She would deliver the willow to the healing house. Already tainted by this disease, further exposure would make no difference now.

The Elves heard Nayla's arrival at the door long before she appeared. Her inflamed lungs caused her to cough and hack as she breathed. Her steps were heavy and sluggish as she fought the ravages of the fever as it burned and spread through her body.

Ignoring the orders of the Elves to lie down with the others infected by this virus, Nayla stumbled back to her steed. Valtar watched as she struggled to pull herself onto the saddle as the fever sapped what was left of her waning strength. She seemed to waver dangerously to and fro with the rocking motion of her mount as she urged the steed on to the east gate of the city.

Nayla's vision began to blur as she fought to guide her horse through the dimming light, back to Joval's cottage. Leaning forward, she rested against her mare's neck, hoping the steed could make her own way home as the last of her energy and will dissipated from her being.

The warm glow of light from the cabin looked so very far away as the Nayla began to lose consciousness. As she finally slumped forward in exhaustion brought on by the arduous trek and the raging fever, she slipped from the saddle. Plunging into a deep black abyss, she suddenly landed into Valtar's outstretched arms as he caught her.

Concerned by her condition when she departed from the healing house, by the time he retrieved his steed, Nayla was already gone. He followed her back, and none too soon.

"Joval, open the door!" hollered Valtar, kicking it with the toe of his boot.

The door flew open and to Joval's surprise, there stood his best friend with Nayla in his arms.

"What happened?" asked Joval, motioning Valtar in.

"She has caught the infection," explained Valtar, stepping inside the cottage with Nayla's limp body.

"Over here," ordered Joval. "Place her on my bed."

Valtar lowered her onto the counterpane.

"I cannot stay, my friend," stated the Elf. "When I knew she was stricken by this illness, I brought back some willow with me. You shall have to prepare the remedy yourself."

"That I can do," replied Joval. "Thank you for bringing her back. And please, do not utter a word of this to Lord Treeborn."

"But Joval, Lord Treeborn has the right to know of his daughter's condition. If she has fallen ill, especially if she should die, Lord Treeborn should be told," argued Valtar.

"She will *not* die," countered Joval. "And believe me, he gloats far too much about Nayla's so-called weak mortal blood. This shall only feed his contempt for her."

"Joval –"

"Valtar, as your captain, I wish for you to comply with my order," insisted Joval.

"Damn it, Joval! I hate it when you use your rank to force me to do your bidding."

"Please, Valtar," pleaded the Elf, 'then do it as my friend."

"Very well. I know nothing of her or her condition," responded Valtar. "You shall be the one to deal with Lord Treeborn if she should die."

"Fair enough," replied Joval, as he showed Valtar out.

Joval watched as Valtar turned Nayla's steed into the stable before heading back to the city. Turning his attention to Nayla, he set a candle on the nightstand by the bed.

Her teeth were chattering uncontrollably as her small body shivered with cold. Joval touched her forehead with his hand. Beneath the beads of perspiration, she was entrenched in a raging fever. He noticed her raiment was drenched in sweat as her body attempted to counter the fever however, in this weather, this cooling was taking place much too rapidly.

Joval worked quickly, peeling the bark off the willow and steeping it in the kettle of water boiling over the fire. As he waited for the medicine to brew, he gathered towels and a blanket from a chest.

"Nayla, wake up! Can you hear me?" He shook her by the shoulders.

Struggling feebly to push him off, she whispered through her chattering teeth: "So cold… So very cold..."

"Nayla, wake up. You must get these wet clothes off immediately. It will only make you worse to wear it," said Joval, slapping her face to bring her around.

His abrupt actions did nothing. Nayla slipped back into unconsciousness. She was totally oblivious to the Elf's desperate plea.

Joval had no choice but to remove her raiment. He unlaced her boots and slipped them off. Working quickly, he stripped her down, peeling off layers of damp clothing. It was no wonder her body was so cold, even with this fever. He used the towels to dry her body, rubbing her briskly to increase her circulation. His hand touched her forehead, and then her stomach. Her skin still felt so very clammy and chilled. Her flesh was raised although her face burned like an inferno.

For the first time, he noticed that though Nayla was short in stature like a Taijin woman, her toned, lithe body was like that of an Elf maiden: completely devoid of body hair. He gently slipped her beneath the counterpane, drawing it up around her neck.

With the willow sufficiently steeped and the liquid adequately cooled, Joval lifted Nayla's head, slowly tipping the concoction into her mouth. Stroking her head, he prayed the medicine would take hold soon to battle the fever, but she continued to shiver. It was clear to Joval the warmth from the fireplace and the extra layer of blanket he had thrown over the counterpane did nothing to stave off the chills.

"Nayla, I mean to keep you warm. I am going to lie here with you, by your side," explained the Elf.

She did not respond to his voice or words.

Joval quickly removed his own apparel. He lay next to Nayla's side, drawing her small body close to his. With her back against his bare chest, he wrapped his arms around her shoulders as his legs entwined with hers; he used the energy of his own body heat to warm Nayla's shivering form. As he held her next to his naked skin, the strange irony that somehow this was not the way he ever imagined she would share this bed with him flashed through his mind. He shook his head to dispel this thought.

As Nayla's body fought back against the fever, Joval could do nothing more than keep her warm and comfortable. He listened to the gentle sound of her breathing as the shivering slowly began to subside. He cursed inwardly as he thought upon her refusal of eternal life and the fact she would have been spared the affliction of such an illness if she had. All her skills with the sword and her courage on the battlefield did nothing to prepare Joval for the realization this warrior maiden was a mortal with all the frailties that comes with being part human. This knowledge saddened Joval deeply.

The glare of the brilliant winter sun penetrated the curtains still drawn across the windows. As the light flooded into the room, Nayla stirred from her long sleep. Her eyes drowsily opened as a cool, damp cloth pressed gently against her cheeks and forehead. She blinked hard as the familiar surroundings came into focus.

"The worst of the fever is over now," said Joval. Dipping the small cloth into a basin of cold water, he wrung it out before placing it back on her forehead. "You are still burning with fever, but you were far worse last night. I swear you were on the brink of death."

"I do not recall coming here," whispered Nayla, her throat ruined by the bouts of coughing as her lungs attempted to throw off the infection. "The last I remember was delivering the willow to Valtar in the healing house."

"It was Valtar who showed up at my door with you in his arms," answered Joval, reaching for the willow bark tonic.

"Valtar?"

"Do not sound so surprised, Nayla," said the Elf. "I know you have many preconceived notions about him, but he is not as bad as you would like to believe. He even delivered enough willow to treat you when he realized you had been stricken with this illness."

"I recall none of this."

"Of course you would not remember any of last night. How you even made the return trip is beyond me. You were delirious with fever. When Valtar delivered you to my bed, you were burning up, and yet, your body was visibly shivering. Chilled to the bones you were. It was as though this influenza wreaked havoc with your entire body. If Valtar had not brought you here when he did, and if I had not taken the measures I was forced to, I have no doubt you would have passed on last night."

"Measures? What measures?" questioned Nayla, as she took in a mouthful of the willow *tea* from the earthenware cup Joval handed to her.

"You were shivering with cold so violently, I had to strip you of your raiment, and then I, too, removed my clothes and lay by your side to warm you."

Nayla's eyes grew wide open in shock as the liquid she had in her mouth spewed out in a fine spray right into the Elf's surprised face.

"You did what?" she coughed and sputtered.

She was absolutely mortified as she lifted the counterpane to peek beneath. True to his words, she was indeed naked.

"You were absolutely freezing, Nayla," explained Joval, snatching the cloth from her forehead to blot his face dry. "You were out in this foul weather with a raging fever, wearing raiment that was drenched in sweat. Short of throwing lumps of coal into the bed with you, it was the only way to warm you quickly."

"You did not do anything *funny*, did you?" queried Nayla, as she drew the counterpane tightly around her neck.

"What do you take me for?" His indignation flared as he snapped at her. "It was all quite innocent, I tell you. I was a perfect gentleman, and besides, I take no gratification in having my way with a woman who is about as lively and frigid as a dead fish!"

The deadly pandemic passed as quickly. Though it claimed the lives of many, mostly the very young and the old who were too weak to fight the fever, surprisingly, even the most unlikely victims succumbed to the viral infection. Mekai, the largest and in Nayla's opinion, the most belligerent of the young Kagai Warriors in Anshen did not survive his bout against the deadly virus.

Nayla was surprised and devastated upon receiving word of this warrior's passing, lighting a single candle and a stick of incense in the sanctuary to commemorate Mekai's short life and unexpected death.

By the beginning of the new year, the training hall and the warriors' quarters were returned to its former use. With the last of the infirmed to be sent on home to finish his recovery, the warriors that were housed here returned after the quarters were aired out and all the cots stripped of its beddings. Freshly cleaned linen, boiled and air-dried to remove any lingering traces of the infection and death, made the quarters useable once more.

Nayla made a hasty recovery after enduring the worst of the fever and in no time, as fear of the influenza passed and life returned to normal, she resumed with her role training the next generation of warriors.

With word of her skills and reputation spreading far and wide, more young men eagerly took up the call to arms; anxious to learn from the warrior maiden they had heard so much about. No longer met with the same level of resistance by those questioning her skills and ability, for her victories in the field of battle and the confidence her warriors had in her leadership spoke for itself.

As usual, the training was conducted outdoors and though mentally taxing and physically grueling, the men took to the sessions with great enthusiasm. After a long week of hard training, Joval, Valtar and other senior warriors made plans to partake in libation at the local drinking establishment as was the weekly ritual for the men.

With the weapons stored back in the training hall, Nayla waited for the last of the men to leave so she could close up the building. As Joval turned to join the others, Valtar glanced over at Nayla as she proceeded to slide the door closed.

"Why do you not join us this eve, Captain Treeborn?" asked Valtar. "Come share in drink or two."

She was momentarily stunned by his invitation. Staring at the Elf through narrowed, suspicious eyes, she questioned him: "What are you up to, Valtar Briarwood?"

"I do not know what you speak of, captain," replied Valtar, trying his best to appear wounded by her doubtful words.

"I have never been invited to an outing with the men before. Why now?" she asked.

"Why not?" He answered her question with one of his own.

As Nayla scrutinized the Elf, Joval stood behind her, frantically waving his hands for Valtar to desist – to decline his invitation. His animated gestures went ignored by Valtar.

"I just felt as a captain, you should take the time to become better acquainted with those in your company; join your men for a bit of merriment," responded Valtar, glancing over Nayla's head to see Joval repeatedly sliding his index finger across his neck as though he was going to slash his friend's throat if he did not revoke the invitation.

Nayla quickly turned to spy a wide-eyed Joval abruptly drop his hands to his sides. Turning his gaze skyward, he did his darnedest to look innocent. She knew immediately Joval did not want her to accompany them on this outing.

She smiled at Valtar as she took him up on his offer: "I would love to join you and the others for a drink. Just give me a moment to lock these doors."

"Very well, Captain Treeborn. It shall be good for you to socialize with these warriors rather than constantly beating on them and bullying them about," stated Valtar, dodging Joval's hand as the Elf tried to cuff him on the back of his head for instigating this. "We shall wait for you in the courtyard."

"Are you daft, Valtar?" asked Joval, thoroughly annoyed by his friend's decision. "What was the meaning of that?"

"You never invite her so I thought I would take the opportunity to do so," answered Valtar.

"For good reason," grumbled Joval. "Suppose she cannot hold her liquor? How do you think she shall come across if she is falling-down-drunk before the men she is expected to lead into battle? It is hardly an image that would garner respect. Is that what you want?"

"Come now, Joval! Where is your sense of fun?" cajoled the Elf, eager to see what the night would bring.

"I believe you intend to have some *fun* at Nayla's expense," growled Joval, angry his friend was setting Nayla up to humiliate herself. "You know in all likelihood she will respond to drink about as well as the mortals do."

"You do not know that, Joval," argued Valtar. "But perhaps this eve, we shall find out for ourselves."

"I swear, Valtar, if she finds herself in trouble because of you, you shall pay dearly for it," warned Joval.

"Let us go, men," said Nayla, excited to be part of the group. "I shall buy the first round!"

"First-timers *always* buy the first round," explained Valtar, as he led the way.

"Ah, that explains why he was so eager to invite me," whispered Nayla to Joval.

Winding their way through the gray haze of pipe smoke and the cloistered maze of tables and chairs, Valtar claimed several tall stools at the bar. Nayla hoisted herself onto the stool, sitting between Joval and a Taijin warrior as Valtar sat next to Joval.

"So what will it be, Captain Stonecroft?" The innkeeper tending the bar shouted to be heard above the noise of the drunken revelers.

"Ale all around," requested Joval.

Nayla stopped the innkeeper as he turned away to fill the order. "Make mine wine, please."

The man took a second look, realizing the request came from a woman. "Of course, young miss! I shall not be long."

True to his word, the innkeeper served Nayla first, placing a goblet of red wine before her, and then passing the pewter mugs of ale on to the men. Nayla passed him some money, enough to cover all the drinks and still provide the innkeeper with a generous tip.

"Where have you been hiding her, Captain Stonecroft? You should bring this young lady more often," smiled the innkeeper, as he pocketed the change.

"Perhaps you are right my friend. Lady Treeborn does not leave the confines of the palace often enough," replied the Elf, observing his Taijin comrades quickly quaff down their ale.

"Lady Treeborn!" repeated the innkeeper, gasping in surprise. "I am so pleased to meet you! My son speaks highly of you, Captain Treeborn. He made his first foray to the north to do battle with the enemy last summer. He is proud to be a member of your battalion."

"It is kind of your son to speak well of me," smiled Nayla. "I am the one to be honoured. It is a privilege and a wonderful opportunity to work with such fine, young men."

"Fine, young men indeed!" laughed the innkeeper. "I would say you have changed these reckless, young rogues and scallywags into well-mannered, disciplined young men – men their parents can be proud of!"

"They were in need of a little guidance, that is all," assured Nayla, taking a sip of the carmine liquid.

"This one is on me," offered the innkeeper, topping up her goblet.

"Thank you," she replied graciously.

A loud squeal of delight pierced the air as several women, obviously local courtesans, recognized Joval and Valtar at the bar. They eagerly pushed their way through the inebriated crowd to fling themselves at the Elves, shoving and jostling for position.

"Captain Stonecroft, where have you been hiding of late?" queried one of the Taijin women. She gazed wantonly at him as her well-manicured fingernails played teasingly with Joval's long hair.

Nayla watched the interaction with bland interest as the woman maneuvered around so she was standing between her and the Elf.

"Have you found another woman to tend to your needs? One better than me?" questioned the courtesan. "Or perhaps none come calling to your home with that *half-caste woman* there."

"If you leave now that *half-caste woman* you speak of will not be there," grunted Nayla, speaking over her shoulder.

The courtesan turned to face her as she retorted smugly: "And how would you know that?"

Nayla gazed into her eyes as she gave the woman a wicked smile.

"It is you!" gasped the courtesan. The sudden spark of recognition ignited in her eyes. She smacked Joval on his arm as she harped: "What is *she* doing here?"

"I would think it is safe to assume Captain Treeborn is drinking wine," responded the Elf, shrugging with indifference as he returned to his ale.

"*She* is here with *you*? Did you invite her?" groaned the courtesan, glaring at Nayla with mounting envy and contempt.

Joval merely shook his head in response, pointing his thumb at Valtar as being the guilty culprit. The Elf, too preoccupied to notice Joval's accusing digit, had his arms around the other two women. Valtar was surprised when the courtesan slapped his back with her silk purse.

"What was that for?" grumbled Valtar, turning with a start to face his assailant.

"That was for bringing *her*!" she hissed, raising her fist to strike the Elf once more with her purse.

Nayla reached over, yanking her away from Valtar before she could accost him again.

"Is it posted somewhere I am not permitted entry into this establishment?" asked Nayla. "I am here because I wish to have a drink, nothing more."

"Really now?" replied the courtesan, nuzzling against Joval's body as her hands fondled his shoulders. "So it matters not if I do *this* to him?"

She rubbed her body up against the Elf in a sensuous manner, like an affectionate feline rubbing up against one's leg.

"Do you mind?" grumbled Joval, leaning away from her amorous attention. "We are in a public place."

"You never minded before, Captain Stonecroft." She continued to eye Nayla, watching for signs of jealousy.

"I believe you have *rubbed* him the wrong way," mocked Nayla. "Obviously, he minds now."

"I was not addressing you, you little witch!" shrilled the courtesan.

"I do declare! You feel threatened by my presence, *harpy*!" announced Nayla, speaking with all certainty.

The woman's smoldering brown eyes burned with hatred. She gave Nayla's braid a hard, deliberate yank.

"You silly fool, you chose the wrong girl to pick a fight with, if that is your intention," growled Nayla. Hopping off her stool, she confronted the courtesan.

"Cat-fight!" Valtar announced with obvious glee as he leapt from his stool. He snatched his ale from the bar, backing away with the two other courtesans still on his arms.

"Now see here, ladies," said Joval, hoping to put a stop to the hostility before it erupted into a full-blown altercation. "There is no reason why we cannot all just get along."

"Shut up!" Nayla and the courtesan both screamed at him as they squared off, causing the Elf to shrink back from their harsh tone.

"Perhaps Captain Stonecroft has had good reason not to bed the likes of you," snapped Nayla.

"Well, if he has chosen *you* over *me*, it is only because you are the only *thing* that comes close to resembling an Elf-woman in these parts," spat the courtesan, her index finger jabbing the little warrior in her chest. "And you are a poor substitute for one at that!"

"Ooooh! That was nasty!" commented Valtar. Hoping tempers would flare and lead to an all-out fisticuff, he goaded Nayla on: "I will have you know, Captain Treeborn will not stand for such insolence. Will you now, captain?"

Both women glared at Valtar, upon which he immediately ceased his jabbering and took half a step back from their wrathful stare.

"This Elf is mine!" railed the courtesan, thrusting her face directly into Nayla's. "If it were not for your constant presence, I would be called upon more often!"

"Did it ever occur to you that Captain Stonecroft has simply lost interest in you?" queried Nayla. "Perhaps he found another more fair, without your ugly demeanor."

"*Ugly*? How dare you call me ugly?" she shrieked like a demon.

"You do not listen very well, do you? I said you have an ugly-"

Before Nayla could finish her sentence, the angry courtesan lunged. Her shaped and lacquered talons lashed out at the warrior maiden's face.

Nayla merely angled her body out of the way, causing the woman to stumble forward into Joval's chest. The Elf caught her as she crumpled into a helpless, pathetic heap in his arms. With exaggerated sobs, she cried to him: "How can you allow her to hurl such cruel words at me! Do you not care for me as you once did?"

Joval scowled at the little warrior as he scolded her: "Enough, Nayla! You know she is defenseless against one such as you."

"Do not underestimate her, Joval. I am confident she has the *fangs* to match those *claws* of hers," grunted Nayla.

"I suggest you two keep your distance on this eve," recommended Joval. He guided the teary courtesan away from the bar to a table in the corner of the room.

Nayla hoisted herself back onto the stool as Valtar reclaimed his seat at the bar. Gazing over at her, he noticed her eyes following Joval as he comforted his mistress.

"I cannot believe you allowed that wench to get away with it," commented the Elf. "You could have beaten her soundly with both hands tied behind your back."

"There is no gratification in fighting one as defenseless and dim-witted as she," argued Nayla.

"Still, it would have made for great entertainment," answered Valtar, wistfully.

"Are you insane? Had I broken her fingernail or put a single strand of hair out of place on that perfect little head of hers, she would have swooned in agony, collapsing into Joval's arms. What sport is that?"

"I suppose only men can appreciate these rare and special moments: Two women rolling about on the ground. Wrestling, engaging in some hair pulling, a little slapping…" sighed Valtar, as he watched the other two courtesans join their friend at the table with Joval.

"Dream on, Valtar! You sound like a mortal when you speak like this. I cannot belief an Elf would take pleasure in such a base act."

"I may be an Elf, but I am still a man," said Valtar, smiling coyly at the women in Joval's company.

"What Captain Stonecroft sees in her is beyond me," grunted Nayla, shaking her head in disgust.

Valtar shrugged his shoulders as he responded: "She merely fills a need."

"Then Joval must be one *needful* Elf if he settles for the likes of that trollop," remarked Nayla, taking a sip of her wine.

"Come now, Captain Treeborn, a little hedonism does not make one needful," argued Valtar. "In fact, it is natural to respond to desire. It is no different than quenching one's thirst."

"I suppose it depends on how *thirsty* one is," countered Nayla, as she watched the courtesan fawn over Joval.

Valtar motioned for the innkeeper to deliver another pint of ale. "Would you care for some more wine?"

"I have more than enough, thank you very much." She placed her hand over the still-full goblet as an inebriated warrior staggered to her side. He leaned heavily against her, throwing a drunken arm around her shoulders.

"Cap'n Treeborn, fancy meetin'… meetin' you here," he slurred between hiccups.

"Do you mind?" Nayla pushed him off.

"Checkin' out the men, eh? Lookin' for a little fun are you?" determined the intoxicated mortal.

"*Men*? All I see are a bunch of drunken *boys*!" Nayla muttered in disdain, leaning away from him.

"Be nice, cap'n," slurred the Taijin warrior, his tongue numbed by too much ale. "And believe me, I ain't no boy. A boy don't carry a sword like this!"

His hand dropped down to grab his crotch in a lewd display.

"My! You are vulgar when you are drunk," noted Nayla, cringing in disgust.

The warrior chuckled in his alcohol-induced haze as he hiccupped: "I am… I am… not drunk. And I assure you, my dear, I wouldn't be bo… bo… boastin' if it were not so."

"I am not *'your dear'*, and yes, you are most definitely drunk. So drunk in fact, you do not even know it," grumbled Nayla, shoving the man off again.

He took another swig of ale as he gave her a lecherous smile and a wink, followed by an offer: "So whaddaya say, cap'n? Wanna check out my *sword*?"

"Now see here, you inebriated sod! Show some respect," ordered Valtar, as he scowled at the inebriated man. "This is Captain Treeborn you are speaking to."

"Ah, come now, Elf! She ain't workin' right now," he slurred. "She's here like the rest of us – here for a little fun. So whaddaya say dearie?"

Valtar seized the unruly warrior by the scruff of his neck to physically remove him from their presence. To his surprise, Nayla stopped him.

"You know, Valtar; he is so boastful perhaps he does not exaggerate. Perhaps he is every bit a *man* as he brags to be," said Nayla. A wicked smile curled her lips as she hopped off the stool.

"What are you suggesting, Captain Treeborn?" asked Valtar, his fists reluctantly unclenching the drunken warrior.

"He is correct, I am not on duty. I am here for the same reason as you and all the other warriors are here for. I am here to relax, have a drink and have some fun," she replied.

"Thadda girl!" said the wobbly warrior. He turned to his drunken comrades sitting at a table, giving them a wink and a *thumb's up* as notification of his soon-to-be latest and greatest conquest.

Valtar leaned in close to Nayla, cautioning her: "He means to make a fool of you; to take advantage of you."

"We shall see about that," she answered with a wink of her eye as she linked arms with the drunken warrior. Even in his less than lucid state, this warrior still possessed rakishly good looks. "Besides, if he insists on boasting about his *sword,* then I want to see if he truly does have something worth boasting about."

She escorted the warrior to the door as he puffed his chest out and swaggered for all to see he had won this captain's favor with his charm and manly attributes. As she guided the warrior past Joval's table, the Elf glanced up to see Nayla leaving on the man's arm. She barely took notice of him as the courtesan threw herself on Joval to divert his attention.

Nayla took the warrior's hand and led him to a secluded back alley just behind the inn. He backed her against the wall of the building, his hands comin up by either side of her head to cut off her escape as he leaned in close to kiss her. Before he could steal away with a kiss, she pushed his face away as she ducked beneath his arms.

"Let us cut to the chase, shall we? Show me this mighty *sword* you have been crowing about," insisted Nayla.

"Oh, you're my kind of girl," said the man, smiling in approval. "Want to get right down to business."

"Time is important to me. It may not be to you, but it is to me. So stop wasting my time." Her tone was laced with impatience.

"Fine! Fine! I assure you, it has made many a woman swoon with delight, for there ain't none here endowed with a larger, more powerful *weapon* than mine," bragged the warrior.

Nayla laughed inwardly. It was evident he was becoming aroused by his own self-delusional thoughts as his erection strained against the seams of his trousers.

"Oh, it better be bigger than any weapon I have ever handled or I will be mighty disappointed," replied the warrior maiden.

"It has a shaft that's as strong as steel, one of such girth you'll barely get your fist around it!" promised the warrior, struggling to maintain his balance as he proudly dropped his trousers before her.

A self-satisfied grin plastered his handsome, but drunken face as he swayed. With his hands on his hips, he stood vainglorious before Nayla to show off his manhood.

"Behold!" he announced, thrusting his hips forward for the warrior maiden to admire.

Nayla's eyebrows arched up more so in disappointment than surprise, and then she stooped for a closer look.

"This is it?" she groaned in pity.

Back inside, Valtar ordered another pint of ale as he sat down, joining Joval as his table.

"Where was Nayla going?" asked Joval, as the courtesan continued to cling to his arm as a warning to her friends the Elf was hers for the evening.

"Let us just say she will not be sleeping in her own bed tonight," replied Valtar.

"Are you telling me that she has elected to go off with that inebriated warrior? She is fraternizing with a subordinate?" gasped the Elf.

"Feast your eyes on this, cap'n! Did I not warn you?" boasted the warrior, as he fought to remain upright as his downed trousers effectively hobbled his ankles. "I wasn't lyin' my dear!"

"Oh, you most certainly did lie. In fact, even your lie was bigger than your manhood," mocked Nayla, her voice sounding rather deluded. "That is no *sword*; it is nothing more than a *paring knife*. And it is definitely not as big as mine."

She drew her long sword. With a flick of her wrist, the silver blade flashed by his eyes and swung down to his rampant member.

The warrior squealed a high-pitched scream that could have easily been mistaken for a girl's cry as the rush of air from the wake of her sword swept past his haughty erection. The blade came dangerously close to circumcising him.

Overcome by alcohol and absolute fright, the warrior's eyes instantly rolled to the back of his head as his knees buckled beneath him. He toppled to the ground in an unconscious heap.

"It is definitely not bigger than my sword," confirmed Nayla, with a confident nod of her head.

Casually sheathing her weapon, she stepped over his prone body as his erection withered away as quickly as a delicate blossom in the scorching heat of the midday sun.

"Did you hear that?" shouted Joval. He leapt up in alarm upon hearing a scream of fright.

"I heard nothing," answered Valtar, placing his half-full mug of ale down upon the table.

"I heard a girl's scream!" insisted Joval, rising up from the table. "Nayla may be in trouble!"

The courtesan latched onto Joval's arm as she pleaded: "If that is so, just leave her be! She can fend for herself!"

"She is a fellow warrior. She may be in need of assistance," argued Joval, peeling the courtesan's tentacle-like grip from his body.

"Come now, Joval. There is no need to worry. Captain Treeborn is capable of taking care of herself," stated Valtar.

"What were you thinking of, allowing her to leave with that drunken fool?" growled Joval, thoroughly annoyed by his friend's indifference.

"Though she is *stunted* need I remind you that she is a grown woman? And who am I to tell her whom she may or may not bed? Remember, I am her subordinate," argued the Elf.

"If Nayla is in trouble, I shall personally throttle you, Valtar!" promised Joval, as he pushed the courtesan away.

Racing to the door, Valtar followed close behind him. As they stood in the cool, evening air, Nayla was nowhere to be seen. All was quiet until a low, mournful groan caught their attention. Following the pitiful sounds, they entered the back alley. To their surprise, there lay the warrior in an alcohol-induced sleep, his trousers still around his ankles, his privates exposed for the whole world to see.

"This is truly a pathetic sight," groaned Joval, in sympathy as he gazed down at the unconscious warrior. He gently prodded the man's ribcage with the toe of his boot to test his sobriety.

"What the hell did Captain Treeborn do to him?" asked Valtar, scratching his head in thought.

"As far as I can tell, except for his dignity, he still looks rather intact," answered Joval, giving the man a rousing shake. The warrior merely groaned in response. "We should get him inside."

"Can we not just leave him here?" asked Valtar.

"He is a brother warrior, Valtar," admonished Joval. "We will not leave him in such an undignified state.

"Very well," he responded sheepishly.

"Quickly! Hide his shame," demanded Joval, his arms around the warrior's chest as he hoisted him onto his wobbling legs. "Pull up his trousers."

"Why do I have to be the one to do this?" questioned Valtar, his nose wrinkling as he grimaced in disgust.

"Because I am –"

"I know. You are my captain," finished Valtar, with a disheartened sigh.

"Yes, and let's be quick about it. Get him inside before the rains come," ordered Joval.

It was well past the midnight hour when Nayla woke from her peaceful slumber. The steady, gentle patter of raindrops on the thatched roof lulled her into a blissful sleep also served to muffle the sounds of Joval as he crept into the cottage with the courtesan. It was not until their whispering and lustful moans of passion wafted up to her quarters did she open her eyes.

Nayla peered down from her loft to spy upon Joval and his mistress in the midst of coupling. A jagged bolt of lightning lit up the stormy sky, filling the room with a blinding flash of white light. The little warrior could see the play of light and shadow reflecting off the naked bodies. The pale skin of the courtesan's buttocks glowed a ghostly white as she raised herself on her hands and knees, presenting herself to the Elf.

Joval knelt behind her, moving inside her flesh as the courtesan sighed with pleasure. With his hands, he grasped her hips, pulling her towards him. He thrust himself deep inside her, causing the courtesan to release an audible, throaty moan. She did not care if the sounds of their lively fornicating disturbed the warrior maiden. In fact, she *wanted* Nayla to know she was there, sharing this Elf's bed.

Nayla sank back into her cot, drawing the counterpane over her head and holding it tightly over her ears to squelch out the noises of their lovemaking. The more she tried to ignore them, the louder the courtesan became, crying out in ecstasy as she pushed back to meet Joval's every thrust.

Unable to withstand another second of their noisy coupling, Nayla reached for a sandal on the floor near her bedside. With accuracy and precision, she lobbed the footwear at the courtesan. The wooden sole of the sandal smacked unmercifully against the woman's buttocks, slapping her so hard it bounced off, striking Joval in his chest. The courtesan shrieked in both rage and pain.

The Elf's passion immediately wilted as he bellowed: *"NAYLA!"*

The little warrior snickered. Clambering back into her cot, she smiled to herself as Joval's mistress hastily dressed.

"Unless you get rid of her, you shall never be afforded my company again!" she raged, struggling to wrap the long sash back around her gown.

"Now be reasonable," pleaded the Elf. "Do not rush off!"

As Joval begged the courtesan to stay, Nayla listened as the angry woman stomped to the door.

"This is war! You hear me?" she screamed up to the loft at her nemesis.

"Then surrender now," replied Nayla. "You shall only lose if you are foolish enough to go up against me."

"You choose, Captain Stonecroft! It is me or her!" she ranted, her eyes wild with anger and loathing for Nayla.

"You want me to choose this instant?" gasped Joval.

"I am waiting!"

"I cannot just throw her out into the rain," protested Joval.

"Then I am leaving!" she shrieked, yanking the door open.

"At least let me see you home," offered Joval, attempting to pacify the courtesan.

"Until you be rid of that horrid, little wench, you shall never indulge in my pleasures again!" she hissed as she flung her cloak over her shoulders.

"But –"

Before the Elf could say another word, the door slammed soundly in his face. He stood stark naked in the center of the room, his anger mounting. Climbing up the ladder to the loft, he peered over the top. He spied Nayla's small form hiding beneath the counterpane. The quilt was visibly quaking as she tried to stifle her laughter.

"That was downright nasty and totally uncalled for, Nayla!" shouted Joval.

Nayla peeked out from beneath the counterpane. Her brown eyes innocently blinked at him. She noticed the veins lining his temples and neck were distended as he raged. Seldom had she ever seen the Elf this angry.

"So I interrupted your little tryst! You were interrupting my sleep!"

"I am not angry about that! I am angry that you could have hurt her. Sometimes you do not even know how dangerous you are. She shall be left with a nasty welt for some time to come, thank you very much!" growled Joval.

"I am sorry. So my aim was a little off this time!" protested Nayla, in her own defense.

"Do not lie to me! Your aim was perfect. It went exactly where you had intended, you horrid, little monster! You, of all people, should be mindful of your powers and your posting as a warrior and a captain: So much for protecting the weak and the innocent!"

"Weak she is, but innocent? I think not!" argued Nayla.

"You know what I mean," growled Joval, as he made his way back down the ladder. "There are times when you push your welcome here."

"I said I am sorry!"

"It is not me you should be apologizing to," grunted the frustrated Elf.

"I would much rather poke my eyes out with a dull stick than to apologize to that trollop!"

"I thought as much," retorted Joval.

The door slammed to the adjoining room. In the dim-light, Joval grabbed the full urn of water, stepping into the empty tub. He slowly poured the entire content over his head, feeling the chilling brace of the water as it ran down his face and body. The cool water served to temper his rage and effectively squelched any desire left inside of him. Snatching up a towel hanging from a wooden peg on the back of the door, he briskly dried himself off.

Nayla heard the door open, followed by the creak of his bed as the Elf lay himself down. He bunched his down pillow beneath his neck as he rolled to his side in search of some sleep.

She was more upset that Joval was mad at her than she felt guilty for accosting his female companion. Nayla lay in her cot, staring at the ceiling as the rain continued to pelt down on the roof. Just as she closed her eyes, a cold, wet drop splashed down upon her forehead.

"Damn it! The roof is leaking!" she announced to Joval.

"I shall repair it in the morning, now go to sleep!"

Another cold, fat drop of rain fell, hitting her dead-on between the eyes.

"Can you not do something now?" Nayla whined as she shrank down in her cot to avoid the next drop.

"You are more than welcome to go up on the roof now if you cannot wait until the morn," offered the Elf. "Just be careful of the lightning."

As if the next droplet of water knew she had relocated, it rolled down the ceiling a ways before coming down with another cold splash on Nayla's forehead.

"I cannot sleep like this," she groaned as her legs swung over the edge of her cot.

Joval could hear her dragging the bed away from the wall and the leaking hole in the roof. Climbing back under her quilt, Nayla closed her eyes to settle back down to sleep once more. After a brief moment of silence, with nothing more than the steady fall of rain to be heard, Nayla squealed in surprise as a waterlogged portion of the roof came away. A clump of soaking wet straw followed by a small cascade of rain that had pooled high above came down with a *splash*, landing smack-dab in the center of her cot.

Nayla sat up, staring dismally at her misfortune. The wet straw and small puddle of water was quickly soaked up by the down quilt.

"Nature conspires against me!" she groaned loudly in a bid to solicit sympathy from the Elf.

"Serves you bloody right!" grunted Joval, unmoved by her dilemma or discomfort.

It was not the response she was hoping for. Removing herself from the cot, once more she dragged it across the loft, away from the rain penetrating the thatched roof. Placing a bucket where the cot once was to catch the rainwater, Nayla resolutely crawled back into her bed. She lay on her back; her legs splayed wide apart to avoid the spreading wetness as the bedding drank up the moisture. It was cold and clammy against her skin as the silk nightdress she wore absorbed the excess water the rain-soaked counterpane could not.

"My bed is drenched! The rain continues to drip through," groaned Nayla. "It is unbearable up here."

"I believe in divine intervention," responded Joval. "The powers that be have chosen to chastise you for your less than proper behavior."

Nayla sighed in defeat: "I was merely trying to sleep and all the noise you two made was making it difficult to do so."

"Well, I shall keep that in mind the next time," grumbled Joval. "Perhaps you would prefer if I went elsewhere?"

"That would be considerate."

"Like bloody hell! I cannot believe you would drive me from my own home!" groaned the Elf.

He pulled the pillow over his face as though he wished to smother himself than to endure listening to any more words from Nayla. After a moment, he heard the gentle patter of bare feet cross the room heading toward his bed.

"It is so wet up there, Joval. Please, may I sleep here tonight?" pleaded Nayla, her small voice a pathetic whimper.

"Pardon me?" asked the Elf, lifting the pillow off his face to glare at her. "Are you asking me to trade places with you?"

"Only if you are offering to do so. But no, I do not mind sharing your bed."

"Well, I do!" snapped Joval, wishing desperately for her to just go away as he rolled over onto his side.

"Please?" she begged.

It was obvious she would not be going away any time soon.

"Very well," Joval answered reluctantly as he moved to the far side of his bed. "Just stay on that side."

"Thank you."

As another flash of lightning filled the room with white light, Joval watched as Nayla's shadow was cast against the wall. He could not help but notice she was slipping her nightgown off over her head.

"What do you think you are doing?" asked Joval, turning away as he averted his eyes.

"My nightgown is wet with rain. I am not about to get your bed wet, too," explained Nayla, as she slipped beneath the counterpane. "Besides, what is the big deal? It is not as though you have not seen me naked before."

Joval rolled over onto his back. His finger drew an invisible marker down the center of the bed. "Do not cross this line. Is that understood?"

Nayla lay her head down upon the pillow, bunching the down-filled quilt up around her neck. Joval was silent as he lay motionless by her side, trying to ignore her presence.

"Do you hate me?" asked Nayla. Her voice had the innocence of a child.

Joval propped himself up on his elbows as he sat forward to gaze at her. In the faint, intermittent light of the moon penetrating the cloud-cover, her eyes were liquid, shining softly in this pale light.

"I do not *hate* you. I hate some of the things you do," clarified the Elf. "There is a difference you know?"

"If it is of any consolation to you, I am truly sorry I acted so childishly," apologized Nayla, in a small voice. "I did not mean to make you so mad."

"My anger will pass," replied Joval. He lay back down, his hands locked together behind his head as he stared up at the ceiling.

Nayla rolled over onto her stomach, propping herself up on her elbows as she rested her chin in her hands. Her long, raven tresses tumbled down around her shoulders making her skin look as pale as fine porcelain. In the deep shadows, Joval's eyes penetrated the darkness to see the soft, round curves of her breasts as she lay pensive, momentarily lost in her thoughts.

She stared over at the Elf, and finally she asked: "Why do you engage in such activities with your mistress? It seems clumsy and it sounds rather painful with all that moaning and groaning that goes on."

Joval shook his head in dismay at Nayla's naivety.

"It is obvious you have never been with a man who can please you," he stated bluntly.

Nayla laughed at his comment: "Joval, do you honestly think any man would dare become intimate with the likes of me?"

He did not respond, watching as her dark eyes saddened.

"I am cursed many times over."

"That is not true," argued Joval.

"Yes, it is! No man wants to bed a woman they fear. No man, Elf or mortal, would want to be seen with a half-caste like me. And I am the daughter of Dahlon Treeborn. That alone is enough to make most men blanch and flee at the very sight of me."

"Are you telling me that you have *never* been with a man?" asked Joval, in an incredulous tone. "Honestly?"

"No, never," admitted Nayla. Her voice sounded meek, almost embarrassed.

"What of Hemashe? I thought he had plans to wed you?"

"Hemashe? That was all very innocent," she answered wistfully. "He, in true Taijin fashion, wished to wait until we were bound in matrimony. As you can see, it never went that far."

Joval was shocked by her admission. "Well, I find this hard to believe a woman like you does not have a hundred men wishing to court you."

She smiled at the Elf, knowing he was attempting to lift her spirits. "You, Joval, are a true enigma."

His curiosity piqued, he rolled over onto his side, leaning on his elbow as he gazed down at Nayla.

"An enigma? How so?"

"One minute, you can be shouting angrily at me. The next, you find it in your heart to say something kind. You expect me to hold my own as a warrior and yet, when I least expect it, you show gallantry and chivalry beyond measure as you come to my defense. You seem so stern and commanding, and then at a moment of levity you find humour in the simplest of things," observed Nayla. "And you have shown me compassion when others would not."

Joval listened to her heart-felt words, touched that she was aware of his *humane* qualities.

"You seem to believe there is little kindness and compassion in this world," noted Joval.

"Do not get me wrong. There is kindness and compassion. I am rarely the recipient of it, that is all," she answered bluntly. "There are times when I truly believe I shall leave this world unwanted and unloved. I have spent my entire life coming to grips with this knowledge, and learning to accept this fate."

It was difficult for him to believe she would be loved by none, for deep down inside, he could feel his own soul being drawn to her wild heart, those smoldering brown eyes, and that sultry smile. Surely, there were other men who could see these same attributes and qualities he secretly admired. Her Taijin/Elven blood created this exotic beauty he felt was profoundly appealing and yet, it was an appearance she seemed to find abhorrent. And though she was a fierce warrior, he also knew of her softer side, hidden beneath her warrior mentality and weapons.

"Do not be so sure of that, Nayla," said Joval, smiling kindly at her.

"Alas, I am doomed to die in battle or diminish of old age as the only virgin in this whole world," she lamented.

"That is not quite true. I understand, the mortals – the holy men in western Imago take an oath of celibacy so they can dedicate their lives to the Maker of All."

"That is odd. And yet, the ascetic priests such as Medaru Saibon and his forefathers all married and had families," noted Nayla.

Joval laughed as he recalled a conversation with Chusai Saibon from long ago.

"Medaru Saibon's grandfather once told me the priests, all the religious leaders who fled to western Orien, married and had families like any other man. They believed if they did not truly understand and appreciate all the happiness, sorrow and angst of the human condition, how were they to effectively administer and counsel to the needs of their followers? Master Saibon also said, and I quote: *'If God meant for holy men not to engage in the act of procreation, He would have made us all eunuchs'*!"

"Chusai Saibon said this?" asked Nayla, in amazement.

"None other."

"But holy men to the west choose this lifestyle. They choose to be celibate. I do not choose this for myself."

"There is nothing wrong with keeping your virtue intact. It is greatly desired by Taijin men looking to marry."

"That is fine if one intends to wed a Taijin, but as I said, I have no intention of wedding. Nor will any mortal in his right mind want to bind himself to the likes of me," stated Nayla.

"Do not speak in this manner. You are still young. Much can happen in your life."

"Young? I have outlived most of my brother warriors."

"Young, relatively speaking," corrected Joval.

"Is this so of the Elf maidens? Are they expected to be chaste?"

"It is a matter of choice. The Elf maidens are free to *discreetly* seek out partners, mostly because our kind is so long-lived. There is nothing worse than to bind to one who is not fully compatible in every respect. After all, once bound in the sanctity of matrimony, then that is it. It is a bond to last an eternity. It is unheard of for such a bond to be broken. Besides, I suppose the risk of impregnating a mortal woman is far greater whereas Elf women can only conceive for the three days leading up to and during the full moon."

"How can that be?" queried Nayla.

"It is said the moon affects the tides and it is believed it has the same affect on the Elf women, controlling their cycles and determining when they are most fertile. However, with mortal women, when they are fertile seems to be a matter of chance. It would appear they could potentially conceive at any time."

"If that is the case, are you and the other Elf men not concerned these dalliances may lead to conception?"

"There is an unspoken law that if we indulge in such activities with a mortal woman, we must use a degree of self-control," stated Joval.

"What do you mean by *'self-control'*?" queried Nayla, wishing to learn more.

"Withdraw before the *troops* can storm the battlements, if you get my meaning?" explained the Elf.

"No, I do not."

"Withdraw before the lava erupts from the volcano," answered Joval, becoming flustered by her ignorance.

Nayla looked just as puzzled by this analogy.

"You know, before the *seeds* of our labour can be dispersed onto the tilled soil!" exclaimed Joval, his hands flailing before his nether regions in exasperation.

"Oooh, I see…" the little warrior nodded in understanding.

"Thank goodness," the Elf breathed a sigh of relief.

They both lay in silence, listening to the diminishing patter of rain falling on the thatched roof.

Nayla spoke again: "An eternity! That is longer than long. I cannot imagine ever being married to one person for this length of time."

"I suppose if one is truly in love, an eternity of bliss is easy to endure," responded Joval. "That is why it is important for both partners to be absolutely compatible in all respects before they take this vow."

"Why did you never marry?" questioned Nayla.

"About one hundred years ago, I was told I was *'much too grumpy'* to be a suitable partner for any woman. Remember?" answered Joval. An impish grin crossed his face as he recalled Nayla's insult.

She slapped him on his shoulder as she scolded him: "Only a fool would listen to a child. Now seriously, why did you never wed?"

"Do you see scads of Elf maidens in eastern Imago?" he replied, his voice tainted with sarcasm. "Most have retreated into the Twilight, retiring to the Haven. The ones that remain are old enough to be my mother, and if they are not, they are already pledged to another."

"Are you in love with your mistress?" asked Nayla, still brimming with questions.

Joval frowned at her, and then he laughed: "Goodness, no! That is an odd question!"

"Then why do you engage in this activity with her?"

"It is like any other urge to be answered. When you are hungry – you eat. When you are thirsty – you drink. When you feel the desire to…" his voice trailed. "Well, you get my meaning."

"Hmm… I suppose," sighed Nayla. She rolled onto her side as she gazed at the Elf. She propped herself up on her elbow, looking at him with great earnest. "Joval, although I am responsible for training your men, in many respects, you have become my mentor, would you not agree?"

"I suppose that is true," admitted Joval. "There is much for you to learn of the Elf-kind."

"Then, as my mentor, help me to understand this. I want to know how it feels, what it is like to couple with a man," asked the warrior maiden.

"What are asking of me, Nayla?" Joval slowly sat up.

"I want to know. I want to understand this feeling. Besides, if I should die in battle tomorrow, I do not relish the thought of dying knowing I will die as the oldest virgin in Orien."

"Believe me, there are far worse distinctions than that!" reasoned the Elf. "Besides, you are a daughter born to a high house. I am merely a warrior, with no other rank or distinction than that of being a captain of an army."

"But we are of the same rank. We are both captains," argued Nayla. "It is not as though you will be fraternizing with a subordinate."

"In our vocation, yes, but our standings in life differ greatly," countered Joval.

"Yes, but you are also my friend and my mentor. I hold you in the same esteem as my teacher. I am asking you now; teach me," she pleaded as she sat up to meet his gaze.

The counterpane fell away to expose her naked body. Her skin looked luminous, glowing gently in the dim-light. Joval averted his eyes from the perfect form of her breasts peering through the dark tresses that cascaded from her head, tumbling around her small shoulders and down her back.

"Nayla, what you ask me to do…"

"If you are not in love with your mistress and you so willingly indulge in this activity with her, why would it be any different with me? I am not asking you to love me, I am asking you to teach me," insisted Nayla.

"You know I would do anything for you, but this? How can you even ask this of me? It is… It is…" he stammered.

A single teardrop rolled down her cheek as she felt the cruel sting of Joval's rejection.

"It is unthinkable?" she concluded his sentence. "Am I that unworthy? Am I that unfit not even you dare touch me?"

The Elf railed against his own growing anger as his true feelings for her that he had kept safely buried, surfaced. His desire for Nayla was undeniable, and he knew he would regret the day he should act on his longing for her. Joval gently brushed the tear from her cheek as he whispered: "It is not that at all, Nayla."

"If you are ashamed of me, then tell me now. I will never ask this of you again," she sobbed.

His arms embraced her tiny form, holding her close to console her. He could feel the palpitations of her heart beating against his as Nayla's arms wrapped around his neck as her chin rested on his shoulder. Joval breathed in the sweet scent of her raven tresses, feeling her body trembling against his chest. He felt the warmth of her gentle breath against his neck as her lips slowly caressed his skin, plying soft, barely-there kisses along his throat. His eyes closed as the scintillating sensation of nerves sparking to life filled his body from her touch alone.

"Nayla, please… Do not seduce me," pleaded Joval. "Do not allow me to give in to this temptation."

His words went ignored as her soft, full lips traveled up his throat to his chin. She could feel his chest heaving as his heart began to race as the tiny pads of her fingertips gently traced the outline of his shoulders and softly caressed the muscles on his broad back.

He could hear and feel the soft jets of her breath in his ear and on his flesh as she teasingly kissed and nibbled his ear lobe. His muscles began to tense and he could feel his toes curl as her gentle ministrations sent surging, pleasurable pulses of energy through his body, like the static building in the air just before a great thunderstorm. It coursed throughout his entire being as she continued to ply him with warm, soft kisses.

"Nayla, I beg of you. Do not do this to me," he gasped, as he peeled her arms off him.

As he held her by the wrists, he could see her breasts rising and falling with each breath she drew as her heart pounded in her chest with unbridled passion. Her eyes were dark and liquid, luring him into these deep, limpid pools, causing him to drown in his own desire.

She gazed into his eyes as she whispered: "You want this as much as I do."

Joval pulled her towards him. He drew her close as his mouth met hers, hungrily seeking out her soft, sensuous lips. He kissed Nayla slowly and deeply. There was tenderness and a passion in his touch Nayla had never witnessed before when Joval would engage in this activity with any of the courtesans. Now, in retrospect, she knew these other women were merely the recipients of obligatory gestures of foreplay.

They sank down into the bed as Joval continued to kiss Nayla, his tongue entwining with hers as he stole her breath away. His hand slowly caressed the length of her supine body, feeling every gentle dip and soft curve as it traveled down her tiny waist and over her rounded hips.

Nayla's hands followed the hard, flat sheets of muscles over Joval's chest, down the length of his torso. The hairless, smooth skin covering the firm muscles beneath felt like warm satin to her touch. There felt to be so much power in his body, for even with the most-subtle movement, she could feel hard muscles flexing and tensing beneath her hands. She could feel an incredible surge of energy emanating from the Elf's body as she caressed him.

Taking her hand into his, he placed it over his swollen manhood. Nayla was at first startled, and then she was enchanted, as it seemed to pulse with life. Even under the lightest stroke of her fingertips it would throb in response. She marveled at the silky smoothness of this skin that sheathed this engorged member as her fingers wrapped around the turgid shaft of his erection. A small moan of pleasure escaped Joval's lips as her hand slowly slid down the entire length, admiring the rigid form of his desire.

He kissed her with great passion, reveling in the sensation of her touch. Nayla slowly pulled away from his body as she knelt on her hands and knees, presenting herself to the Elf so she may be taken from behind.

She had always noticed the birds and beasts mate in this manner. And it was how he would always couple with the other women. She was unaware Joval was fulfilling nothing more than a physical need. He never wished to become emotionally attached to any of his mistresses, always distancing himself by avoiding face-to-face, intimate contact.

"Not like this," he whispered softly to her. His hands came up to her shoulders, turning her over onto her back. "I want to see your face. I want to see your beautiful face."

For a moment, Nayla was stunned to hear him speak these words, for never had he ever complimented her in this manner. Their mouths met again as his lips pressed down on hers. He kissed her fervently, as though she was the very essence of life itself. He moved slowly over her body, between her parted legs.

Nayla felt herself being swept up in a growing tidal wave of emotions and the arousal of strange, new sensations. Her legs instinctively wrapped around his hips, drawing him down upon her body. Her eyes flew open in surprise as she felt the initial burning pressure as Joval slowly moved onto her flesh, penetrating into her.

He stopped momentarily as he met with resistance as the tip of his manhood pressed up against the maidenhead. He knew instantly Nayla was indeed as chaste as she had claimed. His heart pounded in his chest as he fought the urge to forge on, to tear through the hymen that partially impeded his path. The prospect of being the first man to enter this heavenly realm of earthly delights only served to heighten his desire to an all-new level. He moved ever so slowly and gently, but as Nayla gasped at the unexpected pain, Joval began to withdraw.

"No," she moaned in disappointment. "Do not stop."

Her legs immediately folded tightly around his body as the heel of her palms pressed down on the small of his back. She forced Joval down upon her trembling form as she raised her hips to meet his. Her breath seemed to catch in her throat with the sharp pain delivered as he burst through this thin barrier of tissue, penetrating into her.

For an instant, Joval froze. Then slowly, his movements gentle and paced, he sank down into her hot, moist core, delighting in this sensation as her taut, inner muscles engulfed him.

Nayla lay there motionless, feeling Joval filling her, moving deep inside her body. At first, her mind panicked, thinking she would burst, unable to take him in fully. Her muscles involuntarily tensed as though to squeeze him out. To her astonishment, the Elf moaned in ecstasy, throbbing in response. As she exhaled and relaxed; he thrust himself in deeper still. Her muscles wrapped around the shaft of his engorged manhood in an undulating sensation causing Joval to gasp in both pleasure and surprise. Again, his member swelled and throbbed in response. It suddenly dawned on Nayla that she had this mysterious power – an unspoken control over this Elf. This knowledge only served to arouse her all the more, stoking a fire deep inside her soul.

Joval withdrew almost completely, and then he slowly and deliberately plunged the entire length of his shaft into her body until his hips pressed down against the soft pad of her pubic mound. Nayla's breathing hastened with his movements. Her heart raced as never before as she felt an intense sensation spread from the very core of her body, rippling and growing like a mounting tidal wave coursing through her entire being as she experienced her first orgasm.

"What are… what are you doing to me?" she gasped, her nails sinking into his shoulders.

Unable to maintain control any longer, Joval's movements became more urgent as he felt an incredible sensation pooling in his loins and expanding through his body. Panting hard, his heart was pounding loudly like a drum as he moved on her flesh. Nayla raised her hips to meet his every thrust, taking him in fully each time. She delighted in this new sensation that was welling up inside as Joval delivered her to another plane of existence within this realm. Her responsive movements drove him absolutely mad; the feelings of pleasure so intense, it border-lined on torture.

Rummaging in this dark, secret font of carnal delectation, he suddenly withdrew until only the tip of his rampant member remained inside Nayla. A loud moan escaped Joval's lips as he sank back down, deep inside her. The shaft of his erection suddenly seemed to expand in girth and harden like a pillar of rock as he felt his essence course through his manhood. With a final, powerful thrust, his passion erupted as he jetted his seed deep inside Nayla's body.

Nayla trembled beneath him as his body convulsed in spasms of ecstasy. She felt her body carried away on another intense orgasmic wave as they climaxed simultaneously. Joval groaned as his body shuddered in the final throes of passion as the inner rings of muscles engulfed him in strong contractions as Nayla squeezed the very life from him, sapping the last of his strength. Now, completely spent, Joval collapsed by her side, floating on a sea of absolute rapture. Never had he experienced such intense, erotic pleasure.

For a moment, both said nothing as the feeling of euphoria swept them away, body and soul. The only sounds were their ragged breathing and the mad beating of their hearts. This swirling energy that delivered her to dizzying new heights, making Nayla feel more alive than ever before, slowly dissipated. Coming back down to earth, she rolled over to her side. Other than the heaving of his chest, the Elf lay motionless, as though his entire body had gone limp after this encounter. But even with his eyes closed, Joval could sense her staring intently at him. Nayla leaned over to kiss him on his lips.

"That was absolutely amazing! Can we do it again?" she pleaded as she began to ply soft kisses along his throat and down his chest.

His eyes flashed open in surprise.

"*Now*?" gasped the Elf, still attempting to quiet his racing heart.

"Yes! Of course, now," answered Nayla, kneeling before him like a starving cat waiting to pounce on its prey.

"You may as well go flog a dead horse," protested Joval, his breathing still rushed. Even to lift his head from the pillow was an effort. "It will be like trying to resurrect the dead."

"I believe I can create a miracle," insisted Nayla. She lustfully considered the Elf, her hands wandering over his body.

"Good god, I have created a monster!" groaned Joval, sinking beneath the counterpane to escape her rapacious eyes and insatiable appetite.

17

too many farewells

The years dissolved, one into the next. With the passing of time, Nayla watched the mortals who touched her life come and go like the passing of the seasons. Many of the young warriors she trained were fortunate enough to survive a number of battles, succumbing later in their life to illness or old age. Others were not so fortunate. And with each passing year, a new generation of warriors would rise up to fill the ranks. Nayla would be the one to initiate them on the battlefield when they were called to fight for the lives and safety of the citizens of western Orien.

War continued to be commonplace, almost a way of life, but these periods were also interspersed with times of peace. It was during these golden moments, when the earth did not quake in fear under the pounding of thousands of footsteps marching into battle, the people of western Orien flourished. These rare and tranquil periods coincided with the change of heir to the title of Emperor, or when the Imperial Army had faced another devastating loss, their ranks so decimated they had to curtail their military actions until their numbers were such they could advance in volume once again. These times of peace were sporadic at best and never very long-lived.

Since the beginning when these mortals first arrived by crossing an archipelago of islands from their ancestral lands of Taija did problems first surface. Two brothers, the sons of Emperor Orien Darraku, led the expeditions for those seeking a fresh beginning and the promise of prosperity in these new lands across the Arashe Sea. The course of destiny was forever altered when a devastating earthquake reshaped the face of the world. The land bridge used to cross the northern sea sank beneath a massive tidal wave.

Not ocean-going people, the Taijins dared not make the long and treacherous expedition across the open waters. With the stepping-stones of islands that once provided safe harbors and protected shoals now gone, none would risk crossing the Arashe Sea. The brave but foolhardy souls that did, never reached their final destination, to be lost forever on this dark and forbidding expanse of water.

The two brothers, already trained to lead their people, soon fell into conflict. The eldest of the princes believed in ruling the lands and its people with compassion and justice. He allowed them to practice religion and share in the wealth of the crown to assist his subjects as they established themselves in their new homeland that was secured in the name of their father, the Emperor Orien.

Until his death, Prince Kosai governed the lands fairly and the people prospered. When his younger brother, Prince Takume ascended to the throne upon Kosai's death, Takume ruled the people with an iron fist. The ones to prosper from his reign were his cronies, reaping the benefits from the blood and sweat of others by levying numerous taxes on the people. Money donated by the citizens to build temples to practice their religious teachings was circumvented and funneled back to Keso.

Instead, this money was used to line the pockets of the younger prince as he made every effort to quash religion and religious practices, for he felt it was a waste of monetary funds; money better spent on glorifying his reign.

With the royal house so severely divided, through the centuries, the rule and temperament of the land swayed from one extreme to the other with the ascension of each new Emperor.

As was the custom of their people, the crown and title was passed on to the eldest son in line. War was inevitable when Prince Takume's descendants were installed into this seat of power. The people were forced to weather this bitter storm.

Peace and civil order returned only when that Emperor died and the eldest son of Prince Kosai's bloodline ascended to the throne. It was during these times that Eldred Firestaff would be ousted from his position as advisor to the royal family, to be driven far from Keso. In retribution, the Sorcerer would go on a rampage, venturing into western Orien on his own personal vendetta, venting his wrath on the Elves and the free people they aligned themselves with. Eldred would abruptly appear to burn forests, raze villages and then mysteriously disappear again.

During these times of peace, Nayla continued to train the next generation of warriors in preparation for war. When not dispensing the knowledge and skills of the Kagai Warrior, she and Joval would spend their time hunting down the elusive Sorcerer, journeying into the treacherous terrains of the Furai Mountains.

When called to war, they rode into battle on many occasions, riding side by side as captains, but once the threat of war had passed, Joval and Nayla's relationship would take on an added dimension, as they became clandestine lovers.

Although many speculated they were much more than merely friends and fellow warriors; this opinion would often come into debate, for it was not unusual for them to be at odds with each other, bickering about the most inconsequential things.

The only time they were not engaged in verbal jousts was when they were on the battlefield. Being consummate professionals when leading the men into war, Nayla and Joval conducted themselves like true warriors in the public eye; off the battlefield, they were always very discreet in their relationship. And it was this need for discretion and constant self-control that seemed to only heighten their passion when they did come together.

Though their long-standing relationship was marred with conflict and turmoil, for both were equally strong-willed, they still found great comfort in each other's arms. And through the years, they forged a bond that could not be broken by time or distance. With Joval by her side, he helped her to weather some of the most difficult and troubling times in her life.

In the late summer, just over twenty years since she first departed Anshen to reside in Nagana, Nayla had led the army for a confrontation in the north. Two summers had passed since the Imperial Army last set foot in western Orien. Confirmation was received from sympathizers to the east that the Emperor was once again coerced by the Sorcerer to mount another attack, to destroy those who refused to pay their taxes and continued to support religious centers flourishing in the west.

Fearful these religious teachings would filtrate back into the east, causing greater friction and chaos by inciting those still secretly practicing religion to rise up in rebellion, the Emperor conspired with the Sorcerer. This time, an army, the largest ever to be deployed, was due to arrive in the Magare Valley in the late summer.

During this time, the ranks of the Kagai Warriors and those from Nagana had swelled, numbering well over two-thousand. The past victories, accomplished with minimal casualties as the warriors became more adept in the art of war, allowed their forces to grow in strength.

At the age of forty-eight, Keodai Saibon was now the leader of the Kagai Warriors. His father, Medaru was much too old and weak to engage in war at this point of his long and illustrious life. On this occasion, Keodai would lead his men, including his own two sons into battle.

His eldest son, Maisai had first seen battle two years earlier, fighting alongside his father as they defeated the Imperial Army in the Hebeku Valley. Since that time, only small scouting parties of fewer than fifty men dared to sneak into western Orien, hoping their small numbers would go undetected.

The Kagai Warriors, ever vigilant, would quickly and efficiently dispatch these unwelcome intruders. Maisai was always close at hand to learn all the intricacies of their craft, watching diligently as his father would orchestrate the assaults and nighttime raids.

Kashe, Keodai's youngest son, had been training for this moment since he was a boy, yet he was still giddy; anxious as the threat of war loomed on the horizon. For the first time, Kashe was to go to war alongside his Kagai brothers and the warriors from the south, guided by Joval and Nayla.

With word that Eldred Firestaff led the procession northward, Keodai had devised a strategy that would take his men well into enemy territory. Previous battles would lure the Imperial Army to engage in war in the pine forest, or in the Hebeku Valley and on the very rare occasions, just inside the Magare Valley. This time, Keodai prepared his men to do battle deep within the Magare Valley, where not even the Sorcerer would ever suspect an attack would be mounted.

Since arriving in the late spring, the warriors from Nagana worked feverishly with their Kagai brothers to develop elaborate traps and snares, even diverting the course of several mountain streams, damming them so the waters pooled into a small, man-made, alpine lake.

A huge arsenal of arrows was also made to arm twelve specially modified catapults. These unconventional weapons were not designed to hurl heavy boulders but instead, to launch one hundred or more arrows simultaneously. Smaller and lighter than traditional catapults, these weapons were cleverly hidden along the mountain slope on both sides of the valley. Even in the light of day, untrained eyes would not be able to detect these weapons.

Word spread rapidly of the approach of this massive army from the east. The warriors bided their time, waiting and watching. With the Kagai Warriors manning the catapults and snares, Joval's keen-eyed Elven marksmen armed with their longbows were hidden low on the slopes. Behind them, Nayla's warriors, those of the infantry stood by with swords at the ready.

With such a large contingent to move, the soldiers arrived at the eastern mouth of the narrow Magare Valley as dusk settled upon the land. With the Sorcerer by his side, the captain shouted orders for the soldiers to break rank and prepare for the coming of the night. With reassurance from Eldred the Kagai Warriors never venture this far into their territory, that they had only ever mounted attacks in the western front of the valley or deep within the safety of their own territory, the nervous soldiers readied with haste. They pitched their small tents and organized their rations for the night.

Eldred instructed the captain to post soldiers all along the perimeter of camp as a precaution as he journeyed on through the valley into western Orien. He would scout it out for possible obstacles and traps, as was the case before in the pine forest and in the Hebeku Valley. As the Sorcerer mounted his ebony steed to disappear westward into the growing darkness, the apprehensive soldiers felt some sense of relief the Sorcerer was to forge the way ahead, to clear their path as they ventured into the *haunted* forest.

As the soldiers settled for their evening meal under a canopy of twinkling stars shining brightly from a deepening night sky, they were totally oblivious to the many eyes watching from the forested slopes surrounding them. They were lulled into a false state of calm as Keodai and the other Kagai Warriors filled the evening air with the gentle calls of the nightingale, giving the soldiers a sense that all was right in the world.

As a half moon climbed high into the sky to bathe the land in its cold light, the sounds of the nightingale ceased as the call of a gray owl echoed mournfully across the valley.

"Did you hear that?" gasped one soldier to his captain.

"That was nothing more than an owl! It's a harmless bird for pity's sake," stated the captain, in a dismissive tone.

"Nothing more than an owl, you say? I will have you know owls only come around to collect the spirits of the dead," warned the soldier. "That is why they only show themselves after the sun has retreated from the sky."

"That is a bunch of superstitious nonsense; absolute malarkey!" snapped the captain. His eyes nervously scanned the slopes of the surrounding mountains.

"You say that now, but mark my words, captain, the owls forewarn that the dead walk amongst us!" argued the soldier.

"Are you dead? Do I look like I am dead?" argued the captain, his arms flailing over his head in frustration.

The soldier grunted in annoyance, humiliated by this public, verbal lashing.

"Enough of this nonsense! It shall only serve to frighten the others," rebuked the captain. He raised his hand to strike the soldier when a single arrow ripped through his throat.

Before the soldier could scream in fear as his captain fell dead, the air was filled with the whine of hundreds of arrows raining down upon them. In absolute panic, the soldiers snatched up their weapons and shields. The second in command shouted orders for all to fall in line and close their ranks. As another volley of arrows cascaded down, the soldiers held their shields aloft to deflect the projectiles.

As soon as the shields were raised up, Joval's Elven warriors emerged from the shadows of the surrounding forests to release a torrent of arrows horizontally to down the soldiers along the perimeter. With this assault, shields were lowered only to have another volley of arrows hail down from high above.

To stem the rising tide of panic, the senior ranking soldier ordered the others to attack. The massive, black swarm divided. Spreading out, they charged toward their invisible foes hidden in the forests on the north and south slopes.

Joval and his warriors continued their assault as the Kagai Warriors dispensed deadly arrows from their modified catapults. Although the enemy numbers were thinning, the soldiers were still many.

Charging toward the slopes, screams of agony filled the night air as soldiers ran headlong into concealed pits lined with a multitude of deadly, wooden stakes. Caught up in the maddening rush and hysteria, soldiers forced those on the frontline to meet their demise. The men who were not impaled on the stakes were smothered and trampled by the crazed soldiers continuing to press forward. As the pits filled with bodies, the soldiers merely marched over their fallen comrades, continuing onward in pursuit of their enemy.

Joval gave the order for his men to fall back. As they retreated, dissolving into the deepening shadows of the forest, the angry soldiers charged after them.

More screams filled the air as the soldiers on the frontline stepped directly into snares that whipped their bodies into the air, smashing them against the surrounding stands of trees.

The soldiers came to an abrupt halt, confident other traps now lay in wait for them if they chose to proceed. Uncertain whether they should advance, they were momentarily frozen in fear.

They gasped in surprise as Keodai released an ear-splitting call that echoed across the valley. To their horror, warriors poured down from the slopes, emerging from the shadows of the dark forests.

Surrounded on all sides, the soldiers instinctively retreated back into the open valley. With a deafening crash, the earth quaked beneath their feet as they collided headlong into battle.

Keodai charged on ahead as his sons fought side by side. Maisai urged his younger brother to fight as the soldiers stood their ground, battling back. Stunned by the initial onslaught, Kashe reacted only after an enemy blade flashed past his eyes. It jolted him back to reality, angling out of its way as Maisai hollered: "Fight, Kashe!"

The young warrior roared, adrenalin coursing through his veins as he countered the attack. He parried, and then slashed at the soldier.

Maisai smiled proudly at his younger brother, confident he could now stand on his own. And as his father did before him, doing battle by his closest friend Hemashe, now Maisai would also take up arms alongside Hemashe's son, Tadashe.

As the battle raged around them, Nayla cut through the mayhem. Her sword, now bathed in blood, struck down any enemy soldier who dared stand in her way. With the soldiers still so many, she knew it was going to be their bloodiest battle yet. She watched as Keodai, sitting high on his steed, careened through the middle of the battlefield, cutting down those in his path.

Above the cries and the crashing of swords and halberds, Nayla heard Kashe scream out in fear. As she slashed her way through the crowd, she could see the inexperienced warrior rolling from side to side, avoiding the deadly blade of a halberd as a soldier attempted to hack at him.

Unarmed and surrounded by fallen bodies, Kashe was hampered in his movements as he tried in vain to maneuver closer to his sword that lay on the ground. As the soldier hefted his halberd aloft to dispatch Kashe, the young warrior gazed up in fear.

As the halberd came down, the soldier stumbled forward, collapsing onto his knees. Kashe rolled to his side, narrowly missing the great axe as the man fell over dead.

Nayla was relieved to see Maisai had come just in time to spare his brother's life. She turned away to aid another warrior fighting against two soldiers.

As Kashe reached up to grab his brother's hand, Maisai fell against him. Kashe stared in horror as a soldier wrenched his sword free from his brother's back. Maisai crumpled to his knees, trembling before his brother.

"Fight, Kashe! Get up and fight!" he ordered.

Taking up Maisai's sword, Kashe raised the weapon to deflect the blow as the soldier swung down to decapitate his brother. He blocked a second blow and with a circular motion, his blade swept horizontally from his left to right. The soldier howled in agony as his entrails spilled out before him.

Enraged by the assault on his older brother, Kashe brought his sword down again. The blade sliced cleanly through the soldier's throat as a painful scream gurgled out, muted by the rising blood flowing from this fatal wound.

Nayla rolled over her shoulder, coming up onto one knee as a soldier slashed unmercifully at a young Kagai Warrior. With one swift swipe of her blade, she slashed through the tendons on the back of the soldier's knees.

Unable to bear his weight, the soldier toppled over onto his back. He was met by Nayla's sword. It came down with blinding speed as she rammed the blade through his throat. Gazing up as she yanked her sword free, she was momentarily taken aback when the warrior thanked her.

Two years had passed since she had last seen this young man, and now he was the spitting image of Hemashe. Tadashe looked exactly as his father did when Hemashe was a young man still in love with her. He had the same handsome face and kind, brown eyes as his father did.

"Move!" shouted Nayla, drawing a throwing dart from her vest pocket.

As the weapon left her hand, skimming past Tadashe, he dove to the ground. The small weapon struck its intended victim directly in the throat. The soldier collapsed. He died even as he struggled to remove the poisoned dart.

Rising up, Nayla's foot pushed against Tadashe's shoulder, promptly knocking him backwards as she stood over him. With her long sword in her right hand, she quickly drew her short sword with her left. Crossing her blades as she raised her arms, she intercepted a blow meant for Tadashe. Locked together, sword against sword, the soldier bore down on Nayla with all his might.

Just as it appeared she would buckle beneath his force, she suddenly sidestepped to her right. The counterweight of the soldier's sword pressing down on hers caused the tip of her weapon to spring up. It slashed the man from below his left ear, diagonally across his throat.

As she spun away from his falling body, her short sword slashed the soldier clean through his breastplate, slicing through flesh and bone.

Without missing a beat, Nayla's wrists twisted about, flicking off the blood from her swords. Armed with a weapon in each hand, she advanced to her next victim as Tadashe struggled to his feet. Using the long sword to block the incoming blade, Nayla used her short sword to quickly dispatch the enemy. Turning about, she was confronted by three soldiers. They pressed in to surround her.

With swords raised, they closed in on the warrior maiden. Nayla stood before them, prepared to meet her fate. Simultaneously, all three soldiers rushed her, bringing their deadly blades down. With precision timing, Nayla dove between two soldiers. As she rolled over her shoulder, she stood up, turning to face her assailants.

Hemashe and his son Tadashe stood by Nayla's side, prepared to take them on. All three charged toward the soldiers. With swift, deliberate movements, they made quick work of the enemy, but as quickly as they did away with them, there were still others to contend with.

At the height of this battle, a horrific scream pierced the darkness as the Sorcerer came charging from the west. With the glowing orb of his staff held low, he unleashed a fireball.

The great, fiery orb slammed into the ground in a thunderous wake of heat and flames. It sent all flying with its percussion as it exploded.

Nayla hurled a lethal dart at an enemy soldier as he shouted instructions for the soldiers to keep fighting. With her dart well placed, the soldier slumped against his steed's neck. She yanked him down. Throwing herself into the saddle, she guided the stallion through the mayhem to meet the Sorcerer head-on.

She had no choice but to hold him at bay; to keep him off the battlefield. She knew Eldred was insane enough to sacrifice his own men to see the Elves and Kagai Warriors brought down in defeat, allowing all to be consumed in his element.

Eldred released a ball of fire in Nayla's direction as she charged at him. Yanking hard the reins, she steered the horse away from its path, turning the steed back on a direct course toward the Sorcerer. As her mount veered away from another fiery blast, Nayla drew ever closer to Eldred. Behind her, she could hear Joval shout instructions to Valtar to approach from the south as he steered his horse around to attack from the north in a bid to surround the Sorcerer. All around them, the dry grasses began to crackle and burn at an alarming rate as a westerly breeze fanned the flames toward the battlefield.

Nayla's steed raced toward Eldred's ebony stallion. Just as they were about to intercept each other, she drew her sword, sweeping it over her head and down to her left. She missed Eldred's staff by a fraction of an inch as his steed abruptly stopped, rearing up.

Urging her stallion about to face the Sorcerer once again, she charged at her nemesis. Through the growing flames, from the corner of her eye she could see Valtar racing towards the Sorcerer as he called out.

Eldred glanced in Valtar's direction, but it was not long enough to distract him. Just as Nayla attempted another bid to rid the Sorcerer of his staff, the madman aimed his crystal at her. With insufficient time to draw on his full powers, Eldred was able to invoke only enough magic to discharge a surge of energy from the crystal orb. Like a blue bolt of lightning, it crackled as it struck Nayla, throwing her forcefully from the saddle. As she crashed down onto the hard ground, her panicking steed almost trampled her underfoot.

Nayla felt her heart racing as the powerful surge of energy coursed through her body. Struggling to catch her breath, she lay on the ground convulsing, immobilized by the Sorcerer's magic. All around her, the fire was closing in, the flames licking into the night sky and before her was Eldred Firestaff.

The Sorcerer knelt before Nayla. Drawing his dagger with his right hand as his left seized her by the crown of her hair; he yanked back on her head. Weakened and dazed, the paralyzing powers of his magic made it impossible for Nayla to fight him off. She was rendered totally helpless.

"Two decades ago, you left me with a scar on my neck. Now, my time has come!" hissed the Sorcerer. His eyes were aglow, shining a menacing red as it reflected the flames that continued to burn. "This time, it is my turn to leave my mark on you, Treeborn! You will no longer be needing this."

He crouched over her prone body, lifting her head up by a fistful of hair. His dagger was poised at her neck to make its first incision to decapitate her.

Eldred shrieked as Valtar grabbed him from behind, wrestling the dagger away.

Nayla fought to stand as the flames licked ever closer. She watched as Valtar and Eldred grappled over the weapon, locked in a deadly struggle to overpower each other with brute force.

As the numbing sensation began to diminish from her body, Nayla struggled to her feet. In the distance, Joval shouted orders to break the dam as his steed charged forward. Stumbling toward Valtar, she could hear Eldred curse, conjuring his dark magic as he slammed the Elf into the ground.

Valtar, on his hands and knees, strained to reach his sword that was knocked from his grasp. Just as he seized his weapon, Valtar screamed in agony.

And then there was nothing.

He could not feel his legs or the dagger the Sorcerer had driven low into his back. Unable to move or fight, Valtar knew he was done. It was over.

As the Sorcerer raised his dagger again, Nayla staggered forward, lunging at Eldred. Still weakened by the assault, the Sorcerer merely batted her away, knocking her to the ground as he turned his attention back to the Elf.

Valtar could feel the earth quaking beneath his chest as a thunderous noise filled the air and the pounding of hooves reverberated through the ground. Just as Eldred was to sink the dagger into his back again, Joval charged through the rising flames. Leaping from his saddle, he tackled the Sorcerer.

Nayla watched as Joval and Eldred went tumbling through the burning grasses. Orange sparks scattered, dancing high into the night sky. She crawled to Valtar's side, rolling him over onto his back.

"My legs! Can't feel my legs!" cried Valtar; alarmed by this numbing sensation.

Wrapping her arms around his chest, Nayla struggled to drag Valtar away from the flames creeping toward them. As she pulled, the islands of fire surrounding them from the north were suddenly extinguished as the sounds of distant rumbling grew ever louder. She immediately knew the Kagai Warriors had broken the dam to send a torrent of water rushing down across the valley floor.

Holding on to Valtar, she braced herself. The water crashed down the mountain, sweeping across the open valley. Nayla maneuvered Valtar, turning her back to the wall of water to absorb the brunt of the force as it slammed into them. Instead of fighting the tide, she held onto the Elf, allowing the water to carry them away.

Predicting the Sorcerer would engage the powers of his element, Keodai deliberately planned for this flood, putting an end to the wildfires by drenching the grounds so it would cease to burn.

As the water drained away down the other side of the valley, Nayla struggled to her feet. She gazed about to see the massive volume of water had squelched the fires. In the distance, the battle was over. She could see the warriors silhouetted against the still-dark horizon.

Joval ran to their side, kneeling next to Valtar.

"I cannot feel my legs, Joval," groaned the Elf.

Joval nodded in understanding.

"Nayla, see to the others," ordered Joval. He turned his friend over onto his stomach to assess the damage to his back. "I shall heal Valtar first, and then I will join you."

"The Sorcerer… Is he dead?" asked Nayla.

"No. Water is his enemy, but this time it saved him," stated Joval, setting to work on repairing Valtar. "He was ripped from my hands as the water coursed through the valley. The Sorcerer managed to escape. He has disappeared yet again."

Nayla did not waste any time. She standing on her shaking legs, she headed to the battlefield. With the tingling sensation in her body subsiding, she hastened her pace, but as she neared, a sense of urgency filled her heart as she glanced at all the war-weary faces of the surviving warriors. In the midst of all the carnage, she found Keodai. Her heart sank as she gazed into his eyes dulled with grief. He cradled his eldest son in his arms as Kashe knelt by his father's side, weeping for his brother. Maisai was dead.

How can that be? Nayla wondered as she looked upon this grim sight. *He was alive when I last saw him. He was fighting by his brother's side.* Unable to bear anymore of this sadness, Nayla turned away.

Just a few yards from Keodai, she heard the mournful cries of another warrior. Pushing her way through the crowd, Nayla gasped in shock. Before her, Hemashe lay dead. His son, Tadashe clutched his father in his arms, rocking him to and fro as he begged him to wake up.

Nayla knelt down by Hemashe's bloodied body, her hand gently touching his cold face. There was a look of utter peace about him, the type of serenity that can only be found in death during these times of war.

She blinked back her tears, closing her eyes for a moment to remember Hemashe as the young man she once loved. The gray strands peppering his raven black hair disappeared and the fine lines lightly creasing his still handsome face all but vanished as she remembered him as he once was. Overcome with sorrow, great tears tumbled down her cheeks as she listened to Tadashe's heart-wrenching plea.

"Father! Please, wake up. It is time to go home now. It is over. The war is over. Please get up," begged Tadashe, giving Hemashe's body a shake.

"Tadashe, come with me," urged Nayla. "Your father will not be coming home."

"What do you speak of, warrior maiden?" asked the young man. "My father is just weary. He is resting. That is all."

"No, Tadashe. Your father is dead."

"No! He will be fine!" argued the young warrior. "My father is fine…"

He lifted Hemashe's limp body, holding him close to his chest. No longer able to deny the obvious, Tadashe began to weep, his body shuddering with great sobs as he surrendered to his grief.

"Please, Tadashe, listen to me. I am truly sorry, but your father is gone," said Nayla. One hand wiped away her tears as the other rested gently on the young warrior's shoulder. "He is dead."

Tadashe shrugged off her hand, glaring at Nayla as he began to rage: "Where were you, warrior maiden? Where were you when my father needed you? He always told me the great Takaro Bansho kept him safe during times of war! Where were you?"

Nayla recoiled from Tadashe's angry stare as his harsh words pierced her heart. She could feel the eyes of the all warriors turn on her, scrutinizing her as she backed away. Nayla began to tremble as her own words echoed in her mind, haunting with the sad truth: *Hemashe is dead. He is dead...*

It was all so final.

Her soul was like a wounded bird tossed into a raging storm of sorrow, grief, and guilt. Overwhelmed, she was blinded by her own tears, colliding into Joval as he returned with a horse upon which Valtar steadied himself.

Catching Nayla by her shoulders, he could feel her trembling. Her soul was crumbling beneath the crushing weight of her despair.

"Nayla?" He stooped to gaze into her face. The color had all but drained away. He was stunned to see her eyes, wild with rage and sorrow, as bitter tears streamed down her cheeks. "Nayla, what happened?"

Yanking away from the Elf's grip, she grabbed the reins of a horse away from another warrior. Throwing herself into the saddle, she sank her heels into the steed's flanks. The horse reared before bolting westward. Nayla charged past the warriors and on through the blood-soaked battlefield. Joval watched as she disappeared, swallowed up by the shadows of the night.

Riding hard, Nayla threw her head back, screaming in anguish. Her cry was long and loud, as though it was the only way she could exorcise the demons of guilt now crushing her heart and smothering her soul. Her voice resonated through the valley, echoing from mountain to mountain. All knew her sorrow was great.

Working through the somber, gray dawn, the Elves healed the many wounded. Not one warrior emerged unscathed from this battle as injuries ranged from minor lacerations to gaping, bloody wounds and shattered bones to amputated limbs. Although they were victorious once again, the casualties were greater than ever before as this was the largest battle to be fought yet.

Joval released the souls of the dying Elves so they could enter the Twilight to live eternally in a land free of the sorrow and grief brought about by the conflict of war. Keodai set aside his own personal grief long enough to dispatch his warriors so the wounded wishing to relinquish their lives may end their suffering. Once the men were taken care of, all set about the grim task of disposing the corpses. Mass graves were prepared for this purpose.

As dusk settled on the lands, the warriors retreated from the pine forests as they journeyed back to Hebeku Valley. With the coming of the night, as the Elves and weary men settled for an evening meal and to rest by the comfort of the many campfires, Nayla was nowhere to be seen. Like a wounded animal skulking off to die alone, Joval could sense she had no desire to be found. And even if he did find her, the Elf was confident his presence would offer little, if any, comfort during this time of mourning.

Instead, Joval remained with the other warriors. He tended to the wounded souls of the young warriors fortunate enough to survive their very first battle; offering them words of comfort and encouragement.

As the night wore on, Joval made another attempt to relieve the pain still coursing through Valtar's body. Although he was able to mend his broken back and partially severed spinal cord so Valtar was able to walk again, this Elf had been assaulted by a dagger wielded the Sorcerer and blessed by the forbidden arts. Had it been a weapon forged by the hands of a mortal man, Joval knew Valtar would have healed completely. Now, his friend would be forced to endure the pain and discomfort of this injury for the remains of his days in this realm.

By the end of their second day of travel, the Kagai Warriors returned to the tranquil haven of Anshen. With the help of Joval's men, the wounded and the dead were brought back to the village.

As night quietly stole away with the light of day, the sounds of mournful wailing and heart-rending sobs filled the air as families claimed the bodies of their loved ones for cremation. Among those who wept was Medaru Saibon. The old warrior, weakened by old age, leaned heavily on his distraught son. Keodai steadied him as he viewed his grandson's lifeless form.

From out of the growing darkness, Nayla emerged from the shadows. As she dismounted from her horse, the grief was so rampant she went unnoticed by all except Yumai who ran to greet her.

"Takaro! Where is Tadashe?" asked Yumai, her eyes frantically searching through the crowd. Nayla could not ignore how her face and soul had aged over the years. Though in her mid-forties now, Yumai's dulled eyes revealed a heart tortured by the anguish of sending her first-born son off to war.

"Tadashe is alive, Yumai," answered Nayla.

"Thank goodness!" exclaimed Yumai, throwing her arms around Nayla in a grateful hug.

"Yumai, I am sorry to be the bearer of sad tidings."

"What do you speak of, Takaro? My son is alive," replied Yumai. Her eyes darkened in fear as she listened. "You said Tadashe is alive."

"It is not Tadashe I speak of," said Nayla, her voice breaking with undeniable grief. "Hemashe…"

"What of my husband, Takaro?" asked Yumai, her eyes staring into hers, watching as a sad trail of tears streamed down Nayla's face. "I do not understand."

"Hemashe… He is dead," cried Nayla. Falling to her knees before Yumai, she humbled herself, praying for forgiveness.

"No, Takaro! That is not so. Hemashe is not dead," she whispered, embracing Nayla's trembling body.

Yumai held her close, feeling Nayla's body racked by great sobs. Panic filled her heart as she gazed up to see her son. Hemashe was not by his side.

"Tadashe, where is your father?" asked Yumai, slowly rising to her feet.

"He was killed, mother," answered the young warrior, in a sad whisper. "Father is dead."

"*NOOO*!" wailed Yumai, collapsing into Tadashe's arms. "No! That cannot be!"

"I will tell Chusai and Taiko," said Tadashe, trying desperately to console his mother.

"No, Tadashe! Do not tell your brother and sister. Not yet! You could be wrong. This may well be a mistake," cried Yumai, wiping the great tears from her eyes as she tried in vain to compose herself.

"I was there, mother," replied Tadashe, holding her close. "He was overwhelmed by soldiers. There was nothing we could do. Not I, not even Takaro, could have saved him."

Nayla's tears fell fresh upon hearing the young warrior's words. It was cold comfort knowing Hemashe's son no longer held her accountable for his father's demise.

Tadashe led Yumai away, delivering her to the litter upon which Hemashe's body rested. As the shroud was peeled back to reveal his corpse, Yumai fell to her knees, throwing herself over her husband's cold body. Overwhelmed with despair, she wailed uncontrollably. The sound of Yumai's mournful cry pierced Nayla's wounded heart.

Joval knelt before Nayla, his hand gently lifting her chin so their eyes could meet. It was as though the fire was now extinguished from them as the tears flowed endlessly. Without a word, the Elf placed his arms around Nayla's shoulders, guiding her away from the sad crowd.

With the coming of autumn, the warriors prepared for the long trek back to Nagana. Keodai arrived late in the afternoon, seeking Nayla.

"Father is in failing health, Takaro," stated Keodai. "He wishes to speak to you before you depart with your men."

"Of course, Keodai," replied Nayla, gathering her horse's reins to follow him.

"I am afraid with Maisai's passing, father has lost his desire for living," explained Keodai, leading the way to Reyu Falls. "He always believed his life would be spent long before that of his grandson's."

"And what of you? How do you fare, Keodai?" asked Nayla, sensing the warrior's sadness. Though he was only forty-eight years of age, it was as though the calamity of this last battle aged him greatly, both body and soul. His once black hair was now streaked with obvious gray strands and the lines of worry were now more evident on his proud face.

"I am as well as can be expected after losing both a son and a dear friend," answered Keodai, his dark, vacant eyes gazing up to the pale blue sky. "I will miss Maisai and Hemashe immensely and I pray the passing of time will ease the pain of my loss. I suppose that is the very worst of it, Takaro. The mere thought that I live, while my son died, is a terrible burden to bear."

He led the way into the cottage Nayla once occupied. Having turned it over to Yumai and Hemashe upon her departure from Anshen, Medaru now shared this home with his daughter and son-in-law. Too feeble to care for himself, Yumai tended to her father in his twilight years.

"Father," called Keodai, patting Medaru lightly on his shoulder. "Takaro is here. I shall leave you two alone to speak." He quietly closed the door behind him as he departed the cottage.

Nayla sat on the edge of his bed, taking the old warrior priest's lined and weathered hand into hers.

"Takaro?"

"Yes, master," she said in a whisper. "How do you fare today?"

The old man's eyes opened upon hearing her gentle voice. His gaze turned toward her, but Nayla could see his eyes were now clouded with cataracts. She was probably nothing more than a blur of light and shadow before him.

"Ah, my child, the seasons change once again as the cool breath of autumn turn the leaves to gold," smiled Medaru. "The air smells crisp and clean as a beautiful sun shines down on this small piece of heaven."

"Yes, master, it is a beautiful day indeed," agreed Nayla, as she gave his hand a comforting pat.

"Yes, it is the perfect day to die; to pass from this realm of existence," stated Medaru; his words matter-of-fact.

Nayla's hands tightened around his as he spoke these words.

"As surely as one is born, one must also expect to die," said the old warrior priest. "I have lived for almost ninety years and now I find myself asking God if I had been willing to shorten my existence in this realm, would He have extended Maisai's life in exchange."

"Master, I have never known our God to make deals such as this, but I do believe we are all placed in this realm for good reason, no matter how brief our existence may be," replied Nayla. "I wish to believe there is a divine reason for everything, including how much time is doled out to us, and that we must make the best of the time we are allotted."

Medaru smiled as he reflected on her words: "Ah yes, our Kagai credo: Live life to the fullest…"

"And that you did, master, just as your grandson did in his short life. As you once said to me; how *long* you live is not as important as *how you choose to live*," reminded Nayla.

She could see the tears welling in the corners of Medaru's eyes.

"What is it, master?"

"How you choose to live…" he repeated Nayla's words, its meaning now hollow. "Sometimes, one has no choice. Sometimes, the choice is made by others."

"I do not understand."

"There are times when life's choices are dictated by others," said the old warrior, his voice tightened with shame.

"What do you speak of, master?"

"Throughout my long mortal existence, I have known you since I was a small child. I have loved you as a sister and now as a daughter," whispered Medaru, his quaking hand patting Nayla lovingly on her cheek. "I ask you now, before I die, do you have the compassion and grace to forgive this old man?"

"There is nothing to forgive, master," assured Nayla, with a gentle smile. "You, your father, and your grandfather, each of you embraced me into your family, treating with respect, love and compassion; the three things I have not experienced since the passing of my mother. Whatever you speak of shall never sway my loyalty and love for you and your kin."

"I am so ashamed, Takaro," whispered Medaru, his tears falling from his eyes. "I have done you wrong. I had done something I believed in my heart was in your best interest, but in the process, you ultimately suffered because of my decision. I can only pray you will understand what had compelled me to do this."

"Do what? What is it?" asked Nayla, her heart began to race as she listened to his words.

"If I remember correctly, it was about twenty-five years ago when Hemashe came to me, asking for your hand in marriage," replied Medaru.

"Yes," responded Nayla, wistfully. "And then he declined his proposal, forsaking me to wed Yumai."

"No, my child, it did not happen quite like that," confessed the old warrior. "Hemashe pleaded to me. He begged to be bound to you, but it was his parents and I who refused to bless this betrothal. I know you think me cruel, I know you might blame me for dashing your hopes for love and happiness with Hemashe, but understand this Takaro: You are not mortal. You remain youthful while those around you succumb to old age. When Hemashe died, he was fast approaching his fiftieth year while you remain a woman still barely in your twentieth year. To allow you to plight your troth to this mortal man would have sealed your fate. You would have been bound to a pledge that would see you, a young woman, forced to share the bed of a tired, old man."

Nayla's mind reeled from the blow of this revelation. She blinked back her tears as she cried: "I loved him! With all my heart, I loved Hemashe. It mattered not if he had aged. My love for him was such it would have been eternal; it would have withstood the test of time."

"Look at me, Takaro. When you first came to Anshen, I was a mere boy of eight. Gaze upon me now, I am well into the winter of my life," stated Medaru, desperately trying to reason with the warrior maiden. "Though you have lived far longer than I, look at me – at the ravages of time. The last page in the story of my life is about to be turned. There is no more. But for you, your life still unfolds. Your whole life is like a great book with many chapters still before you."

Medaru drew in a long, weary breath as his mind wandered for a moment.

"In all honesty Takaro, could you see yourself bound in wedlock to an old man? Had Hemashe lived, even if he lived as long as I, you would still be the mortal equivalent of a young woman in your mid-twenties. There would be those who would mistake Hemashe for your grandfather rather than your husband. And think of the indignities he would have been made to suffer as an old man no longer able to satisfy his young wife's wants and needs."

"It mattered not. I loved him," she replied in sad whimper.

"And had you children, no doubt the blood of the Elf-kind would bestow them with long life too, forcing Hemashe to enjoy his children as a decrepit, old man, unable to live long enough to watch them grow to adulthood," explained Medaru.

"Why do you tell me this now?" groaned Nayla, her chin dropping to her chest as she lowered her head in sadness.

"Because I cannot leave this realm with a clear conscience knowing you believe Hemashe had forsaken you for Yumai; that his love for you was never genuine. Although you knew as well as I did my daughter loved this man, too, I felt it was in the best interest for all, you included, that Hemashe wed Yumai," confessed Medaru. "It was with great reluctance he agreed to do so. And Hemashe only did this to spare you."

"Spare me? Spare me from what? His love?" cried Nayla, her hands releasing Medaru's from her clasp.

"No, Takaro. Hemashe meant to spare you from a life in exile. I had threatened to deploy you permanently to the Magare Valley for as long as he was willing to fight for his love for you," admitted the old warrior, his hand reaching out blindly to her.

Finally, sad tears spilled from her eyes as she gasped: "For so long I had been bitter to Hemashe, forced to watch as he built a life with another and now it is too late. He died believing I blamed him, that I was angry with him."

"No, he did not, Takaro. Hemashe requested that if he were to predecease me, I was to reveal to you what had happened, so your mind may be put to rest. Just as he was to reveal the truth to you had I died first," stated Medaru. "I just never imagined it would be me to be the one to tell you this. Please forgive me, Takaro. Please find it in your heart to forgive this meddling, old fool."

As though the cruel hands of fate had thrust yet another knife into her heart, it pained Nayla to know this man she had loved as a father had also betrayed her, yet she was torn. She knew his motives were driven by his need to act in the best interest of Yumai, Hemashe, and even her.

"Do you forgive me, Takaro?" asked the old man, his voice pleading as his hand reached out for her.

Nayla folded against his chest, weeping. Medaru's weak arms embraced her in a fatherly hug as he, too, wept. And it was only after hearing her whisper: *'Of course, I forgive you, master'*, did the old warrior finally find the peace of mind that had eluded him for over two decades.

That evening, as the light of day surrendered to the coming of the night, with his family by his side, at the ripe old age of eight-seven, Medaru Saibon quietly passed from this realm.

Since the passing of Medaru and Hemashe, the next fifty-six turbulent years were marred with ongoing battles and sporadic times of peace as the powers shifted in eastern Orien. During this period, Keodai Saibon passed on his skills and teachings to other young men wishing to become one of the legendary Kagai Warriors.

Nayla was there to witness Keodai's surviving son, Kashe step into the role as the new Kagai leader and she watched as Keodai's grandsons and great grandson faced the perils of war. And Nayla was there by Keodai's side when he, too, succumbed to the years, passing into the next realm at the age of ninety-one.

Together, Joval and Nayla would ride into war many times. They determined strategy, led their men into battle and always remained close, fighting side by side. And when the battle was done, they would nurse each other's wounds; and when alone, found solace and comfort in each other's arms.

For Nayla, Joval's constant presence, his loyal friendship was invaluable. He was like a safe harbor from the storms she was often forced to weather in her life. And most of all, Joval was a safe haven from the callous words and cruel treatment cast by her father, Dahlon Treeborn.

During this period, whenever they were afforded times of peace, Nayla and Joval would make excursions into the treacherous terrains of the Furai Mountains in a bid to hunt down the Sorcerer. Convinced a large troop heading into the mountains would only serve to warn Eldred Firestaff of their coming, Nayla and Joval ventured forth alone, in secret. It was during one such expedition did they come across the Sorcerer's secret lair.

"I dare say," whispered Joval, motioning Nayla to follow; "I believe we may have finally stumbled upon that murderous fiend."

Drawing her sword as she followed, Nayla ducked into a low, narrow opening that gave way to a large chamber. In an instant, they were consumed by the deep shadows, surrounded by the damp, musty air that hung heavy in this foul place. It was almost suffocating. At the far end of this cavern was a tunnel illuminated by a series of torches. For a moment, both stood in the gloom as their eyes adapted to the dim light.

"This way," whispered the Elf, the tip of his sword pointing ahead. "It would appear the Sorcerer is home this time."

As they crossed the large chamber, weaving between the limestone deposits that accumulated over an eon from the dripping stalactites suspended from the ceiling, Joval's sensitive nose wrinkled in disgust. He drew the edge his cloak over his nose and mouth.

"This foul stench could be the Sorcerer's rotting remains," hoped the Elf. "Perhaps he met his demise."

"We should be so lucky," replied Nayla, her nostrils burning from the malodorous scent tainting the oppressive air. "Unfortunately, it is bat you smell."

"*Bat*?" repeated Joval. Baffled, he frowned in her direction as his eyes began to water. "It must be one very big, dead bat wasting away in here to create such a putrid stench."

Nayla drew her cloak over her nose, filtering out the burning odor of ammonia as she explained: "It is better to say, this horrid smell arises from the bat droppings."

"What?" gasped Joval.

His eyes suddenly dropped to the floor of the cave. To his horror, the earth beneath his feet undulated; popping and crunching with each step he took. "What the…"

A thick carpet of black beetles and fat, wriggling maggots were feasting on the generous layer of bat excrement as well as any unfortunate bat that fell from the ceiling high above. The entire floor of the cave squirmed with life.

"My God!" Joval shrieked in absolute disgust.

His voice rang through the cavern, reverberating off the walls, ceiling and numerous stalactites.

"Damn it!" cursed Nayla.

Grabbing Joval's arm, she thrust him against the wall of the cave as his voice launched hundreds of small, brown bats into the air. Exploding into frenetic flight, the panicking creatures careened through the dark recesses of the chamber. The beating of thousands of leathery wings was deafening. The frightened bats swirled before them, all circling in the same direction like a black cyclone gaining in velocity as the little creatures synchronized their movements to avoid colliding in mid-air. After several sweeping passes, they funneled out of the cave into the light of day.

As quickly as the bats had erupted into this frenzied flight, they were gone.

Joval breathed a sigh of relief as he picked his way through the chamber, trying his darnedest to tread where there was the least amount of life squirming beneath his feet. Nayla followed behind him. Unbothered by the crunching of insects underfoot, her eyes focused on the corridor before them.

"How far do you think this tunnel goes?" asked Nayla, her sword poised before her.

"Your guess is as good as mine," answered Joval. "I would not be surprised if Eldred Firestaff guards the gates of Hell, biding his time while he keeps the likes of the Dark Lord Beyilzon company."

The pair pressed on. Following the trail of torches deeper into the bowels of the earth, their shadows danced against the walls illuminated by the flickering flames. The farther they journeyed, the hotter it became. The temperature climbed steadily as churning, oozing pools of molten lava bubbled around them, bathing their surrounding in an eerie red glow.

"I think we shall be knocking on the gates of Hell soon," whispered Joval. "The air is tainted with the foul stench of brimstone and the heat; even for an Elf is becoming rather uncomfortable. How do you fare, Nayla?"

She wiped the beads of perspiration from her forehead as she responded with a nod, "Proceed, I can endure for awhile longer."

Joval cautiously crept forward, his keen eyes constantly scanning the deep shadows and recesses of this subterranean labyrinth. Finally, the tunnel terminated, the floor of the cave abruptly dropped away.

Peering down, Nayla and Joval gazed upon a massive chamber. Forty feet below them, huge columns of stalagmites rose up from the ground as great, conical daggers of stalactites loomed high overhead. They hung down like great fangs of a colossal beast waiting to snap down on any unwanted intruder. Vats of boiling lava pocked the floor of the chamber, belching and steaming noisily as gases escaped from deep within the earth's core.

"This looks none too inviting," whispered Nayla, her eyes staring down the sheer face of the cliff wall.

"Neither does that," replied Joval, in a hushed tone. He pointed across the vast chamber to the far side.

Nayla's gaze followed the Elf's finger. Her eyes stopped on what appeared to be a massive boulder partially blocking the opposite entrance of the chamber.

"A big rock…" noted the little warrior.

This dark form moved; expanding and then slowly shrinking as it exhaled a long, slow breath.

"Rocks do not breathe," noted Joval. "*That* is a dragon."

"You jest, right?" responded Nayla. Her eyes strained to focus on the object, for never before had she seen a dragon, dead or alive.

"I have seen that beast before," replied the Elf.

"When? Where?"

"It was long ago when your father led his army to war with my father by his side," answered Joval. "Eldred mounted an attack using that dragon. The creature almost killed Dahlon, dropping him to earth from on high."

"He never told me about this."

"Can you blame him? I was there. I truly believed Dahlon was going to die that night. It was the event that forced his hand, giving him no recourse but to guide his people to find sanctuary in the fortress city."

"But what is that creature doing here?"

"This may be the Sorcerer's lair, but it is also the dragon's keep," determined Joval. "That beast is guarding something."

"This is frightfully extreme," declared Nayla. "Why could he not use a vicious guard dog instead of a dragon, of all things?"

"Nothing can live down here except such a beast," noted Joval, removing a coil of Elven rope from the leather pack slung over his shoulder. "And whatever it is the creature is guarding, no doubt it has great value to the Sorcerer. He means to keep it safe. Stay here, Nayla."

"Are you mad?"

"We have come this far, I will not turn back now," stated Joval, as he secured the slender, silken cord around the broken remains of a stalagmite.

"No, I mean, are you mad to think I would allow you to venture forth alone?" corrected Nayla. "I am going down with you."

She reached for the coil of rope from her bag, securing it tightly to a small, rocky outcrop.

Joval knew better than to argue with her. "Just be warned, if the dragon wakes from its slumber; *do not run*."

"What do you mean by that? I am to stand there and be eaten alive? I think not, my friend," grumbled Nayla.

"This creature has exceptional hearing, but it is cursed with poor eyesight. It is drawn to movement. Sudden, quick movement means food. It also has a blind spot just as horses do. If you stand directly in front, close enough to feel the heat of its breath on your face, it cannot see you," advised the Elf.

"How do you know this?" queried Nayla, taking the rope into her hands as she leaned out over the cliff wall.

"I was told by a fellow Elf who had close encounters with dragons in the past," answered Joval, lowering himself down.

"So he lived to tell of such confrontations?"

"Actually, he died about a century ago," responded Joval.

"Killed in battle?"

"Truth be told, he was killed by a dragon when he fled."

"Well, that is comforting to know, Joval," groaned Nayla, as she rappelled down to the floor.

"He had miscalculated just how close he should be standing before the beast to *vanish* in its *blind spot*. He panicked. He ran. Need I say more?"

"Thank you for sharing," said Nayla. "I shall keep it in mind in case we are pursued by that behemoth."

"Just be extremely quiet as we pass. And for once, take heed of my warning: *Do not run*," ordered the Elf, speaking in a whisper.

Nayla nodded in understanding. Stepping ever so lightly, she followed behind Joval. They remained close to the wall of the great chamber, giving the dragon's body a wide berth until they stood before its massive head blocking the way. Joval motioned for her to squeeze by. He pressed up against the wall of the cave, skirting past the creature's snout into the secondary chamber.

Standing before the colossal reptile, Nayla was surprised to see the dragon's jaws. A rusted metal cage had been secured to prevent the beast from opening its well-toothed maw or releasing a deadly blast of flames. Around its body and huge, leathery wings, heavy iron chains engulfed its scaly form, effectively hobbling the great beast so it could not take flight. For a lingering moment, Nayla took pity upon this once magnificent creature as it slept, oblivious to her presence.

Joval peered around the corner. Flexing his index finger, he gestured for her to keep moving.

Nayla cautiously sidestepped to pass the dragon. She felt the humid jet of air snorting from the beast's right nostril. Another quiet step placed her directly before the great reptile just as a loud blast of gas vented into the air from a nearby pool of lava.

The dragon's ears flickered to life. They flattened against its head in annoyance, bothered that its sleep was interrupted.

Nayla froze in her tracks as Joval pressed up against the cave wall.

The creature's eyes snapped open to reveal the third eyelid. As the thin, cloudy nictitating membrane slowly retracted obliquely across its eyes, the red orbs with the black, slit-like pupils glowed in the dim-light.

Nayla held her breath, attempting to calm her racing heart as the creature's eyes stared straight ahead. She stood motionless, standing right before its snout. She was so close she could feel the blast of spent, rancid air exhaled from its nostrils.

The usual sounds of bubbling, churning lava lulled the dragon back to sleep. Its heavy eyelids gradually closed once more.

Joval peered around the corner again, motioning Nayla to move now. She wasted no time, creeping with great stealth past the dragon. Wandering deeper into this smaller chamber, they spied a tall, stony throne carved into the wall of the cave. The Elf removed a burning torch, holding it forth as they ventured on. As they neared the Sorcerer's throne, to the right stood a great pedestal of black stone.

"What is that?" whispered Nayla, peering up at the object resting on this stone pillar.

Joval stood before the pedestal. His hand brushed away the layer of dust that had settled upon the object. It was a leather-bound book, its cover was branded with characters from an ancient dialect so old, Joval had difficulty deciphering the runes.

"It appears to be a book of spells… incantations," answered Joval.

Passing the torch on to Nayla, he cautiously cracked opened the cover to reveal a volume of tattered parchments yellowed with age.

"Can you read this?" whispered Nayla, staring at the unfamiliar characters.

"It is an ancient dialect no longer used by the Elf-kind," noted Joval. "I recognize some of the characters, enough to know these spells are meant to conjure great evil. Look here." His finger pointed to some runes.

"What do you think it means?" queried Nayla.

"This has to do with awakening the souls of the dead," translated the Elf. "I believe it is used to capture their souls to do his bidding."

"Firestaff is truly no longer the Wizard of the East. He is a Sorcerer, through and through," decided Nayla.

"He is deeply embroiled in the black arts. There is no doubting it," whispered Joval, closing the book shut. "Nothing good will ever come of this book. We must destroy this evil."

"Wake up, you stupid beast!" An angry voice sounded from the dragon's keep.

Joval snatched the book off the pedestal before joining Nayla against the wall of the cave.

The dragon remained unmoved. Its eyes remained closed, choosing to ignore the angry words hurled in its direction. He snorted loudly in defiance.

"Damn you!" cursed the Sorcerer, whacking the dragon sharply on its snout with the end of his staff. "You should be minding this keep while I am out, not sleeping!"

The dragon slowly stood up, its head tipping back as a pathetic groan rumbled from its clamped jaws.

"You would not be wearing this muzzle now if you had minded where you snap those teeth of yours to begin with," rebuked Eldred, unsympathetic as he dragged a large, dirty burlap sack toward the dragon. The sharp scent of fresh blood wafted up into the beast's nostrils. It emitted a guttural rumble, excited at the prospect of food.

"Here you go," muttered the Sorcerer. "There was only one in the snare today. It will have to do."

The dragon knelt before his master like an oversized dog waiting for a treat. Nayla and Joval moved swiftly. Clinging to the shadows of the opposite wall, they crept steadily closer to the entrance. They watched in horrified silence as Eldred dumped a dismembered body from the bag. He picked up a man's leg. Amputated at the hip, he wedged the bloodied mass thigh first into the partially opened maw. Unable to open its mouth wide enough to bite and chew, the Sorcerer hewed the bodies of his hapless victims into dragon-size servings, forcing it into the beast's mouth. The dragon inhaled the morsel, tipping its head back to allow the leg to drop down into its gullet.

Eldred stuffed the other leg into the dragon's mouth. As the beast tilted its head back to swallow, Joval noticed for a brief instance the nictitating membrane closing over the creature's eyes. This third eyelid served to protect the reptile's eyes from flailing limbs as it fed, but it also temporarily blinded the dragon in the process. He pulled Nayla closer until they stood beside the dragon's massive hindquarter that partially blocked the mouth of the cave. They watched in silence as Eldred's shadow moved, cramming a pair of severed limbs into the dragon's awaiting jaws.

Again, the dragon tipped its head back, allowing the arms to tumble down into its throat. The third eyelid slipped over the burning red orbs of the dragon's eyes, concealing its menacing, black pupils.

"One more bite," announced the Sorcerer, as he propped up the bloodied torso.

The dragon snorted in appreciation as its jagged, yellow incisors almost delicately plucked up the corpse by its head. Joval spied the grisly scene from the creature's shadow, watching as it pressed down on the body to wedge this much larger mouthful into the restricted gape of its jaws. A ghastly moan escaped from the dead man's mouth as the pressure exerted on his body forced out the last of the air still trapped in his lungs.

Just as the dragon raised its head to force down the dead body, Joval grabbed Nayla's hand. He guided her around the creature's hulking form as Eldred entered his lair.

As the dragon struggled to swallow this large clump of meat, Nayla and Joval dashed behind a column of stalagmites. Peering behind, the Elf motioned Nayla to advance toward the cliff wall as the great beast remained preoccupied with consuming its meal.

"*WHERE IS IT? WHERE IS MY BOOK?*" shrieked Eldred. His

angry voice echoed through the cave.

Eldred's black form swirled out of his lair. The crystal orb on his staff crackled with energy, fueled by his rage.

"*RUN*!" hollered Joval.

"But you said not to," gasped Nayla, a look of confusion etched on her face.

"Forget what I said! Get out of here! Run!" ordered the Elf, shoving her forward. He knew the dragon was still choking down its meal, blinded to what was happening.

"Ha!" shouted the Sorcerer, spying the two fast-moving figures. "Who do we have here? If I am not mistaken, it is Lady Treeborn and Master Stonecroft. Why not stay awhile? So rarely do I get visitors not already dead."

"Go, Nayla!" shouted the Elf.

"Tsk! Tsk! Not so fast," growled Eldred. "You have something that is mine."

"Then come and get it!" retorted Joval, dashing behind Nayla as he struggled with the large, cumbersome book. It was as though it was weighed down by evil.

The Sorcerer lowered his staff in the Elf's direction. Joval could sense the energy building up rapidly in the orb, waiting to be discharged in a bolt of fire and light to destroy him. Then just as suddenly, Eldred drew back his staff. He was unwilling to sacrifice his precious book of incantations along with the Elf. Closing his eyes, he summoned the powers of the forbidden arts, uttering ancient words beneath his breath.

Sprinting to the cliff, Nayla took up her rope, advancing up the steep wall quickly and confidently. Peering down, she could see Joval struggling to keep his grip on the book. As though an unseen force was attempting to wrench it free from his grasp, Joval wrapped his arms tightly around it, refusing to let go.

"Give it to me!" bellowed the Sorcerer, pointing his staff at Nayla as she neared the ledge, almost within reach of safety. "Give it to me or I shall kill the half-caste wench."

"Stop!" ordered Joval. "It is yours! The book is yours!"

The Elf advanced cautiously, holding it forth for Eldred to take.

The Sorcerer's lips slowly curled into an obscene smile as he reached for his precious collection of spells. Joval could see the red glow of the molten lava reflecting on his lifeless, dark eyes.

"Yes, it is yours for the taking," offered Joval, inching toward the Sorcerer. Holding it out for Eldred to take, the Elf suddenly pitched it into a bubbling cauldron of red-hot lava.

"*NO*!" screamed the Sorcerer, his wild eyes following the book as it fell with a loud *'sploosh!'* onto the gelatinous surface of the quivering ooze.

Joval ran to join Nayla as Eldred frantically danced around the edge of the churning pool. He watched in horror as the edges of the book curled, burning with the intense heat. As he desperately attempted to fish his book out of the lava with the end of his staff, he bellowed at the dragon: "Attack! Kill them!"

No longer wrestling with its meal, the dragon lumbered toward Nayla and Joval. Its hulking mass prevented the creature from advancing with any great speed. It moved slowly and deliberately, its heavy gait shaking the entire cave as it drew steadily closer. Its large strides soon delivered the creature almost to the cliff wall where Joval raced to climb up the sheer face.

Nayla lay on her stomach, her outstretched hands straining to reach the Elf.

"Do not look back! Climb, Joval! Faster!"

As the dragon neared dangerously close, Nayla armed her bow, releasing an arrow. The dragon stopped momentarily as the projectile ricocheted off its large, plate-like dorsal scales. She took up another arrow, this time taking aim at the Sorcerer screamed in agony. He plunged his hand into the molten lava in a desperate bid to reclaim his book before it perished, sinking from his grasp.

As she drew back her arrow, Joval clambered over the ledge to safety.

"Go, Nayla! Forget about him!" ordered the Elf, waving her on to follow him.

"I can take him, Joval," argued Nayla.

As she took aim, the dragon turned, whipping its mighty tail about to strike against the cliff wall. Nayla plunged down as the earth beneath her crumbled away. Joval dove to the ground, seizing her by her left wrist. With all his strength, he swung her back onto the ledge. In absolute fury, the dragon smashed its armored head against the cliff to send rocks, boulders and earth cascading down.

"Quickly, Nayla!" shouted Joval, pulling her to her feet.

As they dove into the tunnel, the dragon's massive head lunged toward them, narrowly missing Joval as he pushed Nayla ahead.

The dragon was insistent, wedging its large snout deeper into the tunnel until the metal restraints clamping its jaws shut snagged onto the rocks and boulders lining this passage. With a guttural cry and an angry hiss, the dragon yanked back with all its might to free its trapped head.

Nayla and Joval dashed away as the ground beneath them shimmied. The creature's actions served to trigger an earthquake. Rocks and earth crumbled down around them.

Racing through the subterranean maze, the rush of air made by the collapsing chamber *'whooshed'* loudly behind them, extinguishing the torches lighting their way. As they forged on in the growing darkness, they could make out daylight far ahead.

They gagged as they entered the large chamber. Now devoid of bats, it was still very much alive with beetles and maggots scattering as the ground quaked. Dashing madly through the chamber, they dove through the mouth of the cave into the blinding light of day.

Tumbling down the slope, they came to a crashing halt. Joval threw his body over Nayla's as the explosive force of displaced air gushing through the network of collapsing tunnels and chambers sent rocks and earth blasting out of the mouth of the cave.

When the dust finally settled, Joval and Nayla peered up at the mountain slope. The entrance was demolished.

"Do you think the Sorcerer is dead?" asked Nayla.

"One can always hope, however, I have my doubts," answered Joval, lifting the little warrior onto her feet. "I know of not one animal dwelling underground, whether it be a mole or a badger that does not have more than one exit from its burrow. My intuition tells me that Eldred Firestaff is no exception."

The journey back to Nagana seemed longer. Joval was quiet as he rode alongside Nayla. For several days he was withdraw and pensive, lost in his thoughts. As they neared the city, Nayla rode on to the cottage they shared as Joval reported to Dahlon Treeborn and the elders of their findings and their harrowing escape from the Sorcerer's lair.

When Joval returned to his cottage, the sun had long since retired from the sky. Nayla was already in bed, waiting for the Elf to return. Though weary from the long trip, Joval still summoned the energy to make love to Nayla, but this time it was not their typical heated, intense encounter of unbridled passion to quench their desire. Instead, there was something very tender and loving as Joval moved on her body.

He held her close as her spirit slowly spiraled down from this state of absolute euphoria he would send her soul soaring to. She listened to his heart beating loudly as she rested her head against his chest.

"You have been so quiet these past few days, Joval," said Nayla, in a gentle voice. "What troubles you?"

She felt his chest slowly rise, and then fall as he breathed a weary sigh, but he did not speak.

"Tell me, what is on your mind?" She peered into his gentle blue eyes for an answer. "Is it the Sorcerer?"

"No, it is not the Sorcerer. Mind you, his actions did trigger this need in me," responded the Elf.

"What need? What do you speak of?" asked Nayla.

"I feel a need to protect you."

"I do not understand, Joval."

"For over seventy-five years we have been lovers, keeping our relationship secret from all. During this time, you have gone to war by my side. Although you are a great warrior, I must admit each time we go into battle, a little more of me dies every time you get hurt or nearly killed," responded Joval. "And the prospect of losing you in such a manner becomes more unbearable."

"But I survive," replied Nayla, her small shoulders shrugging with indifference. "I always do."

"Yes, you do. And I care for you too much to subject you to such a hard and dangerous life anymore, Nayla."

"So what do you suggest I do with my life?"

"Retire your sword. Lay down your bow," answered Joval, his fingertip tracing the soft lines of her face; "and become my wife."

"So your desire is to wed me so you may remove me from the battlefield and retire me as a captain?" teased Nayla, smiling sweetly at the Elf.

"I wish to keep you safe, to spare you the treacheries of war, but my desire to wed you is because I am in love with you."

"Surely you jest!"

He whispered as he held her close: "I am serious, Nayla. You know I love you. I love you more than -"

Nayla's finger pressed against his lips as she pleaded: "Do not speak these words, Joval."

"Why must you always do that? Why do you not allow me to speak my mind where you are concerned? You always turn away from me when you hear me speak of my love for you," scolded Joval, wounded by her rejection. "Why do you spurn my words?"

"I cannot bear to hear them," answered Nayla, her voice barely audible.

"But I speak the truth," whispered Joval.

"That is why I cannot bear to hear them."

"Is it because you do not love me?" asked the Elf.

"Do we not share the same bed?"

"That is not the same thing, Nayla! Do you not love me? Answer me that," ordered Joval.

Nayla pulled away from his touch. He could see the incipient tears as her eyes misted over.

"All my life, Joval, you have been the one constant, stable factor: a safe harbor in a sea of storms. You have shown me kindness and compassion in times when others would not. You have been the only person to have the courage to confront my father, to spare me from his abuse. I am forever indebted to you."

"But do you love me?"

"You have been the consummate friend and a loyal companion," replied Nayla.

"Answer me!" demanded Joval. "Am I nothing more than a friend that you willingly share this bed with, or is there more? Are you in love with me, or do you love what I mean to you?"

"I love.... You are..." stammered Nayla, searching desperately for the words to express her true feelings for him. "You are my closest and dearest friend, Joval."

"But do you love me?" asked Joval, his eyes darkened as his voice tightened. "Do you love me as I love you? Do you love me as a woman loves a man?"

"You are my sanctuary – my home," stated Nayla.

"I am not a *home*, Nayla. A home does not feel! I am of flesh and blood. I am a man," rebuked the Elf, "a man in love with you. Now, I ask again: Is this love returned?"

Nayla sat up before him, wrapping her arms about his neck as she whispered: "Joval, I owe my very existence to you. I would willingly lay down my life for you. I have pledged my allegiance to you."

"But do you pledge your love to me?" asked the Elf, his words now sad and bitter.

Nayla was silent.

Joval peeled her arms off him. Holding her by her wrists, he stared into her dark, liquid eyes. Nayla's heart began to race. Her body trembled as he forced her to look upon his face as great tears tumbled down his cheeks, leaving a damp trail of sadness. She was overcome with guilt, for she never believed a man, mortal or Elf, could ever feel the crushing anguish of heartbreak. For the first time in their long history, she was made to bear witness to this great and noble Elf's descent into sorrow, watching as he wept in despair for love lost.

Releasing his grip on her, Joval rose from their bed. Dressing quickly, without a word, he slipped out the door. Nayla peered out the window, watching as he mounted his steed, riding off into the darkness toward the fortress city, no doubt to seek the company of his best friend, Valtar Briarwood.

Late next morning, under a somber, gray sky, Joval returned home, playing over in mind what he would say to Nayla. There was an unnatural quiet shrouding the room as the Elf stepped into the cottage. The bed was made. The room was tidy. Everything was in its place.

Joval closed the door behind him as he called for her.

The displaced air caused a small piece of parchment to float off the table top onto the floor before him. He stooped to pick up the note and as Joval read, his tears fell fresh once more.

My dearest Joval:

I never meant to hurt you; to cause such anguish and sorrow in your life after all you had done for me. I am eternally grateful for your friendship and kindness of which I shall cherish the memories for the remains of my days.

I have already sent word to the elders of my resignation. Do not come looking for me. I am a Kagai Warrior so you know I will not be found if I choose not to be. Do not waste your time or life on me.

With much respect and gratitude, farewell.

Nayla

18

the beginning of a long journey

Not long after Nayla's sudden departure from Nagana, Dahlon Treeborn reassigned Joval's commission, removing him from the post of captain. Though Joval never revealed to him his true relationship with his daughter, Dahlon was not blind to the fact this Elf was pining in her absence. He could sense Joval's growing despondency and woe brought on by his concern for Nayla. It went well beyond that of one warrior for another. And Joval's fears and anxiety would escalate with each rumored sighting as she accepted dangerous missions in eastern Orien or when she would organize daring raids with her Kagai brothers to the north.

For his part, Dahlon was quite relieved to be rid of Nayla. With her gone, so too were the bitter feelings that would surface whenever she was present. Though Dahlon had little concern for what became of her, his worry for Joval, whom he regarded as a son, continued to grow.

Time and again, Joval's journeys to the north proved fruitless as Nayla, in true Kagai form, would silently and deliberately vanish upon his arrival. The Elf would also make perilous excursions into the east whenever he caught wind of her exploits. And during times of peace, he wandered the lonely mountains in search of her whenever he received word of the warrior maiden's presence in the vicinity. And always, there was that glimmer of hope he would come home to find Nayla waiting there for him.

Dahlon decided to put an end to these missions and Joval's wasteful pining by appointing him to the role of Stewart of Nagana. Made to live within the walls of the palace, Joval was now forced to tend to the administrative needs of the fortress city and the surrounding villages. No longer made to lead armies to do battle in the north, it was Dahlon's way of preventing Joval from seeking Nayla out as she continued her warfare against the enemy.

With the passing of time, Joval grew to accept his new responsibilities, allowing Dahlon greater opportunities for more leisurely pursuits as he limited his precious time to advising the senior members on council. Joval was left to oversee the security of the city in Dahlon's absence, especially during the fifty-two years of peace brought about since Shekata Darraku ascended to the throne.

During this period, Dahlon made numerous excursions to the royal palace in Keso. He worked closely with Emperor Shekata to ensure those loyal to his brother, Tisai Darraku, were kept in check. Tisai, a royal upstart who favored a more self-serving dictatorship over sharing prosperity and wealth with the people, skulked about. He was forced to wait in his brother's shadow for his chance to take over the throne.

For Tisai Darraku, the prospects were good, for his brother was twenty-two years his senior. With Shekata's advancing age and failing health, the likelihood of a male heir apparent was dismal. Tisai for the most part, quietly bided his time, exiled to the royal residence in Shesake, north of Keso.

During this time of peace, Nayla returned to Anshen, living amongst the descendants of the original Saibon clan. Though the atmosphere was light and the carefree days devoid of the evil specter of death that loomed in the shadows of war were cherished, Nayla continued to work with Keodai's grandson and great grandson to train and hone the skills of future generations of Kagai Warriors.

The long-lived citizens of Orien came to know that peace was a temporary state, as in constant flux as the politics to the east. Nayla was not about to allow these people to become complacent, jeopardizing their lives by taking up arms only when ill prepared and forced to do so.

For Nayla, it was also an opportunity keep the traditions and teachings of the Kagai Warriors alive. During all these years, she remained here, living peacefully amongst the mortals. Not once did she return to Nagana, nor did she ever speak of Joval Stonecroft again, learning only of him when he or Dahlon Treeborn would send messages to the Kagai leaders of potential strife or other news that could directly affect those to the north.

It was during Emperor Shekata's fifty-second year in power that hopes for prolonged peace sprung anew when Empress Metasu, the emperor's second wife gave birth to a much-desired son. The birth of Prince Tokusho was greeted with great jubilation, for the people believed he would mature to become a kind and just ruler like his father. The only one who did not embrace this news was the prince's uncle, Tisai Darraku. Fearful for the life of his only son, Emperor Shekata prayed for the powers that be to come to his aid.

Six months after the prince's birth, rumors of a mysterious and powerful being arriving in Keso late one night sent ripples of fear through the country. Whisperings of an evil, of unnatural powers descending upon the palace caused growing anxiety. Palace staff was shocked to learn that a being gifted with the powers as great as any Wizard had crafted a tomb-like vault in the throne room. Encased in stone and sealed by a massive door of granite, only the combination of Shekata and Metasu's palm prints inlaid into the stone would unlock the vault.

In this room, a treasury of gold, silver and precious gems relied upon during lean years to see the people through were safely stored away, along with the emperor's crown. Fearful that his brother would plot against Prince Tokusho, Emperor Shekata sealed the vault to prevent Tisai Darraku from plundering the riches belonging to the people as well as the crown meant for his son. Only the descendant from Shekata and Metasu's bloodline would have access to this great vault.

With news of this mysterious entity's presence in Keso, those to the west feared it was the Sorcerer Eldred Firestaff. Some believed Eldred resurfaced after all these many years, arriving in disguise to dupe the emperor.

Nayla journeyed eastward with several Kagai Warriors to investigate this strange appearance, but then an unsettling event changed the course of history for the people of Orien. Summoned to attend an official gala in a prefecture to the north, a tragic accident claimed the life of the emperor and empress, as well as those in their company when a freak storm washed away a mountain road they were traveling.

Though all fingers pointed to the emperor's brother, none could prove Tisai Darraku was directly responsible for the calamity.

With this news, Nayla's journey was drastically altered. Having only arrived at the palace in Keso when official word was received of the tragedy, she and her men spirited the infant prince and the staff loyal to the emperor away from the Imperial Palace. They were provided with a safe escort to the royal residence in Shesake.

To the warrior maiden, it was not a mere coincidence this estate was already vacated by Tisai Darraku, who was more than willing and eager to take on the role as the Regent of Orien until Prince Tokusho was of age to ascend to the throne. With all eyes watching the new

Regent, Tisai was reluctant to act on his plans to subvert the young prince, but while he was to reign, he was going to take full advantage of his new title and power.

By the spring of the following year, Eldred Firestaff reappeared in Keso to offer his wisdom and counsel to the Regent. In response, Tisai Darraku amassed a huge army to attack western Orien. Once again, the lands were immersed in war.

"Takaro!" called out the Kagai leader. He waved at the warrior maiden to catch her attention as she steered her horse toward Reyu Falls. "Takaro! A message arrives for you from Nagana."

Nayla turned her steed about, racing back towards the village. The Kagai priest held it up high for her to see.

"Master Saibon, perhaps you are mistaken," said the little warrior, as she dismounted before him.

"Oh no, my child," responded Hunta Saibon. "This is indeed for you. It is from the Stewart of Nagana."

Nayla's brows furrowed in curiosity as she wondered: "What could Joval Stonecroft want with me?"

"Read and find out," suggested the warrior priest, holding forth the parchment.

Captain Treeborn:

Your presence in Nagana is urgently requested. Please leave with the greatest expedience.

Joval Stonecroft,
Stewart of Nagana

"Hmph," sniffed Hunta, reading the note over Nayla's shoulder. "He is not one for great detail however; I do detect a tremendous sense of urgency in his words."

"I have not set foot in that city for over fifty years. I have no desire to go now," answered Nayla, crumpling the note in her hand.

"Perhaps your father is dying?"

"People like Dahlon Treeborn do not die." Her voice was tinged with sarcasm. "They linger on forever."

"Perhaps the Stewart of Nagana is dying?"

"He is an Elf. He would pass into the Twilight, retiring to the Haven before he would die in this realm," answered Nayla.

"Then perhaps he plans to enter the Elf Haven," continued Hunta.

Nayla studied the warrior's face. He had the same dark, spirited eyes his great, great grandfather, Keodai Saibon once had; lively and so full of curiosity.

"You believe I should go, do you not?" queried Nayla.

"Indeed, I do, Takaro," admitted the warrior. "I hardly think Master Stonecroft would make such a request if it was not of dire importance. And are you not curious yourself?"

"I believe *you* are more curious than I am," answered Nayla. "I have no desire to see Dahlon Treeborn or to face Master Stonecroft again."

Hunta smiled as he stated judiciously: "If it is your past you fear, you can run but it will catch up to you one day, most likely when you least expect it."

"I do not fear my past…"

"Nayla, you have often heard me say *'where you end in life depends on how you begin'*, yes?"

"Yes, master."

"We are all shaped by the events of our past and you have come so far in your life. From such austere beginnings you chose to rise above your grief and woes, channeling your energies to become a great warrior. You have found the courage to take the path less known than to take a road well traveled. And yes, it is true that how we begin in life can have a great influence on the final outcome; ultimately, it is how we choose to deal with these events that shall determine our destiny."

"Well, I am determined my destiny will not take me within one hundred leagues of that forsaken city."

"You dread the memories of this place, not the city itself," corrected Hunta Saibon. "The ghosts from your past only haunt you if you allow it."

"Some of these ghosts you refer to are very real, master."

"Perhaps you are right, Takaro," agreed the warrior priest; "but never before have you allowed '*ghosts*' to dictate how you live, what you do or whom you chose to become. You would boldly go where many dare not tread and now, you seem reluctant to go home."

"Nagana is not my home," corrected Nayla, wadding the parchment into a tiny ball, crushing it in her hand.

"You can squeeze that note as small as you wish, but I assure you, like Nagana, it shall not vanish because you wish it so," pointed out the warrior priest. "Perhaps it would be wise for you to choose to meet the future than to avoid this part of your past.

"But that will still take me to Nagana."

"Yes, but perhaps from a fresh perspective, you shall not be confronting your past so much so as boldly embracing your destiny, to meet your future head-on so to speak," stated Hunta Saibon.

No longer faced with the threat of war after the Imperial Army's latest defeat in the Magare Valley, Nayla made the long, arduous trek back to the fortress city, returning once more as the cold breath of winter descended upon the lands.

Warriors stationed along the stairs leading up to the palace bowed in recognition as this famed Kagai Warrior strolled past them. Making her way through the courtyard as a gentle fall of snow began to blanket the grounds; Nayla recalled her first training session in this very courtyard over one hundred years ago. Climbing the stairs to the meeting hall, she stopped as a once familiar voice called out to her.

"Lady Treeborn."

In the vestibule stood Joval Stonecroft. He smiled kindly, pleased to see her after all these many years. Nayla approached, gazing up at the Elf.

Joval dropped down on one knee before her, bowing his head as he whispered: "The warrior maiden returns to her high house."

"Rise up, Joval, there is no need for this," said Nayla, her hand touching his head.

Joval peered up to look upon her face. She still looked beautiful in his eyes, but he could see she had aged twice as fast as he had. In the fifty-three years that had passed since she left him, where he had aged the mortal equivalent of perhaps two years, appearing to be a man of thirty-seven or thirty-eight years, Nayla had aged about five mortal years during this same time. She now appeared to be the equivalent of a mortal woman approaching her late twenties.

"You have kept yourself well, Joval. Your role as the Stewart of Nagana suits you," praised Nayla, admiring his rich attire befitting one with such a prestigious title.

"And you look well," responded Joval, rising up before her. "You have barely changed at all."

"You have never been good at lying to me, Joval. Do not start now," teased the little warrior, with a grateful smile. "I have aged before your eyes while you have remained unchanged with the passing of time."

He smiled back as he responded: "You have not aged, matured perhaps, but you have not aged. In mine own eyes, you are still beautiful."

Nayla could feel her heart and her soul melt as the Elf embraced her in a warm hug and whispered: "I have missed you dearly, Nayla Treeborn."

"And I, you," admitted Nayla. A relieved sigh escaped her as she listened to the familiar beating of Joval's heart as he held her close to his chest. She could sense their friendship still endured, and if there was any bitterness Joval felt for her, it had mellowed with the passing of time.

"I wish your return to Nagana was under happier circumstances," whispered Joval, gazing into her eyes. "The elders summoned you as the threat from the east continues to grow."

"The Regent…"

"Yes, Tisai Darraku has forged an alliance with the Sorcerer. Together with Eldred Firestaff we will be forced to face an even greater threat," confided the Elf, giving Nayla's small hands a gentle squeeze. "Lord Treeborn and the elders anxiously await your arrival."

"Let us not keep them waiting," said Nayla, turning to enter the meeting hall.

It was just as Nayla had anticipated. Dahlon Treeborn gave her his usual cool reception, for he had been forced to call upon his daughter's services by those who sat in power. He was civil as he introduced her to the new council members.

As always, three mortals, Taijin descendants of the elders of the past, greeted the legendary warrior, the daughter of the famed Kareda Bansho. The one elder who spoke on behalf of the others, Maiyo Sonkai, was most lavish in his praise of the warrior maiden's courage and bravery. Nayla smiled modestly at his kind words.

"If this is your attempt to woo me to do your bidding where securing justice and peace is concerned, it is not necessary, Master Sonkai," replied the little warrior. "I am willing to do what I can to help your people."

"Forgive me, Lady Treeborn. It was not my intention to coerce you into this assignment through flattery," responded the elder, apologetically. "You are above that."

Nayla considered the mortal. His raven hair was liberally peppered with gray strands and his dark brown eyes reflected a soul burdened with woe. He appeared to be in his late fifties, she was sure he was younger than he appeared. Her gaze strayed over to her father, sitting next to Master Sonkai.

Dahlon had remained unchanged during her absence, as typically the case, the older the Elf became, the aging process also slowed. The high Elf was silent, but Nayla could sense his contempt and disgust as he gazed back at her. She knew what he was thinking: that her Elven blood, *tainted* with that of the weak mortal's kind, was causing her to age before his very eyes. The warrior maiden released a dreary sigh as she came to realize the only other thing that remained unchanged about her father was his arrogant, condescending demeanor.

"What is it that you require from me, Master Sonkai?" queried Nayla.

"As the threat from the east grows and the Regent rallies a following of bloodthirsty warlords and power hungry landowners, we fear our only hope for long-term peace will be destroyed," answered the elder, his hands wringing in woe.

"This long-term peace you speak of, would this be the late emperor's son, Prince Tokusho?"

"Yes, Lady Treeborn," replied Sonkai. "Your father had claimed that only one as skilled as you can see this mission through successfully."

"I see. And what would this mission entail?"

Dahlon rose up from the table as he spoke: "I – *we*, require you to establish a network of spies within Keso and Shesake, to determine who can and cannot be trusted with the life of the prince. You are to infiltrate the royal circles; become acquainted with palace staff; sniff out those loyal to the prince from those whose interests are to serve the Regent, and in turn, endanger Prince Tokusho's life."

Nayla studied the faces of those before her as she considered her father's request. The elders averted their eyes from her unyielding stare as she scrutinized them.

"You need not do this, Nayla," whispered Joval, as he leaned in close to her.

Dahlon's keen ears detected the Elf's hushed words.

"Need I remind you, Master Stonecroft, our security, and that of her people to the north are in great peril if we do not find a way to weather this storm until the prince can take his rightful place on the throne?" reminded Dahlon. "How do you think the Kagai Warriors will take to another fourteen years of war? Especially now as Eldred Firestaff becomes more obsessed and demented in his dealings with our kind and the Taijins to the west."

"And how do you propose I establish this network?" asked Nayla, leaning back against her chair.

"You are reputed to be the greatest spy and assassin trained by the Saibon clan to ever rise out of Anshen," stated Dahlon, his piercing blue eyes staring down at his daughter. "Let us see just how great you truly are. Put your training to the test, if you dare."

"You should never *dare* me, my lord," responded Nayla, her voice devoid of emotion. "I will do it."

The elders were elated and grateful for her decision. After further discussion to determine her plan of action, the council dispersed from the meeting hall.

Joval shook his head disapprovingly as he gazed at the warrior maiden. "You did not have to accept this mission, Nayla. Whatever compelled you to take this on?"

She offered him a smile as she answered: "I am not one to shirk off a challenge. Dahlon Treeborn *dared* me."

"In all these years, you have not changed one iota," admonished Joval, shaking his head in dismay.

"And that could be a good thing," she said with a giggle, laughing at her own plight.

As she followed the Elf from the meeting hall, a young Taijin woman greeted them. She immediately bowed upon seeing Nayla and Joval.

"Lady Treeborn, I am here to escort you to your quarters," offered this mortal, as she bowed in respect and greeting.

"My quarters?"

"Yes, Nayla," responded Joval. "You shall be staying in the palace during the term of your mission."

"What of your cottage?" questioned Nayla.

"Since my commission as the Stewart of Nagana, I am required to dwell within the walls of the city. My cottage is vacant and has long since fallen into disrepair," answered the Elf. "With your anticipated return, Master Sonkai felt it would be most appropriate for you to reside in the palace. He had your former bedchamber refurbished –

hopefully, to your liking."

"Yes, my lady, I am confident you will be pleased," added the young woman, leading the way through the corridor. "And I shall be at your service."

"And you are?" asked the little warrior, scrutinizing this young woman.

"Nayla Treeborn, this is your lady-in-waiting. Her name is Nakoa," introduced Joval. He opened the door to Nayla's room, motioning for both to enter. "And on this note, I shall be taking my leave."

"Hold on here, Joval! My lady-in-waiting? Whose idea was this?" asked the warrior maiden. "You know how I feel about this matter!"

Joval rolled his eyes as he recalled the other women assigned to this post, all of whom Nayla had scared off. They were women whom Dahlon Treeborn appointed to undertake the task of ensuring his daughter, this *savage* warrior, was taught the finer points of being a lady in a position of honour and prestige, the daughter of a high Elf.

"Master Sonkai wishes to make your stay as comfortable as possible," answered Joval, turning to flee her wrath.

"Now see here, Joval!"

"I shall see you in the morn. And please, for once, do not offend the palace staff. You shall have me to answer to if I see Nakoa fleeing the grounds because of you!" declared the Elf, disappearing down the corridor.

Nayla closed the door. She gazed around the once familiar surroundings. Adorned with new furniture and bedding, it did not look like the room she once inhabited. All memories of her childhood were stowed away, gone from her sight. Where her small collection of dolls once sat, there now rested a sword stand. Nayla removed her weapons, placing the long and short swords carefully upon the wooden stand, turning the handles so they could be grasped by the right hand.

During these times of war, it was customary for the Kagai Warrior to keep his weapons at the ready, so it can be quickly removed and drawn at a moment's notice. She gave her long sword a gentle pat, as though it was a trusted friend she was laying to rest.

"My lady, I have drawn your bath," said Nakoa, calling from the small, adjoining room. "I have tested the water. You should find it adequately warmed."

Nayla wandered into the room. Immediately, the delightful fragrance of dried rose petals, resuscitated back to life by the rejuvenating water, wafted through the air. The scent seduced her senses, body and soul.

Without a word, Nakoa proceeded to disrobe the warrior maiden.

Nayla leapt away from her hands as she growled: "I am perfectly capable of doing this myself."

Nakoa bowed politely, and then again, proceeded to remove Nayla's cloak.

"Do you mind?" snapped Nayla, backing away from the young woman.

"I am sorry, my lady," apologized Nakoa, "but I must follow orders. Please allow me to do my job."

"And what are these orders?"

"As your lady-in-waiting, I am required to administer to your day to day needs and care; to dress you as a lady should dress, and to insure you understand the protocols and adopt the manners becoming of a lady of your high standing," answered Nakoa, stubbornly yanking at Nayla's cloak.

"Now see here, Nakoa, this is totally unnecessary," declared the little warrior, as she turned away from the room. The young Taijin woman maneuvered around her, blocking her exit.

"Please disrobe and get into the tub, my lady," coaxed Nakoa.

"You are not my keeper!" growled Nayla, standing defiantly before the young Taijin woman.

"That is true, my lady. However, your behavior leads me to believe you are in need of one," replied Nakoa, unmoved by this warrior's pointed words.

"Why you insolent little…" muttered Nayla. "Do you even know who I am?"

"Indeed, I do. You are someone in dire need of manners, and I shall be the one to assist you with your deportment, or lack thereof," answered the lady-in-waiting, her composure intact.

"Now I know why you are called a *lady-in-waiting*. You are waiting for me to toss you out of this room!"

"I have been warned about you, my lady," said Nakoa, standing her ground with just as much defiance. "And I mean no disrespect to you, but I intend to serve my tenure in this position. I cannot afford to be removed from this posting. You will not drive me away as you have the others, nor shall I be forced to quit."

"So, who has been speaking to you?"

"Master Stonecroft, my lady. He instructed me not to be bullied or intimidated by you; to use whatever measures I would deem appropriate to gain your cooperation," confided Nakoa, her arms now crossed boldly before her as she stood steadfast.

Nayla scrutinized the young woman who stood no taller than she as

Nakoa glared back at her. She was probably no more than twenty years of age, and yet she had the poise and confidence of one much older.

"Now please, my lady, into the tub," urged Nakoa, her toes tapping impatiently on the floor.

Nayla attempted to push past the small woman only to have Nakoa shove her back. She gasped in surprise as her lady-in-waiting abruptly hurled the remaining water from the urn into her face. The cold water drenched Nayla from head to toe.

"If you refuse to disrobe and bathe, then I shall be forced to douse you with more water until you are adequately cleaned, my lady," cautioned Nakoa. "So what will it be?"

Nayla was absolutely dumfounded. She stood motionless; dripping wet in her raiment. Never before had any of the past ladies-in-waiting ever had the audacity or gall to confront her in this manner.

Nakoa dipped the urn into the tub of water, poised to throw it at her mistress as she asked once more: "So what will it be, my lady, by urn or by tub? It makes no difference to me."

Without another word, Nayla quickly disrobed, turning her back to Nakoa as she slipped into the tub of warm, floral-scented water. Inwardly, she was pleased this young woman did not gasp in horror or utter one word of question as her eyes were cast onto the bold, dark tattoo adorning her right shoulder blade and the multitude of long, silvery scars lining her back. These painful reminders of old wounds were blatantly obvious, and yet, Nakoa casually went about the business of washing Nayla's long, raven tresses.

From that moment on, Nayla's newfound respect for this young Taijin woman evolved into a lifelong friendship.

For the next thirteen years, Nayla made numerous excursions into eastern Orien, always in secret, always on her own. And during these years, she would be unwittingly invited into the homes of the powerful warlords aligning themselves with Tisai Darraku.

Using various disguises, from cook to courtesan and gardener to nanny, she was a lethal force to contend with. More often than not, her victims met with an untimely demise under most mysterious circumstances. The cause of death was usually deemed as an unfortunate accident or a tragic illness that had led to sudden heart failure. Only the warrior maiden knew how they died as she carefully determined the most appropriate method by which to dispense with the enemy. And all the while, Nayla moved like a spirit, coming and going like an elusive phantom.

Each time she returned to Nagana, Joval was relieved to see she had survived yet another mission. Although she and Joval never resumed their past relationship as lovers, they renewed their long-standing friendship. The Elf once again championed her causes, paving the way for her to execute her daring schemes as well as easing her burden when coping with Dahlon Treeborn's insufferable demands, cruel treatment and spiteful comments.

For her part, all Nayla could offer in return was her devoted friendship and loyalty as Joval's soul found some vicarious adventure, as well as respite from the doldrums of life in the city, through her passion for life and good-humour as she always seemed to find something amusing in even the most dire of situations, particularly when she was in the midst of the controversy.

With the passing of time, as Nayla observed from a safe distance, Prince Tokusho matured. And as the young prince grew, so did the hopes of all those wishing to displace the corrupt Regent. However, these hopes were soon over shadowed as a new threat from the west stormed down the Iron Mountains.

During the autumn to leading up to the one-thousandth year of the Second Age of Peace by the Elven calendar, the unthinkable happened. For the first time in history, battalions of soldiers loyal to the Dark Lord Beyilzon breached the northern range of the Iron Mountains, leaving in their wake, death and destruction.

Driven back by Hunta Saibon and the Kagai Warriors to the north, it was only a small taste of what was to follow with the passing of winter.

Once again, the council reconvened. For the first time, Nayla noticed the signs of age and genuine worry etched on her father's face as he presented his case to those present.

"Never had I believed this evil would follow us into eastern Imago," sighed Dahlon, his shoulders slumping from the burden of this disturbing news.

"How dire is this situation?" asked Nayla.

"Five months from now, as the world braces for the return of the spring, it shall be a black spring indeed. We will not be welcomed with a time of renewal and growth. Instead, we shall be immersed in a war that will make all of our past wars against the Imperial Army only pale in comparison."

"According to Master Saibon, these soldiers were not skilled in the art of war. The Regent and his armies pose a far greater threat," noted Nayla.

"Oh, the soldiers of the Dark Army are a definite danger," averred Dahlon. "They may lack the skills of our opponents to the east, but I was there. I was present to witness the hordes awaiting us on the Plains of Fire in Talibarr on the day that decided the fate of man and Elf in this realm."

"Aah," groaned Maiyo Sonkai, wringing his hands fretfully. "Another enemy that we can ill-afford to face. Though we have been able to defeat those to the east, our numbers are seriously depleted. We have barely enough warriors to drive back the Imperial Armies that invade our lands."

"Perhaps the Dark Army's presence was a mere coincidence," reasoned Joval. "Perhaps the soldiers that breached the Iron Mountains were merely scouting parties, soldiers set forth into our lands to determine the feasibility of mounting such an attack."

"No, Joval, the Dark Lord plans once again to hold dominion over all in Imago. Beyilzon will strike down mortals and Elves on both sides of the Iron Mountains. One-thousand years incarcerated in a Hell of his own making has only served to make the Dark Lord even more vengeful than ever before," warned Dahlon, his mind churning with fear as he relived the horrifying memories of the great war. "We were forewarned by the Three Sisters, the Watchers of the past, present and future. Lady Eliya predicted evil would rise once more."

"They may be wrong," hoped Maiyo Sonkai, as the remaining elders nodded in agreement.

"They have never been wrong," stated Dahlon. "Upon the first day of spring, the stars will begin their alignment. With the next full moon, it shall appear blood red in the night sky and the coming of the dawn shall bring with it a sun that will grow cold and black. With these events, Beyilzon shall be unleashed from his underworld prison. These soldiers are merely the harbingers of the dark days to come. The Dark Lord Beyilzon will lead them to war. They will come. More than we can hope to repel."

"Are you saying we are doomed?" asked Joval, rising up from his chair. "That this is the end of life as we know it?"

"Yes," said Dahlon.

"Then we must summon for help," decided Joval.

"We stand alone!" declared Dahlon, his voice trembling as the prospect of war filled his heart with fear and woe. "Where there was once an alliance of Elves and men; it is no more. We are now forced to stand alone."

"My Kagai brothers to the north drove back the incursion, killing many. The few that escaped shall only return to their leaders to warn them death will be imminent if they choose to return," stated Nayla.

"You do not understand!" snarled Dahlon, angered by her ignorance. "They shall return and they will do so in unprecedented numbers! We are doomed. We do not stand a chance once they breach the Iron Mountains. We are destined to perish."

"Lord Treeborn, what of this alliance you spoke of?" asked Sonkai. "Can they not be called upon once more?"

Dahlon folded onto his chair, already accepting defeat: "As I said before, this alliance no longer exists. And if it does, we are no longer a welcome party to it."

"But surely, if this is a peril we must all face, does it not stand to reason those to the west shall come to our aid? That they will stand by us if we in turn pledge to aid them during this time of war?" reasoned Nayla.

"There is only one who can decide our fate, if we dare attempt to call upon old alliances to see us through," stated Dahlon. "Kal-lel Wingfield the Lord of Wyndwood, the king of Elves, first forged this alliance to bring the Dark Lord down in defeat. If King Kal-lel is indeed still alive and continues to exist in this realm, he will be the one to determine whether those to the west shall answer our call to arms."

"He is a high Elf. Surely he will have the compassion to come to our aid during these desperate times," said Joval.

"Do you forget that he was the one to drive my people, we *dark* Elves from Wyndwood. I hardly think King Kal-lel will come to our aid now," responded Dahlon.

"But we are still Elves," argued Joval. "Surely he has some empathy left for those who once shared his domain."

"That has yet to be seen," snapped Dahlon, rising up from his chair. "And besides, how do you propose we get word to the king? None of our falcons have ever ventured into the west. None know the way to Wyndwood," stated Dahlon, his fingers now drumming impatiently on the table.

"We shall send forth a small battalion to escort a messenger!" suggested Maiyo Sonkai. "We shall send a messenger!"

Dahlon's eyes rolled in exasperation: "Now see here, Master Sonkai, to send forth a small force of warriors will not go unnoticed by those in Talibarr, and besides, we shall require every able-bodied man and Elf to do battle, especially if both the Dark Army and the soldiers of the Imperial Army arrive at our gates simultaneously."

"Perhaps you are right, Lord Treeborn," conceded the elder. "But what if, instead of sending forth a messenger protected by many warriors, we send forth only two or three warriors to deliver the message to Wyndwood?"

Dahlon sat back, his brows clenched deep in thought as he considered Maiyo Sonkai's idea.

"Certainly two or three warriors shall have a far easier time slipping past the enemy than an entire battalion. And it will be more prudent to spare several warriors for this task than a small army..." determined the high Elf, as he thought aloud.

"So you would consider this?" asked Joval.

After a reflective pause, Dahlon nodded his head in approval.

"Very good!" exclaimed Sonkai. "So be it! At the first opportunity when the winter passes, we shall send forth three warriors to deliver word to the King of Wyndwood to muster those of the alliance to come to our aid."

"I shall be prepared to leave with the coming of the spring," declared Joval.

"No, you will not, Joval," ordered Dahlon. "Instead, I shall have to return you to your post as captain; to lead our warriors into battle."

"Then who do you propose will lead this expedition to western Imago?" asked Joval. "I hardly foresee you volunteering to return to Wyndwood."

Dahlon said not a word as his gaze fell on Nayla. Joval was momentarily stunned.

"No, my lord!" gasped the Elf. "Not Nayla, not for this mission!"

"She is the most logical choice, Joval!" retorted Dahlon, rising up before him.

"Damn it! Not this time!" protested Joval, rising up to challenge the high Elf.

"Then who would you suggest?" growled Dahlon. "Who is better prepared for a mission of this nature? Name one warrior more skilled and better trained than she!"

"By God, Dahlon Treeborn, only you would send your only daughter to be slaughtered on the pretense this is what she has been trained to do!" snarled Joval. He lunged at the high Elf, grabbing him by the lapels of his vest. "The only time I hear words of praise coming from that mouth of yours where Nayla is concerned is when you willingly offer up her life for such deadly missions! To justify your actions!"

Maiyo Sonkai jumped from his chair, his hands waving about in a desperate bid for calm to prevail as he sided with Dahlon: "Master Stonecroft, think on it! Lady Treeborn *is* the best candidate for this task. And though you believe Lord Treeborn's words are motivated to justify his decisions and actions, we on council, my brothers and I are well aware that Nayla offers us the best chance of success."

"This is insanity!" argued Joval, releasing his grip on Dahlon.

"I do not relish the idea of sacrificing the life of any of our warriors in this manner, but consider this, Master Stonecroft: our backs are pressed well against the wall as we face potential enemies from both the east and west," explained Maiyo Sonkai.

"He means to see her killed!" argued Joval.

"Think logically! Think of what will happen if we do not select wisely in whom we send forth on this mission!" countered the elder. "The lives of many shall depend on the skills and experience of the one warrior we choose to lead this expedition! Knowing what we are up against, what does logic dictate? Personal feelings aside, in your heart you know who is the best warrior for this mission."

Joval slowly slumped back down in his chair. His soul was shaken by the elder's statement, for he knew his words to be true. He could not find it in his heart to look at Nayla – to gaze into her eyes.

The warrior maiden had been silent throughout this exchange. It was no surprise to her Dahlon would offer her up for this service. Although, she was aware her father's motives were two-fold, she also understood the elders had complete confidence in her abilities. She knew Master Sonkai truly believed that if anyone could do this, it would be her.

Nayla rose up from the table. She proceeded to leave the meeting room.

"We are not done yet, Nayla! Where do you think you are going?" Dahlon demanded to know.

"Apparently, I am going into the west."

With the impending winter, Nayla prepared to leave at first light. She would make the long journey to Anshen. Here, she would wait out the storms of this season most foul and to await instructions to advance westward at the first sign winter was about to let up.

Already stationed to the north, her excursion would be shortened by at least twenty-eight days had she been forced to make the run from Nagana. From Anshen, a weeklong journey would bring her to the Iron Mountains. A mountain pass would deliver her into western Imago and on to Wyndwood.

As her steed was made ready, Nayla said her farewells to Nakoa and the elders who came to see her off. Joval arrived with a scroll in hand to deliver to the warrior maiden.

Maiyo Sonkai and his two comrades bowed in respect to Nayla, wishing her well: "All our hopes shall be riding on you, Lady Treeborn. We shall pray our God will keep you safe."

She reciprocated with a bow, and then she turned to give Nakoa a hug as her lady-in-waiting wept openly.

"Please be careful, my lady," said Nakoa, between her sad sobs. She clutched Nayla tightly in her arms as though it may be the last time.

"Always, my friend," answered Nayla, hugging her back.

"I shall be awaiting your return," promised Nakoa, blotting away her tears on a kerchief.

Joval stepped forward and offered her the scroll as he explained: "Your father said you will be needing this. It is the map of western Imago. He had traced the fastest route for you to take that will deliver you to Wyndwood."

"Thank you, Joval," said Nayla, accepting the scroll.

"I have already sent forth word to Master Saibon to expect your return to Anshen," added the Elf.

"Did you use Tori?" asked Nayla. "She is the swiftest, most competent of our falcons."

"Indeed, I used Tori. You shall see her in Anshen," promised the Elf.

As she turned to claim her steed, Joval suddenly pulled her close, embracing her in a great hug. Nayla could feel a worried sigh escape his heavy heart as he held her tightly to his chest.

"If anyone can do this, it will be you," stated the Elf, with the greatest confidence. "We shall meet again, Nayla."

Mounting her steed, she glanced over for one final look at those coming to wish her well. Dahlon Treeborn was nowhere to be seen, but to her surprise, marching across the courtyard were the warriors of Orien, led by Valtar Briarwood. In a final gesture of respect, the warriors knelt down, bowing before her as Valtar wished her a safe journey.

Reciprocating with a bow, she promised: "I shall return. Help is imminent. Those of the old alliance will come."

With those final words, she steered her mount to the west gate, ducking beneath the portcullis as several warriors cranked the massive winch to raise the heavy iron grate. As the elders retreated back to the palace and the warriors dispersed from the courtyard, Joval raced up to the battlement.

From high atop the windswept rampart of the fortress city, he watched as Nayla charged northward, becoming a dark speck on the long road before her.

"Stay safe, little warrior," whispered Joval, his voice carried off by the wind, "until we meet again."

Racing against time and the elements, Nayla pushed her steed on. Just three days outside of Anshen, the first snows of winter blanketed the land, embracing it in a shroud of white to muffle the sounds of a now-sleeping world.

Hunta Saibon greeted Nayla, knowing full well she would arrive just as Joval Stonecroft had said.

For Nayla, it was good to be home again although this stay was to be the precursor to the deadly task awaiting her early in the spring.

The winter seemed to pass slowly as Nayla prepared as much mentally as she did physically for the mission she was to undertake. Much time was spent with Hunta and the Kagai Warriors, discussing strategies as how best to fend off an attack if the Dark Army should breach the Iron Mountains should the enemy to the east arrive simultaneously.

During this period of long, dark nights and short, cold days, Hunta Saibon selected the two warriors to accompany Nayla on this perilous mission.

For the Kagai leader, the reasoning for sending only three on this quest made perfect sense. Choosing two of his best warriors, known for their great stamina and fighting abilities, Hunta prepared them for this grueling and dangerous quest. When they were not perfecting their warrior skills, Nayla would work with the young men, studying the map so they would memorize even the minute details of western Imago. It was critical they become absolutely familiar with the map, for if Nayla should fall to the wayside, the other two warriors would be forced to press on without her.

With the cruel hands of winter releasing its icy grip on the lands, Nayla prepared to leave Anshen in the company of the two warriors. On this day a cold, pale sun illuminated the stark landscape made barren by winter's chilling breath.

As Hunta Saibon, his disciples and the families residing in Anshen congregated to wish the trio well, the warrior priest embraced Nayla in a hug.

"It is with great trepidation I send you forth into the unknown, my child," said Hunta. "However, soon we shall be braced in war; made to face the new enemy with the coming of spring. May our God and the spirits that aid Him watch over you and protect you. I shall pray you be granted safe passage into the west."

"Thank you, master. We shall do everything in our power to deliver word to the Alliance of our dire situation. You will see! Help shall be forthcoming," promised Nayla.

Hunta smiled confidently as he responded: "Yes, help will be forthcoming, Takaro."

He and the villagers watched as the trio rode away, heading westward to disappear behind the waters of Reyu Falls.

Nayla led the way through Hebeku Valley and then northward past her mother's ancestral home of Saijun. They stopped briefly, only long enough to forewarn the villagers of the impending evil destined to crest the Iron Mountains. Well-known and respected by these people, the citizens took heed of her warning, preparing to fight, and when necessary, flee into the surrounding hills or southward to Nagana to escape danger.

It was during the fifth day of travel to the west of Saijun that Nayla and her warrior brothers followed the plumes of distant campfires as the gray smoke curled into the ever-darkening sky. Following the sounds of horses and many voices speaking in the common tongue, they came across a large encampment of soldiers. An army, two thousand strong consisting mainly of foot soldiers, was in the midst of settling down for the night.

Concealed in their vantage point, Nayla assessed the situation. For the first time she spied upon the mortals of western Imago. These soldiers from Talibarr were much taller than the Taijins, most were as tall as the shortest Elf and many were as tall as the average Elf, standing six feet tall or more.

"Takaro, there are far too many for us to take on," whispered Kansai. "Shall we head back to Saijun? Warn the villagers of the Dark Army's approach?"

"They have already been forewarned," answered Nayla. "Our presence shall not make a marked difference. The villagers will make good use of their traps and snares. They shall fight while they can and then they will flee."

"They will not be prepared to take on such a large troop," noted Edomu. "Surely there is something we can do?"

"There is, but we shall wait until the soldiers have retired for the night," said Nayla. "Only when the guards posted to sentry duty remain shall we make our move."

"What do you propose?" queried Kansai, his dark eyes following the movements of the enemy soldiers.

"As you said, there are far too many of them to confront head-on. If we cannot do away with them using our bows or swords, at the very least, I shall find another way to thin their numbers and hamper their movements," advised Nayla. She reached into her leather pack, extracting a small ceramic vial to show her brother warriors.

"Tomorrow morn, the first soldiers to rise for a drink of water or tea shall also be the first to die. I will need you and Kansai to divert attention away from the camp while I poison their water supply. And then, I will do away with the fencing to allow their horses to escape," stated Nayla.

Kansai and Edomu nodded in understanding. The three waited in the shadows of the forest until all was quiet.

While Nayla inched closer to the camp, Kansai and Edomu headed deeper into the forest. She smiled to herself as the two warriors began to rustle about in the darkness, groaning like a wounded bear. She watched as one soldier ordered four guards to follow him into the forest to investigate the source of these strange noises. They were to do away with the creature lest it entered their camp to wreak havoc. The three remaining guards were to stay behind, watching over the encampment in case the animal circled back around.

As soon as the five soldiers disappeared, following the sounds of the *wounded animal*, Nayla kicked over a large rock, sending it crashing through the undergrowth down the hillside. The three soldiers glanced about nervously, peering through the vegetation as the rock tumbled away, sounding much like a person dashing madly through the dense shrubs.

"Who goes there?" one soldier demanded to know.

"You fool! Do you really believe the enemy would make himself known to you?" scolded another soldier. "For all you know, it could be a deer."

With the other soldiers already heading in the opposite direction to hunt down the mysterious creature, the three soldiers had no choice but to forge on ahead to investigate the sound. The third soldier waved the other two on to follow him down the hill.

Crouching low in the undergrowth, Nayla watched as the soldiers' boots passed right by her as they moved swiftly down the hill, following the rustling of bushes. Silently emerging at the edge of the camp, she cautiously wove her way between the tents. Over the still-smoldering campfire, a large iron pot filled with water was suspended over the glowing embers of wood. Quickly and quietly, she uncorked the vial, pouring in a small quantity of poison. The white powder hissed and darkened as it made contact with the water, and then slowly disappeared as it dissolved.

As Nayla made her way through the encampment toward the corral of horses, she tipped a bit of poison into other pots and kettles of water. The poison she used was so potent, she knew only a small amount was needed to do away with many of the soldiers, at least enough to make a significant difference in their war efforts against her people.

Nayla silently made her way to the makeshift corral. It was thrown together rather carelessly with small trees that were cut down and laid on its side. She shook her head in disgust knowing full well that any of these horses could easily jump the fence line if spooked. She moved cautiously so as not to frighten the animals as she lowered one of the tree trunks to encourage and hasten their flight from the corral.

The call of the nightingale alerted Nayla that her brothers had doubled back, awaiting her return in the deep shadows. In the distance, the five soldiers retraced their steps back to camp. The warrior maiden's sharp ears could make out their muted grumblings as they voiced concern for the mysterious creature that seemingly vanished into the night.

Nayla joined Kansai and Edomu. Snatching up some rocks in their hands, she motioned them to climb into the trees. As the soldiers neared the camp, the little warrior hurled a rock, striking the rump of a stallion. The horse whinnied in alarm, bucking at its invisible foe and instead, kicking out at the mare standing directly behind.

Kansai and Edomu joined Nayla, pelting the horses with rocks. Soon, the quiet night air was shattered by the high-pitched squeals and whinnies of protest as the horses panicked, sailing over the downed fence of this flimsy corral.

The soldiers raced back as frightened steeds stampede past them, almost bowling them over as they charged off into a valley to the north. As the soldiers called out for assistance to capture the horses, men stumbled out in a confused daze from the many tents. The captain began shouting angrily for the soldiers to retrieve their mounts.

In the midst of the chaos, Nayla and her warrior brothers climbed down the tree. Silently, they headed westward, satisfied the Dark Army's advance would be slowed and by morning, their numbers significantly thinned.

On the seventh day of their trek, under the fast-dimming skies, the trio came to rest at the foothills of the Iron Mountains.

"Takaro, dare we venture any further on this day?" asked Kansai, the warrior's eyes taking in the inhospitable terrain.

She quickly assessed the steepness of the slope and the condition of the trail awaiting them. Though some portions of the path they were to take was hidden by large outcrops of boulders or were concealed by walls of rock, Nayla knew where her keen vision would allow her to negotiate this craggy, desolate terrain in the darkness of night, these mortals would be putting their lives at risk if they were to follow her.

"No," decided Nayla. "Darkness will descend shortly. We will not even make it a quarter of the way up the mountain before we are forced to stop."

"So we will rest here for the evening?" asked Edomu, dismounting from his steed.

"Yes, let us rest and let our horses take in sustenance through the night, for it promises to be a long and treacherous journey to reach Deception Pass," suggested Nayla.

Kansai's eyes stared up to the summit of the mountain. Heavy, gray clouds latched stubbornly to the jagged pinnacles of the highest range in all of Imago.

"Deception Pass…" Kansai's voice echoed her words. "Why is it named so?"

"According to Dahlon Treeborn, he named it Deception Pass

because storms seem to blow in from nowhere, consuming the mountains in its deadly embrace, and then just as suddenly, the foul weather disappears. It is deceptively calm one moment, and then deadly the next," explained Nayla.

"I take it that is the only route, the only passage into western Imago?" determined Edomu.

"If you recall the map, the only other possibilities are hampered by impassable glaciers, steep crevasses or treacherous rivers. It would be much too dangerous. At least at the summit, if our luck holds, there is an opportunity to pass safely."

"The nights are still bitterly cold, Takaro. Would it be safe to build a small fire?" asked Kansai.

Nayla gazed at the two warriors in her company. Although she was able to withstand extremes in temperature better than these full-blooded mortals, even she could feel the cold bite of winter still lingering in the air.

"A small fire," she conceded.

As the lands were cloaked in blackness once again, Nayla took the first watch. So close to the great land barrier that divided Imago in half, she was not about to risk being taken by surprise by the enemy. Hours later, under a still-dark, pre-dawn sky, she was relieved by Kansai. She would sleep for several hours before resuming the next leg of their perilous journey.

"Takaro! Wake up!" shouted Kansai, giving her shoulder an abrupt shake.

Nayla instinctively snatched up her sword. She bolted up from her bedroll, her eyes still half-closed with sleep as she asked: "What is it?"

"While you slept, Edomu ventured forth. He went on ahead to scout out the area; to find the most direct path to take us to the mountains," answered Kansai, his voice strained with worry. "He said he would not be long, but now, a good measure of time has passed. He has yet to return."

"Quickly! Ready our horses, let us be off!" ordered Nayla.

Leading the way, she followed the hoofprints left behind by Edomu's steed. It brought them ever closer to the slopes of the mountains, but still, there was no sign of the warrior.

"Look!" Nayla pointed to the ground.

Amongst the many hoof prints were scattered footprints left by the enemy. Broken vegetation and the disturbed earth told her immediately Edomu had been taken by surprised. He was overwhelmed and captured.

"What is that?" gasped Kansai, pointing to a bloodied handprint left on an old tree stump. Scattered about the base of this stump were dismembered fingers and thumbs: Edomu's fingers and thumbs.

"Good heavens!" groaned the warrior, reeling from this morbid and sinister site.

"We must leave immediately," whispered Nayla.

"Well, what do we have here? Gonna leave behind a fellow warrior so you can scurry off in fear, eh?"

Nayla and Kansai spun their horses about to face the voice coming from the shadows. To their horror, the captain of the Dark Army emerged from the forest with their comrade. Edomu's face was ashen; his eyes dulled with pain. The edge of a dagger was thrust to his neck. With his wrists tightly bound before him, Edomu's hands were a frightful mess as the blood continued to flow from the wounds of his missing digits.

"Surely you weren't gonna leave your friend behind, were you?" mocked the captain, shoving Edomu towards Nayla and Kansai.

Edomu shouted out in Taijina: "I am dead! Escape if you can!"

The wounded warrior suddenly howled in pain as the captain squeezed his maimed hands as he ordered: "Shut your mouth! An' if you wish to speak, speak in the common tongue!"

Kansai urged his steed forward to confront the captain when a dozen soldiers emerged before him; swords drawn and spears at the ready.

"Takaro, be ready to flee! I shall hold them at bay," said Kansai.

"Speak so I understand!" demanded the captain, motioning his men to close their ranks as he interrogated the strangers. "Who are you? What are you doin' in these parts? Where's the rest of your army?"

"There is no army. There are but two of us warriors. We were sent to patrol the borders, to warn our people of your arrival," answered Kansai, speaking in the common tongue.

The captain stared suspiciously at Nayla as she wrapped her cloak around her body, concealing her weapons and battle raiment.

"An' what about her?" grunted the captain.

"This woman?" asked Kansai, pointing to Nayla with obvious disdain. "She is nothing more than a whore we picked up in Saijun. The nights are still long and cold. She keeps us amused as we are forced to bide our time in this forsaken place."

"Really now?" snorted the captain, eyeing the small woman before him.

"I have no further need of her. She is yours for the taking if it pleases you," offered Kansai, giving Nayla a dismissive wave of his hand.

"How odd," noted the captain. Clenching a fistful of hair, he yanked back on Edomu's head. "Your friend here says nothing, even as we removed his fingers, one by one, still refusin' to answer our questions. An' then you willingly prattle on, tellin' me what he wouldn't."

Kansai glanced at the dozen soldiers encircling them. They closed in tighter, their weapons poised towards them.

"Hmph! You sing like a bird an' yet, your comrade is willin' to die than to speak," grumbled the captain. "I can only guess what secrets you're willin' to divulge with the right type of *persuasion*."

"Be ready to flee, Takaro!" ordered Kansai, speaking in Taijina.

"Speak in my tongue! Speak so I understand!" demanded the captain. "Dismount! Both of you!"

Edomu's bloodied fists struck out at the captain, slamming into his bearded jaw. As the captain stumbled back, soldiers moved in to pounce on the warrior. Edomu dove from their grasp, kicking another soldier in his midriff as he came up onto his feet before Kansai.

As Kansai drew his sword, he shouted to Takaro: "*NOW*!"

Throwing herself back into the saddle, Nayla's heels sank into her steed's flanks. The panicking stallion reared up, striking out at the soldiers trying to contain them. With a loud snort, the steed bolted through the melee. As the six soldiers left standing attacked with their swords, four others mounted their steeds. They gave chase as Nayla careened between the trees, charging westward to the mountain trail that would take her to the summit.

Distant screams of agony echoed off the mountains. Kansai and Edomu fought valiantly until their dying breath. Nayla's raced on, her heart shaken by her warrior brothers' courage and valor as they sacrificed their own lives so she may continue on.

With even greater determination, she rode on. The thunder of the fast approaching steeds closed in behind her. As she urged her stallion up the mountain trail, blasts of steam jetted from the horse's nostrils as it expelled the spent air from his great lungs. With a coat now drenched in sweat and muscles quivering from exhaustion, the steed struggled up the mountain.

A spear flew directly in front of the horse's path causing the frightened animal to rear up. Already on an angled slope, gravity worked against the stallion. The animal to toppled backwards. With fifteen hundred pounds of bone and muscle coming down on top of her, Nayla leapt from the saddle. The stallion came crashing back, sliding along the trail toward the enemy soldiers. As Nayla fell to the side of the trail, her arms flew out to break the initial fall, but the deadly terrain caused her to tumble down, skidding directly toward the sheer face of the mountain.

The ground abruptly disappeared beneath her. Nayla plunged downward. As she went over the cliff, her gloved fingers raked into the earth as her hands seized the very edge of the world. Her heart was pounding like a drum in her chest. Her muscles ached as her hands struggled to maintain their hold as she strained to hoist herself to safety.

Without warning, the rocks and earth beneath her hands crumbled away. Nayla plummeted straight down.

The soldiers gathered along the edge of the cliff, gazing down on her body. She had landed on a small ledge about twenty-two feet below them. The captain shoved his men aside. He stared down at her, determining her condition.

Through half-closed eyes, Nayla could make out his form in the blur of shadow and light.

"Forget about her, she's nothing but a worthless woman," grunted the captain.

"Shouldn't we see to it that she's dead?" asked a soldier, staring down at Nayla as she groaned in pain.

"If the fall doesn't kill her, the cold night will!" snapped the captain, his impatience mounting.

"But, cap'n…"

"What don't you understand? You heard me! Time is wastin' away. Move out. *NOW*!" hollered the captain. With these final words ringing in the Nayla's ears, her world went black.

"I said, NOW! Move out before the next storm descends upon this forsaken place! MOVE!"

This unfamiliar voice echoed in Nayla's mind as her eyes snapped open only to be greeted by utter darkness. The frozen ground beneath her seemed to quake as the pounding of thousands of feet marched past her. Enshrined in a tomb of ice and snow, she was safely concealed from their eyes.

Exhausted from her long, arduous climb to Deception Pass, she had fallen asleep while waiting out the brunt of the storm that had trapped her here. Now, in the darkness of her makeshift shelter, she fought to calm her racing heart that was overwhelmed by memories of the past that had led her to this terrible, dreaded place and predicament.

She remained motionless, listening to the sounds of an army marching by. Far ahead, leading them eastward, the captain continued to shout orders for the soldiers to advance. Amidst the loud grumblings of protest, the men marched on; some cursing loudly as they tripped over the frozen bodies of long-dead soldiers buried beneath the fresh mantle of snow.

Eventually, the air grew still and quiet.

Nayla listened again. Her ears strained to hear through the insulating blanket of snow. There was nothing, only the eerie whisper of the wind swirling through the pass. Her cold, weary muscles still ached from the short, but difficult climb up the cliff from the ledge she had landed on. Followed by the all-day ascent up the trail that delivered her to the summit of this treacherous mountain; her entire body felt painfully stiff.

Using her shoulder against the frozen sheet of snow-encrusted cloak, Nayla pushed the walls of her shelter away. Her eyes blinked hard, adjusting to the dazzling glare as crystals of ice and snow sparkled like flecks of diamond, glistening against the weak light of a pale sun. Rising up from her shelter, she slowly stretched, stomping her feet a few times to stimulate the circulation of blood in her tired body. Picking up her leather pouch, she slung the strap over her left shoulder so it came to rest on her right hip.

Nayla edged over to the mouth of the pass. She crept to the top of the trail, cautiously peering down the winding, steep path that meandered along the mountain slope. To her relief, there was no other sign of advancing armies heading her way. Suddenly, a small shadow silently glided over her. Glancing up, to her surprise, it was a falcon. The bird's keen eyes scanned the landscape; it spiraled down closer for a better look, circling past Nayla.

"Tori," she called out, holding her arm out as a sign for the falcon to land.

Although this bird was trained to fly to specific points in western Orien to deliver messages, she was also trained to scour the lands in the general direction Nayla traveled to search for her master. Never did Nayla think her falcon would seek her out in unfamiliar territories.

The bird circled overhead once more to ascertain this person's identity. Suddenly, the small raptor descended toward the outstretched arm at a frightening speed, only to land lightly on her master's forearm.

"Good girl, Tori," praised Nayla, scratching the bird on the back of its head.

She set the bird down on a rock as she removed the sealed vial attached to the falcon's leather jesses that hung from its ankles. Emptying the small piece of parchment from inside, she unrolled it to read:

Takaro:

Saijun has fallen. Soldiers heading south – after the Elves.
All flee to Nagana. You are our last hope.

Hunta Saibon

With no ink or writing quill, she lanced the tip of her left index finger, squeezing some blood out into a small depression on a stone. Cutting a small bit of her hair, she fashioned it into a paint brush that she dabbed into her own blood, working quickly before it could coagulate. On the other side of the parchment she wrote:

King Kal-lel:

Dark Army has breached the Iron Mountains. Please help.
Send Alliance to answer our call to arms. Without your aid,
we shall perish.

Dahlon Treeborn.

Rolling the parchment tightly, she inserted it into the vial. Fastening it back onto Tori's jesses, she pulled tightly on the thin straps of leather. Speaking in Elvish, Nayla whispered to her falcon: "Follow the sun, Tori. Head westward, may the winds guide you to the great Elf kingdom."

Stroking the bird's soft breast feathers, she then held the falcon aloft, raising the bird up to the brooding sky.

Tori launched off Nayla's arm, her wings fully extended as she swooped down the face of the mountain. A great thermal caught the bird, carrying her upwards on a rising bank of warm air. The falcon floated up past her master, suspended on this invisible hand of God, and with a loud *'scree!'*, she set off to follow the faint glow of the sun veiled behind growing cloud cover.

"Go, Tori! Fly straight and true! Do not diverge from this path!" shouted Nayla. On a wing and a pray, the small, graceful falcon quickly ascended into the sky, flying westward to the fabled forest of Wyndwood. "If I do not make it, I pray you will."

As her eyes followed the falcon until it disappeared from her sight, her gaze took in the vast and unfamiliar lands of western Imago that sprawled out before her against an infinite horizon. Far off in the distance, gray smoke curled into the dismal sky, no doubt a village that had fallen victim to the Dark Army. From her high vantage point, she could make out the small, unassuming land formation of Mount Hope. Beyond this small mountain was the Valley of Shadows where a large army was massing along the forest that skirted the Plains of Fire. Already, her most direct route was impassable.

Silhouetted against a bleak and somber, early spring sky, her deep brown eyes searched for the landmarks she had memorized from the old map her father had provided her. It all seemed strangely surreal.

Nayla drew in a deep breath as she took her first few, attentive steps into this new land. With time now her enemy; she would be forced to travel harder and faster than she ever did before. As impossible as this mission now seemed, her pace hastened and her heart was no longer burdened with despair. It was as though the invisible hands of fate itself guided her on and forced her to act as the familiar whine of arrows sliced through the air. The projectiles skimmed by her, shattering or ricocheting off the surrounding rocks and boulders.

Nayla immediately ducked. Dropping down on her knees, she pressed her body against a large boulder. Cautiously peering up to the pass, she caught a glimpse of a dozen soldiers arming their bows and preparing to take aim. Hugging the stony wall, the warrior maiden inched her way down the trail.

"There she is!" shouted a soldier.

With no other choice but to run, Nayla began to sprint down the treacherous path, hoping against hope her Elven blood and Kagai teachings would give her the stamina and skills to negotiate this steep trail.

Now, whether this journey ended with success or in utter failure, Nayla knew she had no choice but to forge on alone, for somewhere to the west, her destiny awaited. This was to be the first step in the beginning of a long journey.

pronunciation

Places and Names

In the language of the mortals of Orien,
the following vowels are pronounced as follows:

symbol:	keyword:
a	f**a**t
â	**a**pe
ä	f**a**ther
ê	m**ee**t
i	b**i**te
ô	g**o**
yoo	**u**nited

Anshen:	än-shên
Anzan:	än-zän
Arashe:	a-rä-shê
Borai:	bô-râ
Chusai Saibon:	chyoo-sâi sâ-bôn
Edomu:	ê-dô-myoo
Esshu:	ês-shyoo
Furai:	fyoo-râ
Hebeku:	hê-bê-kyoo
Hegashe:	hê-gä-shê
Hemashe:	hê-mä-shê
Hetai:	hê-tâ
Hunta Saibon:	hyoon-ta sâ-bôn
Kagai:	kä-gâ
Kaisheke:	kâ-shê-kê
Kansai:	kän-sâ
Kareda Bansho:	kä-rê-da bän-shô
Kashe:	kä-shê

Keodai:	kê-ô-dâ
Keso:	kê-sô
Magare:	ma-gä-rê
Maisai:	mâ-sâ
Maiyo Sonkai:	mâ-yô sôn-kâ
Medaru Saibon:	mê-dä-ryoo sâ-bôn
Medore:	mê-dô-rê
Mekai:	mê-kâ
Metasu:	mê-tä-syoo
Nagana:	nä-gä-nä
Nakoa:	na-kô-a
Nome Mewaku:	nô-mê mê-wä-kyoo
Orien:	ô-ri-ên
Reyu:	rê-yoo
Reyuzan:	rê-yoo-zän
Saijun:	sâ-jyoon
Shekata:	shê-kä-tä
Shesaiji:	shê-sâ-jê
Shesake:	shê-sä-kê
Shenyu:	shên-yoo
Tadashe:	tä-dä-shê
Taija:	tâ-jä
Taijin:	tâ-jên
Taijina:	tâ-jên-a
Taiko:	tâ-kô
Takaro:	tä-kä-rô
Tisai Darraku:	ti-sâ där-rä-kyoo
Tokusho:	tô-kyoo-shô
Yaruke Saibon	yä-ryoo-kê sâ-bôn

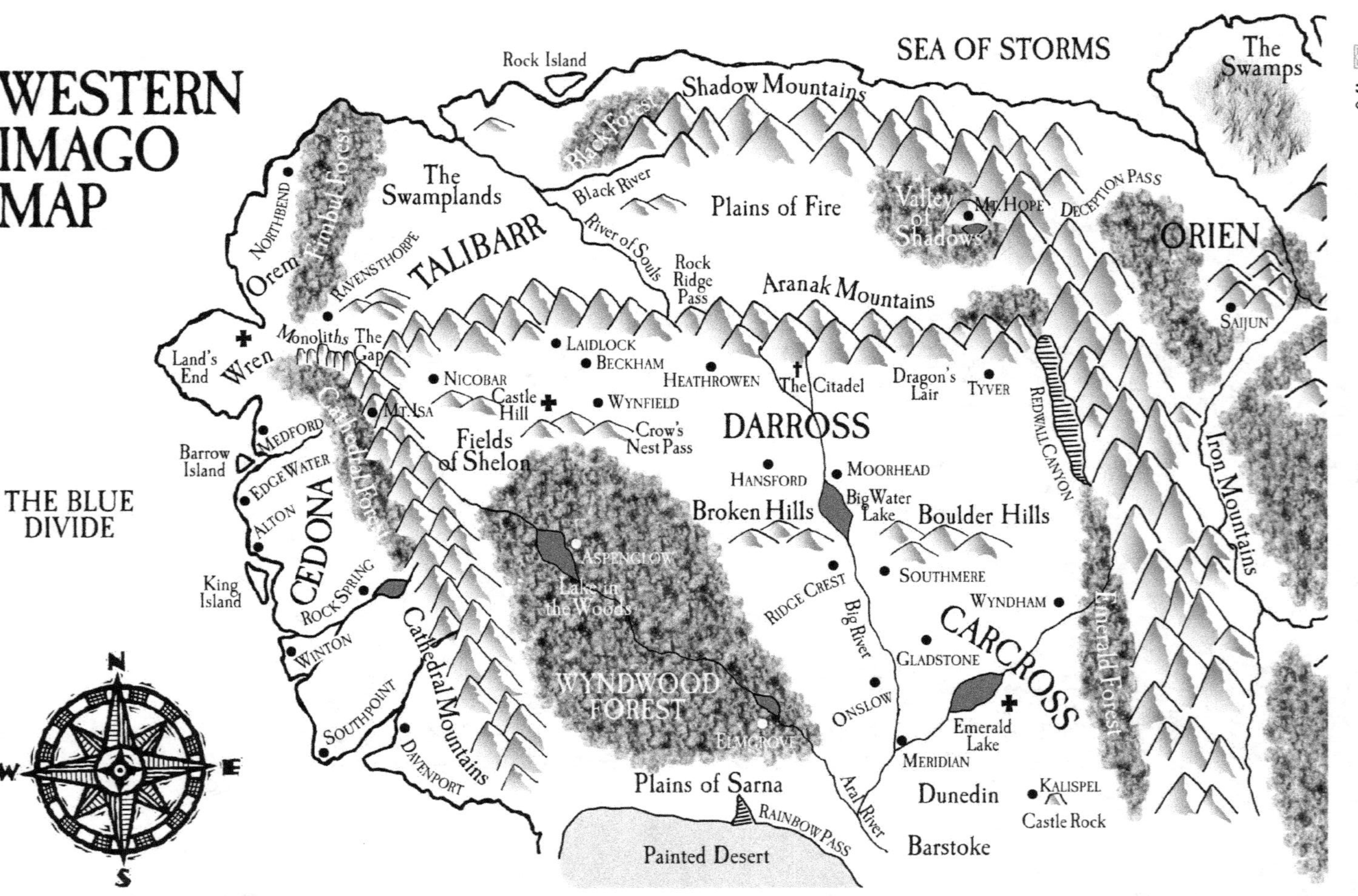

WESTERN IMAGO MAP
THE BLUE DIVIDE
Rock Island
SEA OF STORMS
The Swamps
Shadow Mountains
Black Forest
Black River
Plains of Fire
Valley of Shadows
MT. HOPE
DECEPTION PASS
ORIEN
SAIJUN
The Swamplands
Fimbul Forest
NORTHBEND
Orem
RAVENSTHORPE
TALIBARR
River of Souls
Rock Ridge Pass
Aranak Mountains
Land's End
Wren
Monoliths
The Gap
LAIDLOCK
BECKHAM
HEATHROWEN
The Citadel
Dragon's Lair
TYVER
REDWALL CANYON
Iron Mountains
NICOBAR
Castle Hill
WYNFIELD
MT. ISA
Crow's Nest Pass
Fields of Shelon
DARROSS
MEDFORD
Barrow Island
EDGEWATER
Cathedral Forest
CEDONA
ALTON
HANSFORD
MOORHEAD
Big Water Lake
Broken Hills
Boulder Hills
ASPENGLOW
Lake in the Woods
King Island
ROCK SPRING
RIDGE CREST
SOUTHMERE
WYNDHAM
Emerald Forest
Big River
CARCROSS
GLADSTONE
WINTON
Cathedral Mountains
WYNDWOOD FOREST
ONSLOW
SOUTHPOINT
DAVENPORT
ELMGROVE
Emerald Lake
MERIDIAN
Plains of Sarna
Aral River
Dunedin
KALISPEL
Castle Rock
RAINBOW PASS
Painted Desert
Barstoke
N
W
E
S

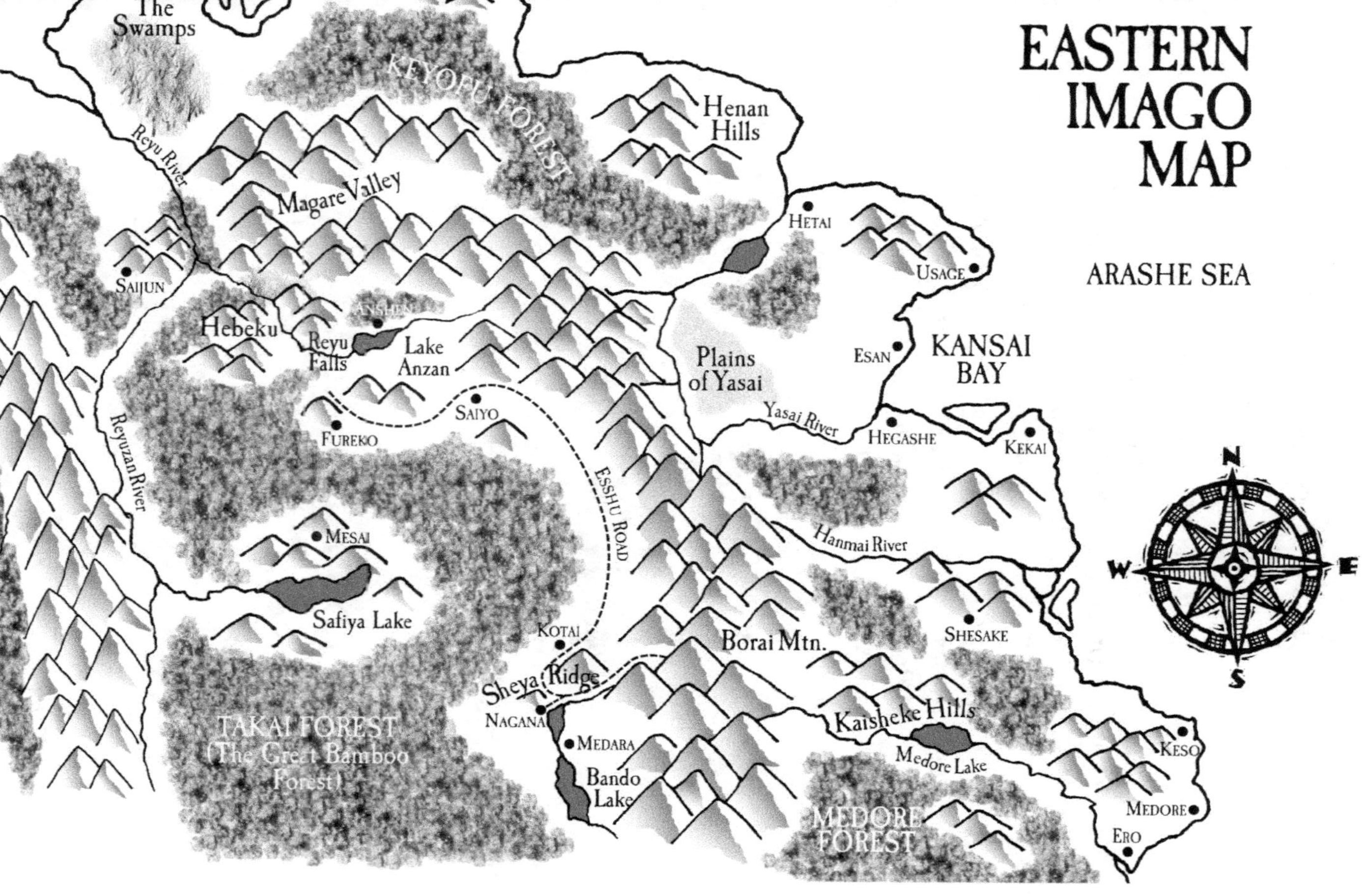
EASTERN IMAGO MAP
ARASHE SEA
N
W
E
S
The Swamps
KEYOFU FOREST
Henan Hills
Reyu River
Magare Valley
HETAI
USAGE
SAIJUN
ANSHEN
Hebeku
Reyu Falls
Lake Anzan
Plains of Yasai
ESAN
KANSAI BAY
SAIYO
FUREKO
Yasai River
HEGASHE
KEKAI
Reyuzan River
ESSHU ROAD
MESAI
Hanmai River
Safiya Lake
KOTAI
Borai Mtn.
SHESAKE
Sheya Ridge
NAGANA
Kaisheke Hills
TAKAI FOREST (The Great Bamboo Forest)
MEDARA
Medore Lake
KESO
Bando Lake
MEDORE
MEDORE FOREST
ERO

adult fantasy series

(in reading order)

Imago Chronicles: Book One, A Warrior's Tale
Imago Chronicles: Book Two, Tales from the West
Imago Chronicles: Book Three, Tales from the East
Imago Chronicles: Book Four, The Tears of God
Imago Chronicles: Book Five, Destiny's End
Imago Chronicles: Book Six, The Spell Binder
Imago Chronicles: Book Seven, The Broken Covenant
Imago Prophecy (Prequel to Imago Chronicles series)
Imago Legacy (Sequel to Imago Prophecy)

YA fantasy series

(in reading order)

The Dream Merchant Saga:
Book One, The Magic Crystal

The Dream Merchant Saga:
Book Two, The Silver Sword
(Publication date: 2011)

about the author

L.T. Suzuki is a fantasy novelist, script-writer and a practitioner and instructor of the martial arts system, Bujinkan Budo Taijutsu; a system incorporating six traditional samurai schools and three schools of ninjutsu.

For more information, please check out L.T. Suzuki's official website at: ***http://web.me.com/imagobooks***

www.ingramcontent.com/pod-product-compliance
Lightning Source LLC
LaVergne TN
LVHW020646110826
845149LV00012B/1933

* 9 7 8 0 9 8 6 7 2 4 0 2 2 *